ETERNITY'S END

"Full of that good old-fashioned science fiction *stuff*, man! This is the sort of thing that got me reading science fiction in the first place!"   —Craig Shaw Gardner, bestselling author of *Dragon Burning*

"[Legroeder] finds true love, cognitive dissonance, divisions among the enemy, ambitious schemes, another mission—this one deeper than anyone has ever gone before into the substrata of the Flux—and a final resolution that leaves the reader both breathless and satisfied."   —*Analog*

"After his escape from the notorious Kyber pirates, star rigger Renwald Legroeder finds himself on trial for his freedom by those he had hoped would protect him.

"Accused of collaboration and treason, Legroeder accepts a perilous mission to recover the starship *Impris*, a vessel lost in the timelessness of Flux space, in the hopes that he can vindicate himself and halt a comspiracy that permeates the colonized worlds. Carver ("*Chaos Chronicles*") continues his series of novels set in the Star Rigger universe with a mesmerizing tale of human perseverance and courage under pressure that updates the legend of the flying Dutchman."   —*Library Journal*

"A real treat."   —Melissa Scott

BOOKS BY JEFFREY A. CARVER

*The Infinity Link
*The Rapture Effect
Roger Zelazny's Alien Speedway: Clypsis
From a Changeling Star
Down the Stream of Stars

THE STAR RIGGER UNIVERSE
Seas of Ernathe
*Star Rigger's Way
*Panglor
*Dragons in the Stars
*Dragon Rigger
*Eternity's End

THE CHAOS CHRONICLES
*Neptune Crossing: Volume One
*Strange Attractors: Volume Two
*The Infinite Sea: Volume Three

*denotes a Tor Book

ETERNITY'S END

JEFFREY A. CARVER

TOR®

A TOM DOHERTY ASSOCIATES BOOK
NEW YORK

This is a work of fiction. All the characters and events portrayed in this book are either products of the author's imagination or are used fictitiously.

ETERNITY'S END

Copyright © 2000 by Jeffrey A. Carver

Edited by James Frenkel

A Tor Book
Published by Tom Doherty Associates, LLC
175 Fifth Avenue
New York, NY 10010

www.tor.com

Tor® is a registered trademark of Tom Doherty Associates, LLC.

ISBN: 0-812-53443-3

First edition: December 2000
First mass market edition: October 2001

Printed in the United States of America

0 9 8 7 6 5 4 3

For my family, with love—
Allysen, Alexandra, and Julia

Acknowledgments

This book took four years to write: forever, it seemed; an impossible task. But at last it is done. I owe more than the usual debt to those who helped me through it, and this is where I get to thank them publicly.

It's customary to save one's family for the end in this sort of thing, but I'm going to break with custom and start with the very best: my wife Allysen, without whose love and support this book would never have been written. Thanks for that and so much more. And what better fans could any writer ask for than my own smiling daughters? They've spent more time in my office than anyone but me, and I doubt they've known what a wonderful, continual encouragement they were to me. (Note to A. and J.: I look forward to many more years of having you peer over my shoulder asking, "Are you almost done yet, Daddy?") And thanks to my brother, Charles S. Carver; he knows why. (Note: if you happen to be in the fields of personality or social or health psychology, you may know his books, too.)

Next in line comes my dauntless writing group, more than twenty years old now! Mary Aldridge, Richard Bowker, Craig Gardner, Victoria Bolles. Three times—and more!—they read this book through, in all of its stages of semi-intelligibility. They helped me think through many a complex twist of plot and character, and circled the dumb parts so you wouldn't have to. I am forever grateful. Whatever the flaws in this book, you can't blame them.

Nor can you blame my friend and editor, Jim Frenkel, who waited patiently, patiently, while I wrote, rewrote, and rewrote some more. Thanks, Jim—and not just for that, but for the hard editing, too. And while I'm at it, thanks to Tom Doherty and the rest of Tor Books, and my agent Richard Curtis, for letting me take the time I needed, not just to finish the book but to finish it right.

A special note of thanks is due to Freeman Deutsch and Noel Friedman, for their generous contributions to the Big Sisters auctions. I hope you enjoy your namesakes' appearances.

And finally, there's you the reader. Some of you are new; some of you have been waiting a *lonnng* time for the next book. Some of you, in the CompuServe and SFF Net forums, helped me search for a title. Well, here it is, and welcome aboard! Thanks for waiting, and for all the letters and emails that helped me persevere. You can't imagine how much they meant to me.

Now, enjoy.

Arlington, MA
August, 1999

ETERNITY'S END

PART ONE

Time is the Image of Eternity.
—Plato

They who see the Flying Dutchman never,
never reach the shore.
—John Boyle O'Reilly

Prologue

GHOST SHIP

STREAMERS OF light seemed to coil in slow motion through the corridors of the starship.

The passengers and crew moved in great straining ripples as they walked through the ship, carrying on the business of living, if living you could call it.

The passengers breathed and ate and slept, and socialized after a fashion. And the crew carried out their duties, seeing to the needs of the passengers, repairing machinery, and tending the makeshift hydroponics gardens that supplied the nutritional needs of the five hundred-plus souls on board. The riggers on the bridge continued to search the skies for a way home, peering into the bewildering mists of the Flux and wondering what in the name of creation had gone wrong. Their lives consisted of ennui and bewilderment, interrupted at long intervals by heart-pounding excitement when they sighted another ship . . . followed inevitably by piercing despair, when their efforts to make contact ended in failure.

It was a strange and terrifying limbo, here where the starship floated, trapped in some enigmatic layering of the Flux, exiled from the "normal" regions of the Flux—never, it now seemed clear, to restore contact with the universe of its origin. Time had ceased to flow in a rational or comprehensible manner. It wafted through the ship unpredictably, a drafty breath sighing through unseen holes in the walls of eternity.

Among the passengers was the Jones couple, married on the ship two days after departure, who now passed their time in each other's arms—not in perpetual bliss as they had once imagined, but huddled despairingly in their cabin where time, through some twist of fate, had slowed to an even more glacial crawl than elsewhere on the ship. There they found, if not hope, then at least a hint of sorrowful consolation in each other's company, as their bodies lay entwined in near-stasis.

In the lounge one level down, a pair of old men played the same game of chess they'd been playing for who knew how many years. Had they ever gotten up to eat or sleep? No one could quite remember. The ship's captain seemed always to be nearby, moving more speedily than the chess players and yet without aging, stumping up and down the corridors, muttering to himself like a tormented Ahab of the stars.

And in his own cabin, the tailor stared for the thousandth time at a slip-needle and bind-thread as though he had just now found them in his hand. His movements stretched out in ghostly projections; he felt as if his life were hardening in amber. He could not fathom what was happening, and had long ago given up trying. And yet, even as he worked, his thoughts reached out to his sister and her family. It was their homeworld he had been bound for, their home lost now across the twin gulfs of time and space. He no longer held any hope of seeing them again, but he could not stop wondering how much time had passed on the outside, and whether anyone he had known off the ship was still alive.

With a prolonged sigh, the tailor drew the slip-needle in a slow, glittering slide down the shoulder seam of the coat he was altering. The seam split, and came together again a centimeter to the right. He studied the results for half a lifetime . . . and then, with great deliberation, moved on to the next stitch.

Chapter 1
ESCAPE FROM CAPTIVITY

RENWALD LEGROEDER'S eyes darted frantically, scanning for traffic as he guided the scout craft away from the spacedocks. His heart pounded with fear. No general alarms yet, thank God; but how long could that last? The scout's flux reactor hummed, alive and ready. The rigger-net would spring to life at his command; but first he had to get clear of the outpost.

The raider outpost loomed like a threatening mountain cliff over his back as he powered the tiny ship away. The spacedocks were an enormous, malignant structure, blotting out most of the view of the Great Barrier Nebula that stretched across the emptiness of space behind him. He felt terribly alone.

He snapped on the intercom. "Maris—if you can hear me, we're away from the docks!" She couldn't answer, and probably couldn't hear. She was the only other person aboard—the only one with the guts to flee with him.

Guts—or insanity? Don't be distracted. Switch over now . . .

He lurched out of the pilot's seat and climbed into the rigger-station, yanking the secondary maneuvering controls into position over him. The scout crawled toward the departure area; he dared not go faster. *Don't draw attention.*

Had they been spotted yet?

Their only hope was stealth. Any of a dozen ships of the pirate fleet could destroy him at a moment's notice. Clear of the docking zone, he popped thrust toward the inner marker. *Gently!* He ached to punch full power . . . to sprint away . . . *Keep it slow, keep to the traffic patterns, don't arouse suspicions . . .*

About ten minutes had passed since their shootout with the guards at the maintenance docks. Only a miracle would get them away from here and out of pirate space alive.

Was Maris alive even now? He risked a glance, toggling a monitor to the first-aid compartment. Maris lay in the med-unit, eyes closed, arm flung across her chest. Neutraser burns ran down her neck and shoulder. Life signs flickered on the screen . . . URGENT: SHOCK: IMMINENT NEURAL FAILURE . . . He'd started the suppression-field; there was nothing more he could do.

The com blasted, jolting him back: *"SCOUT SIX-NINER-SEVEN. STATE YOUR CLEARANCE."*

His breath caught as he jabbed down the volume. He stalled, keyed the mike, held it as Departure Control repeated its demand through the static. Every second took him a little farther out. If stealth didn't work, confusion might.

He drew a ragged breath. "Departure Control, Scout Six-Niner-Seven, emergency departure Bravo Eleven Alfa. No delay, please—answering an emergency call from sector—"

Something lit up behind him, and he choked off his words. A blaze of lights in the central docking region, and at least one large craft moving out. After him? He scanned hastily. Weapons arrays were coming to life at three key defense points.

"SCOUT SIX-NINER-SEVEN, TERMINATE YOUR VECTOR AT ONCE. WE HAVE NO EMERGENCY CLEARANCE ACTIVE. BRAKE TO DEAD STOP! PREPARE FOR INSPECTION! REPEAT—"

Legroeder cursed, shut his eyes for an instant, and hit the fusion thrusters.

The scout ship rocketed past the marker buoys, shot across traffic lanes, leaving a plasma trail in its wake. Scan ahead, behind . . . The weapons arrays on the station were opening fire now, a cluster of neutraser bursts glittering against the dark of space. He veered far out of the departure path, away from the direction they'd expect him to flee, and aimed for the guard field that flanked the channel, all energy and spatial distortions. A neutraser beam flashed over his screen.

Hold tight, Maris!

Another blaze of neutraser fire caught his port-side sensor, partially blinding him. He veered left, then down, and right. The ship tumbled as it hit the guard field. The hull shuddered, and he nearly lost control. Then he was through the field, into the Dead Man's Zone that enclosed the departure lanes.

Clouds of plasma swirled over the ship's prow. There was a reason for this place's name. The spatial distortions were nearly impossible to maneuver through. But if he could manage it, pursuit should be impossible.

A neutraser burst leaked through the field and spun weirdly around the ship. His viewscreen and console began to glow with St. Elmo's fire. He couldn't wait any longer. He slammed the maneuvering controls shut, drew a deep breath, and closed his eyes. At his silent command, the rigger-net billowed out into space, a shimmering sensory web. He caught some fragmentary words on the com: *"—Going under in the Zone—must be crazy—!"*

And then he reached out with his arms in the net like wings on a plane, and banked the ship down out of the fiery cauldron of normal-space and into the chaos of the Flux.

THE STAR rigger's Flux: a higher-dimensional realm where reality and fantasy became strangely merged, where landscapes of the mind intersected with the real fabric of space, where space itself flowed and surged with movement—and where a rigger's skills could vault him across light-years, or send him spiraling to his death.

Legroeder was flying in a thunderstorm, wind shear and lightning buffeting and rocking him. His senses stretched through the net into the Flux, as though his head and torso were the bowsprit of the ship. His arms embraced the storm, mists of streaming air coiling through his fingers. He drew around him the only image he could think of: a stubby-winged airplane bouncing through cumulonimbus, stubbornly refusing to surrender.

The craft bucked violently. It was hard to keep a heading in the turbulence—but he had to, if he was going to get through the Dead Man's Zone and out the other side. The raiders had sown mines throughout the Zone, which was almost redundant; the place itself was a natural minefield. Everything was distorted here, normal-space and the Flux alike. A fragmentary remnant of some ancient violence of creation, it was a perfect place of concealment for the raider base. Only a maniac would try what Legroeder was trying now . . .

He fought back a rush of fear as he skidded through the wind shear. Why had he thought he could do this? *It's impossible!*

No sooner had he thought it than the turbulence grew worse. He realized why, and fought to control himself. His mere thoughts could reverberate disastrously into the Flux; he dared not allow panic or fear.

Stay calm!

He drew a long, slow breath and tried to refocus the image. *Keep flying the ship. Whatever happens, we're away, better off than before.*

What lay ahead? Mines. Treacherous shoals. Dead ships. But where? *Change the image: make it transparent.* Sooner imagined than done; the energies swirling before him were too powerful to easily remap. He blinked once to alter the contrast, and now he could make out distant flecks of darkness against the glowing whirlwinds of the storm. Shipwrecks? He couldn't tell.

WHOOM!

Something blazed off his port-side, a mine exploding. He veered hard, avoiding damage. His heart raced. The explosion had opened a path through the storm, a shadowy tunnel in the clouds. A way through? It wouldn't last long. He circled back, scanning for pursuit. Nothing: maybe they'd given him up for dead. Fly, now—*fly!* The currents were tricky; he had to scull with his arms to bring the ship back.

As he banked into the tunnel, the winds seemed favorable—but at once he sensed his mistake. *A trap.* He banked hard the other way, back into the current. It was too strong now—it was pulling him into the passage. He cursed and hit the fusion motors—dangerous in the Flux!—and continued thrusting until he'd veered past the opening. At that instant the passage twisted closed, then erupted with a belch of fire. The blast caught his wingtip and snapped him head over heels.

The storm clouds spun around him. By the time he pulled the ship out of the tumble, he'd lost his bearings completely. He felt a rising panic.

And then he heard a voice softly, distantly, in his mind. *You must keep your center . . . stay calm. Legroeder, you'll find the way through. Aren't you the one who showed me, after all?*

His heart stopped as he recognized the voice-from-memory, his old shipmate Gev Carlyle, as clear as if Gev were right here looking over his shoulder. Keep your center . . . stay calm . . . how often had he said those things as the younger Carlyle had fought to master his instincts and fears?

Keep your center . . .

The storm clouds tossed the little vessel like a wood chip on a pounding sea. He again breathed deeply and focused inward, and then from his center focused outward—and as he did so, the clouds shimmered to transparency, just for an instant. He drew another breath. *Center and clarify . . . illuminate . . .*

For a moment, he felt the almost tangible presence of his old friend. The feeling was so powerful, it drove the fear back a little more, and the storm clouds grew pale. Through the twists and turns of the moving currents, he began to glimpse a path: a fold in the Flux, and a current slipping through . . .

THE ESCAPE had happened so fast Legroeder had scarcely had time to think. For seven years since his capture, he'd looked for a chance to make a break. But the guard was too

tight, the fortress impregnable and light-years from anywhere. No one had ever escaped alive; that was what they
said. Everyone said it; everyone believed it. A few had tried:
they were dead now, or being tortured, in solitary.

And yet . . . even as he'd piloted their raider ships for
them, preying on innocent shipping in the wilds of Golen
Space, even as he'd worked for the bloody pirates, to stay
alive, he'd never stopped watching, planning, ready to bolt
if the opportunity ever arose.

He never dared talk about it with the other prisoners. But
he'd sensed that Maris was of like mind. He'd had a rough
time among the pirates, but she'd had it worse. At least he
hadn't been raped and abused, in addition to being forced
into labor. She was a tough woman and an angry one. He'd
thought often of Maris as a friend he'd not really gotten to
know.

When the chance finally came, he had just seconds to
make up his mind. They were coming off a ship-
maintenance detail in the outer docks—Jolly, Lumo, Maris,
and Legroeder—when a Flux capacitor in the main docking
room blew, spewing a jet of blazing plasma across the room.
Two of the guards, caught in the discharge, went sprawling.
Several other workers helped the injured out of the compartment, leaving two guards with four conscripts. Through
the haze and confusion of the leaking plasma, Legroeder
spotted a fallen handgun lying under a console. He glanced
at Maris, who stiffened as she saw it, too.

Legroeder thought furiously. The remaining guards were
occupied by the plasma leak, and behind Legroeder and the
other prisoners, just down a short corridor, a small ship was
docked, its airlock doors open. His crew had just finished
checking it over; it was ready to fly.

Maris's eyes met his; they both shifted to the far side of
the compartment, where the guards were shouting, trying to
cut off the plasma discharge. Maris gave a shrug that
seemed to ask a question. Legroeder nodded. He looked at
Jolly and Lumo, standing to one side watching the plasma

jet. Neither was likely to be of help. When he glanced back, Maris was moving toward the gun.

One of the guards finally noticed. "Hey, what are you doing?" he shouted, unslinging his neutraser rifle. The plasma plume partially obscured his view, but it wouldn't block his shot.

Legroeder barked a warning.

Maris came up with the gun.

A crackle of neutraser fire: Maris cried out and spun around, wounded. But not too wounded to fire back: from a crouch, she fired three times. A shriek of pain told Legroeder that she'd hit one of the guards. She dropped the gun, staggering.

Legroeder snatched it up and caught her by the arm. The second guard was coming around the end of the dying plasma jet. Legroeder aimed and squeezed. There was a flash: the guard staggered back. Jolly and Lumo were flattened against the wall, dumbfounded. "Come with us?" Legroeder yelled.

Jolly shook his head. Lumo was frozen with fear.

Legroeder squeezed several bursts into the guards' com panel. "Then don't try to stop us!"

Jolly nodded, terrified.

"Let's go," Legroeder grunted, straining to support Maris with his shoulder.

" 'Kay," she gasped. "Let's go." Her face was taut with pain, but she was already struggling toward the airlock.

It took about five minutes for him to get them both onto the scout, seal the airlock, secure Maris in the med-unit, and get to the bridge to power up.

A lifetime.

THE SCOUT ship dashed out of the Dead Man's Zone like a fish through a broken net. Legroeder steered furiously, searching for currents leading away from the raider outpost. They were past one danger, but hardly in the clear.

BAROOOOOM!

The ship shuddered violently.

He kept flying as he scanned for the source of the explosion. The crimson and orange clouds of the Flux billowed past like foaming surf over the prow of a submarine. But he needed to stay fast and maneuverable. He reshaped the image to one of a jet fighter, fast and sleek, streaking through the misty clouds. He veered left and up, then right and down, trying to make them a difficult target if anyone was aiming. They were back in the main channel, on much the same course a raider ship might take in leaving the area. If the raiders were still pursuing . . .

BAROOOOOM!

Light flashed in the clouds to the left, and Legroeder banked hard away. Three raider ships burst out of the clouds in pursuit. Hell's furnace! he thought. They'd been waiting to see if he made it through the Dead Man's Zone. He was damn sure he'd surprised them.

He barreled over into a steep dive, pulling away, but only momentarily. They'd never get out by the main route—which left just one other way.

Maris! he shouted into the intercom. *We're going out through the Chimney. If you can hear me, hold tight!*

Ignoring the lurch in his stomach, he pitched his dive past the vertical, undercutting his own flight path, then rolled the ship upright for a view of the raiders that were coming around in pursuit. They were not quite as desperate as he was, or as crazy, and they took a wider turn. They were firing, but accomplishing nothing but lighting up the clouds. Legroeder rolled inverted again to search the clouds below, and finally spotted a region of shadow that marked the opening of the Chimney, a passage so narrow and hazardous it was known as the Fool's Refuge. He stretched himself into the longest, fastest fighter plane he could imagine, and aimed straight down into the murky darkness of the Chimney.

Pounding waves of energy suddenly assailed the net. *TURN BACK! TURN BACK! OR YOU WILL DIE! . . . DIE! . . . DIE!* The raiders were broadcasting into the Flux.

It was the booming of a steel kettle drum, projected so

as to come right up out of the Chimney, reverberating through the very fabric of the Flux and booming into the rigger-net as though he were inside the drum. Legroeder knew the source of the thunderous noise, knew it well—he'd used it himself, against others—and yet, even knowing that it was only a trick to inspire fear, he couldn't help being shaken. He *was* doing something insane.

WILL DIE . . . WILL DIE . . . WILL DIE . . .

There was no escaping the echoes. He could only try to ignore them. Try not to be afraid.

A deep, dark fissure was opening in the clouds below. That was where he had to go—and if he had any doubts, they were erased by bright flashes of light behind him—neutrasers and flux torpedoes. He took a sharp breath and spun down into the fissure. Into the Chimney. From this moment on, the pursuers would be the least of his worries. If they were stupid enough to follow, maybe they would all die together . . .

DIE . . . DIE . . . DIE . . .

Suddenly he was in darkness—midnight in the Chimney. Glints of light flickered in the cloud walls ahead. Deadly Flux-abscess, or other terrible ways to die.

He glanced back. *Damn.* They were still coming after him. No time to worry; he was dropping at tremendous speed through a shaft of raging turbulence. He fought vertigo as the cloud walls flashed abruptly light/dark/light/dark, until he could scarcely focus on them at all.

Something flashed past him from above, a coruscating veil of light that turned and rose back up toward him like a vast fishnet of energy seeking to ensnare him. He grunted and narrowed the rigger-net to a needle and arrowed straight down. The fishnet veil billowed up and around him again with a twinkle and a *whump*. The ship bucked but kept moving—until a blast of secondary turbulence hit him.

With a shriek, the ship lurched out of control and careened sideways toward the deadly Chimney wall.

Chapter 2
INQUEST

THE RIGGERGUILD hearing room was dead silent.

Its domed ceiling was coated with a multi-optic laminate that made it glitter like stars against darkness. Legroeder let his gaze wander along the ceiling, and for an instant the stars were transformed into the luminous features of the Flux.

Skidding toward the Chimney wall, pulsing with light: pockets of quantum chaos, where images could distort without warning. The ship plummeted through, and suddenly the landscape was strobing with stark reversals of light and contour. Behind him was the sparkle of weapons fire. Before his heart could beat twice, a spread of flux-torpedoes exploded, triggering a cascade of distortions that sent his ship spinning . . .

The holograms of the three panelists sat at the curved table at the front of the room. Legroeder sat with his young, Guild-appointed counsel, a Mr. Kalm-Lieu, facing the panel from a smaller curved table at the center of the room. Despite the expansive design, the room was designed to keep the inquest panel and its subjects rigidly separated. Only Legroeder and Kalm-Lieu were physically present.

From the front bench, the holo of the RiggerGuild inquest chairwoman was speaking. Her voice seemed hollow, devoid of inflection. Legroeder couldn't remember her name, had never met her in person. "Rigger Legroeder, please remember that there are no charges being considered in this hearing. Our purpose is not to determine guilt or innocence, but rather to determine if you should be represented in this matter by the Guild of Riggers. We hope you understand the distinction."

Legroeder shrugged in disbelief, staring up at the dome . . .

The pocket of Flux-abscess turned itself inside out with the torpedo blast, hurling him into a sudden opening that he felt rather than saw, a breach caused by the blast. Steering by an intuition that seemed almost supernatural in its accuracy, he threaded his way through . . . and by the time he caught his breath he was coasting free in the open Flux, well away from the Chimney, away from the raider outpost, and apparently free of pursuit.

Spying a current leading away from that place, he rode it for a long time, until he could decide on a destination world. The choice in the end was made for him; there was only one major world within his reach that was free of pirate influence: Faber Eridani, well beyond the borders of Golen Space. Not an easy flight in a small ship; but if he wanted to be free, really free, he had no choice but to risk the distance. Checking frequently on Maris, still in near-stasis in the suppression-field, he rigged their ship toward a new life and new hope for both of them. Toward the protection of the Centrist Worlds and the RiggerGuild, their own people . . .

Legroeder trembled with anger. He avoided looking at the inquest panelists. To have escaped from the raiders and gotten Maris to a hospital here, only to be put on trial for collaborating with pirates in his own capture? It was impossible! Who would have believed it?

"Counsel, may we take that as a yes?" asked the voice of the inquest chair.

Kalm-Lieu glanced uneasily at Legroeder. "Yes, Ma'am."

"In that case, Rigger Legroeder, we will put the question to you again. Please describe your actions, seven years ago, leading up to the taking of *Ciudad de los Angeles* by the Golen Space pirates."

Legroeder felt as if he were standing outside of his own skin, watching himself—a small, olive-skinned man with gloomy eyes, trying to comprehend the trap he was caught in. He sighed and rubbed his temples, forcing himself to suppress that image.

"Let me understand," he said slowly. "I've just escaped from forced servitude with interstellar pirates, and I've come to you for sanctuary and offered to tell you everything I know about the pirates' operations. But all you care about is what happened when my ship was *attacked* seven years ago—and whether you can pin something on me for it?"

"Not at all, Rigger Legroeder. But we must have the facts before us."

"Including facts about the ghost ship? About *Impris?*"

The voice of the court inclined her virtual head. "You may describe your capture in whatever way you feel is appropriate. Now, if you please . . ."

Legroeder closed his eyes, summoning the events of seven years before. The beginning of the nightmare . . .

THE *CIUDAD* de los Angeles was a passenger/cargo liner, a good ship carrying a modest but respectable manifest of fifty-two passengers and twenty-four crewmembers, including the rigging complement of seven. Legroeder was among the more seasoned of the riggers, three of whom were stationed in the net at any given time. Legroeder's specialty was the stern-rigger station, the anchor; he was to be the maintainer of good grounding and common sense, especially if the lead and keel riggers became carried away with the imagery of the Flux. He was known as a rigger with a a dark outlook, but solid reliability.

Ciudad de los Angeles was en route to Varinorum Prime—a little close to the edge of Golen Space, but on a route considered fairly safe from pirate attack. It was Legroeder who first sighted the other ship in the Flux, flickering into view off to the portside of the *L.A.* It appeared to be on a course parallel to theirs. The sighting of any other ship in the Flux was such a rare event that the image was branded on his memory: the ship long and pale and silver, like a whale gliding slowly through the mists of the Flux.

He didn't just see it, but heard it: the soft hooting of a distress signal so thin and distant as to be nearly inaudible.

Take a look off to the left, and tell me if you see what I see, he said, alerting his rigger-mates to the sighting. He strained to get a better reading on the distress signal. He couldn't quite make it out, or decipher where the ship was going; it seemed to be passing through a layer of the Flux that was separated from the *L.A.* by a slight phase shift, though he couldn't quite discern a boundary layer.

I see it, too, said Jakus Bark from the keel-rigger position. *Is that a distress signal? We'd better call the captain. Bridge—Captain Hyutu—?*

When Captain Hyutu checked in, he reported that he could just make it out in the bridge monitors. By now, the distress beacon had become more audible. The codes didn't match anything in the *L.A.*'s computer, but soon they could hear voices calling across the gulf: "This is *Impris* . . . *Impris* calling . . . please respond . . . we need assistance . . . this is *Impris,* out of Faber Eridani . . ."

Legroeder and the rest of the crew were stunned.

Impris.

The legendary Flying Dutchman, the ghost ship of the stars? Impossible! Officially, *Impris* was nothing more than a legend—a ship that vanished into the Flux during a routine voyage, well over a hundred years ago. *Impris* was hardly the first, nor the last, ship to vanish during a voyage, especially in time of war. What made her the stuff of legend was the recurring rumor of ghostly sightings—not just by one ship or two, but by generations of riggers. None of the sightings was clear enough to constitute proof of her continued existence, but the number of alleged sightings was enough to keep the legend alive.

It was as though *Impris* had faded into the Flux, never to reemerge into normal-space; and yet neither had she perished. So the tale in star riggers' bars grew: that she was like the Flying Dutchman of old, the legendary haunted seagoing ship whose captain and crew were doomed to sail through eternity, lost and immortal and without hope.

Myth, said the Spacing Authority's archives.

Real, said the riggers in the bars.

In the Flux it could be hard to tell the difference.

Not this time, though. Legroeder saw the ship moving through the mists of the Flux, and his crewmates saw it, too. Captain Hyutu of the *L.A.* was no rigger, but he was an experienced captain who could read the signs in the monitors as well as any. When he heard the distress call, he gave the order to the riggers: *Make slow headway toward that ship. See if you can bring us alongside.* An announcement echoed throughout the *L.A.* They were preparing to render assistance to a vessel in distress.

The *L.A.* closed the gap between the ships.

And that was when the Flux began to light up, the misty atmospheres around the *L.A.* suddenly flashing like a psychedelic light show. *What the hell—?* muttered Legroeder.

And then the sounds . . . *DROOM! DROOM! DROOM!* . . . like booming kettle drums, drowning out the distress call. Legroeder's heart pounded as *Impris* turned toward the *L.A.*, and for a few seconds he thought the sounds were coming from *Impris* herself.

Are they turning to dock? called Jakus, from the keel.

They're on a collision course! cried the lead rigger. *Hard to starboard! Captain, sound collision!*

Legroeder's stomach was in knots as he struggled, in a Flux that had suddenly become turbulent and slippery, to bring the stern around. Captain Hyutu intoned, *Steady as she goes! Steady, now!* The riggers obeyed, Legroeder holding his breath. And then Legroeder saw what Hyutu must have seen in the monitors: the other ship was shimmering and becoming insubstantial. As she closed with the *L.A.*, turning, the front of her net cut across the portside bow of the *L.A.*'s.

And for just an instant, Legroeder felt the presence of the rigger crew of the other ship, heard their cries of anguish and despair, felt their awareness of *him* . . . and then *Impris* and her crew became altogether transparent, and suddenly were gone.

Gone.

A heartbeat later, another ship emerged from the mist in its place: a spiky and misshapen ship with a grotesque, leering face on its bow and weaponry bristling down its side. *What—?* Legroeder breathed, along with the others in the net, and then someone cried, *Golen Space pirates!* The booming crescendoed: **DOOOOM! . . . DOOOM-M-M! . . . DOOOM-M-M!** The Flux came ablaze with light, and it was all coming from the marauder ship. It had been hiding behind *Impris,* using the doomed ship as a shield.

Away! Legroeder cried, and they tried to turn the *L.A.* away to flee, but it was already too late. The pirate riggers had spun threads of deception and fear, and they seemed to have a command over the stuff of the Flux that the *L.A.*'s crew did not. Within minutes, the two ships were bound together in coiling, distorted currents of the Flux, and then the marauder ship was pulling them up through the layers of the Flux into the emptiness between the stars. As they emerged into normal-space, light-years from the nearest help, the emerald and crimson haze of the great Barrier Nebula obscured even the sight of the distant stars that had been the *L.A.*'s destination.

The boarding was a brief, violent affair. The liner, carrying some limited armament against the perils of Golen Space, was hopelessly outmatched. Her fighting potential lasted about ten seconds, and by then half a dozen members of the crew were dead. To Legroeder it was a blur—emerging from the net and staggering out onto the bridge, he was met by armed raiders and herded through the ship's passageways at gunpoint, through clouds of noxious gas and smoke. From the airlock, he was shoved through a passage tube to the raider ship—and then into a hold with about thirty other people; and his life as a free man came to an end.

THE COURT panel interrupted him, stating that they would get to his "captivity period" at a later time. Legroeder fell silent, gazing at the panel. "We'd like to know," said a man sitting to the right of the chairwoman, "if you can tell us a little more about the fate of others from the *Ciudad de los Angeles*." This man represented the Spacing Authority, the enforcement agency that dealt with pirates. Why was *he* here, if Legroeder wasn't on trial? "How many would you say were taken prisoner, and how many executed by the pirates?"

Legroeder stared at the man. "That's hard to say. I didn't see it all."

The man wore a pained expression, as though he hated asking such questions. "But what would be your best estimate?"

Legroeder turned to Kalm-Lieu in frustration.

Kalm-Lieu's soft, boyish features were twisted into a frown as he rose. "My client does not have that information, if it please the panel."

"Counsel," said the chairwoman, "we're only trying to complete our picture of the situation. If your client would give his best *estimate* as to the number captured, and the number executed by the pirates—"

Kalm-Lieu glanced at Legroeder and shrugged.

Legroeder sighed. "If I had to *guess*, I'd say that maybe half to two thirds of the crew and passengers were taken prisoner, and the rest killed during the boarding. Is that what you mean by executed?"

"Wouldn't you call it an execution to kill innocent people in the process of hijacking a ship?" asked the man from the Authority.

"Sure," Legroeder said. "I would." But in his seven years, he'd seen people summarily executed who weren't doing anything at all to resist. The thought of it made him ill, even now. But as for casualties in the boarding, he had never really known the true number, because most of them he never saw again—including Captain Hyutu. But he had the oddest recollection about the captain, one that had stayed with him all these years. In his last glimpse of Hyutu, he had seen on the captain's face an expression of outrage and indignation, as the raiders stormed through the ship. This would have seemed exactly right on another man's face. But not on Hyutu's: the man had always looked stiff and expressionless when he was angry. Legroeder had always wondered about that.

"I see," said the panelist.

The chairwoman of the panel spoke inaudibly to the other two. Then: "That will be all for today, Rigger Legroeder. Thank you for your cooperation."

KALM-LIEU ACCOMPANIED Legroeder to the Spacing Authority holding center and waited while Legroeder made a call to the hospital. No change in Maris's condition. Returning to join his counsel in the small visitors' lounge, Legroeder shook his head. Maris had been in a coma since their escape, and was now under intensive care in the hospital. Legroeder was torn between gratitude that she was alive and guilt that she lay in a coma because he'd encouraged her to flee with him. It wasn't just the wounds; the pirates had put implants in the back of her head specifically programmed to deter escape. The doctors here were at a loss as to how to remove them without killing her. Legroeder wondered if they'd ever even *seen* an implant, much less a booby-trapped one.

"I'm sorry," Kalm-Lieu said, handing him a cup of coffee—real coffee, supposedly, not like what they'd had at the raider outpost.

"Not your fault," Legroeder murmured, taking a sip. It burned going down.

"The news is on," Kalm-Lieu said, pointing to the holo in the corner of the room.

"News," Legroeder whispered. How long had it been since he'd seen news—uncensored journalism about what was happening in the rest of the world. Rest of the world, hell—the rest of the known galaxy. He cradled his coffee and watched.

". . . Discussions toward improved trade relations with the Narseil homeworlds hit a snag today with revelations of a preferred status offered to Clendornan traders by the Narseil merchant coalition. Reports suggest that the Faber Eridani Trade Minister would be unwilling to open further doors to Narseil business interests without some clear, reciprocal action on the part of the Narseil. This seems to contradict earlier predictions that the Faber Eridani government would actively court increased trade with the Narseil . . ."

Legroeder sipped the hot liquid, letting the reporter's words drone on. These concerns felt so alien—Narseil, Clendornan, interstellar trading relations.

"You know," Kalm-Lieu said, shaking his head. "I wonder how long they'll go on pretending we don't need decent relations with the Narseil. It's not as if we have to *like* each other. We could still work with them."

Legroeder glanced at him, slightly dazed. *Who cares?* he thought. *The politicos have always hated the Narseil.*

"Stagnation," Kalm-Lieu said. "That's what's happened to our society. And it started a long time ago . . ."

"You still trade with other worlds, don't you?" Could things have changed that much?

Kalm-Lieu darted a glance at him. "Sure—of course we trade. But mostly just among humans—and Centrists, at that. In a lot of ways, we're a very isolationist society. But it's been so long, now . . ."

Legroeder squinted, trying to absorb what the lawyer was saying. He'd been away from civilization for seven years, and Faber Eridani wasn't his homeworld, anyway. But now that he was here, he supposed he'd better start learning . . .

The holo broke into his awareness again. "In other news from the offworld front, a preliminary RiggerGuild inquest has been looking into the strange case of a fugitive star rigger who arrived on this planet ten days ago, after a harrowing escape from Golen Space raiders—"

Legroeder choked on his coffee.

"Seven years ago, Renwald Legroeder served aboard the interstellar liner *Ciudad de los Angeles* when it was captured by raiders. Spacing authorities reportedly suspect Rigger Legroeder of collaboration in the capture, quoting sworn testimony that the rigger deliberately steered the *Ciudad de los Angeles* toward the pirate ship. Rigger Legroeder, through his Guild-appointed attorney, denies all such allegations. Questioned by the press, Spacing Commissioner Ottoson North issued the following statement."

The reporter's image was replaced by that of a well-groomed man wearing a dress tunic with a gold, interlocking-ring insignia over his breast. "Let me make one thing clear: this Spacing Authority will never tolerate collaboration with pirates. However, Rigger Legroeder *must* have the opportunity to defend himself in a court of law. He has found his way to Faber Eridani after a death-defying escape from a pirate outpost, and he has every right to expect fair treatment. As long as Ottoson North is commissioner, he will get that fair treatment. For all we know, the man may be a hero."

The commissioner was interrupted by a reporter shouting, "What about allegations he was responsible for the loss of *Ciudad de los Angeles*?"

Commissioner North waved his hand to acknowledge the question. "We're *investigating,* as is our responsibility. All allegations will be examined. But there has been no guilt established yet—and it's the job of the Spacing Authority to determine *facts*, not allegations. It's also the job of the RiggerGuild to protect and defend the interests of riggers everywhere, and that includes Rigger Legroeder, as well as his colleagues. So let's allow the investigation to move forward, and let the evidence speak for itself, shall we?"

The holo cut away from North and back to the news desk, where the anchorwoman continued, "Despite these words of reassurance from Commissioner North, potentially damning testimony by the rigger himself was released by the RiggerGuild . . ."

The image cut to Legroeder saying, "We steered toward the other ship—" cut to "—the captain told us to maintain our course—" cut to "—we were headed directly toward the pirate ship—"

The holo cut again, to the panelist asking how many had been killed and captured, then to Legroeder snorting, looking with apparent disdain toward the ceiling. Then just his voice, answering, "Hard to say . . ."

And finally an echo of Commissioner North's voice: "— let the evidence speak for itself . . ."

Legroeder's coffee cup fell and rolled across the floor. He stared at the holo image, scarcely hearing as his attorney repeated, "That's not the way you said it. We can challenge that. Don't worry, we can challenge that . . ."

"THE PANEL has reached its decision," the chairwoman said, with the barest of opening prelimaries.

Legroeder drew a sharp breath. *Reached its decision—?* He turned to his attorney.

Kalm-Lieu was already on his feet. "Madame Chair, this is highly irregular! My client has not yet concluded his testimony."

"Irregular it may be," said the chairwoman, with a severe expression. "Nevertheless, the decision is made."

"May I ask *why* the rush to judgment?" Kalm-Lieu demanded.

"This is not a *judgment,* Counsel, merely a decision as to the RiggerGuild's involvement in the matter." The chairwoman sounded chiding. "The full legal proceedings have yet to begin."

"Nevertheless—"

"However, I will inform you that the reason for the timing is a request from the Spacing Authority that we move quickly so that the full investigation *can* begin. This matter is viewed very seriously by the Spacing Authority, and it is the wish of the RiggerGuild to cooperate to the fullest extent possible."

The chairwoman stared down, clearing her throat. "Now, then. It is the finding of this panel that your actions while serving aboard the *Ciudad de los Angeles* did in all probability bring harm to the passengers in your care, and to the shipmates with whom you served. Such actions are therefore in violation of RiggerGuild Code—"

Legroeder grunted in disbelief and tried to turn to his lawyer, but his head felt frozen in ice.

"—we find a high probability of conviction for dereliction of duty in Spacing Authority Court, and therefore have determined that the Guild of Riggers should not represent you in this matter."

"Madame Chairman, I object!" he heard his counsel protesting, miles away, it seemed. "My client has not even been permitted to present his full case—"

"Mr. Kalm-Lieu, please be seated. I repeat, the purpose of this hearing is simply to determine whether the RiggerGuild should take a role in the matter. We have determined that the Guild should not become involved."

The attorney was clearly flustered. "I really must—I mean, what about the circumstances? What about starship *Impris*? You have released misleading information to the press, and have given us no opportunity to—"

"Please be silent, Mr. Kalm-Lieu, while I finish reading the decision. You will have an opportunity to make a statement at the end."

The attorney stood for a moment, shaking with frustration. Finally he sat down beside his client.

Numbness was overtaking Legroeder. He stared at his thumbs and listened impassively as the rest of the judgment was read.

"Thank you. Rigger Legroeder, your service aboard *Ciudad de los Angeles* was a sacred trust. If you had acted with greater care and wisdom, you might have saved many passengers and crew from death or captivity at the hands of Golen Space pirates. Instead, in your belief that you had seen the legendary ship *Impris,* you pursued a phantom. As a result of those actions, your ship was boarded, and all hands taken or lost."

"Objection! He was hardly the only crewmember involved in the actions! What about the captain—?"

"Mr. Kalm-Lieu, silence! Rigger Legroeder was not the only one, perhaps, but he is the only one to stand here before us."

There were locked, silent glares for a half dozen heartbeats.

The chairwoman went on, "There remains the question of Rigger Legroeder's complicity with the society of raiders, in captivity. That we leave to the Spacing Authority to determine. But by his own admission, he participated in as many as fifty or sixty acts of piracy—"

"Before he had the opportunity to escape!" protested Kalm-Lieu.

Was it Legroeder's imagination, or was his counsel losing spirit?

"—in those acts of piracy, uncounted innocent people may have lost their lives. Therefore, it is the judgment of this panel that Rigger Renwald Legroeder's membership in the Guild of Riggers shall be suspended, and he shall not be granted the protection of the RiggerGuild in this matter or any other."

Legroeder sat rigidly silent as the chairwoman concluded, "Mr. Kalm-Lieu, your vigorous defense of your client has been admirable. However, you will not be continuing in this role. Mr. Legroeder, following the conclusion of this hearing, the Guild legal offices will no longer be available to you. You will be remanded back to the Spacing Authority, for their judgment in the matter of your alleged complicity with the Golen Space raiders.

"And now, Mr. Kalm-Lieu. If you or your client would like to make a final statement, this is your opportunity."

Kalm-Lieu rose slowly, obviously struggling to find words to express his disbelief. "Ma'am, I can only reassert that this is a blatant violation of my client's rights. I ask for a moment to confer." He turned to Legroeder. "If this were a trial, I could file an appeal. But under the Guild rules—" He raised his hands helplessly. "This is extremely irregular. I had no idea this was coming."

Legroeder did not look at his lawyer, but slowly raised his gaze to the holo of the chairwoman. He was beginning to feel his anger burn through the numbness, but he had no target for it. He knew, as certainly as he knew his own name, that this panel could not possibly be acting on its own. It was just too irrational. But who were they acting for? He couldn't even guess. Finally, he glanced at his attorney.

"Do you want to voice your personal protest, for the record?" asked Kalm-Lieu.

"You've said it all already," said Legroeder. He raised his voice to fill the room. "It's clear this hearing has been a fraud from the start. So why belabor it?"

Kalm-Lieu grunted. He rose unsteadily, glanced back at Legroeder twice before speaking. "My client . . . protests the injustice of this hearing, Madame Chairman. He has nothing further to say." Kalm-Lieu sat again, fidgeting.

With a motion of her hand, the chairwoman sealed the judgment in the computer. "Then this hearing is adjourned." A moment later, she and the rest of the panel shimmered and vanished.

Legroeder forced himself up, a tightness in his chest.

"I'm sorry," Kalm-Lieu said.

So am I. "What's my next step?"

Kalm-Lieu's eyes darted around the room uneasily. "I'm sorry, but I am no longer permitted to advise you. They've taken me off your case."

Legroeder felt his breath go out. "You mean I'm just left to twist in the wind?"

Kalm-Lieu gestured awkwardly. "That's not the way *I* want it, but—"

"But that's the way it *is*, isn't it?" Legroeder gestured toward the empty hearing table, the fury rising at last in his voice. "You mean you can't even tell me what's supposed to happen next? Who do I get to represent me with the Spacing Authority? What am I supposed to do now?"

"You're free to hire counsel, of course." Kalm-Lieu lowered his voice, and looked as though he were going to shrink away altogether. "Perhaps I could recommend someone—"

"Hire counsel?" Legroeder thundered. "I've been a prisoner in Golen Space for seven years, and I have nothing

but the shirt on my back, and you tell me I can *hire counsel?*"

"I understand how you must feel—"

"Oh, do you?" Legroeder snapped. He shouted toward the front of the room. "Do you understand what it's like to be *betrayed* by the people who are supposed to be defending you? Do you understand that?"

"Please. This won't help."

"Then what will? Sitting here arguing RiggerGuild code, instead of trying to find out why they're blaming me for what a band of pirates did to my ship?"

Kalm-Lieu's face was filled with remorse. Two security agents had appeared at Legroeder's side. "I'm afraid," Kalm-Lieu said, "you'll have to stay in confinement with the Spacing Authority until your hearing. Unless you can post bond . . ." His hands fluttered helplessly.

Legroeder snorted in disgust. Post bond? With what? Even his back salary from the owners of *Ciudad de los Angeles* was in escrow until the matter was settled. He shook his head once—and without another word, strode out of the hearing room, the guards close behind.

Chapter 3

HARRIET MAHONEY

ONLY A few people were being held at the Spacing Authority holding center at the time of Legroeder's arrival: two small-time smugglers and an orbital tug pilot being held for a license violation. It was rare for a rigger to be kept there, since riggers usually fell under the protection of the Guild; if they were detained at all, it was generally at RiggerGuild quarters. Legroeder felt humiliated, being held like a common criminal.

At least it wasn't a cell. They'd put him in a small room with a bunk, granting him some privacy and a com-console linked to the center's library, but few amenities beyond that. The primary amenity it lacked was freedom. He spent the first few days exercising until he ached, trying to regain muscle tone after the long journey cooped in the scout ship. The guards looked on, bemused, as he cycled the exercise machines over and over through their full range of movement: stretches, lifts, crunches, steps . . . until he was puffing with exhaustion. When he wasn't working out, he was mostly lost in grim thought, worrying about Maris, and trying to understand how an escape from the pirates of Golen Space could have brought him to this.

How could he possibly be accused of trying to give *Ciudad de los Angeles*—"City of the Angels"—into the hands of the pirates, even if he had made an error in judgment while rigging? How could he have known that Golen Space raiders were hiding behind the phantom ship, waiting to strike? He hadn't even been in command. Captain Hyutu was the one who'd given the order to approach *Impris*.

And yet, he found himself almost beginning to doubt his own actions. Many had died; and many more had endured, and continued to endure, captivity among the Golen Space pirates. Few if any would escape as Legroeder had. He could only hope, forlornly, that those remaining behind would not suffer reprisals because of his escape.

By the end of his third day of confinement, there was still no word on the beginning of his hearing. Kalm-Lieu was gone, and Legroeder had done nothing about finding new legal assistance. He did spend some time on the com-console, running searches through the RiggerGuild finder service to see if any of his old rigger friends happened to be on Faber Eridani. The closest he found was a stopover six months ago by a rigger he'd known casually ten years before. It didn't look as though he would find help from any friends here.

Faber Eridani! he thought. *Why'd I have to pick Faber Eridani?* But really, where else could he have gone?

All this mulling was getting him nowhere. He dumped his cup of cold coffee into the sink and returned to sit at the tiny desk beside his bed. He stared at the seascape holo on the wall, a painting of a ship in a storm, and thought, *Ghost ship. It wasn't a damn ghost. But who will believe me? Who—*

"RENWALD LEGROEDER!" A voice outside in the hall.

Legroeder sat up, blinking. What the hell time was it? Morning . . . he didn't even remember getting into bed, much less going to sleep.

"Rigger Legroeder!" repeated the voice, closer now.

Legroeder stared at the locked door. "Yeah! What is it?"

The door clicked and opened. Vinnie, the tall, skinny guard, stepped in. He was half human and half some kind of Trakon hybrid, built like a rail with bulging hips and shoulders. A weird-looking alien guard dog stood at his side, rumbling from the back of its throat. The guard claimed it was just a purr, but Legroeder had never wanted to test the claim. Vinnie grinned. "Wake you up?"

Legroeder shrugged.

Vinnie chuckled, tugging at a strand of cordlike hair. "An easy life, eh—sleeping in whenever you want? Well, it's coming to an end. Gather up your things. You're leaving."

"Leaving?" Legroeder struggled to his feet. "Why, are they transferring me somewhere?"

Vinnie's laugh sounded like a twang. "The hex, no. You're free on bail."

"Bail? I haven't posted any bail."

"Someone did it for you."

Legroeder stared at him, uncomprehending.

"What's the matter? I thought you'd be happy as a pig in the dew."

"I *am* happy. Don't I look happy? Who was it?"

The guard unclipped a compad from his breast pocket

and consulted it. "Says here the name's Harriet Mahoney. Friend of yours?"

"Never heard of her." Legroeder blinked in bewilderment. "Who is she?" His mind raced through possibilities and came up blank. Could it have been some forgotten affair, from years ago? Ridiculous. He'd only been on this planet a few times, and certainly had never had an affair here.

Vinnie seemed to read his thoughts, and winked. "Well, she's a real looker, if you ask me."

Legroeder frowned, then shrugged. Out was out, so what did he care? He grabbed the duffel bag a kind soul at the Guild had given him, and began to pack. It didn't take long.

"Ready?"

Legroeder shouldered the bag, stepped carefully around the guard dog, and nodded.

"Let's go."

As LEGROEDER was being processed out through the Spacing Authority lobby, he peered around for anyone he might recognize. It wasn't until he had passed through the security barriers and filled out six or seven forms without reading them that he heard the name Mahoney again, and turned to see who was attached to it. He followed Vinnie into a small room off to one side of the lobby. An older woman rose from a plastic chair to greet him. Her face, lined with years, was slightly reddish as though sunburned, and her hair was mostly silver, with streaks of black. She wore tastefully designed chrome-rimmed glasses. She was old enough to be his grandmother. Legroeder glanced at Vinnie, who winked. *A real looker.* But she moved with an energy that Legroeder did not associate with older women. "Renwald Legroeder?" She extended a hand. "I'm Mrs. Harriet Mahoney. I've arranged for your release."

Legroeder shook her hand. "Pleased to meet you. And— thanks, I guess. Will you think I'm ungrateful if I ask, *Who are you?*"

She smiled. "I may be your only friend at the moment. If you would consent to join me for breakfast, I'd be happy to explain. I've been over your release forms, and they're all in order."

Legroeder stared at her. "Are you a lawyer or something?"

Mahoney adjusted her glasses. "That is correct. It's my understanding that you need a lawyer. Yes?"

"Well—"

"I've posted your bond, and you're free to leave. You're prohibited from leaving the planet, however, pending your hearing with the Spacing Authority. Is that satisfactory to you?" She peered intently over the tops of her glasses.

Legroeder shrugged. "Do I have any choice?"

Mrs. Mahoney's eyes twinkled. "None that I can see. Shall we get out of here and have breakfast?"

Legroeder pursed his lips. "Can I visit a friend in the hospital first?"

HE GAZED down at Maris for a long time. She lay motionless in the hydro-bed, the scars on her face and neck not looking much better under the clear bandages than they had when he'd first brought her in. But it wasn't the scars that bothered him; it was the stillness. Whatever had most damaged her was invisible. According to the doctors, her basic physiological signs were strong; but with the raider implants controlling certain basic cortical functions, they couldn't predict when—or if—she'd return to consciousness. "We just don't have much experience with these augmentation devices," one of the doctors said. "It's hooked so deeply into her autonomic nervous system that we don't dare meddle with it—not without knowing more. But if there's no activity in a week or so, we'll try some cortical stimulation and see what happens."

Legroeder touched Maris's forearm. Fellow prisoner. Comrade in arms. He knew little about her life before her capture by the pirates. She was taken from a ship he didn't know the name of. They'd served together a few times on raider missions. But really . . . it was those two or three minutes on the maintenance dock, when they'd made the decision to trust each other, that had bound them together. He gripped her limp hand and leaned close to her ear. "You did well, Maris. We're out. We're away from the pirates. You'll be free, just as soon as you pull yourself out of this. Just one more escape." He hesitated. "I have to go and . . . do some things. Try to clear up a mess. I'll be back . . . as soon as I can."

He straightened with a sigh. Rejoining Harriet Mahoney in the hallway, he walked out of the hospital, into the late morning sun.

HARRIET TURNED out to have a good knowledge of coffee shops in the area, and they settled on one that featured a holosurround of a desert, complete with spike bushes, umbrella trees, and a proliferation of desert flowers. A spring ran past their table—real rock and real water—and for the first time in years, Legroeder had the feeling that if he stayed in this place long enough, he might conceivably begin to relax. Or he might, if he weren't bristling with questions. He held most of them long enough to wolf a plate of waffles and drink a mug of—not just real coffee, but *good* coffee. He had forgotten what the aroma of good coffee was like, filling the air around his head.

Finally he said, "Mrs. Mahoney—or should I call you—?"

"Harriet," she said, resting her teacup in its saucer. "Please. I hate formal names. They make me feel old."

"All right. Harriet. Is there a Mr. Mahoney?"

"There was. He passed away almost twenty years ago."

"I'm sorry."

A smile twitched at her lips. "Don't be. I think he was glad to get away from me. I was a hard person to live with, back then. Probably still am." She chuckled. "And tell me, how do you prefer to be addressed, Rigger Renwald Legroeder?"

"No 'Rigger' anymore, it looks like." He grunted, feeling a surge of anger. "Just Legroeder."

"Then Renwald is your surname?"

He shook his head. "Legroeder is just what people have called me since I was about five. My friends, I mean."

"Very well, then—Legroeder. You'd like to know why I bailed you out." Harriet reached up to her right ear, as though to adjust her earring. A holo a dozen centimeters high sprang up on the table between them. It was a boy, six or seven years old, sitting on a lawn with a pet Althasian minibear. The boy was smiling and waving at the camera. "Have you ever seen this young man?" Harriet asked, and for the first time since they had met, Legroeder heard a tremor in her voice.

Legroeder bent to study the image. "Should I have?" He looked up at Harriet. "He looks a little like you. A relative?"

"My grandson," she said. "My only grandson. He was a passenger on the *Ciudad de los Angeles* when she was lost." Her voice caught. "When you were attacked by the pirates."

Legroeder's throat tightened as Harriet gazed somberly at the holo. "His parents were separated, you know. His father—my son—was killed in a building collapse here in Elmira. Bobby was on his way to join his mother on Thrice Varinorum. On the *L.A.*" Harriet touched her earring again, and the image disappeared. "For years, we didn't know anything, except that the ship had failed to arrive, and was presumed lost."

Legroeder said nothing.

"Until two years ago, when we first heard that the *L.A.* had been taken captive . . . by the gentlemen pirates of Golen Space."

Legroeder laughed hollowly. "Gentlemen?"

Harriet reached for her teacup, but her hand started shaking, and she pulled it back. "By the murdering, cutthroat bastard pirates of Golen Space," she whispered.

Legroeder closed his eyes, willing the memories away.

"I'm sorry," Harriet said. "You suffered, too. I can see it in your eyes. Are you sure you never saw Bobby? You have no idea what might have happened to him?"

Legroeder shook his head. "I never really saw the passengers, even during the flight. And after we were taken prisoner, they split most of us up. I don't even know what happened to most of my crewmates. I just never saw them again."

Harriet's gaze narrowed. For some reason he suddenly felt uncomfortable under her scrutiny. He squinted past her, across the broiling desert that landscaped the coffeehouse. "Not even Jakus Bark?" she asked.

"*Jakus?*" Legroeder started at the name, and blinked down at the table, and a holo of Jakus Bark, the keel rigger who'd been in the net with him at the time of the pirate attack. But in this picture, he looked . . . older. "Where did you get this picture?" Legroeder demanded.

"I'll tell you in a moment. May I ask, when did you last see Rigger Bark?"

"Well, I—" Legroeder's voice caught, as he remembered being marched off the bridge of the *L.A.* with the other riggers. Jakus had been visibly shaking with fear; he'd looked even more scared than Legroeder was. Legroeder cleared his throat. "We were both pulled off the *L.A.*, onto the raider ship. But we were taken into separate holds."

"Did you see him again?"

"Just once. A few weeks later, I guess. At the raider outpost. We'd been going through nonstop indoctrination, telling us if we wanted to live we had better learn to cooperate." Legroeder swallowed, feeling the familiar pain. "In the case of the riggers, that meant flying their ships for them." He struggled to put words to the memory. "Jakus— that one time I saw him—I got the feeling he'd adapted more than most. I was still pretty resistant—not outwardly, but in here." He tapped his chest. "But Jakus . . . *wasn't*. He didn't seem as angry as the rest of us. After that, I never saw him again."

"Would it surprise you to learn," Harriet asked, rotating the image to better display Jakus's face, "that he's here on Faber Eridani?"

"*Here?*" Legroeder was stunned.

"Right here in Elmira, in fact. He's been here for two years. I talked to him not long after he returned."

"But—" Legroeder stammered "—they said at the inquest that no one else from the *L.A.* had returned. How could they—don't they know he's here?"

"They not only know," said Harriet, "but it was his testimony, in large part, that led to their decision against you."

Legroeder stared at her in bewilderment. "But that's not— I didn't hear anything about any testimony—"

"No. You didn't," said Harriet. "And isn't that interesting—especially given the damaging nature of his testimony?"

Legroeder opened his mouth again. "*What* damaging testimony?"

"I can show it to you later, if you like. The fact that they hid it from you is something we can use in your defense. I assume the testimony will be brought into an actual trial. But in this preliminary inquest, they didn't need it; all they wanted was to deny you the support of the RiggerGuild. But someone pretty high up must be scared about something. Or at the very least, dismayed by your sudden arrival here. Dismayed enough to use hidden testimony against you, apparently in hopes of shutting you away forever. Why do you suppose they would do that?"

"I don't know. Why?"

Harriet sighed, frowning. "That's what we have to find out. I think there's a lot more to this than meets the eye. But right now, all I have is suspicions." She studied Legroeder for a moment. "It wasn't easy to get you freed on bail, you know. I think the only reason they *set* bail for you was that they weren't expecting someone like me to come along and help you." She pressed her fingertips together in concentration. "You know, if you're convicted of setting up the *L.A.* for capture, you could be mindwiped, or locked away for life."

Legroeder tightened his lips, but said nothing.

"I'm sorry—you didn't need to hear that." Harriet attempted a smile. "So, Rigger Legroeder . . . would you like me to represent you?"

"Well, I don't have any m—"

"There's no fee up front, just a percentage if we ever go for damages and collect anything. We probably won't. I'm not in this for the money."

Legroeder was having trouble focusing; his head was filled with questions. "Did Kalm-Lieu bring you in on this? Are you a *good* lawyer?"

Harriet grinned. "Does it matter? I'm the only one you've got. But yes, I think I'm a pretty good lawyer. And no, Kalm-Lieu didn't bring me in—though I think he was *relieved* that I stepped in." Her grin vanished, and she looked deadly serious. "When I spoke with Kalm-Lieu, he seemed—*scared*, is the only word I can think of. Though he tried to hide it, I'm sure he's glad to be off the case."

Scared? Frustrated, Legroeder would have thought. Angry. But why scared? "Why are *you* doing this? If it scared Kalm-Lieu?"

Harriet steepled her fingers. "I've been following your case with great interest—along with everything else I can find that's related to the *Ciudad de los Angeles*. As I said—there's a *lot* going on here beyond procedural irregularities—but I'm just beginning to put together what it is. I'm hoping we can help each other find out, and get you exonerated."

"But *why*? Why are you helping *me*?"

"Because somehow there's a connection between what's happened to you and what happened to Bobby," she said softly. "And one way or another, I am going to find out what it is."

Impossible. Bobby's in Golen Space. He's gone, Legroeder thought, shutting his eyes. He took a deep breath. "What chance is there of learning anything about your grandson? Realistically."

"Maybe no chance. Maybe it's hopeless. Maybe I'm just a crazy old lady, and I wouldn't blame you if you thought so. But I want to know if Bobby is alive or dead. *I want to know what happened.*" For a moment, she seemed surprised by her own vehemence. Then she poured some tea from the insulated pot into her cup. "And I want to make sure everyone else knows, too. Would you like some more coffee?"

Legroeder's head was spinning. He felt as if a real sun were beating down on his head, here in this holodesert in the midst of the cafe; he could feel the heat like the blast of an oven. "Yes, sure," he muttered. "More coffee would be wonderful. . . ."

Chapter 4
COMRADE IN ARMS

THE RECORDING of the testimony was a bit muddy from imperfect decryption. Access to it had been restricted by the RiggerGuild office, and two years ago Harriet had paid a PI to snag an illicit copy off the datagrid. According to the private investigator, the copy he'd intercepted was being transmitted to a location known to be a datastop for an extremist political group called Centrist Strength. What Centrist Strength had to do with a RiggerGuild inquest on a five-year-old lost ship, the PI had been unable to say. Centrist Strength was new to Legroeder. According to Harriet, it was a group headquartered here on Faber Eridani, but active on a few other worlds as well, which was known for an almost fanatical advocacy of new human expansion into the galaxy. Their philosophy was laden with heavy overtones of what they called "Destiny Manifest"—a belief that the stars, all of them, were destined for human conquest and habitation. Though lip service was paid in their pronouncements to cooperation with other species, the overall tenor of their activities seemed to be one of a human supremacist movement.

Harriet remained silent as Legroeder watched the initial part of Jakus's testimony. It was a fairly straightforward account of the raider attack, with one critical omission: any mention of the sighting of the lost starship *Impris*. Legroeder stared, tight-lipped, waiting to see how his old shipmate would explain the *L.A.*'s entrapment by the pirate ship. The Jakus on the recording looked like a different person from the one Legroeder had served with on the *L.A.* For one thing, he seemed far more tentative and cautious, and—Legroeder thought—*old*. Or perhaps not so much old, as *worn*. His time in servitude with the pirates had taken a heavy toll. A datachip implant flickered on his left temple—a gift of the pirates, no doubt. Legroeder wondered how he'd been received here on Faber Eridani with that implant; there was a lot of prejudice about that sort of thing on many of the Centrist Worlds—or at least there had been seven years ago. Not for the first time, Legroeder uttered a prayer of gratitude that he had been spared that particular indignity.

Eventually someone on the inquest panel had asked Jakus why the *Ciudad de los Angeles* had slowed enough to make it vulnerable to attack in the first place.

"Watch Jakus's face here," Harriet murmured.

The haggard-faced man on the screen hesitated before answering. Jakus looked as though he were running two or three possible scenarios through his mind. Twice, he seemed about to speak, before biting back words. He scratched at the implant on his temple, cocking his head slightly. Finally he answered in a gravelly voice, "It was because of a bum image from our stern-rigger. He had some kind of crazy idea he'd seen a vessel in distress." Jakus seemed to be trying to laugh at the idea; but the laugh couldn't quite get out. "The rest of us and the skip—we saw right through that. It was just a clumsy deception thrown up by the pirates to confuse us."

"And were you confused?" asked an offscreen voice.

"Well, *yeah*—things got pretty damn hairy pretty fast." Jakus barked a laugh, almost a cough. "But still—"

"What?"

"Well, you know. If our stern-rigger hadn'ta fallen for it,

we could've steered clear. The pirates didn't come after us 'til after we'd slowed."

"But if you and the captain saw through it, couldn't you do something?"

Jakus shook his head. He seemed to gain a measure of self-confidence, now that the lie was out. "You got to understand about rigging—it's a team thing. It only takes one person pulling the wrong way, or getting confused, to bring the whole thing down around you. And that's what happened—we got bad input from the stern, 'cause our guy there kept sayin' he saw something. And even though the *skip* said—well—" Jakus's voice faltered. "Well, he said to stay right on course, but we couldn't—couldn't do it—"

"Because of the stern-rigger?"

"Yeah."

"And his name was—?"

"Oh, uh—" Jakus hesitated, swallowing. "Groder, I think it was. Is that right?"

A different voice from the panel: "There was a Renwald Legroeder listed on the rigger crew. Is that who you mean?"

Jakus's voice shook a little. "That's it."

"Thank you—"

"Legroeder," Jakus repeated, his voice gaining strength. "It was Renwald Legroeder."

The recording ended.

Legroeder stared at the blank screen. "I'll be a Goddamned son of a monkey."

Harriet turned off the monitor and settled into the wing-backed chair behind her office desk. The sunlight coming in through the window was turning golden orange with the approach of sunset. "What do you think?"

"I think," growled Legroeder, "that I'd like to have a talk with my friend Jakus."

"Well, I'm not sure *that* would be very productive." Harriet lowered her glasses to hang from the chain around her neck. "That was two years ago. The inquest is history now. But if we could *prove* that there was falsification—"

"Prove it? The sonofabitch lied through his teeth because

he thought he'd never have to answer to me." Legroeder tried, with difficulty, to keep his anger under control. "You don't happen to know where he lives, do you?"

"I haven't really kept track—"

"You aren't going to bullshit me now. My lawyer?"

Harriet scowled. "All right. As your lawyer, I strongly recommend that you not attempt a personal confrontation. You're out on bail, if you haven't forgotten."

"I haven't forgotten. But something rotten's going on, and we aren't going to find out what by sitting here. So do you know where Jakus is, or not?"

Harriet stared at him for a moment. "Let me see what my PI's latest files say." She put her glasses back on, tapped on a small screen on her desktop and studied it before looking back up at Legroeder. "According to this, he lived for a short time in a RiggerGuild complex on the outskirts of the city; then he left the Guild and moved out into a small condominium. He hasn't flown since, though he's done some work for a maintenance outfit at the spaceport." She studied the screen again. "What would a rigger do for a maintenance company, I wonder."

Legroeder rubbed his chin, remembering many days on maintenance details at the raider outpost.

"Whatever it is, he spends a lot of time at it. According to this—and I must commend my PI for staying current—he's moved out of his condominium and is spending *all* of his time with that maintenance outfit."

"You mean he's sleeping at the spaceport?"

"Apparently so." Harriet closed the screen again. "The question is, what should *we* do?"

Legroeder rose, shaking, and not from the coffee. "I know what *I* have to do."

"That's not what I meant, Legroeder. Will you please let me do this *right*—and keep you out of jail? Let my PI make the contact."

Legroeder closed his eyes, as the memory of all that had happened to him welled up, bringing his rage with it. He struggled to push the rage back under. "I'm sure you're probably right. But this . . . is something I have to do my-self." *Jakus Bark. My friend. Backstabbing bastard.* He forced a smile at Harriet. "I'll be good. I'm not going to start a fight with him or anything. But I am going to talk to him. I mean, we used to work together. That counts for something, right?"

"Legroeder, please—"

"And after this, I'll follow your advice. I promise."

THE SPACEPORT field was a sprawling place, bordered with countless hangars and repair shops and administration build-ings, and few signposts for strangers. Legroeder had trav-eled in and out of this port before, but he still had trouble finding his way around; the place had changed in seven years. They'd taken his RiggerGuild ID away from him, but as it turned out, security was nonexistent on this part of the field.

Legroeder stood at the edge of the decayed plasphalt pavement of a parking lot and squinted across the complex into the setting sun, trying to figure out from Harriet's notes just where the maintenance hangar might be. He was at a remote corner of the field, and it looked more like a down-at-the-heels industrial park than a spaceport.

Harriet's words echoed in his mind. *What are you going to do if he won't talk to you?* She'd given him a good, long stare. If his own grandmother had still been alive, she couldn't have conveyed greater sternness.

He hadn't had an answer, and still didn't. But he knew one thing: pushing paper wouldn't get answers out of Jakus. He had to confront the man himself.

The line of hangars just across the way looked promising. He started across the crumbling tarmac, clenching and un-clenching his fists. When he realized what he was doing, he pressed his open hands to his sides.

The shop he was looking for was the last one, marked by a dusty sign: CAVANAUGH AND FARHOODI RIGGER SYSTEMS. The hangar door was shut, so he tried a small door to one side. It opened with a creak and banged shut behind him as he entered. Inside was a dingy outer office, with a scarred counter and one dirty chair; behind the counter was an inner office, with a light on. A voice—a woman's—called out: "Who's there, eh? We're closed!"

"Hello!" he called, and moved around the end of the counter to peer into the office.

A thick-waisted woman in a faded jumpsuit stood behind a desk, holding a dusting wand. "That door was supposed to be locked," she said, sounding annoyed. "They're closed here."

Legroeder showed his empty hands. "I'm sorry—I'm not here on business, exactly. I'm looking for someone named Jakus Bark. I heard he worked here."

The woman's eyes narrowed suspiciously. "Yeah, I guess he does. What d'you want with him?"

The words came reluctantly. "We used to . . . rig together. I haven't seen him in years, and I, um, wanted to say hello. I'm . . . interested in getting into his line of work."

The woman squinted at him, obviously processing his words slowly. He couldn't tell if she recognized him from the news or not. Perhaps she wasn't someone who watched the news. "I'll check," she said. She touched a com switch on her collar, spoke subvocally for a moment, then nodded. "What's your name?"

He told her, and she relayed the information. Her eyebrows went up once, as she listened to a reply. Finally she shrugged. "It's okay, I guess. He's in the, what do you call it, sim'lator three, out back." She hooked a thumb over her shoulder, indicating a door behind her. "Don't touch nothin', though, 'cause you probably shouldn't be in here." She muttered under her breath for a moment before adding, "and be quick, eh? I don't want to get in no trouble."

"I'll be careful," Legroeder assured her. "Thank you." He passed through the door into the hangar and paused to let his eyes adapt to the gloom. There were several modest-sized spacecraft in the hangar, with various bays and panels open for servicing. One small craft was in an advanced stage of disassembly. Legroeder had to skirt around the front of the first ship just to find a path back through the hangar. Two ship-lengths back, against the righthand wall, he saw three giant grey eggs. They were rigger-station simulators, used for testing repairs to the flux-reactors and rigger-net equipment. As he walked back alongside the ships, Legroeder saw a flicker of actinic light on the far side of the hangar. Someone was working with a photonic torch on the underside of a third ship.

The door was slightly ajar on simulator three, letting light escape. As he approached, he could see a full bank of controls and monitors—and the back of someone's head. Suddenly the door slid the rest of the way open, and the couch rotated, and his old comrade Jakus Bark blinked up at him from beneath the brim of a battered duckbilled cap. "Legroeder," he said, rubbing his left temple. An implant glittered beneath his fingertip. "Wha'd'ya know?"

Legroeder's voice caught. "Hi . . . Jakus."

Jakus squinted. "Shit, man—good to see you. I heard somethin' on the news that you got out. Man, I didn't think *anybody* would ever get out of there. Way to go!" His voice trembled as he peered up at his former crewmate.

Legroeder had to reach to find his own voice. A host of feelings were welling up inside him, most of them violent. "*You* made it out," he said finally. "Imagine my surprise to hear about it."

Jakus's eyebrows went up a fraction of an instant, and then he laughed—a nervous bark that echoed in the little chamber.

"They didn't seem to remember it at the RiggerGuild," Legroeder said, with forced evenness. "About you coming back."

"Well, heh—that's the RiggerGuild for you."

"Yeah," Legroeder said. "So how'd you get out?"

Jakus shrugged. "I was on a raider ship that blew up, a couple of years ago. I was the only one to get out alive. How about you?"

"Escaped," Legroeder said. "Not a fun story."

"I bet not." Jakus gave another nervous laugh. He gestured at the simulator panel. "You like my new job?"

"Yeah, real nice place here." Legroeder looked around at the hangar, then back at Jakus. "I get the feeling you're not too happy to see me—if you don't mind my saying so."

"Well—no, it's not that, man. Shit—let me get out of here—" Jakus lurched forward out of the reclining seat of the rigger-sim and grabbed the edges of the doorway "—I been sittin' awhile." He hauled himself out of the giant egg and stood upright, towering over Legroeder by half a dozen centimeters. His hair looked thinner than when Legroeder had last seen him, and his face more chiseled. "I just wasn't expectin' you to turn up here out of the blue, that's all. How the hell'd you find me, anyway?"

Legroeder ignored the question and glanced around again. "What is it you do here, anyway?"

"Pretty much what it looks like." Jakus shrugged. "Refit ships, test 'em out for the customers. It's not too fancy a shop, but it's better than some places we've seen, right?"

Legroeder didn't argue. No doubt it was better than the raider outpost, where every moment was a battle between fear and despair. But how had a rigger like Jakus wound up in a place like this? He'd been a good rigger in his time. Before the pirates . . .

"So what's up, Renwald?" Jakus leaned back against the simulator shell. "You didn't drop in just to say hi, I guess."

Legroeder felt his gaze narrow. "No. I didn't." A knot was tightening in his stomach. "I came, actually, to ask you about your testimony before the RiggerGuild."

"Testimony?" Jakus grunted.

"Yeah. Testimony. About the *L.A.* You want to tell me about that? About why you lied to the Guild about what happened to the *L.A.*?"

Jakus looked away. "Don't know what you're talkin' about," he said, rubbing his nose. "I didn't give no testimony."

Legroeder snapped, "I saw the recording of it, Jakus. You blamed *me* for what happened to the *L.A.*"

Jakus gave that nervous laugh again. "Nah, I didn't really.

I remember now. I didn't know what you were talking about at first."

Legroeder drew his lips back. "You said you and the captain tried to tell me that *Impris* wasn't real—and that *I* was the one who put the ship in danger."

Jakus looked down at the floor. "Yeah, well—isn't that what happened?"

"You sonofabitch!" Legroeder slammed the side of his fist against the shell of the simulator. "You saw that ship just the same as I did! And it was Captain Hyutu who gave the order to move in, and you backed me up when I made the identification!"

Jakus's eyebrows went up. "Did I?"

"Yes. You damn well did." Legroeder let his breath out with a hiss. "What'd those pirates do to you, Jake? Back then, I could've trusted you to tell the truth. Instead of lying to protect your own little ass—"

Jakus jerked a little.

"—or whatever the hell it is you're protecting."

Jakus said nothing. His right eye had begun to twitch, and he rubbed at the tic with his finger. As Jakus shifted his head, Legroeder noticed that a second implant behind the man's right ear was alive with a tiny, erratic red flicker. Was Jakus connected to something or someone right now? Or was he just thinking?

"The *truth*," Jakus said slowly. "Easy word for you to use. What exactly do you mean by it?"

Legroeder snorted. "Do I have to explain the word 'truth' to you?"

Jakus worked his mouth for a moment, then cocked his head toward the glowing interior of the rigger-sim. "Well, hell, Renwald, we're both riggers, right? We both know that half the time there's no way you can tell what's real and what isn't, in the Flux."

"Don't bullshit me, Jakus. Is that thing whispering so loud in your ear you can't even hear yourself think anymore? You and I know what we saw."

"Not real," Jakus said, with a shake of his head. "Not real."

"You know it was real!" Legroeder shouted. "You heard the distress call. Hyutu wasn't even in the net, and *he* heard it! If anyone was responsible, it was him."

"Show some respect," Jakus said, with a shiver. "A little respect for the dead, okay?"

Legroeder was drawn up short. "Who's dead?"

"Hyutu." Jakus make a throat-slitting motion with his finger. "The pirates did 'im. You and me, we were lucky to get out with our skins."

Legroeder scowled. "How do you know? Did you see it happen?"

Jakus shrugged. He tapped the silver disk on his temple. "You had one of these Kyber things, you'd be able to see things a whole lot better. Understand stuff you don't know now."

Legroeder felt a chill at Jakus's words. *Kyber things?* "Is that it?" he whispered. "Is that what took your—" he struggled for the right word "—*integrity* from you? The implants?"

That brought a sharp laugh from the other man. "We gonna talk about *my* integrity now? Oh, yeah, Renwald— you must've had loads of integrity, the whole time you were pilotin' pirate ships, burning innocent people. Oh, yeah."

Legroeder's face grew hot with bitterness and shame. "I did what I had to, to survive. I don't deny that I rigged ships for them." There had been no choice, if he'd wanted to live. And it was only his exceptional skill as a rigger that had kept him free of an implant; he'd persuaded his captors that he could rig better without those things in his head.

"Yeah, Renwald, that's right. We did what we had to to survive. You and me both. Maybe if you'd taken a chip you wouldn't be so high and mighty about it now." Jakus sneered. "Listen, it was sure nice of you to stop by, but I've got work to do."

Legroeder realized he had allowed Jakus to derail him from his point. "You lied to the Guild, Jake. Thanks to you,

I'm losing my certificate and getting framed for what happened to the *L.A.*"

"I'm real sorry about that," Jakus said.

"Sorry enough to go back and tell the truth? Tell them we both saw *Impris?* Tell them it was real?"

Jakus shook his head. "I told you already—there's no way to know what was real and what wasn't. You thought it was real, and I didn't. Neither did the captain. I ain't gonna change my story about that."

"The pirates were real enough, weren't they?" Legroeder growled.

"Oh yeah, they were real." Jakus glanced over his shoulder, as though worried that someone might overhear. "Listen—we're both damned lucky to have gotten away at all. Maybe you're losing your certificate—not that I have one anymore, either—but at least you got away alive. Isn't that more important than your certificate? You can still work."

"Work? More likely, they'll lock me away for life. If they don't mindwipe me instead."

Jakus shrugged. "Whatever."

Legroeder glared into the oppressive gloom of the hangar, his thoughts burning. "So that's it? You're going to let them frame me?"

Jakus shrugged. "If you want to put it that way. Now, like I told you, I gotta get back to work."

"Yeah." Legroeder made no attempt to hide his disgust. "You get back to work. See you around, Jake." He turned away.

"You don't know what the truth *is!*" Jakus called after him. His words were punctuated by a loud metallic slam.

Legroeder glanced back; Jakus had climbed back into the sim and slammed the door shut. Legroeder angrily strode away, alongside the half-assembled spaceships. What the hell was going on here? Why was it so important to *someone* that he take the fall for the *L.A.*? It was obvious this wasn't just Jakus's doing. It seemed to be coming from somewhere in the Spacing Authority. But what conceivable connection could there be between the Spacing Authority and a lowlife like Jakus?

As he made his way back toward the front of the hangar, he also began wondering what sort of a shipping firm would use the services of a place like this. He couldn't *imagine* a respectable company letting a contract here. He stared at the ships for a moment, then realized what was bothering him. They looked . . . armored. A glint of light from a single overhead lamp reflected off the hull plates with a greenish sheen, almost the color of oxidized copper. It wasn't obvious, and he might not have noticed if he hadn't just spent seven years around raider warships. But that looked like arnidium hull armor, very hard and resistant to radiation. With a surreptitious glance around, Legroeder crouched to peer beneath the nearest ship.

Not much to see—a number of closed bays on the underbelly of the craft. He looked beyond, to the next vessel; he could see the feet of a worker moving around with a work light. With a mechanical hiss, a bay door opened beneath the far ship. Legroeder squatted lower, trying to get a good look. The feet moved left, then right. The light flickered. For an instant, he caught a glimpse into the just-opened bay. *A weapons compartment.* He caught sight of three slim shapes—dark, sleek and oily-looking. Then the light moved away, leaving darkness. He heard the hiss of the bay door closing.

Legroeder rocked back on his haunches, letting his breath out slowly. Those were flux-torpedoes, he was nearly certain. Now, what the hell was a ship like that, in a place like this, doing with flux-torpedoes? The vessel bore no markings of police or navy. So what was it? Undercover? Criminal? Right here at the main spaceport? How could the Spacing Authority let that kind of thing slip by their security . . . unless they knew?

Legroeder rose silently from his crouch. The sooner he got out of here the better. As he started walking again, he saw the worker with the photonic torch moving between the two ships; that must have been the man who'd opened and shut the weapons bay. The man looked at him without friendliness, and stared as Legroeder walked on, heart pounding, toward the front exit.

As he paused near the office door, Legroeder heard footsteps, then a bang of metal. An unfamiliar voice shouted Jakus's name; Jakus shouted back. Legroeder stood in the darkness, listening. As the voices rose in heated argument, he bit his lip. *What have I done?* Without quite knowing why, he started edging back the way he had just come. Moving alongside the nearer ship, he tried to make out the conversation. He caught his own name—then Jakus yelling, "—didn't tell him anything!" The voices became more muffled. He strained to hear the rest of the argument, thought he heard the word *Impris*. The anger in the voices was unmistakable, and made the speech hard to understand. Then . . . there was a bone-jarring thump and a prolonged moan. That was followed by a third voice in a language Legroeder didn't understand—Veti Alphan, maybe. There was another thump, and the cry of pain cut off. Then footsteps, moving away. What the hell was going on?

Stay out of it, Legroeder.

But he couldn't just walk away, could he? Someone had obviously overheard his argument with Jakus.

God damn it. He looked around for something, anything, that he might use to defend himself. Nothing. Cursing silently, he crept back toward the simulator pods. The door to the third sim was open, light pouring out. He pressed his lips together. Maybe he could act as if he'd come back for something he forgot. "Jakus, you still there?" he called softly. No answer; but a door slammed shut way in the back of the hangar.

"Jakus?" He peered into the sim pod. It was empty, but the controls were still on, the screens flickering with a simulation in progress. On the floor was Jakus's hat, its brim bent. Legroeder picked it up and examined it in the light of the sim chamber. There was a dark, wet stain along the headband. Blood, it looked like.

Legroeder looked around nervously. The hangar seemed completely deserted now. He bent to peer under the ships. No one. Now he heard distant doors and vehicles outside. Someone leaving? With Jakus, maybe? Legroeder circled around the stern of the third ship, toward the rear of the hangar. There were spacecraft maintenance tools scattered all over, and the smell of ozone and vacuum-grade lubricants. In the far corner, a dim hallway led away from the hangar area. He hesitated, before moving toward it. The hallway was short. A dim emergency light glowered, revealing two doors on the right side, and one at the end.

Legroeder drew an uneasy breath. This was stupid. What would he do if he found someone? Still . . . he'd come this far. He stepped into the hallway. What were these—storerooms? Offices? Armories? One of the two doors bore a dirt-encrusted warning sign: CAUTION—STAIRS. He tested it cautiously: locked. He exhaled softly. Beyond the end door, he heard traffic sounds. It was a steel door with a push-release, and a security panel beside it. With a nervous glance at the security panel, he pushed the door open.

Cool night air greeted him, along with the sound of a truck whirring past. He stood at the top of a short flight of steps: early evening darkness, some empty loading docks; not much else. Spaceport lights glowed in the distance. If Jakus had walked or been carried out, he was gone now. Legroeder started to turn back through the door.

"Far enough, chump—"

He saw only a blur. Then the club slammed into the side of his head, and he tumbled backward down the steps. His head hit hard on the tarmac, and he rolled, as he heard the words, "Come back again and we kill you." Then the sound of the door slamming. He raised an arm dizzily to ward off further blows, but none came.

When he managed at last to push himself up to a sitting position, he saw that he was quite alone in the night, outside the locked building.

Chapter 5
HARRIET'S WAY

"YOU'RE LUCKY they didn't kill you," Harriet said, examining the wound on the side of his head. "They probably just didn't want to have to deal with your body. For Heaven's sake, will you hold still?"

Legroeder grunted as Harriet used an antiseptic cloth to clean the dirt out of the scrape on the side of his cheekbone. She shook her head, spraying the area with a bandage mist. "I'm a lawyer, not a doctor," she muttered. "There, I hope that holds."

"Thanks," Legroeder managed, testing the spot with a fingertip. "I can tell you were a mother once."

"I still am," Harriet said, tossing the sprayer back into her office first-aid kit. "A lousy one."

"Oh—well—"

She went back around behind her desk and snapped open her compad. "Now, do you want to tell me why you did such a damn fool thing? It wasn't bad enough you had to go talk to Jakus. You thought you had to snoop around in the dark, too?" Harriet rocked back in her chair, eyeing him. "I suppose, since you did go back in an effort to prevent mayhem, I will refrain from remarking about fools I've had for clients."

Legroeder sighed. He *felt* like a fool. Worse, he didn't know what to do next. "There's still the question of what they did with Jakus. I wouldn't be surprised if they killed *him*." It was obvious Jakus had been lying on someone's orders. And if he'd been overheard arguing about it . . .

Legroeder was mad as hell at the guy, but he didn't want

him dead. For one thing, there was always the chance that he might recant and exonerate Legroeder. A dwindling chance, to be sure.

"I wouldn't be surprised if he was killed, either. If you still had the bloody cap, we'd have more to go on," Harriet pointed out.

Legroeder grunted. He wasn't sure if he'd dropped the cap where he'd found it, or lost it when he'd gotten clubbed. The bash in the head seemed to have clouded his memories.

"Of course, now it has your finger oils on it as well as Jakus's blood," Harriet said. "So I suppose it's not something we necessarily want turning up right away."

"Look, I'm *sorry*. But isn't there something we should do? Call the police, at least? What if they've got his body in there or dumped it nearby?"

Harriet sighed. "Given the circumstances, and the frame-up that you yourself are experiencing, I'm not entirely sure who I trust. That hangar is probably under Spacing Authority jurisdiction."

"But—"

"Still, I suppose I could contact my PI and ask him to phone in an anonymous report. He could say he heard reports of a fight. Hang on a moment." She touched her throat com and swiveled her chair away. "Peter? Harriet Mahoney. I need you to do something . . ."

When she was finished, she swiveled back to Legroeder. "Don't get your hopes up," she cautioned. "And don't expect them to find armed ships, even if they look. If you know what I mean."

Legroeder raised his hands and dropped them. "All right. So we've done our duty. What next?"

"I'll ask Peter to keep his ear to the ground, to see what he can find out about possible covert military, or paramilitary, operations. Or who knows what—there could be a dozen explanations for those ships you saw. And yes—given Jakus's involvement, it's probably something we should find out about. But that's Peter's job, not yours. As for what *we* will do next . . ." Harriet lowered her glasses on their chain and studied him again. "Are you ready to take the advice of your attorney?"

He sank back in defeat. "I promised I would, didn't I?"

"I'm glad you remember." Harriet smiled faintly. "Then I think it's time we learned all there is to learn in this city about starship *Impris*."

He spread his hands in question. "Where are we going to do that? The RiggerGuild and Spacing Authority libraries had nothing."

Harriet snapped her compad shut. "We're going to start by getting some sleep. I've got a place where you can stay. Unless you've got someplace else in mind—? Good. Then first thing tomorrow, we're going to pay a visit to the public library."

"The *public* library?"

"Believe it or not, Legroeder, riggers are not the only people interested in knowledge . . ."

AN ORANGE-TINGED sun woke Legroeder before the knock on the door. He was up on one elbow in bed, staring out the window at rooftops, when a velvety voice purred, "You wanted to be up at six, Mr. Legroeder-r-r?" It was Harriet's housekeeper, Vegas.

"I'm up," he called back. He dressed and stepped out of the guest quarters. It was actually a small cottage, set back twenty meters or so from Harriet's house. By the time he'd crossed the garden to the back door of the main house, Vegas was there to open it for him. Vegas was a Faber aborigine who looked like a cross between a swan and a very slender, very white-skinned humanoid woman with small vestigial wings. She led the way to the dining room.

Harriet was seated at the table with a cup of tea, studying her compad. "Good morning. Did you sleep well?"

Clearly Harriet was a morning person. Legroeder was not. And he had not slept well; he'd awoken constantly during the night. "Couldn't have been better. Have you already gotten started?"

"I checked the Guild library files on *Impris*, and as you

said, there's not much. So I thought I'd try the main files at the public library. I must say, they don't have a lot, either." Harriet fiddled with the compad screen. "Just a summary about the similarity of legend between *Impris* and the old stories of the Flying Dutchman. Judging from this, you wouldn't think that *anyone* took it seriously."

"Even here in its home port? You'd think they'd have more information here than anywhere in the galaxy." Legroeder pulled out a chair to sit, and looked gratefully at Vegas, who had just appeared with a tray bearing a thermal coffee pot and cup.

"Well, it's been a hundred and twenty-four years since she was lost, during the war. And after the war, a lot of the early records disappeared." Harriet turned the compad around. "Here, take a look."

Legroeder poured a cup of coffee and stirred in some yellow-tinged cream. He sipped it as he read the entry.

Impris. Interstellar passenger liner operating out of Faber Eridani during the years of the War of a Thousand Suns. *Impris* reportedly disappeared during a routine flight in the final year of the war. No official explanation was ever provided for the ship's loss; however, unofficial and highly controversial reports attributed the loss to surprise hostile actions on the part of the Narseil, theretofore considered allies of the Centrist human worlds. (For a historical overview, see <u>NARSEIL: PARTNERSHIP WITH CENTRIST WORLDS: BREAKDOWN IN RELATIONS</u>.)

Legroeder grunted. He hadn't associated the Narseil with *Impris*. The amphibious Narseil were relatively rare—and not always welcome—guests in human society. But their riggers were among the best in the known galaxy, and the Narseil Rigging Institute was without peer in the study of rigging science and technology. Legroeder had always suspected that the Narseil could teach the human rigging community a thing or two, if they were given a chance. He didn't know much about the historical relationship of the human and Narseil worlds—history had never been his strong suit—but he couldn't imagine why the Narseil would have destroyed *Impris*.

He drank more coffee and read on.

Accurate information concerning *Impris* disappeared, along with a host of other records, during post-war turmoil on *Impris*'s homeworld of Faber Eridani. She might well have been forgotten by history were it not for the lasting political repercussions against the Narseil, which among other consequences, served to delay continued exploration of deeper space (see also GALACTIC EXPLORATION: COLLABORATIVE EFFORTS: LOSS OF WILL IN THE POST-WAR ERA). In addition, curious legends arose in the rigging community during the following decades, referring to *Impris* as "the Flying Dutchman of the Spacelanes"—a ship and crew doomed to sail the Flux forever, haunted and immortal.

No objective evidence has ever been found to support these legends. Nevertheless, myth has it that the ship, in the more than one hundred years since her loss, has reappeared on numerous occasions to riggers during routine passages through the Flux. Typical reports have the Ghost Rigger sighted only fleetingly, sometimes transmitting a distress call, but never responding to any attempts at contact. Variations on the legend attribute the loss of other ships to unexplained, deadly encounters with *Impris*; but such claims similarly lack substantiation.

Though the legends are considered meaningless for purposes of rigger navigation, a significant body of folklore has grown up over the years regarding not only *Impris* but also other ships of similar reputation, notably *Devonhol* and *Totauri*. (See PURPORTED GHOST SHIPS: SPACE and FLYING DUTCHMAN

LEGEND: LITERATURE AND HOLO: FACT VS FICTION.)

Legroeder swiveled the compad back to Harriet. "This doesn't help much."

Harriet shook her head. "I said this was just a beginning, remember?" She buttered a scone from a tray Vegas had set between them. "Have something to eat, and then we'll go down and see what we can find."

"Go down?" Legroeder asked. "What's the point?"

Harriet smiled and took a bite of her scone.

THE ELMIRA Public Library was a tall-towered affair, originally designed as a mayoral office building and later converted to its more prosaic (in some views) role as library. As they walked from the hoverbus, Harriet told Legroeder that she loved the place, not for its auto-retrieval capabilities (she could do just as well from home or from a coffee bar) but for its collection of hard-copy books. Paper, mylar, parchment . . . she didn't care what they were printed on. "I like the permanence, the texture, the smell of old books—"

"The dust, the dust-mites—"

"Heavens, don't be so dreary." Harriet led the way up the steps and into the central hall of the library. "My dear Legroeder, sometimes you find information in hard-copy, or even from people, that you just don't find on the net."

Legroeder grunted.

"Well, you may turn out to be right. We'll see." She stepped forward briskly. They walked through the main reading room, past a small gallery of pastels on paper— aboriginal artwork. They came to a solid wood door at the back of the reading room, which let them into a hallway lined with offices and special study spaces. Harriet knocked on the door of the third room on the right. A Fabri aborigine female looked up from the desk. To Legroeder's eye, she looked identical to Vegas.

"Quoya, Mrs. Mahoney," the woman said, with a musical chuckle. "Nice to see you."

"Good morning, Adaria," said Harriet. "I wonder if you could help us with a problem today."

"Ha, but I always tr-r-ry, do I not? What will it be today? Exotic cuisines frrom the Gar-r-rssen mountains? Animals from the cirrr-cus-es of the known galaxy? Architectural drawings from Old Earth?"

Harriet smiled. "Not today, thank you. My friend Legroeder and I are looking for some old information that has passed out of circulation, and I thought perhaps if we searched some of the original paper records, we might find something."

"Of course," chuckled Adaria, with a toothless smile; the Fabri had a pair of curved plates, not teeth, in their mouths. "What can I help you find?"

"Well . . . we were hoping you might have some in-depth information on *Impris*, the legendary starship. Faber Eridani was its home port, you know. But I'm having trouble coming up with much."

Adaria rocked back slightly. "Ffff. There was nothing in the main records?"

"Not to speak of. That's why we thought perhaps the original materials—"

"Ahh. Those may be a tr-r-rifle difficult to locate. But if you would like to wait—?"

The librarian rose with a flutter and disappeared down the hall. When she returned, a few minutes later, she seemed agitated. "I've spoken to the archives director. Those were very old papers, and I'm afraid they were removed from the collection some years ago." She puffed a few times.

Harriet cocked her head curiously. "I'm sorry to hear that. Is anything wrong, Adaria?"

"What? Ffff—no. That is, I don't think so. It's just that the question seemed to disturb the director for some reason. I don't know why." The librarian nervously fluffed a vestigial wing.

"I see," Harriet said, frowning. "Would you happen to know why the papers were removed?"

Adaria looked uncertain. "Lack of demand, is the usual reason. If no one was interested, they wouldn't be kept forever."

Legroeder stirred. "That seems odd. It was a Faber Eridani ship. Wouldn't *someone* be interested in the legend—for tourist value, if nothing else?"

"An inter-r-resting question," said the Fabri. "I recall there were some private press items written on the subject. But they never generated much interest. We don't even have copies here."

Harriet rubbed her chin, as the librarian shrugged. "Tell me. When the materials were removed, would they have been destroyed?"

"Well—fffff—that's difficult to know. It's been years."

"If they weren't destroyed, what would have been done with them?"

Adaria clucked thoughtfully. "It's possible they were passed on to a smaller, more specialized collection. That sometimes happens with outdated mater-r-rials."

"And would there be a way to find out who they might have been passed on to?"

Adaria consulted her compad. "Ffff—herrre's a thought. Those small prrress items I mentioned? Several of them were wr-r-ritten and published by a R-r-robert McGinnis."

Harriet turned her hands up. "Do you know this man?"

"I know *of* him," Adaria said. "He is a p-r-rivate collector of archives, with a special interest in materials dating from the War of a Thousand Suns. He has a reputation as a r-recluse, but his collection is well regarded. Let me see if his location is available . . . Fffff, yes. Would you like it?"

"Please," said Harriet. She placed the ring on her right hand against the edge of the librarian's compad. Then she nodded. "Thank you, Adaria. You've been most helpful."

The librarian rose, her wings fluttering. "It's always a pleasure, Mrs. Mahoney. Perhaps next time we can rrre-search some, ffff, Iliution gems. We have some wonderful new materials on them. Wonderful materials."

Harriet smiled. "Perhaps next time." She gestured to Legroeder. "Shall we?"

Legroeder nodded politely to the Fabri librarian and followed Harriet back through the halls and out of the building. "Was that worthwhile?" he asked, squinting in the bright midmorning sun, now bluish in tint.

"We'll find out, I suppose." Harriet hummed for a few moments. "Adaria is a dear, and *always* helpful. I've done some work for her people, you know—the Fabri natives have problems from time to time with our brand of civilization—including extremist groups like Centrist Strength encroaching on their land and bothering them because they can get away with it. I've been able to give them some legal advice on occasion."

Legroeder glanced at her, surprised. "You get around, don't you? And so does Centrist Strength, it sounds like."

Harriet shrugged, frowning. "There's a *lot* that goes on that you wouldn't suspect—even if you were here for more than just the occasional port of call." Before he could react, she waved him around a corner. "Would you like to look in on your friend in the hospital? I'll see what I can learn about Mr. McGinnis, and we can meet in that lovely coffee shop around the corner from the hospital . . ."

LEGROEDER SAT motionless, his hand resting near Maris's arm. He watched her sleep in the hydrobed, thinking, *Sleep. She's asleep. Better to think that than the other. That she's in a coma. Being slowly suffocated by those damned implants.* The burns on her face and neck leered at him from under the clear bandages. *She got me out of the raider outpost alive. She slowed up the guards for us—even with the shots she took herself.* He shook his head grimly.

He wished he could give her a chance to escape now. Escape from this hospital room. From the shadow of death. He rested his head back against the hospital room wall and closed his eyes, willing away the feeling of helplessness—not just about Maris, but about whatever was behind his own troubles. *How many enemies can one guy have, anyway?* He hated to think.

"Mr. Legroeder?"

He opened his eyes. "Yes?"

It was an attending robot. "I'm sorry, but your visiting time is up."

He rose with a sigh. "You'll send word if there's any change?"

"Of course, sir."

Legroeder uttered a silent prayer in the direction of his companion, and walked off in search of Harriet.

HE FOUND her at a back table in the coffee shop, her compad plugged into the wall. "Ah, there you are," she said. "I was starting to worry. Don't sit down, we're leaving."

"Huh? Where are we going?" He'd been looking forward to a good strong Eridani coffee with marsotz cream.

"To the aircar rental."

Legroeder blinked in confusion.

Harriet rose, packing her compad. "I've rented a flyer to take us for a visit to our Mr. McGinnis."

"That was fast. Have you talked to him?"

Harriet shook her head. "Mr. McGinnis doesn't have a listed com number. But I've made a few inquiries. Very reclusive man, it seems—but respected by those who know of him. He's a former space-marine." She urged Legroeder toward the door. "He also has the planet's most complete set of archives from the War of a Thousand Suns. Besides which, he has a special interest in rigging history." Harriet smiled grimly. "Let's just hope he doesn't mind surprise visitors."

Chapter 6
HISTORICAL TRUTHS

THE MCGINNIS estate was located four hundred and thirty kilometers northwest of the Elmira spaceport, a little over an hour's flight at the speed of a rental flyer. The countryside flowing beneath them was wooded and green. The autopilot seemed confident of finding the address, so Legroeder and Harriet didn't have much to do except drink their coffee and worry.

Legroeder asked Harriet why, if she had been so obsessed (her word) with this case for the last seven years, she had never researched the history of *Impris* before.

Harriet looked at Legroeder with amusement. "You aren't accustomed to solving puzzles, are you, dear?"

"What's that supposed to mean?"

"Well, think about it. How would I have known, until you came back, that *Impris* was even involved? I'm almost as interested in knowing why that information was taken from the library as I am in knowing about the ship itself. Was it innocent, or was someone deliberately hiding it? And if the latter, why? Once we know *that*, I think we'll be closer to understanding why *you* were framed."

Legroeder shrugged. "The librarian said if the documents weren't being used—"

Harriet laughed. "If you don't mind my saying so, you must have made a very poor pirate."

Legroeder felt his face redden.

"Oh, don't take it as an insult. It's a compliment. You don't seem to have a duplicitous bone in your body. But I'm reasonably sure those papers were removed because someone *wanted* them gone. Now we just have to find out if someone *else* wanted them preserved."

"Someone like Mr. McGinnis?"

"Let us hope so." With that, Harriet closed her eyes to rest, and Legroeder drank his coffee in silence. He gazed out the window, watching a winding river snake to and fro beneath them. Scanning for traffic, he saw another craft, higher in altitude, following a parallel course, and a couple of others crossing their path like fast-moving bugs against the sky.

It wasn't much longer before he felt the flyer begin its descent. He searched for their destination, nestled somewhere in the wooded land below. The flyer began to bank and turn for its approach. There was the glint of the river again, a smaller stream to the west of it, and the occasional rocky bluff poking up out of the woods. The flyer seemed to know what it was doing, but Legroeder kept checking the console map to verify the course. The position readings seemed right. As he sat back, he realized that Harriet was watching him with amusement. He tried to feign unconcern.

Out the window on Harriet's side, he saw another flyer, a little higher, apparently also circling to land. "Look," he said, pointing to the other craft, which was trailing a little behind now, and falling back out of his view. He couldn't tell if it was the same one he'd seen before, but he felt a prickle of unease. "They look like they're headed to the same place."

Harriet craned her neck to see. "What's that puff of smoke?"

"What puff of smoke?" Legroeder leaned over Harriet to look out the far window. The other craft had dropped even farther back, and something was shooting forward from it, leaving a contrail of smoke. It was arcing directly toward them. *"Jesus Christ, Harriet!"*

"What?"

"Hang on!" Legroeder shouted, groping for the autopilot release. The flyer lurched and nosed down abruptly as he grabbed the yoke. He wasn't used to this kind of craft, and it dove alarmingly as he struggled to regain control. Legroeder banked hard to the left, then started to bring up the nose. The missile streaked past and exploded with a *whump!* The flyer slipped sideways, bucking. Legroeder cursed, fighting with the damaged controls. They were in a steep left bank and spiraling steeper.

He fought to level it out of the bank, then gradually pulled up the nose. He didn't want to crash, but didn't want to stay an easy target, either. "Look for a clearing!" he shouted. "Any clearing! And see if you can find that other ship!" They were dropping like a stone now, the power inductors losing strength. In less than a minute, they were going to plow into the forest.

"There!" cried Harriet, pointing to the right. "There's a clearing! No, you're turning away from it!"

He didn't answer. He was too busy trying to bring them around. As he glanced up, he saw the other flyer circling.

"There it is again!"

Their turn had brought the clearing back into view. A large house stood in the middle of it—probably the McGinnis estate. "Good—good—" Legroeder muttered. He fought to control the descent. They had too much airspeed and were in danger of overshooting.

"Legroeder, I think that flyer's attacking again!"

He shoved the nose down to drop them fast and hot toward the clearing. The other craft was coming around . . .

They skidded sideways as he banked left, then right. He thumbed the com. "Mayday, Mayday, Mayday! We are under attack!" He glanced backward at the other flyer, just in time to see it peel off at high speed. Apparently its occupants didn't want to be seen by witnesses.

"We're not going to make it," Harriet said nervously.

"Yes, we are," Legroeder said, as they careened over the house and low over the forest again. He began a new turn, trying to coax some additional power out of the propulsion. The inductors wheezed a little, then slowly oozed back to life. He banked in a slow hundred-and-eighty-degree turn, back toward the clearing. He had just enough power to maintain control. "Good . . . good . . ." he murmured, leveling onto a straight course for the clearing. There was some crosswind. He compensated, then brought the nose up a little, and settled into a final approach. That was when he noticed the faint glitter of a forcefield over the clearing. *Oh shit.*

The com blared to life. *"Unidentified craft approaching McGinnis estate, identify and state your purpose!"*

He thumbed the com and rattled, "This is the flyer, Legroeder and Mahoney aboard. Mayday! We're disabled, sinking fast, and your clearing is the only place to land."

"I just tracked a missile. If you're in a fight, take it elsewhere."

"Mr. McGinnis, we're falling out of the sky! We didn't come to fight! We urgently request clearance to land!"

There was a pause that lasted forever. *"Very well, you may land. But I warn you, my defensive lasers are charged."*

Legroeder was too busy flying to answer. Harriet pressed the switch on her side and said, "You'll get no trouble from us. We were attacked, and we don't know by whom. We need your help!"

"I'm shutting off the forcefield. Land to the west of the house. It's smoother there." The sparkle of the forcefield vanished from the air, and a man came running from the house, waving them toward the far side of the clearing.

The ground was coming up fast. Legroeder ballooned the power from the inductors, and they slowed, wobbling. They slammed, bounced, and lurched to a stop. He cut the power, and looked at Harriet. Her face was pale as she gasped, *"Damn,* Legroeder—that was good flying! Thank you."

"You're welcome," Legroeder whispered, his throat dry. He glanced out at the approaching man. "I don't think this gent is too happy about it, though." Legroeder popped open the door and allowed fresh air to blow across them before he released the seat restraints.

As they climbed out, the man was scanning the sky, shading his eyes with one hand. A large brown dog, some kind of retriever, had come to join him, and was standing alertly at his side.

Legroeder, too, studied the sky. He saw no sign of their attacker. Keeping a wary eye on the dog, Legroeder greeted their host—a short, stocky man with black eyebrows that set off his grim features. "Robert McGinnis?"

"Yeah. That flyer that shot at you took off toward the west." McGinnis pointed over the treetops, where the edge of the forcefield was glittering; evidently he had switched it back on already. "Mind telling me what the hell's going on?"

"We're not quite sure," Harriet said, breathing hard. "But thank you for allowing us to land."

The retriever, ears raised, was sniffing the air around them. "That'll do, Rufus," McGinnis said, snapping his fingers. The dog, lifting his nose one last time, circled back to McGinnis's side. "Well . . . I didn't seem to have much choice." McGinnis rubbed his chin. "Except to let you crash in the woods."

"We're grateful you didn't," Harriet said.

"No doubt you are. No doubt you are." McGinnis pointed to the side of the flyer near the main inductor cowling, where a meter-long burn mark showed the lasershrap hit from the exploding missile. "I'm not overjoyed at having missiles fired over my property. Is there an explanation for this?"

Legroeder bent to inspect the damage, sobered to see just how close they had come to being blown out of the sky. "We'll tell you what we know. But it's not much." He hesitated, then stuck out a hand. "I'm Renwald Legroeder, and this is Harriet Mahoney."

"Legroeder," McGinnis said grimly, resting his own hands on his hips. "*Rigger* Legroeder?"

Legroeder let his hand drop. "You've heard of me?"

Harriet forced a chuckle. "You've been in the news, Legroeder. I'm sure even out here, Mr. McGinnis has heard of your case."

"Well," McGinnis said. "I don't pay a lot of attention.

But I have heard of you." He cocked his head. "They say you were responsible for handing over a ship to Golen Space pirates."

Legroeder felt a flash of anger, but Harriet put a calming hand on his arm. "That is what I am *accused* of," he said grudgingly.

McGinnis barked a laugh. "Well, I didn't say I believed it, did I?" He stared out into the woods for a moment. "Did you all come out here to see me? If you did, it was a risky thing to do."

"Apparently so," Legroeder agreed.

McGinnis turned to Harriet. "And your name was—"

"Harriet Mahoney. I'm assisting Legroeder in trying to prove his innocence." Harriet adjusted her glasses as she returned McGinnis's gaze. Either she had recovered quickly from the trauma of the attack, or she was hiding it well. "We undertook this . . . visit . . . because we were hoping you could help us."

"Is that so? And what gives you that hope?"

As McGinnis cocked his head, Legroeder observed that the man's left eye was synthetic; then he realized that a good portion of the man's *face* was synthetic. Legroeder's glance did not go unnoticed, but McGinnis said nothing.

"I apologize if we were mistaken," Harriet said. "But your name came up in some research we were doing. You are known as a collector of historical materials on the subject of rigging—particularly materials dating back a century or so. As it happens, we are very much in need of information from that period."

"In order to prove Rigger Legroeder's innocence?"

"Precisely." Harriet patted her forehead with a handkerchief. "Mr. McGinnis, do you suppose that we could step out of the sun somewhere? I'm feeling rather faint, after that close call we just had."

McGinnis grunted, not answering. He bent to make a closer examination of the scorched side of the flyer. When he straightened up, he had a troubled look on his face. He again gazed up into the sky, as though struggling with some decision. And then, as quickly as the cloud had come over him, he relaxed. "Yes, of course. I'm being a poor host. You both must be shaken up. That was a very fine landing under the circumstances, Rigger Legroeder."

"Thank you. Just Legroeder will be fine."

"Legroeder, then," said McGinnis. A smile worked at his lips. "I guess there's someone out there who doesn't like you much. Or maybe doesn't like lawyers," he added with a glance at Harriet.

Harriet's eyes gleamed. "Did I mention that I was a lawyer?"

McGinnis looked startled. Another shadow seemed to cross his brow. "Now that you mention it, I don't recall. I—suppose I must have seen your name in the . . . news, too. Let's go inside, shall we?"

As they walked to the house, he spoke to his dog. "Stay and watch out here, Rufus." The retriever trotted to take up a position under a tree, and stood alertly as the humans made their way across the lawn to the side door.

"IF YOUR attackers come back, my security field should keep them out," McGinnis said, leading them into his living room. The place looked like a converted hunting lodge. The living room breathed with space; it had an open-beam ceiling and wood-paneled walls. A ceremonial sword and several sidearms were mounted on the walls, along with half a dozen holos of military spacecraft.

"May I ask how you happened to have a forcefield around your house?" Legroeder said. "Not that I'm ungrateful, mind you."

"You can ask." McGinnis gestured toward a cluster of seats near a large stone fireplace. "Make yourselves comfortable while I fix something to drink."

Legroeder sank into a seat near the fireplace. A crackling fire billowed up with a soft rush. Legroeder closed his eyes, forced himself to try to relax . . . to focus on the warmth of the fire, the smell of the wood smoke, the crackle of flames. His thoughts drifted inevitably to the weapons fire of attacking pirate ships, and missiles in the air—and he winced, opening his eyes. He twisted around in his chair.

Harriet had seated herself on a small sofa facing a broad wooden coffee table. Her compad was out. She beckoned to Legroeder, and he moved to the seat opposite her. When McGinnis returned, carrying a tray with three tall drinks, Harriet lowered her glasses on their chain. "Is there some way I could make a call from here? We need to order a replacement flyer, but my signal can't seem to get past your forcefield."

McGinnis rested the tray on the table. "Of course. I'll see to it in a moment." He passed out coasters and glasses. "I think you'll like this. It's an infusion made from the leaves of the nascacia tree."

Legroeder held his glass up, peering through a reddish amber liquid and several ice cubes. He took a cautious sip, then another. The drink had a sharp tang, with a hint of sweetness. He nodded appreciatively.

McGinnis didn't respond. He was standing with his eyes closed, concentrating. "Hmph," he muttered, looking annoyed. Returning to the bar, he tapped at a control panel. "Try your transmission now," he called.

Harriet touched her earring, then typed at the pad.

"Are you getting through?"

"I'm afraid not."

McGinnis did some more fiddling, then returned to join them. "Whatever's wrong, I've got my house system checking into it. It should let me know when it finds the problem." He looked preoccupied as he took a seat at the end of the table. But rather than speaking of whatever was troubling him, he leaned forward with his elbows on his knees. "All right, then—you've come a long way because you think I can help you. What is it you want? And why did someone want to shoot you out of the sky to keep you from getting it?"

Harriet cleared her throat. "What we want is information about an old rigger ship. As for why someone would kill us to keep us from talking to you . . . well, I was rather hoping *you* might be able to tell *us*."

McGinnis inclined his head. "Really. What ship are you interested in?"

"If you've seen the news reports, you probably already know. The passenger liner *Impris*. The Flying Dutchman of Space." Harriet paused, waiting for a reaction. McGinnis said nothing, but his eyes seemed to narrow. "Oddly enough," Harriet continued, "we've found very little information about her in either the RiggerGuild library or the public library."

"That *is* odd, isn't it?" McGinnis said, in a gravelly tone that suggested he didn't find it odd at all.

"But we heard—rumor, I guess you would have to say— that some of the original reports on the ship had been removed for safekeeping." Harriet scrutinized McGinnis's face. "Would you, by any chance, know anything about that?"

McGinnis's eyes closed, and an expression of pain crossed his face, unmistakable even through the synthetic skin. For a few heartbeats, he seemed removed from their company, as if his thoughts were occupied far, far away. Legroeder watched him, wondering what inner struggle was going on in this man. And what did it have to do with them? He also wondered, suddenly, what augmentation McGinnis had beneath that synthetic skin. And was that augmentation one of the reasons McGinnis lived out here like a hermit?

When McGinnis's eyes blinked open, he exhaled suddenly, as though a great tension had been released from his body. His voice sounded husky. "Why, may I ask, are you interested in this . . . ship?" His gaze shifted from one to the other, and came to rest on Legroeder. "You weren't thinking of *looking* for her, or something . . ."

"As a matter of fact," Legroeder answered softly, "I've already seen her."

"*You—*" McGinnis said with a start, and then cut himself off. "Please continue."

Legroeder nodded, feeling a band of tension in his forehead. "I've seen it. And I've heard lies about it. And I need to know the truth—to *prove* the truth. This has great personal importance to me. So if you—" He paused, realizing that McGinnis's hand was trembling.

McGinnis placed his half-empty glass on the table and stared at it, as if it held answers to his questions. His gaze caught Legroeder's. "Tell me," he whispered.

"If you've seen the news reports, you must know—"

McGinnis shook his head. *"Tell me."*

Legroeder glanced at Harriet. What nerve had they struck here? Drawing a deep breath, he told McGinnis the story. The *Impris* sighting. The pirate attack. His years of captivity and servitude. His escape. And finally, his framing by the RiggerGuild inquest panel. Even in brief, it was a tortuous tale. When he finished, he sat back with a sigh, trying to push the reawakened memories back into their bottle.

McGinnis rotated his glass in his hands, contemplating. "Well." He gazed up at the ceiling. "You're right about my having information about *Impris*. Nobody's looked at it in years. I probably have the closest thing there is to a complete record. As complete as there *can* be, considering that we never learned what happened to her. Except—" he paused, looking down"—you've just confirmed reports I've heard over the years, that she's being used by present day pirates as a lure for unsuspecting ships." He shot a piercing glance at Legroeder. "You might want to think about what that means, in terms of your being framed."

Legroeder opened his mouth wordlessly.

Harriet spoke sharply. "Would you be willing to share the information you have with us?"

McGinnis pressed three fingertips to his forehead, scowling. *"Yes,"* he hissed . . . but as though he were speaking to someone else.

"Mr. McGinnis? Are you all right?"

Pain flickered across the man's face. "I'm . . . *fine.*"

Harriet exchanged alarmed glances with Legroeder. "Is there anything we should—?"

McGinnis blinked his eyes open. *"No.* I'm fine now. Really." He grimaced. "I don't . . . know much more than you about the present state of *Impris*, I suspect. But if you're interested in knowing the truth of her past . . . I'll show you what I have." He seemed to have difficulty getting the words out. He pressed his hands to the tabletop, as if steadying himself. His chin jutted, eyes challenging them. "Not many people are interested in the truth, you know."

"The truth is what we're here for," said Harriet.

"Then I have what you need. The whole reason I've kept these documents here . . . is to keep the truth alive. Truths. Not just about one ship, but about a larger historical matter—" he paused, as though gathering strength "—that for over a hundred years has been nothing but a lie."

Legroeder shook his head in confusion. "What—?"

"You came here to ask about a ship. But what you really need to know about is dishonor and betrayal between *worlds*—in wartime *and* in peace." McGinnis's voice hardened to a knife edge. "A betrayal that continues to this day—unrecognized, and written right into our history books." He sighed. "The disappearance of *Impris* was one of a great many mysteries left at the end of the War of a Thousand Suns. Most of them remain unsolved, and forgotten. But for some—like *Impris*—answers were fabricated, and perpetuated, for reasons that have nothing to do with the facts. But there *are* real answers . . . if you want to know them." He glared in the direction of the crackling fire, his black eyebrows knitted together. "If you want to read them for yourselves."

Harriet seemed taken aback by his ferocity. "Yes, we do—very much. But may I ask something first? Why was this information removed from the public record? Was it deliberately suppressed? Is there some *raider* influence here?"

McGinnis barked a laugh. He slapped a fist into his open palm and sat trembling. His lips barely moved as he whispered, *"Get . . . out of my . . . you little shit!"* With a shiver, he said a little too loudly, "Sorry—oh yes—it was suppressed."

McGinnis looked to Legroeder as if he were about to explode. "Who suppressed it?" Legroeder asked.

McGinnis spoke in halting words, as if against some resistance. "I cannot—tell you that—now. But I can tell you why—the lies were told—a hundred years ago, and still are, today."

"Yes?"

McGinnis's breath rasped. "Blame the enemies of the Narseil."

"Excuse me?"

McGinnis seemed to gain strength, and his voice became almost normal. "Back then, there were those who wanted the Narseil blamed for the loss of a prized ship. It could have been any ship. But when *Impris* disappeared, the perfect excuse presented itself. Look at the Narseil and the Centrist Worlds. They were allies against the Kyber in the War of a Thousand Suns—until the end of the war, when *suddenly they weren't, anymore.*"

Legroeder frowned. "That's what the RiggerGuild library says. That it was suspicion that they'd destroyed *Impris* that ruined relations with the Narseil. But *Impris* wasn't destroyed—I've *seen* it! It's out there!" His pulse was racing now, with hope that he might finally learn what was behind the RiggerGuild lies. But why would anyone have betrayed the Narseil, and what could it possibly mean now, one hundred years later? What connection did it have to pirates using *Impris* as bait?

"Perhaps," said McGinnis, "this would be a good time to show you what *was* known, until it was buried under the lies. Would you like to see the report of the inspector who investigated the ship before it disappeared?"

It took a second for the words to register. *"Before—?"*

"That's right. *Impris*'s troubles started well before the time of her disappearance. Excuse me one moment." McGinnis returned to the control console near the bar. He worked for a moment, muttering under his breath. Rejoining his guests, he said, "The materials will arrive shortly."

* * *

When the library robot rolled into the room, bearing a large carton, McGinnis quickly cleared the table. "Some of this used to be on the public library systems, but it was purged long before the originals came into my possession. I was given these materials for safekeeping—"

"Why you?" asked Harriet.

"That," McGinnis said sharply, "is something I'm not at liberty to speak about. Let's just say they were safer with me." He lifted a set of folders from the carton. "I've reloaded all of it on my own system, but these are the originals. Or as close as one can get. These are certified copies of the original investigation by the Space Commission—they were the forerunners of the present Spacing Authority—into the disappearance of *Impris*. And along with it, the old RiggerGuild investigation. They don't entirely agree with each other—but neither one ascribes any blame to the Narseil." McGinnis opened the top folder and took out several sheaves of mylar paper. "In fact, they don't even mention the Narseil."

Legroeder picked up the RiggerGuild document and held it gingerly, as if it might burn his fingers. What could possibly be in these old documents that would explain what had been done to *him?* For no clear reason, he felt a tingling sense that he was teetering on the edge of answers. Rigger intuition?

"If you're wondering how the Narseil got implicated," McGinnis continued, "it happened in a special report to the planetary governor—written by a political committee with virtually no rigging or spacing expertise. That's in here, too."

"Would you mind," asked Harriet, "if we made copies of some of these documents?"

McGinnis hesitated, his brow furrowing again. "Copies," he murmured, straining. "There are reasons . . . why I have not . . ." His breath caught, and for several heartbeats, he seemed unable to continue speaking. Then he hissed suddenly, "Yes, I'll give you the whole damned collection on a cube before you leave. "But—" his gaze caught them sharply "—be aware, your possession of the information could make you a target."

"It would seem that we're already a target," Harriet said dryly. McGinnis inclined his head in acknowledgment.

Legroeder touched an unopened folder. "What's this?"

"That's the Fandrang report."

"Fandrang. That name's familiar."

"Gloris Fandrang. He was a shipping inspector, very highly regarded, before and during the War of a Thousand Suns. Later, he went into politics, but not here on Faber Eridani. He moved to the Aeregian worlds. Died in a flyer accident about ten years after he wrote this." McGinnis shrugged. "At least, they called it an accident."

Legroeder glanced at the paper. "And his report—?"

McGinnis opened the folder and laid out a number of holos, as well as a long text document. "This was never released to the public. It was the result of his investigation into the disappearance of *Impris*. But not just her disappearance. Fandrang had been looking into anomalous events reported by her riggers a dozen voyages before her disappearance."

Legroeder felt a chill of fear. Why should a century-old event frighten him? "I hadn't heard anything about that," he whispered.

"I know. And when you read this, you're going to wonder why you never had access to this information. Because there was something going on—probably is *still* something going on—that every rigger ought to know about."

"Meaning—?"

"Dangers out there that you know nothing of. And yet you face them every time you rig."

"If you're talking about the raiders—" Legroeder heard his own voice trembling "—I think I know more about them than you'll ever know."

"Maybe." McGinnis's gaze didn't waver. "But no, I'm not talking about the raiders."

"Then what—"

McGinnis gestured to the table. "Read the report."

Chapter 7

THE FANDRANG REPORT

ROBERT MCGINNIS watched with both dread and satisfaction as his two visitors settled in to study the materials. At last, it seemed, someone had come along to whom he could reveal the truth—and perhaps, entrust its safekeeping. There was no way to be certain, but his heart wanted to trust these two. And if they were being persecuted by the Spacing Authority and the Guild, then his heart probably knew best. Let them study the facts first, and delay as long as possible opening his own thoughts to them. Of course . . . there was no way they could possibly understand the danger they were stumbling into, and no way he could warn them without risking a total collapse of the charade he'd been carrying on all these years.

"You can read the text here if you want—" he touched a switch under the edge of the table, and two compads opened out of the tabletop for Legroeder and Harriet "—and then compare with the documents. Afterward, we can talk. Now, why don't I go fix us a light dinner? I always eat early." Legroeder and Mahoney nodded; they were already absorbed in the materials.

McGinnis retreated quietly, not so much to prepare dinner as to prepare himself for the next attack, which surely would come. All the signs were there: the anonymous message from the Elmira library just a few hours ago, advising him that two people had been looking for information on *Impris*; and a separate warning, direct through his augments, that if a Rigger Legroeder and his lawyer came snooping, he was to turn them away. It had been years since he'd allowed himself to think much of the *Impris* investigation, and he'd found the warnings jarring at first—and then terrifying, once he'd examined the implications. Was the *Impris* matter about to be thrown wide open? Maybe he had insulated himself too well here in his enclave. He had indeed recognized Legroeder's name from the news, but in his determined insularity had paid little heed to the actual reports.

Now he recognized his error. It seemed likely that the confrontation he'd long dreaded was—quite without warning—at hand. Absolute caution and attention to control were essential.

He walked to the kitchen, just down the hall from the living room. He focused on his breathing, keenly aware that his thoughts could slip at any moment. He'd managed to keep his deepest intentions isolated from his augment network, but several times in the last hour, he'd almost lost the struggle. If only he weren't so dependent on the network for his own memories and thoughts!

The other side no doubt had their suspicions, but they could not be sure. The forces testing him from within were growing stronger; the instructions from those who would be his masters came with greater and greater urgency. If he had been complacent these last years, so had they. But no longer.

He stood before the cookmate, trembling, fingertips pressed to the countertop, trying to focus on what he could cook. And then the power hit him from within, like an ocean wave—slamming and lifting him as though to hurl him head over heels. His breath went out in a terrible gasp . . .

Stop it, don't let it past . . . FIGHT IT!

The fingers of the augments were reaching downward, trying to discover his innermost thoughts . . .

▫ *Let us see, let us see—!* ▫

He fought back with a grim will, clamping his thoughts down until his mind was almost totally blank . . . leaving only the familiar, abstract struggle of mind against circuitry. *("Out! Get out, you bastards—out!")* He reeled, losing ground. The eyes and ears of the augment, and of those who controlled it, were like a tiger at his tent, clawing at the thin flap that protected him, roaring to be let in . . .

(You may not, they are my thoughts, you may not have them . . .)

Even as he hissed his protest, the barrier was shredding, the claws tearing the canvas; in a few more heartbeats he would lose the struggle. When that happened—and he could smell the tiger's breath now, almost upon him!—he would be torn open like a gutted fish. He would spill everything he knew, everything he was about to do. And then it would be over and they would have won . . . they would have defeated him.

OVER MY DEAD BODY!

Like a rubber band snapping, the fear gave way to utter determination. Almost as if he were a rigger, he put all of his focus into that inward battle. And suddenly the canvas of the tent transformed itself to crystalloy steel—and the tiger raged and howled, but could not get through. It clawed and hurled itself against the barrier, in vain; and finally in frustration it stalked away, leaving him gasping.

McGinnis struggled to focus his eyes on the kitchen counter. His heart was pounding with the terror . . . and with the jubilation of having won one more time.

Always one more time. But the augments were not without deeper resources; and he knew their masters would be infuriated by his victory, his discipline and determination, and yes, his superior mental strength. Once the battle was truly joined, he couldn't win forever. He was weary, so weary. Soon the tiger would gain entry, and then his part in this war would be over. He'd bought a little time. But how much—a day? An hour? He hoped it would be long enough to do what he had to do.

The supreme irony was, he actually shared many of the *stated* goals of the hated masters of his augments—he too longed for humanity to reach out again to the more distant stars. But this collaboration with pirates . . . never. *Never.*

And now . . . out in the other room were two people he prayed he could trust—two guests who had fallen like angels into his life, to carry on the fight. Perhaps once they had the information and understood it, he could pass the burden at last. *So weary* . . .

But he had to give them time to absorb the knowledge, to begin to comprehend it before he dared open his own thoughts to explanation. He had to buy his guests a little more time.

He let his breath out slowly and ran his finger down the menu list on the cookmate. His guests might be angels, but they still needed to eat.

LEGROEDER ADJUSTED the screen of his compad, and started with the Fandrang report. It began with an investigation of certain piloting reports from *Impris* of difficulties in navigation. The outcome, according to the abstract, was uncertain. Legroeder read the introduction:

. . . into circumstances surrounding the loss of the passenger starship *Impris*, owned and operated by Golden Star Lines of Faber Eridani. Once considered the "Princess of the Starlanes," *Impris* disappeared en route from Faber Eridani to Vedris IV, in the thirteenth week of the year 217 Space. This was in time of war; however, no evidence of hostile action has been found.

Indeed, this report will examine certain troubling events noted prior to the final journey, events investigated by the author and his associate, Mr. Peñ Lee. The investigators traveled aboard *Impris* three times prior to her disappearance, observing and interviewing her crew. By chance, the author left the ship immediately before her last fateful journey; however, Mr. Lee remained aboard and is presumed lost with her passengers and crew.

The nature of the earlier events is difficult to summarize, and about them no firm conclusions can be drawn. They certainly call for a fuller investigation; they may present clues to rigging hazards that all would do well to understand. A fuller study may clarify the nature of that hazard—representing as it does the latest of the uncertainties and perils that have accompanied peoples of all kinds for as long as men have "gone down to the sea in ships."

This much is known about the final voyage of *Impris:* she departed Faber Eridani on the last day of the twelfth week of 217 Space (local date: Sunday, Springtide the thirty-fourth), at 2635 local evening time, bound for Vedris IV. She carried a full complement of 74 crew, under Captain Noel Friedman, and 486 passengers, including Mr. Lee. Her itinerary called for a brief layover at Vedris IV, before continuing on into the Aeregian sector.

Impris never reached Vedris IV. No communication was ever received from her. No evidence of her destruction has ever been found—though wreckage in interstellar space is notoriously difficult to locate. Though she traveled in time of war, she was far from areas of active conflict. Hostile action cannot be completely ruled out, but neither is there evidence to support . . .

Legroeder scratched his head. "There's no mention of piracy as a possible explanation for her disappearance."

Harriet glanced up from her viewer. "This was written just after the end of the war. If I'm not mistaken, there wasn't much piracy, even in Golen Space, for at least a decade after that."

"That's right," said McGinnis, who had come back into the room and was working at the bar. "The raider culture developed after the war—though you can trace much of its origin to the war and its fallout. I'm surprised you don't know that."

Legroeder felt a flash of irritation. "All right—so I flunked history. Give me a break, will you?" During the seven years of his captivity, he'd come to know a lot about the raider culture and its ways of operating, but very little about its past.

McGinnis inclined his head in apology, and Legroeder read on.

In the two years since her disappearance, several reports have been made to the RiggerGuild of purported sightings of *Impris* by riggers flying in the same region of the Flux, though not on identical routes. Upon investigation, these reports were dismissed by Guild authorities as imaginative constructs by riggers who, it must be said, are preselected for an ability to create vivid imagery. Nonetheless, these reports did bear certain similarities to the earlier reports by *Impris*'s own riggers, which triggered the initial phase of this investigation.

The statements from the *Impris* riggers will be examined in detail in the main body of this report. In brief, however, they concerned two distinct, but possibly related, classes of phenomenon: 1) a series of unexplained sightings of ships in the Flux; and 2) a series of difficulties experienced by the crew in returning from the Flux into normal-space.

The sightings, three in number, came to be referred to by the *Impris* crew as "ghost ship" sightings. The ships, while bearing markings of known worlds, appeared only briefly and did not respond to efforts at communication, nor could all riggers in the net confirm the sightings. The riggers came to describe these events as sightings of the "Flying Dutchman"—a reference to ancient legends of a haunted seagoing ship, a vessel doomed to sail through eternity with neither port nor rest nor hope.*

Was this a whimsical designation, reflecting the imaginary nature of the sightings? Or was it a truthful and accurate observation of a ship or ships caught in some dreadful layer of the Flux, unable to reach port or even respond to communication?

*References to the Flying Dutchman are hardly new to star rigging. The legendary ship *Devonhol* has long been a part of rigger lore, despite the lack of historical evidence for the existence of such a ship.

Most of this material was familiar, so Legroeder skipped ahead to the main body of the report. Fandrang and Lee had conducted extensive interviews with her rigger crew and captain. Fandrang noted that even after in-depth analysis, he found it impossible to draw conclusions. Nevertheless . . .

We found surprising consistency in the sightings, even when reported by different sets of riggers on separate occasions—similarity in the sudden but fleeting manner of the other ships' appearances in the Flux, in the reception of faint distress calls, and in the subjective impressions of there being *something wrong* aboard the ghost ships—specifically, a sense of a "living presence" within the ghost ships, as though there were live riggers in the other ships' nets straining to reach out to make contact . . .

Captain Friedman regarded these sightings as significant in terms of the psychology of his own rigger crew—thus his request for outside consultation—but he discounted their reality in physical terms. (See Appendix A: "Captain Friedman Interview.") It was the captain's belief that a pattern had developed within the rigger crew's imaging, predisposing them to "see" things like ghost ships during certain kinds of Flux transition. His concern was more for the possibility of group hallucination among the rigger-crew, with attendant risks to the safety of the ship.

Our own survey of the *Impris* rigger-crew supported no such concerns at the time—though of course now, with the disappearance of the ship, we must reconsider all possibilities. (See Appendix B: "Rigger Interviews 1–17.") We found all members of the crew to be clear minded, cooperative, and helpful—at least within the bounds of normal rigger variance. Several were rather private individuals, a common enough trait among riggers, and several exhibited low levels of anxiety concerning our presence and the matter we were investigating. However, none of these observations caused us to consider detaining the ship in port or to request replacement crew. Indeed, we felt that it was a fine crew.

What did concern us was the possibility of some *physical* effect arising from repeated passage through the interstellar Flux. This is a vaguely stated concern, but it is difficult to be more precise without further data. Could problems be traced to certain regions of the Flux? If so, why were similar problems not noted on other ships? Were the difficulties experienced in exiting the Flux (Appendix C: "Prior Navigational Anomalies") somehow related to the sightings, real or imagined, of the ghost ships? These were among the questions we sought to answer.

Legroeder read with growing interest. The navigational difficulties Fandrang referred to mostly seemed to involve transient conflicts of imagery in the net. Shared imagery, of course, lay at the core of flight with a multi-rigger crew. One rigger had described a *tenuous* feeling in the net, a temporary difficulty in finding anchor points in the Flux. This reference was not to physical points in space or time, but rather intuitive compass points in the minds of the riggers. Without such anchors, riggers would find it impossible to make navigational connections back to normal-space.

Legroeder skimmed ahead, looking for an explanation. He found, not an answer but a suspicion, farther into the text.

"What's he talking about with these EQ levels along starship routes?" Harriet asked, peering over the top of her glasses. Apparently she had reached the same section.

"EQ is an old mathematical expression for energetic turbulence leaking into the Flux from black holes, star formation, matter annihilation, that sort of thing. No one uses the term much anymore. It was an approximation for something no one quite understood."

"Do they understand it now?"

"Well—we're using different measurements now. It's still an imperfect science. From what I hear, the Narseil come closest to having a good theoretical understanding."

"So maybe they should have been brought in on this investigation?"

Legroeder stared back at her reflectively. "Yeah, maybe. Except . . . they got blamed for it, right?"

"Ah. Yes," Harriet said.

Legroeder continued reading.

. . . in comparing the flight histories of *Impris* with those of other ships flying well-established routes, we found *Impris* crews experiencing a 37 percent higher-than-mean EQ exposure. In fact, the very stability of the crew during her final year resulted in even greater EQ exposure than the "average" *Impris* crew over the ship's lifetime.

Tables followed, which Legroeder only glanced over. He hadn't looked at this sort of thing in a long time, and it hadn't gotten any easier to read over the years. He pushed ahead to the conclusions.

No intimations of carelessness or negligence should be inferred from these findings. All flights appear to have been conducted within lawful limits; nevertheless, the fact emerges that the flight paths of *Impris*'s normal runs did expose her to areas of relatively high EQ.

One important factor may turn out to be the star-birthing region of the Akeides Nebula—a navigational "caution point" along the route between Karg-Elert 4 and Vedris IV, and a sightseeing attraction for passengers. Though unquestionably a beautiful sight, one must ask: is the nebula also a hazard to those who pass by it? This report draws no conclusions, but we believe the matter deserves further study—not just with respect to the Akeides Nebula, but EQ exposure in general. More will be said about this in Section 4 . . .

At this point, the report shifted to a history of the Fandrang/Lee investigation, including logs of the observation flights. Legroeder flipped through the pages awhile, then sat gazing into the fire in the fireplace, lost in dark thought on the possibility of there being something in the Flux, something unidentified, that could so drastically interfere with a rigger's ability to find his way among the stars.

"Legroeder? What do you make of it?" Harriet had a troubled expression on her face.

He turned from the fire, shrugging. "I wish I knew."

"Well, you're the rigger. Does this stuff seem plausible?"

"Which? The ghost ship sightings? The EQ readings?"

"Any of it. All of it."

Legroeder sighed. "Who can tell? But if any of it is true, then riggers need to know."

"Excuse me," Harriet said pointedly. "If it is true, then *we* need to know. It could constitute objective evidence that *Impris* is still out there."

"Oh. Yeah." For a few minutes there, Legroeder had lost sight of his own troubles. "But Fandrang doesn't seem to have come up with any answers."

"Well—" Harriet pressed a finger to her lips. "If *Impris* is still out there—and we know it is—then we're back to the question of why someone, aside from the pirates, wants nobody else to know. Wants it badly enough to hide evidence of a danger to *all* riggers." She tapped the compad screen and looked around. "I wonder where our host—oh, there he is."

"What do you think?" McGinnis said, coming through the door.

"It's damn sobering," said Legroeder. "But if this Inspector Fandrang was so well respected, why weren't his suspicions ever investigated further?"

McGinnis sat down heavily, his face creased with the now-familiar pained expression. "Why, indeed?"

"And why were these documents removed from public access?" asked Harriet. "I can only think of two plausible reasons. One is that they were discredited upon examination."

"I've found no evidence of that." McGinnis clasped white-knuckled hands in front of himself.

"Then the other is that they endangered someone's position, power, or money."

McGinnis made a clicking sound with his tongue, and almost smiled. He riffled the documents in his hands.

"What are we talking about?" Harriet asked. "A cover-up by the shipping line?"

McGinnis shook his head. "None that I could see. Oh sure, there might have been a wish not to alarm potential passengers—and perhaps liability concerns. Certainly, for the Golden Star Line, it was preferable for the public to think that the ship was destroyed by the Narseil than that it didn't come back because its riggers had . . . how shall we say, *faded into the Flux.*"

"Well, that right there—"

"But that's not all there was to it," McGinnis interrupted. "That much would have come out eventually, if there hadn't been someone who wanted it hidden, badly enough to see to it that *history was rewritten.*"

"And who might that have been?" Harriet asked.

McGinnis rested the documents on the table with care. "I don't know—if I can tell you—that." He seemed to be struggling again, a grimace creasing his face. "I can show you *what* information was hidden. But by whom is . . . difficult." He drew one slow breath after another, until the grimace faded. "If we had the time, I could take you through some of the ways the truth was obliterated in the public record—or altered enough that it might as well have been obliterated. But to really understand that time period . . . you'd have to visit a historian I know."

Harriet cocked her head with interest.

"A Narseil. By the name of El'ken."

Legroeder stared at McGinnis in astonishment. *The Narseil historian El'ken.* Even Legroeder had heard of him. "But if the Narseil were framed for the loss of the ship—"

"You won't necessarily receive a warm welcome. Even a century later, El'ken hasn't forgotten, or forgiven. The breach has never really healed. But for reasons of his research, El'ken lives here in this system, out in the first belt. Asteroid named Arco Iris. I'll give you a reference, if you like."

"But why would someone go to such trouble to discredit the Narseil? It makes no sense."

McGinnis, eyebrows raised, seemed about to nod in agreement; then his movement froze, and he squeezed his eyes shut in obvious pain. A warbling chime sounded somewhere, and he seemed to be struggling against an urge to turn his head.

Harriet reached out her hand. "Mr. McGinnis—"

"No," he whispered, his face pale. The chime continued, insistently. McGinnis stood up awkwardly. "If you'll . . . excuse me . . . for just a moment . . ."

Legroeder felt an inexplicable urge to reach out, to stop him. He felt his hands clench as McGinnis disappeared into the hallway. A moment later, he heard the sound of a door locking.

He and Harriet stared at each other. Legroeder's heart was hammering; he didn't know why. He swallowed and picked up the Fandrang report again. Across the table, Harriet did likewise. But neither of them could read long without their gazes being drawn to the back of the room.

ROBERT MCGINNIS locked the door to his office and tested it with a shaking hand, then lowered himself into his desk chair. He drew a slow breath as he turned on the neural-interface panel. His head was throbbing from the inner struggle. The chime had been a summons from his security monitor. He was under assault, this time not just from his own implants, but from the outside. The enemy had been blocking *his* outside transmissions earlier; now they were trying to force their own way in through his security shields. Not a physical attack, of course. No, this was much worse . . .

There was so much he had wanted to say . . . about criminals in government, and the Kyber, and their meddling with all of space commerce . . . but he couldn't risk it, because the barrier he'd built between his thoughts and the implants was beginning to fail. And now it was too late to say it directly to Legroeder and Mahoney. But perhaps there was another way.

This was all happening far faster than he'd anticipated. The enemy must have glimpsed enough through his mental barriers to at least suspect his intentions. Now they would do everything in their power to stop him—everything short of revealing themselves to the rest of the world. But he, McGinnis, was expendable. This was the battle he had been dreading. A battle to the death.

It was a battle he could not hope to win. The augments had always been stronger, but he had been protected by their owners' desire for secrecy, and their belief that he would remain valuable as a guardian of information, and a powerful agent at need. He doubted they cared much about his value now.

But perhaps he could still win the war. For himself. For those two out there. For the rest of civilized space. For his last thirty years of effort.

□ *Open link . . . access requested . . .* □

Denied. Denied. Denied.

The noise level in his skull was ballooning. He could feel the rictus on his face, the twitching of his eyes. If he could just keep control a little longer . . . keep the compartments of his mind separate, the barrier between the artificial and the natural, the augment and the McGinnis. If he could keep the implanted chips at bay long enough to get his guests out of here and the information with them . . . before the intruding signal took command and turned him, as he knew it would, into a machine that would ruthlessly kill the very people he was trying to help . . .

And long enough for one more thing.

To find a way to preserve the information in his own thoughts . . . in spite of the tremendous power of the augments. He heard Rufus barking somewhere outside, was aware of Rufus's presence at the edges of his mind, the chips that he himself had implanted in his dog, linked to his own. *Rufus,* he thought, *can I do this to you?* It would be risky; it could kill the dog. But what else could he do?

He could feel the augments searching like a roving eye, trying to discover what he was doing. *I'm sorry, boy. Whatever happens . . . I need you to do this for me . . . one last service . . .*

He made an adjustment on the interface board, hesitated only a moment, then closed the circuit. With one part of his mind, he felt a projection channel opening into the living room. In another part, he felt a burring sensation, and then something that felt like great stores of grain slipping away, down a long, long shaft . . .

LEGROEDER WAS not even aware of the sound of the dog barking in the distance until he heard a sudden yelp—and the barking abruptly stopped. Then he heard a loud, sharp voice:

"You must leave at once!"

Legroeder looked up with a start and saw a holoimage of McGinnis standing in front of the fireplace. A faint flicker of the fire could be seen through the image of the man.

"What's wrong?" Legroeder asked.

"You must leave at once!" the image of McGinnis repeated. *"You are no longer safe here!"*

Legroeder and Harriet exchanged alarmed glances.

"Excuse me," Harriet said. "We can't leave. Our flyer is disabled."

The image faltered for a moment. *"Christ, that's right."* It seemed to freeze, and then spoke again. *"Take my flyer! I'm releasing the controls to you now. But go. GO! Take this cube and take all the documents and HURRY!"* With that, the image blinked out.

A small compartment opened in the top of the coffee table. In it was a datacube half the size of a human fist.

Legroeder stared at it in astonishment and indecision, then

snatched up the cube. "Gather the documents!" he commanded, jumping to his feet. Pocketing the cube, he hurried to the door. He peered cautiously up and down the hallway. "McGinnis!" he shouted. "McGinnis, do you need help?" There were several closed doors. Did he dare go searching? *You are no longer safe.*

"Take the documents and go!" boomed McGinnis's voice again, from hidden speakers. *"If you delay, you'll lose everything!"*

Legroeder cursed, returning to Harriet. "I don't know what kind of trouble he's in, but I don't think we can help him. Let's do what he says. Let's get this packed up!"

Harriet stuffed the last of the folders into the archive box. Her voice shook. "Legroeder, what do you think is happening?"

His own breath was tight with fear. "I don't know," he whispered, picking up the box. "But remember Jakus? And the missile? All I know is McGinnis wants us to keep this stuff safe! *Let's go!"*

THEY CAME upon McGinnis's dog Rufus outside the house. It was lying on its side, glassy-eyed—twitching, as if with a seizure. Legroeder crouched by the dog. "Look at that!" He pointed to a tiny implant flickering rapidly behind the dog's ear. He looked up, scanning the estate and the tree line. Was the house under attack? If so, it was by an invisible foe. Legroeder rose. "I don't think we can do anything for him, either. I don't know what's going on, but we'd better get out of here."

As if in answer, Rufus yipped twice, then was still.

Harriet's face was white. "Which way?"

"Around back." They hurried past the damaged rental car to the rear of the house. McGinnis's flyer was a high-powered Arcturan sports model, for which Legroeder was grateful as they climbed in. Whatever was going on, he wanted all the speed he could get. "Strap in," he said, scanning the controls.

As the power came on, he squinted, shading his eyes from the glare of the setting sun. No sign of anything in the air; nothing moving within the security field. He wondered if he should use the autopilot. Probably not; better to risk unfamiliarity with the controls. He took a deep breath. "Lifting off." He pushed the power forward, and the flyer shot into the air. Before he had it fully under control, they were already climbing out through the forcefield boundary and were well above the house and clearing.

The com suddenly crackled, and they heard McGinnis's voice:

"You will have the only copies. Keep them safe! Get to El'ken if you can!

Legroeder exchanged glances with Harriet, then banked the flyer in a circle around the clearing to find his bearings.

McGinnis fought for control as he watched his guests' departure on the remote scanner. He was in a life-and-death struggle now to retain the functioning of his own brain. The chips had not yet decided to kill him; they were still trying to keep him from doing what he was doing, but they were not yet certain what that was. It had taken all of his strength to give Legroeder and Mahoney their chance to get away, and to keep that information locked away from the augment-mediated portion of his brain.

His hand shook over the control board. Jesus; he was losing it. He shut his eyes, opened them in time to see his finger press the stud to power up the defensive laser. *"Damn you, no!"* he whispered. It was not *him* aiming, but the augments. Shuddering, he wrenched control back, and in the instant that the laser fired, he deflected the aim. A lance of death stabbed up from the house . . .

It missed the departing flyer.

He slammed the power off to the laser and swiveled from the board, shaking. The information was still pouring from his mind, but not reaching his augments, not yet. *Iron will. You must keep an iron will.*

The information about the *Impris* conspiracy was out now, and what was done with it was up to others. Maybe, with luck, they'd live long enough to follow the trail to *Impris* and back again to the bastards who had ruined *his* life and were using the ship in their web of lies. But the augments didn't know yet, not for certain. And it was crucial for the protection of Legroeder and Mahoney that they not learn—or at least not transmit the knowledge out. Their masters might suspect that he'd betrayed them in the end, but they wouldn't know, at least not until Legroeder and Mahoney were on their way.

The thought was lost in a flash of pain that seemed to come from a million miles away. The fun and games were over; they were going to torture him to break down the barrier. He clenched his teeth and turned back to the console. Gasping, he struck the console once with his fist. It was time for the final action. He had always known this moment would come; he was well prepared. The circuits were ready. It took several steps, no mistakes: switch cover up, button jammed down, laser charged.

And then . . . the code, painfully typed in, grim desperation on his lips, focusing, focusing, *over my*: D-E-A-D-B-O-D-Y . . .

Shaking with pain, he fired the laser.

This time, nothing happened . . .

. . . except the deliberate overload in the laser capacitors, exploding in the basement. A half-second later, the pyrotechnics beneath the first floor erupted—and then billowing fire roared to life in the center of the house. There was no escape now, not with the fire-arrest system disabled, not with the door lock sealed.

He seized the interface input cable from the console control. Reaching behind his right ear, blinded by pain, he lifted the flap of hair and jammed the connector into the augment socket. A wind howled through his brain.

He keyed the next sequence of switches. A message on the screen began flashing:

ARE YOU SURE YOU WANT TO DELETE
MAIN MEMORY MODULE?
TYPE "YES" FOLLOWED BY NAME AND I.D.
TO CONFIRM.

He could barely type now, his hand was shaking so hard. He used his left hand to steady his right, as he typed with one finger. He paused for a heartbeat to cry out a silent command, *Rufus, run for safety—take what I've given you—keep it safe until . . . Jesus, why didn't I send you with them? Look for them when you can.*

Crying aloud, he pressed START. *Good-bye, my friend . . .*

The erasure current was like a balm of flowing water in his skull. The pain subsided as the programming of the augments faded, as the waters washed away all of the jointly stored memories of the last thirty years, all of *his* memories as well as the augments'. It lasted only an instant, but an instant that seemed to go on forever . . .

. . . as all that was Robert McGinnis, all the memories that were his life, slipped away like sand through a broken hourglass. And when it was all gone, there would be light, as the fire roared, and peace . . .

Peace.

Chapter 8

FURTHER TRUTHS

"DID HE just *shoot* at us?"

Legroeder glanced over his shoulder. He thought he'd seen a laser flash. "If he did, he missed by a mile. He couldn't have been aiming for us." But if McGinnis hadn't aimed for the flyer, what *had* he aimed for? Legroeder scanned, but couldn't see any other craft in the sky.

"Look down there!" Harriet shouted.

He was just beginning to break out into a southerly heading; he banked back into an orbit around the house instead. "What is it?"

"I thought I saw something. Fire, I think. In the house!"

"Jesus!" He banked steeply, ignoring Harriet's gasp, and peered down at the house. There was no mistaking it: smoke was curling from a second-floor window. "The whole place is going up!"

"We've got to do something!"

"We can try to get back down, but I don't—"

Whoop! Whoop! A light flashed on the console with the audible alarm, and the flyer lurched sickeningly. He fought to steady it.

Harriet's voice was tight with fear. "What was that?"

"His forcefield. It won't let us back in! We *can't* go down!" Legroeder snapped a series of switches on the console. Finally he found a remote for the forcefield, but it blinked: ACCESS DENIED. "It's demanding a password. Harriet, I don't think there's any way we're going to get back in there."

"Let me try." Harriet began keying in everything they

could think of: *McGinnis. Rigger. Impris* ... After the fifth attempt, the screen flashed: UNAUTHORIZED ACCESS ATTEMPT! SECONDARY OVERRIDE CODE REQUIRED! "Oh, hell. Legroeder—"

"Yah." He strained to watch the house as he maneuvered outside the forcefield. Unfortunately, the barrier was hard to see. The alarm sounded and the flyer bucked again. He took them farther out, but lower. If he could bring them down near the edge of the clearing ... maybe the forcefield ended before the start of the forest. "I don't know what kind of a shield this is. I wonder if it would let us *walk* through ..." He interrupted himself as he saw something ahead and below. "What's that?"

"It's the dog!"

Rufus was running in a zigzag toward the edge of the clearing. Legroeder slowed the flyer, watching, as the dog burst through the forcefield with a sparkle, bolted in alarm into the woods, then reemerged and tried to run back in through the security field. It half-slid, half-bounced off the invisible barrier. Terrified, it disappeared into the woods again. This time it didn't come back.

"Hell!" Legroeder pulled the flyer into a savage climb. "We're not going to get in that way, either. Harriet, there's not a damn thing we can do."

"My dear God," whispered Harriet, pointing at the house.

There was a flicker of flame inside the windows now, and a thicker plume of smoke curling into the air. Legroeder cursed. "Let's get some altitude and see if we can call for help." He flicked the com switch. "Can you handle that?"

Harriet didn't waste time answering, but starting calling out a Mayday. She got only static in reply. "Can you get us farther from the house?" Whatever had been blocking their com-signal before was apparently still doing so. Legroeder boosted them quickly to five hundred meters altitude. Harriet finally got through and reported the fire to a regional control center. An emotionless voice told her that units would be on their way at once. She glanced at Legroeder. "Should we wait for them to arrive?"

Legroeder hesitated, scanning the sky for other craft. The question kept running through his mind: Why had McGinnis told them to flee? And what had started the fire? Was McGinnis under attack, and if so, by whom?

"Legroeder?"

He shook his head finally. "I think we'd better get the hell out of here, like he told us to. I don't know what started that fire, but if someone was coming after him, then they're pretty damn sure to come after us, too. I'm glad you didn't broadcast our names just now."

Harriet was silent.

"Look," Legroeder snapped. "I don't like leaving him, either. But he wanted us to take these documents and keep them safe. And we aren't going to do that if we get caught by whoever decided to take him out."

"Okay," she said quietly.

Legroeder was already turning the flyer away from the estate. He took one last look back. It wasn't going to make much difference when rescue teams arrived, he thought; if that forcefield didn't go down, the rescue workers would be as helpless as he and Harriet had been.

He shook his head, pushed the throttle out to full, and was jammed back in his seat as the sport flyer accelerated.

THE LINK broke with a jarring twang, but not before Major Jenkins Talbott caught the image that McGinnis had projected back into the link: *fire . . . destruction . . . termination.*

Talbott cursed violently, trying to reestablish the contact. C'mon, c'mon . . . But there was no longer any carrier signal from the implants, even on the lowest level. The screen in front of him had turned to static—how the hell?—and all of the house monitors had shut down. Damn! McGinnis had somehow silenced his personal implants. There was only one way Talbott could think of to do that.

The man had taken his own life. Deliberately, and probably premeditatedly.

That can't be . . .

Talbott leaned back and hollered to the tech on the other side of the cramped control room. "Jerry, 'd you do something to cut the signal from McGinnis?"

"Not a thing," came Jerry's drawl. "What's wrong?"

Talbott didn't answer. He scrolled back through the log. It took a few minutes of searching, but there it was, hidden in the noise: McGinnis issuing a *termination* command—on himself. *Jezu.* How could he have done such a thing? And why? Mr. Big Ex-Marine had never rebelled before—at least not until he'd let that rigger and his lawyer onto his property. What the fuck . . .

Talbott hit the controls; the display in front of him switched to an overhead satellite view. It zoomed in with quick jumps until McGinnis's house emerged from the forest, smoke and flames billowing.

"Talbott—what's going on with McGinnis?" squawked a voice in his headset. His commanding officer.

Crap. Talbott cut from the remote link and switched over to the local.

"Major?"

"He killed himself and his house is burning down," Talbott snapped into the com. Christ, was there anything else that could go wrong with this operation? Maybe he'd at least taken Legroeder and the lawyer with him.

"What?"

"You heard me."

"Don't move."

Talbott wasn't about to move; he was glued to his seat. He pulled back a little on the satellite-zoom. About the time Colonel Paroti showed up to lean over his shoulder, he saw what else could go wrong.

"What's that flying away from the house?" Paroti asked, stabbing at the lower left corner of the display.

Talbott was already reaching for the e-com to call in backup. But he knew it was too late. "That's McGinnis's flyer," he muttered.

"I thought you said McGinnis killed himself."

"He did—I think."

"You think?"

"Well, I don't have the body, for chrissake. But yeah, I'm pretty sure. That may be the rigger and the lawyer, taking his flyer."

Paroti growled. "Can we bring 'em down?"

Talbott shook his head. "Assuming they're heading back toward the city, it would take maybe fifteen minutes to intercept." He looked up at the colonel. "They'll be in patrolled airspace by then—"

Paroti swore. "We *can't*, then. Too much chance of being seen."

"No shit. Wait a sec' . . ." Talbott paged back in the satellite imagery; the replay took a few seconds to load. "There." He pointed. "Yeah, there's the woman and Legroeder getting into the flyer. I wonder if McGinnis sent them away."

Paroti smacked a fist into his hand in fury. *"Damn it to shit!"* He swung back to the screen. "Did they get away with any information? Or did it all go up in that house?"

Talbott yanked off his headset and sat back angrily. All the equipment they'd gathered, all the organization, the men, the ships ready to go when the call came—and they couldn't fucking stop an unarmed flyer. "How would I know? But I'm guessing they took the records. The implant logs are garbled pretty bad, but I'm thinking McGinnis was planning to hand the records over."

"What a fuckup! How could this happen? Christ, Jenk— what made McGinnis do it? Did he do *anything* we told him to?" Paroti clawed at his sideburns in agitation. Finally he moaned, "We're gonna have to tell Command. And I suppose North, too."

Another risk of exposure. *And who's gonna take the heat? Not Command. Not North.* Talbott scowled up and down the console. God, he wanted a drink right now.

"What do you think about picking them off in the city?" Paroti asked.

Talbott glared up at him. *Why is this idiot in charge?* He drew a breath. "We can't take chances like that, Colonel.

Going after them out in the wilderness was risky enough. This is supposed to be an undercover operation, remember?" *And now we screwed it up royally.*

"Don't be a wise ass. Give me some options. What about that other rigger, or whatever the hell she is. Legroeder's woman. Can we do something with her? She probably knows some things that would be useful."

Talbott rocked back in his chair, surprised by his commander. "There's a thought now. That rigger might not be so eager to spill his guts if we've got his girl. We'd probably have to have Command pass on it first. And I suppose we'll need to see what Hizhonor North has to say. But grabbing her just might be a way to pull our nuts out of the fire on this one."

"Then get on it . . ."

"YOU KNOW," Legroeder said, between glances at the instruments and the autopilot, "we're flying what could easily be construed as a stolen craft. Plus, we've got a box full of documents that were probably known to have been in his archives. We might want to do some thinking about how that's going to look."

"I have been thinking," she said softly. "And I don't like what I'm hearing."

"You think they're going to come after us?"

"I think the police will probably want to have some words with us."

"Which raises the next question. Are they in on this frame-up business?"

Harriet bit her lip. "Maybe not. Whatever's going on at the RiggerGuild—and whoever *they're* colluding with—I haven't seen a reason yet to suspect the police."

"But do we trust them enough to go back to Elmira? Will we be safe there?" They were flying on a southerly heading at the moment; Elmira was to the southeast.

Harriet scowled in concentration. Clearly matters had gone beyond anything in her experience. "Seems to me, if anything, we're probably safer in the city. At least there we have some control, and we can use the legal system. Peter has good security, and whoever these people are, they don't seem eager to reveal themselves."

"They might not have to, if they can frame us for McGinnis's house burning."

"Yes, but we *were* shot at before we landed there."

"Which will be hard to prove, until someone gets through the forcefield and looks at the rental flyer."

"Well, nothing's easy," Harriet said. "You know, McGinnis knew more than he told us. I think he was expecting us."

"Why do you say that?"

"For one thing, he knew who we were. Remember his remark about whoever shot at us not liking lawyers? Only I didn't tell him I was a lawyer?"

Legroeder grunted. "I was wondering about his reconstructive surgery. I didn't see any datachip markers on him, but that doesn't mean he didn't have implants."

"Meaning—? What are you thinking?"

"I don't know." Legroeder rubbed his jaw. His guess was, anyone with implants was suspect on this world; but that didn't mean he was guilty of anything. "I'm just thinking Jakus had them, and gave every sign of being under their influence. And we know where *he* got his implants."

Harriet was watching him over her glasses. "Golen Space?"

Legroeder nodded. Implants made him uneasy enough in and of themselves; but in the pirate culture, they were designed without safeguards, and were used for control as much as for enhancement. He shuddered, remembering how close he had come to having them in his own head.

With a deep breath, he set a new course for Elmira.

THEY LANDED at the edge of the city shortly after sunset, in a driving rainstorm. They sat in the grounded flyer, listening to the rain pound on the roof, while Harriet called for Peter to send a car to meet them, and made arrangements for the flyer to be garaged outside the city. Then they piled into Peter's associate's car with the box of documents. It was a gloomy ride to Harriet's office, in the rain and the darkness. They were greeted outside by another of the PI's men, already on watch.

When they walked into the office, shaking off the raindrops, Legroeder was surprised to see a woman sitting at Harriet's desk, poring over Harriet's com-console. The woman's face looked familiar. "Hi, Mom," she said. "I was starting to worry."

"We had a few problems, dear," Harriet answered, showing Legroeder where to put the box. "Like someone trying to shoot us out of the sky, and then a house burning down. Legroeder, this is my daughter Morgan. Morgan, Rigger Legroeder."

They shook hands. Morgan appeared to be in her mid-thirties, a good-looking woman with a narrower and more angular face than Harriet's, but with her mother's greenish eyes and intensity of expression. She looked alarmed as her mother bustled around the office, turning down lights and closing shades. Then Harriet told her about the visit with McGinnis.

"Christ, Mother! You need to get some security. Do you think they'll attack you here in the city?"

Harriet sank into an overstuffed chair with a heartfelt sigh. "I don't think so. But Peter's on his way over now. We'll do whatever he says."

"But what about Mr. McGinnis? Do you have any idea what's happened to him?"

Harriet looked grim. "I have a pretty good idea, yes, though I hope I'm wrong. I'll ask Peter to send someone up there as soon as possible. But in the meantime, McGinnis gave us some extremely sensitive materials to safeguard. This stuff could be major armament for Legroeder in his case with the Guild and the Spacing Authority. What else it will do, I don't know." Harriet got up with a groan and pried the lid off the box. "Somebody is awfully afraid of what's in there. So let's get busy making backup copies. We'll want one in a bank vault, one in free-float storage on the net, and maybe a couple in other places. Let's copy the cube first, then scan in all the hardcopy."

"Let me clear a space here," Morgan said. A smile flickered on her lips. "Jeez, mother, I haven't seen you look this alive in years. Maybe you should have people shoot at you more often." The smile disappeared when it became apparent that neither Harriet nor Legroeder could make light of the situation. "Sorry. Let me see if I can get this going for you."

"Any calls while we were gone?"

"*Yes*—I almost forgot. There was a call for Legroeder from the hospital. It was sealed, so I saved it for you." Morgan tapped on the phone pad and turned the viewer toward Legroeder. "Do you want to take it in private?"

Legroeder shook his head. Did Maris wake up? he wondered hopefully. He keyed the call and saw the face of the attending physician.

"Mr. Legroeder," said the doctor, "I'm calling to let you know that Maris O'Hare is about to be transferred out of our facility. Some of her relatives came by and made the arrangements. I know you were concerned about her, and I hope this reaches you before she's gone. Please give me a call back. It's now nineteen hundred hours."

Oh, sweet Jesus. Legroeder looked up at Harriet in fear. "Somebody got to Maris." He checked the time. It was 2430, getting late in the evening.

Harriet hurried to his side. "What happened?"

He shook his head and pressed the callback button.

The phone blinked on, displaying the face of the duty nurse. Legroeder asked for Doctor Goldman and was promptly put on hold. He fumed helplessly until the doctor came on. "Mr. Legroeder—I was just on my way out. I'm not sure if Ms. O'Hare is still here. They were supposed to come for her a little while ago."

"*Who* was?"

"Their names were—ahh, MacAffee and Squire. Man and woman. As I said in the message, they were family. Half-siblings, I believe."

"Doctor, she doesn't *have* any family on Faber Eridani! She told me her closest family was on Gamma Ori Three. That's about as far away as you can get and still be in the same galaxy! There's no way they could be here now even if they'd been sent word!"

The doctor leaned away from the phone, frowning. "Well, that's very strange. They had all the proper credentials. Are you sure? From what you told me, her knowledge of her family was years out of date."

Legroeder shook his head vigorously. "No—this isn't right!" His heart was sinking.

"Well, it was all according to procedure—though I did argue against moving her. I said she was better off here—"

"Wait—doctor—where did they say they were taking her?"

"They had papers from a private hospital in another city, where there were physicians they knew. Legally, since she was stable, I couldn't refuse."

Legroeder's grip tightened on the phone pad. "Is she gone yet?"

"Hold on, let me check. I'm not on that floor right now."

Legroeder asked Harriet, "How fast can you get me to the hospital?"

Harriet touched her earring and began muttering urgently.

Dr. Goldman returned to the phone. "Apparently they arrived just a few minutes ago to check her out."

"Stop them!"

"Well, I can try, but I—"

"You *have* to! I'm on my way. *Don't let them take her!"* Before the doctor could reply, Legroeder lunged for the door.

"Wait, I'm coming with you!" Harriet called. "Morgan, keep copying this material!"

The ride to the hospital with Peter's man took ten frantic minutes. Legroeder jumped out ahead of Harriet and dashed through the lobby and up to the third floor. "Maris O'Hare! Is she still here?" he cried, running past the front desk.

"Sir! Just a moment!"

Legroeder ignored the shout and rounded the corner to Maris's room. He stopped, panting, inside the doorway. *"Maris?"* he shouted. The bed was empty, stripped. He turned. "Where is she?"

"Sir!" A nurse was behind him, followed by a robot security guard. "Please come this way. If you want to talk to—"

"Dr. Goldman! Where's Dr. Goldman?"

"Dr. Goldman's not—"

"I'm right here," said a voice from down the hall. The doctor hurried into view. "I tried to call you. I wasn't able to stop them."

"What?"

"I'm very sorry—they were gone by the time I got downstairs."

"Damn it to hell!" Legroeder clenched his fists, fingernails biting into his hands.

"I really am sorry. But they identified themselves as closest kin. They had the right to insist. I simply had no legal authority to hold her here."

"Damn the legal authority!"

The doctor drew back. "Excuse me, I know you're upset . . ."

Legroeder took a deep breath, trying to calm himself. He could feel the blood pounding in his head. It would do no good to scream at the doctor. "I'm sorry—what hospital did you say they were taking her to?"

The doctor checked his compad. "Symmes. In the town of Arlmont in the Northern Province."

"And you did verify that this hospital was expecting her?"

"Mr. MacAffee showed us the admission order, yes."

"But did you call the hospital?"

The doctor looked pale, both defensive and frightened. "There seemed no need. All of the documentation was in order. Mr. Legroeder, are you *sure* that—"

"I'm telling you those people were not her family! I don't *care* about their documents. They were not her brother and sister!" Legroeder turned with helpless fury to Harriet, who had finally caught up.

"Then who were they?" Dr. Goldman shook his head in dismay. "If this was an abduction, we'd better call the police at once." He turned to the robot guard. "Check the door security. See if there's a record of the vehicle that Ms. O'Hare left in."

Harriet spoke quickly. "We'll need that, and we'll need all of the purported documentation." She pulled at her earring and spoke subvocally for a moment.

"May I ask who you are?" Dr. Goldman said.

"Harriet Mahoney, attorney at law," she said brusquely. "Doctor, there will certainly be a legal investigation into this matter, and it is paramount that all of the documents be preserved. We'll need to examine them for evidence of forgery."

The doctor's alarm deepened visibly. "Yes, of course. But hadn't we better concentrate on getting the police on this?"

"Absolutely. Please do that. We'll be in touch. But right now, we must see if we can put a pursuit on that vehicle."

"They told me they were headed for the Northern Province," Dr. Goldman said.

"Then they probably aren't. Legroeder, let's move quickly. Thank you, Doctor." Without waiting for anyone to reply, Harriet seized Legroeder above the elbow and propelled him down the hall toward the lift and the exit. "If there's any more to learn here, Peter and his people will learn it. I don't think we want to be here when the police arrive."

"Are we going after the car that took Maris?"

"Peter's getting someone on it right now. But Legroeder—understand there's very little chance of catching them. If they could produce papers to fool the hospital, then they aren't going to be waiting around for us to catch them."

"But we've got to do everything we can—"

"We will, Legroeder. We will." Harriet steered him out a side exit onto the street. In front of the hospital, a police flyer's lights were flashing. As they strode away quickly, she added, "But we'll let the people do it who can do it. *You*, my friend, have other business. And no time to delay, before the police start to suspect you." She shook her head worriedly. "And what am I doing? Helping you to become a fugitive? God. There's the car . . ."

LEGROEDER SLUMPED in a chair in Harriet's office, picking with a pair of chopsticks at a nearly empty carton of Fabri takeout food. An hour ago, he had been starving; now he had no appetite.

Morgan glanced at him sympathetically. She was still busy copying and scanning the hundreds of pages of material they had brought from McGinnis's house. The data on the cube had already been encoded and distributed for safekeeping on the net.

Legroeder started as Harriet snapped off her phone; he must have dozed off. "You were right, Legroeder. There *is* no Symmes Hospital in the town of Arlmont. The town itself is nothing more than a trading post for lumbering interests in the northern forest."

Legroeder grunted, unsurprised. Maris really was gone, then. Either dead . . . or in the hands of the same people who had tried to kill him.

"Peter will give a report to the police, of course. But I doubt they'll be able to do much." Harriet consulted her notes, then continued grimly, "We need to think very carefully about what your next move should be."

"Meaning—"

"Meaning, whoever these people are, they seem to have connections in more places than I'd guessed. We may not be safe here for long." Harriet ran her fingers through her hair in agitation. "But who the hell *are* they? Someone in Spacing Authority? Some outside group? There's a note here from Peter. It seems that spaceship hangar where Jakus Bark worked is owned indirectly by Centrist Strength. I wonder if they're involved."

"Centrist Strength again! Where do these people *come* from?" Legroeder asked in annoyance.

Harriet looked as if she had a bad taste in her mouth. "Mainly Faber Eridani, though there've been rumors of off-world connections outside their own organization. It began years ago as a particularly strident, and racist, lobbying group—then they started getting into paramilitary activities. Their members all have military-type ranks and titles. And they've got wilderness training camps—which is where they're causing that trouble with the Faber aborigines I told you about. Lately, they seem to have been trying to improve their public image, but I haven't heard of any change in their human-supremacist outlook."

"I wonder how Jakus got mixed up with them."

"Good question. And I wonder how, or if, they're connected with your problem."

Legroeder grimaced. "May I make a suggestion?"

"By all means."

"We're not going to solve this by wondering. Let's contact that Narseil historian that McGinnis told us about. El'ken. Maybe he knows some things. And we've got to read the rest of this material. What are we doing for security?" Legroeder looked around, as if terrorists might leap out of the closet.

"Peter is proofing my house right now," Harriet said. "I think we'll be safe there for the time being. He's the best in the business. Morgan, you're staying with us."

Morgan nodded, sorting pages.

"Then let's study while we can. And let Peter do his work."

PETER MET them at the office to escort them to Harriet's house. Among humans, Peter was the only name he used. He was a Clendornan—a silver-blue-skinned humanoid with a wedge-shaped head, wide and flat on top. His nose was all angles, and his eyes looked like clear orbs with luminous steel wool at the backs of the eyeballs. He smiled only once, briefly—a zigzag smile beneath an angular brow, and then was all sober concentration. He had two body-guards with him—a long-armed, almost tentacled Gos'n named Georgio; and a Swert named Pew, a brawny individual with a head like a horse's and an astringent smell. "We take no chances from now on," Peter said, after introductions. "We've scanned your house, I'll leave Georgio and Pew to look after you for the night, and I'll stay in touch with them, but I have many investigations to undertake tonight. Are you ready to go?" The words spilled out of his mouth like marbles out of a bag.

"We need to get these spare copies stored safely," said Harriet, showing him the datacubes.

"The bank vaults won't be open at this hour. But if we each keep a cube, that will give us a measure of security. You've dispersed a copy on the worldnet, right? Good—and the originals?"

"Right here. Peter, we might need to make a trip to the asteroid belt. Can you arrange that?"

Peter blinked; the effect was like a lighted sign going off and on. "I can arrange it if necessary." He peered at Legroeder. "Is it your intention to become a fugitive?"

"Could I be more of a fugitive than I am now?"

Harriet cleared her throat. "I believe Peter's reminding us of your bail conditions—namely, that you won't leave the planet. And of my responsibility, as your attorney, not to encourage you to violate the law. Is that correct, Peter?"

The PI turned up his long-fingered hands. "I'm not trying to tell you what to do. But I wanted to remind you, not just of Mr. Legroeder's bail, but of the fact that he is a potential suspect in both the disappearance of Jakus Bark and the possible death of Robert McGinnis. It would not appear to help his case for him to vanish from the planet. That is the sort of thing that fugitives do, no?"

"You're absolutely right, Peter," said Harriet. "But frankly, we're in some pretty deep manure here. Whatever is going on, I'm convinced that someone in the Spacing Authority is involved. And maybe Centrist Strength—who knows? We certainly can't trust the RiggerGuild, and the police are less and less likely to believe us, as all this circumstantial evidence piles up. I hate to say it—you can't *imagine* how much I hate to say it—but I'm afraid if we follow all the rules, we're going to wind up squashed. The same way I believe Mr. McGinnis has been squashed. Have you learned anything more about him?"

Peter's eyes flared with light. "Nothing, really. We can't get near the house, and all the regional authorities will tell me is that the fire's still burning inside the forcefield, and they can't do a thing until the forcefield generator fails." He shrugged and tilted his large head. "With all the smoke, they can't even tell me if the rental flyer is still intact."

"The rental flyer is the least of our worries," said Legroeder.

"The rental company won't think so," Peter chided. "Anyway, the burn mark from the missile may be about the only evidence on your side in this entire business."

Legroeder grunted.

"So one or more of us should go to visit this El'ken," Harriet said.

"And you would be taking Rigger Legroeder with you?" Peter asked.

"Damn right she is," said Legroeder.

"The reason being—?"

Legroeder answered irritably, "I'm only going to beat this by finding out what the hell's going on. And what it all has to do with *Impris*." He paused a moment. "Someone wants it kept quiet pretty badly. Badly enough to frame me. Badly enough to kill and kidnap people. I can't help Maris directly, it seems. So where would I rather be—out in the asteroid belt looking for information, where at least it'll take them a while to catch up with me—or here, waiting to be arrested?" He looked at Harriet. "If anyone should stay here, it's you."

"Why do you say that?" she asked quietly.

"You'll become an accessory if you come with me. Aren't you a little old to become a criminal on the run?"

"I could go with him," said Morgan.

Harriet turned and squinted at her daughter.

"That way, you could keep working here. And if he needs legal advice while he's there—"

"Are you a lawyer, too?" Legroeder asked.

"Most of a lawyer. I never took the planetary bar." Morgan stared at her mother.

"You're both missing the point," said Harriet, "which is that we have an urgent need to gather this information, and I need to hear it for myself. And I'm probably better at digging for it than either of you. Now, the fact that I may well lose my legal license is neither of your concerns."

Legroeder and Morgan exchanged glances. "Then I'm coming along to keep an eye on you, Mother," said Morgan. "You might be smart, but you think you're invincible, and you need someone to guard your back. And you'll probably need some legal advice of your own, before you're done." With that, Morgan turned away and busied herself with the last of her work.

Harriet stood silent, frowning into space.

"If that's settled, are you ready to gather up and head home?" Peter asked mildly.

BY THE time they reached Harriet's house, they all realized that they were dead tired, and probably the best thing to do was get some rest. Legroeder tossed and turned on his bed in the little guest house for what seemed hours. The last thing he remembered thinking was that, having snatched Maris, his enemies were not likely to wait long before trying to snatch him, as well.

It was the middle of the night when he awoke from a dead sleep to a thumping on the door. He sat up with a start. "Who is it?" he demanded hoarsely.

"Peter. We need to see you in the house. Hurry, please."

Legroeder let out the breath he'd been holding and pulled on his clothes. He stumbled across the lawn to the dining room door, rubbing his eyes. Everyone was gathered around the table, including the Fabri housekeeper, Vegas, who apparently had been roused to make coffee and was clucking unhappily as she offered some to Legroeder. "What's going on?" he murmured, accepting a steaming cup.

Harriet gestured to him to sit. "I think Peter had better tell you."

The Clendornan's eyes were flickering like a thunderstorm. "I've just heard from a friend in the police department. They're drawing up a warrant to bring you in on suspicion of murder. And since that business at the hospital, they're moving even faster. They could be here within the hour."

Legroeder's head was spinning. "Just which murder do they think I've committed?"

"Two counts," Peter said. "One—Robert McGinnis. The house has burned to the ground. The forcefield is still holding, but scanners have identified a human body in the rubble."

Legroeder said nothing, but felt a sudden, fresh weight of sadness and regret.

"I'm sorry," said Peter. "By the way, they're considering arresting Harriet on that one, too."

Legroeder looked up. "Why Harriet?" he asked Peter.

"Because she was with you, obviously. And it was she who put in the call about the fire. And she who stored McGinnis's flyer. It didn't take them long to find it."

"But she didn't identify herself when she called in the fire."

"Which is a strike against her. The com had a transponder ID, and they've confirmed the voice recording. I might add that my friend indicated that the department is under some pressure from the outside to act against you."

"The outside? Who on the outside?"

"He wouldn't say."

Legroeder sighed. "What else, then?"

"Your old friend Jakus Bark."

Jesus. "They found him? How was he killed?"

Peter tipped his top-heavy Clendornan head. "They have *not* found him. But they did find a series of holo recordings, starting with the two of you arguing, then you skulking around in the back hallway of that hangar, and finally Jakus lying unconscious and bloody on the floor of the basement. Oh, and they found Jakus's bloody cap, which indeed has oil traces from your hands on it."

Legroeder stared at the PI. "But they don't have a body?"

"No."

"Then it's all circumstantial, right?"

Peter gestured to Harriet, who was lost in thought. "Harriet?"

She looked up with a start. "What? Yes—but unfortunately, they probably have enough to bring you in. Under Fabri law, they don't need a body, or even proof of a murder, to arrest you under suspicion. They have the circumstantial evidence, plus one piece of material evidence. It wouldn't be enough for them to convict you—but they could hold you indefinitely."

"Indefinitely?"

Harriet nodded.

Morgan, who had been sitting quietly at the end of the table, said, "Faber Eridani is not a signatory to the Danii Convention. So the laws are a little different here. It goes back to the days after the Thousand-Sun War."

"But that was over a hundred years ago!"

"Yes—and there was near-civil-war here, afterward," Harriet said. "The war took a big toll, you know—in money, personnel, ships. There was a nasty dissident backlash. Coups, attempted coups, martial law. By the time things settled down, civil liberties were in the toilet along with a lot of other things. A few revolutionaries have worked for change over the years, but . . ." Harriet shrugged.

"Mom being one of those revolutionaries."

"In my younger years, dear. Back when I had fire," Harriet said. Morgan rolled her eyes. "But the upshot is, they *can* arrest you. So let's concentrate on keeping us out of jail—and alive."

"Which we will do how?"

Harriet looked pained, and frightened. "As your attorney, I have a hard time saying this—but you're not going to be able to clear your name from inside a prison cell. And I don't think *I* can do it without you, even if I stay out of jail myself. And—" she glanced at Peter "—the fact that they're being pressured to arrest you on so little evidence, in spite of the attack on you, *in spite of your having brought them a captured pirate ship*, suggests to me that—" she hesitated, clenching her teeth "—that we'd better get the hell off the planet at once. Right now. Before that warrant is issued."

Legroeder was stunned.

"At the moment, you'll be breaking your bail agreement, but you won't be fleeing arrest. This is probably our last chance to get away. *If* Peter can get us a ship."

"We'll know in a few minutes," said Peter.

"Have you heard from El'ken yet?" asked Legroeder.

Harriet shook her head.

"So we head there anyway? Because we're good at dropping in unannounced?"

"Something like that."

Legroeder sat back, staring up at the ceiling. Fleeing from bail would virtually guarantee he'd be finished at the RiggerGuild. But his career would be at an end anyway, if he couldn't prove his innocence—not just in the deaths of Jakus and McGinnis, but in the loss of *Ciudad de los Angeles*. "All right," he whispered. "I'll go get my bag."

Harriet glanced at her daughter. "Are you ready to go?"

"Whenever you are."

"I'll do what I can here, while you're gone," said Peter.

Vegas, gathering up the empty coffee cups, made a soft chuckling sound. But she did not look happy.

"LET'S GO, let's go!" Legroeder heard, as he snapped his bag shut. He ran back into the house. Peter was at the living room window, peering out, a com-unit pressed to his ear. He turned to Legroeder. "Georgio says three patrol cars are on their way up the hill. We've got to go *now*."

Legroeder piled into Peter's flyer with Harriet and Morgan. Peter took the controls, and they lifted straight from Harriet's drive pad, with running lights dark. At the same time, two of his men climbed into a ground-car and roared off down the hill, in the direction of the approaching police. With a little luck, they'd be able to distract any pursuit.

Legroeder peered down from the flyer and saw flashing blue lights, just a few blocks from Harriet's house. The police had stopped the car with Peter's men. Legroeder flopped back in the passenger seat, breathing heavily.

Peter flew them directly to the southeastern edge of the spaceport, farthest from the main building. Piling out onto the tarmac, they got their first look at the ship they'd be traveling in. It was a small corporate-size craft, pretty old from the look of it. Peter had hired it from a company on Faber Eridani's largest moon—a company whose officers were looking for ways to generate some revenue from their expensive equipment. They probably weren't paying too much attention to what was going on at the Elmira spaceport, or with the spacing authorities or the local police. Legroeder wondered if Peter had mentioned that their passengers-to-be had an unfortunate tendency to bring trouble along with them.

A drizzling rain obscured the field. It was comforting to be surrounded by banks of mist in the midnight darkness, knowing that the police would be looking here soon. They hurried to the spacecraft and were greeted by the pilot, Conex, a dark-skinned Halcyon whose face, while humanoid, was extremely narrow, with an almost reptilian snout. Conex and Peter exchanged words and dataslips, before the Clendornan turned and said, "I'll be off, then. I'll learn what I can here. You be careful, yes?"

The Clendornan's eyes sparkled with light as Harriet thanked him. Then he glanced across the field, where the flashes of police flyers were piercing the night. "You'd better get going," he murmured. He hurried to his flyer and disappeared into the mist.

Conex escorted them through the entry portal and up to the passenger compartment. Once their bags were stowed, and everyone secured in their seats, Conex rejoined his co-pilot in the cockpit.

Five minutes later—an eternity—a tow descended and coupled to the ship. Flanked by the soft glow of the tow's Circadie space inductors, they accelerated up through the rain clouds and out into the star-flecked blackness of space.

Chapter 9
TO THE ASTEROIDS

THE TRIP out to the asteroid belt took three days from the time the tow released them on a fast outbound track. The sleeping compartments were scarcely larger than closets, so Legroeder, Harriet, and Morgan spent most of their time together in the cramped passenger compartment. Conex and his copilot Zan, also a Halcyon, kept to themselves most of the time, joining their passengers only at mealtime.

As a passenger on a spacecraft, Legroeder felt like a third leg. He kept wanting to go forward and help pilot the ship, never mind that they were simply traveling through normal-space and there was no rigging involved. Instead, he and the others pored over the data from McGinnis, absorbing details about the *Impris* investigation, and pondering the questions that McGinnis had never had a chance to answer. From time to time, they would go to the lounge's observation port and peer intently back at Faber Eridani, as if they might glimpse pursuit by the police, or by their unknown enemy.

After a time Legroeder, overwhelmed by the minutiae of the hundred-year-old investigation, simply sat and gazed out the port into the depths of space, his thoughts wandering among the stars. He found himself longing wistfully for a set of pearlgazers he had once owned, before they were stolen by his pirate captors: gems with psychogenerative powers that he had often used as a focus for meditation. Now, missing them, he began to lose himself in his memories . . . glimpses of lost friends, lost hopes and dreams . . .

"Penny for your thoughts, Legroeder."

He blinked and turned his head.

Morgan Mahoney had settled into the seat beside him. "You haven't moved a muscle in the last hour. I was afraid we were losing you." She peered at him for a moment, frowning. "I didn't mean to intrude."

"No—no, it's fine." It wasn't fine at all. But he would talk; he could do that.

"You're worried about your friend?"

He shrugged. "What am I *not* worried about?"

"I know what you mean. I've been wondering whether we'll get there before the authorities turn us around and haul us *all* in. I have to admit, I've never been on the run like this before. It scares me."

Legroeder rocked back and squinted up at the ceiling of the little lounge. It glittered. Now, who the hell would put *glitter* on their ceiling? "Yah," he murmured, thinking, When was I last *not* on the run?

A chime sounded, and the younger Mahoney got up to retrieve a fresh pot of tea from the galley. Returning with cups, she said to Legroeder, "I hope you don't mind my asking, but you know, I haven't heard much of anything about your life before."

"Before—?"

"The pirates. Where did you come from, how did you start rigging . . . what was your family like?"

Legroeder felt a sudden roaring in his ears. He closed his eyes, trying to shut it out. *Before the pirates . . .*

"I'm sorry—did I—I'm sorry, I didn't mean to pry."

"No . . . no . . ." he whispered. Life before the pirates . . . eons ago. Another world. Another universe. At this moment, he couldn't begin to recapture it. Any of it. He felt as if he'd *had* no life before the pirates. Just the effort of reaching back into the fog made him dizzy. Claire Marie, where he was a child; then New Tarkus a little later. He had never really had a home planet as an adult, though for a while, Chaening's World came as close as any. Finally he managed, "Why would you want to hear about that?"

"Well . . . I guess to get to know you better," Morgan said, looking a little puzzled. She handed him a cup of tea. "Isn't that the usual reason?

Legroeder accepted the cup. "I guess so. But I don't recall your telling me anything about *you*. You know, before you met me."

"Oh." Morgan cleared her throat as she sat back down. "Well . . ."

"What's wrong? Did I say something wrong?"

Across the tiny lounge, Harriet looked faintly amused, as Morgan foundered for words. "Well, I don't know. There's not that much to say."

"Why? Because your life is too dull, or too interesting?" Morgan blushed.

"Oh, just go ahead and tell him," Harriet said.

"About what?" Morgan snapped. "The failed marriage? Or the three different attempts at a career?"

"Listen," Legroeder said. "I didn't mean to start anything—"

"It's perfectly all right, Legroeder," said Harriet. "Morgan is just being hard on herself. She's had career troubles for perfectly good reasons, and I haven't noticed her giving up. As for the marriage—well, it's not as if she had a great role model." As Morgan glared protectively at her mother, Harriet shrugged. "Her father divorced me when she was seven. And for good cause. I was too preoccupied with my career—and, I am ashamed to admit, somewhat neglectful of my two children."

"Are we going to bring out all the dirty laundry now?"

"I'm sorry, dear. I don't mean to embarrass you. But you did open the subject."

"I did not. I just asked—"

"Look," Legroeder interrupted. "Would it help if we cut out all this feel-good history crap, and I just told you what it was like to be with pirates? That ought to bring everyone down to earth."

Harriet, startled, opened her mouth to answer. She was interrupted by a buzz from the intercom and Conex's voice: *"Mrs. Mahoney, we've received a message from Mr. El'ken, addressed to you. Would you like to come forward to view it?"*

"Thank you, yes!" Harriet set her cup of tea on the sideboard. She rose and disappeared through the door to the bridge.

Legroeder sighed, glancing at Morgan.

"Don't mind my mom."

"I like your mother," Legroeder said. He looked toward the bridge, wondering what El'ken's reply was.

"Well, she has good taste in clients," Morgan said, busying herself with the pot of tea. "Sometimes, anyway. I'm sorry if I made you uncomfortable. I asked out of genuine curiosity. But if it's something you'd rather not talk about—"

"Which—my life before? Or the seven years in a raider stronghold?" Legroeder shrugged, as if the distinction were inconsequential. But there was a tension rising between his shoulders, and he knew that it was going to be a long time before he could talk about either. Strangely, he felt more inclined to discuss the pirates now. It was no worse than sitting here wondering how soon he would wind up in prison. "It was—"

"Difficult?"

He chuckled. "Yeah—it was difficult."

"That was stupid of me. What I meant was, when you had no freedom and your life was always being threatened, wasn't it hard to keep a sense of your own identity?"

"Well, yeah. I suppose the hardest thing was being forced to rig ships for them. Not so much when we were just flying transport. But when we were out prowling—" he shook his head, as if that might somehow keep the memories at bay "—when we went out to attack other ships, and we knew they were going to capture or kill innocent people . . ."

Morgan winced.

Legroeder shrugged, trying to ignore a buzzing in his head. "There was nothing we could do—we either flew where they said, or *we* would be killed, or brainwiped. And not just us—"

"What do you mean?"

"They always had hostages on the ships—and they wouldn't just kill *us* if we disobeyed, they would kill *them*, too. And it wasn't an empty threat."

Morgan was silent.

Legroeder frowned in thought. "Except for that one time. There was . . . one . . . occasion . . . when I actually managed to keep them from capturing a ship."

"*Really?* How?"

He wanted to laugh, but couldn't. "We were attacking a ship—and we made contact with the other rigger crew. And . . ." He had to struggle to keep his voice steady; the memory was rising with incredible power. It was about four years ago; the three riggers on the raider ship had cast an oversized net around their intended victim, and were drawing it in like a fishing net. Something in the other net struck him as oddly familiar, and he risked opening a private speech channel, disguising it as a dark crease of cloud billowing over the landscape. "I couldn't believe it. It was an old friend of mine, an old shipmate, flying the other ship! Along with some kind of alien, catlike thing."

Morgan's mouth dropped open.

Again, a half laugh rose in his throat. "His name was Gev Carlyle—one of the most innocent guys you ever met in your life. I mean, painfully innocent. When I *flew* with him, I had to watch out for him. A good rigger, but young— naive." He shook his head, pressing his lips together. "I'm not sure what came over me—but I just *couldn't* let them capture him . . . or kill him. I couldn't." Aboard the raider, a team of commandos was preparing to board the target, and another crew stood ready to blow it to pieces if it tried to escape or fight back.

Morgan's voice was husky. "What did you do?"

"I was scared. Real scared. But I had to hide that." His heart was pounding with the memory. "We were coming in—lights flashing in the Flux, drums crashing, boarding party ready to go. If you've never been under attack in the Flux, you can't imagine how terrifying that is. We were already grappling, net to net, drawing him in. But I was able to sabotage the net imagery . . . just enough. Made it seem like a fluctuation in the net." In fact, he'd been incredibly lucky. The only people who could *really* see what was happening were the riggers. He reshaped the image just enough: they already had the two ships enveloped in a flaring thunderstorm, and when an eruption of turbulence loosened their grip and clouded the image, it seemed almost natural . . .

Legroeder remained silent a moment, reliving the memory. He'd kept the covert channel to Carlyle open just long enough to yell, *Gev, go!* . . . and then let the two ships slip apart as though he'd lost his hold in the turbulence.

"And—?"

He swallowed. "I was able to give him time to break free and vanish. I couldn't have gotten away with it if Rusty, one of the riggers in *my* net, hadn't been willing to look the other way." He laughed, this time for real. "And if the other guy hadn't been so dumb. Rusty was a captive like me, but the second guy . . . he just didn't catch on."

"Dear God," Morgan whispered. "Weren't you afraid they'd kill you?"

"Sure—afterward. At the time, I just reacted. Pure instinct." It made him shudder now to think of the peril he'd put himself into. "Why'd I do it then, and no other time? I don't know. If I'd *thought* about it, I don't know if I would have had the nerve *then*." He closed his eyes, feeling vaguely ill. "You know something? I've never told anyone about this. Not until now."

"It sounds like a very tough business," Harriet said. She was back in her seat with a small printout in her hand.

Legroeder blinked. "When did you come back?"

"Just now. I didn't mean to eavesdrop." Harriet folded

the paper and then reopened it, with uncharacteristic nervousness.

"That's all right. What did El'ken say?"

Harriet chuckled without humor. "That since we were halfway there, he wouldn't turn us away. But if we were anything less than serious students of history, we shouldn't expect much. It's not what I'd call a friendly note. But since El'ken is one of the Narseil's most honored scholars, I guess we're fortunate to get to see him at all."

Legroeder hmph'd noncommittally. "Well . . . McGinnis wasn't eager to see us, either. But we won him over."

"That's true."

"Of course, he's dead now."

"That's also true. Legroeder, dear, this is starting to sound depressing. Can we go back to talking about your life among the pirates, and see if we can cheer ourselves up a bit?"

Legroeder managed a laugh. "To be honest, most of it was crushing boredom and frustration, and chronic anger—interrupted by periods of extreme terror." Harriet looked away, and Legroeder suddenly realized that, despite her remark, Harriet probably didn't much want to talk about life with pirates. Not with her grandson—if he was still alive—almost certainly enduring similar hardship at this very moment.

Legroeder cleared his throat. "I don't really know what it would have been like for a young boy—if Bobby was even at that outpost. I wish I could tell you, but I just don't know."

Harriet nodded, stirring her tea. Glancing at Morgan, Legroeder could see appreciation in her eyes. He sighed again and fell silent.

Morgan brought him back to his story. "What happened after you let your friend go?"

"Well . . ." Legroeder scratched the back of his head. "I have *no* idea what happened to Gev Carlyle. He seemed to get clear okay. Funny thing was, he was flying around trying to put an old crew back together—including me. He managed to get that much across in the half second we had to talk. And here I was, in the net of a pirate ship. I can't imagine what he thought."

"But you did risk your life to let him go."

"Yeah. But I never got the chance to tell him why I was there in the first place."

Morgan frowned. "What happened to *you* afterward?"

Legroeder let out a slow breath. "No one except Rusty seemed to suspect that I'd done anything deliberate. If they had, I doubt I'd be alive now to tell you about it. But it was clear *something* had gone wrong, and I told the captain that a Flux anomaly had caused us to lose our hold on the other ship. I'm not sure he really believed me—but how could he tell?" Legroeder chuckled darkly. "On the other hand, he definitely thought I'd blown a sure capture. Or he thought *we* had, and thank God Rusty was willing to take some heat for me, rather than blowing the whistle."

He reflected a moment longer. "But I must have done a pretty good job of making it look real, because they never did come down on us, except to say, 'You stupid lowlifes— couldn't you see it *coming?*' The third guy, Joey, who was sort of a favorite of the captain's, helpfully volunteered how *amazing* it was—and said it with such conviction, the captain made a note about it in his log." Legroeder laughed. "Poor Joey! He was a terrific natural rigger—could take just about any image and sail right down it—but he didn't have a clue about much of anything else." He shook his head. "We were just damn lucky."

At that moment, Conex appeared in the doorway. "We'll be making a course adjustment soon, to start our final approach to Asteroid Arco Iris. For safety, please secure yourselves."

Morgan collected the cups and saucers, while Legroeder turned the seats into position. Five minutes later, he watched the stars turn as the ship rotated end over end. As he waited for the vibration that would tell him that the acceleration had gone from two gees to five, he let the emotions from all that had come before wash over him like a tide coming in over a sandbar. Maybe this time he really was on the way to reversing his fortunes.

AT FIRST the asteroid was a sparkling point of light whose motion was barely visible against the star field. As they drew closer, it began to take form: disk-shaped structures of shiny metal poking out here and there, and along one edge the profile of a silver dome. A large golden helix floating just beyond the asteroid looked like a Narseil Flux antenna.

A private Flux-wave transmitter? The average planet usually only had a couple to serve the whole world. They were not only horrendously expensive; there was a bandwidth limitation before transmissions began to interfere with rigger ships moving in and out of a system. But the Narseil had a reputation for looking out for their own needs when they lived among humans. And with the technology of the Narseil Rigging Institute at their command, they did it remarkably well.

"The Narseil own the asteroid," Harriet remarked. "They hollowed and outfitted it themselves. El'ken is their most famous resident, but there are at least a few hundred Narseil living here."

Conex came on the intercom to inform them that they would be docking in several minutes, and if they had any second thoughts, now was the time to voice them. Harriet and Morgan chuckled, but Legroeder remembered their reasons for coming, and felt anything but amusement. If he'd been at the controls of a rigger ship, he'd have taken them straight down into the Flux and on until sunset . . . or until he found a place where no one had ever heard of pirates, or of Renwald Legroeder.

AS THEY passed through the airlock into the asteroid's interior, they plunged into humid air filled with the smell of the sea. An alien sea. The corridors, with their long stretches of bare stone wall, seemed at once tidy and musty. The walls felt damp to the touch. As they walked along, Legroeder tried not to think about mildew. Nevertheless, he was intrigued. He had never entered a Narseil habitation before, and only on a few occasions had even seen a Narseil rigger.

They were greeted by a pair of the amphibious Narseil. They were tall and vaguely reptilian, with dark green, finely scaled skin like an iguana's. Their eyes were humanoid except for the shape: vertical ovals with similar-shaped pupils. Their faces seemed long and hollow, with mouths but no nostrils. Breathing was accomplished through fan-shaped gill openings on the front of the neck. Tailless and bipedal, the Narseil had long, flat dinosaur-like crests or neck-sails running from the backs of their heads to their lower backs. They dressed in wide, crisscrossing bands of fabric and carried long, thin compads. Their speech was a mixture of their own rendition of Anglic and synthesized translation, in about equal measure.

"Please ssstate your business on our world," hissed the Narseil on the right, as the other examined their ID tabs.

Harriet answered calmly, though the sight of the Narseil towering over her must have felt intimidating. "We are here to visit El'ken the historian."

"Jussst the three of you?" asked the second Narseil.

"Yes, plus our pilot and copilot—" Harriet gestured back up the corridor toward their ship "—who will be waiting for us for the return trip."

The second Narseil made a noise somewhere between a grunt and a hiss. "They may stay on their ship. If they need assistance they may make a request."

"We have permission to visit Academic El'ken," Harriet replied. "We wondered if you might direct us to his quarters."

"*Kkhhhh*—we will get to that." The first Narseil busied himself making entries on his compad, while the other motioned to the visitors to follow. "Come. First you must pass through customs."

Customs consisted of a complete multiscan examination of their persons as well as their possessions. They were assured that the radiation levels were almost undetectable, but Legroeder could not help thinking that the Narseil looked to him as if they had very different tolerances for radiation. Or as if they'd already had way too much of it. *Don't be racist,* he chided himself. But their cool demeanor was starting to wear on his nerves.

As they were led from customs through the inner asteroid, they saw the occasional human face, and one Swert; but the vast majority of those they encountered were Narseil. They came at last to a short passageway with a door at the end. A nameplate on the wall listed a name in Narseil script, beneath which was engraved in Anglic: *El'ken.*

"Do not expect to stay long," said their escort. "He is a very busy *tophai.*" The escort deliberately used the Narseil word, which Legroeder recognized as a high Narseil honorific. He opened the door and they walked in.

They were suddenly beneath the stars again. El'ken lived under a dome. His quarters were a large, twilit cavern, about half the size of a human gymnasium. Perhaps two-thirds of the ceiling was dome; the rest was a dark stone overhang. On the near side of the cavern a long, curving desk or counter, a trifle high by human standards, was built into the stone wall. The far side of the cavern was dominated by a pool carved out of stone. A bordering strip between the two sections was covered with gravel, and held two bench seats.

Legroeder peered around in the gloom. He exchanged glances with Morgan, who was also turning around. "Is anybody here?" she asked.

There was a splash, and then a husky voice from somewhere in the darkness of the pool. "What do you want?"

"Academic El'ken?" called Harriet. "I'm Harriet Mahoney. This is my daughter Morgan and our client, Rigger Renwald Legroeder."

There was a ripple in the water, and a head appeared over the top of a stone island in the center of the pool. "I know who you are," said the Narseil, his eyes gleaming in the twilight. "I asked what you want."

"Truth," Harriet answered. "What we want is truth, if you have it and are willing to share it with us."

The Narseil made a sound remarkably like a dog's bark. It was hard to tell if it was a laugh or a snort. "Humans from Faber Eridani come to a Narseil in search of truth? Just what manner of truth were you hoping to find?"

Legroeder sighed. "Truth about a rigger ship from a century ago, and truth about why the Narseil were blamed falsely for her disappearance. We'd hoped to put an end to a longstanding lie. But if you don't have it, or don't want to share it—"

"Legroeder," Harriet interrupted, giving him an annoyed look.

Don't blame me, Legroeder mouthed.

"I see," said El'ken. "If it's *Impris* you want to know about, and if you were sent here by Robert McGinnis, as your message said, then perhaps indeed we can talk." The Narseil's head vanished with a splash. A few seconds later, he reappeared at the near edge of the pool. "No need to hang back. You may approach."

The three walked across the gravel border as El'ken rose to his waist in the water. "I have not been able to reach Robert McGinnis, these last two days. Do you know if something is wrong?"

"Very wrong, I am sorry to say," Harriet answered. "He died in a fire at his estate, three Fabri days ago. We believe the fire was deliberately set. But we don't know by whom."

El'ken stared at her with dark eyes. "That is most distressing news." A flutter went down the crest, or sail, on his neck. His eyes sharpened as he studied Harriet. "You knew him well, then?"

"We had only just met."

"But even so, he sent you here to see me?" El'ken angled a glance at Legroeder, and seemed to focus on the rigger for a long moment.

It was Harriet who answered. "He said, if we wanted to know the truth about what had happened between the Narseil and Centrist Worlds, we should go see El'ken the historian."

El'ken continued to study Legroeder appraisingly. "And why do you wish to know these things?" He sank slowly up to his neck again in the water, as if he might dismiss them.

Legroeder lost his patience. "Because no one believes in *Impris!*" he exploded. "And I'm being framed for piracy because of it! Your people were blamed for the loss of *Impris*—but I've seen her! I know she's alive!"

El'ken suddenly rose again, dripping. "Yes? And what about the history books?"

"Damn the history books! Even the Fandrang report doesn't say a thing about the Narseil and *Impris*."

"You've read the Fandrang report, then?"

"Read it? We *have* it!"

"You have the Fandrang—"

"McGinnis gave it to us for safekeeping. He also told us to come to you if we wanted to learn more."

Harriet added, "Mr. McGinnis seemed to be expecting trouble. He sent us away with some urgency."

"I might add," interjected Morgan, "that someone on Faber Eridani seems extremely upset about all this. They tried to kill my mother and Legroeder."

El'ken's eyes gleamed in obvious fascination as he shifted his gaze from one speaker to the next.

"We would be happy to make a copy of the report available to you," said Harriet.

"Unnecessary. But thank you."

"You already have it?"

"Let's just say that I have *seen* it." The Narseil stepped suddenly out of the water and onto the gravel floor. As he stood dripping, a soft whoosh came from the floor, and he remained still as a warm draft of air dried him. "I think," he said, pulling a silken, split-backed robe over his shoulders, "that it is time you told me all that you know. And then, perhaps, we can talk about what you would *like* to know."

Legroeder felt a chill as he gazed back at the Narseil. There was a glint in El'ken's eyes that suggested that what he had to say would not be reassuring, not at all.

Chapter 10
EL'KEN THE HISTORIAN

EL'KEN SENT away the Narseil guides and pointed to the bench seats. Harriet began the story, but after laying the groundwork, turned the narrative over to Legroeder. El'ken was not a patient listener; he kept interrupting and asking for more information—first, about their trip to McGinnis's, why they had gone there, why their visit had been so abruptly terminated. Then about *Impris*. And about the pirates, and Legroeder's escape.

Legroeder had not expected El'ken to be especially interested in his time with the pirates, but in fact the old Narseil's eyes seemed to grow clearer and more intense as he came to that part of his story. El'ken leaned forward, his paper-thin neck-sail rustling in the air. "You must tell me more about this pirate culture," he said, seeming to forget all about what his guests had come to ask him.

"Well, certainly, but"—Legroeder hesitated —"later, perhaps? Right now, we're very concerned about *Impris*, and what the loss of that ship meant to the Narseil."

El'ken stared at him for a moment with his large, green-yellow eyes. Then he made a wheezing sound and said, "Very well. I will do the telling, for now."

For a moment, there was hardly a sound in the chamber except the chuckling and stirring of water in the pool. The old Narseil leaned back and looked up through the dome at the stars. "So much history," he sighed. "So many years, and so much . . . truth lost." He peered at Legroeder, his eyes burning. "Do you want to know the truth—not just about *Impris*, but about why my people and yours were the losers in the War of a Thousand Suns?"

Legroeder frowned in puzzlement. "I'm not sure what you mean. I always thought that the Narseil mostly kept out of the war. Wasn't it just between human worlds? McGinnis implied there was more to it, but he never finished telling us—"

El'ken interrupted him with a loud hiss, his sail quivering with anger. "Your *ignorance* is *appalling*."

Legroeder drew back, stung.

"But at least you are willing to admit it, and that is in your favor," the Narseil added. He rose, shaking like a leaf on a tree. "I will tell you what I can. Since Robert McGinnis seems to have paid for it with his life."

Legroeder took a shallow breath, saying nothing.

El'ken walked alongside his desk, touching bookends and compad controls. He made a sound through his gills that was equal parts rumble and sigh. "I have spent my life trying to establish the truth, and to record it so that others may one day benefit from it. Too many of my own people don't even know it. But your people—" The Narseil turned back to his guests. "The only human I ever knew who cared about the truth of those days was Robert McGinnis. And he struggled against terrible obstacles to keep his work alive. *Terrible* obstacles. Do you know what I refer to?"

Legroeder shook his head.

"He did not tell you?" El'ken said. "No, I suppose he would not. Or could not. Something happened that kept him from finishing with you. Hssss." The Narseil returned to his bench seat. "Let me tell you a story about Robert McGinnis, and how as a young man he served in the Centrist Worlds Navy."

"As a space marine, yes?" Legroeder said.

"Hssssh, do not interrupt! This human named Robert

served on a warship that was sent to fight against an incursion of pirates in the region of the Great Barrier Nebula. In those days, there was an effort to combat the pirates—back before the Centrist Worlds lost their spine and integrity, and surrendered the region to the raiders. Young Robert's ship engaged the pirates and fought a great battle—but in the end, they were outnumbered and outgunned. They were neither captured nor destroyed, though. Instead, they were left adrift. And their ship drifted into a region of the Flux known as the Sargasso."

"I know that area," Legroeder said. Seeing incomprehension on Morgan's and Harriet's faces, he explained. "In the Flux, you know, space itself flows in currents, like rivers and streams—which is how rigger ships move, as well. But the Sargasso is a dead zone, where almost all motion ceases. It's deadly for ships, because you can be stranded—just like old-time sailing ships that were sometimes becalmed, and left drifting helpless in the middle of an ocean."

"That is correct," said El'ken. "And that is where the pirates left them. Only a handful of crew members remained alive on the warship, and they subsisted for a long time on the remnants of the ship's stores. Eventually, they drifted to the edge of the region, but at that point they had no functional net controls."

"Jesus," said Legroeder.

"Exactly," said El'ken. "They were nearing the end of their supplies when a ship appeared. Robert—who had received severe head wounds in the battle—lost consciousness and knew almost nothing of what happened from that time until much later. But he never saw his crewmates again.

"The next clear thing he knew, he was on a ship coming into port—Faber Eridani, to be precise. He had been treated for his wounds, and his facial structure had been rebuilt. He had also been given neural implants. Though the implants helped maintain his brain function, his rescuers did not install them for altruistic reasons."

Morgan stirred at the mention of implants. "Like your friend Jakus?" she asked Legroeder.

"I do not know of this Jakus, nor do I know why you people insist upon continually interrupting," said the Narseil. "But yes, he'd received implants of considerable sophistication. It was, I imagine, like having a robot intelligence constantly interacting with his own intelligence. They provided much memory support to replace cognitive faculties he'd lost due to his injuries. But they also, at times, tried to control him." The Narseil paused. "Yes, I know—that's what worries you about *all* implants. An understandable, but not entirely accurate, worry. At times, Robert's appeared dormant, benign, and he could almost forget that they were there. But they never stopped working."

"Working for whom?" asked Legroeder.

El'ken gazed at him piercingly. "I think you know."

"The pirates? He didn't look like a man who was under the control of Golen Space pirates."

"I did not say he was 'under the control' of the pirates. I said that the implants *tried* to control him. But he fought them—subtly, so as not to be in obvious rebellion. For thirty years he fought them! You wonder why he secluded himself, why he lived in a small fortress in the wild? It was because he dared not let others see the struggles he fought. At times, it was a near thing. At times, he almost succumbed to their control. Indeed, he had to do some of their bidding to persuade them of his usefulness. But ironically, it was partly because of his torment that he was so devoted to gathering and preserving information. His passion for the truth was his own private bulwark against the encroachment of this other power." El'ken paused, and for a few moments his eyes and thoughts seemed focused on something very far away.

"But why didn't he have the implants removed?" asked Morgan.

"Ah," said the Narseil. "The implantation was too thorough. The augments were bonded, not just to his cerebral cortex, but also to his—what is the word?—autonomic nervous system. He went to several specialists, but in the end they determined that the integration was so complete that there was no way to remove the implants without killing him in the process."

"Just like Maris," Legroeder muttered. "The bastards."

El'ken gave a stiff-necked nod. "And so he lived, and fought his silent, lonely battle, all those years. Until, presumably, the day you came to visit. Now, perhaps, he is at rest."

"But what did they want with him? Why did they bother?" Legroeder asked.

"Indeed," said El'ken. "Did they send him back as a spy? As a weapon to be held in reserve for some future need? Probably both."

"Then," said Morgan, "in a way it might have been a blessing that he died in the fire."

"That may be," El'ken said. "But a very sad blessing, nevertheless."

Legroeder's thoughts flickered back to McGinnis's last cries to them . . . to their escape from the house, somehow under attack . . . the dog shuddering in a seizure, as though *it* were under attack . . . and the smoke and fire billowing under the impenetrable security field. The memory was profoundly disturbing.

El'ken rustled his neck-sail. "What's important now, I think, is not what drove McGinnis, or drove against him—but the information he fought so hard to preserve."

"Which is now entrusted to us," Harriet said.

"Yes. Not just to preserve, but to *use*. Would you excuse me a moment?" The Narseil walked along the gravel pool perimeter, until he stood under a stone overhang. A soft spray of water came on, misting him. He made a sound like a weary sigh, then came back to sit again on the bench seat. "Forgive me. It is my skin. It grows dry, these days. But Robert sent you to me to learn about what really happened in the War of a Thousand Suns. And so I will tell you."

"Is there a connection to what happened to him?" Legroeder asked.

"In a way there is. Yes . . ."

* * *

THE OLD Narseil knew far more about human history than Legroeder did—probably more than all three of the humans put together. He spoke softly, almost as if addressing a group of students.

The War of a Thousand Suns (he said) actually involved between thirty and forty human worlds. It was in many respects a conflict between two divergent elements of starfaring humanity: the so-called Kyber worlds and the human Centrist Worlds. The Kyber had embraced highly sophisticated neural implants of all kinds—and as a people, had all but subsumed their humanity in a maelstrom of cybernetic consciousness. The Centrist Worlds, on the other hand, espoused separation from cyber-consciousness, declaring this to be an essential foundation of human reality.

"But the Centrists won," said Legroeder, realizing even as he said it how thin his knowledge was.

"Did they, now?" asked El'ken. "Do you really know what happened to the Kyber—what they were then, and what they've become?" The Narseil hissed softly. "I thought not," he said, and continued his explanation.

The Kyber were a frantically creative and yet dangerous element of humanity. Though they resided largely in off-planet locations, such as asteroids and artificial habitats, they sought leadership over a proposed, massive, migrational movement inward through the galaxy, toward rich clusters of promising star systems. Indeed, it was for this region of space that the war was named—though in fact the war had as much to do with racial prejudice and economic position as it did dreams of far-flung colonies. Still, the Kyber claimed ludditism on the part of the Centrists, a claim not without some justification. But neither were the Kyber innocent victims. Arrogant and ruthless, they commanded the finest technology in the human realm, including weapons technology.

And yet, despite their technological advantage, the Kyber lacked the numbers and the internal cohesion needed to fight effectively against the joined forces of the Centrist Worlds. In the end, they lost the war. But they exacted a terrible price from the Centrist Worlds, in destruction and social disorder.

"But what does all this have to do with the Narseil? You said that—"

"We were betrayed—yes!" barked El'ken, eyes glinting. "A betrayal which to this day has never been acknowledged—though it changed the course of both human and Narseil history."

Throughout most of the war, the Narseil were allied with the Centrist Worlds—not because they particularly wanted to be involved in the conflict, but because they thought the Centrist Worlds were the most stable. The riggers of the Narseil Rigging Institute had long been developing interesting new synergies with the riggers of the Centrist Worlds, something the Kyber worlds found a threat to their own hoped-for dominance in starfaring science. "But in the end," El'ken said, and his voice tightened until it was clear that his words were underlain by a very old anger, "the Centrists decided that a fragile alliance with a *nonhuman* species was less important to them than ending the costly war. They broke their alliance with the Narseil, in exchange for concessions from the Kyber. On the surface, the Kyber surrendered the fight—but in reality, the Centrists weakened themselves, without even realizing they had done so. Without the shared skill and knowledge of the Narseil, they could never reach the Cluster of a Thousand Suns—not in a practical way. They're too distant; the undertaking too expensive. But by the time the Centrists realized this, the will to attempt such things had withered away in the long aftermath of the war."

"But why such an abrupt shift—if the Narseil were allies—?"

El'ken waved away the question. "There were numerous small events, and much racially-motivated suspicion. But what finally provided the excuse to break the alliance was the disappearance of *Impris*." El'ken gazed up through the star-dome for a moment, then continued with a sigh. "The Narseil were accused of hijacking the ship in order to obtain details of strategic technologies supposedly carried by one of the passengers. There was never the slightest evidence of any such technical secrets, on or off the ship. But most of humanity was all too willing to believe the accusation. You might find some of the writings of that period interesting. They could teach you a lot about your own people."

Legroeder wasn't sure he wanted to know.

"By blaming the Narseil for the loss of *Impris*, the leaders of the Centrist Worlds were able to justify excluding my people from the colonizing effort that everyone assumed would follow at the end of the war. And by doing *that*, they unwittingly strengthened the position of the Kyber worlds— the very people they were fighting. Such was the price of the peace."

"I don't see—" Morgan began, but was silenced by a sharp nce from El'ken.

"That was the end of collaborative rigging between the Narseil and the Centrist Worlds. It left my people impoverished from the collapse of trade, and the Centrist Worlds a parody of their former power and vision. And history was written to perpetuate the lie." El'ken's voice grew even sharper. "Who knows what technologies went undeveloped, what areas of knowledge untapped, because of the breakup of that alliance—particularly *rigging knowledge*, which not only might have taken us to new star clusters, but might also have helped to explain such mysteries as the disappearance of *Impris* herself? Who knows! And yet, look at the Kyber worlds, which supposedly lost the war. Their expansionism was restricted, for a time. But they have not remained idle—no."

"But we hardly even hear about most of the Kyber worlds anymore," Harriet said.

"Perhaps not. But they haven't gone away. They've changed some of their names, to be sure. And they work in other ways now. But they are not idle." El'ken laced his long, green fingers together and gazed down at his folded hands, in contemplative silence.

He looked up again. "It was a shrewd maneuver by the

Kyber leaders. They would have lost the war anyway, had they continued to fight. But by breaking the Narseil-Centrist alliance, they crippled the growth of the Centrist Worlds' power and influence, even while appearing to cede victory to them."

"You mean, by undercutting the Centrists' joint explorations with the Narseil?"

"Of course," said El'ken. "But it wasn't *just* a matter of lost technology. The collaboration had served as a catalyst, inspiring new efforts. Now, with that gone and the real costs of the war hitting home, many of the Centrist Worlds became insular, more concerned with their own economies than with huge investments in exploration, which might not pay dividends for decades. Many, like Faber Eridani, went through their own post-war upheavals, further undermining the preservation of truth. You can read my own writings on the subject, if you wish to know more about it." El'ken's eyes again seemed to focus elsewhere. "Among my people, bitterness lingered long after the war's end. For many years, the Narseil drew away from humanity."

"But there's commerce now," said Harriet.

"Yes—*now*. But not nearly what we once had. Tell me—how were you greeted, when you arrived here?"

"Like dogmeat," Legroeder said.

"Not with great friendliness," El'ken conceded. "Yes, commerce has been renewed, haltingly. But how much has been lost between the cultures as a result of the betrayal? How much trust? Intellectual exchange? How much fruit of cooperation? What knowledge might have been gained if we had explored the Cluster of a Thousand Suns? It is incalculable."

El'ken abruptly stood up. Breathing huskily, he returned to his mist unit, where he stood facing the pool. Legroeder watched Harriet making notes in her compad. When El'ken seemed in no hurry to return, Legroeder got up and walked to the edge of the cavern dome and peered out into space. It all seemed so changeless out there. But he knew it was not. Though it was invisible to the eye, the expanse of interstellar space was laced together by the powerful currents of the Flux. *Impris* is out there somewhere, he thought. The Flying Dutchman of the Flux . . . marooned in eternity.

El'ken returned at that moment, picking up as though he had never paused. "It is my belief that descendants of the Kyber are using *Impris* even now, for their own purposes."

"Meaning—?"

"Do you have to ask? You, of all people?"

Legroeder's voice caught. He had never, in seven years with the pirates, been privy to information about *Impris*. But he'd heard rumors—as had McGinnis. And he had his own capture as evidence. "I know what *I* think. I want to know what you think."

"Fair enough. But first, let me ask—do you know who the pirates of Golen Space really are?" The Narseil turned from one to another, his gaze probing. "Any of you?"

Harriet remained silent, though obviously troubled by the question.

"I can tell you who they are," Legroeder said savagely. "They're scumbags who prey on the innocent and practice slavery. You want their names? I could give you some, but it wouldn't do you any good. They're a long way away."

"So they are," said the Narseil. "But that's not what I meant. I meant, who are they as a people? Where do they come from?"

Legroeder shrugged. "All over the place. A lot of them start out as captives, and get converted, or tortured into co-operating—or—" he tapped his temple "—they get implants, and they don't have the strength to resist the way Robert McGinnis did."

"Indeed. But I'm talking about the core population. Do you not know? I'm talking about the Free Kyber—the descendants of the Kyber revolution."

Legroeder's mouth opened, but it took him a moment to find words. "Free Kyber? Are you saying that the *Kyber* worlds are the sponsors of the *pirates?*" He suddenly remembered Jakus saying something about the Kyber. Kyber implants.

"Some of them. Do you not know the term 'Free Kyber' from your period of captivity?"

Legroeder shook his head in bewilderment. "No—but I was in one outpost the whole time. I never learned much about the pirate movement as a whole." He did know that the early pirates had split off many decades ago from other spacefaring worlds, and gone to live in hidden fortresses lost in places reachable only through the Flux.

"Well, there is substantial evidence that several of the old Kyber worlds heavily support the present-day piracy movement." El'ken raised his hands. "Not all of them. There are doubtless many honest Kyber, and Kyber worlds that are no more a part of piracy than you or I. But others are not innocent."

Legroeder absorbed that silently. "And *Impris*?"

"Ah," said the Narseil. "At last we come back to *Impris*. I have long believed that the so-called Free Kyber—the pirates—have known exactly where *Impris* is. They knew where she was seven years ago, when they used her to entrap your ship, *City of the Angels*. And they no doubt have done the same with countless other victims."

Legroeder clenched his fists. "That's exactly what I've been trying to say!" He swung triumphantly to Harriet, then back to El'ken. "Can you help us prove it?"

"Not directly, no," El'ken answered.

Legroeder's heart sank.

"It is only a strong suspicion," El'ken continued. "The trouble is, none of the victims ever make it back to testify. Or they haven't, until now. You are unique, Rigger Legroeder."

Legroeder shut his eyes, thinking of Jakus Bark, who could have told the truth but didn't. Had others made it back—but under the pirates' thumbs, like Jakus? Or framed, as he was?

Harriet was tapping furiously on her compad. She looked up. "It's a very provocative assertion—if we can prove it. Academic El'ken, I'm afraid Legroeder is in a terribly difficult position. Not only has he violated his bail by coming here, but he's fled from possible prosecution for two murders he didn't commit—including, I fear, that of Robert McGinnis."

El'ken's eyes closed in sorrow. "I would very much like to see the killers of Robert McGinnis brought to justice."

"Well, I can assure you that Legroeder is innocent. I was with him the entire time. Academic—it is clear that there is a conspiracy on Faber Eridani to conceal the involvement of *Impris* in the *L.A.*'s capture. And it would seem that to unmask the conspiracy, we must first prove the continued existence of *Impris*."

El'ken touched his fingers to the front of his robe. "That is indeed the problem, isn't it?"

"We were hoping you'd be able to help us," Legroeder said.

El'ken's neck-sail fluttered. "Unfortunately, I do not know where *Impris* is."

"But I thought you said—"

"Let's just say that the Narseil Rigging Institute has been hard at work trying to answer questions related to her disappearance."

Legroeder waved his hands in frustration. "Such as?"

"Matters related to obscure conditions in the Flux, conditions that can interfere with a ship's movement in and out of certain interdimensional layers. I am no rigger, and cannot explain it to you. May I assume, however, that this line of research is of interest to you? If it is, perhaps you would like to stay here as my guest for a day or two, while I acquire some information for you."

"Thank you—yes. We would appreciate that very much."

"Excellent." El'ken gave a great, inhuman sigh. "In that case, my friends, I must ask you to excuse me. I am unused to so much company. If you could return first thing in the morning . . ."

"I THINK he knows more than he's saying," Morgan said, pouring herself some pale-violet Narseil wine and passing the bottle to Legroeder.

"Well, of course he does," Legroeder said. "The question is, why? Is he just teasing us? Or does he want something?" Harriet barely looked up from her notes, which she had been studying almost continuously since they'd been escorted to the dining room. Legroeder held out the wine bottle, but she ignored it.

"What about this connection between the Kyber worlds and the pirates?" Legroeder said, pouring himself a refill. "I wonder if we could get evidence on what the pirates are doing with *Impris* by going to one of the Kyber worlds. Do you know anything about them?"

Harriet peered up from her compad and removed her glasses. "Not much. I've heard rumors on occasion that some of the old Kyber worlds are supplying some of the pirate outposts. But there's enough innate suspicion between the Kyber worlds and us—the wired and the unwired, you know—that it's hard to know what to believe."

"But if there's even a grain of truth to it—" Legroeder turned the wine glass slowly, studying the purplish liquid "—there are probably people on those worlds who have information."

"Meaning what—you want to take off to one of the Kyber worlds?" Morgan asked. "And make yourself an interstellar fugitive, instead of merely an interplanetary fugitive?"

"Well—I'm not saying that, exactly. But still—if you want to go fishing, you have to go where the fish are, right?" He took another sip of the tart wine, aware that the alcohol was layering a soft fuzz around his thoughts. Despite his confident words, he felt considerable uncertainty.

"Yeah, right," Morgan answered. "But this isn't a fishing expedition. This is your freedom and your career."

"Exactly. Which is why I'm considering it." Never mind that he had no idea how he would get to a Kyber world, or how he would gather information if he did go. "It all depends on what El'ken can tell us, I suppose. I don't want to go off half-cocked, but I'll do whatever I have to."

Morgan looked unconvinced.

"Here comes dinner," said Harriet, closing her compad. "Fortunately, we don't have to make any decisions this instant. Are you two going to hog all of that wine?"

AFTER A dinner consisting of oversalted roast feasting bird and unidentifiable greens, plus a second bottle of wine, they left the tiny dining room. Morgan suggested that they walk around a bit to clear their heads. "Dear," said Harriet, "I'm not sure we're really invited to wander—"

"It'll be *fine*. Legroeder?"

He groaned at the thought of moving. Nevertheless, they followed Morgan through the winding stone corridors. Eventually they came to a domed area that appeared to be a common lounge. It was empty—except for the stars.

"It's glorious!" Morgan exclaimed, turning about under the dome. They were on the opposite side of the asteroid from El'ken's cavern, and here the display of stars was a spangle of light across blackness. The dust lanes of the Milky Way arced across the dome like a welcoming carpet of luminosity. Far off to one side, a bright blue dot floated, the distant world of Faber Eridani. A handful of moving points of light were visible: spacecraft maneuvering nearby. At the edge of the dome, the outer surface of the asteroid curved away like the dark slope of a volcano.

Legroeder walked along the edge rail, absorbed by the

spacecraft activity. One ship, just near enough for its shape to be distinguishable, was approaching the asteroid. Another, much closer, flew up suddenly from below the horizon, startling him. It lifted away with glowing maneuvering inductors.

"Impressive," Morgan said, coming alongside him.

Legroeder suddenly stiffened. He pressed his hands to the crystal dome. "That's our ship!"

"What did you say?" Harriet asked.

"That's our goddamn ship!" Legroeder pointed, trying to project the flight path. "And that other ship out there is turning to meet it."

Harriet stood with her mouth open, as Morgan swore under her breath.

"Excussse me, please," said a voice behind them.

They turned, as one. A very tall Narseil approached them, holding out a slender envelope. "May I ask, which of you is Mrs. Mahoney? I have a message from your pilot." The Narseil handed her the envelope, gave a stiff bow, and walked from the room.

"What's this all about, I wonder," Harriet muttered, opening the envelope. "Oh, by God in Heaven."

"What? Mom, what is it?"

Harriet fumbled with her glasses and finally read the message aloud. " 'Mrs. Mahoney, greetings. We are sorry, but circumstances have forced us to leave Arco Iris. We have received word that a Spacing Authority cruiser, waiting outside diplomatic limits, carries warrants for your arrests. Our vessel will be impounded if we attempt to transport you. I am afraid we must leave you to find alternate transportation home. Apologies for the inconvenience. —Conex.' " Harriet crushed the message in her hand.

"Why, those—" Morgan began, then caught herself. "No, it's not their fault. So what do we do now?"

Harriet muttered to herself as she smoothed the paper out to read it again. She was clearly struggling to maintain her professional dignity. "Hope we can get diplomatic protection from the Narseil, I suppose."

Diplomatic protection? Legroeder began pacing under the dome. If the Spacing Authority was ready to arrest them the moment they left the Narseil asteroid, then they were effectively prisoners here. Unless he could find some other way to leave—not for Faber Eridani, but perhaps another star system. The Narseil probably had diplomatic ships here. It was a long shot, but they did have some goals in common.

But what about Harriet and Morgan?

"What?" Morgan said, peering at him. "What are you thinking?"

"I'm thinking," he said, "that we need to talk to El'ken again. How long's the day in this place?"

"Eighteen hours," said Harriet. "It's the middle of the night now."

"Then we'd better get some sleep. Morning will be here real soon."

THEY FOUND the historian busy at his desk. He looked as if he had been awake for hours.

"Have you ever heard of a group called 'Centrist Strength'?" El'ken asked, before they had a chance to say a word. He turned from the long desk-shelf that lined the wall of his cavern, and dusted his hands together.

"Yes, certainly," Harriet said. "Why?"

"Then you're familiar with their view that the Centrist Worlds should reclaim their mantle as leader of the galaxy and strike out in a colonizing movement? 'Destiny Manifest,' they call it. 'Timid no longer—ours the stars!' is one of their slogans."

Legroeder answered impatiently, "Yes, but—"

"Interestingly enough, this group is reported to have ties with several of the old Kyber worlds—and maybe even with the Free Kyber. *Adversaries* of the Centrist Worlds. I only bring them up as a possible factor behind your current problem."

"Which just got worse, last night," Legroeder said.

"Yes, I heard." The old Narseil pressed his fingertips together in what seemed a very human gesture. "That was most unfortunate, the arrival of the Spacing Authority and the departure of your transportation. Perhaps there is something I can do to help you—beyond bestowing temporary diplomatic protection."

Legroeder blinked. "I'm listening."

"Yes. Well, I doubt you can fight them on their own territory. But suppose I could get you to a place where you could gain information far beyond what I have to give you."

"I would appreciate that very much," Legroeder answered.

"And would you be interested in trying to gain information directly from the Kyber?"

"I certainly would."

The Narseil stood very still, gazing at Legroeder. "Then we must get you out of the Faber Eridani system. There may be a way . . ."

"Yes?"

"You would travel aboard a Narseil naval vessel, with diplomatic immunity. From there, you could join in with certain efforts of our own."

"Yes?"

"But I must tell you . . . you would eventually be entering a—how shall I put it?" El'ken paused, touching his oval mouth with one finger. "Hostile environment."

Legroeder felt a ripple of fear. "More hostile than I'm facing here?"

"I would think so. Although you would be in the company of Narseil naval officers, so the risk would be shared."

"Are we talking about . . . the Kyber worlds?"

"In a manner of speaking." The Narseil's face contorted in an expression of discomfort. "I suppose there's no easy way to put this to you." El'ken looked away for a moment, then whirled back, his robe billowing. "If you want to know more about *Impris* and those who follow her, you must go to a place where such matters are pursued."

"You mean the Narseil Rigging—wait a minute." Legroeder caught himself. "What *are* you saying—"

"That if you want to go fishing, you must go where the fish are, yes? An old human saying?"

Legroeder pressed his lips together in anger. *So much for private conversations.*

El'ken waved a hand. "I apologize for any intrusion."

Legroeder let his breath out slowly. *Forget it; let it go.* "So where . . . do you propose that we go to do this fishing?"

"To an outpost of the Free Kyber Republic."

"The—?"

"Free Kyber." El'ken coughed delicately. "The raiders."

Legroeder felt as if he'd been kicked in the stomach. He stood stunned, struggling to draw a breath. Finally he managed, "Do you know how long I spent *getting away* from the pirates?"

"Yes, I do," El'ken said. "Nevertheless, my offer is to send you back into the lion's den. To a pirate stronghold." He held up a hand to forestall protests from Morgan and Harriet, then tugged the closures of his robe together. "To fully explain, I must reveal certain things that are classified as secret. Before I can do that, I require an oath of secrecy from you. All of you."

Back into the lion's den. Legroeder shook his head to dispel the buzzing sensation in his head, and a surreal feeling of disconnection from the world around him.

"I do not suggest this lightly. And I assure you—I would not send you back to the place where you served your captivity."

"Then what exactly would you do?"

El'ken drew himself taller. "Are you willing to take an oath of secrecy? All of you?"

Legroeder laughed harshly. "Who would we tell?"

"Perhaps no one. But that is not the question. There are others involved, and I must be able to assure *them* of your sincerity."

"I'll take your oath," said Harriet, echoed by Morgan.

Legroeder shrugged. "Okay. Sure."

"Very well." El'ken brought his hands to his chin. "There

are preparations underway, through the Narseil naval undercover services, to mount a mission to infiltrate a pirate outpost. The goal is to gain intelligence—about pirate operations and about, as it happens, *Impris*."

Legroeder was speechless.

"It is not only human ships that fall prey to pirates, you know. My own people are victims, all too often." El'ken's gaze shifted for a moment to the emptiness of space, beyond the dome. "And now we have made plans to do something about it."

"But *how?* By attacking a raider outpost? You can't be serious!"

"I did not say attack. A Narseil ship is being readied to go undercover, in search of information."

Legroeder blinked uncomprehendingly.

"The intent is to be captured. Or to *seem* to be captured."

"You must be joking."

"I am not. There will be danger, obviously. However, considerable preparation has gone into the mission. We have found—" El'ken hesitated, and his eyes closed to vertical slits for a moment "—sympathetic connections within the raider organization, which lead us to believe there may be hope of success. But clearly the mission would benefit from the assistance of someone who has spent years among the pirates, and who knows much about their methods and systems." His yellowish eyes widened again, which had the effect of making his entire face seem to glow.

"No doubt it would," said Legroeder. "But how would this be anything but a death sentence for me? I'd not only be an infiltrator and a spy, I'd be a returning escapee."

"To put it mildly," Morgan interjected. "Legroeder! You'd have to be crazy!"

"Perhaps he would," El'ken agreed. "However, a great many Narseil naval personnel are crazy too, perhaps. Because they are preparing, even as we speak—and the mission will soon be off."

"Forgive me, Academic," said Harriet, "but this is a rather sudden proposal—and not one that I feel at all—" she struggled to find the right word, and finally shook her head "—happy with."

"None of us is *happy* with it, Mrs. Mahoney."

"No, but I'm here to advise and protect my client's interests. Before I could even *think* of allowing him to do this, I'd have to know a lot more. Academic, what hope is there *really* that this mission will succeed—and that Legroeder would come back alive?"

El'ken pressed his hands together and took a seat on the bench. "I will tell you what I can." He glanced from one to another; no one was breathing. "You see, it seems there may be an *underground* within the pirate organization. Our contact has advised us that we might, surprisingly, have some needs in common. Interests to be shared. You would not *altogether* be walking into a hostile situation . . ."

EL'KEN TALKED for a long time, even calling for refreshments midway through their discussion. He described a daring (far-fetched?) plan for penetrating a raider stronghold—one well away from the area of DeNoble, the outpost from which Legroeder had fled. Legroeder listened, but distractedly. He cared about the particulars of the plan, and yet in a sense, he didn't. A part of him was willing to trust the Narseil to put together a viable scheme—it was either completely crazy, or wasn't, but he doubted that he would have much to add to it one way or another.

He wondered which was the crazier prospect: embarking upon a dubious Narseil undercover operation, or turning himself back over to the Faber Eri Spacing Authority, who would lock him up and throw away the key. Which would give him the better chance of proving the existence of *Impris* and still being alive at the end of the exercise?

". . . and so you see, we will be depending upon stealth, meticulous planning, and judicious use of connections within the Free Kyber organization. Rigger Legroeder, are you following me?"

Legroeder blinked and nodded to the Narseil. "Get captured, get information, get out."

El'ken rocked slowly on his bench. "Put simply, yes. You understand the steps leading to it?"

Legroeder shrugged. "More or less. It sounds like an astronomically long shot to me. But maybe not absolutely impossible."

"It sounds insane to me," Morgan said.

"I would have to agree with Morgan," said Harriet. "And yet—"

"*What?*" Morgan asked, in disbelief.

"Well, if his only alternative is to surrender to that Spacing Authority cruiser out there . . ." Harriet lowered her glasses and rubbed the bridge of her nose. "Academic, is there no other option? No way you could get Legroeder out of the Faber Eri system to go searching for information, short of going back to the pirates?"

The Narseil rose and walked to the edge of his pool. He turned back. "No other way that I know of. No way to get him protected on one of our ships, without his participation in the mission. I'm sorry."

Harriet sighed. "What do you think, Legroeder? We're talking about your life, here."

Legroeder nodded without answering. He had no answer. For a few moments, the only sound was the chuckling of water in El'ken's pool. Finally Harriet spoke again. "I think this is a decision not to be made in haste. Academic, could we have some time to think, and talk, about it?"

"Of course," said El'ken. "But not too much time. We can stall the Spacing Authority for a while. But once diplomatic pressure is brought to bear . . ." He raised his hands in something like a shrug. "Thank you for considering the proposal. I will await your choice." And with that, he stepped into the water and vanished beneath the surface.

LUNCH WAS a somber affair. Legroeder had more or less made up his mind, without voicing it. He went through the pros and cons with his friends, perhaps hoping to be persuaded otherwise. But so far, nothing led him away from the inevitable choice.

He was depressed by the conclusion he had come to, but he didn't see any other way. "Whatever happens," he said, "I'm not going to be able to do much to help Maris. Promise me that you'll do everything you can for her?"

"You know we will," Harriet said. She peered at him, frowning. "You've decided to go, haven't you?"

Legroeder saw Morgan's eyes widening, and he looked away, staring at nothing for a few moments. "I guess we should go tell El'ken."

"Legroeder, you're not—" Morgan began, then caught herself as he smiled at her.

"What else can I do?" he asked gently. He turned to Harriet. "I promise I'll try to find out about your grandson."

Harriet nodded. She fiddled with her glasses, trying unsuccessfully to disguise her anxiety. "Legroeder, if I knew another way . . . even giving yourself up to the authorities . . ."

"Forget it, Harriet. There is no other way. By the time we get the evidence we need on Faber Eridani, they will have brainwiped me six ways from Tuesday." He drew a breath and bared his teeth. "So . . . can we please smile, everyone?"

EL'KEN WAS unavailable that afternoon, but sent a message to Harriet, informing her that the Faber Eridani authorities had made an initial filing for Legroeder's and her own extradition with the Narseil government. Time was growing short. He would speak to them first thing the next morning.

Legroeder retired to his room to think; to sleep, if he could. Instead he ended up pacing round and round in the tiny, stone-walled bedroom. Memories of the pirate outpost kept surfacing in his mind: the slamming of gates, shouts as new captives were brought in . . .

The door hummed. He stopped pacing and tried to force that mental image out of his mind. "Who is it?"

"Me. Morgan. May I come in?"

He turned and swung open the stone-and-metal door. "I thought you'd gone to bed."

"I thought so, too. But I have a message for you. Mother was going to bring it, but I offered to." She took a folded mylar paper out of her breast pocket and handed it to him. "It's from El'ken."

Legroeder opened the paper.

"Barrister Mahoney:

I have been in contact with appropriate elements of the Narseil Navy. They are willing to accept Renwald Legroeder as a member of the special services undercover mission, provided he agrees to certain temporary, but essential, surgical alterations and augmentations. We are to transmit an answer by 0900 tomorrow. In the event Rigger Legroeder does not wish to accompany the team, the three of you may remain on this asteroid as our guests until such time as the extradition negotiations have run their course.

With all due regards—El'ken."

Legroeder looked up at Morgan. "You've read this?" She nodded, her eyes troubled. Legroeder looked at the note again, then closed his eyes. *Surgical alterations and augmentations . . .* Visions of Robert McGinnis and Jakus Bark danced before him. Had he avoided cyber-implants all these years, only to be trapped into accepting them now?

Morgan perched on the edge of his bed. "Is it the augmentation part that worries you?"

"Good guess."

She seemed to suppress a shudder. "I wish we could just send you the hell away from all of this. Someplace where no one's ever heard of you." Her eyes seemed to say she didn't really want him to do that. Was she feeling attached to him? Personally?

"Yeah, well . . ." Legroeder managed a laugh. "I guess my mistake was picking Faber Eridani as a port of refuge in the first place."

Morgan caught his hand and gave it a squeeze. He was startled; he liked the feeling.

"Of course," he said awkwardly, "I wouldn't have met you and your mother then. But . . ."

"Legroeder?"

"Yeah?"

She tightened her grip on his hand. "I . . ." Her eyes seemed to be welling up. *"Oh hell."*

Legroeder cleared his throat, trying not to seem obtuse. He hadn't had much practice reading women in recent years. Or even paying attention to his own feelings. Here he was, alone in a bedroom with Morgan, whom he found quite attractive in an understated way. He liked Morgan; he liked her warmth, and the intelligence that shone through her eyes. As he thought about it, he realized it wouldn't take a lot for her to seduce him right here and now—in spite of everything that loomed over him. Was that what she wanted? Was it what *he* wanted? He wasn't likely to have too many more chances—with Morgan, or anyone else. He returned the pressure on her hand.

"Since you're not jumping in to fill the awkward silence," Morgan said with a nervous laugh, "I guess I should."

He drew a silent breath.

Her voice fell to a near whisper. "I like you, I want to help you, I want you to come through this." She pushed her hair back with her free hand. "And I feel like a complete fool right now."

Legroeder squeezed her hand harder. *Yes? So do I . . .*

"But if . . . there's anything I can do . . ." Morgan met his gaze. "If you'd like me here with you tonight . . ."

Legroeder smiled, or tried to, past the lump in his throat. He tried to speak, but could only think, *Want you . . . do I . . . so rushed? I don't know; give me more time. I need more time! Will I ever have another chance?*

Morgan continued, looking away, "I don't even know if you and . . . Maris . . . or if the two of you . . ." She frowned. "I'm sorry—here I am, and we don't even know if she's still alive, or what's happened to her."

"That's all right," Legroeder said softly. "You can't help about Maris—not right now. Anyway, she was a friend—

is a friend. But we weren't—lovers." He tried to stop thinking about Maris. What she might be going through right now.

Morgan's grip tightened again.

"But I—" Legroeder's voice caught, and he suddenly found himself breathing harder. Did she want him to kiss her? He envisioned her in his arms, and a confused part of him suddenly yearned for that. Without quite consciously deciding, he leaned to kiss her. Her breath went out with a strained sigh, and her lips met his, tentatively, and then softened against him. She leaned into him, slipping her arm around his waist. For a moment, he focused only on the pressure of her lips, and her breath, and the warmth of her body pressing against him. He felt a powerful stirring of arousal; but it was confused, uncertain. He wasn't sure what he was feeling. He kissed her more urgently, felt her tongue flicking at his. Her hand started to move over him; he drew a sharp breath and touched her breast, reveling. And then hesitated. It didn't feel right; he didn't know why.

Both their eyes blinked open, and their gazes met. Morgan pulled back from him, head cocked. Her face reddened with embarrassment as she seemed to read his thoughts. "You don't . . . really want that, do you?"

"No, I don't mean—it's just that—Morgan, I don't—you're very beautiful—"

"Shh. Stop." She put a finger to his lips. "I'm *sorry*. I shouldn't be doing this. I should be helping you, not messing you up when you've got so much on your mind." She stood up, readjusting her blouse.

He followed, his emotions churning. "Morgan, don't—"

"No, look—"

"Don't *you* apologize. I'm the one who—"

"I wasn't exactly—"

"Yes, you were." Legroeder suddenly burst into laughter, and then she did, too. He hugged her tightly. "I'll see you in the morning, okay?"

She nodded and pulled away toward the door. "Call me if you need . . . to talk . . . or whatever."

"I will. Good night."

The door clicked shut, and he stared at it in dumb bewilderment, before mentally kicking himself. *Idiot . . .*

THEY FOUND the Narseil historian swimming back and forth in his pool, his neck-sail cutting through the surface of the water like a shark's fin. He lifted his head, spotting them, but did not stop until he had finished swimming his laps. When he stepped out of the pool and into the soft whoosh of the dryer, he was breathing hard, with a whuffing sort of sound.

"My apologies," he said, joining them in the dry section of the cavern. "I am old. If I do not keep up my daily exercise, my mind and body will both fall into decay. Have you decided?"

"I have," Legroeder said. "When do we leave?"

El'ken bowed in acknowledgment. "I am pleased, and grateful. You will be an invaluable addition to the party. If you will excuse me for just one moment, I will begin making the arrangements." He turned toward his communications console, then paused. "Regarding Mrs. and Ms. Mahoney . . ."

"What about them?" Legroeder asked, before either of the women could speak.

"Well, since you will not be accompanying Rigger Legroeder, and you have problems in terms of getting back home . . ."

"I was hoping you could help them with that."

El'ken visibly suppressed his annoyance at the interruption. "I can offer hospitality here, as long as necessary. Perhaps once the mission has been completed, and security for it is no longer an issue, we will be able to assist you—"

"No," said Legroeder.

"I beg your pardon?"

"If you keep them prisoner here, the deal's off."

El'ken spread his long-fingered hands. "I assure you, they would not be *prisoners*. They will be very comfortable."

"They have important work to do, back on Faber Eri. If you don't let them go, they're prisoners."

"Legroeder, wait," said Harriet.

"No—it's that or nothing." Legroeder rubbed his jaw. He hadn't realized until just now that this was part of his decision. "Look, Academic—if I'm going to entrust my life to your people, then you have to trust my people. Quid pro quo. Isn't that what they call it, Harriet?"

Harriet opened her mouth, then closed it.

"Yeah, that's what they call it. Look," he said. "Maybe you see this in just one dimension, which is your secret mission. Well, my friends won't peep a word about it. You can trust them. And I'm not only concerned about their freedom. They have work to do while I'm gone, and I'm hoping you can help them. I expect to return to find that I've been cleared of all charges back on Faber Eridani."

Everyone else seemed at a loss for words, so Legroeder kept talking. "I notice your eyes narrowed just a bit at the word *return*."

The Narseil winced slightly.

"I thought so. Maybe you don't think I have all that much chance of returning. But you wouldn't be undertaking this mission if you thought it had *no* chance, right? And you will offer me the same prospects for safe return as your own people, won't you?"

He was aware of Morgan stirring uneasily beside him, but he kept his gaze on El'ken's.

Finally the Narseil said, "Your chances are exactly the same as any other member of the crew. I hope very much for your safe return."

"Good. Then what can you do to help my friends on their way?"

El'ken hesitated a long moment. "I suggest a cooling off period, at least until the Spacing Authority cruiser leaves. Then perhaps I can arrange for a diplomatic transport to take them back to Faber Eridani. Barrister Mahoney, can you perform your duties from within the Narseil Embassy in Elmira?"

Harriet looked surprised. "Better than I could do them from here, or in prison, I suppose."

El'ken bowed. "Then I will endeavor to arrange it. And I would very much appreciate it . . . if you would do all in your power to learn who was responsible for the death of a good man."

"McGinnis? You have my promise."

"Thank you. Before I make the call to my people, Rigger Legroeder— when can you be prepared to travel?"

Legroeder shrugged. "I'm ready now."

"Excellent. A transport will be standing by."

"And its destination?"

"That, I cannot tell you." The Narseil stretched out his hands. "I suggest you make your appropriate farewells in the next few minutes. You will not hear from him again until he returns. Go and make your preparations, and come back when you are ready."

LEGROEDER FELT like a body being viewed at a wake. "Look—I'm not dead yet, okay?"

Harriet nodded miserably, and Morgan was too busy leaking tears to say anything. Legroeder tossed his bag over to the door of their little dining room. "It's not as if I'm never going to see you again. So for chrissake, how about showing me a smile. Morgan, you were terrific in bed last night."

Harriet's eyebrows went up. Morgan made a choking sound, and for a second he didn't know if she was going to laugh or sob. She smacked him on the shoulder—hard— then burst into tears. "Asshole," she muttered.

Legroeder sighed. "Doesn't anyone have a sense of humor around here?" He knew he was just making it worse, but couldn't help it. "Look—I'm sorry—you were awful in bed last night. *Terrible*. In fact, you weren't even there. Harriet, she wasn't—*ow!*" Morgan had just hit him twice as hard. Now she was covering her face, making hiccuping sounds.

He sighed again. "Morgan, I'm just trying to make you a little less funereal, okay?"

"No, it's not okay," she said, voice muffled by her hands.

"All right. But look—don't be so scared for me. Be happy that I have a chance I didn't have before." He moved awkwardly to put his arms around her. She grabbed him in a sudden, powerful bear hug. They embraced for a long time, before stepping apart. Morgan wiped at her eyes.

"Good-bye, Legroeder," said Harriet, putting her arms around both of them. "Take good care, dear—and come back safely, so I can collect my thirty percent, okay?"

Legroeder struggled to answer, as Morgan shook, hugging them both. "All right, you two," Morgan said hoarsely. "Can we please get moving, before I go to pieces again?"

Legroeder picked up his bag, and they walked off together, back to El'ken's chamber.

Chapter 12

NARSEIL MISSION CENTER

ONCE MORE, Legroeder rode as a passenger, this time on a Narseil diplomatic transport three times the size of the corporate ship that had brought them to the asteroid. And this time, traveling through the Flux, he fairly twitched with frustration, wishing he could get up there on the Narseil bridge and see what rigging was like among these amphibious star travelers. Eventually he sent a message to the captain, asking for a visit to the bridge. He received a polite rebuff: forget it, while they were en route to the secret base.

He chafed at having nothing to do but sit and wonder what the hell he was doing, and what would become of his friends. Where was Maris by now? And what would happen to Harriet for helping him? Was her grandson Bobby alive? *Gah.* He was going to be cooped up way too long to spend all his time fretting.

Eventually, a crew member pointed him toward the ship's library, where he occupied himself delving into the Narseil files on *Impris*. At first he read grudgingly, to kill time. Soon, though, he became fascinated reading about the ship from the alien perspective. Inspector Fandrang was mentioned only fleetingly. Considerably more space was given over to the propaganda campaign that was launched against the Narseil, blaming their navy for the loss of *Impris*. Various searches of the Narseil's meticulously kept naval archives, over the years, had turned up no record of any engagement with such a ship—or any ship even remotely close to *Impris*'s course. It was clear from the sheer volume written on the subject that *Impris* remained a sore point with the Narseil.

Legroeder browsed for writings by El'ken, and found quite a lot; he was a prolific and respected chronicler of Narseil history. There was nothing by him on the subject of *Impris*, though, except for a third-level footnote in one article—the Narseil loved footnotes—mentioning that *Impris* was to be a subject of future research. Legroeder closed the file, feeling unsettled at having recognized himself as a tool in the august historian's "future research."

As the days wore on, he found himself reflecting on how far one could travel in a dangerous and possibly quixotic search for truth. He also found himself reflecting on the irony of his own worlds' failure in space exploration—no vision, no courage, no willingness to sacrifice and take risks—and how strange it felt knowing that he was, in some sense, in accord with those he so utterly despised. What if he were given a chance to participate in deep-space exploration, but only in the company of pirates, or the likes of Centrist Strength? *Jesus.* Would he do it?

No . . . *no* . . . he wasn't that desperate to go. Not yet . . .

* * *

By day four, the feelings of isolation were starting to close in around him. He finally found some company in the crewman who had shown him the library, a young Narseil named Korken. Korken was interested in learning about humans. He had never been to a human world, but had studied the major Earth-standard language, Anglic, and talked when he could without the assistance of the implanted translator. "The closssest I ever got was the asssteroid where we gathered you," he said ruefully.

"Well, that makes us even," answered Legroeder. "I've *seen* Narseil riggers, but that asteroid was the first time I'd ever been on your turf."

Korken nodded, causing his neck-sail to flutter. His crest was considerably larger than El'ken's, framing a smaller and rounder face. Was it his youth, or simply a personal characteristic? Legroeder was finally becoming able to tell one Narseil apart from another. When he'd first come aboard, they'd all looked the same to him.

"Have you ever rigged?" Legroeder asked, pouring himself a small beaker of juice from the refreshment center.

Korken poured himself a larger beaker. "No, but I hope to, one day. I am—what would be the word in your language—an *apprentisss* to the riggerss of my ship. I study their inssstructionals—and one day, when I have passed their tests, I may be permitted to enter a rigger-net with the crew." He paused to sip his drink. "That will be a proud day for me."

"I'm sure it will," Legroeder said glumly. When Korken looked quizzical, he sighed. "Sorry, I'm just not used to being cooped up like this. Not able to see where we're going—it makes me nuts."

"Ah, I underssstand," said Korken. "I wish I could show you, but I'm afraid that my superior here—" he gestured to a Narseil officer who had just walked in "—would take away my job. Yesss?"

"Yes," said the officer. "But in fact, I came to tell Rigger Legroeder that we have made better time than expected. We will soon be entering the restricted zone, and then you'll be able to see."

"Huh? I'll be able to see the *restricted* zone?"

The Narseil waved a bony hand. "We're not concerned about your seeing the base itself. It's the location of it we need to protect."

Legroeder spirits rose. "When?"

"I would think, by dinnertime. Would that be sssatisfactory?"

"That would make my day," said Legroeder.

Korken beamed, his face distorting nicely into a mask of apparent pain.

THE NARSEIL base consisted of a chaotic array of disk-shaped structures—like an assortment of pancakes stacked in parallel planes, but shuffled out of alignment. Legroeder pressed his face to the viewport, trying to take it all in. "I'm a little surprised," he murmured to Korken.

"Why? Did you think we would have large weapons and thhhreatening battle fleetss?"

"I thought you might have a few ships. But I didn't think it would look just like a holo of typical Narseil architecture from *Galacti Geographic*."

"Ah," said Korken. "I guesssss, when a design works, one stays with it."

Soon they were docked and Legroeder was being escorted onto the station. He wasn't sure what he was expecting— maybe something like El'ken's asteroid. Instead, he found an interior that mirrored the smoothness and asymmetry of the exterior: smoothly curving grey walls, soft greenish-white lighting, the occasional expansive viewport, and pools everywhere. Some of the pools were occupied by Narseil; others were empty and still. An air of quiet efficiency pervaded the station.

Accompanied by a pair of officers from the ship, Legroeder was whisked to a meeting room that might have been any human conference center, except for the French-curve walls and a large, brightly lit pool in which half a dozen Narseil were carrying out some sort of underwater training exercise.

"This way, please."

Legroeder followed a Narseil to the far end of the meeting room, where he was introduced to an array of officers, only three of whose names he remembered—Fre'geel, Cantha, and Palagren. He stared at each for a heartbeat, trying to fix names with faces.

"Welcome to our team," said Fre'geel—tall, green-eyed, and businesslike. He was the mission commander, dressed in a shiny, forest-green uniform that seemed all straps and belts; he was, Legroeder had learned, a veteran of several forays against Golen Space raiders. "If you're ready, we'd like to brief you immediately on the mission. You've shown great courage in joining us."

Legroeder twitched, but said nothing.

"We'd like to go over our objectives and strategy, to determine where you might best fit in. We welcome any ideas you might have for improving the chances of success."

"I'll do my best," Legroeder murmured.

"And then of course we must get you to the surgical theater to begin the alterations to your physical appearance—"

"Uh?" Legroeder blinked. "So soon?"

Fre'geel looked surprised. "Well, of course. We launch in just a few days. You knew that, didn't you? And you know we're equipping you with augmentation?"

"Well, I . . . did want to talk to you about that, actually . . ."

One of the others spoke up—Cantha, the stockiest of the Narseil. Dressed in a dull khaki uniform, he had an extremely thick neck crest, almost a ridge rather than a sail. His face was fuller and craggier, and he had greenish-brown eyes. "It's essential that you be fully equipped. As a human, you may have more opportunity to gain useful information in the stronghold than we do—but it may be necessary for you to blend with the locals—"

"Right, I understand."

"—and equally important, to record your findings."

"Yes, but—"

Suddenly they were all staring at him, as though wondering what his problem was.

He stirred, self-conscious. "Well, it's just that . . . I'm not really sure I can function properly with augments." *Because I'm terrified of them.* He gestured awkwardly. "The pirates didn't put any in me because they thought I'd have trouble functioning in the net with them." *Or at least I managed to convince them of it . . . and I was a good rigger without . . .*

"Ah."

Fre'geel turned to Palagren, a slender, grey-eyed Narseil who was dressed in a grey robe that shimmered with occasional iridescence—a trademark attire of Narseil riggers. Palagren answered, "I will be the lead rigger, and I will train you very carefully, to make certain that we can work together with your augments. We have considerable experience in that area, so I wouldn't worry."

Legroeder opened his mouth to answer, but Palagren continued, "In any case, it is necessary, so there's no need to discuss it further."

Legroeder closed his mouth.

"If I might add," said Cantha, "since our intent is to penetrate a raider stronghold—and, we hope, to gain useful information from their internal datanets—you'll need to be able to interact with those nets." Cantha paused, as Legroeder reflected on the fact that, in all his years of captivity, he had managed to remain quite disconnected from the raider intelnets. "Our analysis," Cantha continued, "suggests that with you assisting us with full augmentation, our chances of success rise significantly. That is to say, our chances of getting out with the information. Or at least getting the information itself out."

Legroeder cocked his head at that. "Tell me something. What *do* you estimate our chances are of getting back in one piece? El'ken was a tad vague on that question." *And yet I listened to him. So who's the fool here?*

The Narseil exchanged glances among themselves. *This is the mighty human warrior come to aid us?* he could imagine them thinking. Fre'geel, the mission commander, answered, "That's impossible to know, really. El'ken told you we have had contacts with people in the Free Kyber society?"

"Yes."

"That is one of our reasons for considering this mission worth attempting. But of course, there is a chance that the team will not return, that our lives will be traded . . . for useful information. Did you not understand that?"

Legroeder tried to conceal his annoyance . . . and fear. "Well, yeah—I knew there were serious risks. Obviously. But I have no interest in going on a suicide mission. I assume you have some actual plans for getting us in, and getting us out again?"

Fre'geel clapped his hands together in apparent irritation. "Of course we have plans, and we will brief you on them. Appearing to be captured will be our first challenge; penetrating a raider stronghold will be the second; gaining information, the third; and getting out again, the fourth—and most difficult. Our minimum goal is to transmit out information useful to the Narseil Navy."

"Information such as—?"

"Information on *Impris*, of course. Data on the nature and location of the outpost, and information on the command structure of the enemy." Fre'geel's eyes glinted. "Understand, we have tried before to strike out at the pirates. The cost has always been greater than the reward. Three times we have seized raider ships, only to watch them self-destruct before we could learn anything from them. We have yet to locate a single raider outpost. If we enable our navy to find, and possibly neutralize, even one outpost as a result of this mission, we will have succeeded." The Narseil commander blew out a breath from his mouth. "But the risk to those of us on the mission . . ." He turned his long-fingered hands outward.

Legroeder tried to nod, but felt himself scowling instead.

"All right, look—here's *my* feeling on the subject, if you care. All these noble ambitions are fine, but I've already lived as a prisoner in a raider outpost, and I don't intend to do it again. If I go into another one, I *plan* on coming back out. If you don't think we can do that, tell me now."

Fre'geel stiffened. It was Cantha who answered, "I have heard that is a common human approach. Our way is different. Our way is to plan on giving all, including our lives. To *expect* to have to give our lives. If we find that we come away alive, so much the better. A happy surprise."

Legroeder stared at Cantha. I always knew there was something wrong with you people, he thought. Finally he shrugged. "Well, at least we know where we stand with each other. But if you want my *help*, as opposed to just my warm body, then I trust you'll take my needs into account here. Yes?"

He saw several neck-sails flutter. Then Fre'geel bowed. "Indeed, you shall have a voice. And soon we'll discuss strategy in detail. But first we must see to those alterations you will need."

Legroeder frowned. "Why first?"

Fre'geel's mouth stretched in an expression he couldn't identify. "Because we must have your absolute commitment before we can discuss details. And what better way to show your commitment than to go ahead with the operation, yes?"

Sarcasm? Triumph? Legroeder tried to think of a good answer—or a way out. *You've already committed*, he thought. Finally he shrugged. "All right. Let's go . . ."

His Narseil hosts took him to the medical center, which looked like a cross between an aquarium and a physiological stress lab. There were sunken pools in the center of the room and raised glass tanks around two sides, several containing placidly floating Narseil surrounded by medical instruments. There were also cots and tables, and banks of unidentifiable equipment.

Legroeder was introduced to the chief medical officer, a surgeon named Com'peer, a female Narseil dressed in flowing green robes. Her neck-sail was maroon-tinged, and edged with a striking gold ridge. Legroeder found himself wondering, irrelevantly, if those colors were real. Did Narseil color their neck-sails?

Com'peer wasted no time. "This is what we'll be installing," she said, holding out a tray for his inspection. It contained four small metallic buttons and two large syringes with real needles, not sprays. "We'll implant the disks by subcutaneous insertion, but the internal wiring will be established by programmable nanoscale microsurgeons." She tapped the first syringe. "That will be phase one."

Legroeder studied the tray unenthusiastically. "What's phase two?"

"We'll alter your physical appearance—a precaution, in case your image and vital statistics have been circulated among the raider outposts. After all, you may be on—what is the term?—a 'wanted' list."

I'm sure I am, Legroeder thought.

"Do we have your permission for the changes, Rigger Legroeder?"

"Well, uh—are you planning to leave me human, at least?"

"Of course. And you will have an opportunity to preview all of the changes before they're made."

He let his breath out very slowly. "Well-l-l . . . all right, I guess. As long as I see every step before it happens."

"Excellent. Then let us proceed with phase one."

"Just like *that?*" Legroeder was startled to realize that all the others, except Cantha, had disappeared. And Cantha was examining his long Narseil fingers, pretending to ignore the entire conversation.

"We are ready. You are ready," said the surgeon. "And you will need time for adaptation and training." Com'peer studied him for a moment. "Why delay?"

I can think of a thousand reasons, Legroeder thought with a shiver. "All right . . ."

* * *

FOR THE operation, Legroeder received a partial anesthesia, which left him conscious but spacey, filled with a disembodied awareness of what they were doing to him—guarded not so much against physical pain as neural disorientation. When they implanted the disks, he felt a brief stinging sensation—four times, once on each temple and once behind each ear. Within minutes of the syringe injections that followed, he began to feel an inner tickling as the microprocessors that had just been released into his bloodstream burrowed into his nervous system, building interfaces between the implants and his brain.

"Am I—" he murmured dreamily "—going to be able to have these taken out after it's all over?"

"Why would you want to?" asked the bemused surgeon, rustling about beside him. "You'll be far more intelligent with these inside you."

"Wonderful . . . but will I still be *me?* With this . . . stuff . . . I won't know who's in charge."

Com'peer made a hissing and clucking sound. "You humans—you are so insecure about your personal identities!"

"What the hell do you know about humans?" Legroeder muttered, just aware enough to be annoyed.

The Narseil gave a chittering laugh. "Quite a lot, actually. How much time have *you* spent on Earthhome?"

Legroeder blinked in amazement; with the anesthesia, the action occurred in slow motion. "You've been to Earth?" Earth, to him, was hardly more than a legend. He had never been within a hundred light-years of the place.

"Indeed I have. I did my post-post-training on Earthhome," said Com'peer. "Columbia Interspace Medical Center, in Old America."

"Huh . . ." said Legroeder. He wanted to ask more, but just then the surgeon stepped away, humming softly. A moment later, his thoughts were obliterated by a sudden rush of sensation from the inner network construction . . .

It was a little like feeling a spiderweb being pulled through his nerves, veins, and sinews. The sensation was partly physical, and partly an *image* being drawn through his consciousness. It was growing and he had no power to control it, to slow it or stop it. He had a sudden feeling of being caught in traffic in a city, trapped and choked, and forced to move where traffic moved him, or held where it held him, caught in a living web that was part of something greater than himself.

And then darkness flared over him, and all sensation flickered out, and he no longer knew whether time was passing slowly or quickly. But he knew that it was somehow *altered* . . . and he retained just enough awareness to realize that the new network was somehow integrating itself with brain centers associated with time perception . . .

. . . and then without warning there was a jarring sensation, as if his own inner system were being *reset*. Immediately a rush of information followed, to and from the implants. He had no idea of the actual content of the information; it was as though the system were testing itself, and felt no need to involve him in the process.

And then, just like that, the physical alteration was done. But not the readjustment; that was only beginning. There were things linked to his brain now: knowledge systems. It was a little like being hooked into a rigger net; but the kinds of data he sensed were very different, more like a library connection. He was dimly aware, as he lay motionless, of the Narseil medics moving around nearby, but most of his attention was drawn inward; the knowledge systems were stirring, and offering their services to him. He wasn't sure what he was supposed to do.

A series of connections flickered open briefly, in succession. Some were to databases, others to analysis engines. Still others, to the outside—or would be, later, when he needed to join with ship systems, or libraries. Or . . . the pirates' intelnet.

He became conscious of Com'peer moving around, humming. When the surgeon leaned over to peer into his eyes, he yelped involuntarily; there was a mutant iguana staring at him. His vision squirmed for a moment, then refocused to reveal the Narseil's face.

"Good," said the surgeon.

Legroeder struggled to make his mouth work. "Wha' d'y' mean, *good?*" he managed. "You scared . . . living b'jesus . . . out 'me."

The Narseil laughed, the sound of a zipper going up. "I was applying a small input to your vision system to see if you would react. I was not disappointed."

Legroeder closed his eyes, praying it would all go away.

"Don't worry if all this seems a bit disconcerting," Com'peer went on. "We'll have you trained before you actually go into action."

"How're you—?" Legroeder started to say, but before he could complete the thought, a new rush of inputs came over him. He was suddenly swimming in a surrealistic landscape, floating over glowing orange lava beneath a blood-red sky. He felt a rush of fear, and then annoyance and confusion. Finally it occurred to him that perhaps he could control this the way he would control a rigger net. He tried to wish the volcanic landscape away. When that didn't help, he tried to command it away. There was still no effect, except that the lava seemed to glow hotter, rising toward him with its sulfurous fumes. With a silent mutter, he focused his thoughts more sharply. In his mind's eye, he formed his right hand into a painter's brush. He stroked at the sky. The blood-red softened to pink, and then to a pale violet. *Ahh* . . . With a sweep of his brush, he erased the lava and turned the surroundings into a cool blue place with a ceiling over his head . . . and finally back into the Narseil medical center.

He glared up at the Narseil surgeon.

"Very good," said Com'peer. "You seem to have a knack for this. Of course, as a rigger, you should."

"As a rigger," Legroeder growled, "I don't like having my mind messed with. If I don't know where input is coming from, and I can't control it, I can't rig. That's why I didn't *want* these damn things!"

"I understand," said the surgeon, in a tone of sandpaper, probably meant to be soothing. "That's why we're training you—so you *will* be in control. You're off to a good start.

I expected it to take you far longer to pull out of that image just now. My congratulations."

Legroeder swore under his breath. "You might have given me some warning."

Her laugh sounded like crinkling cellophane. "Next time. Next time we will give you warning. Now, would you like to rest before we move on to phase two?"

Legroeder rolled his head on the padded table. "Phase two? *Phase two?* Yes, I would like to rest! Can I get off this damned table?"

The surgeon helped Legroeder sit up. "You are feeling well enough to walk? Good! Then my associates will take you to your room and get you something to eat before you sleep. Try to make yourself at home and I'll see you tomorrow."

Legroeder wobbled as he slipped off the table onto rubbery legs. "Thank you."

The surgeon acknowledged with a nod, then motioned to one of the medical assistants to come forward. "Now, do not be surprised if you find yourself . . . interacting . . . with your new implants as you sleep. It is nothing to worry about."

"Nothing to worry about?" Legroeder asked suspiciously.

"You may have dreams."

SLEEP PROVED hard to come by, and when he did drop off, Legroeder found himself on a roller coaster of night visions. His inner world flickered with images and movement; he ran in his dreams, trying to find his way down a maze of corridors, trying to escape from he knew not what, or to catch up with something very much like it. His breath became ragged; his pulse raced.

He woke up, alone, in a small room. He was lying on a pad on the floor. The Narseil had worried that he might fall off one of their high beds, and his tangled bedclothes suggested that they were right. He sat up, dazed, trying to bring back the confusing welter of dream images that had preceded his awakening. He felt a need to identify them before he could push them aside—to clear his mind of them before he could trust his senses in the waking world.

A Narseil aide appeared, calling him to breakfast. Already? It felt like the middle of the night. He dressed and followed the aide to a nearby room, where he sat alone and ate cereal with rice milk, and drank something like coffee. Finally he was taken back to the medical center. Com'peer greeted him cheerily, asked how he'd slept, and led him to a console. "Please study," she said.

On the display were six faces. The first snapped to full screen as he sat down. It was his own face: dark, olive-tinted skin in a narrow, slightly pinched face. All right—he knew what he looked like. He could stand to be a little handsomer, but he'd lived with this face for a long time, and figured he could keep on living with it. The screen flicked to the second face, and it was . . . his face, but different. It was longer and thinner, almost more like a Narseil. His features were recognizable, but only because he was looking for them. It was a very good disguise. It was also a remake of his entire facial structure. "Just how would you do this—by putting my head in a vice?" he asked, looking up at Com'peer.

"Nothing so crude," said the surgeon. "But in a sense you are right. We would have to redo the bone structure of your face. It would involve some pulverizing and reconstituting."

"Jesus," Legroeder said, feeling faint. "What else have you got?"

The next image was just the opposite effect: it looked as if an anvil had been dropped on his head. The face was recognizably human, but barely. "Oh, that's great," he said. "Christ Almighty."

"All right, no need to worry," said Com'peer, beginning to sound just a little tense. "We'll keep showing you possibilities."

"I can just imagine! *Christ!*"

Com'peer was quiet for a moment. "Could I ask you a personal favor? Could you not curse in those terms, please?"

"What?" He looked up at her, startled.

The Narseil's voice changed in tone. "I am a Christian," she said, "and it troubles me to hear His name used in that manner."

Legroeder stared, open-mouthed. "You're kidding."

"No, I am not." The Narseil looked at him oddly. "Why would I kid?"

"You're a *Christian?* I thought you Narseil were all Three Ringers."

Com'peer's neck-sail quivered a little. "The Three Rings is the predominant faith on my world. But not the only one, no. Forgive me for the digression. About these images—"

"I'll be damn—I mean—"

"It is all right. Now, if you will look at the images again . . . I think you worry too much about these changes. If you do not want us to alter your fundamental bone structure, we will not. There is much that we can do, short of that."

Legroeder shifted his gaze from the surgeon to the screen. The next image looked like a face that had stood in the path of a desert sandstorm. The features were scoured and smoothed, the eyebrows almost entirely missing, the angularities of his nose and cheekbones rounded and softened. It seemed almost feminine.

"Next!" he grunted.

The next was a lot more like his real face, except that at first he scarcely saw it, because his hair was so drastically altered. It cascaded out in a thick, overhanging umbrella, and was cut sharply inward at the bottom, in a downward angle to his head. The eyes were changed, too—dulled from the dark intensity that he normally saw in the mirror. *"Ug-g-ly,"* he grunted. "But better than any of the others, that's for sure."

"This would require far less in the way of organic change to your facial bones," Com'peer said. "But we're not sure that the change is sufficient to disguise you." She hesitated. "At the risk of offending . . . I must confess that most human characteristics look universal to most Narseil. Even after considerable exposure. So we must depend somewhat on your judgment in the matter."

Legroeder tried to look more offended than he actually felt, then realized that the expression was probably lost on the Narseil, anyway. "It would fool me," he said. "You got any others?"

There was one more, which looked like his face molded from putty. Legroeder shook his head. "Nope. If it has to be one of these, give me the umbrella-head."

Com'peer and several other Narseil conferred, then Com'peer said, "Very well. That is what we will do. Do you have any requirements before we begin the procedure?"

Besides packing my bag and leaving? Legroeder sighed heavily. "I guess not. You mean, *now?* Let's get it over with, then."

They put him back on the padded table, and this time put him under a light sleep. He started to protest—did he trust them to do this right without his oversight?—but it was already too late. The sleep-field slipped over his thoughts like a fine, downy comforter and his thoughts drifted away.

He dreamed of rows of corn growing on the top of his head, and the wind sighing through his hair.

Chapter 13

MISSION AWAY

HE AWOKE feeling clear headed, and asked to see a mirror.

"Dear God, how long was I asleep?" he gasped, when they led him to a seeing wall. His face was white, and his hair had turned light grey and been shaped into a wide, snub-topped cone, extending about four inches out from the sides of his head. It was at least ten inches longer than it had been when he went to sleep. He touched it hesitantly;

it felt synthetic. But it wasn't; it tugged at his scalp roots as he moved his head from side to side.

"About fourteen hours," said Com'peer, walking into the room. "How do you like it?"

Legroeder was having trouble breathing. "My skin! I'm bleach white!"

"Well, it's not quite that—"

"Fish-belly white! You didn't tell me you were going to do that to me!"

Com'peer waved her hands. "We felt that it was necessary."

"For *what?*"

"To ensure your anonymity. The other changes seemed insufficient, when we saw them."

Legroeder patted his skin, scowling at himself and at the surgeon in the reflection. What the hell was wrong with this mirror, anyway? Then he realized that the surgeon, who was standing to his right, was also to his reflection's right. It wasn't a mirror; it was a projection of his image, without left and right reversal. Damned disorienting. He shut his eyes for a moment. "What else have you done?"

Com'peer made a husky sound. "Well . . . we did change your DNA slightly—just enough to fool a scan."

Legroeder gulped. "You changed my—"

"Only in your gonads. According to our reports, that's where the raiders like to do their testing."

"What?" His hands went instinctively below his belt.

One of the other Narseil said, "Apparently it is more accurate there."

"Not more accurate," corrected Com'peer. "Just more humiliating. It is a method of theirs." She lowered her gaze as she studied her human patient. "That is something you needed to be warned about, in any case. You must be ready."

Legroeder stared at her, appalled.

Com'peer seemed to relax a little, having delivered the bad news. "We can change you back if—forgive me, *when*—you return safely. And we only changed genome segments listed as inactive or cosmetic. So it's not really a big thing."

Speak for yourself.

"Good," said Com'peer. "Now, if we're through with the inspection and everyone's happy, let's get started with your training. Shall we?"

Shaking his head, Legroeder followed the others out of the room.

IF HE thought they were going to give him time to acclimate to the changes, he was wrong. Before he could blink, he was being subjected to lectures on combat and undercover operations, interspersed with physical training in everything from hand-to-hand combat to deep-cyber penetration of shielded intelligence systems.

The basic plan of action was simple enough. Their ship, posing as a passenger liner, would put itself in harm's way, in a region of space known to be patrolled by ships of a certain raider tribe. Upon contact with a raider ship, the Narseil would be prepared for a diplomatic encounter if it occurred—but if attacked, they would attempt to capture the pirate ship, and then use it as a cover to make their way to its home base. Once at the raider outpost, their goal was to gather intelligence through the local networks, contact the underground, and get out as quickly as possible.

It was a risky plan, obviously. They were counting on a combination of Narseil fighting skill and potential assistance from their contacts in the raider organization. Indirect messages received from this outpost had suggested a possible interest in opening lines of communication with the outside. The problem was, the messages were of uncertain reliability; however, it seemed possible that they represented a genuine underground movement within the Free Kyber organization.

To the Narseil Command, it had seemed a risk worth taking—especially if, in the long run, it might lead to a reduction of hostilities.

"Academic El'ken is more hopeful about that than I am,"

Mission Commander Fre'geel said during one discussion. "I doubt we'll find this particular leopard changing its spots, as you might say. If someone is looking for us and wants to talk, we'll talk. But I am operating on the assumption that this will be an undercover intelligence mission, from beginning to end. We can hope that any underground element that wants to find us, will. But we have no way of looking for them; we must *assume* that we are on our own. If we're in a fight, we intend to win it. And not just win, but take captives and a flyable raider ship. That could be the hardest thing of all."

"Except, perhaps, getting out again afterward," Legroeder pointed out.

"Well, yes—there is that. And that is why everyone, including you, Rigger Legroeder, must be trained in all phases of combat. We might have to fight our way out."

It was hard to argue with that line of reasoning, and Legroeder threw himself wholeheartedly into the training. After two days of lectures, rigger-sims, and hands-on training with Narseil weaponry, he was brought to a large cavern the size of a sports arena. From a balcony, he looked down on Narseil commandos in training—in one corner storming an office complex, in another working their way through a jungle setting (*a jungle?*), and in still another making their way deck by deck through a mockup of a ship, opposed by holographic adversaries. At one end of the balcony, he peered through a window into an enormous zero-gee chamber, where spacesuited teams were rehearsing a ship-to-ship assault.

"This way, please!" his trainer called. Legroeder turned from the window and dutifully followed to the suit-up room. Having gear fitted to him took two hours—and for the next two, he ran and climbed and shot—and tried not to *be* shot—all with a heavy pack on his back, and holo-enemies popping up like targets on an arcade game. At the end of a long obstacle course, he found himself being urged into a pool for water-borne hand-to-hand combat training.

That was where he reached his limit.

"Swim yourself!" he gasped, and threw himself down, wheezing for air.

"What's the matter?" asked his trainer, a Narseil weapons specialist named Agamem.

"I'm not an amphibian, and I don't want to drown, that's what's the matter!" Legroeder snarled. He had never been a strong swimmer. He had nearly drowned once as a boy, when he'd lost his footing in the shallows of a river beach, and gotten caught in an undertow. The memory still haunted him, twenty years later. "Why the hell should I train in water combat, anyway?"

"We want you prepared in all environments," said Agamem.

"Yeah, well, we're trying to penetrate a pirate outpost. Unless I wind up falling into the local pirate Y pool, I don't think I'll have to fight anyone in the water. *Comprendo?*"

Agamem looked puzzled, but perhaps recognized that an alien species might have different training requirements. "Very well, then. How about another round of corridor fighting?"

Legroeder nodded. That he would do. It was entirely plausible that there would be fighting in corridors. Although he had little interest in or native talent for fighting, he did have a survival instinct. He would take all the training he could get.

"Let's go, then."

"Give me a moment to rest, okay?"

"Will your enemy give you time to rest . . . ?"

THE IMPLANT training was another matter altogether. The Narseil had embedded what seemed at times a controlled madness in his skull, and he had to learn to master it. The knowledge bases, the processing enhancements, the memory caches . . . none was impossibly difficult in isolation, but taking them as a group was like trying to herd a group of drunken pirates.

During commando training, he'd mostly kept them turned off. But in rigger training, his teachers insisted that he practice using the implants. His trainers seemed puzzled by his difficulties; but Legroeder felt as if his head had become a cage full of wild animals, and his confusion and frustration were overlaid with fear that the augments were gaining the upper hand.

Palagren and Cantha led him to a sim-room filled with rigger-stations that looked like giant clamshells propped open at a forty-five degree angle. Legroeder climbed into the opening of one and lay back on the soft body of the clam—a neural hydrocushion. The clamshell snicked closed, leaving him surrounded by darkness and silence, except for a reassuring whisper of circulating air. He tried to relax, alone with his thoughts . . . and his implants. A minute later, the com and the net came alive. Cantha was at the control center on the outside. Though not a rigger himself, Cantha was an expert in rigger theory, having done advanced research at the Narseil Rigging Institute. He would be overseeing much of the training.

"Are you ready?"

"As ready as I'll ever be." A moment later, Legroeder's head filled with voices: library inputs, head-up data displays, com status reports on everything from the rigger-net interface to his own kidneys. He tried to corral the voices into the background, but the only thing that seemed to work was to turn them down to near inaudibility; and that left him with an annoying and useless low-level buzz. In the end, he simply tried to ignore the voices, droning in the background.

First Cantha let him fly alone, to regain the feel of being in a net and to acclimate himself to the Narseil equipment. Though he wouldn't have mistaken the sim for the real Flux, the net responded well as he "flew" virtual currents of wind and sea. After a while, Palagren joined him, and then another rigger, named Voco. For the rest of that day, they flew programmed sim voyages, polishing their skills together along both familiar and unfamiliar star-routes.

The next day was more of the same.

Legroeder struggled with the difficulty of rigging with

aliens in an alien environment, and of adjusting his flying
style to theirs. The Narseil were restless riggers—using a
lot of sea imagery, but also changing images frequently in
an effort to gain new leverages or insights. When Legroeder
invoked his implants for assistance, he found himself
quickly overwhelmed by inputs. It didn't take long before
he had the whole crew struggling to maintain control of
their virtual ship. He was thankful that these were only sims;
the Narseil probably thought he was a hopeless incompetent.

"You must *control* your augments—be their master,"
Cantha urged. "You are their master. You are like the con-
ductor of one of your human symphony orchestras, and you
must think like one." Legroeder felt more like a musician
trying to produce a concert on a synthmixer, but unable to
control anything except the master volume while a gaggle
of musical voices rippled through his skull.

The breakthrough came on day three of his training. The
night before, he'd tossed and turned in his sleep, dreaming
of struggling with the strings of a dancing marionette, and
thrashing helplessly in a tangle of threads. He'd woken up
trying to remember what had followed that dream; it was
something important. Were the dreams part of his training?
They certainly felt similar. The first sim of the day gave
him a tangle of maneuvers to perform, with full input from
his internal nav-libraries. The streams of data nearly overwhelmed him. But he was determined to overcome it.

He was flying down a cataract—a simulation of a region
of the Flux known as the Hurricane Flume. Palagren and
Voco were at the keel and stern, with Legroeder in the lead
position. He was having trouble keeping the ship centered
in the flow. It was a white-water rapids, fast approaching a
sheer drop into a waterfall. The dashing water tossed the
ship from side to side, threatening to capsize it. Legroeder's
head reeled with data from the nav-library, suggestions from
the augments' tactical advisor, and warnings from Cantha
on the outside. It was too much; he was losing control. If
he didn't shut off the implants, he would crash for sure.

A memory of the dream jumped into his mind: the helpless feeling of swinging in a tangle of marionette strings . . .

As he was about to turn off the augments, the scene around him blinked out and he heard Palagren shout: *We've lost sensory input! We're on internal nav only.*

Legroeder cursed. Cantha had thrown a simulated emergency at them, forcing him to use the implants. He was already failing. *Focus, damn it, focus!*

And then he remembered, like a punch to the stomach, the dream that had followed the marionette dream. All those strings had turned to streams of water, erupting in a complex of geysers that towered into the sky . . .

And the image of Com'peer's lava storm came back to him, and he remembered how he had controlled that image by treating it not as an inner switch, but as a landscape feature of the Flux. He realized now what he needed to do. He *could* master the welter of inputs—not with the built-in controls, maybe, but by changing it all to image and letting his subconscious take charge. Let it *all* be streams of water. He didn't need to conduct an orchestra; he needed to rig through his own mind.

As though in response to his thoughts, the white water image sprang back, and a great gusher of spray went up. For a frozen instant, as the ship dashed through the water, he saw—like a mushroom cloud at the center of his mind— a thundering wave of foam that was not a part of the white water of the Flux at all. It was datastreams from the augments gathered together in a curling wave. He could see, glimmering in its interior, the silver threads of a dozen or more individual inputs. He touched the streams and they bent to his touch. With difficulty at first, then with growing skill, he reshaped them into forms that curved toward him when he wanted them, and out of his way when he didn't.

He felt the ship coming back under his control. He quickly damped out the back-and-forth yawing, and felt the Narseil behind him slipping into a closer coordination. The three riggers and their ship shot down the Hurricane Flume and out, dropped along a dazzling white waterfall, and spun away downstream. Legroeder laughed in triumph and heard

the Narseil hissing their approval, and he knew that he had
finally won the lesson, and it was one he would not soon
forget.

FOR THE next two days, his training accelerated to a blur.
Battle sims were added to the basic rigging practice, and
soon Legroeder was steering the fictitious ship as frantically
as he had once piloted a scout ship out of the mine-strewn
fortress of Outpost DeNoble. It was something he was good
at, and he'd certainly done enough battle flying in captivity,
but now he was being tripped up by something altogether
different.

It was his rigger-mates, the Narseil.

He had always known that the Narseil had some kind of
weird time sense, which was one of the things that made
them exceptional riggers; but he'd never encountered it first-
hand. They called it, in their own translation to human
speech, the *tessa'chron*, or extended time. A form of temporal persistence, it enabled them to see the "present" as a
smear of time fore and aft, ranging from about a second,
under ordinary circumstances, to several seconds under
stress. Battle, even simulated battle, seemed to bring it out
in them. No doubt it was useful to them to have a continuing
momentary glimpse into the future; but for Legroeder it
meant always feeling half a step behind. The implants
helped; they couldn't give him the same time sense, but they
could reinterpret some of the information that the Narseil
were pouring into the net. But that meant adjusting to a
whole new level of implant function.

It was going to take practice. A *lot* of practice.

In the meantime, the rigger crew racked up a score of six
victories to three losses against programmed enemies, all in
encounters in which they were outnumbered and outgunned
by their adversaries. Mission Commander Fre'geel pronounced their progress satisfactory, and decreed additional
exercises.

* * *

"We're ready to go," announced Cantha at breakfast a day later. "We'll be boarding this evening, and departing during the night."

The announcement stunned Legroeder.

"Is this a problem? Don't you feel ready?"

"Well—not to invade a stronghold, no." Legroeder suddenly felt a desire for a few more days of commando training. He suddenly felt hazy on the actual strategic plans. He suddenly wanted to go lie down in a meadow.

The Narseil chuckled, an almost musical sound. In the days they had spent together, Cantha seemed to have developed a pretty good understanding of Legroeder's feelings. "None of us feels quite ready, either. Don't worry, we'll keep training on the ship. But you know—beyond a certain point, our strategy is going to have to unfold on the fly. If things go according to plan, you and I won't have to fight; we'll just follow the marines in."

"Yeah, well, that's a nice thought—"

"And between your knowledge of the raiders, and our own skills, I'm hopeful of acquiring some good intelligence and transmitting it out before we're discovered and destroyed." Cantha's tall, amphibious eyes seemed to glimmer with an almost human humor.

"Very funny. Could you please refrain from using the word *destroyed* when you talk about our chances?"

"If you insist," said Cantha. "Look, this is our last day here. What would you say to breaking training and having some of our excellent—" he struggled for the correct word "—the closest thing to it, I guess, would be your beer. Do you like beer?"

"I like beer."

"Then let's celebrate, my friend."

IT TURNED out that all the Narseil involved in the mission were celebrating that day. It also turned out that the average Narseil had a much higher tolerance for alcohol than Legroeder did. He was fairly woozy after just half a glass of what was definitely a fermented beverage, but seemed to him a cross between coconut milk and something called beermalt that was popular in rigger dives. Not only did it carry a kick; the Narseil served it in liter-sized flagons.

Legroeder began nursing his drink, watching the celebration from the sideline. He still wondered what made these Narseil tick, but he had grudgingly come to enjoy the conviviality of their company. Cantha turned out to be something of a singer, and while the singing sounded to Legroeder like the moaning of a walrus, it was well appreciated by the other Narseil. Legroeder sipped his drink and chatted with Korken, the young Narseil who'd been friendly with him on the trip here, who wasn't coming along on the mission but wished he were; and with Com'peer the surgeon, who wasn't coming along, either, and didn't appear the least bit sorry.

After the celebration had gone on for a while, Fre'geel called for silence. A Three Rings priest stood up and spoke for a few minutes in a kind of singsong that might have been a prayer, or poetry, or both; and then Com'peer rose with a Bible in her hand and offered a prayer in Legroeder's tongue. It sounded vaguely familiar to Legroeder, though he had trouble placing it. A psalm, perhaps?

> . . . When I consider your heavens,
> the labor of your hands,
> the celestial bodies you have created,
> who are these beings that you are mindful of them,
> mortals that you care for them?

The other Narseil listened in respectful silence as Com'peer read several other psalms, then concluded with a benediction. Legroeder found himself unexpectedly moved by the offering. A moment later, Fre'geel returned and delivered an address that sounded more like a eulogy than a pep talk—except that he then broke into what could only be called a song and dance, jittering across the front of the room, waving a wand that was apparently some sort of data storage device, but looked to Legroeder like a wooden cane.

Cantha, noting Legroeder's amusement, came over and confided that when Narseil departed on a difficult mission, especially one with a high degree of risk, they liked to send themselves off with a rousing good time—to taste, if briefly, the good times that they might not live to see if things went against them. Legroeder nodded. "Not so different from us," he said.

At the end, all the Narseil sang an anthem together, swaying to and fro as though their arms were linked (they weren't), their neck-sails flopping from side to side in perfect rhythm. Legroeder tipped his glass to finish his beverage, and realized that he was drunk. As the Narseil anthem came to an end, he sighed deeply, thinking that maybe it was time he offered a bit of human something to this gathering of lunatic aliens. He stood, clearing his throat self-consciously—then raised his empty glass and cried, "Hip, hip—hooray!" and when all eyes turned toward him in curiosity, he yelled it again. "HIP, HIP—HOORAY! Say it with me! Shout it!"

The Narseil stirred in uncertainty, but Cantha and one or two others joined him . . . and then more, until the whole roomful of Narseil was thunderously shouting, *"HIP, HIP—HOORAY! HIP, HIP—HOORAY!"*—cheering the celebration to its conclusion.

Legroeder returned to his quarters to rest for a few hours before boarding the ship. Lying on his mattress on the floor, he stared at the ceiling and tried not to be sick. He thought of what the Narseil had turned him into, and realized that he really did not want to go on this mission at all; and then he remembered Harriet and her grandson, and Maris, and why he had to for himself—and he closed his eyes mournfully and let all of his thoughts drain out of his mind. Eventually he drifted off to a sleep that was neither long enough nor restful.

AS THEY gathered to board the ship, Legroeder stood off to one side of the crowd. His head hurt, and he didn't want to talk to anyone.

◻ *Your condition can be self-correcting.* ◻

Legroeder blinked and looked around, just to be sure the voice had come from within. It was one of the implants.

(All right, I give. How do I correct it?)

The answer appeared silently, and he realized that he could use the same technique he had applied to the control of the implants themselves. He closed his eyes and focused inward, and cast a golden cloud around himself, which slowly penetrated him with its ghostly glow. After a moment, he let it evaporate. When he opened his eyes, the headache was gone.

(I'll be damned,) he said to the voice.

He turned and saw Com'peer watching him. "What?" Legroeder asked.

"You're learning, aren't you—and you will continue to learn," said the surgeon. "Rigger Legroeder, you will be a formidable member of this crew. And I believe you will find your implants useful for more things than you can imagine."

"Well, they worked pretty well on my hangover," Legroeder conceded.

Com'peer rested a long-fingered hand on his shoulder. "May God go with you, Legroeder. And who knows? Maybe even your desire for a safe return will come true." She laughed, a sound like a saw cutting wood. "I look forward to hearing your report."

"Too bad you're not coming," Legroeder said. "You could remake everyone on the ship."

"I almost wish I could. I almost really do," Com'peer said, none too convincingly. "But my orders keep me here."

The boarding began then, and Legroeder got in line.

THE SHIP'S NAME was *H'zzarrelik*, which roughly translated meant "Javelin." But Legroeder found himself referring to it mentally in the Narseil tongue; it seemed more appropriate somehow. She looked like a luxury liner, at least on the outside—long, silver, and sleek as a shark. Her departure was silent and unheralded, marked by little more than a vibration in the deck in the middle of the night. The celebration was a fading memory now, and the official mode of operation was stealth and efficiency, even in departing from Narseil Naval Command.

Legroeder's cabin was, to his surprise, more pleasantly appointed than the one he'd had at the naval base. The ship looked like a passenger liner on the inside, too. His cabin had smoothly curved walls, like those back at the base, in a cool off-white, with charcoal-gray trim. It was fitted with a respectable bunk and a small bath alcove. He wondered what class he was traveling in—business class, maybe?—not perfect luxury, but far better than steerage.

Soon enough, he grew weary of being alone with his thoughts, and went out for a walk around the ship. Everything seemed to convey the illusion of this being an innocent passenger vessel. But surely it was not so innocent, if one probed beneath the surface. It wasn't long before he encountered Cantha in the corridor. "Are you unable to sleep?" asked the Narseil.

"Who can sleep, when we're just getting underway?"

"I think there are many of us who feel that way," said Cantha. "That's why I'm up. I'm not on duty right now, either."

"How about showing me around, then?"

"Happily. What would you like to see first? Shall I show you where the weapons are hidden?"

"Well—"

"We're not as harmless as we look, you know," Cantha said, blinking his elongated Narseil eyes. "Come on. You might as well see where everything is."

They were near the midships exercise room and pool, so Cantha took him there first. It was an impressive facility, and already in use by several of the crew. Cantha took him past the pool to the equipment lockers. He released a catch and the backs of the lockers opened to reveal numerous rows of small arms. "Enough for half the crew right here. If you count up all the different storage locations, we have several weapons for everyone on board, including you."

"So this isn't the only stash?" Legroeder briefly examined one of the Narseil neutrasers. A week ago, he would not have known which end to hold. Now it felt almost comfortable in his hand.

"Hardly. I'll show you the other stores as we come to them." Cantha closed up the lockers and led him back out past the pool. "Oh—by the way, there are antipersonnel weapons sealed into the bottom of the pool. They're remotely controlled, so if you get involved in a fight in this area, beware."

"Terrific. I'll remember that the next time I go for a late night swim."

Cantha peered at him, as though trying to decide how to interpret the remark. "A sense of humor is a good thing to have," he said finally.

Legroeder followed Cantha out of the room and up the corridor toward the bow of the ship. Three more times, Cantha pointed out locations of concealed antipersonnel weapons. The Narseil *really* did not want the pirates taking control of this ship. They stopped just aft of the bridge, at the access portal to a large, round compartment. "Flux reactor?" Legroeder asked in surprise. "This close to the bridge?"

"Standard on our ships," Cantha said. "This is also where the external armaments are concealed."

Legroeder peered around, but saw nothing remotely resembling weapons. "Where? Inside the power room?"

"Almost. You won't find them without tearing the ship apart. They're embedded in the walls, inside the shielding."

"That's handy. How do you load them?"

"They were loaded when the ship was built. Reloading could be a problem, though." Cantha gave a whistling chuckle. "No, if they're used at all, it's one shot per tube." The Narseil raised a hand and traced the slight cylindrical bulge of ventilation ducts near the ceiling. "Those go radially out toward the skin of the ship. They really are ventilation ducts. But they have special linings, waveguides, and shunts. If we need to fire torpedoes, that's where they go out, through concealed openings in the hull. And the internal power couplings"—he pointed to smaller bulges—"carry high capacity op-fiber barrels, for the beam weapons."

Legroeder frowned, following it with his eye. All very clever, he thought. But would it work? It wasn't as if they'd be able to keep this stuff hidden from the pirates for long. "Interesting," he said finally. "But Cantha—isn't this over-kill, for a stealth mission? I mean—maybe we can blow a pirate ship out of the sky with all of this, but that's not what we want to do, is it?"

"Indeed not," said Cantha. "If all goes well, most of this weaponry will never be used. We hope that stealth will be our greatest weapon. But pretending to be vulnerable carries obvious risks. Hence our preparations for defeating the enemy right here on our own decks, if necessary."

"But what about these supposed contacts in the raider underground? What if they meet us, looking for a parlay?"

Cantha looked uncomfortable. "We were hoping for a confirmation message from the underground, some indication that a nonhostile contact could be made. Unfortunately, it never came. Therefore we must assume—" Cantha spread his hands wide, in the Narseil equivalent of a shrug.

"In other words, we really don't know *what* the hell we're doing."

"That is an exaggeration," Cantha said.

Legroeder grunted. "So, look—have you got anything to show me that *isn't* a hidden weapon?"

"Indeed, I—" Cantha paused and raised a finger. "Listen."

An instant later there came a call on the intercom: *"Rigger Legroeder, please make your presence felt on the bridge."*

Cantha seemed to straighten a little. "Yes, indeed. I will show you the way to the bridge. If I am not mistaken, they are planning to put you in the net before much longer."

"That's more like it."

* * *

THE NARSEIL bridge was large, with rigger-stations in a row, and nearby, a post for the captain, who apparently always stood while on duty. Captain Ho'Sung, the ship's master, was present along with Fre'geel, the mission commander. Ho'Sung's job was the safety of the ship and crew; Fre'geel's was the success of the mission. How the two commanders reconciled their responsibilities and authority was a mystery to Legroeder, but it didn't seem to trouble the Narseil.

The captain nodded a greeting. "Welcome."

Legroeder acknowledged and looked around eagerly. A glance at the viewscreens told him that the ship was still in normal-space, probably still navigating out of the region of the Narseil naval base. The stars were visible in a thin, wide band that stretched across the front of the bridge. The view of the stars was moving in a slow, continual scan up and down. For the Narseil, with their tessa'chron view, it no doubt worked just fine. It gave Legroeder a headache.

"Rigger Legroeder," said Ho'Sung, "We will be entering the Flux shortly. I thought you might like to observe."

Legroeder felt a twinge of excitement in his fingertips. He had not been in a real net in the real Flux since his escape from the pirates, which seemed a very long time ago. "Where would you like me to stand?"

Ho'Sung made a burring sound. "Stand, indeed? I would like you in rigger-station number four, over there." He gestured with both hands, the sleeves of his robe billowing like a priest's.

Legroeder felt an involuntary smile spread across his face. He hurried to climb into the clamshell rigger-station. He sank back, watched the shell close over him, and sighed with pleasure as his senses flowed out into the living matrix of the net.

THE NARSEIL riggers greeted him with quiet salutations. *Welcome,* said Palagren. *First time lucky, we always say. You may take the top position.*

Legroeder moved into the spot at the top center of the net, where he felt like a rifleman atop an ancient horse-drawn stagecoach, in classic holos. After he'd settled in a bit, that image gave way to a feeling of being top lookout in the bubble of a fishing sub, as the three Narseil riggers crafted a starting image for the voyage: a misty, copper-green sea beneath them, with long, smooth waves rolling in toward their bow. The rigger-crew was preparing to dive.

Will you let me stay in my bubble here for a while, or am I expected to sprout gills to keep up with you fish people? Legroeder felt better than he had in a long time. The net was a powerful euphoric drug.

For our poor, nonaquatic human friend? Palagren answered. *Of course we will allow you your hull filled with air. Perhaps we can even tow it on our backs. Are you ready, crew?*

Voco at the stern and Ker'sell on the keel echoed their assent. The captain, his voice whispering from the outside com, said, *Riggers, you may take to the Flux.*

The Narseil riggers responded with a hiss of approval. An emerald light welled up from the sea below. Legroeder felt a familiar rush of adrenaline, and a less familiar tingling from his implants, as the three Narseil took the ship down. The watery mists of the Flux closed over their heads, and Legroeder put out his hands, sighing with pleasure at the movement of the current through his fingers.

The sea and the mist were at once real and imagined; everything around him was a blend of mind and reality—his imagination, and the Narseil's imagination, and the actual multidimensional energy-flows that would carry them across the light-years. He knew that the images would change many times in the coming days, as they passed out of the realm of the Narseil and the Centrist Worlds, and made their way toward the no man's land of Golen Space. He knew that his skills would be tested, and his courage, and that of the Narseil, as well.

But for now, Legroeder was content simply to be sailing on the streams of space, even if they were making their way toward danger, even if they were heading back toward the seas of mist where none but pirates ruled.

PART TWO

*In what ethereal dances
By what eternal streams ...*
—Edgar Allan Poe

Like glimpses of forgotten dreams.
—Alfred, Lord Tennyson

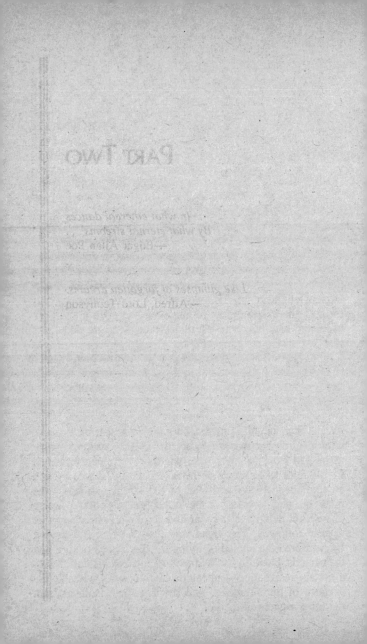

Prologue

PIRATE PATROL: FREEM'N DEUTSCH

RIGGERS, TAKE her down.

The voice of the raider captain crackled through the net with cold authority. The lead rigger obeyed with a tilt of his head and a flash of input from Augment Foxtrot. The acknowledgment of his two flank riggers came silently through the net, augment to augment, and with a swift coordinated kick they sent the raider ship *Flechette* down into the Flux like a spinning bullet.

The start of the patrol began as it always did—with a sideways dance through the maze of Flux currents that isolated raider Outpost Ivan from those who might come spying.

Lead rigger Freem'n Deutsch had been on more pirate patrols than he could count, but still he began each patrol with an almost inexpressible dread. He felt it as keenly now as he had from the very first, when he had been forced to fly missions as a captive of the raider colony. It was a dread compounded of rage and fear, of a desire not to attack the innocent, and—perhaps if he looked deeply enough—also of a secret delight in the fear and smoke and mayhem that usually followed. The dread was always there. But having been offered the choice of flying for the pirates or dying at their hands, Deutsch had learned to approach his duties with a certain resignation—managing his emotions with the assistance of the augments, and keeping them isolated from the other riggers in the net.

It would all change, once they were genuinely on the prowl. But for now, there was only the dread, like a weight in his belly—and the discipline to keep it concealed.

Though far from the largest or most powerful raider in the fleet, *Flechette* was a formidable threat to any ship. She bristled with flux torpedoes, beam weapons, and flux-distortion antennas to deceive and confuse any enemy. She carried a boarding party of twenty-four pirate commandos, of varying degrees of biohumanity. Her captain, Te'Gunderlach, was himself more cyborg than human, and was known for never retreating once a battle was joined—a trait that made him a fearsome warrior. Deutsch sometimes imagined that it might also make for a disastrous failure if one day *Flechette* met her match.

Today Deutsch flew with, if anything, a greater-than-usual sense of unease. A premonition? He couldn't say. He'd felt a premonition of trouble on the day, nine years ago, when his Elacian freighter was attacked by pirates—and by the end of that day, his life had changed forever. But he'd also felt his share of premonitions that had come to nothing.

Lead rigger, we seem to be going a little fast here. Is there anything I should know before we hit the chute?

Deutsch brought himself back to the present, carefully concealing his surprise at the speed with which the ship was moving toward the exit point, where they would leave the clouds that kept the fortress concealed in the Flux. He sent a signal to the other riggers to reduce speed, then answered the captain with a breezy, *No difficulty, sir. We are simply eager for the hunt.*

Very well, said Te'Gunderlach. *That is good. I feel that this will be a fruitful voyage.*

Indeed, replied Deutsch.

Take us away, then.

Aye, sir.

The ship roared left, then right, and leaped into the chute. It was like the first big hill of a v'rticoaster—screaming, hurtling down a streamer of energy that crackled as they dived—and finally, with a great gout of fire, spat them out into the freedom of the open Flux.

THE EARLY part of *Flechette*'s voyage was routine, a passage through a little-traveled no man's land where the currents tended to be weak and unpredictable. It was a challenging enough region to rig through in its own right, requiring a thorough knowledge of the terrain; but the main reason few outsiders came this way was that these currents didn't really go anywhere, in terms of normal-space destinations. That, of course, was what made it a perfect place for hiding a pirates' fortress. Few would come looking, and if anyone did, the chances were excellent that they would lose their way. Golen Space in general was a risky place for the unwary rigger; this particular pocket of Golen Space was avoided even by raiders from other outposts.

Rigger Deutsch led his crew through an atmosphere of oddly swirled clouds, seemingly frozen against the sky. The clouds appeared unmoving; and yet within their coiled vortices were narrow ribbons of movement, and it was along those ribbons that *Flechette*'s riggers threaded their way. Gradually, the clouds thickened and became more solidly sculpted, and the strength and visibility of the currents picked up. They were beginning to move out of the no man's land of secret places, toward regions where starship traffic might be found.

Deutsch was not privy to the exact nature of their mission; the captain was as tight-lipped as ever. But rumors had been whispered that their orders were somehow different this time, that they were going after an unusual prey . . . that they were searching for a *particular* prey, and they might allow others to pass unimpeded. If so, this was a significant change from the norm. On the other hand, it was possible that the rumor was nothing but wind and vapor.

They would just have to wait and see what the captain revealed, at the moment of contact.

* * *

DROOM. DROOM.

The low rumble quivered through the net, and fire began to flicker around the edges of Deutsch's vision.

The morale programs.

Deutsch hated them, but there was no escape, for him or anyone else. He could resist their effects for a time; but in the end, they were a foolproof system. They were channeled through both the augments and the net itself, and if the augments found insufficient effect, the morale input was increased automatically. As program images emerged in the net, they came to seem a part of the natural landscape, part of the larger vision, and the riggers formed and shaped them as they banked through the energy streams of the Flux.

Fire. Flames coloring the energy streams.

Droom. Droom.

They were the flames of the hunter on the prowl, the flames of the corsair. Soon the flames would spread, and would reach out into the nets of other ships; they would strike fear into the heart of the prey. Already, Deutsch could feel his own adrenaline starting to pump. There was no ignoring the beat; it was like a military march, an orchestration driving the blood lust of a hunt. It was primal and inescapable, tapping somewhere into the reptilian brain. After the first few minutes, Deutsch and his fellow riggers no longer wanted to stave it off. Resistance, revulsion, and fear gave way to inexorable desire.

The flames would soon lick higher still. Higher, and fiercer, and hotter. But not yet. Not until *Flechette* had found her prey. Then and only then would they burn their true burn.

Chapter 14
PIRATE SEARCH

DID YOU hear something back there? Legroeder glanced behind them through the eerie undersea passage. They had been gliding through an endless, watery corridor, irregular and enigmatic, like an abandoned structure from some lost civilization.

Voco, the phlegmatic stern-rigger, answered, *Just an echo. Always echoes in places like this.*

Oh, said Legroeder, straining to peer back through the mists.

If the Narseil mission plan still made him uneasy, their riggers had nonetheless impressed him with their prowess in the Flux. They seemed to have an uncannily clear sense of where they were going, so clear that it left Legroeder a little breathless. They were prowling like rangers on a patrol through a wilderness. They seemed to notice signs in the Flux that Legroeder could not begin to fathom, subtle changes in current patterns that his implants translated for him as "smell" and "feel," but only after the Narseil had pointed them out.

Lacking any specific knowledge of where to look for pirate ships, they were trying to find their quarry by acting like prey. The plan was to shadow the shipping lanes that grazed the boundaries of Golen Space, lanes where the risk of pirate attack had lately been on the increase. It was a region where few ships would ever have ventured, were it not for an accident of astrography that put Golen Space squarely between two long arms of more civilized and heavily traveled space. Shippers journeying between the two arms faced a choice of a dangerous passage skirting Golen Space, or a much longer way around, as the Flux currents went. Many, indeed, took the long way. But there were always shippers—and passengers—who deemed the risks worth taking, in exchange for shorter travel times. Some even went *through* Golen Space for the fastest trips; but the majority chose pathways just outside the boundaries, which offered at least the illusion of greater safety, combined with speed. It was in such a passage that *Ciudad de los Angeles* had been attacked.

H'zzarrelik, however, was well to the galactic south of where that attack had occurred. The Narseil hoped to attract the attention of a different band of pirates, by seeming to have lost their way along the edge of Golen Space. They had, for a time, kept *H'zzarrelik* on a flight path such as an ordinary liner might have taken; but a few days ago, seven days into the journey, they had slipped off into the borderland, where ships losing their way might blunder. And where, presumably, raiders might lurk. They hardly needed to pretend. One mistaken twist in a current could easily send them off course. It had taken no great effort for Legroeder to imagine them actually lost.

A couple of days after their passage into the edge of Golen Space, they had entered a region that seemed particularly murky and mysterious. The undersea imagery was a natural, almost inevitable, choice. The submarine image had given way to a sleek forcefield that flowed back from the lead rigger, and up and over Legroeder's head, so that he could sit in a cross-legged yoga pose, facing the oncoming stream. It was purely an illusion—his real body was reclining, motionless, in the clamshell rigger-station—but it felt as real as flesh to him. His main job, just now, was to be alert for features that the Narseil, with their alien perceptions, might miss.

They continued gliding through the olive-oil-green seafloor structure, the ship stretched out behind them in a sinuous ribbon of silver. It seemed to Legroeder that the foreboding eeriness emanated not just from the surroundings, but also from Ker'sell, in the keel station. Ker'sell was the one Narseil rigger who seemed suspicious of Legroeder, and seemed drawn in general to darkly moody images—a trait with which Legroeder, ironically, could empathize. Legroeder couldn't do anything about Ker'sell's moods, so he concentrated on smoothing out their movement as they glided down channels and corridors and tunnels, like ghostly miners pursuing memories in a flooded coal mine, or archaeologists pursuing the past.

Twice now he'd thought he had heard sounds in the passageway, sounds not from their own ship. In all likelihood the Narseil's explanation was correct: he was probably hearing disturbances of their own passage, altered and reflected as echoes in the net. Still, he felt a nagging unease, wondering if something might be out there, shadowing them. If so, it was concealing itself well.

H'zzarrelik slowed and, rocking slightly, slipped around a corner in the tunnel. Another drop lay ahead; the tunnel had been descending in a long series of steps, each drop affording only limited visibility ahead. *Do we have any idea where this will end?* Legroeder asked.

Not really, said Palagren, his head turning from side to side as he scanned the edges of the tunnel. *I've never been able to hold such a structured image so long before. I'd guess that the hard-edged form will end of its own accord before much longer. It must be associated with a dense nebula or some such thing.*

The ship slipped downward over a sharper step, then another. *Pinga-ping.* There was another faint sound—like a distant, clanging buoy. The current seemed to be speeding up. Legroeder felt a sudden chill of fear, as he imagined a submarine shadowing them through this labyrinth, torpedoes ready to fire.

Don't let your imagination run away with you, he cautioned himself. Still . . . *Was that our own echo I just heard?*

Voco answered from the stern, *I heard it, too. I think it was our own, yes.*

And I think, said Palagren, *that I see the end of this tunnel.*

Legroeder peered ahead, past the Narseil, where he glimpsed a shifting of light. Yes, now he could see the labyrinth opening. *What's that up ahead?* he murmured. Before anyone could answer, the ship picked up speed and shot out of the tunnel like a bird out of a chute.

The undersea image evaporated, and the ship sprouted long, slender wings as it flew into a cloud-filled sky. Legroeder could feel the craftsmanship of Palagren and the others at work on the image, but really they were just refining what was here: a skyscape of great, sculpted clouds, and currents slipping among them like dancing breezes. The clouds looked like top-heavy savanna trees leaning with the wind; sunlight glowed on their tops, and great caverns of open air yawned in their shadows, where complex and convoluted Flux currents wound among the cloud bases.

While the Narseil riggers conferred on a direction, Legroeder stretched his arms out in the net and felt the wind whisper through his fingers. He rocked the wings a bit. Off to the left, and a little behind, he glimpsed a flicker of lightning among the clouds.

What is it, Legroeder? Anything wrong? asked Palagren.

I guess not—just a flash of something back there. Just some weather, probably.

The other riggers seemed puzzled.

Didn't you see it?

No, I didn't— began Palagren, but was interrupted by a distant rumble of thunder. The sound seemed to echo among the clouds for a few moments, then faded away.

You may be right about the weather, Voco said from the stern. *I see a thunderhead moving off to the port side. We'd better keep a watch on it.*

Palagren began a wide turn away from it. *Wait,* Legroeder said. *Do you mind if I do this for a moment?* he asked, nudging them back toward the left.

I sense a difficult passage in that direction, Palagren said cautiously.

I just want to check something, Legroeder said, banking the ship a little more sharply. He thought he saw something dark among the shadows under the clouds; something darker than the shadows . . . *I'm not sure . . . hold on a sec' . . .*

What is it?

Legroeder thought he heard a faint booming sound. Maybe it was just a reverberation of thunder, but he felt a little shiver of apprehension; he wasn't sure why. But the view had changed now and he saw nothing. Shrugging, he returned the ship to the right bank that Palagren had initiated, and gave control back to the Narseil.

He remained unsatisfied, though. Closing his eyes, he searched back in his memory, analyzing the sound and feel of the thunder. His stirring of apprehension turned into genuine fear as some connection clicked into place, some pattern in the sound. Opening his eyes, he said softly, *Don't be alarmed, but we need to change the image and see if we can get a clearer view under those clouds.* He hesitated. *Palagren, I think you should inform the captain and the commander.*

The ship became rounded, a domed flying saucer, with all-around visibility. The clouds began to change in color and density as they shifted the image through different combinations of filters. *Inform them of what?* Palagren asked.

To ready their defenses.

He felt Palagren's surprise, then heard the soft mutter of the Narseil passing his words on to Ho'Sung and Fre'geel. And the captain's voice: *What exactly have you seen, riggers?*

Legroeder answered, *Nothing I can explain easily. But it's the lightning and thunder. Somehow I have a sense—*

Before he could finish, there was another flash, like heat lightning in the clouds ahead of them. As he listened to the rumble of thunder, he felt that there was something not quite natural in the sound. He felt the recognition as a tightness in his chest. To the left and astern, he saw a fleck of darkness moving against the underside of a cloud. His stomach dropped. *Mother of stars . . .*

Legroeder, Palagren said, *what are you sensing? It does not seem—*

Legroeder interrupted. *It's behind us, port side and thirty degrees above! Prepare for attack. This is it!*

He felt Palagren's puzzlement as he sent the message on to the captain. The Narseil didn't feel his certainty; but then, they had never rigged with pirates. *Expect a lot of light, and a lot of—*

I hear it. Coming now—! Palagren called.

A second later: ***B-D-DOOM-M-M! B-D-DOOM-M-M!***

The sound crashed through the net with a dissonant rumble, as if reverberating from all directions at once, a hundred echoes arriving out of synch with each other. The Narseil riggers looked jarred and confused—too many inputs funneling through the tessa'chron. Legroeder called, *This is the beginning of an attack! Don't let it shake you!*

Palagren, recovering, called back, *I'm all right. Captain, we are under attack!*

Audio attack only, so far, Legroeder added. *No sign of weapons fire yet.*

Very well, came Ho'Sung's voice. *Let's act like victims, until we determine their intentions.* His voice became more distant, probably directed elsewhere on the bridge. *Let's have that hail ready.*

Act confused but don't *be* confused, Legroeder thought.

B-D-DOOM-M-M! B-D-DOOM-M-M! B-D-DOOM-M-M-M!

The reverberations shook the net, making it harder to steer a level course. They were hitting turbulence, as waves of sound crashed over them like a pounding surf. The fleck of darkness that Legroeder had spotted was gone. It was impossible now to localize the direction of the sounds.

The pattern was familiar enough to Legroeder—did all raider bands use similar tactics?—but it also felt different enough to reassure him that his pirate ship was from an outpost other than DeNoble. It was not his former captors.

The captain's voice rang through the net: *All weapons*

and stations are on full alert. Is the attacking vessel in sight?

Palagren answered, *Not yet. Legroeder—do you see it?*

Negative. He'd lost it in the clouds. The pirates could make their approach from any of a dozen directions. The terrain of the Flux was so convoluted here, the number of places to lurk almost limitless.

Sending our hail now, Ho'Sung said.

A moment later, a recorded voice echoed into the Flux. *THIS IS NARSEIL STARLINER H'ZZARRELIK. PLEASE IDENTIFY YOURSELVES. REPEAT, PLEASE IDENTIFY YOURSELVES.* The message repeated, in five different languages.

Legroeder waited, holding his breath.

B-D-DOOM-M-M! B-D-DOOM-M-M!

The sounds were growing louder and more frightening. Legroeder shut his eyes, trying to suppress the memories of countless raids that were welling up in his mind. He felt himself begin to shake. He thought of all those weapons hidden within *H'zzarrelik*'s structure and imagined them coming to life. He thought of the weapons carried by the pirate ship, and began to shake harder. He had never gotten used to combat, and his stomach was knotted. (Calm . . . calm. . . .) he whispered to himself.

◻ *Use an image to quiet yourself,* ◻ one of the implants suggested, vibrating to life. It offered an image of waves lapping on a shore.

He seized on it gratefully; even as more thunder shook the net, he felt his trembling abate slightly. He scanned the shifting mists of cloud. *There it is!* he shouted, spotting a flicker of light ahead of them and off to the left.

Moving this way, said Palagren.

The object turned toward them with a flare, and accelerated toward the Narseil ship with remarkable speed—either riding a powerful sideways draft of turbulence, or using internal fusors to drive it across the streams of the Flux. As it flew toward them, a great curtain of red fire lit up the clouds behind it. The fire grew into an enormous canopy of

flame spreading outward and forward like great outstretched
wings. In the space of half a minute, it curled around
H'zzarrelik as though to engulf them. It seemed to shout a
warning: *Fire . . . death . . . destruction . . .*

Steady, Legroeder murmured. *It's just an effect. Slow and
steady as we wait.* His heart was pounding, and he had to
remind himself that the effects were not nearly as powerful
as they seemed. Their greatest power was to frighten.

The thunder was now an incessant din . . . *DOOM-M-M . . .
DOOM-M-M!* . . . making it hard to think or communicate.
The Narseil crew and Legroeder kept *H'zzarrelik* on a
steady course, turning neither to flee nor to attack. Steady,
steady, like an unarmed ship . . .

With a blast of static, the net suddenly came alive with
a yammering of voices, crying in a cacophony: *SURREN-
DER! SURRENDER! THERE IS NO ESCAPE! THERE
IS ONLY DOOM-M-M . . . DOOM-M-M . . . DOOM-M-M!*
From the clouds there came an enormous, rumbling thunder
like the sound of a tornado passing; and the nose of the
oncoming ship spat half a dozen bursts of neutraser fire,
which lit up the clouds on all sides of *H'zzarrelik* with dazzling green light.

Multiple thunderclaps followed each of the firebursts. The
net of the Narseil ship shook and sizzled with energy. Legroeder gritted his teeth. If one of those bursts had truly
connected with *H'zzarrelik*, they might all be gone now in
a blaze of energy. But the pirates didn't come out to destroy;
they were here to capture, to pillage.

Legroeder, what's your assessment? Ho'Sung asked quietly through the net.

Legroeder drew a harsh breath. *Captain, I don't think
they're out here to* talk. *They're trying to frighten us into
submission. This is a standard attack pattern.* And damned
effective, even against those who knew the strategy for what
it was.

You don't believe this is a pretense? Ho'Sung asked.

Hell no, I—

Protect yourselves! cried Palagren.

Their words were cut off by the flare and crackle of a fresh neutraser burst, directly in front of *H'zzarrelik*'s bow. Fire blazed through the net. Legroeder cried out in pain. It felt as if they had passed through a wall of fire. The Narseil net was sputtering and crackling with energy. It took several seconds for the energy to dissipate, leaving the net tight and sluggish. That was more than a warning shot; it was intended to disable.

The pirate ship was coming into full view now. It was a menacing-looking frigate—not the largest Legroeder had ever seen, but powerful enough to challenge even a naval cruiser. Ripples of fire danced through her net, outlining the ship, and flashing at node points that probably represented the positions of her riggers. Legroeder imagined the crew of *H'zzarrelik* targeting those rigger-stations with their concealed weapons, and for an instant, he felt a pang. Those riggers who were attacking him—how many of them were captives as he had been? He drew a sharp breath and forced the thought away.

A powerful drum beat was growing in the Flux now, booming through the net like the rumble of kettle drums. Then a braying voice:

HEAVE TO! HEAVE TO OR BE DESTROYED! NO DELAY! THERE WILL BE NO SECOND WARNING!

To punctuate the words, two more bursts of neutraser fire flared off the bow of the Narseil ship.

Ho'Sung's voice reverberated in reply: *THIS IS THE NARSEIL H'ZZARRELIK. WE ARE SETTING OUR STABILIZERS AND PULLING IN OUR NET! WE REQUEST A PARLAY. REPEAT, WE REQUEST A PARLAY.* Then he ordered in a more muted voice, *Riggers, shut down and withdraw!*

The net rocked with laughter, broadcast from the other ship. The three Narseil and Legroeder pulled the net close around the ship, set the autostabilizers, and withdrew. The last words Legroeder heard in the net were: *THIS IS FLECHETTE. STAND BY FOR BOARDING . . .*

* * *

Legroeder emerged from his clamshell to a scene of deadly calm on the bridge of the Narseil ship. The captain and commander were each at com posts, murmuring instructions. The weapons control panels were alight. The Narseil weapons crew, led by Agamem, were stone faced, motionless, awaiting orders.

Ho'Sung conferred in a low, hissing voice with mission commander Fre'geel, then turned back. His manner was intense, but he seemed very calm. "Riggers, stand by to return to your stations on my order!" He spoke into the ship-to-ship com. "*Flechette*, our net is down. We have unarmed civilians aboard—"

One, anyway, Legroeder thought.

"—please do not shoot again! What are your orders?"

The answer was a staticky shout: *YOU WILL OPEN YOURSELVES TO BOARDING, OR WE WILL BLOW YOU OUT OF THE FLUX!*

Ho'Sung stood silent for a moment, then looked at Legroeder. "You're the expert in human behavior. They're not responding to the prearranged signal. Do you see any reason not to regard this as a hostile contact?"

Legroeder shook his head, swallowing. "I think we have a fight on our hands."

Ho'Sung gestured a go-ahead to Fre'geel.

There was no further communication from the pirate ship, now framed in the long, narrow band of the monitor across the front of the bridge. The raider was nearly bow-on to *H'zzarrelik*'s flank, presenting the smallest possible target while keeping its bow weapons trained on the Narseil ship. Three lines fired out from the frigate, snaking through the glowing mists of the Flux to attach with a thump to the hull of *H'zzarrelik*.

A company of small, suited figures emerged from the side of the raider ship. The pirates moved with alarming speed along the lines between the vessels. They would be at the airlocks in less than a minute, and they would be none too concerned about whatever damage they might cause boarding the ship. "Open the airlock hatches," ordered Ho'Sung.

Legroeder stared at the screen, fighting back memories of a pirate boarding, long ago . . .

"Pinpoint all targets," said Fre'geel, to Agamem and the weapons crew.

Legroeder held his breath.

"Ready," said Fre'geel calmly, as the pirates approached the ship, "to destroy targets, fire . . . *now*."

The screen erupted with light. The sides of *H'zzarrelik* blazed as the concealed neutrasers fired. The beams were too fast for the eye to follow, but Legroeder saw the nose of the pirate ship seem to explode, and smaller, multiple explosions zip like lightning along the boarding lines. Cinders that had been suited raiders were blown off into the Flux like so much pepper.

Before anyone could exult, the raider ship released a blossom of return fire against *H'zzarrelik*. The deck shuddered beneath Legroeder's feet as the first blast hit, but by the time he had caught and steadied himself, Agamem and his crew had pinpointed and destroyed those weapons on the pirate's flank.

H'zzarrelik was yawing in the grip of the raider net. She was damaged—how badly Legroeder couldn't guess—and Ho'Sung was shouting commands for damage control. But what about the enemy ship and its riggers? Legroeder couldn't tell. This was a perilous moment: the Narseil had eliminated the nose weapons on the *Flechette*, plus a couple of side weapons. But the fight was just beginning; the raider captain had most likely just revised his plan from "capture" to "destroy." *H'zzarrelik* held a momentary advantage due to surprise. It was possible they could even destroy the pirate ship right now, if they wanted—but maybe not without destroying themselves in the process. The ships were too close together to use the torpedoes. And that wasn't what they had come for.

Ho'Sung and Fre'geel were snapping out orders. Deep in the belly of the ship, Narseil fighters were preparing for their own assault. If *H'zzarrelik* could survive long enough to get them on their way over to the enemy . . .

"Maneuvering fusor! Portside stern, hard!" Ho'Sung shouted.

A loud groan passed through the hull, and in the long screen—part of which was now dark, knocked out—Legroeder could see that the Narseil ship was rotating away from the raider, into a more protected nose-on position. But hardly had the maneuver begun than Legroeder heard a shout of *"Torpedoes in the Flux!"* Three jets of light streaked from the pirate ship. Three missiles shot away into space, and then looped back, bearing down on *H'zzarrelik*.

"They're mad!" hissed Palagren. "They'll kill us both!"

Agamem already had the Narseil defenses in action. A flash of neutraser beams took out one of the torpedoes with a splash of light, and a second went spinning away. The third streaked inward unhindered, until with a shudder, the side of *H'zzarrelik* vomited a torpedo of its own. The two connected about a kilometer from the ship, near the edge of the enemy's rigger net. The torpedoes exploded together in a curtain of fire.

An explosion in the Flux was not like an explosion in the vacuum of normal-space. The energy from the explosion blossomed like a jellyfish, enveloping the two ships. Some of the energy flared outward into the Flux, but much was focused inward, drawn to the nets. The Narseil net was withdrawn, but the pirate's net was fully deployed, and it blazed up like a sparkler. A moment later, it went dark, dropping its hold on the Narseil ship.

"Maneuvering power!" Ho'Sung shouted. "Riggers, return to your stations!" The Narseil captain darted across the bridge, giving orders to his crew. Legroeder and the others scrambled to their rigger-stations.

If the curtain of fire from the explosion did not hit the ship directly, the waves of turbulence in the Flux did. The ship had begun to lift and turn, shaking horribly. Legroeder was halfway into his rigger-station, the clamshell still open, when the strongest wave hit. In the screen across the bridge, he saw the ship turn sideways to the pirate ship, then begin to tumble. He drew a fearful breath as the clamshell closed around him.

Reentering the net was like pulling on a tight bodysuit of unraveling fabric. The net had been seared, even in its withdrawn position; but it was still workable. He shouted, *Ready!* as he strained into position and stretched his arms into the Flux. The other riggers joined him, and they began expanding the net.

It was like sticking his hands out from a spinning raft into the base of a waterfall. The Flux had taken on the look of a cosmic maelstrom, and across the whirlpool of light, the raider ship was a chip spinning on a swirling stream. The pirate captain had badly miscalculated in firing those torpedoes. The two ships were some distance apart now, but the currents seemed as likely to slam them back together as to carry them farther apart. It was probably a good time to counterattack, while the other ship was helpless; but *H'zzarrelik* was nearly helpless, too. Maneuvering was going to be very difficult.

Ho'Sung clearly understood that. *Get us out of here, but keep the enemy in sight if you can,* he ordered.

Let's steer out toward the edge, said Palagren. *I'm going to change this to an undersea image—*

Legroeder cried out, without even thinking, *No, not the undersea! It's a whirlpool of light; it's a galaxy; I can keep the raider in sight if you let me form it for you.*

Startled, the Narseil leader gave Legroeder the con over the net. Legroeder worked quickly, repainting the churning mists into a vaster, grander picture of violently exploding nebulas and spinning stars. The ship was being pulled hard, and it took all of their strength to keep them in a current moving in the direction he wanted—downward, and to starboard. The Narseil riggers, confused at first, gradually understood what he was doing and found the leverage points to help him, moving *H'zzarrelik* away from the center of the maelstrom. At last they were able to turn and watch the raider ship, a small black dot caught in the currents of light.

I think their net was shredded by that blast, Legroeder

said. *It might well have killed their rigger crew.*

They're helpless, then, if we want to go after them? Ker'sell asked, from the keel position. It was a moot question, because *H'zzarrelik* was now riding a stream away from the raider.

Although the image looked like a disrupted galaxy, the power of the stream dissipated fairly quickly. As the riggers brought the ship around in the slowing current, the captain called: *Are we in a position to go after them?*

Palagren took a quick poll of his team, his gaze at last coming to rest on Legroeder. *You're the expert on pirates. Can we do it?*

Legroeder thought hard, staring out at the small black object still spinning in the stream, disabled by its own weapon. *No*, he said at last. *I don't think we should go in and risk getting caught in that turbulence again.*

But isn't this is our best chance to get them? asked Palagren.

Yes, it is. But not by going in. Legroeder grinned at Palagren across the ghostly veil of the net. *I think I know where he's going to come out. And I know right where we want to nail him when he does.*

Chapter 15
CAPTURE!

ALL RIGHT, *we'll follow your lead on this. Go ahead, Rigger, and—* The captain interrupted himself in the middle of his communication. Legroeder could hear him shouting to someone on the bridge. *"What do you mean they got into the airlock? Do you have it under control—?"* There was a moment of silence, and then he came back with: *Get us clear, riggers! But stay ready to engage!* Then he was gone—light-years away, it seemed.

Palagren looked to Legroeder to see what he had in mind.

Take us deeper into the Flux, Legroeder said, praying that his certainty was not misplaced. *Now. While they can't track us.*

But we'll lose sight of them, Palagren protested.

Didn't you bring me along to tell you how the pirates think? We'll pick them up again.

Palagren reluctantly complied, stretching out the battered fabric of *H'zzarrelik*'s net to draw the ship deeper into the multidimensional layers of the Flux. As the glowing mists darkened and became less focused, Legroeder explained his reasoning. It was likely that the pirate ship had suffered severe damage to her rigger-net when the torpedo had exploded. There was no way to know how much damage, or how long it would take to repair, if it could be repaired. But Legroeder knew what most raider captains would do, in a case like this. *They'll try to sink into the deeper levels and get out of the turbulence.*

Palagren sounded skeptical. *There's not much movement down there. Are you sure they'll try it, without a working net? It'd be hard enough to steer there normally.*

Legroeder nodded, scanning the surroundings. They were sinking into a level of the Flux that was comparatively sluggish. Ordinarily no one would choose to enter such slow-moving currents, but he had learned, with the raider fleets, that the underlayers made good hiding places at need. *This is far enough, I think.* Legroeder could still perceive the whirlpool shape of the region they had left; it looked ghostly now, on the verge of vanishing. For visual clarity, they viewed it as a cloud stretched overhead.

What now? asked Palagren.

Well—they're in serious trouble. And if their captain is anything like the ones I knew, they're going to try to slip into hiding while they make repairs. Even without their net, they can move into deeper layers by manipulating their flux reactor, just like a submarine flooding ballast tanks.

The usually stolid Voco sounded surprised. *This is true? They would do that?*

Oh yes, Legroeder said, scanning the ghostly region. *It sounds primitive, and you need careful coordination between the flux reactor and the net sensors, or you can lose control and wind up so deep you'll never get out. But it works.*

They had lost sight of the raider vessel. The turbulence in the levels "above" had not affected this layer at all. There was a slow, steady movement of current away from the point at which they had entered. Legroeder pointed ahead and to the left. *If we take a looping path around, it'll bring us back to where we can intercept them when they drop to this level.* The Narseil riggers agreed, and they took *H'zzarrelik* in a slow arc, searching out currents one by one until they had achieved the sweeping movement he wanted—almost an orbit around the place where he guessed the raider would come out.

So far so good. They hadn't heard back from the captain or anyone else on the bridge for a little while now. Legroeder assumed that Ho'Sung and the rest of the crew were busy with emergency repairs. They had taken a couple of good hits from the pirate ship, and some of it showed in the sluggishness of the rigger-net.

We're on the verge of losing maneuverability, Palagren warned, as they slipped unevenly through a transition layer.

All right, Legroeder said. *Let's edge back upward a little. If we hug those clouds, we should still be in good position to spot them.*

Stretching their arms out, they worked to nudge the ship upward. The clouds sparkled more brightly, and they felt the streams of the Flux stir around them with a little more force. Beneath them, the gloom of the deeper layers remained quiet, scarcely moving.

I'M CONCERNED about what's happening on the bridge, Palagren muttered. *No one's answering—*

There he is! Legroeder interrupted. A small, grey shape

had just dropped out of the clouds toward the darker under-derlayers.

Captain, we have the adversary in sight, Palagren reported.

There was still no answer from the bridge. Legroeder found this worrisome, but there was nothing they could do about it now. The riggers focused on carrying out their last orders, bringing the ship into position for an intercept. They climbed a bit more, for mobility and for greater cover in the light-and-dark lanes of the misty whirlpool. At the same time, they scanned for currents that could carry them to the enemy more quickly than the pirate could move away. Legroeder's plan was to approach with both speed and stealth.

Palagren continued calling to the captain. As they drew closer to the pirate ship, now from above rather than below, they could see that it was still tumbling slowly; its crew had not yet regained control. But that didn't mean it was harmless. If Legroeder and the Narseil were to attack successfully, to take out the enemy's remaining weapons, they would have to coordinate closely with *H'zzarrelik*'s gunners. The moment they were in a position to strike, they would become a target, as well.

Palagren tried once more to raise the captain. Finally he said, *Ker'sell, take a look outside the net. See if the com is down.*

The keel rigger acknowledged, and vanished from the net.

In the instant he disappeared, there was a momentary outcry—from Ker'sell—followed by an alarming silence.

POPPING THE clamshell of his rigger-station, Ker'sell was surrounded by noise and smoke and chaos. Lights flared, and he heard the crackle of beam weapons. He cried out in alarm, and rolled forward out of the rigger-station—just as a laser beam slashed across the open clamshell. He started to shout to the captain, but someone grabbed his neck-sail, yanking him sideways and down, behind a bank of consoles. It was Agamem, the weapons officer. "Enemy boarders on the bridge!" Agamem hissed. "They got in through the air-lock!"

"How is that possible?" Ker'sell protested. "I thought you hit them all."

"We did, too. But they were fast. They killed our guards at the airlock. We didn't know any had made it on board until they were halfway to the bridge." Agamem was cradling a neutraser, waiting for a target to appear. Across the bridge, a raider commando was firing from behind the cover of another console, keeping several of the Narseil pinned down. "There were two of them. I don't know where the other is. They disabled the door, so right now we're—"

The flash of an energy beam cut off his words.

Ker'sell whispered an oath. What a disaster. Leave it to these two-ringed humans to engage in such treachery. "What about ship's weapons?" he whispered to Agamem. "We're coming into attack position on the pirate right now. What does the captain want us to do?"

Agamem's eyes flashed. "The captain's dead. We're trying to keep the weapons panel protected here—but we can't possibly—"

A figure of rippling silver leaped overhead, sparkling with laser and neutraser-light. Agamem twisted to follow, firing his neutraser, but the commando was too fast, taking cover again behind the rigger-stations. There were shouts, Narseil voices, somewhere in the smoke-filled room.

Ker'sell glanced over at the rigger-stations, like boulders looming out of a fog. He was useless out here; he needed to get word to Palagren, if he could do it without being killed in the process. "Com to the net—is it down?" he hissed.

Agamem nodded.

"Then I must get back in the net, to warn the others."

"I'll cover. Be fast," Agamem said.

Ker'sell hummed his understanding and crouched to spring to his station. But before he could move, he saw in a tessa'chron blur another flash of silver as his station exploded in fire.

* * *

WE'D BETTER hear from someone soon, Palagren said to the others. *H'zzarrelik* had moved into a downwelling current that was taking them in an arc toward the raider ship. In a minute or two, they would be in a perfect position to fire.

Legroeder fretted at the shout they had heard from Ker'sell as he left the net. Clearly there was trouble on the bridge . . . and if they made a run on the raider without weapons, it would be suicide. *Do you want me to take a quick look?*

As he spoke, the raider ship below them was rolling its full flank to them, presenting a broadside target. *Yes! Tell them to fire right now if they can!*

Legroeder started to pull out of the net.

WAIT!

Palagren's shout brought him up short. He saw the reason at once: the pirate ship was glittering with neutraser fire—aimed at them.

Take the keel, Legroeder! Palagren was already twisting the net sharply, to bring them about. *Into the clouds! Back up into the clouds!*

The first neutraser beams burned through the Flux below them, lighting up the keel of the net just as Legroeder reached down. A searing pain flashed up his hands as he reached through the sparkling fire at the keel. He gritted his teeth and held on, warping the keel to help bring them around and into an upwelling. If they could get just a little higher, the boundary layers would block the enemy's weapons.

The next shots grazed the net, sending another flash of fire up his arms. They were nearly out of range now. The bottom layers of mist curled around, then closed under them. The neutraser shots glowed beneath them, dissipating in the clouds.

All right, Legroeder—take a look outside. But don't leave your station!

Legroeder took a deep breath and dropped out of the net. A wave of dizziness swept over him, and his eyes went dazzle-blind as he opened the clamshell. He heard a scream and leaned forward. "Sweet Jesus!" He rocked back as a laser beam flashed in front of his face. The bridge was full of smoke and ozone.

"Legroeder, get back in the net!" he heard. It was Ker'sell, shouting from somewhere in the smoke and confusion. "We have no weapons! My station's destroyed! Call off the attack!"

Before he could respond, there was a bright flash to his right, and a silver-suited raider commando spun in the air, firing everywhere. Something else made of silver was flying toward it . . .

Legroeder snapped the clamshell closed and dropped back into the net so abruptly that it buzzed like an electric cloud around him. *Boarders on the bridge!* he cried. *No weapons! Abort the attack!*

Palagren's voice was soft with dismay. *Boarders! Rings alive—*

They heeled the ship over in a slow curve through the clouds, trying to keep the raider located through breaks in the cloud, while keeping themselves out of sight. They were going to have to dance through the clouds, praying that the enemy was hurt more than they were. In fact, the raider ship seemed nearly helpless in the Flux. But though Legroeder and his companions held the flying advantage, he could not escape the thought that just outside the plastic shell that enclosed him, enemy soldiers were trying to kill him. For all of their power over the movement of the ship, he and Palagren and Voco were as helpless as babes in a crib.

KER'SELL, CHOKING in the acrid smoke, saw the enemy figure whirl as a bright mesh sailed through the air toward it. The enemy fired at the mesh, but it might as well have been trying to shoot a fishnet. The mesh caught the raider and enveloped it, and there was a moment of struggle—and then a blinding flash. A sharp retort cracked the air, as the net discharged into the raider's suit. The raider fell to the deck.

"He's down! Get him out of here!"

"Get the fans going!" someone else shouted.

Soon the air began to clear, and it became possible to see what was going on. The raider was indeed down, his forcefield disabled, his hardsuit smoldering. He appeared dead, but two of the Narseil fighters, taking no chances, were dragging him away. Someone had gotten the doors to the bridge open, and a handful of Narseil soldiers rushed in. Was that raider the only one left on the bridge? Ker'sell hoped so.

He hissed with dismay as he rose, taking stock of the mayhem. Several Narseil were down, possibly dead. A lot of people were trilling and hissing. Who was in charge now?

"Ker'sell!" someone called behind him. "If you're free, can you help me get this console turned back on?"

Ker'sell half turned, waving a negative reply. "I must know who is in command!" he shouted. "Can this ship fight?"

Several of the crew turned toward him. "Do you think we have not been fighting?" one of them asked, neck-sail fluttering as he bent over the still form of the captain.

"We're closing with the enemy ship!" Ker'sell shouted. "We need weapons, *now!*" He pushed his way to the weapons console, where several injured crewmembers were just getting to their feet. "And we need com to the net!"

One of those staggering to his feet was Mission Commander Fre'geel, aided by Cantha. Fre'geel was bleeding maroon blood; his neck-sail was half torn off. He looked as if he had been knocked across the bridge in the fight. "You heard Ker'sell," he rasped, struggling to stand. "Do we have weapons?"

Agamem was working at the weapons console. "Soon, I hope." He glanced at the front of the bridge. Only one short segment of the external monitor was working. In that narrow window, for just an instant, there was a glimpse of the raider ship, visible through swirling mists. "I need power restored to this console—"

A bright flare of light made everyone duck and turn. "Enemy on the bridge!" someone shouted, as a second raider commando was suddenly flushed out of hiding. The raider swung around to lob a grenade toward the rigger-stations. One of them was already smoking. Ker'sell's breath froze. There was another flash of silver in the air. Before the raider could complete his throw, someone had tossed a shock-web into the air, curling toward the raider. The grenade hit the web and detonated—and with a **whump!** the raider was knocked backward toward the exit. The explosion must have shielded the raider from direct contact with the web, because in an instant he was back on his feet. He fired one last shot, then fled from the bridge, pursued by two Narseil soldiers.

"Holy spirit of the mist!" Fre'geel gasped. Wincing with pain, he held up a hand to Ker'sell. "Report on the net! Are we maneuvering?"

"Yes—but com to the net is out! When I left, we were on an intercept course to the raider. We've got the advantage, if we can fight! If I could just get back in!" He gestured toward the shambles of his rigger-station, and suddenly realized that the next one was smoking, too.

Fre'geel hissed with alarm. "Damage teams—weapons console and net communication! We need them now! Is Ho'Sung alive?"

"He's dead. He was one of the first hit," someone reported from across the bridge.

"Then I have command. Get me an intruder report. I want that raider subdued, and I want to know if any others got in through the airlock." Fre'geel glared around, silently urging the crew back to their stations, regardless of their injuries.

Ker'sell wished desperately that he could get back to his. But his rigger-station was gone, and this one . . . there was a laser hole in it, venting smoke. He pressed the override release and opened the station. A cloud of noxious smoke billowed out. Ker'sell peered in—and wept at the lifeless form of Voco, burned through the head by the raider's last shot.

* * *

VOCO! PALAGREN was shouting. *Voco!*

The stern-rigger had uttered a silent, wordless screech, then vanished abruptly from the net. Legroeder reeled from the wave of pain; it echoed like a death cry.

Voco's gone, Palagren said, stunned. *You and I must do it now. I've lost sight of the raider. Do you have it?*

No, Legroeder grunted. They were now in a dance of desperation. Two riggers down: Ker'sell unable to get back to the net and Voco—what? Dead? Sweet Christ, they'd *had* the raider ship; they could have ended it that instant. And now he and Palagren, straining like two oarsmen trying to steer a wallowing ship, were bringing *H'zzarrelik* around through a layer of mist, struggling to stay in concealment while keeping track of the enemy's position—and all the while frantic to know what was happening on the bridge. It seemed insane to think of engaging the pirate ship; but they had no order to retreat.

Legroeder saw something moving through the mists. *There!* he called. The raider was slipping along, just at the edge of sight. He and Palagren had climbed and circled, and now were overtaking the enemy again. Another minute or two and they would be in perfect position to drop and fire. If they had something to fire with.

Legroeder, keep a fix on it, said Palagren. *I'm taking a fast look on the bridge.*

Legroeder barely moved a muscle. Palagren glanced back, and their eyes met for an instant before the Narseil vanished from the net. Legroeder's hands were stretched out far into the Flux, serving as both keel and rudder. He just had to steer straight . . . straight and level . . . and pray that when the time was right to bank over and dive, like an old-time fighter plane, it would be more than just him in the net, waving empty-handed at their foe.

"STAY, PALAGREN! Wait!"

Ker'sell raised a hand to the lead rigger, who had just opened his station. "Voco's dead—com's still down—" Ker'sell turned his head back to Agamem, hissing in frustration at the weapons console. Suddenly Agamem made a shrill sound of satisfaction and slapped a hand on the console. Ker'sell glanced at Fre'geel, who made a click of approval.

Ker'sell shouted to Palagren, "We have weapons! We have monitors on keel and starboard bow only. If you can put us where we can see the enemy, we'll fire when we can. Go!"

Palagren's station slammed shut.

LEGROEDER HAD started a banking turn to the right, but changed his mind when Palagren explained the situation. *Keel and starboard bow? This won't work,* Legroeder said, as Palagren returned to the lead-rigger position. *We'll need a different angle of approach.*

What's your recommendation? asked Palagren, peering around at Legroeder's refashioned image for the ship: an ancient, tiger-nosed fighter aircraft. An ancient fighter with extremely modern weapons.

Bring us a little to the left, and extend our run out ahead, Legroeder said.

We'll lose him.

No, we won't, Legroeder said, glancing down as the pirate ship disappeared beneath the mist. *As long as their net's still down,* he added silently. *We'll be making our dive to the right.* He was falling back on maneuvers he'd learned years ago in flight wargames.

He waited impatiently, watching their progress; then he called, *Now!*—and with Palagren's help, heeled the ship over into a steep, diving right turn.

They were now dropping not just vertically but also deeper through the dimensional layering of the Flux. He could feel his implants trying to help him coordinate the rush of data; but, afraid of the distraction, he kept them at the edges. His thoughts narrowed with concentration, as he let all of his instincts and experience flow to his fingertips. The plane/ship flew like a bird of prey, swooping down . . .

Spirit of the mist, let them have those weapons working,

Palagren breathed, as they gathered the deeper layers of the Flux around them, building momentum for the sluggish currents ahead.

Legroeder's gaze swept the parting clouds. He spotted the pirate ship, drifting below. The enemy had almost pulled out of its tumble, but as it grew beneath them, Legroeder saw the tattered sparkle of a rigger-net and knew they were still mostly dead in the water. He drew a breath. *Keep them on your right, Palagren, and let me face them as we pass.*

They hit the slower current like a swimmer hitting a cold layer. He'd tried to prepare for it, but it was jarring . . . and the moment was now for turning, and they banked hard over, putting the enemy off their lower right bow . . .

The neutrasers blazed from the *H'zzarrelik*, dancing like ghostly laser beams on the other ship. The raider's nose and net flared and darkened. There was a *sput sput sput* in the Narseil net, and three torpedoes twirled out and away from *H'zzarrelik*, curving wide, then back in toward the enemy's weapons bays.

Legroeder and Palagren pulled away, exposing *H'zzarrelik*'s belly for a moment but also aiming the one remaining sensor for the benefit of their own gunners on the bridge. Legroeder saw a flicker of neutraser fire as they twisted away from the enemy—the pirate ship firing back wildly. And then three blazing flashes, as the flux-torpedoes exploded. He was pretty sure at least one had connected.

Let's move off and take a look, Palagren said. They approached the cloud layer overhead and wheeled around in a circle, peering down at the enemy ship. The raider's net was dark, and there were several black holes in her hull. One neutraser on the side of the pirate ship was firing erratically into empty space.

Should we make another pass?

We don't want to destroy her, Palagren answered.

Better her than us, Legroeder thought silently.

The net crackled with static, and Legroeder nearly jumped out of his skin. A voice was trying to reach them—

inaudibly at first, and then becoming clear. *This is Fre'geel ... can you hear me in the net?*

The two riggers cried out at once, then Legroeder shut up and let Palagren report to the commander.

Keep a safe distance, said Fre'geel, *while we discuss terms of surrender.*

For a moment, the two riggers stared at each other in breathless amazement. Legroeder had never in his life heard of a pirate ship surrendering. So who, he felt himself wanting to ask, was surrendering to whom?

MISSION COMMANDER Fre'geel was leaning over the com unit, shouting to make himself heard over the static. "To whom am I speaking?"

Ker'sell listened for the reply. The voice that answered was human. Ker'sell was no expert, but he thought the voice sounded shaken. *"My name is ... Deutsch,"* rasped the voice over the short-range fluxwave.

"And you are—?" demanded Fre'geel.

"... lead rigger ..."

Fre'geel snapped to Ker'sell, "Call Legroeder out here at once." As Ker'sell obeyed, Fre'geel continued on the ship-to-ship, "Why is a rigger answering? Let me speak to your captain."

"... captain is dead ... most of the bridge crew dead ... all of the other riggers," said the distant voice, straining. *"I have the con ... am prepared to surrender."*

As Legroeder climbed out of the rigger-station, Ker'sell pointed to Fre'geel, who motioned the human over. Fre'geel barked into the com, "Say that again. I could not quite hear ..."

AT THE other end of the bridge, Agamem was working furiously to bring the rest of the weapons and internal security systems back up. There was a flicker on one of the screens. He muttered an oath, and then finally had an image on the internal security monitor: a sweep of the ship's corridors, some of them empty and some with crew members running.

Pressing the augment-link to his temple and focusing his thoughts, he set the system scanning for intruders . . .

The monitor flickered and froze, displaying the portside main corridor, amidships. There was a streak of silver, almost too quick to see; it was the escaped raider commando, suited and heavily augmented, darting into hiding. Agamem focused again: that was a replay, two minutes old. Where were his own soldiers?

"Security," he hissed into the intercom. "Intruder is—" Then he saw four Narseil crew running into view of the monitor, pointing weapons and searching. He keyed the intercom again. "Port Corridor Two—intruder has gone into—" he checked the location data "—the exercise room. Proceed with caution."

The Narseil acknowledged and gathered around the closed door. One of them opened the door, and two of the four darted inside.

Agamem switched to the monitor inside the exercise room. At first, he didn't see the pirate. Then he did. "Rings," he hissed. His men were moving cautiously along the edge of the pool. And there was the enemy—underwater in his armored spacesuit, about two feet below the surface, close to the pool wall where the soldiers couldn't see him. Weapon up, ready to fire up through the water the moment someone peered over the edge.

Agamem keyed the intercom again. He'd wanted to capture the pirate alive, if possible. But his people were too close—and he hadn't forgotten Voco and Captain Ho'Sung lying dead on the bridge. "Get out of the room and seal the bulkhead door," he ordered.

His crew moved quickly, obeying without hesitation. Agamem pressed the augment-link to his temple again, and focused. It took half a second to arm the weapon at the bottom of the pool, and another half second to confirm. Then he shut his eyes, sending the command to the security system.

Whump!

In the monitor, water shot up in a geyser. And with it, a silver-suited figure, twisted and broken.

A TREMOR shook the deck. Then stillness.

Legroeder looked up in alarm, and saw that he was not the only one. Fre'geel was already asking for a report. "The antipersonnel weapon in the pool," Agamem answered. "The escaped raider has been subdued. No further casualties on our side."

Fre'geel acknowledged and turned back to Legroeder, with a muted hiss. For the first time, Legroeder realized how much pain the commander must have been enduring; his metallic green neck-sail was practically shredded from the battle on the bridge, and was crusted with clotted purple blood.

Moving and speaking abruptly, Fre'geel said to Legroeder, "What about a rigger in command of the other ship? Can we believe that?"

Legroeder had listened to the ship-to-ship communication. "It might be true," he said. "Those shots could have killed the riggers in the net, certainly—and quite possibly the rest of the bridge crew. If the ranking officers were killed, the lead rigger would take the con, yes. Assuming some miracle had kept him alive."

"And would he be in a position to surrender?"

"He might even *want* to, if he's a conscript like I was. The problem is—"

"What?" Fre'geel towered over him, green eyes flaring.

"Well—if there are still commandos aboard, they're *not* going to want to surrender."

Fre'geel hissed, looking at the front monitor for a moment. The pirate's main power appeared to be down. Its sole remaining gunner had ceased firing. But there was no telling what other weapons they had left. Fre'geel turned back. "How many commandos would you expect on a ship that size?"

Legroeder frowned. "Hard to say. They're usually organized in squads of twelve. Two squads, maybe three."

Fre'geel spoke into the ship-to-ship com. "How many crew do you have aboard? And how many commandos?"

There was a short pause, before the rigger on the other ship said, *"We started with thirty-four ship's crew, and twenty-four commandos. I don't know . . . how many are still alive. But all of the commandos went out. I think you . . . killed them . . ."*

Fre'geel shot Legroeder a questioning look.

"That's plausible," Legroeder said. "Did you get a recording of the attempted boarding? If you knew how many were—" His voice caught, as he thought of the commandos blown off into the Flux. What was it like to die, adrift in the Flux, slowly suffocating if the neutraser didn't kill you? It was said that a prolonged naked-eye view of the Flux drove men mad.

"Cantha is checking now," Fre'geel said. "But if you look around, you will see that it was not merely an *attempted* boarding."

Chagrined, Legroeder nodded as he looked around the bridge. Bile rose in his throat at the sight of the bodies, and the shambles. He gazed at Ker'sell's destroyed rigger-station, and the small laser hole that had killed Voco—and he turned away with a shudder.

"Captain Ho'Sung is no longer with us," Fre'geel said. "We have lost others, as well. I don't know if you knew that."

Legroeder shook his head.

Fre'geel gave an almost human nod, then spoke again into the com. "Hear this, raider ship *Flechette*. Any remaining commandos and all gunners will gather in your main airlock and prepare to exit, without weapons. If any fail to comply, or if any of your crew resist, your ship will be destroyed. Is that understood?"

"Understood," said the voice from the enemy ship. *"I do not think there are any of the boarding team left on our ship. But I am checking now."*

"Very well." Fre'geel turned to Cantha, who was reviewing the monitor log. "Are you getting a count of boarders?"

"Almost. Yes—Captain, it appears that there were—I count twenty-four suited boarders leaving the raider ship. It is difficult to verify how many were destroyed by our weapons—possibly as many as twenty-two. And we know that two were killed aboard our ship."

Fre'geel turned back to the com. "*Flechette?* Have you made your determination yet?"

It was another minute before an answer came.

"*I am told there are no commandos left aboard. I have instructed all weapons operators to suit themselves and to prepare to exit the ship, unarmed—as soon as I can assure them of safe passage.*"

"Safe passage?" Fre'geel hissed under his breath. "If they do not resist, they will not be harmed—provided that the rest of your crew cooperates, as well. Otherwise, we will burn them down. That is your safe passage."

A momentary hesitation. "*Agreed,*" rasped the com.

Fre'geel raised a hand for attention on the bridge. He keyed the shipboard intercom. "*H'zzarrelik* crew, we are about to take possession of the enemy ship. Commando teams, prepare for boarding."

Fre'geel turned to Legroeder, his vertical green eyes glinting in his reptilian face. "Rigger Legroeder, good job so far. Now, get back to the net. You and Palagren will bring both ships out to normal-space."

Chapter 16
OUT OF THE ASHES

FOR FREEM'N Deutsch, the nightmare had come true. He surveyed the remains of the raider *Flechette*'s once-proud bridge. The captain and most of the bridge crew had died instantly when the massive neutron burst had flooded the nose of the ship, with the failure of the net and the forcefield protection. What had Te'Gunderlach been thinking, firing torpedoes at such close range? Stars knew how many men were dead now. And the ship? Most of her weapons were shot out; and her rigger-net was dead, burned out by flux-torpedo and neutraser fire.

It was their own damned arrogance that had killed them—Te'Gunderlach's arrogance, assuming that the Narseil commander was going to roll over for them. Well, this time they had met their match. From the moment that torpedo explosion ripped through their net, nearly killing *Flechette*'s rigger crew, they were crippled; and it was just a question of which damaged ship would recover first. That question had been answered soon enough. The only reason Deutsch himself was alive was that he'd been off the bridge, assisting with an emergency adjustment of the flux-reactor.

Te'Gunderlach and his blood-lust: he was dead now, and there was some justice to that. How ironic that as lead rigger, Deutsch—forced servant of the Republic—was now in command. During the pitch of battle, the augments had kept him burning with an adrenaline fever; but that had faded in the aftermath, leaving him with a cold, weary uncertainty. He'd felt something terribly strange during the battle; for an instant it had felt like a priority command message through his augments. (An order to break off the fight? That seemed unlikely.) Whatever it was, it had been swept away in the heat and chaos of fighting. And then his external-control augments had gone silent, when the central control in the ship's computer was destroyed.

Acting on his own judgment as ranking officer, he had made the determination to surrender. Ironically, it was what he had long ago abandoned hope for—a chance to give himself up and escape from the Kyber Republic. Now that he faced the prospect, he found it frightening.

"Ganton," he said, floating on his levitators toward a young smoke-begrimed ensign awaiting orders. "Go to the muster deck and make sure all of the weapons crew are there. I want you to inspect them, and see to it that they're suited and unarmed."

"But Rigger Deutsch," protested the ensign, "they won't stand still for *me* inspecting them, will they?"

Deutsch gazed at him grimly. Ganton was a promising young spacer—reasonably intelligent and if anything, excessively loyal. He probably had no idea how despised the Kyber were in the rest of the galaxy; he probably thought the Narseil had attacked them for no reason. He would learn; but there were small lessons to be learned as well as large ones. "Ensign," Deutsch said, "they *will* stand still for it, because I have given the order, and I am in command." He almost added, *Because our captain is dead.* But there was no need; the captain's body lay in plain sight. The ensign grimaced, saluted, and hurried away.

Three crewmen arrived on the bridge, and Deutsch waved them over as they looked around in horror. "You three— get this bridge cleaned up. Take the bodies to—" he had to stop and think "—the starboard airlock." As he pointed to the bodies, caught in various expressions of agony, he suppressed a shudder of his own. The stench of death had nearly overcome him earlier, even with his autonomic nervous system augments.

As the crewmen trudged forward to obey, Deutsch closed his eyes and connected to his inner com. "Narseil ship," he muttered low in his throat, "we are gathering crew as ordered. Do you have further instructions?"

The answer came quickly. *"Flechette, prepare for normal-space."*

Normal-space? Deutsch thought. If he were Te'Gunderlach, he would have seized on that as one last chance to level the playing field. He hoped none of the crew would have ideas of that sort. He wanted this to be a clean surrender. "Understood," he replied.

He turned to the pilot standing watch over the bridge controls. "You have the con. Keep the ship stable, but do nothing more. Cooperate with the Narseil and be polite if they speak to you. I'll be on the muster deck."

Deutsch rotated in mid-air, and glided off the bridge and down the smoky passageway.

THIS WOULDN'T be easy, with only two in the net. Legroeder and Palagren brought *H'zzarrelik* alongside the pirate ship. Its hull was dotted with craters where the remaining weapons had been carefully eliminated. *Close enough?* Legroeder asked, feeling as if he could reach out and touch the pirate ship's hull with his hands.

I think so, Palagren answered. *Let's extend the net and see.*

The glittering spiderweb of the net expanded as they drew more power from the flux-reactor. The net had suffered damage in the explosion of that first torpedo, and they dared not stretch it too far, or too fast. And yet, they needed to encircle the other ship. It would have been impossible if the net had not been overdesigned with this mission in mind.

All right, Legroeder—reach under. See how far your arm can stretch.

The net gave, as Legroeder stretched his "arm" all the way under the raider ship and up the other side. Palagren reached over the top. Their fingers met on the far side of the pirate vessel, and interlocked to complete the grapple. After checking the strength of the net, they began drawing the two ships upward through the shifting, sparkling layers of the Flux. It was a hard labor, with the increased mass and just the two of them in the net. Soon Legroeder was straining, and having difficulty focusing his efforts.

□ *Let us help . . .* □

Before he could respond, he felt strength flowing to him from within, from his Narseil-installed implants. He was startled for a moment, then realized that they were not providing actual power, but simply helping him to channel the strength flowing into the net from the flux-reactor, like a surge of electricity. The two ships rose, turning like a lily petal on the surface of a pond, as the clouds of the deeper Flux gave way to the expanding circlets of light of shallower layers—and finally the cold dark of interstellar space, dotted with the fires of a million distant suns.

The two scorched ships floated, bound together, a ludicrous emblem of human and Narseil power against the majesty of the universe.

Normal-space, Palagren reported to Commander Fre'geel.

THE MUSTER deck was full of shocked and sullen crewmen when Acting Captain Deutsch arrived. About half were suited for vacuum, and the rest were standing around waiting for orders. Ensign Ganton was just completing his inspection. He handed Deutsch three sidearms removed from crew members. "They all check," the ensign said softly. "Except for . . . Gunner Lyle. He refuses to give up his weapon."

Deutsch looked down the line of crewmen. Lyle was an older crewman, a veteran of dozens of buccaneering flights, a former commando, now a ship's gunner. He was silver-suited, but with his forcefield turned off. He sneered as Deutsch approached. "Gunner Lyle, surrender your weapon," Deutsch said, holding out his hand.

"I don't *surrender,*" Lyle said, glaring down at the rigger. He stood about half a meter taller than Deutsch.

"I see. Do you obey orders?"

Lyle's head jerked a little. "I answer to the captain. And you aren't the goddamned captain."

Deutsch rose on his levitators to gaze straight into the eyes of the pirate. "I am now. Are you planning to dispute my authority?" His voice was beginning to sound ominous, echoing from the twin speakers on his armored chest.

"Captain Gunderlach—"

"Is *dead,*" Deutsch said, letting his voice turn to hardened steel. "As you will be, if you do not obey your *new* captain."

"The captain," Lyle snarled, "would never give his ship up to *Narseil.*" He jerked a thumb over his shoulder. "And he wouldn't give up his crew, either."

"That's right," Deutsch said softly. The beating red flame of anger that drove him so effectively in the net was beginning to rise again in his thoughts, and he didn't try to keep it from his voice. "He wouldn't have. The captain thought he was invulnerable. And that's why he and a lot of your friends are dead right now. And if *you* don't obey *my* orders, a lot more will join them." Deutsch beckoned to Ensign Ganton. "Ensign, remove this man's weapon."

He could see fear in the ensign's eyes. He also saw Lyle's hand moving toward the sidearm at his waist. Deutsch caught Lyle's defiant gaze—and an instant later, Deutsch's telescoping left arm shot out to twice its normal length, and he caught Lyle's gun hand in a hydraulic vice-grip. Lyle's face went pale.

Deutsch chose not to break the man's wrist. Instead, he used his network of fingertip sensors to locate the faint aura of nerve pathways in Lyle's wrist; and as Deutsch smiled at the man, he searched his augmented memory-stores for the image he wanted. He sent it out, amplified: an irresistible image of a crushing force closing on Lyle's wrist, a vice slowly splintering the bone, and pain like nothing the man had ever dreamed of . . .

Lyle sank to his knees, trembling. His breath escaped with a gasp, and then a curse. Deutsch released his wrist unharmed. But Lyle remained on his knees, cradling his right arm in agony.

Deutsch motioned Ensign Ganton over. "Remove his weapon." The terrified ensign obeyed, taking care not to touch Lyle's arm. Deutsch accepted the gun and amplified his voice as he spoke to the other stunned crewmembers. "We have already paid the price of our failure. We paid it in blood. But it's done. As your acting captain, I command that no more shall die needlessly."

At that moment, he heard a small inner voice, providing an update from the bridge. He acknowledged, then linked to the intercom and announced ship-wide, "We are now in normal-space. All suited personnel move into the airlocks and open the outer doors. You are to offer no resistance to the Narseil. Essential systems crew only, remain at your stations."

Deutsch watched as the suited weapons crew flicked on

their silversuit-forcefields and moved into the airlock. Lyle rose, silent with rage, and activated his silversuit. A sneer crossed his features an instant before his face turned to a blank mirror. Then he followed the others into the airlock. Deutsch waited until the inner door closed and the outer door opened, then turned his attention to the rest of the crew.

LEGROEDER HAD a clear view from the net as the Narseil boarders, looking like large metal insects, floated across space to the pirate ship. They moved efficiently, but more cautiously than their raider counterparts had. Their first priority was to scan the suited pirates who had come out of the *Flechette*'s airlocks and to secure them as prisoners before entering the pirate ship itself. Who knew what traps might await them aboard *Flechette*? Legroeder did not envy them their job.

As he watched, along with Palagren, Legroeder sensed a chromatic flicker in his vision, and certain chimelike inner sounds; and he realized that his implants were busily recording, buzzing with analysis and observation. Their progress was displayed to him as streaks of color-coded light at the edges of his inner vision. He exhaled slowly, trying not to let it distract him.

In the space between the two ships, the Narseil commandos were corralling the silversuited pirates into groups. Others were preparing to move into the enemy ship. Something didn't look right to Legroeder, and he nudged Palagren and pointed to one of the clusters of pirates.

Is that raider commando moving out away from the others? Palagren asked softly.

Yah. Legroeder realized that three of the Narseil commandos were already moving to encircle the figure. But before he could even distinguish what was happening, there were two flashes—and one of the Narseil went tumbling backward. An instant later, the fleeing raider dissolved in a cloud of sparkling silver particles, expanding into the darkness of space.

* * *

DEUTSCH SAW it happen on the monitor. Saw his man—had to have been Lyle—pull out a concealed weapon, take one idiotic vengeful shot, then overload his forcefield suit as the Narseil fired back. An instant later, he was ionized dust. What the hell was he trying to do, take a Narseil with him to show how brave he was? And maybe take all of his shipmates, when the Narseil decided to exact punishment? *Lyle, you stupid sonofabitch bastard.* Deutsch turned and shouted to the roomful of men, all of whom had seen it on the monitor. "Listen up! If any of you is thinking of doing some brainless asshole thing like that, tell me and I'll put you out of your misery right now. If we don't all get killed for what Lyle did." He glared across the room. No one moved. "Good."

Shaking his head furiously, he linked his primary implant to the ship-to-ship com. "*H'zzarrelik*, this is *Flechette*."

"*This is H'zzarrelik*."

"About what just happened, Commander—"

He never finished, because at that moment the first wave of Narseil marines erupted through the airlock door—and there were more weapons than he could count, aimed at him and all of his men.

A REPORT came back from Ker'sell, who had remained outside the net, on the bridge. *It looks as if there was one rogue pirate who didn't want to surrender. Our marine was not seriously injured.*

Legroeder growled to himself, thinking, Just one rogue pirate? Or will there be more?

Ker'sell continued, *The airlock deck has been secured, and the raider's acting captain insists that all his crew have been ordered to cooperate. But the boarding party is taking nothing for granted. The commander says to pull the net in. We're backing to a safer distance.*

Legroeder peered over at Palagren as they drew the net in. The Narseil rigger seemed to be regarding the pirate ship thoughtfully, as though wondering whether it had been worth the price they had paid for it. Legroeder wished he knew himself.

EXPLOSION ON the Flechette! There's been an explosion.

The call from the bridge filled the withdrawn rigger-net like a jolt of electricity. Legroeder and Palagren extended the net instantly, ready to dive away from the pirate ship at the commander's order.

The silence that followed seemed to last forever.

Although *H'zzarrelik* had pulled back from the raider, Fre'geel had left the riggers in their stations as a hedge against the unexpected. There was always a chance that he would have to order a fast retreat in an emergency—such as a suicidal self-destruct of the pirate ship. Their quickest escape would be straight down into the Flux—though of course they would leave behind a lot of Narseil marines that way.

They waited.

How long had they been in this net, anyway?

The pirate ship floated, silent and enigmatic, off their port bow. Whatever was happening aboard it was invisible to the eye.

The com hissed. Cantha's voice: *Riggers, withdraw from the net.*

Legroeder stared at Palagren in surprise. *Did he just say to come out?* he said in a whisper, afraid to shatter what might have been an illusion.

Let's go, said Palagren, and winked out of sight.

Legroeder followed.

He rubbed his eyes, looking around the bridge. Although the place was a shattered mess, a good deal of cleanup and repair had been done already.

Fre'geel, his neck-sail encased in a clear gel bandage, turned from the center console. "We had one last holdout on the raider. He blew up an engine compartment, and himself and a shipmate with it. But we had no casualties, and the raider ship is now secured." He touched his long fingers together thoughtfully. "It occurred to me that you might be ready for some relief." He gestured to a pair of Narseil backup riggers, standing by to take the stations. "I think they can get us out of here in a hurry as well as anyone can. But I doubt it will be necessary." Fre'geel's mouth remained slightly open, and for a moment his noseless face looked as if it were wearing a human smile.

Legroeder stared at the commander in amazement. He felt relief, and dread, and a dozen other emotions he couldn't yet sort out. They had captured a pirate ship. And now they were going to . . . what? Fly it back to its owners.

For all of his tangled feelings, when he glanced at Palagren, their eyes met in satisfaction. For this moment at least, satisfaction.

Chapter 17
FABER ERIDANI

"YOU *SURE* we're on course?" the man asked, checking the satmap display for the thirteenth time. The aircar had covered hundreds of kilometers over forested terrain since they'd left Elmira, and he still wasn't sure they'd passed over the right landmarks. His personal augments weren't calibrating properly on the data streaming to him from the flyer's instruments; apparently his realignment to Faber Eridani standard hadn't quite taken. He couldn't make heads or tails of the ground below or the visual display.

His partner rolled her eyes as she scowled down over the rolling woods. *"Ye-e-es,"* she said, "we're going the right way. It's another ten, twenty kilos."

"What about the woman? She okay back there?"

His partner sighed and punched a couple of buttons on

her compad. "This says she's alive and in a coma. Does that count as okay?"

The man shook his head in annoyance, wishing for the hundredth time they'd gotten clearer directions from command on this operation. . . . *Secure and transport the woman . . . observe evasive protocols . . . keep secure for further instructions . . .*

Further instructions. He had no idea why this woman was important, just that she was. And that others would soon be looking for her. But who? It was a hell of a way to run an undercover operation.

"Any idea who they've got meeting us up there?"

"We'll find out when we get there, won't we?" his partner said irritably. A couple minutes later: "Looks like we're coming in." A town was beginning to emerge from the woodland ahead. "You ready to take over?"

He grunted. The aircar was descending now over street breaks in the forest cover; the autopilot was bringing them down into the outskirts of the town. "You got the directions to the rendezvous?" he asked, kicking off the autopilot. Gripping the yoke, he glanced at his partner.

"Look out!"

"Why, what—?" He saw the car come out of the blind spot to his left just as his manual controls kicked in. With a squawk, he jerked the car hard over, trying to avoid the other vehicle. There was a slight, glancing impact, putting them into a skid, about five meters above the ground. He fought the controls until the car straightened itself out and dropped the rest of the way to ground level. *"God damn these Faber cars!* How the hell are you supposed to—"

"You just ran that guy off into a field," Lydia said, looking back. "*Christ*, Dennis. Get us out of here before the police show up!"

"Well, don't blame *me!*" Cursing, he careened down the nearest side street and slammed the power to the floor, hoping their human cargo was still in one piece in the back seat.

* * *

EL'KEN INCLINED his head as the human woman Harriet bowed to him. "Academic, I am grateful for all of your assistance," she said gravely.

"And I for yours." El'ken gestured toward the stars overhead in his dome—in the general direction, he hoped, of where Legroeder had disappeared two weeks ago. His expression of gratitude was quite genuine. He wished he could have kept Harriet here longer, but his concerns were somewhat allayed by the recent departure of the Spacing Authority cruiser.

Harriet appeared to understand the gesture. "Let's hope some good comes to both our peoples from that venture. But now it's time for us to get on with our investigation. We can't let Legroeder do all the work."

"May I inquire how you hope to proceed?" El'ken asked the question out of genuine curiosity.

Harriet fiddled with the eyeglasses hanging from a chain around her neck—a peculiarly human mannerism. "We hope to find the trail of Legroeder's friend Maris. And find out who killed Robert McGinnis. And why Legroeder was framed." She paused, looking reflective. "And with your generous offer of transportation and diplomatic protection, we might actually stay out of jail long enough to do these things."

El'ken regarded her with a certain inner tension. He desired to tell her more, and yet he couldn't, without violating the conditions of his contact with the other side. He was not wholly certain of his knowledge, in any case. He hissed a breath through his gills and consoled himself with the thought that it would be worse to pass on wrong information than none at all. "You have people to help you, yes?"

Harriet nodded sharply. "Oh, yes. Peter, my PI, is quite good. A Clendornan. He may need to work miracles, though. Maris could be anywhere now—if she's alive at all. When we find her kidnappers, I suspect we will have found the people who killed McGinnis."

El'ken hesitated before speaking. So many deaths and possible deaths—all, in a way, the result of Rigger Legroeder's escape to freedom. Ironic. But it presented great possibilities, as well. El'ken hoped he had not erred in sending Legroeder to join the undercover mission. But the Narseil urgently needed intelligence about the Free Kyber—and they even more urgently wanted to find *Impris*, and not just for the sake of clearing their names in history. With Legroeder they had a better chance of accomplishing both than without him.

El'ken focused on Mrs. Mahoney again. "Do not be certain that her kidnappers are the same as McGinnis's killers," he said finally, deciding he could say that much, at least. "And do not presume that you won't find her alive." And how would you know that? he thought to himself rhetorically. "I . . . *feel* . . . that you might find good news about this. I cannot exactly say why." Nor could he exactly say why Robert McGinnis had died; he wanted to know that, too. He drew a soft breath and added, "And if you do learn more about these matters, I hope you will send word to me."

"I will," said Harriet. "Thank you. And good-bye."

"Safe journey back," El'ken said, extending a downturned palm. "To you and your daughter."

Harriet nodded, and hurried away. After she was gone, the Narseil sank back into his pool and settled slowly to the bottom. For a time he just rested there, staring up at the shimmering surface of the pool, and imagining the stars that lay beyond, out through the dome . . . and wondering if he had done the right thing.

"WELL, ARE we off?" Morgan asked, looking up as her mother returned to their room.

"We are off." Harriet went to put her last few things in her bag, then glanced back at Morgan, who was moving restlessly around the room. "Is something wrong?"

"No," Morgan snapped.

"What is it?"

"Nothing. I just told you."

Harriet sighed. "How long have I been your mother?"

Morgan shrugged and snapped her bag closed. "I don't know. Seems like forever."

"My. What's eating you?"

Morgan sighed. "Nothing. I'm sorry. I'm just worried about Legroeder, that's all."

"This is professional concern, I assume?"

Morgan let out an exasperated sigh. "No, mother—I'm carrying his child. Jesus. What do you think?"

"I don't know, dear. I was just wondering if you'd developed an emotional attachment, that's all." Harriet raised her eyebrows, then turned to snap her own bag shut. As she was finished, she looked back at her daughter. "Are you?"

"What?"

"Carrying his child."

Morgan snarled softly. "*No*, mother. I am not carrying his child." She grabbed both bags and headed for the door. "Let's go, shall we?"

"Testy, testy." Harriet followed her out of the room, chuckling.

THE NARSEIL embassy ship was both more comfortable, and less, than the corporate ship that had brought them to the asteroid. It was larger and more luxuriously appointed, with comfortable, private compartments—at least two of which had been adapted for human occupancy. On the other hand, for all of the comforts, it felt *alien* to Harriet. All of the surfaces seemed either too smooth or too rough, and the light was too green, and everywhere the ship seemed to have little pools and streams that looked like instant catastrophes in the event of loss of gravity. The Narseil crew were courteous, but left them alone.

That gave them plenty of time for planning; the Narseil ship was making a leisurely trip of it back to Faber Eri, in hopes of attracting less attention from the Spacing Authority. They knew from Peter's last communication that Harriet, at least, would be subject to arrest if she set foot outside of Narseil diplomatic territory. She was wanted on suspicion of complicity in the murder of Robert McGinnis, as well as suspicion of aiding and abetting the escape of Renwald Legroeder. She still had enough friends in influential places to have some assurance that the Narseil diplomatic protection would be honored, at least for a time. But she was going to have to come up with evidence of her innocence fairly soon—which could prove difficult, locked in the Narseil embassy.

She was more grateful than ever for Peter's assistance. She was also determined not to stay locked up one day longer than necessary.

RATHER THAN landing at Elmira Spaceport, the embassy ship docked in low orbit with a small diplomatic shuttle, which took them planetside and landed directly on the roof of the Narseil embassy compound. Morgan and Harriet were led inside and met by an assistant ambassador, a tall Narseil named Dendridan, who conducted them directly to their quarters. They were given adjoining bedrooms, plus a work room that already had been outfitted with a secure com-console. "We have been in touch with your investigative representative—the Clendornan?—and have set up a secure com-link for your use," Dendridan said.

"Thank you." Harriet looked around, surprised and touched by the Narseil's thoughtfulness. Apparently El'ken's recommendation carried some weight here.

Dendridan touched his embassy robes absently. "Officially, our reason for granting you asylum is to facilitate investigations crucial to the righting of historic wrongs against our people. Naturally, if you need to locate certain persons, or pursue information *tangential* to that investigation—purely as stepping stones, of course—we find no reason to disallow that." He gave a small bow, and said, "If you require nothing else just now, we will leave you to your work."

Harriet returned the bow. As soon as the Narseil was gone, she activated the console. She brushed past the security confirmations. "Peter? We're here. What do you have for us . . . ?"

* * *

PETER, SHE was sorry to learn, had little on the McGinnis case. The security forcefield had finally gone down, but only after the house had burned to the ground. The police still had the property cordoned off. But Peter *had* learned a few things about the disappearance of Maris. Security-cam records from the hospital had produced a description and partial registration number for the vehicle in which her abductors had driven off. That was enough to identify the vehicle as a rented aircar, later returned in another city, Bellairs, two hundred kilometers to the west of Elmira. However, the same vehicle had earlier turned up in Forest Hills, a town four hundred kilometers to the *north* of Elmira, where it had been involved in a minor traffic incident, but had fled the scene. Peter had investigators working in both cities, but his money was on Forest Hills.

"One more thing," he added, before ending the call. "You remember, they never found Jakus Bark's body?"

"For all the good that did us, yeah. Do you have something more?"

"Possibly. Someone fitting Bark's description was seen leaving the planet two days ago. On a ship registered off-planet, but suspected of being connected to Centrist Strength."

Harriet whistled. "Very good—I think. Any hard evidence we can use?"

"Unfortunately, no. If it was Bark, he traveled under an assumed name. We're still checking, though."

"Well, good work, Peter. Keep on it."

Not long after, another call came in. This time it came through the regular embassy switchboard. On the com was a stern-looking woman who began, "Spacing Commissioner North, to speak with Harriet Mahoney . . ."

"COMMISSIONER, I don't know what you expect me to do. It is true that my client has left the star system, against my desires—" which wasn't *quite* a lie "—but that doesn't change his basic dilemma, or mine. The fact is he was framed on patently trumped-up charges. And your office hasn't done a thing to dispel those charges."

"Mrs. Mahoney—please believe me—" Commissioner North spread his hands in appeal "—we are conducting a thorough investigation, right here at the highest level. If we find *any* evidence of unfair treatment, I can assure you that heads will roll."

"Commissioner, I would dearly love to believe you—"

"Well, then, let's talk." North placed a forefinger against his temple, and seemed to be searching for conciliatory words. "I believe if I speak to the D.A., I might be able to arrange for you to be free on bail. It's not in my hands, obviously—but you certainly have a long-standing reputation in the community, and if you want to make a gesture of good faith by meeting me, say, at the police station—or any neutral location you would care to suggest—I might be able to prevail upon my colleagues at Justice to give you some breathing room. Wouldn't that be better than staying holed up in the Narseil embassy?"

Harriet hesitated before replying. She had no certain knowledge of where in the Spacing Authority the corruption lay. It was possible that North was innocent. But she would have to be out of her mind to take a chance.

"Mrs. Mahoney?"

Harriet shook her head. "I can't do that."

"But surely you realize—"

"Commissioner, look at it from my point of view. My client, who not only escaped from a pirate outpost, but *brought you a captured pirate ship*, was framed for a crime he didn't commit. Then, while in my company, seeking information on a matter related to his defense, he narrowly escaped an attempt on his life. On *both* our lives. Finally, to top it off, we were both framed for the death of Robert McGinnis, who sent us away in his flyer because he knew he was coming under attack. Now, what would any intelligent person's response be to a pattern like that?"

North looked troubled. "That depends on whether it's all true, doesn't it? I hardly have to tell you how the police see it. You lack physical evidence for your assertions, and the fact that you left a burning house with a dying man inside, taking the man's flyer, is problematical. Unless you can produce evidence of your explanation, of course."

"We're searching for the physical evidence now, Commissioner. I expect we'll be finding some as soon as there's a thorough examination of the McGinnis property."

North scratched his sideburn. "Well, we're all eager to see what turns up there. But Mrs. Mahoney—I'm concerned that you're making your case worse by your insistence on taking refuge with a bunch of—well, I mean, with the Narseil." He leaned forward. "The thing is—from the point of view of the prosecutors—how do they know that you were at McGinnis's house just to discuss *Impris*?"

"What else would we have been—?" Harriet caught herself, struck by a sudden realization. "Who told you we were discussing *Impris*?"

North's gaze sharpened. Was that a flicker of dismay in his eyes? "Well, your statement—"

"Did not specify the content of our discussions with McGinnis. It said only that we were seeking historical information."

North was silent for a moment. "I guess I must have assumed . . ."

"Yes," said Harriet. "You must have assumed." *Or you knew from the start, because your people had their hooks into McGinnis.*

"Well," North said brusquely, "let's not get sidetracked on that. Mrs. Mahoney, if you change your mind and want to talk, you know where to reach me. Yes?"

"Yes," Harriet said, reaching forward. "Thank you—" she cut the connection and finished in a mutter "—*for your concern.*"

She sat mulling the screen.

"Mother?"

She looked up at Morgan, who had entered the room halfway through the conversation. "Yes, dear?"

"What was that all about? Was he just asking you to turn yourself in?"

Harriet blinked and slowly returned to the present. "Yes. Yes, I guess he was."

"You didn't consider it or anything, did you?"

Harriet sighed. "Well, if I *had* been thinking of it, he just ensured that I won't. Ever."

Morgan rested a hand on her mother's shoulder. "Good. I want to know that I can trust you to stay put here, when I leave."

"Leave?"

"There's no arrest warrant out on me. And if someone's going to go looking for Maris, there's a good chance they'll need some legal advice—especially if they can't prove that those hospital release papers were fraudulent. If you're stuck here, that leaves me."

Harriet stared open-mouthed at her daughter. She'd been so busy wishing that *she* could get out and be useful, she'd failed to consider what her daughter could do—besides put herself in harm's way.

Morgan hugged her. "What, did you think I was going to stay here and serve you tea the whole time?"

"That's *exactly* what I want you to do," Harriet said, laughing uneasily.

"Mother—"

"At least until Peter assures me it's safe . . ."

IRV JOHNSON liked working for Peter, the Clendornan PI, but there were times when he wondered what he was getting himself into. For the better part of the last two days, he'd been hanging around the grounds of the McGinnis estate, chewing on the stems of weeds, waiting for the fire investigation team to finish up so he could ask about their findings and maybe take a look himself. Fair enough. But this business about the dog . . .

When Peter had told him to keep an eye out for McGinnis's runaway dog, he'd had that glint that he sometimes got in his eye. In Peter's case, the glint was real: Clendornans had a sort of steel-wool fuzz at the backs of their eyes, and when it lit up, you noticed. What it meant, as far as Irv could tell, was: my intuition is telling me something and I'm not sure what it is, but I think it's important. Peter's intuition was pretty exceptional, and when he got that glint, there was usually good reason.

The client, Mrs. Mahoney, had said that McGinnis's dog had run away from the burning house and gotten out through the forcefield. It was probably somewhere in the woods right now, starving. Peter had been quite clear in his instructions: find the dog if he could, and bring it in.

Dogs made Irv nervous, and he had no idea what to do if he saw the animal. Whistle and hope for the best, he supposed. He spat out his weed and walked along the edge of the clearing. The house was a charred ruin. There was nothing anyone could have done to save it. With the forcefield up on internal power, the fire crews had had no choice but to wait until it burned down into the basement and destroyed the forcefield generator from the inside. By then, about all they could do was sift through the ruins and carry out the bones of the lone inhabitant. The remains were being examined at the regional coroner's office, but there wasn't much doubt as to whose they were. McGinnis's implants were pretty readily identifiable.

The fire inspectors were on the far side of the house now, looking for evidence of foul play or electromechanical malfunction. They'd told Irv they suspected some kind of power feedback in the house wiring. But until they were done he was to stay out of the way. That was fine with him. The smell of the charred remains was sickening, even way over here. The sooner he headed back to Elmira, the happier he'd be.

He'd already gone over the rental flyer and taken pictures of the lasershrap burns on its side. Earlier today, the regional authorities had trucked it away for further analysis. That left looking for the dog.

Irv sighed, picking his way along the edge of the woods. Here, doggy doggy. He scanned the trees, thinking he'd seen something moving in there. Maybe a bird or two. But no dog.

He yawned, remembered the thermos of coffee in his flyer, and started walking that way. After a few steps, he heard something and glanced back.

The dog leaped up, missing his nose by about an inch.

"Gah!" He jumped back, heart pounding.

The dog darted skittishly away. "No, wait! Come back! Good boy!" Irv stepped nervously toward the dog, snapping his fingers. "Come back here. Good dog! You snuck up on me. How did you do that? Huh, boy?"

The dog circled, making a low growl. Irv wasn't sure whether he looked fearful or aggressive. Irv drew a slow breath, studying the animal. It seemed to fit the description Mrs. Mahoney had given. Dark brown, medium-haired, long muzzle. It was panting, and looked hungry and probably thirsty.

"Good boy," Irv murmured, wishing he'd brought some food.

The dog stopped growling and stepped toward him.

Now what? Irv thought. Don't hold its gaze; he remembered Peter saying that. But the *dog* was holding *his* gaze. There was something damned peculiar about this dog, something intense, even for a starving, homeless animal. He tore his eyes away with a shiver.

The dog barked, piercingly.

"All *right*, damn it! C'mere, boy." He held out a hand again. "*C'mere*, for chrissake." The dog sniffed at his fingers, but when he tried to grab its collar, it backed away.

It barked again, making a mouthing, quavering sound. Damn if it didn't sound like it was trying to *talk*.

Irv squinted. "You want to come back with me? Smart dog."

The dog stared back warily.

Irv lunged, just missing. The dog sprang away with a yelp, tearing into the woods. Irv lit out after it, yelling. Then, realizing he was being stupid, he slowed to a walk. "Come on back!" he called. "I didn't mean to scare you!"

The dog's face peered out at him through some bushes. It was panting frantically, and making little whimpering sounds.

Irv whistled.

The dog just stood there with its tongue hanging out and its chest heaving.

"Listen—lemme go see if I got something I can give you to eat." Irv backed away, moving along the edge of the clearing toward the flyer. The dog trotted after him, still keeping its distance.

Across the way, the investigators seemed to take no notice of him or the dog. When he reached the flyer, he opened the gull-wing door and leaned inside. Maybe he should call in; maybe someone could tell him how to catch a dog. He hoisted himself into the seat, keeping an eye on the dog through the open door.

"Peter? Is Peter there? Yeah—I found the dog." He leaned forward, making sure the animal was still nearby. "That's right, Mrs. Mahoney's dog—I mean McGinnis's. Yeah. I'm having trouble catching it, though. What do you think's the best—*yoww!*" He rocked back, startled.

The dog gouged his lap with its nails as it sprang into the flyer, scrambling over him to get into the righthand seat. It sat there, panting like a steam locomotive, peering around wildly. It gave a long whine.

Irv stared at it, mouth open. He gulped and yanked the door closed. "You want a sandwich? Wait a minute." As he rummaged through his pack, conscious of the dog's hungry stare, he remembered the com and thumbed the key. "No problem here. Look, I'm bringing the dog in, Peter. Just like you said. I'll see you soon."

Finding a half-eaten roast beef sandwich, he tossed it to the ravenous animal. Then, taking a deep breath, he fired up the motors and took to the air before either of them could change their minds.

Chapter 18
MEETING OF MINDS

FOR SEVERAL shipdays, intensive repair efforts had been underway on both *H'zzarrelik* and *Flechette*. On the pirate ship only a bare skeleton of the original crew remained; the rest were in confinement aboard *H'zzarrelik*, undergoing interrogation. Nine Narseil had died in battle—a spiritually significant number in the Narseil Rings religion—and the atoms of their bodies were cast to the interstellar winds with ceremony and mourning. Of the raiders, something on the order of forty were dead; and the atoms of their bodies were scattered, too, with considerably less ceremony.

For a time, it was unclear whether the mission would be able to proceed. *Flechette* was badly shot up, and no one knew if it could be made to fly again. If not, *H'zzarrelik* would return to base with prisoners and no doubt a great deal of useful information from a thorough examination of the Kyber ship—but with the primary mission unfulfilled. On the other hand, Legroeder had seen the Narseil engineers at work, and had a healthy respect for their capabilities. Even so, he was amazed when, three days after the surrender of the pirate ship, he was ordered to report to *Flechette* to help test its rebuilt rigger-net. It was Cantha who brought the news, and when Legroeder rose to follow, thinking he might be gone for a few hours, Cantha chuckled. "You must bring all your things, my friend. We are moving aboard, you and I. Fre'geel has called a strategy session for later in the day."

Legroeder blinked with astonishment, followed by a chill of apprehension. They were going forward with the original plan, then. He ought to have been prepared, but it was a jolt to realize that it was really happening.

Gathering his gear, he joined Cantha at the main airlock. Enveloped in a forcefield silversuit, he hooked his tether to a cable that joined the two ships and jetted toward the pirate ship, weightless and reeling from vertigo. He had never felt quite so exposed to space as he did during that crossing, surrounded by an awesome myriad of stars, suspended untold light-years from the nearest world. The net felt nothing like this, even when he was looking at the same view. In the net, he was anchored and secure; here, he could fall forever. He floated into the airlock of the raider ship with a gasp, and when the airlock door sealed behind him, he uttered a silent prayer of gratitude.

The air on the pirate ship assaulted him with the residual stink of smoke and burned insulation. But walking through the ship, he was struck by the ubiquitous repair work—fiber panels and plasteel patches and jury-rigged pumps and field generators. He peered down a corridor sternward and saw a maze of cables snaking through a blown-out wall. Shaking his head, he followed Cantha forward to a meeting room amidships, where he found Fre'geel, Palagren, and much of the crew he'd worked with on *H'zzarrelik*. They had all moved into quarters on the pirate ship.

"Rigger Legroeder," said Commander Fre'geel, "there is someone you need to meet, as soon as you've gotten settled."

"I thought you wanted me to work on the net."

"I do. As soon as you've spoken with—"

"Their rigger crew—?"

"I would be pleased to have you not interrupt me. Yes, with their lead rigger and acting captain. Deutsch is his name. I want you to establish a relationship with him."

Legroeder let out a silent breath. "Excuse me?"

"You are to establish a relationship. Make friends, if you can," said Fre'geel. "And you might as well get used to the idea," he added, noting Legroeder's incredulous reaction. "Everything's going to be different now."

* * *

"YOU CANNOT be serious!" boomed the synthetic voice of the pirate rigger, Deutsch.

"But we are," said Commander Fre'geel, sitting tall on the other side of the meeting room table. "You are to lead us back to your base."

Legroeder watched the exchange with confused emotions. Curiosity, trepidation, hatred of what the pirate stood for, and, to his own surprise, sympathy. Freem'n Deutsch was a stocky man-machine. Legless, he moved around by floating in the air; a round, brushed-titanium housing where his hips should have been apparently contained the levitators. Around his chest was a complex assortment of armor and cyborg-augmentation, including speakers for his voice. His round face was one-third chrome, with glowing cyberlink connectors on his temples, and four lenses—two hemispherical mirror lenses over his eyes, and two smaller ones mounted on the sides of his cheekbones. Presumably the four eyes gave him enhanced peripheral vision; they also made it nearly impossible to read his emotions.

Legroeder suddenly realized that Fre'geel was waiting for him to say something. "We'd have thought you'd be glad to go back," he said, with a shrug.

Deutsch made a low ticking sound. He rotated one way and then another, as though to see who was listening. "I am not eager to return to the outpost with a chain around my neck," he said finally. "Truthfully, I would prefer not to return at all."

Legroeder frowned, realizing what his opening question should have been. "Were you—how shall I say?—not a volunteer in the raider fleet?"

The pirate made a metallic cawing sound, which Legroeder took to be laughter. "Volunteer? Are you mad? I am a captive! Can you understand that?" *Tick tick tick.* "It has been so long that I sometimes have trouble remembering. But having been forced to serve, I—" there was a slight catch in his voice "—well, I have tried, I suppose, to serve well."

Legroeder replied softly. "You might be surprised what I can understand." He didn't care at all for this man's looks, or for the memories that Deutsch's presence stirred up; but he found himself unable to hate him, either. A fellow captive, impressed into pirate service—apparently far more assimilated into the raider culture than Legroeder had become. But what would *he* be like, if he hadn't had the opportunity to escape, or if his captors had forced him to take implants?

"I was planning to ask for asylum when you took us back to your worlds," Deutsch said.

Fre'geel eyes contracted to narrow, vertical slits. "That will not be an option," he said. "Unless, of course, you help us in the completion of our mission, and come away with us."

Rigger Deutsch gazed at the Narseil commander for a long moment. "Why do you want to do this? You will be killed—or if not killed, taken prisoner and forced into service." He lowered his voice. "There are not many live Narseil captives in the Republic. I . . . understand they don't incorporate well into the system." Deutsch looked at Legroeder as if to say, you're human, you at least should have some sense.

Legroeder sat silent, his stomach churning.

Fre'geel answered, "It is not our intention to be taken prisoner . . . exactly." He seemed to consider his next words carefully. "Tell me something. Are you aware of a movement within the Kyber organization—a movement that wishes to make contact with the outside worlds?"

Deutsch took a deep breath and let it out slowly. Something seemed to flicker across his face, some expression, but the mirror-lensed eyes made it impossible to tell what it was. "No," he said.

Fre'geel glanced at Legroeder, who stirred uneasily. Legroeder had no idea whether Deutsch was telling the truth, if that was Fre'geel's unspoken question.

Fre'geel said to Deutsch, "If you hear any information of such a movement, you will inform us at once."

Deutsch cocked his head.

"Please," Legroeder added.

Fre'geel's gaze seemed to sharpen at that, but he said nothing.

Deutsch nodded slightly, moving his gaze around the room. Clearly, while he did not feel free to challenge the commander of the ship that had just nearly destroyed his own, he found all of this incomprehensible.

"Now, then," said Fre'geel, "I know you two riggers have a great deal to discuss—rigger paths to the outpost, and so on. I will leave you to your work." He gathered the other officers, leaving Deutsch and Legroeder alone in the wardroom with a single Narseil guard.

The two riggers sat staring awkwardly at each other. Vanquished and conqueror. Would-be refugee and would-be infiltrator. Legroeder cleared his throat. "I note that you seem fairly well equipped with augments."

Was that a slight flicker in the lenses covering Deutsch's eyes? "How did you guess?" the raider said finally, his voice modulated and dry.

Legroeder chuckled silently without answering. He blinked as Deutsch's right arm suddenly telescoped out a meter and a half to the end of the table and plucked a cracker out of a bowl there. The metal arm retracted silently back into its fabric sleeve, and looked more-or-less natural as Deutsch took a bite of the cracker.

"Yes, I have many augments, supplied by the technical units of the Free Kyber Republic," Deutsch said finally, and this time, Legroeder clearly detected the sound of sarcasm in his voice.

Legroeder nodded in acknowledgment. "Tell me—do you ever let those lenses go clear so we can see your eyes?"

"These *are* my eyes."

"Oh." Legroeder frowned, more uncomfortable than ever. "I guess I might as well tell you—I was also a guest once of the—what did you call it?—Free Kyber Republic? They didn't use such a fancy name at DeNoble, where I was a prisoner."

Deutsch tipped his head slightly, and the shifting glint of

the ceiling light on his lenses made it seem as if he were somehow tracking movements all around him as he listened to Legroeder. "You rigged . . . for the Kyber?" Deutsch asked, his voice a whisper. If his eyes didn't convey emotion, his voice did. "*DeNoble*. I have heard of the outpost . . ."

Legroeder felt a sudden heaviness in his chest, remembering. "The reason I ask about the augments . . . is that I need to know if they are critical to our getting back to your base."

"I would find it difficult without," the pirate said.

"Then I may require some coaching from you."

Deutsch leaned slightly, as though to examine the side of Legroeder's head. "Unless I am mistaken, you appear to have augments of your own."

"That is true. But they're new. I haven't used them long."

Deutsch's mouth curled with an unreadable expression. "You rigged well enough in combat with us. You and your people . . . fought very well. While we fought—recklessly?"

Legroeder cocked his head.

"You fooled us completely. We were not expecting you to fight back. You disguised the nature of your ship well." Deutsch's voice held no hint of reproach. "I must say I did not expect Captain Te'Gunderlach—" Deutsch hesitated, as if wrestling with some thought or other "—to launch a flux torpedo at point-blank range." His voice was grim and matter-of-fact.

Legroeder did not argue. It *was* foolish, what the raider captain had done.

"I always knew it would end this way," Deutsch said.

"What? That you would be defeated? Or that someone would come after you?"

Deutsch shook his head slowly. "That Captain Te'Gunderlach would destroy us with his pride. He seemed more machine than man—*much* more machine than I am—and yet a machine with pride, a machine that could not accept the possibility of defeat. Or retreat. If he had retreated from your trap, and taken time to recover, we would still be out there on patrol. You would still be looking for your mark, and we would not be . . . begging for mercy."

Deutsch laughed again, with a caw. "But then . . . here we are. You've captured us, and you want to *turn yourselves in*—to the gracious governance of the Kyber command."

"Well, not quite. We hope to be somewhat cleverer than that."

"I'm sure you do." Deutsch's mouth closed in a frown, and he shook his head a little. It struck Legroeder as odd the way Deutsch's mouth displayed expression even as his words came from the speakers. "I don't know what you hope to do there, but you'll have to be mighty clever indeed. And in case you fear that I might act to expose you once we're there—"

"The thought had crossed my mind."

"You're probably right, I would." Deutsch stared at him again, and his face had become utterly expressionless again. "But mainly out of the small hope of lessening the penalty my crew and I will pay for *our* failure."

Legroeder nodded. The Kyber security systems were formidable, as he well knew; he also knew that they were not invincible. "You know," he said, "there may be a way to do this that will help both of us." It would take smart work and luck. But he had beaten the Kyber before.

The captured pirate only stared at him with those indecipherable eyes.

THE RIGGER systems had been transformed into a crazy-quilt network of Narseil and Kyber equipment. Narseil repair crews had labored long, replacing burned out components and bringing the flux-reactor and net-generating equipment back up to power. "It's amazing," Legroeder said to Palagren, with real admiration. He waved Deutsch closer. "You don't have to keep a respectful distance, way over there. We're going to need your help." When Deutsch didn't reply, he tried joking, "You'll be teamed up with the best. It could be the high point of your rigging career."

Deutsch said stiffly, "This is where my crewmates died.

I do not think that flying on this bridge again will be a source of pleasure to me."

Legroeder opened his mouth, shamed by the rebuke. He had quite blotted from his mind the fact that Deutsch might have had friends here on the bridge, regardless of how he felt about the Kyber regime.

Fre'geel spoke up. "Pleasure or not, you will still rig." He said it in a husky tone that might have come across as a threat to Deutsch; but Legroeder knew it to be a tone of understanding, and even compassion. Fre'geel had lost friends, too.

Deutsch levitated to his assigned station, and Palagren and Legroeder went to theirs. As there were two each of Kyber and Narseil-designed stations, Legroeder had a choice. He chose the Kyber. No time like the present to check out their design specs.

He energized the net and stretched out into the starry sky. Palagren was already there, and Deutsch joined them a few seconds later. There was a moment of awkwardness as Palagren assigned Deutsch, the former lead rigger, to the stern position. Deutsch took up the place without comment, but there was a dull reluctance to his presence in the net. Legroeder knew that it would be up to him to talk to the pirate rigger if there was a problem, but for now he decided to let Deutsch decide on his own how to cooperate.

They began a series of tests of the net, stretching out in various directions, and dipping the fringes of it into the beginnings of the Flux. Deutsch did what was asked of him, but no more. And that, Legroeder decided, was probably okay for the time being. They were not yet ready to fly— there were many repairs still to be completed. But the time was drawing near.

Riggers, if you are satisfied with your test, please come out, said Fre'geel, on the com.

I find no problems, said Palagren. *Legroeder?*

Seems okay.

Rigger Deutsch?

Legroeder turned to Deutsch, resting in silence at the

stern. *You must give your judgment. You are the one who has flown this ship.*

Even in the net, Deutsch's glass-lensed eyes gleamed enigmatically. *Yes,* he said at last.

Then let us meet on the bridge, said Palagren.

THE DEBRIEFING was conducted over a light meal in the galley; afterward, Fre'geel dismissed them for the night. Legroeder, mindful of his assignment, approached Deutsch. "Is there someplace we can go to talk in private?"

Deutsch stared into space. "Talk about what?"

Legroeder shrugged. "We're going to have to work together. I have to know if I can trust you. And you have to know if you can trust me. So I thought—at least, we ought to know something about each other. Know what we're capable of. What to expect."

Deutsch's expression was utterly unreadable. Disdain? Dismay? Embarrassment? He answered in a soft voice, "In order that we may take you to your imprisonment that much sooner?"

"If you want to put it that way."

Reluctantly, it seemed, Deutsch turned his hand up. "We can use my cabin, if you wish. Your commander magnanimously allowed me to keep it."

"All right. Let's go, then." Legroeder spoke to the Narseil marine assigned as guard, and asked him if he would keep his vigil outside Deutsch's cabin.

Behind the sliding, metal-composite door, Deutsch's quarters were small but well appointed. The walls had many curtains and hangings, as if in counterpoint to the mechanically hard shininess of Deutsch's own person. An odd sort of reclining seat occupied one side of the room where a bunk might have been; on the other was a desk and a flat-seated stool, plus a straight-backed chair pushed back against the wall. On the desktop, a clear case held half a dozen luminous, faceted shapes, each glowing a different color in the light of the desk lamp. Legroeder felt a rush of wistfulness. "Meditation crystals?" he asked. Just the sight made him long again for his pearlgazers.

Deutsch's eyes gleamed. "You know them?"

It had been so long. "I had pearlgazers once. I lost them when my ship was—when I was taken prisoner." In his early years of rigging, the pearlgazers had been a valuable training tool, a focus for image-creating. Later, they'd been a comfort in times of loneliness. His sessions with the pearl-gazers had been rather like a prayer time.

Deutsch floated over to the desk, opened the case, and lifted a ruby-red crystal into the light. "Mine were taken also. I bought these a couple of years after. They were my first purchase when they put me on a cash rating." He peered over at Legroeder. "Without them, I think I would have gone mad long ago."

Legroeder didn't answer. When he lost the pearlgazers, he'd lost the meditative habit—not that he'd had much op-portunity for quiet reflection as a prisoner, anyway. But now, as he stared at Deutsch's crystals, it all came back in a rush.

Deutsch seemed to be reading this thoughts. "Would you like to try them?"

Legroeder started, then shook his head reflexively. Losing himself in a meditative trance in the presence of a just-conquered enemy was probably not the best way to establish authority. Bad enough he was having to do this at all. What was his purpose here—to win Deutsch over? Or to find the pirate's weak spots, so he could be controlled? Legroeder hated this, hated being someone's handler, which was more or less what Fre'geel wanted him to be.

"If you haven't tried it with implants, you may be un-derestimating their value." Deutsch gazed at him probingly. "You said you wanted comunication."

Legroeder blinked. "So?"

"Well, they're good for solitary meditation, of course. But they can also interact. Your augments could mediate that—if you want." Deutsch hefted the crystal in one hand.

Legroeder frowned. He hadn't thought about *communi-*

cating with these. But he was the one who'd said they needed to learn about each other, to gain trust. Maybe Deutsch had a point. If they were to have even a prayer of penetrating the raider fortress, they needed to have some understanding of the place ahead of time. It would be better yet to see it through another's eyes. Still . . . there was an intimacy to this sort of joining; it was something you did with friends. Good friends.

"No need, if you don't want to." Deutsch replaced the crystal in its case and floated to his recliner. The levitator housing that passed for his hips settled into a recess in the seat, and the entire apparatus tilted back about fifteen degrees. It looked as though it reclined fully for sleeping.

"Perhaps—" Legroeder began, driven more by some inner momentum that he didn't understand than by logic "—perhaps a short session *would* be useful. At a moderate level."

They were not friends. And yet, they were already linked in a way that reminded him of his bond with Maris— brought together by circumstance, by the condition of being fellow prisoners. Could the same bonding force work here? Was it something that could be summoned? In the back of his mind, stirred perhaps by his own implants, he felt a growing curiosity about Deutsch.

Deutsch gazed at him assessingly. "You might find these somewhat more powerful than your pearlgazers." He said it as though they were two men standing in a shop talking about the latest innovations in meditation gear, the tensions of the recent battle forgotten.

Legroeder nodded. "May I?" He reached out to touch the tip of a long, blue crystal. Deutsch's arm telescoped out and picked the crystal out of the case and handed it to him. Legroeder sat back in the desk chair and held the sapphire-like gem up to the light. It appeared to have its own inner fire: threads and facets of self-contained light.

"We start separately," Deutsch said. "The interaction between the crystals will come, as we meditate. If that's a problem . . ." His silver eyes peered at Legroeder. Legroeder shook his head. "All right, then." Deutsch held the ruby crystal almost reverently in his hands.

Legroeder allowed his gaze to drift downward into the depths of the crystal. It already felt different from the pearl-gazers: more active, more alive. And yet the approach was the same, to let his thoughts flicker inward . . . to let them settle into the object's inner fire, until the stirrings of the subconscious sent them swirling in a new direction.

He heard his augments urging him on; then they melted out of sight.

Slow, deep breathing . . .

He felt himself slipping downward, drawn by the crystal. His thoughts came together in sparkles of cerulean blue, like plankton in the sea . . . or particles of knowledge in a da-tanet, forming threads of light, commingling and joining. Voices chattered in the distance. His own thoughts? The implants?

He became aware of droplets of light moving against darker surroundings, sketching zigzagging paths outward. The augments, reaching out . . . as if they knew what they were doing, even if he did not. He watched, hypnotized by the patterns drawn in liquid light . . .

Only gradually did he become aware of crosstalk be-tween crystals, voices murmuring distantly. So many inner voices . . . asking why he was doing this. Why he was doing the mission.

Because I must.

But why?

For my friends . . . for me . . .

A tangled vine of voices, his own inner voices, curling around the knots of questions.

To strike at piracy . . . to find truth . . .

But who'd appointed him a seeker of truth and justice?

There was a strange shifting sensation in his mind, as the voices wrapped around and around . . .

To learn the truth of Impris . . . to find answers among the Kyber . . .

Shift . . .

There may be others interested in these questions . . .

He felt a sudden confusion. Not all the voices were his, or his implants' . . . and he noticed certain color patterns that had come together, ruby and cerulean reflecting and joining in halos . . . and the implants, his and Deutsch's, were skittering and handshaking and opening tiny dialogue boxes of thought . . .

(Is it your thoughts I'm hearing?) he said to Deutsch.

(Didn't you know?)

He hadn't been sure, at first. It wasn't threatening, so much as startling. *(It's strange,)* he whispered. They were joining across a distance: he and Deutsch standing on two stages in darkness, each spotlighted, calling out to each other. To share? Through stories on stage?

The Kyber rigger shut down half the lights on his side, and turned the rest to standby illumination. *(You can darken or illuminate what you want. For a rigger, it should be easy.)*

Legroeder practiced flicking lights on and off, revealing and unrevealing. *(Perhaps,)* he said thoughtfully, *(it would be useful to share some history.)* He found himself going back in time, his subconscious spinning an image, which sprang to life on his stage like a holo projection.

A ship under attack . . .

*

It was the *Ciudad de los Angeles*, caught in a surprise attack by the raider, pummeled by Flux distortion and wails from the pirates' amplifiers. A torpedo exploded, threateningly close.

And then, with a subconscious edit, the image cut to:

The bridge—officers shouting, captain trying to raise the pirates on the ship-to-ship fluxwave (this image a little blurry, but Legroeder hadn't been there; he'd been in the net at the time; this was a reconstruction).

Cut to:

The rigger-net, where terror and bewilderment raged like a forest fire. They were under assault and their captain was wavering. Should they fight? Flee? Lightning flared in the

Flux, indistinguishable from the fire of weapons.

Then word came through from the bridge:

Let the raider ship grapple them . . . the battle was over . . .

*

(Your ship?) murmured a faintly metallic voice.

(Yes. "Ciudad de los Angeles," she was called. "City of the Angels.")

(Bad . . .)

*

Bad enough, but it wasn't over . . .

His imagination supplied the images he hadn't witnessed personally—the battle raging, a nightmare uncorked—terror in the corridors, commandos overrunning the ship, killing in reaction to the slightest resistance, seizing passengers and crew without mercy, without concern for age, mothers and children alike . . .

Cut to:

A small boy, Bobby Mahoney, hauled screaming from his cabin, terrified and kicking; finally shot with a stunner and dragged off to the hold of the pirate ship . . .

Cut to:

Riggers stumbling out of the rigger-stations to face armed commandos, then herded off to similar holds . . .

And later taken back to the raider fortress, and forced into service as riggers aboard pirate ships that would go out and start the same thing all over again . . .

*

The final image quivered on the stage, until Legroeder breathed it away with a sigh. It was a terrible burden, and yet a relief to let it out. He had tried so long not to think of it.

On the facing stage, Rigger Freem'n Deutsch was mulling over what he had seen. *(Very disturbing,)* he said, with an inflection of uncertainty. *(Would you mind if I—?)*

His voice faded into silence. The lights came up on his stage.

*

For several heartbeats, nothing.

And then, in the spotlight glow, a lumbering freighter—and coming alongside it, a raider. There was no contest, once the firing began—except, unaccountably, on the bridge of the freighter, where the captain lost his head and screamed to his men to resist . . .

Like Legroeder's image, this one had the hazy outlines of reconstructed memory. Deutsch was just coming out of the net when the fighting on the bridge began. It didn't last long, just enough time for shouts of outrage and several bright flashes of laser fire, and then . . .

Searing pain, followed by numbness . . .

Deutsch fell, aware of his legs no longer holding him up. Blackness . . .

*

He came to, twice. Once, for an instant, to the corridors bumping past at a dizzying sickening angle; something felt very wrong, but he didn't know what, it was a mind-wrenching blur. Then blackness again.

The next time was in a narrow infirmary cot, with ghostly sensations and nothing else where his legs used to be. And in his head, the buzzings of his new augments, testing the connections to the auxiliary equipment being integrated to his body . . .

*

Legroeder was stunned. (*They saved you? The ones who took me would have left you there to die.*)

(*These would have, too, except my crewmate José . . .*)

(*Rigger-mate?*)

(*Yes, he carried me like a sack; told them I was the best rigger in the fleet; they couldn't lose me. He risked his life, insisting.*)

Legroeder marveled at the courage. Would he have done that? (*Where's José now?*) He felt a sudden chill. (*He wasn't . . . on the bridge here . . . ?*)

Deutsch's thoughts darkened, the lights lowering on the stage. (*He died, his first flight out with the raider fleet. I think he wanted to, by then. He was sorry he'd saved me;*

sorry any of us lived to be put to this kind of work.)

I'm sorry too, Legroeder tried to whisper.

(It was bound to end one way or another. Those who live by the sword . . .)

*

The raider ship *Flechette*, coursing through scarlet-glowing clouds of the Flux, joining battle. Nose flickering, lightning flashing, booming sounds reverberating through the Flux. On her bridge, a cyborg captain bent on leading them into conquest.

And in Deutsch's head, a tiny jangling, an implant or an instinct telling him something was not right. When the captain ordered them in for the kill, the jangling got more insistent, as though he should do something to stop this. For an instant, he imagined a Priority One command message trying to get through; but within seconds, it was lost in the chaos and confusion . . .

Cut to:

Blinding flare of a flux-torpedo, and the wrenching upheaval of the Flux shearing the net. Smoke and ruin on the bridge. People screaming; the captain glaring, eyes blazing, against the back wall—dead. Crewmen crumpled from the radiation burst.

Deutsch, staggering from the fluxfield chamber, where fate and the chamber shielding had protected him from the burst. He surveyed the devastation in horror and disbelief . . . and finally numbness as his implants shut down the worst of the awareness so that he could function. But they could not shut out the sight of his fellow riggers, smoking in their stations . . .

Cut to:

Darkness.

*

Legroeder felt his own darkness welling around him, felt himself mourning Deutsch's friends. What a strange feeling.

From across the gulf of darkness: *(We were both forced into service. Your story could have been mine. We have both suffered great loss.)*

(Yes. And you thought you were dead—and then hoped you were free. And now you wonder . . .)

Deutsch stared across at him from his stage. Questioning with his eyes the scenario that Legroeder proposed: returning to the very heart of darkness, the pirate outpost.

Legroeder thought he sensed a flicker of something—some inkling of hope, or maybe destiny, that even Deutsch didn't recognize.

(You can show us the way in, and the way out. And how to find the information we need.)

Deutsch's image shook its head. He didn't have to say: Why should I? If he helped the Narseil and got caught, he could be hung, or tortured, or mindwiped . . .

Legroeder searched for that flicker of hope again; perhaps he had only imagined it.

But the connection with Deutsch had become compelling. He wanted to keep the momentum alive. *(There are other things I can show you,)* he whispered . . .

*

A more neutral memory: crewing a ship called *Lady Brillig*, with three riggers named Janofer, Gev, and Skan. A happy crew, for a time. But though all three of the men were smitten with Janofer, only Skan found the way into her heart, and even that didn't last. It seemed almost inevitable that the chemistry could not hold, and in the end it didn't.

Later, much later, he saw Gev Carlyle again; but this time Legroeder was flying under duress for the raiders, and Gev Carlyle was the prey.

(And was your friend captured?) Deutsch asked.

Legroeder remembered the terrible risk he had taken, to fake unexpected turbulence in the Flux. *(I found a way to free him.)*

The next image was of the stinging rebuke he and his fellow riggers received—and yet, they persuaded their captain that it was bad luck that had caused them to lose their quarry. Now, recalling the moment, Legroeder wondered why he'd never found the courage to save others the same way he'd saved his friend.

Deutsch seemed to recognize the feeling, and for a few moments, there was a subdued silence in the connection. *(It was brave of you,)* Deutsch said finally, and the images that followed seemed to reflect his confusion over how to respond. It was a series of fragmentary images, glimpses of raider society in a bewildering order, all suffused with an emotion that Legroeder had trouble recognizing. Was it regret? Or Deutsch's own guilt for the degree to which he'd allowed himself to be absorbed into the raider culture? Flickering through the images were glimpses of that jangling alarm that Deutsch had heard at the start of the battle with *H'zzarrelik*, and then lost in the confusion.

Legroeder tried, in frustration, to follow.

But rather than clarify, Deutsch changed to images from his more distant past, from times before his capture by the raiders. Learning to fly as a youth, in the balloon fleets of Varinorum Secundus. Later, as a rigger, flying a race down the Grand Canyon Nebula, a strange formation that extended deep through the layers of the Flux. Legroeder sensed echoes of the exhilaration of the race, still alive in Deutsch's memory. It was enough to make him think that perhaps now was the time to raise another subject . . .

*

A mighty and storied ship, soon to be lost in the streams of the Flux, *Impris* gleamed against space, and cut through the mists of the Flux like a speedwhale of Cornice III. Her passengers enjoyed a view that few but riggers usually saw. As she passed by the Great Barrier Nebula, the sight caused even the most jaded of star travelers to draw a sharp breath.

Dissolve to:

The same ship, somehow untarnished by the years, slipping out of the mists like a ghost on a fog-shrouded moor—wailing for help, and drawing the innocent to their doom.

Cut to:

A raider ship closing in on would-be rescuers . . .

Cut to:

Loss. Darkness. And through the darkness a man, Legroeder, searching the skies with a tireless gaze, searching for answers, searching for the lost *Impris* . . .

(I know of this ship,) murmured the other rigger.

Startled, Legroeder cast his gaze to the other stage. *(You do? Can you tell me more?)*

(I know of it. I have not seen it myself.) Deutsch hesitated. *(There is knowledge of it at the outpost.)*

Legroeder suppressed a rush of excitement from Deutsch's words. *(Do you think there might be a way to—)*

(No, no . . .) Deutsch shook off the question, and before Legroeder could rephrase it, Deutsch was speaking again, illuminating his stage, sidestepping the question of *Impris* and offering new memories, new stories . . .

*

They went back and forth for a time, but eventually Legroeder found his focus slipping, and questions he wanted to ask were vanishing from his thoughts before he could raise them.

(We must stop,) he said, and slowly withdrew his thoughts from the glowing interior of the crystal. He rubbed his eyes, bringing them back into focus in the real-time and real-space of Deutsch's cabin.

Deutsch's mirror eyes glinted as Legroeder carefully replaced the crystal in its case. Legroeder couldn't tell if Deutsch was watching him or staring still into his own ruby-colored crystal. "This has been . . . interesting," Legroeder said. "But I must be going. It will be a difficult day tomorrow." He hesitated. "Thank you."

Deutsch remained motionless, as though he had not heard. But as Legroeder was turning to leave, the Kyber's voice rumbled, "You're welcome."

Legroeder made his way back out into the corridor, and then to his own cabin. He was stunned to realize, as he fell into his bunk, that three hours had passed in the company of the Kyber rigger. And he was aware, drifting off, that he was by no means finished with this experience. This was going to be a night filled with dreams.

Many dreams . . .

Chapter 19
INTO THE HEART OF DARKNESS

FREEM'N DEUTSCH remained lost in the world of the gazing crystal for a long time after the other rigger left. His good-bye to Legroeder was generated by a general services augment, which took over the niceties of social interaction when his real thoughts were busy elsewhere.

And busy they were: pondering the visions Legroeder had shown him, and his own memories that Legroeder's had awakened.

He was stunned to realize how completely he had shielded himself from memories of his own life—memories of a time when he, too, had been an innocent rigger, reveling in the freedom and exhilaration of the net. Memories of the time before he was taken by storm, legs burned off, life transformed to the darkness of captivity and forced labor. His story was remarkably similar to recollections Legroeder had shared, and the remembrance had primed his thoughts for the emergence of far darker visions . . .

Right now his augment-matrix was struggling to control those visions, to keep them from erupting and destroying his mental equilibrium. It wasn't quite working; the visions were too powerful to keep out; having begun, they were now an unstoppable force, wracking his mind and body with nausea and revulsion.

It was one thing to have endured an attack as victim; but the other kind of darkness came from living through the maelstrom as an attacker, loosing the great waves of fury that sent the quarry reeling in terror . . .

*

Doom doom doom . . .

The drumming would reverberate in his sleep as long as he lived, even when his protection circuits were supposed to suppress it. And rising from the drumming was the growing din of other sounds . . . the screams, the crackle of weapons . . . gunshots echoing in the canyons of his mind . . .

And the smoldering crimson glow of fire, illumining all of his memories . . .

Deutsch shuddered, struggling to make it stop. Why weren't the protection circuits working? Something was wrong, something gone squirrely, something not keeping the damn memories under control.

Almost as though the augments *wanted* him to remember . . .

*

Before the trade to Ivan, rigging under the flag of Carlotta, it had been even worse than under Te'Gunderlach. *No, damn it, stop.* He didn't want to relive . . .

The attack on the *Melanie Frey.*

They'd savaged the ship like an animal with newrabies, tearing at its own body and its enemy alike, no awareness of boundary between self and other. DeMort was the most bloodthirsty of all the captains he'd served under, and his own riggers had no more certainty of safety from his fury than did his victims. It made them fight harder—out of fear, to deflect the madness outward—at someone else, anyone else.

The *Melanie Frey*'s crew had resisted. Stupid, maybe, but the raiders had come upon them so suddenly that they probably had no time to think. They had fought instinctively, not realizing the futility. The battle destroyed the ship, costing the pirates a prize vessel, plus three quarters of its crew and passengers. Captain DeMort, infuriated by the resistance, sent a berserker impulse through the command-link into the implants of the boarding crew. For a full hour, the commandos ransacking the ship had gone mad . . .

And into the net, to give his riggers a taste for blood, DeMort had fed a live image of the fighting.

Not fighting: carnage.

Of all the horrors, the one that most pierced Freem'n Deutsch's heart was the sight of a young boy set upon by a maddened commando. The boy fought heroically, for the moment or two that he lived, after clawing with his hands at the face of the armored pirate.

That commando, and a dozen others, never emerged from their berserker state and instead had to be ordered into stasis. Whether they were mindwiped upon their return to base, or simply terminated like useless equipment, Deutsch never knew.

None of the riggers were capable of flight for some time afterward. The pirate ship drifted away from its prey, sickened and helpless, like an animal that had swallowed poison.

It was Captain DeMort's last voyage in command of a raider ship. But it was not Deutsch's last as rigger of a raider . . .

*

Under Te'Gunderlach of Outpost Ivan, it was also brutal, to be sure, but Te'Gunderlach maintained at least a veneer of rationality behind his tactics. Still, it was no surprise when Te'Gunderlach's aggressiveness, in the end, put the ship into a trap from which there was no escape . . .

*

P1 alarm, P1 alarm . . .

Deutsch's heart pounded as he relived the memories. He tried to slow it, but his augments resisted his efforts. Why did he keep thinking about a P1 intervention? What was going on here—an autonomic system failure? No, there was a response from his central monitor: ▢ *High heartrate necessary to assist in coping and proceeding . . . we are reanalyzing your memories of a Priority One code . . .* ▢

Deutsch remembered the jangle of an alarm during the fight with the Narseil, and a momentary conviction of wrongness about what Te'Gunderlach was doing. He recalled now an inner maelstrom that had passed too quickly before—voices calling out to him, from or through the augments. He couldn't tell what they were trying to say; but then, the net had taken some bad jolts during the fight. Had his augments suffered damage, scrambling the P1 message?

□ *All circuits are intact; however, there may have been loss of data . . .* □

Loss of data . . . echoes of voices . . . and the oddest resonance between those voices and his sharing just now with Legroeder . . .

He shivered with uncertainty. Where could such a message have come from? The echoes were strangely powerful. And alongside them was the image of what Legroeder had done—something that he, Deutsch, had never found the courage, or the opportunity, to do. Legroeder had risked his life to save a victim from capture.

Risked the wrath of a raider captain.

And now this preposterous plan of the Narseil.

Through the ringing dissonance of the memories, Deutsch found himself asking the question: Would he ever find it in himself to risk his life that way? Would he?

LEGROEDER BLINKED awake from a dream about Bobby Mahoney . . . and about the bosses of Outpost Ivan. *Strange.* He had never laid eyes on Bobby Mahoney in the flesh—and of course, he had never met the bosses of Outpost Ivan. Yet the images—one a reconstruction by his own mind, and the other someone else's memory—were replaying in his mind now with the clarity of real life. The gazing-crystal joining with Deutsch had left a more powerful impression than he would have guessed. Feeling unsettled, Legroeder had a cursory breakfast in the galley before reporting to the bridge.

Fre'geel was there with Palagren. "We're going to get underway today," Fre'geel told him, looking up from the captain's console.

"So soon?" Legroeder asked in surprise.

"We can't keep drifting. We've pulled enough nav data from their library to get us going in the right general direction. How are you doing at persuading our prisoner to help us?"

Legroeder hesitated. "I've started to get to know him a little. He's not eager to go back, that's for sure. And I can't promise he won't betray us if we *do* make it to their base. And yet . . ."

"What, Rigger Legroeder?"

He scratched his jaw thoughtfully. "Well, he has no love of the Kyber, that's for sure. I believe he might actually have some sympathy for our cause."

Fre'geel's eyes gleamed. "Did he tell you this?"

Legroeder shook his head. "Not in so many words. It's something I sensed. A feeling."

"A feeling," Fre'geel echoed. He studied Legroeder for a few dozen heartbeats. "Very well, Rigger. Today we will fly with our own crew and see how we do. But afterward, you will continue in your efforts to secure Deutsch's co-operation." Fre'geel made a burring sound. "And you will report to me on your progress."

Legroeder nodded. "He was a free man taken prisoner, same as me. I think we can talk."

"Let us hope so." Fre'geel turned to the other waiting riggers. "Take your stations, then."

THE TWO ships parted in silence, in the Flux. *H'zzarrelik* fell astern of the captured pirate ship, drifting in the gently flowing current. Soon the Narseil ship looked like a toy model behind them, small and silver in the orange mists.

The Narseil ship, piloted by her secondary crew, would follow *Flechette* for a time. Later, as they drew closer to the raider base, *H'zzarrelik* would vanish into hiding in the mists of the Flux, monitoring *Flechette*'s progress as best they could with long-range instruments. If *Flechette* got into trouble, there was little the Narseil ship could do to help. *H'zzarrelik*'s mission was to await Fre'geel's team's return—or a transmission of data—and to safeguard the information already captured. Efforts to contact the nearest Narseil Navy ship for a transfer of prisoners had proved unsuccessful, so the return of *H'zzarrelik* was crucial. If *Flechette* failed to make contact or reappear, *H'zzarrelik* would slip away like a spirit in the night and carry the existing data and prisoners back to the Narseil authorities.

To say that *Flechette* and her Narseil crew were expendable would have been an extraordinary understatement.

Legroeder tried not to dwell on that, as they flew deeper into Golen Space, and farther from any possible help. Palagren was humming in the net before him, seemingly unconcerned with danger. In the keel, Ker'sell muttered darkly to himself. Neither of them had said a word to Legroeder about their thoughts on trusting Deutsch. But Legroeder could guess what they were thinking.

They flew through streamers of cloud that morphed slowly from something out of a bright, sunny afternoon to a sky full of scattered thunderstorms. They cautiously skirted the dark weather. They were still learning the ways of this ship, and didn't want to push too hard, too fast.

Still, Legroeder was relieved when they set the stabilizers and left the net to the backup crew of Narseil riggers for station-keeping.

ACCORDING TO the guard at the door, Deutsch had not emerged from his cabin since Legroeder had left. "Unless he snuck out through the ventilation system," the Narseil commando said huskily, with an unreadable expression. Humor? Legroeder wondered.

He signaled at the door. When there was no answer, he pressed the handle. The door slid open and he stepped in, blinking in the gloom. The room smelled like a sauna. "Freem'n?" The only light came from the ruby crystal in the hands of the Kyber rigger. Deutsch was sitting exactly where Legroeder had left him; he seemed not to have moved a muscle. But the crystal in his hands was glowing far more brightly than before, casting a blood-red glow over Deutsch's half-metal face.

"Freem'n?"

There was a long pause. Finally he saw a shift in the

pirate rigger's gaze—not the main eyes, but the two peripheral-vision eyes atop his cheekbones. Just behind them, the augments on his temples were flickering erratically.

The voice-speakers crackled, "Rigger Legroeder."

"Yes. Are you all right?"

"No," said Deutsch, with a series of clicks.

"Do you need help?"

For a long moment, Deutsch sat utterly still. Legroeder was wondering whether to call for medical aid when Deutsch spoke again. "How sure are you that you want to do this thing, going back to our base?"

Legroeder turned up his hands. "There are no if's about it. That's why we came."

Though Deutsch's eyes were inexpressive, something in the shape of his mouth conveyed pain. "I do not wish to go back to that life," he said finally.

"Neither do I," said Legroeder. "That's why we're going. To take some action against it."

"And . . . you hope to learn something about that ship, yes? *Impris?*"

"Yes." Legroeder hesitated. "And we have reason to believe there are people at your outpost sympathetic to our cause."

Deutsch's lips pursed. "Your commander spoke of an underground movement."

"Which we hope to contact. But regardless, we'll continue our mission." Legroeder cleared his throat. "I have to know what to tell the commander. Will you cooperate?"

Deutsch sighed. When he spoke, his voice was ponderous, as though he were deep in thought. "It's the strangest thing. I feel as though . . . for reasons I don't entirely understand . . . I may be meant to do this thing with you. I don't know why. Or how. But the feeling . . . comes from deep within."

Legroeder blinked in surprise.

"I've been giving the matter considerable thought," Deutsch continued. "And I've reached a decision."

"And that would be?"

Deutsch's breath came in a strained sigh, even as his voice reverberated from the speakers. "I hope it's not a foolish one. But I will help you get to the outpost. And after that, I'll . . . well, I'm not sure, exactly. Perhaps I can help you gain your information."

Legroeder stared at him in amazement. "What made you change your mind?"

"Don't ask."

Legroeder raised his eyebrows.

"Don't ask," repeated the rigger, his temples pulsing with light.

"I *have* to ask. We have to know that we can trust you."

Deutsch breathed in and out a few times. "Let's just say . . . I think it is intended. And besides—" his facial muscles twitched "—I don't want to be returned as a prisoner. If you win, I want to be on your side. And if you don't—I'd just as soon get it over with. They can smoke us all."

Legroeder scowled as he inclined his head in acknowledgment.

LEGROEDER AND the Narseil kept a close eye on Deutsch in the following days. Legroeder knew that if anyone was going to notice any deceptiveness or backsliding, it had better be him. Deutsch's support seemed genuine, as he guided the riggers in the net—not enthusiastic, perhaps, but determined. While Legroeder wondered at the inner forces that had caused Deutsch to agree to cooperate, the result seemed to be decisive.

In the ensuing days, Legroeder spent considerable time in conversation with the pirate rigger, and began to feel that he was gaining some sense of the man. Deutsch was somber, almost fatalistic in his determination to lead the ship back to port; he somehow looked as if his years of captivity were a leaden weight on his shoulders. Nevertheless, Legroeder had the oddest feeling that Deutsch was a man who, under other circumstances, would probably laugh a good deal. Legroeder found himself wanting to hear Deutsch laugh.

With input from Deutsch on what to expect when they reached Outpost Ivan, the Narseil commander and crew began to refine the plans for their arrival. According to Deutsch, one thing in their favor—if their goal was to get in, get information, and get out—was the modular design of the Kyber docks. It was at least theoretically possible to take control of an isolated docking center and hold it—if they were lucky, without tripping system-wide alarms—while they did their spying and tried to contact the Kyber underground. The hope was for a nonviolent contact, but it was a modest hope. The Narseil commando teams were already in full-scale rehearsal for a docking-port capture, which was how they would proceed if they hadn't made friendly contact prior to docking. Contingency plans were also being shaped up for Legroeder's role in the event the Narseil were captured.

In the net, the riggers continued flying in formation with *H'zzarrelik*. At times, the clouds turned an eerie green, like a sky ripe for tornadoes. Though no whirlwinds actually appeared, Legroeder was constantly aware that this region of the Flux could contain many surprises. When the image changed to a nighttime scene, as it did from time to time, he could just discern the ghostly Wall of the Barrier Nebula towering over them. They were venturing ever deeper into the forbidden realms of Golen Space, farther than he had ever gone in this direction.

He found himself thinking of Maris, and wondering if she was still alive. Had either one of them, in the end, really escaped? It was a sobering thought, and he flew for hours after that in a very dark frame of mind.

THE NARSEIL commander paced back and forth in the briefing room as Palagren and Cantha reported privately on their progress so far. Fre'geel was burning to hear what his own people thought of the work of the two humans together. He trusted Legroeder—mostly, anyway—but had a suspicion that the human might be prone, when in doubt, to presenting an overly optimistic view of his own work. And there had to be *some* doubt about Deutsch, no matter how cooperative he appeared.

Palagren expressed cautious optimism about the performance of the joint rigger crew.

"Nothing to suggest that Deutsch is hiding anything from you?" Fre'geel asked.

"Well, he's not shown us the whole of the route to the outpost. But that would be difficult to do, anyway. He seems to be feeling his way through." Palagren stroked the side of his head with a long fingertip. "I believe him when he says that the Flux is highly changeable throughout the area, and the way in is a little different each time."

Fre'geel blew air through his gills. He resisted an urge to scratch the neck-sail behind his head. Recently out of the gel bandage, his neck-sail was still healing, and it itched ferociously. The makeshift mist-chambers they'd set up on the pirate ship were no substitute for proper Narseil pools. Fre'geel envied the crew still aboard *H'zzarrelik*. He turned to Cantha. "What's your view?"

Cantha, as a rigger-science researcher who was not himself a rigger, had a more objective if less intimate view of what was going on in the net and the Flux, and of what they might expect as they approached their perilous destination. "It appears to me," Cantha said, "that Rigger Deutsch is performing well with our crew. The question is whether he's doing so because he's really decided to join us, or because he's hoping to earn a bonus for turning us all in the moment we arrive."

Which of course was precisely what worried Fre'geel. How could they know whether to trust this man? There were myriad justifications for believing him—he was a captive like Legroeder, he hated the pirates, there could be a link between his augments and the underground, and so on—but what it really came down to in the end was deciding whether or not to trust him. Fre'geel turned back to Palagren. "Could he hide it from you in the net, if he were planning to betray us in the end?"

Palagren answered carefully. "If he were like Legroeder, I would say no. Legroeder has a clearly defined personality, which as far as I can tell has not been greatly altered by his augments. But with Deutsch—who knows? He's been augmented for a long time. His augments may be able to conceal what his natural personality could not."

"That sounds more like blind trust than I care to risk our mission on," Fre'geel said, with some edge in his voice. He turned to see Ker'sell joining them. "What do you think about it?"

Ker'sell didn't surprise him. "I think that he's a human on a Narseil mission, and we can trust him to act like a human." The blandness in Ker'sell's voice belied the distrust they knew he felt—even toward Legroeder, whom he'd had plenty of time to get to know.

"Meaning what?" said Fre'geel.

"Meaning, as far as I'm concerned, there's no *telling* what he'll do," answered the dour rigger.

Palagren's narrow eyes winked shut momentarily. "I see no choice, really. We have to trust Legroeder to be attuned to the possibility of betrayal by Deutsch. If he doesn't detect it, we probably won't, either."

"And that's the real question, isn't it?" Fre'geel asked. "Can we trust Legroeder to observe accurately?"

"Aren't we already trusting him with more than that?" asked Cantha. "If things go wrong, we're practically counting on him to take over the mission for us. I'm sure he's not eager for that to happen. But he accurately spotted the Kyber attack coming before any of us had a clue. And his instincts got us out of trouble in the fight. So shouldn't we trust him to think clearly now?"

Fre'geel puffed his gills and stared off into space for a long time, leaving the question unanswered.

WHEN DEUTSCH reported that they were nearing the general region of the outpost, they signaled farewell to *H'zzarrelik* and watched the Narseil ship slip out of sight behind them. *H'zzarrelik* had sophisticated Narseil tracking equipment, so there was some chance that her crew would know where *Flechette* was, long after the converse was no longer true. While *Flechette* approached the raider outpost, *H'zzarrelik* would be listening—silently, like a sub at the bottom of the sea.

The raider ship, under Deutsch's guidance, flew through a series of gray clouds—and for a time, something like rain came through the air in sleeting gusts. They emerged to find themselves winding along an ocean coastline, at the altitude of a small airplane. Deutsch flew in the lead position at the bow, threading them this way and that along the intricate filigrees of coastline, occasionally obscured by wisps of cloud. *Without my old crew, the whole sense of the place is different,* he said. *I have to feel my way into it.* But a few minutes later, he added, *I think I've found it. I'm looking for an updraft now.*

To look, Legroeder thought, is to find. Soon they were rising through a skyscape of mountain-shaped clouds that gradually stretched out in flattened angles until they looked like outstretched arms of coral. When they finally topped the clouds, they entered a sky filled with streamers of white sunlight, like an artist's vision of Heaven.

There, said Deutsch.

Where? Where's the entrance?

Deutsch almost managed a chuckle. *Think of this as cam-ouflage over the door. You'll see, as we go through.*

The sun bloomed into a sinking, crimson orb, as Deutsch nosed the ship down again. The sky darkened.

We still okay? Legroeder asked.

More than okay. We're going through the door.

The sun gradually diffused to a burnt, reddish-orange, subterranean glow, ominous against the darkness. The change took Legroeder's breath away, and he glanced at Palagren, who was stirring with obvious unease. *We are close now,* said Deutsch.

Legroeder's heart began to pound.

They flew into the glow, with darkness above and darkness below. Legroeder found it comforting to imagine he was gazing through a thick brown beer bottle into a bright candle flame. But as he thought of the danger ahead, the vision turned to a more perilous one, the fire of a smoldering volcano.

Very close, said Deutsch. *Now.* He nosed the ship into a layer of almost impenetrable darkness. Palagren muttered worriedly, and Legroeder wondered if he should intervene. But to do what? He waited breathlessly, in near darkness. Only tiny, gleaming position markers at the edges of the net interrupted the night. *Almost there,* said Deutsch.

And then Legroeder saw it: the burnt-orange glow reappearing from the gloom, but as a series of vertical striations. He had trouble interpreting the perspective: one moment it was a background of dying-fire light, with black columns before it; the next it was columns of living fire, standing watch over passages of darkness; then, with a disconcerting reversal, it was again pillars of darkness guarding passages into great depths of fire.

Are those actual openings in the Flux? Palagren asked softly.

Indeed, said Deutsch.

It's very strange, whispered Legroeder. *Is it a natural formation? Or is it . . . manmade?* He'd seen navigational buoys in the Flux, but never anything as elaborate as this.

A little of both, said Deutsch. *Structure imposed on natural features. You'll see it better soon. Instruct your com operator to be ready to send the authorization code I gave him.*

Legroeder passed on the message to Cantha, with growing trepidation. They were approaching a critical moment, and Fre'geel would likely have to make a split-second decision, depending upon the response to their transmission. Would the authorization code get them the clearance they needed, or would it get them blown to kingdom come? Would the underground pick up on it? The message would contain a reference to an encounter with the Narseil navy.

If the underground was monitoring arrivals, that ought to alert them. But even so, there would be little time for response.

Freem'n, Legroeder said sharply, *where exactly are we now? Have we reached the outer perimeter?* In the last few moments, the structure ahead had brightened until it seemed to vibrate almost to the point of inducing vertigo.

Reaching it now, said Deutsch. *Transmit the contact and ident code.*

Fre'geel acknowledged.

Any answer?

Autoresponse only, reported Cantha.

All right. I'm taking us toward one of the outer docks for damaged-ship arrivals, Deutsch said.

I don't see *any docks,* said Legroeder.

Then watch carefully, if you want to see how this works.

Legroeder grunted. In the keel and top gun, the two Narseil were stirring anxiously. Now was the time when any reasonable scenario would have them bringing the ship out of the Flux into normal-space. Deutsch had told them it wouldn't happen that way, but hearing it described wasn't the same as experiencing it.

As they moved inward toward the surreal column-structures, a few tiny blips of traffic became visible in the distance. Deutsch steered them toward the extreme left opening between dark pillars. Legroeder's augments were abuzz, seething with interpretations of what he was seeing. As their destination grew before them like some glowing, mythical gateway, he finally realized that those columns were not just channel markers; they were physical foundations of the outpost, anchored right in the Flux.

We are *docking in the Flux,* he whispered.

I told you that.

Yes, but . . . He hadn't quite believed it. *Is the whole damn* city *embedded in the Flux?*

It was one thing to have vessels floating in the Flux, but he couldn't imagine the power it would take, and the coordination of riggers, to maintain a city in the Flux. It was inconceivable.

Now you understand, said Deutsch.

I don't understand anything, Legroeder said. *How—?*

There are maintainers who keep it anchored. Like riggers . . . but . . . don't worry, they won't notice us. Deutsch banked farther to the left. *Time to send the second set of codes.*

Cantha reported the codes sent.

Legroeder saw the glint of other ships moving past the strange structures. He worried for a moment about being seen—but they were flying a raider ship, with a pirate rigger in the lead. There were still plenty of ways for them to die; but probably they would be okay on the approach, if the codes passed muster. *(Are you following all this?)* he asked his implants.

□ *We are recording. We are also initializing routines for contact and impersonation.* □

(Thinking ahead. Good.)

The structure grew until it displayed a hundred entry points to a strange, fabulous city, each entry point marked by a set of pillars glowing a pumpkin orange. At the left edge, the pattern was more distended, with wider dark patches in between. The orange gates there were disconnected from the larger structure. That was where captured ships, and damaged ships, came in—ships that might, for example, explode without warning. Deutsch pointed to the last gate on the left. *That's where we're going.* He hesitated visibly, then glanced back at his rigger-mates. *Gentlemen, if you haven't heard yet from your underground, this might be a good time for your commander to set his alternate plans in motion.*

Legroeder swallowed hard as Palagren passed the word.

The entire Flux seemed to vibrate around the net as they approached the fiery pillars marking the last dock. Deutsch called for one last set of codes to be sent—and then made a com-call directly from the net. *This is Freem'n Deutsch,*

*lead rigger and acting commander of Flechette, requesting
clearance to dock.*

Legroeder held his breath.

The pillar of light somehow softened, and opened; and
within it, Legroeder could see a tunnel of indeterminate dimensions, and . . . a docking cradle. *I don't believe it,* he
whispered. He and the Narseil silently withdrew to the innermost part of the net, making themselves as inconspicuous
as possible.

The ship was soon surrounded by a hazy orange glow,
as if they had floated into the interior of a wood-burning
stove. Deutsch guided them smoothly into the docking cradle, peering one way and another as snakelike arms of the
cradle emerged to grapple the ship. Finally he said softly,
Time to shut down the net.

Palagren spoke to the commander, and the order came.

The net darkened, and Legroeder rubbed his eyes as he
climbed out of the rigger-station. He gazed around the
bridge, his heart pounding so loudly he could scarcely hear
what was being said around him. They were now squarely
in the grip of the pirate empire, and the next few minutes
could determine whether they would succeed or fail.

The Narseil commandos were already on the move.

Chapter 20

RAID!

THE RIGGERS stayed on the bridge, watching on monitors
as two commando groups deployed, in full armor. The first
group marshaled in the regular airlock, to confront the Kyber docking crew. The second team was already outside the

hull of the ship, splitting up to make their way to the station's fore and aft emergency access ports.

Deutsch had his implants connected to the bridge console and was doing something that none of them could follow— including Legroeder, who was connected right beside him. Deutsch was linking somehow to the intelnet on the station, but all Legroeder could pick up was flashes of input—a flicker of bitter-red and sour-orange, then a quick, sweet taste of lemon. He didn't know what it meant and didn't dare interrupt Deutsch to ask.

Deutsch turned to Fre'geel. "There are thirty-seven crewmen stationed on the docks. I have informed the intelnet that *Flechette* has battle damage, and only a part of its crew is intact. I have advised we are having difficulty with the airlock and require assistance. That may give you the diversion you need. I will now attempt to interrupt the comlink to the main outpost."

"Very well," said Fre'geel. He waited until Deutsch nodded again, then transmitted the go-ahead to the number-two commando group. In the outside monitors, the Narseil warriors were barely visible, moving along the outer pressure hull of the docking bay in camouflage armor. In the Flux they appeared as little more than momentary, shimmering distortions in the hazy glow. With luck, any Kyber watching from inside the station would miss their movement altogether.

In another monitor, the first group was gathered around the airlock hatch. Presumably, the docking crew working to open the hatch were expecting *Flechette*'s raider crew, injured and weakened—not Narseil commandos.

Fre'geel waited until group two reported ready to begin their breach of the portals. He asked Cantha one last time if there was any signal from the underground. When Cantha answered in the negative, Fre'geel called to the commando groups: *"Go."*

The main airlock ballooned open. Group one moved like lightning, overpowering the surprised docking crew. The first puffs of neural gas left the Kyber crumpled outside the airlock, before any alarm could be sounded. Group one flew into the station in all directions, neural gas billowing ahead of them. By this time, group two had entered the station at both emergency portals and were fanning out, pouring gas into other compartments.

Legroeder's stomach knotted as he waited. Once the commando teams were in the station, direct transmissions were cut off. Would they be able to subdue the entire raider crew before a cry for help went out?

Legroeder glanced at Deutsch, who was immersed in the comlink. Some part of Deutsch was aware of his glance, because he gestured urgently to Legroeder to join him in the link. Complying, Legroeder found himself at the outer fringes of the docking station's local net. He waited while Deutsch connected to security monitors inside the station. Seconds later, the interior view blossomed around him.

At first glance, it was chaos. Narseil commandos raced through the corridors past the crumpled figures of unconscious Kyber crewmen. A handful of Kyber, more cyborg than human, were still on their feet, fleeing or hiding. Several were shooting back. They were soon brought down by gas or neutraser fire—but not before a Narseil went down.

The commandos moved swiftly to secure the com stations. Within the intelnet, Deutsch was working to keep communications with the main outpost cut off. Because an abrupt failure was as likely to attract attention as an alarm, Deutsch was trying to make it appear a momentary glitch, an accidental triggering of safety firewalls. Legroeder's job was to make sure Deutsch did his—as if he could do anything about it, anyway.

By the time Deutsch verified that the com "glitch" was working as intended, the commando action was over. One Narseil was wounded, two pirates were dead and two wounded, and the rest were unconscious. Legroeder dropped out of the comlink to report to Fre'geel, just as word was coming back through the airlock: *The docking station is ours.*

Fre'geel's face was a study in piercing concentration, his

dark Narseil features taut, his vertical eyes flicking this way and that, the gills under his neck pulsing rapidly. He voiced the question everyone was thinking. "Any sign we were detected from beyond the station?"

"I don't believe so," answered Deutsch. "It all looked isolated from here."

"How long do we have?"

"Impossible to be sure. Minutes? An hour or two, maybe? Probably no more."

Fre'geel bobbed his head. "And in your estimation, can you run your intelnet search from here?" His glance included Legroeder in the question, but they all knew who was going to answer.

Deutsch's luminous glass gaze seemed to sweep the bridge. "Better bandwidth from on board the station. And from there, we can use the sweeping tools and storage nodes."

"Go, then. Both of you. At once!"

Legroeder and Deutsch hurried from the bridge.

LEGROEDER'S HEART was thumping like a drum as he raced through the station, his breath rasping steamily in his face-mask. The air was probably clear of gas now, but no one was taking chances. All around them Narseil commandos were busy pulling unconscious and semi-conscious pirate captives out of the corridors. Deutsch led him to a mainte-nance control center, where a half-circle of consoles sat glowing. Deutsch floated before them, studying the controls. "I think this will do it," he said in a metallic whisper. "It should enable access to the intelnet. If we can keep from tripping any alarms . . ."

Legroeder slid into a seat on Deutsch's right. Glancing at an external monitor, he saw a startling image: a great, luminous city stretched out into darkness, into the Flux—with crossmembers and pillars reaching both down and up, and fading away where they appeared to extend out of this layer of the Flux altogether. He felt the implants buzzing with interest as a dozen questions leaped into his thoughts; but there was no time now.

"Yah," Deutsch grunted. He unfolded a pair of shiny extensions from the console and jacked them into metal plates on his chest. "Let's go," he said, his amplified voice turned down to a mutter. "If you can't use these arms, see what else there is."

Legroeder found a headset and adjusted it, as Deutsch was setting up a channel to Cantha, back on *Flechette*. Cantha would be recording everything.

Legroeder took a deep breath and focused his thoughts downward into the link. He entered the station's local data matrix, a dark place full of yelling voices and colored, smoky lighting. The voices were not other users, he realized after a moment, but helper-engines within the system. Banks of flickering strobes pulsed through the steaming murk, churning up a stink of oil and plastic and ozone. They were somewhere in the data sections used by station maintenance. All around him were vague mechanical shapes, connections full of repair specs and technical detail.

(Still receiving?) Legroeder murmured back to Cantha, and received a single-bit acknowledgment in reply.

He wondered if there would be anything useful here in the local section. Up one level, he heard music: a thrumming bass rhythm. Enviro controls? Yes—and what else?

They needed to get their bearings quickly, and move into more useful areas of the intelnet. There was still hope that they could discover a link to the underground; but failing that, their job was to gather strategically meaningful information and get the hell out.

Legroeder sensed Deutsch moving through the matrix like a monkey through a set of climbing bars, graceful and quick, never lingering. With practiced speed and the power of his augmentation, Deutsch was conducting a search of the local node, far more efficiently than Legroeder could have. He didn't linger long; apparently he didn't regard much of it as relevant to their goals. Legroeder followed him into what appeared to be a technical library connection, filled with datastores like tiny, spinning whirlwinds. There was no time to comprehend the material; but as they passed, Legroeder tried to judge by smell and feel, and spun copies of some of them down the line to Cantha, in case there was something useful buried in them.

But where was the important stuff? It wasn't as if data on the defenses of the raider outpost, or on *Impris*, or anything that might lead them to an underground movement, would be laid out for casual perusal.

(We're not finding the tactical and strategic info that Fre'geel wants,) Deutsch said. *(We should get out of here and make the jump to the main intelnet.)*

(All right,) Legroeder answered. He whispered their intentions back to Cantha.

Deutsch was already analyzing the severed links to the city, trying to figure out which might safely be restored. *(Legroeder, you stick out like a sore thumb. Until you can find a way to blend in, you'd better let me handle the approaches.)*

Blend in? Legroeder thought. Fat chance of that.

▫ *We are preparing your camouflage now,* ▫ the implants informed him, holding up his false-ID information with a quick flicker for his approval.

He glanced at it and waved it away. *(Fine, fine . . .)*

Deutsch was unraveling some of the knots he had tied in the links to the main outpost. He tested carefully, leaving as much of the "glitch" in place as he could. Finally he opened a single channel, under the cloak of technical maintenance. They were going to try to slip into the main intelnet using the technical library connection as a gateway. Legroeder felt a sudden movement, like a swiftly flowing current.

(We're passing through the comlink now. Stay close . . .)

Deutsch was following the link like an underground spring, delving toward its roots. It was like slipping down a silver thread into an utterly different world . . .

* * *

DEUTSCH FELT himself driven by an increasing sense of urgency. *(Keep moving, Legroeder!)* He wondered if he was losing his mind, even to be attempting this. Something more than just practical expediency was driving him onward, some sense that this was what he was supposed to be doing. But why? To aid Legroeder and the Narseil in some quixotic blow for freedom? Partly that, perhaps. But there were also those jangling echoes of voices at work in his mind, almost inseparable from his own subconscious. They made him feel as if *he* were, somehow, connected to the Kyber underground.

Ridiculous. But he couldn't deny *wishing* that such a thing could be.

He cast the thought aside. He needed full alertness to get through what lay ahead.

They were in the intelnet of the main outpost now, somewhere deep in the technical libraries. The stream was carrying them through musty-smelling caverns of data, where Legroeder would certainly have gotten lost on his own, and even Deutsch could easily enough have done so. He'd caught Legroeder's mental image of a subterranean stream, exploring the roots of a mountain range, and it was true enough. They were flowing through deep passageways, sniffing and tasting the waters as they went. Deutsch wasn't quite sure where they were going, but he trusted his instincts as he took them from the technical library into the general stacks.

They were no longer alone in the network; others were moving through the datastores on business of their own. None took note of them, and Deutsch did his best to veer quietly away from any that drew too close. He scanned the branch indices: . . . *maintenance, personnel, planning, production, shipping* . . . But what about the ones they really wanted, such as *armament, fleet operations, chains of command* . . . ?

But *were* those the ones he really wanted?

Move on, move on. Somewhere in here, he felt sure, he

would find better information, maybe even a thread leading to the rumored Kyber underground . . .

LEGROEDER STRUGGLED to cope with the massive flow of information.

□ *We are sorting . . . categorizing . . . setting priorities . . .* □

Yes, but what about his own control? They were flying past vast tracts of information, and he was caught between the risk of detection and the danger of missing data useful to the Narseil.

Deutsch seemed to be steering them upward through the layers, moving through one library after another. Legroeder felt a sudden fear that Deutsch was leading him straight into the hands of the enemy, or at least taking him in so deep he could never hope to get out by himself.

As if sensing his unease, Deutsch spoke, softly. *(Are you getting a look here? Some of this might be worth a scan.)*

Legroeder moved in for a closer inspection. Deutsch had found stacks of archived planning sessions; Legroeder paused for a microsecond, perusing them. *(Look at all this talk about expanding the settlement.)* He thumbed and riffled a moment. *(More like building a goddamn empire.)*

(True enough . . .)

Legroeder zipped up a packet and sent it downlink to Cantha.

(Let's keep moving,) said Deutsch.

The earlier image persisted: they were moving upward through the roots of the mountains, searching for sunlight. Shadowy shapes were all around, the repositories of data. But far above were splinters of light that suggested change. Maybe more than change, maybe access to the indices that would let Deutsch run his sweeps. Legroeder held his breath, trying to remain inconspicuous.

There was a sudden flash of light—and then a series of light beams fanning past. Before he could react, Legroeder felt a breathless rush, as though he'd taken a deep lungful of oxygen. He realized dizzily that he had just absorbed a burst of data; his augments were madly trying to interpret.

(Sweep working . . . we're getting somewhere now,) Deutsch said.

More and more splinters of light were breaking through the ceiling. Deutsch's sweep was darting among them. But Legroeder's own implants were signaling for his attention: a sharp aroma of peppermint stung his senses until he allowed a window to open . . .

▫ *Tracking a thread . . . multiple references to* Impris *found . . .* ▫

(Impris?) Legroeder echoed. *(Freem'n, wait—!)*

DEUTSCH WAS a beat behind Legroeder in recognizing the reference. He turned in surprise. *(What's that about Impris?)* He caught the data streaming from Legroeder's implants. *(Yes, I see it now. How did I miss that?)*

He quickly ran his sweeps up the splinter of light that Legroeder had found, and saw a thread that electrified him. *(Take a look at this, Legroeder! It's not just Impris. Do you remember asking me about a Kyber underground? Here it is! In the same stream!)*

(Not really,) said Legroeder.

(It's right here.) This was perfect, Deutsch thought; it seemed too good to be true.

And usually, he realized an instant after he started up the thread, when something seemed too good to be true . . .

KYBER UNDERGROUND? And *Impris* in the same thread? Legroeder sent a flash summary back to Cantha and flew up the thread after Deutsch.

A fraction of a second later, it occurred to him that perhaps there could be more to this than met the eye. Why would a connection to these two things be linked? Was the underground concerned with *Impris*? Or was it a . . .

A new sound came up suddenly in the back of his head— a wiry, nervous sound like a buzz underwater. It came first from one direction, then another, and suddenly grew to a hollow gonging that filled the space all around them. *(What the hell is that?)*

(It's an alarm,) Deutsch answered. *(We may have tripped something. We'd better back off. Fast.)*

Legroeder cursed and hurried after the ghostly, retreating Deutsch. He felt a sudden, terrible suspicion. Had Deutsch triggered the alarm on purpose? Was this all a setup?

Deutsch's voice echoed, *(If we don't get out of here, they'll be down on us in no time.)* Deutsch peered back at him. *(What's wrong?)*

For a heartbeat, Legroeder was frozen with doubt and indecision. Could he trust Deutsch, or should he flee? But where could he—?

(Legroeder, MOVE!)

That snapped him out of it. *(Coming!)* Legroeder fired himself down the thread after Deutsch—his friend, yes?— trying to outrun the buzz of the alarm. Whatever his doubts or fears, they were in this together.

Endless picoseconds later, they were back in the smoky room where they had started, in the docking station's intelnet subsystem. It still smelled oily and metallic, but the bass rhythm was more subdued now, and overlying it was a kind of harmonica sound. A persistent and growing harmonica sound. It made Legroeder increasingly uneasy. *(Freem'n, did we do that? I've got a bad feeling—)*

He shut up when he realized that Deutsch was already scanning all connections into and out of the smoke-filled room. Legroeder could see little rays of light shooting this way and that through the data-matrix, as Deutsch unleashed his inner search machines, trying to localize the alarm. Trying to stay out of Deutsch's way, Legroeder conferred with his implants.

▫ We have stored data to 13% of our capacity, which we are currently analyzing. We believe the sounds you have identified are indeed alarm transmissions, possibly with autonomic blocking attachments. There may be danger. We recommend attending to your personal safety. ▫

(Meaning what? Should I get out of the intelnet?)

□ *Quickly, if possible.* □

Legroeder hissed his breath out into the sudden chill of the data-matrix. Deutsch sensed it and turned. *(What is it?)*

(My implants are telling me to get the hell out. Is there a security squad on the way?)

Deutsch's voice seemed seared by a dark pain. *(I think there might be. I don't know that we can do anything about it. You'd better pull out and warn the others.)*

Legroeder blinked hard. *(Okay,)* he whispered.

So close, he thought. So goddamned close. And now . . .

He pulled out of the intelnet.

"HE'S OUT!" called a Narseil voice.

Fre'geel strode across the room, his face half covered by a transparent breathing mask. "What have you found? There are alarms going off all over! Did that pirate set them off?"

Legroeder gulped air. He felt as if he'd just come out of a cocoon. "Not on purpose. Everything I got went out to Cantha. I got—I'm not sure what all, but—" He closed his eyes for a moment and saw a streaking flash of emerald: an enormous amount of data. But any of it useful?

"Should I tell Cantha to transmit?" Fre'geel demanded.

Breathless, Legroeder tried to think. It might be their last chance to get a message out to *H'zzarrelik*, and at that they would have to be very lucky. But if they did transmit, it would telegraph their presence and their intentions to the entire Kyber defense—if they weren't already known. That would not only endanger them, but would also betray the presence of *H'zzarrelik*, hiding out in the Flux.

"Should we transmit?" Fre'geel asked, his voice suddenly iron. His hand, much larger than Legroeder remembered it, was reaching out as though to seize Legroeder by the throat. "Did we get information worth transmitting?"

Meaning, if they had, this was the time to make themselves expendable. But if not, their next best hope was . . .

Legroeder shook his head, his stomach knotting. "I don't think so. We were just on the verge. *Dammit.*"

"The verge of what, Rigger?"

Legroeder peered anxiously up at the Narseil commander. "Just before we tripped the alarm, we'd found a thread connected to the Kyber underground. There were also references to *Impris*. It could have been a trap, I suppose—but why? Unless there really is an underground out there."

Fre'geel's expression stopped him. He was squinting in the odd sort of way only a Narseil could squint, working at a decision. An army of Kyber troops was about to descend on them. But if they sent what they had, or boarded the ship and tried to flee . . .

No. Legroeder didn't want to die for the sake of a bunch of planning commission reports. "I think there's still a chance we could get what we came for. *Impris*. Maybe contacts that could make a difference if . . ." *If* they could hook up with a Kyber underground. But as captives?

"Are you prepared to take on your role, then?" Fre'geel said with a sharp glance upward. Footsteps could be heard through the ceiling. Fast and hard. *"Rigger Legroeder—"*

Legroeder could barely draw a breath; the thought filled him with dread. Yes, he said, then realized it hadn't come out. He cleared his throat. "Yes."

Fre'geel's gaze snapped around to check the positions of his people, then back to Legroeder. "Very well. Begin your role now. And Rigger Legroeder, I hardly need to say—"

"Yes."

"This radically alters the mission. I will do what I can to protect my people. But you must leave us to whatever happens. The next step is yours." The Narseil's gaze held him like a steel pin. "Deutsch. Will he help you?"

"I think so," Legroeder said softly. He picked up his headset and put it back on. "Dear God, I hope so." And with great deliberation he turned away from Fre'geel.

FRE'GEEL WATCHED with terrible unease as Legroeder returned to the intelnet connection. He had just dropped an enormous responsibility on Legroeder's shoulders. Would the human botch the job and bring the entire mission to an end? Would the pirate rigger betray them all?

It was out of the Narseil's hands now.

Fre'geel turned, touching his com-implant. "Cantha," he said, calling to *Flechette*.

"Here," said Cantha.

"Inform the crew to prepare for boarding and capture. Do not resist. We have turned primary control of the mission over to Rigger Legroeder. Do you understand?"

"Yes," said Cantha, and Fre'geel knew that in that simple word were many emotions that Cantha would not reveal. The officer had developed a great fondness for the human, and was well aware of the risks. "Will there be a transmission to *H'zzarrelik*?"

"No," said Fre'geel. "Store what you can in your augments. Erase the rest." Risk all that they had gained so far, in hopes of gaining more later.

"Understood," said Cantha.

Fre'geel broke the connection. The Kyber troops were in the corridors outside. His voice tightened involuntarily he called to his crew of commandos, "Lower your weapons and prepare to surrender!"

FRE'GEEL'S VOICE echoed in Legroeder's thoughts even after he was immersed in the net. *The next step is yours . . .*

In the data-matrix, everything was so confused that he had trouble even finding Deutsch. Before, the station had been a tech shop stinking of oil and smoke; now there were jets of steam everywhere, and lights flashing behind the billowing clouds of mist. *(Freem'n!)* he called, need overcoming caution.

There was no direct answer from Deutsch, but he heard a *tap tap tap* somewhere on the other side of the dataspace, beyond the clouds of steam. He tried to move that way, and called out again, but there was still no answer from Deutsch. *Tap tap tap.*

(Freem'n?)

A blast of steam shot out in front of him, sending him staggering backward. He cursed, steadying himself. It felt so real, he almost forgot it was just a rush of data, probably a security-sweep protocol. He hesitated, crouching, then launched himself past the dissipating billow, searching for Deutsch. (*Freem'n, where are you?*)

He passed by several darkened pillars. The whole chamber looked different now, and yet was recognizably the same. He came upon a collection of large steel drums, grimy and covered with illegible warning signs. God knew what was in them, or what they represented. He squinted and tried in vain to read one of the inscriptions. As he straightened and moved on, he suddenly saw Deutsch. The man was sitting on a crate, on the far side of the collection, leaning back against one of the drums.

Legroeder hurried to him.

Tap tap tap.

The sound was coming from Deutsch. It was his metal arm, shorn of the garment that had covered it, twitching and vibrating as if trying to move, stuck in a half-extended position. At first Legroeder thought it was tapping against the drum; then he realized that it was the arm jerking against itself in some kind of internal jam.

(*Freem'n, do you need help?*)

Deutsch seemed to gaze directly at Legroeder, but showed no sign of recognition, or any awareness at all. His eyes glowed like tiny light bulbs behind dusty, dark-colored glass.

Jesus, Legroeder thought.

What the hell could have happened?

The implants stirred.

◻ *Likelihood: he may be trapped in an electrocution-web matrix. Any attempt to free him could result in injury to him or to you.* ◻

(*I can't just leave him here. How will he get free?*)

◻ *Likelihood: he will be freed when he is freed. Likelihood: whatever intelnet agent detected and trapped him will release him again when it chooses. There is probably nothing you can do.* ◻

Legroeder circled around, studying Deutsch from various angles. (*Freem'n, if you can hear me—if I knew how to free you, I would. If you can speak, now is the time.)*

Deutsch, unblinking, appeared to drool.

Legroeder made his decision grimly. *(I have to go ahead with the job, then—as we'd planned, in case of problems.)* He hesitated, afraid to say too much. He started to turn, then swung back. *(I'm sorry I doubted you for a moment back there, Freem'n. If I can find a way to help you—inside the intelnet or out—)* He ran out of words. What more could he say?

With a final wave, he rose on the clouds of steam and looked for a place to hide himself while he sorted out what to do next.

THE PLAN, at this point, was of necessity vague. But he could feel, welling up through the augments, a series of datapacks intended to help him.

◻ *We have prepared all the elements of a working ID for you. Are you ready to assume your new identity?* ◻

(As ready as I'll ever be. Do you think it will work?)

◻ *We analyzed the situation while you were exploring. Recommended action: create the impression that you set off the alarm against the Narseil. We can plant tracking indicators in the intelnet to convey this. Shall we do so now?* ◻

He swallowed hard. It was one of the options in the plan—but it was difficult. *(All right.)*

◻ *Please stand by. We will attempt to establish your ID in the system.* ◻

Legroeder held his breath, as a flower of light blossomed out from where he stood and rose into the upper layers of the intelnet interface. Its shoot vanished into the mists like a beanstalk.

A moment passed. There were flickerings of light at the top of his vision—the implants at work in his skull, doing whatever the hell they were doing. He felt a sudden blip between his eyes, and the space around him seemed to brighten suddenly, as though a dimmer switch had been nudged up.

□ *ID established.* □

□ *Attempting to place tracking records. One moment . . .* □

He waited anxiously, as a pattern of streaks shot up and out, twinkling as it spun a spiderweb path through the surrounding matrix. An instant later, it all came back, like a holo in reverse.

□ *Done.* □

He felt a chill up his spine. *(What now?)*

□ *For your own protection, you may wish to inspect your physical surroundings.* □

Physical surroundings. Christ. Legroeder started to back out of the intelnet, then realized he could check from here. A series of windows opened around him like shutters: monitors showing the room he was sitting in and the surrounding corridors.

Full of raider commandos.

Full of Narseil with their hands clasped awkwardly behind their heads. Their face masks had been removed.

And seated at the console, two motionless figures. He recognized Deutsch first, then himself. He had nearly forgotten what he looked like, with his flaring, umbrella-cut grey hair.

Surrounded by the enemy.

□ *Reminder: you have an ID now. You are a member of this society.* □

There was a brief flash of images. When it was over, he knew that according to his ID, he was a raider being transferred to this outpost, by way of having served as a spy on the Narseil ship. It should not be surprising if he had trouble finding his way around the station.

He drew a breath and pulled out of the intelnet. He found four cyborg commandos aiming laser weapons at him. Several others were flashing bright handlight beams around; all but the emergency illumination had been cut off. Beside him, Deutsch sat motionless as a statue, still plugged in. A raider gestured sharply. Legroeder raised his hands and lifted the com-helmet from his head. He glanced around, moving only his eyes. Fre'geel and several other Narseil were being held on the other side of the room. They were watching him closely.

An amplified baritone voice said, "Did you sound the alarm?"

It took him a moment, squinting through the shifting beams of light, to find the raider who had spoken—to make sure he was the one being addressed. He started to answer, then simply nodded, swallowing his words. His gaze drifted back to the Narseil. Some of them knew the role he was to play, but not all of them. Would they believe he'd betrayed them? It was necessary, to be convincing. His face burned as he forced himself to speak. "Yes. I set off the alarm. Along with him." He nudged Deutsch.

"You'll come with us, then," said the raider. "What's wrong with him?" He pointed his weapon at Deutsch.

"He—" Legroeder's voice caught as he tried to formulate an answer "—he got caught in a system loop, trying to help me get the alarm out. He . . . needs to be released. I don't know how." Legroeder hesitated, looking away from his crewmates as he uttered the words of betrayal. "I . . . was planted with the Narseil. Undercover. I'm from another outpost."

"Is that so?" The Kyber made a squawking sound and stepped up to slap his palm to a connector on the console. A second later, Deutsch slumped forward. A pair of guards lifted him effortlessly and carried him from the room. "We'll see to him," said the lead Kyber to Legroeder. "You come with me." He turned and made a sound like a grate opening. The other guards barked commands and raised their weapons—and for a terrible moment, Legroeder thought they were going to kill his friends on the spot. To his relief, they began herding the Narseil from the room.

Legroeder was escorted separately. Out in the corridor, he was pushed to the right, away from the Narseil. He felt a lump in his throat as he turned his back on his shipmates.

□ *It is part of the plan,* □ said a voice in his head.

(Yeah,) he muttered, and after that, the implants were silent.

The raider soldiers marched him through a maze of corridors and finally into a transport capsule set in a large vertical tube. He glanced at the stoic faces of the soldiers and wondered if, with experience, he could learn to read the expressions on those cyborg faces. He suddenly thought once more about what he was doing. It had taken him seven years to escape from a raider stronghold. Now he was walking into another.

The transport doors irised closed, and with an upward surge, they were moving.

Chapter 21

THE KYBER LAW

LEGROEDER FELT felt a steady vibration through his hands, pressed to the back railing of the transport capsule. He couldn't tell where he was going—there were no windows in the capsule—but he could feel it streaking in a great long arc, and he imagined that they must be shooting away from the docking station toward some other part of the Kyber outpost. He glanced around, trying to gain some clue from his three escorts.

There was little expression on any of their faces, nor had anyone spoken to him since they'd left the control room. But the leader was busy talking to someone; his lips were moving silently but continuously, his gaze shifting back and forth between Legroeder and a small control panel near the door. Finally he nodded and touched a control, then settled into an alert stance with his eyes on Legroeder.

After several long minutes, the movement of the transport

slackened. Legroeder gripped the rail as deceleration kicked in. No one stirred until the transport came to a stop.

The door irised open. The soldiers nudged him out into a concourse, brightly lit and full of people. Legroeder was amazed to see people walking around as though conducting normal, everyday business; he felt as if he had just crossed into another universe. This place looked nothing like the raider outpost at DeNoble, where he had been imprisoned; it was more like a spartan version of a space station in the Centrist Worlds.

The soldiers led him through a maze of corridors away from the concourse. They finally stopped at an arched doorway shrouded by a glimmering, translucent privacy-screen. Through the screen, Legroeder could make out the shape of a person sitting at a desk. The leader seemed nervous. "Time to speak to the law," he said.

The law? Legroeder wondered. At DeNoble, the law meant the autocratic rule of pirate bosses, with fear as the strongest motivator, and favoritism the next strongest. Would this be any different?

He followed the guard through the screen and found himself in a small anteroom facing—what? A receptionist? It was a woman—apparently—whose face was a chrome mask grafted onto a natural head, with tightly curled red hair. She had seemingly normal human limbs, but a torso of articulated metal. She sat on a swiveling stool, surrounded by suspended holograms of faces and incomprehensible designs. Most of the holos appeared to be rotating, or changing too quickly for Legroeder's eye to follow. The woman was turning back and forth, touching one holo after another. Each twinkled as she touched it, and she seemed to be subvocalizing at a tremendous rate of speed. What was she doing? Legroeder wondered.

The guard made a soft, guttural sound. For a moment, there was no response, as the woman continued with her silent conversations. Then the holos winked out, and she suddenly focused her attention on the people before her.

"The new arrival?" she asked, her voice metallic and high pitched.

"Yes, Ma'am," the soldier said, and stepped back.

The woman looked at Legroeder. "State your name."

Legroeder froze, thoughts racing. What the hell name had he been ID'd under?

◻ *Is there a problem?* ◻

"Legroeder," said the woman. "Is that your name?"

(Did you ID me as Legroeder, for chrissake?)

There was a momentary hesitation in the system; he imagined the implants blinking at each other disconcertedly. ◻ *We presented the options. You didn't specify another name.* ◻

Legroeder tried to recall the moment, but everything had been chaos. *(You didn't include a picture with that ID, did you?)*

◻ *That is the normal procedure.* ◻ And then, with what might have been a hint of contrition, ◻ *Should we not have?* ◻

(What picture did you use?)

◻ *We took it from your memories.* ◻

His heart sank as he saw his own mental image of himself. It was, of course, Legroeder as he had seen himself most of his life—as he had appeared before Com'peer and the Narseil med techs had remade his features. As he had appeared at DeNoble.

"What's the matter?" said the half-metal woman. "Your ID says Renwald Legroeder."

"Um—yes."

"And you have just arrived from a mission with one of the affiliates?"

"Yes, that's right." His tongue stuck to the roof of his mouth. "Kyber affiliates."

The woman's two eyes pulsed in alternating waves of intensity. Her gaze flicked for a moment to a new holo, another point of attention; it flicked back. "I didn't think you meant Narseil affiliates. You just turned in a shipful of Narseil infiltrators. Is that correct?"

Not trusting himself to speak, Legroeder nodded.

"Good. Then you will be seen for debriefing." Her glance shifted to the lead guard. "Take him in."

The guard gestured to Legroeder to circle around the receptionist, leaving the other two guards to wait. A whole new set of holos sprang up around the woman, who appeared to have already forgotten Legroeder.

A glowing doorway appeared behind the receptionist, and they passed through it into a darkened space. It was a room lit only by the glow of consoles—a great many consoles, lining the circumference of the room, and the ceiling, as well. Some displayed data, others holo-images. In the center of the room was a high-backed swivel chair, turned partly away from the door. Legroeder could just make out a woman in the chair, scanning a bank of consoles. A faint spatter of light seemed to flicker in the air in front of her.

The guard hesitated—and finally Legroeder himself cleared his throat. Before he could speak, a voice broke the silence. *"You may leave him with me and return to your post."* It was a female voice, but electronically distorted. He thought it was the voice of the woman in the chair, but it came through speakers around the room.

The guard nodded, turned, and left the room hurriedly.

"Step forward."

Legroeder circled around to approach her from the front.

The woman in the chair was more human looking than the receptionist, but also more startling. She seemed to have all the normal human body parts—but her face was alight, sparkling with fire. At first he thought it was all reflections from the consoles; then he realized it was coming from her face—rather like a dance-floor laser, spinning out dazzling rays faster than the eye could follow. At first he could not see her actual eyes; then she turned her head and he saw a pair of smoldering embers. He shivered, before realizing that she was wearing some kind of clear mask on her face, and *that* was the source of the dazzling light and glowing eyes.

Legroeder started to speak, but the woman raised a hand,

pressing it against thin air. Her other hand was busy manipulating something on the left arm of her chair. "You are Renwald Legroeder?" she said after a moment.

"Yes."

"I'm Tracy-Ace/Alfa. I've been expecting you."

Expecting me?

She leaned forward, staring at him. "Correct me if I am wrong. It is my understanding that you have come to us, indirectly, from an affiliate Kyber settlement. And that you were—what was the word?—a 'plant' aboard the Narseil ship that encountered *Flechette*. Are those facts correct?"

□ *That is how you were ID'd,* □ his implants informed him.

"Yes," Legroeder answered.

"You look different from your ID photo." Half question, half accusation.

He stiffened. "Yes, I—" He hesitated, then decided that the truth might be as good a cover as a lie. "The Narseil made some changes to my appearance, to conceal my previous identity in case of capture. I'd . . . persuaded them that I'd joined their cause."

Her eyes glowed brighter. "And had you?"

Legroeder's face burned. "They think so."

"Explain."

"I was aboard a Narseil vessel, purportedly to help them defeat the Kyber in battle. I didn't really think they would; in fact, I expected we would be captured. But once the Narseil defeated *Flechette*, I persuaded them to try to penetrate your facility, to gain intelligence."

Tracy-Ace/Alfa studied him for a moment. "And did you?"

"What?"

"Penetrate our facility? Before sounding the alarm, I mean."

Legroeder frowned, and waggled his hand noncommittally.

"I see," said Tracy-Ace/Alfa. "Does that mean a lot, or a little?"

"A little," Legroeder said, with a shrug. "I tried to make a good show of it—and I pretty much coerced your Rigger Deutsch into going along with me—but I really didn't know my way around. We didn't get anything that was very heavily guarded."

Tracy-Ace/Alfa's face sparkled. "I see. I'll accept that for the moment." Though the mask on her face was clear, it was impossible to interpret her expression. "I understand that your *H'zzarrelik* took quite a toll on our ship. A dreadnought, it was supposed to be. Were you unable to . . . shall we say, temper the Narseil counterattack?"

He turned his hands palm up. "How could I? I was posing as a member of their crew. If I had turned against them in battle, they would have killed me at once." He hesitated. Perhaps it was time to put in a plug for his friends. "They are, I must say, excellent fighters."

Shots of light came from her eyes. "Are they, now? You can tell me more, in our full debriefing later. But in view of the disastrous mission of *Flechette*—good Lord, brought in as a captive of the Narseil, all but one of our crew dead or taken by the enemy—we come to the fact that *you* seem to have been something of a hero."

He started to speak, but his voice caught. This was what his ID was supposed to convey, yes?

She cocked her head slightly, and continued, "Against all odds, you brought us a captive Narseil crew. And before they could do too much harm at the docking station, you managed to alert us through the intelnet—thereby saving us untold costs. Fair statement?"

He cleared his throat, amazed that his cover story appeared to be working—though he still wondered what had *really* set off the alarm. He shrugged. "It was all pretty confusing, to be honest. I wouldn't want to take more credit than I was due. But I—hope that my actions were helpful."

"You not only captured the Narseil, you thwarted their attempt at espionage."

"I suppose so," he admitted. In his head, he felt a circle of crimson light expanding like a ripple on a pond. The implants hastened to reassure him, ▢ *You are only confirm-ing what we implied in the traces we left.* ▢

(Right. It's okay.) He felt dizzy. Was it okay? He wasn't contradicting information already in the intelnet; that was the important thing.

"We'll have to decide later on the proper disposition of the Narseil prisoners," Tracy-Ace/Alfa continued, an un-readable shimmer moving across her face. "Execution . . . or whatever. After interrogation, of course."

Legroeder drew a slow breath; he was certain she was watch-ing him for any sign of reaction. "I'm sure," he said care-fully, "that they can prove valuable as prisoners."

"No doubt," she said. "Meanwhile—for our planning pur-poses—I need to learn what you can tell me about the Nar-seil and their treachery. Then, if your debriefing is satisfactory, I will arrange for you to be integrated into our world here."

Integrated? he thought grimly. Or assimilated? But that's what he was here for, wasn't he? To gain information. And how better to do it? He felt the implants suppressing his involuntary shiver.

He thought he heard a cold chuckle. The flickering on Tracy-Ace/Alfa's face began to subside, along with the coal-fire glow of her eyes. "Renwald Legroeder," she said softly, and this time the voice seemed to come from her mouth rather than speakers around him. "I think we can speak face to face." Her natural voice was strong, though mild in comparison to the reverb she'd been using until now.

She reached up and gripped both sides of her face mask, pushing it up and over the top of her head. She blinked her real eyes for a moment and peered at Legroeder. Without the mask, she looked like a fairly normal young woman: with human skin of a pale tan hue, eyes, nose, mouth. Her eyes flared green, just for an instant, before she shifted her head, putting them in shadow. Her face was bejeweled with augments: an array of tiny ones clustered around the outer corners of her eyes, and slightly larger ones stretched back like gemstones along her temples.

Legroeder blinked, his breath catching. He was staring; he glanced away for a moment, then back. There was a hard-edged look to the young woman, and yet in a way, she was curiously attractive. There was a chameleonlike quality to her eyes, her mouth, her entire face. Every little movement seemed to reveal a different quality: one moment, an inquisitor; the next, a potential ally in finding his way in this strange place; the next, something more personal, a . . . what? Friend?

Don't be an idiot.

"In case you think I trust you a little too much," Tracy-Ace/Alfa said casually, "you should be aware that there are no fewer than twelve security lasers focused on the interior of this chamber. All under my direct control."

"Ah," he said, keeping his voice equally casual. "Well—pleased to meet you, Tracy-Ace/Alfa."

She produced a wry smile and leaned forward in her chair to shake his hand. Her grip was wiry and strong. "You may call me Tracy-Ace."

"Tracy-Ace," he echoed. "Is Alfa your last name?"

"Alfa is my node designation." She gestured with one hand toward the profusion of consoles and God-knew-what arrayed around the room.

"Then" he said carefully, "it is through this node, Alfa, that you connect to the intelnet? And through that you—?"

Tracy-Ace laughed, a short bark.

Legroeder swallowed the rest of his question. "What did I say?"

"I do not connect *through* node Alfa," Tracy-Ace said. "I *am* node Alfa. It is a part of my being, and without *me*, that portion of the intelnet would not exist."

Legroeder absorbed that in silence. A part of the intelnet . . .

□ *It is a logical extension. If you wished, we could help to expand you in the direction of such capabil—"* □

He cut off the inner voice with an image of a hand closing into a fist.

"If we have been sufficiently introduced," Tracy-Ace said, "then let's go complete a proper interview. But not here, I think. Are you hungry?"

Legroeder started. This wasn't quite what he'd expected.

"Although we have no insect life here, I suggest that you close your mouth," Tracy-Ace said with dry sarcasm. She stepped out of her high-backed chair. He saw for the first time that she was dressed in black sim-leather pants and tunic, with various belts and attachments in silver. Her black hair was clipped with bangs in front, and to the mid neck in back. He was startled by her height, a good three centimeters taller than he was. "All right," she said with a shrug. "But don't blame me for what you swallow." She beckoned him as she turned and strode toward a door on the far side of the room.

Legroeder closed his mouth and followed.

TRACY-ACE LED him down a deserted corridor lined with a panoramic holo of the open Flux. It was a far broader view of the outpost than he had seen from the ship's net: a sprawling array of glowing and shadowy structures, each apparently separate, but joined together by a spiderweb of luminous, arcing threads that looked more like thought than matter.

Legroeder paused, squinting. He thought he saw movement in those threads, but couldn't be sure. He recalled what Deutsch had told him, about maintainers who kept the outpost anchored and stabilized in the Flux. A swarm of questions rose in his thoughts, but Tracy-Ace was already gesturing impatiently.

"Sandwich and murk okay?" Tracy-Ace asked, turning a corner away from the view.

Murk? *Moke?* He suddenly realized how hungry he was. "Uh, sure," he said. "Fine. Um, where are we going to do the debriefing?"

She glanced back at him, without breaking stride. "Well,

we can do it in an inquisitor's cell, with the truth enhance-ments of your choice—" she paused as he scowled "—or we can do it in a joe shop I like. Which would you prefer?"

He wondered if she was mocking him. He decided to treat it as a straight question. "Given that choice, I'd prefer the latter."

"So would I. Here it is."

They turned another corner and were suddenly walking along a row of small shops—with people moving about, in and out of storefronts. The joe shop was third on the left. Through the door, it was dark; and as Legroeder's eyes adjusted, he saw that it was also dingy and nearly empty. Tracy-Ace chose a booth off to the right, three steps up from the main floor. She slid onto a bench seat facing the en-trance, and motioned him into the other.

Legroeder glanced around. What a strange place this out-post was, nothing like the stronghold of DeNoble. That had been more like a military encampment, with a large popu-lation of prisoners. This seemed a real city, for people with human needs. And yet, evidence remained that it was a pi-rate stronghold. Here and there, he had noticed electronic monitors winking out of recesses in walls. Nearly everyone he'd seen was visibly fitted with augmentation, and many of them carried sidearms. Judging from this joe shop, crea-ture comforts were minimal, but not altogether absent. There was only one other person in the shop, a man sitting in the shadows near the back.

Legroeder faced Tracy-Ace across the table. "Do you mind if I ask a question?" he said, placing his hands on the table.

Tracy-Ace waited, silent.

"Why bring me here for a debriefing?"

"Why? Isn't it good enough?"

"I don't mean that. But it seems more . . . informal . . . than I expected." To put it mildly.

Tracy-Ace seemed to be assessing him. "Let's just say, I like to get a personal sense of people before I download."

"Download?"

"Put out your hands," Tracy-Ace said. "Palms up." As he turned his hands, Tracy-Ace examined them, then grunted in dissatisfaction. Her own palms glittered with connectors. "How the hell do you do it?" She looked up at his face, then leaned sideways to inspect his temples. "There?"

"Do wh—?" he began, and then realized what she was talking about. "This isn't going to be verbal—?"

"Verbal? For a debriefing?" She peered at him incredulously, with silver-green eyes. "Why in blazes would we *talk*, instead of downloading?"

His face burned, as he realized that he was doing a poor job of impersonating a Kyber. He decided, again, to tell the truth—part of it. "Sorry. I'm not used to all this."

Tracy-Ace's eyebrows went up. "What the hell do you *do* with those augments, then?"

"Well, I didn't have them at the other outpost. I got them from the Narseil, so I'd fit in with their crew. I haven't quite mastered them yet."

Tiny lights flickered at the corners of her eyes. "So you're not prepared to give me the download?"

"Uh—" He focused inward. *(Can we?)*

◻ Certainly. We'll be ready in a moment. ◻

"Yes," he said uneasily. "I can do it."

Tracy-Ace looked vaguely relieved. "All right. Where shall I connect?"

◻ Ask her to wait a moment longer. We're preparing something. ◻

Legroeder blinked, raised a finger to ask Tracy-Ace to wait, then thought: *What's that tingling in my arms?* Now it was in the palms of his hands.

"Where shall I connect?" she repeated impatiently.

"Sorry. One second." Legroeder focused inward. *(Are you making connectors in my goddamn hands?)* He saw an interior image of a glowing red ribbon snaking, branching, reaching out into a skeletal hand; suddenly it turned green.

◻ Yes. Try making contact, hand to hand. ◻

(How the hell did you do *that?)*

◻ We simply directed the microrobots. ◻

The microrobots! For godsake, were they still in his body?

Tracy-Ace was scowling. "Look, if you can't—"

Legroeder took a deep breath. "Okay, I'm ready." He opened and closed his hands a few times, then stretched them out, palms up. "Let's give it a try."

Tracy-Ace looked at him curiously, then placed her palms onto his. "All right?"

He blinked, with a heightened awareness of her touch. A few minutes ago, she'd touched him; but this time it was different. A tingle of his inner senses . . .

□ *We are establishing contact. Do you wish us to filter out the emotional component?* □

(What emotional component?)

□ *Your reaction to the contact.* □

(I don't know what you—yes, dammit, filter it out.)

Tracy-Ace was scowling again. "Relax, will you? I'm getting a confusing interface."

He drew a long, slow breath and let it out.

Something was flickering inside him; he couldn't tell quite what. It glimmered twice, three times, then for several seconds was much brighter. Something was stirring in his thoughts, but he couldn't identify it. Then it stopped.

Tracy-Ace lifted her hands and rubbed them together, frowning thoughtfully.

"Couldn't you make contact?" he asked.

For a moment, she simply looked at him. With what: Curiosity? Disdain? Humor? Legroeder experienced a sudden flush of what felt like attraction, as though something meaningful had passed or grown between them, without his knowledge. He felt dizzy. The feeling faded, as her expression changed to one of puzzlement. "I got what I needed," she said finally. "Is something wrong?"

He opened his mouth, closed it, took a silent poll of the implants. *(What did she get?)*

□ *Our report. Exactly as we intended.* □ There seemed to be a slight air of cockiness in the answer. He clucked silently; he didn't approve of cockiness among implants.

Focusing on Tracy-Ace, he forced a smile. "No, no—it's just that it was very quick. I could hardly feel it. I wasn't sure if you'd made contact."

"You," she said, resting her chin on one hand, "are an odd one." She stared at him hard for a few seconds, perhaps processing the information he'd uploaded to her.

He started to answer in his own defense, then realized he didn't know if she'd meant it as an insult or a compliment.

"Would you like something to eat?" Tracy-Ace flicked at the air with her fingertips. A stout, half-bald waiter seemed to appear from nowhere, wiping his hands on a soiled white apron. After reeling off a list of specials in a bored voice, he took their orders for sandwiches and moke, or rather, *murk*. Legroeder stared at the man, thinking he was the only one around here who didn't look like a pirate. But was that a faint glimmer around the edges—?

The waiter belched and winked out.

No wonder he'd appeared out of nowhere. Legroeder looked at Tracy-Ace with raised eyebrows. She shrugged. "Just our way of remembering the home worlds."

Legroeder cleared his throat and looked around the joe shop while they waited. The lone man on the other side of the shop seemed to be watching him. For a moment, Legroeder thought he saw the man *glow*. He rubbed his eyes and the impression was gone. He looked back at Tracy-Ace. She seemed preoccupied, and didn't speak again until a panel suddenly slid open in the wall next to the table.

"Sandwiches and murk," Legroeder heard, and bent to peer through the open panel. The waiter's face was peering back. A tray slid out onto their table, bearing two plates and two mugs. The panel slammed shut.

"Friendly service," Legroeder remarked softly. Tracy-Ace gestured, and he pulled a plate toward himself. He took a swallow of the murk, and shuddered.

Tracy-Ace didn't seem to notice his reaction. "You didn't seem afraid of me," she said suddenly, lifting her sandwich. "Why?"

Legroeder was still working his tongue to get rid of the

taste. "Huh? Why should I have been afraid of you?"

"When you were brought to me. The guards who brought you were scared to death, you know." Tracy-Ace took a bite.

He kept his lips puckered, but in a scowl. "I was wondering about that. Why were they afraid?"

"You really don't know?"

He spread his hands. "I'm new here, remember?"

She chewed thoughtfully, arching one eyebrow, then took a sip of murk. "I wouldn't have thought it would take much explanation. At your old outpost, weren't you nervous when you were brought into the presence of a node holder?"

Legroeder felt a flash of memory: of fear, and hatred, and longing, and . . . He cut it off with an internal throat-slashing gesture. "There were things that made me scared, yes," he said. "But we didn't have . . . node holders."

Her eyes narrowed. "No node holders in Barbados?"

"Well, none where I worked, anyway." *(Barbados? Am I supposed to be from Barbados?)*

▫ *We told you that.* ▫

(You did? Is there such a place?)

▫ *There is reason to think so. In any case, the goal was to avoid connecting you with DeNoble, since you are presumably a wanted man there.* ▫

Clearing his throat, he tried to shift the subject back before he said something provably false. "So then, because you have that name, Tracy-Ace/*Alfa*, they're afraid of you?"

"Oh, yes." Her lips tightened. "Indeed they are."

"Because—"

"Because of certain . . . powers of authority . . . that I am occasionally called upon to exercise." Her gaze seemed intense for a moment, and then the strain seemed to subside from her eyes. One corner of her mouth turned up. "Powers that . . . it does not appear I will have to exercise in connection with you."

Legroeder felt his eyebrows come together. He sat stone still, thinking. Concluding nothing. He raised his cheese sandwich and took a large bite. Finally, when it was clear she wasn't going to continue, he said, "That's good. I guess. Isn't it?"

Tracy-Ace's implants glittered as she peered at him. Abruptly, she laughed out loud. "Yes, it's good. Very good. Now, finish up. Based on our briefing, I think I can make you a useful citizen here. There's a lot I have to show you." She drained her mug. "That's assuming you decide to stay, and we decide not to ship you back to Barbados. But there's plenty of time to decide."

He cleared his throat. "Ah. Well . . . I do want to stay . . ."

There was a sudden movement off to his left, and he saw the shop's other occupant stirring. Tracy-Ace was glancing that way now, and for a moment, her expression seemed to become still, almost frozen. But her implants flickered energetically, and for just an instant, Legroeder had a chilling sense that something was passing between Tracy-Ace and that other man. Legroeder squinted, and saw that the man was bald, and dressed in light colored shirt and pants, and had an unsettlingly *luminous* quality about him. The man nodded in their direction, and Tracy-Ace nodded back. Just as Legroeder started to shift his gaze back to Tracy-Ace, the man abruptly vanished. Winked out.

Another hologram? Legroeder shot an inquiring glance at Tracy-Ace. "Who was that?"

Tracy-Ace shrugged; she seemed slightly uncomfortable with the question. "Just someone I know." She slid out of her seat. "Good. So let's go get you settled. Ordinarily I'd have someone else take you to your quarters, but I'm off duty." She paused, pursing her lips. "You know, you seem like a very interesting man, Rigger Legroeder. I believe I want to oversee your case myself."

He nodded cautiously, wondering if this was a good development or an ominous one.

"Come on. We'll take the flicker-tube."

He took a last bite and dusted his hands together. "What's a flicker-tube?" he asked, braving one last swallow of murk.

"They don't have flicker-tubes on Barbados, either?"

Legroeder thought a moment. They did not, he decided.

Tracy-Ace shook her head. "Rings," she said, "I don't know how your people manage. Let's go."

Legroeder bristled on behalf of his fictitious home, and followed her out of the joe shop.

Chapter 22

OUTPOST IVAN

IT SEEMED, as they walked through the halls, that everyone they passed was moving quickly, as though on urgent business. Even so, Legroeder felt that something was missing, some element of ordinary random bustle. Or maybe it felt emptier than he expected. "I thought there'd be more people around," he murmured, half unconsciously.

Tracy-Ace glanced at him sharply, and he wondered if he'd said something wrong. But she answered calmly enough, "There's been a big shift of personnel lately. More and more people have been sent out into the field, to work in fleet preparations."

Legroeder tried to hide a twinge. "Fleet preparations?" *Preparations for what?*

Tracy-Ace glanced sharply again. Was he being tested? He took a stab. "Are you talking about the pirate fleets?"

That brought a laugh.

"What'd I say?"

"Usually, it's the people who don't like us who call us *pirates*," she said abruptly. "The preferred term around here is *raider*." She was silent for a moment before adding, "Usually defined as 'raiding for that which should be ours.'" She laughed again, in a hollow echo of the first.

Legroeder tried to interpret the sound. Was she making a commentary on the raiding—or on his naiveté? "I guess

I've picked up some of the Narseil's language," he said apologetically. "Most people on the *outside*, you know, do regard the Kyber fleets as pirate ships."

Tracy-Ace cocked an eyebrow at him and lengthened her stride. "Well, that's not the fleet I meant, anyway."

"What, um, fleet *did* you mean?"

"You really don't know?"

He shook his head.

"The colony fleet."

Colony fleet . . . ?

At that moment, they came around a corner into a brightly lit area that looked like a transit platform, except instead of cars, it was filled with clear vertical cylinders.

Legroeder blinked at the sight.

"You'll see later," she continued. "This is where we catch the transport between sectors."

He was struggling to keep up with the cascade of new information. *Transport between sectors . . .* He remembered it had looked as though the sprawled-out structures in this outpost were anchored separately in the Flux. It had seemed an unlikely arrangement.

"The habitats float independently, but they're joined by the flicker-tubes," Tracy-Ace said, as though reading his mind. "It avoids certain instability problems of large structures, and gives us greater safety in the event of an attack."

"Have you ever *been* attacked here?" Legroeder asked, remembering uneasily that part of his mission was to gain intelligence that might permit just such an attack.

Her eyebrows bristled. "No. But that doesn't mean it couldn't happen. And if it did, we could absorb some hard punches and still survive. Our leadership has always been very strong on taking the long view."

As they talked, people were crossing the platform in both directions, stepping in and out of the clear cylinders. Those who stepped into the cylinders sank out of sight through the floor; others emerged from below like slow-rising pistons.

Tracy-Ace led him to a pair of empty cylinders, side by side, and touched the two simultaneously. "We'll be linked.

Go on and get in." She stepped into one capsule as Legroeder stepped into the other. The capsule closed around Legroeder with a puff. "You with me?" he heard.

"Yup." His breath went out with a *whoof*, as the capsule dropped away from the platform. He looked down. They were falling, Tracy-Ace before him, into a glowing, golden tube of energy. It curved downward and away, seemingly to infinity. In the distance, he could see the arc of the tube intersecting with other strands like threads of a spiderweb. Tiny droplets of light were moving through the tubes; he guessed them to be other passenger capsules in transit. It was impossible to judge his velocity.

"So this—" his words came out in a gasp "—is a flicker-tube?"

Tracy-Ace's voice was a chuckle in his ear. "This is a flicker-tube." He could almost imagine her standing beside him. "Okay, now I can fill you in . . ."

"I, uh—" He cut himself off as a shower of images sprang up around him, painted on the blurred inner surface of the tube. The images changed with an almost cinematic flicker as they shadowed him in his glassy chariot. He reeled from the sheer volume and speed: strobing glimpses of faces and ships and places, and fast-changing shots of what looked like space-station construction. "What the hell *is* this?" he breathed.

"It's the flicker feed," Tracy-Ace's voice said. "It conveys news and information to people when they're in transit. It makes use of slack time."

Legroeder wished he had something physical to hang onto. The motion through the tube was a blur, and the images were now a blur, too. "How is this conveying information? I can't make out a thing."

☐ *We are processing . . .* ☐

"If your augments are any good," Tracy-Ace said, "they'll be picking it up and storing it for you. Don't worry about trying to follow it consciously—"

Thank God. Legroeder closed his eyes for a moment. He was startled to find that he was still seeing the images.

(What's going on? I thought it was being projected on the tube wall.)

☐ *Meant to look that way. But no, it's coming through us.* ☐

(Oh . . .)

"—but you are meant to be observing sensations and context, to help you integrate it," Tracy-Ace continued. "It would be better if I kept quiet now and let you watch."

Legroeder breathed slowly and deeply, trying to stifle the thoughts racing through his mind. A hundred images flashed by every second. After a while, he was only dimly aware of the Flux outside the tube wall; he almost came to feel that it was normal to be surrounded by swirling patterns of light woven through with holographic images, and the murmuring of recorded voices, some in languages he could not identify. It was like listening to multiple conversations and understanding none of them—but absorbing it all, so that later, perhaps, he would be able to sort and translate and comprehend. From within, the implants murmured repeatedly . . .

☐ *. . . relax and listen, do not concern yourself with comprehension . . .* ☐

All right, then, he wouldn't . . .

SEVERAL TIMES, they passed tube intersections in a molten blur. And then, at last, he was startled to see a habitat looming over his head and drawing closer; he was ascending headfirst toward a terminus. How in the world had they flipped without his noticing? In other tubes, he could see capsules dropping away from the habitat like beads down a chute. Overhead, Tracy-Ace was disappearing into the building.

As his own capsule decelerated and entered the structure, Legroeder was aware that he had just acquired, in several minutes, considerable knowledge about this Free Kyber world known as Ivan. Not that he could put his finger on any of it this instant, but he knew that it was tucked away somewhere in his cranium. His implants were likely to be working long into the night, sorting it all out.

The capsule came to rest on a platform distinguishable only by color—blue—from the one they had left behind. As he stepped out beside Tracy-Ace, he felt an unexpected pleasure, as if he were glad to see her, an old and comfortable friend. He stopped in his tracks, stunned by the feeling. Why did he suddenly feel as if he had known her for years?

"What?" Tracy-Ace said.

He let out his breath, banishing the thought. "Nice ride," he muttered.

She peered at him with obvious curiosity. "We go this way," she said, pointing to the left.

As they moved on, he began to suspect that she was puzzling over him as much as he was over her. (*Did you pass personal information between us during that download link?*) Legroeder muttered to his implants.

□ *If you mean information about your past, and your true identity, no.* □

(*Good.*)

□ *But there was a certain amount of handshaking involved, and personal protocol exchange. Most of it was strictly augment-exchange protocol.* □

(*Do I hear a "but"—?*)

□ *But there had to be certain personal-preference exchanges to establish how and what would be transferred. To establish "trust," as it were. That could be part of what you sense.* □

He wondered uneasily just how much "personal preference" information had been exchanged. How could protocol exchanges make him feel not just warmth, but a certain actual attraction toward this pirate whom he hardly knew? These augments were beginning to scare him.

□ *We're only here to serve.* □

(*Mm.*)

". . . be staying here in this sector," Tracy-Ace was saying. "This is where we put visitors and people who are . . . between jobs. You know, like unemployed heroes." She flashed a grin at him—and he flushed, realizing that he felt such a palpable attraction that he had to shove his hands firmly in his pockets to keep from reaching out and touching her. He countered the thought by thinking about his imprisoned comrades, and wondering when he might dare to ask about them.

Tracy-Ace had quickened her long-legged stride. They walked, rode lift-tubes, walked some more. When they finally stopped at a closed door, they might have been in the hallway of a cheap apartment building anywhere in the known galaxy. Tracy-Ace pressed her hand to the plate beside the door. "Number 7494," she said. "Remember that." The door paled and she ushered him into a room the size of a crew cabin on a starship. "Your new home."

Legroeder surveyed the place. It was plain but neat: narrow bunk, tiny desk with com, table, sling chair. Perfect for a monk. Heaven, compared to what he'd lived in for seven years at DeNoble. His bag, which he had last seen in his cabin on *Flechette*, was sitting on the bunk. They were efficient here. He could forget about any hopes he might have had about sneaking back one day to transmit a message from *Flechette*.

◻ *That was hardly a serious option, you know.* ◻

(Well, yes, but . . .)

◻ *The underground. Finding the underground is your only real option now.* ◻

(I am aware of that, thank you.)

"You ought to be comfortable here," Tracy-Ace was saying.

"Thank you." He struggled to find words, and hoped she wasn't reading his thoughts. "I guess—it'll take time to learn my way around. And to figure out—I don't know— what I'll be useful for." It was starting to hit him all over again how alone he was here. With the unraveling of the Narseil plan to get in, get info, and get out, it was really all up to him. Suppose he couldn't contact the underground. What then? Sign on to another ship, and try to broadcast a message in flight, before they killed him? *H'zzarrelik* would wait out there for fifteen days before heading back with their prisoners. Once they were gone, there would be nobody to broadcast *to*.

"You'll learn fast," Tracy-Ace said, touching his arm. "I'm going to set you up with some study programs, to get you oriented."

He'd felt an electric tingle at her touch, and was trying to pretend he hadn't.

"We'll find things for you to do, don't worry."

He forced a nervous smile. "Okay—what's next, then?"

"What's next is I go back to work. And you—you look like you could use some sleep. When you're ready, here's where you can call up the study programs." She stepped over to the desk and showed him the controls. "Why don't I come back later to show you around?"

He nodded, covering his surprise. He couldn't deny being pleased by the personal attention. "I guess I could stand to sleep a few hours." He was exhausted, actually, and the adrenaline was starting to wear off. "What time is it? When do *you* sleep?"

Tiny lights sparkled at the corners of her eyes. "It's third-quarter evening. A lot of people will be on sleep cycle during the next six or eight hours. I'll be working, myself; I don't need much sleep. My programs handle REM processing right in the node, so I can pick up sleep functions while I work."

Legroeder didn't know whether to be envious or sympathetic.

"I'll be free in about ten hours. Will that give you enough time? We have to confine you to quarters until your case has been reviewed. But if you get hungry, you can call up some snack pantry items on the com here. Anything else you need?"

Yes, he thought. The com address of the underground. "I guess not. Is it okay if I play with the com system a little?"

She gave him a look. "As long as you don't try to access anything that it wants you to stay out of." She touched his arm and moved toward the door. "Bye, then." He couldn't answer; he was mesmerized by the tingle. "Oh—if you need to reach me, use this code." She turned to the desk com and placed an index finger on the reader-plate. "There, it's stored for you."

As she went out and the door opaqued behind her, he felt a pang of self-recrimination at the pleasure he'd ust felt. *She's the enemy, remember? What the devil are you thinking?*

Sighing, he tossed his bag off the bunk and lay down. He had no idea how long it had been since he had last slept, but he knew it was way too long.

SLEEP, HOWEVER, did not come easily. When it did, it was a troubled affair, blurred with wakefulness. It felt as if his brain were continuing to fire at a scattergun pace—his dreams and the activities of the implants intertwined with one another, synaptic impulses rocketing up and down in a frenetic series of discharges. Even asleep, he was aware of the intense activity . . . dreams coming silently and escaping again, pushed out by the next, and the next, in an unending cascade. Images from the flicker-tubes, from his long-ago past, from battle, from the gazing crystals . . .

He awoke at one point, exhausted but unable to keep his eyes closed. Without thinking about it, he stumbled to the desk and switched on the com. He glanced briefly at the study programs, but found he was too groggy to concentrate. He idly began running searches. After noodling aimlessly for a few minutes, he narrowed his search. *Prisoners . . . Narseil . . . Freem'n Deutsch . . .* He wasn't even sure what he was looking for; he just wanted to know if there was reason to hope for their safety.

The implants flagged him briefly, asking if he really wanted to proceed. He brushed the caution aside irritably; he didn't know why the Kyber trusted him, but Tracy-Ace had said it was okay to play around.

He wasn't making much progress; but somewhere into his third attempt, he finally woke up to what he was doing. *Dear God, what an idiot.* Was he giving himself away, showing his concern about the Narseil? He sat back, feeling sick.

The implants spoke up. □ *Our monitoring did not show you betraying any incriminating data.* □

(*Except my doing the search in the first place. Why didn't you stop me?*)

The answering voice was clearly meant to be soothing. □ *Our programming does not include interference in personal activities, barring clear and present danger.* □

And I assured you it wasn't dangerous, he remembered, rubbing his forehead. What the hell time was it now? *Fourth-quarter two.* What the hell did that mean? He didn't understand the time-keeping system here.

□ *If you like, in the future we will note such activities as dangerous . . .* □

(*Fine.*) He reached to turn off the com.

The implants stopped him with: □ *You have a message waiting.* □

(*What? Where?*)

And then he saw it, a tiny dingbat at the corner of the comspace. He blinked at it, and it expanded, and he heard Tracy-Ace's voice saying, (*Sorry, Rigger Legroeder, that com-search is off limits. But I'll tell you what you need to know, next time I see you. In the meantime, if you can't sleep, why don't you give those study programs a try.*)

For several heartbeats he sat absolutely still, neither moving nor breathing. And then he realized that she hadn't sounded angry or suspicious. Maybe, after all, it was okay for him to wonder what had become of his former shipmates—even if they theoretically were the enemy.

Tracy-Ace wasn't done. (*Someone I know's going to want to talk to both Deutsch and the Narseil crew, by the way. So don't worry about their being executed in the near future.*) She chuckled. (*Now, get some sleep.*)

The message dingbat closed.

Legroeder stared in dumb amazement at the com for a full minute. Then he sighed, rose, and went back to the bunk to try to follow her suggestion.

* * *

IT WAS no use, he thought after a half hour of tossing fitfully in the bunk. Once more, he went to the com console. This time, he brought up the orientation programs, and sat for over an hour listening to droning voices and watching images of station layouts and command hierarchies as the workings of everyday life and lines of authority were explained to him. He was aware, as he followed in a semidaze, that much more was being conveyed through the augments, and that they were going to be even busier digesting the new load of data than any of them would have guessed possible.

As he threw himself back onto the bunk for one more attempt at sleep, it occurred to him that he had just been given, with almost no effort on his part, some of the very information he had come here hoping to steal.

AMAZINGLY, HE did sleep, though not peacefully. He dreamed of mysterious machineries relentlessly thrumming, surrounding him and filling him with incomprehensible activity.

At one point he stirred to the piping of a com signal and he half-woke with the memory of the frenetic dreams fading like a half-forged, coded message. But he didn't quite make it to wakefulness before he drifted back under and this time was swept up by a wave of images and sounds like a breaker crashing in from the sea.

Memories of Golen Space. The Fortress of DeNoble. Barracks of the captives, more a warren than a human habitation. The bunk on which he rotated shifts with three other men, the mattress that smelled of things he tried not to think about. The raider flights. And between missions, days spent working on weapons arrays and flux-modulation reactors. Days spent dreaming of work stoppage, of suicide. And each day, walking past the window of the punishment center . . .

Stop . . . please . . . he whispered, struggling to wake; but the memories were like a surround-holo, relentless. He couldn't move, couldn't shut his eyes or his ears. Prisoners who tried a work stoppage? They were only tortured for a few days with electrosynaptic shock. But those who tried suicide or sabotage? They were strapped into chairs, gnawed by alien parasites, condemned to a lifetime of screaming agony, dying slowly . . . only to be resuscitated by robot life-support systems. They were the examples: suffering the boss's eternal wrath for defying the law of the fortress. According to rumor, the boss had once led a bizarre religious splinter sect, inspired to ever-higher standards of torture by ancient legends of purgatory.

Why do I keep remembering . . . ?

And one other memory: he never knew her real name, but among the prisoners she was known as Greta the Enforcer. A woman of exquisite beauty and deadly malice. What her actual position was in the DeNoble hierarchy, Legroeder never knew, either; but in his one encounter, begun as a seeming invitation to special "favors," he'd been left shaken, dizzy, heart pounding with fear and humiliation. It was rumored that she used pheromones and charm equally as weapons, and just as no man could resist her appeal, neither did any escape the pain that she enjoyed inflicting.

Legroeder, in the depths of sleep, groaned, wondering how he had survived as long as he had at DeNoble, wondering how he'd ever found the courage—or madness—to escape.

And now, to return voluntarily to it all, to new punishments . . . torture and incentive, reward and punishment . . . all in a blur that he could only imagine, shivering . . . struggling to awaken . . . visions of Tracy-Ace/Alfa and the pirates of Ivan strapping him into a chair alongside his Narseil comrades . . .

Bzzzz . . . bzzzzz . . . bzzzz . . .

What was that noise, like killer bees swarming—?

Bzzzzzzzz . . .

He sat upright in bed, shaking. "What—what—?" he stammered.

The door paled and Tracy-Ace strode in.

He shuddered, the aftershocks of the final dream-quakes still rocking back and forth in his mind.

"You're alive," she said, looking as if she were surprised to find him still breathing. "Rings—you look awful! I've been trying to call you for hours. Why didn't you answer? Are you sick?"

He rubbed his forehead, struggling to fight his way out of the dream fog. "Uh—I guess I was really asleep," he said thickly, sounding as if he had marbles in his mouth. "How'd you get in?"

"I overrode the lock." Tracy-Ace squinted at him. "You don't look like you slept very well." She got him a glass of water. "Should I come back later?"

He took a few sips, choking, as he tried to process her question. He thought of his dream and wondered: *Are you the one who orders the tortures here?*

◻ *Hold, please. We're working to compile relevant information for you . . .* ◻

His head reeled. But indeed, some of the information he'd gained was starting to swarm into focus. This outpost was different; they used different methods of persuasion here. He knew more about Outpost Ivan than he'd have guessed possible in such a short time. In the midst of all that dreaming chaos, his implants had been processing the info-dumps that the flicker-tube and the study programs had given him, half a lifetime ago.

◻ *We've been comparing past and present . . .* ◻

(Wait a minute,) he thought with sudden bitterness, *(are you saying that I dreamed all that stuff just so you could analyze it?)*

◻ *It helped us to establish a perspective, yes.* ◻

Perspective, he thought, shaking his head. Christ.

Tracy-Ace was frowning. "Does that mean yes or no?"

He blinked. "Huh? What did you ask? Give me a minute here, I, uh—"

Tracy-Ace cocked her head. "Are you having a flicker-tube hangover, or do you always wake up this way?"

"Flicker-tube . . . hangover," he mumbled. "That must be

it." He squinted, looking around for the time. "How long was I asleep?"

"About fourteen hours. Look, I'll give you a few minutes to get showered. Then I think we'd better go get some breakfast into you."

He nodded, rubbing his eyes. He suddenly realized that she'd changed clothes since he'd last seen her. She looked more than a little sexy, dressed in a short gold skirt over black tights, and a patchwork black-and-gold blouse. Her temple implants were flickering, drawing his eye. Now why did he think *that* made her look good? He drew a sharp breath, thinking of . . . Greta. This is the face of the enemy. Remember that.

"Great," he said huskily. "Thanks."

After she was gone, he tossed off the thin blanket and stepped into the mist-shower, aware of his nakedness as he wondered vaguely: what was one supposed to wear while touring a raider compound with a lady pirate, anyway?

WALKING WITH Tracy-Ace, later, he discovered that the implants had done a pretty thorough job of organizing his headful of new information. He found himself with a silent guide in his head, producing tiny captions for him as they passed through the station.

□ . . . To your nine o'clock, note the flicker-tubes leading to the new docking port construction site. Just under a thousand workers there . . . □

He glanced left. (*New docking port? You mean they're expanding this place?*)

□ And farther to your left, a departure portal to the location of Outpost Ivan's contribution to the Free Kyber colonizing fleet . . . □

Legroeder staggered a little, his heart pounding. He turned to peer back at the flicker-tube portal they had just passed. The colonizing fleet. He had managed to put that out of his mind.

"Something wrong?" Tracy-Ace asked, pausing. She'd been talking all this time, he had no idea about what.

He drew a slow breath. "No," he said, forcing himself to rejoin her. "Nothing wrong."

They continued walking.

Colonizing fleet. He was dying to ask her about it. Terrified of what she might say.

He hardly noticed as Tracy-Ace tugged him faster along the promenade, while he contemplated the thought of the Kyber worlds moving out of Golen Space, colonizing . . . the Centrist Worlds? No, that didn't make sense.

It must be something else . . .

HE ONLY gradually became aware of the tingling in his arm, mostly after Tracy-Ace took her hand away to gesture toward a food-plaza. "Breakfast," she said.

Breakfast. Legroeder tried to think what he had been feeling a moment ago. She'd been touching his arm—but as a polite gesture, or a personal touch—or was she making a data connection? He cocked his head at her. "Were you reading my mind a moment ago?"

Was that a twinkle in her eye? "And if I was?"

That startled him; he'd been expecting a denial. "Usually people ask first."

She gazed appraisingly at him. "What if I said I was letting *you* read *my* mind?"

"Uh?"

Tracy-Ace raised her chin slightly. The gems around her eyes glittered with reflected light from the ceiling. "I thought it might be helpful," she said. "During the download yesterday, I caught a few things about you—"

He drew back.

"Nothing profound. But I sensed you didn't quite trust me. And if we're going to—" she paused "—work together . . . I thought it might help if you knew more about me."

Legroeder felt flattered and puzzled at the same time. *Why,* he started to ask, *would you care if I trusted you?*

Before he could voice the thought, he was startled by the appearance, inside his head, of two converging arcs of ruby light signifying new information about Tracy-Ace. She was twenty-seven years old, Free Kyber standard calendar. No immediate family, but a couple of cousins who might have been real biological relatives. Parents, from one of the old Kyber worlds: came to join the Free Kyber alliance, and died in a border dispute when she was four. *(Oh.)* Raised by the local childcare collective. Adept in the system; rose to the ranks of node administration before most of her contemporaries had even finished school. For three years, Node Alfa.

She was peering at him, emotions unknown.

Liked the challenge and the responsibility—and the proximity to power. Socially unattached, but willing to consider unusual liaisons. Had a fondness for rebels.

He felt his blood rise, wondering if he qualified as an "unusual liaison." Or a rebel.

□ *That part of the analysis is ambiguous. Shall we probe further?* □

(No, thank you.) He cleared his throat. But Tracy-Ace was talking—about *him*—and he'd missed the first part of it. Something about his being useful to the outpost.

". . . have skills we need, and knowledge. Possibly for special operations. I believe my boss will want to talk to you, soon." Tracy-Ace was studying him again. "I see you wondering. But part of my job is to evaluate people and situations, to look for the unexpected. To make judgments for the benefit of the outpost. And the Republic." *And the colonizing fleet?* At the outer corner of her left eye, a tiny red bead glowed for a moment, as though she were photographing him for a security check. A smile flashed across her face. "Besides—I rather like you."

He felt a moment of lightheadedness. Was it the implants, fracturing away all of the normal inhibitions? Everything seemed accelerated here. A momentary vision of Greta the Enforcer flickered across his mind, giving him a shiver.

If she noticed or understood his shiver, she didn't show it. He was still trying to think of a response to her statement that she liked him. *The face of the enemy.*

"Let's get some food," she said. "Then there's something I want you to see."

He followed her through the food-plaza. The choices were some kind of bread, some kind of curd, and some kind of soft cereal. He took a small serving of each, plus a cup of murk. Tracy-Ace led him to a line of tables looking out over a huge balcony. No, not a balcony—a holo.

Legroeder stared out at an enormous view of the Flux. In the foreground were sprawling structures that he hardly noticed, because behind them were swirling gas clouds that seemed vast, almost galactic in scope. They might have been a bright emission nebula, a star-birthing grounds. But this was something different. His rigger's intuition told him: this was a boundary layer. Not the boundary between normal-space and the Flux, which would have been impressive enough for structures to be anchored against. No, this—he felt with absolute certainty—was the transition zone between the familiar layers of the Flux where starships flew, and another place deeper and more mysterious, and far more perilous.

"You know what it is?" Tracy-Ace said.

He opened his mouth, but couldn't speak. *The Deep Flux.* He knew it by name only. It was an underlying region of the Flux so unstable and unpredictable that riggers avoided it, always. He had never heard of anyone flying in it and returning, though the Narseil Institute had reportedly done some experimenting along the border regions. But the Kyber—? Was this just an impression-image, a work of art?

"Is it real—this view?" he murmured.

"Oh yes," she said, gesturing to the lower part of the image, at the indistinct structures in the foreground.

He couldn't quite make out what they were. Man-made, certainly. A station? Docking ports? Ships? He shivered at the thought of man-made structures hovering on the edge of such cosmic instability.

"Let me change that view a little," said Tracy-Ace.

There was a shimmer as the perspective shifted, magnifying the foreground. His breath left him in a rush. It was a fleet of a hundred or more glittering starships, gathered around what looked like a cluster of asteroids. Long, curved limbs like sea-urchin spines arched out from the central bodies to the starships.

Legroeder felt as though his heart had stopped beating. "What is it?" he whispered.

"The colony fleet," she said.

He swallowed. "Headed toward—?" Not the Centrist Worlds, surely.

"New hunting grounds," she said softly, watching his reaction. "What do you think?"

His voice caught. *I am a Kyber, unafraid of bold Kyber initiatives. Unafraid . . .* "It's—" he said, trying not to stammer "—*impressive.* We, uh—don't have anything like this in—Barbados."

Tracy-Ace stared at him for a moment, then laughed out loud. "No," she said finally. "No, I guess you don't."

"Don't have what in Barbados?" asked a familiar metallic voice.

Legroeder turned.

Freem'n Deutsch was floating toward them.

Chapter 23

THE MAINTAINERS

"Freem'n!" Legroeder cried. "Are you all right?"

Deutsch floated to the table. "As all right as ever. Mind if I join you?"

"Please do," said Tracy-Ace.

"We've met before, I believe. Tracy-Ace/Alfa?" Deutsch said.

"Yes. Good to see you again." To Legroeder she explained, "I asked him to meet us here. Since you were wondering about him."

Legroeder opened his mouth and closed it. Finally he let a smile crack through. "How did you—the last time I saw you, you were frozen in some kind of—"

Deutsch waved a cybernetic hand. "Leghold trap. I saw the damn thing coming, but not in time to get out of its way."

Legroeder winced at the memory. "It looked painful."

"Infuriating as hell, I can tell you that," Deutsch said. "When they finally killed the switch, it knocked me out cold. I woke up in the infirmary. That's where I've been until about an hour ago." He nodded to Tracy-Ace. "Thank you for bringing me out. I'm looking forward to getting back to work."

Are you? Legroeder thought. This was a danger point, when Freem'n had to make his own reentry into the Kyber world. Just how closely would his interests coincide with Legroeder's now?

Tracy-Ace was watching them both with obvious interest. Freem'n seemed to be doing an excellent job of acting. He had to persuade his superiors, presumably including Tracy-Ace, that his actions with the Narseil had been taken either under duress or in order to sabotage the Narseil mission. Had he already been debriefed? Legroeder could read nothing from Deutsch's face.

"That's what we were hoping to hear," Tracy-Ace said. "In fact, there might be another job coming your way soon." She glanced at Legroeder, who realized he was holding his breath. He let it out slowly, hoping that Deutsch wouldn't decide to explain what *really* had happened.

Legroeder shifted his gaze back to the holo, momentarily forgotten in the excitement of seeing Deutsch again. The Deep Flux. The waiting Kyber fleet. "Weren't you about to tell me about that?" he asked Tracy-Ace.

"The Free Kyber Republic Joint Fleet?" she said. "What would you like to know?"

"Well—for one thing, why do they *appear* to be poised at the edge of the Deep Flux?"

Tracy-Ace chuckled. "That's right, you don't know about this on Barbados. Well, they're poised there because they have a *long* way to go. I'm not free to discuss the specific destination. But as I said, new hunting grounds. Away from the Centrist Worlds."

Legroeder tried to think through the implications of a vast pirate fleet setting out to colonize new worlds. If the Kyber were going *away* from the Centrist Worlds . . .

Good riddance?

That seemed unlikely.

"But why the Deep Flux?"

Tracy-Ace's gaze was steady. "That's the shortcut our planners have chosen. Too slow, otherwise."

"But . . ." *Shortcut? To slow death?* ". . . the Deep Flux is unnavigable. It's unstable; it's unmappable. I've never heard of anyone rigging it and coming back alive." Or coming back at all. *Where could they be going that it would be worth risking the Deep Flux?* The very thought reminded him, with a shiver, of the way *Impris* had vanished.

Tracy-Ace cocked her head slightly. "All that used to be true."

"*Used* to be?" Legroeder blinked. "Are you telling me that you know how to navigate the Deep Flux? Go in and come back out again? Go where you're supposed to go?" Not possible. Was it? Dear God.

Tracy-Ace gave the slightest of nods. "There are some problems, still. But it does work."

Legroeder glanced at Deutsch. His cyborg friend was sitting silent and expressionless, easy enough to do with those damn silvered lenses for eyes. *"Problems?"*

"Perhaps Rigger Deutsch could explain it better," Tracy-Ace said. "Rigger Deutsch?"

Freem'n whirred for a moment. "You know some of it already, Legroeder. The differences in our rigging techniques—"

"You mean the augments?"

"Of course. In our experience, the main problem with navigating the Deep Flux is the huge range of complex sensory elements that have to be translated and decoded before they can be perceived clearly. For that, we think you need augments."

Legroeder stroked his temple, trying to consider Deutsch's words without seeming to be puzzled. He didn't want to make Barbados seem like a *complete* backwater outpost. He was certainly aware that the augments changed the overall look of things in the Flux; it was one reason for his aversion to them. He didn't *want* the look of the Flux changed from something he could understand intuitively.

Deutsch seemed to read his thoughts. "It *is* one area in which the use of augments is superior." Deutsch paused. "I take it the Narseil, in your observation, haven't made much headway in this regard?"

Legroeder shook his head slowly. He was supposed to have been a spy among the Narseil. He had better be ready to convey intelligence about them. "None that they mentioned to me."

"But they do have their own areas of great strength, and versatility, when it comes to rigging, yes?" Deutsch said.

"Certainly," Legroeder answered, wondering why Deutsch was making that particular point now.

Tracy-Ace interrupted the chain of thought. "So, yes, we do have the ability to go through the Deep Flux. It's not been perfected. But it's good enough ... or nearly so ..." She pressed her lips together with what seemed a flash of pain, looking at the holo.

Good enough to risk an entire colony fleet? Legroeder was stunned by the thought. He wasn't sure which dismayed him more, the thought of risking a whole fleet of ships in the Deep Flux, or the thought of new colonies being started by a band—an armada—of pirates.

"Legroeder?"

He blinked, turning.

"Come back."

He exhaled slowly. "Sorry. What did you say?" He carefully lifted his cup of murk to his lips.

Tracy-Ace angled a curious gaze at him. "I was just wondering—does that view, by any chance, make you think of *Impris*?"

Legroeder choked on the thick, black liquid.

"Are you all right?"

He cleared his throat vigorously. "Yes—" he managed "—it does. I don't, uh, know that much about *Impris*, actually." He tried to control the flush in his face. "But I take it—you do?"

"Well, sure, we track it. Or rather, *we* don't—but we receive reports on it from time to time from the outpost whose rotation it is to follow it." She frowned. "Not very *clear* reports, mind you. If Kilo-Mike/Carlotta weren't so damned chary with their data, I'd be able to show you its location on a chart." Mercifully, she did not ask whether or why they did not have such information on Barbados.

He decided to head off the question anyway. "Really. I've always been interested in the ship—Flying Dutchman of the Stars, and all that—but I was never privy to that sort of information."

"Bosses," Deutsch interjected in a pleasant baritone. "Half of them won't give you the information you need. And then they complain when you don't get the job done right."

Tracy-Ace eyed Deutsch with an unreadable expression. "Careful, there, Rigger Deutsch. You never know what a boss might hear." Her cheekbone implants blinked. "Still, you do have a point. Some bosses delegate responsibility better than others. Certainly the bosses of different outposts do things in their own ways."

◻ *Shall we fill you in on that?* ◻

Legroeder nodded as the internal voice provided details. The outposts of the Free Kyber Republic were joined in a loose confederation of worlds and fortresses—each with its distinctive culture and bosses. Each stronghold made its contribution to the group goals, such as the colonizing fleet;

but rancorous disagreement was more common than not. The bosses made their own rules, treated their own people as they chose, and determined such things as when or how to raid Centrist shipping. Some gave their captains near-complete autonomy, with reward systems for bringing in booty such as captured ships and slaves. Others exercised tight control . . .

"Legroeder, are you *listening?*"

"Uh—yes."

"I was talking about *Impris*. You said you were interested."

"Yes. You say someone tracks her all the time?"

Tracy-Ace peered at him closely, which made him nervous. "Theoretically, someone keeps a ship in her vicinity at all times—though when the rotation changes from one outpost to another, things can go to hell pretty fast. She's been lost more than once."

Legroeder stared at her, wishing he had this conversation recorded.

◻ *You do.* ◻

He bobbed his head, trying not to show any reaction. "Why the, uh—rotation?" he asked, trying to sound guileless. "If you don't mind my asking."

Tracy-Ace shrugged. "It's hardly a secret. When *Impris* is in a participating boss's territory, she makes a powerful bait for drawing in passing ships. It makes for such an easy kill." She shook her head in apparent disdain. "Especially when the captains of the target ships are on the take, as has happened more than once."

Legroeder thought of Hyutu, captain of the *L.A.*

"I never thought it was very sporting, myself," she added. "But some of the bosses love it so much they fight over whose turn it is—especially since *Impris* seems to hop-scotch around a lot, for reasons I don't personally understand."

Legroeder stared at her, blood pulsing, wishing he could be standing in court on Faber Eridani right now, listening to Tracy-Ace repeat all of this under oath. He tried not to let his voice tremble. "Do you know anything about the ship itself? Her crew? Her passengers?"

Tracy-Ace gave her head a shake. "As far as I know, there's never been any contact. It's hard to imagine that anyone's alive on her, though. After all these years?"

Hard to imagine, maybe. But they are alive. I heard their voices, crying out. It was no illusion. I know what I heard. Legroeder swallowed, then said hesitantly, "Would you mind if I—researched the subject a little, while I'm here? It's a sort of . . . well, hobby, I guess you could call it." *A hobby? Christ.*

As Tracy-Ace raised her eyebrows, Deutsch began to stir. Was he uncomfortable with the direction of this conversation, warning Legroeder to back off?

Deutsch pushed himself back from the table. "If you would excuse me—" a sharp glance in Legroeder's direction seemed to confirm Legroeder's fear "—I'm just about due for a meeting with my crew chief. Miss Alfa, thank you for bringing me here. Legroeder, it's good to see you. If you need me, just use my name on the com system."

Legroeder raised a hand in farewell as Deutsch floated away on his levitators. *You're on your own again. Be careful.* If only he knew what being careful meant.

Tracy-Ace was also gazing after Deutsch. "We have to find a place for him. Not routine flights, not after what he's been through. He did a remarkable job under the circumstances."

"Yes, he did," Legroeder said uncomfortably. He looked down and realized that the food in front of him was cold.

"Try the bread," Tracy-Ace said, spreading some syrup on a piece of her own. "It's pretty good." She tucked it into her mouth and chewed quickly.

Legroeder toyed with the bread and nibbled a piece. It was tasteless. "Yah. Listen—um—" The discussion of Deutsch had wrenched another subject to mind, one he'd been avoiding. "There's something I've been wanting to ask you about. What are you—I mean, what's going to happen to the Narseil crew?"

The augments lit up at the corners of Tracy-Ace's eyes. "What do you think we should do with them?"

"Well, I don't—I mean, I—"

Her eyes hardened momentarily. "It has been suggested that we put them out an airlock. They cost us heavily in that battle."

Legroeder felt his face turn pale. He remembered the dream . . .

"I didn't say I was *taking* the suggestion, though," Tracy-Ace said. She looked away, stroking her cheek in thought, then glanced back at him. "I get the feeling that you got to be pretty good friends with some of the Narseil during your time together . . ." She raised her eyebrows.

Legroeder shrugged, but his throat tightened.

"It would be surprising if you hadn't," Tracy-Ace pointed out. "I was thinking, you might be able to smooth the way to getting some information from them." Her eyes changed expression, but he still couldn't tell what the expression *was*. "We would be foolish to waste all that knowledge and talent, after all. And whatever else my boss is, he isn't foolish."

Legroeder nodded uneasily. "Then, I take it . . . it'll be your boss who makes the decision about the Narseil?"

Tracy-Ace cocked her head quizzically.

"You know, they were just—fighting for their ship—and their people," Legroeder said, and instantly regretted blurting it out like that.

"That is true," Tracy-Ace said. "It remains to be seen just what their fate will be—and how the decision will be made." She frowned. "I think you just need to trust me on this."

Trust her? Could he?

"Did you get the message I sent you last night? If you weren't on the com in your sleep?"

"Uh—"

She glanced carefully around before continuing. "There are people who are interested in talking to the Narseil. *Im-*

portant people—who are interested in seeing some changes."

His hands froze in midair. *The underground?* He struggled to act as if he had heard nothing of import.

Tracy-Ace had a smile at one corner of her mouth; her finger stroking her cheekbone. One eyebrow arched slightly. "Why don't you finish eating, so I can show you around some more? My schedule is clear for the rest of the day."

Legroeder felt such a sharp tingle in his nerves, he wondered for an instant if she had a hand on his arm again. But no; her hands were folded in front of her. Legroeder took a last bite of bread and nodded as he swallowed, and whispered silently, yes, I think I'd like to do that very much. I would.

ONE COULD do a lot of walking in Outpost Ivan. Maybe that was how everyone got their exercise—although it wouldn't have surprised him to discover that he could absorb exercise impulses from the flicker-tubes, while riding like a salami from one place to another. For two hours now, they had walked—surely covering the length of the station several times over. Tracy-Ace pointed out this and that, giving him a sense of the general layout of the place. His implants were frantically integrating this new knowledge with the information they had gained during the night and in the flicker-tubes; it was probably just as well that they weren't riding the flicker-tubes again, because he thought he'd absorbed about all he could handle at one time.

For the most part, the implants stayed out of his way and let him observe at his own pace. But he always had the feeling that somewhere in the back of his mind a structure was growing, a steady accretion of bricks and mortar and grains of sand—not just a gathering of factual knowledge about the Kyber and Outpost Ivan, but a basis for understanding how it all worked together. Maybe the implants weren't such a bad thing, after all; without them, he would have spent weeks learning what he'd learned in the last twenty-four hours here.

Perhaps the strangest observation was that life here seemed considerably more like life in the Centrist Worlds than he had imagined. He caught glimpses of citizens performing the necessary work of keeping a world of eleven thousand people running: building and repairing infrastructure, growing food in culture-factories, packaging and transporting it and preparing it for consumption. At one point, they passed a troop of children being herded along by their monitors or teachers, though Tracy-Ace told him that for the most part the children were housed and educated in a different habitat.

There was one question that hadn't been answered yet; it had started as a back-of-the-mind thorn, ignored at first, but steadily growing in his thoughts. Finally he voiced it, as he stood with Tracy-Ace at an overlook to a cargo hub, a kind of indoor railway yard where pallets of food and other goods were being unloaded and sorted. He had not yet seen any visibly oppressed workers. "Where," he asked, framing his words with care, "are the . . . captive workers?" *The slaves.*

As he turned toward Tracy-Ace, he saw her expression darken. For a moment, she didn't answer; and then her voice took on a distant quality as she said, "The . . . nonvoluntary workers are mostly out in the fleet preparation area."

He waited for elaboration; she looked as though she had more to say. But she turned without meeting his eyes and said, "Let's go this way."

He had to hurry to catch up with her, and by the time he did, she had her outward expression firmly under control and began pointing out other sights of interest: the corridor toward enviro-controls, security, medical. Finally Legroeder interrupted to say, "Should I not have asked that, back there?"

Tracy-Ace jerked her head toward him, her implants firing rapidly. Frowning, she shook her head, her hair swinging violently back and forth. "I can't talk about that right now. This is a time for you to see what we have; it's not a time for you to ask about our policies."

"But I wasn't—" he began, and then shut up. *Don't push it.* "Okay," he said. "I won't ask."

She nodded sharply. "Good." She closed her eyes for a moment, and seemed to be coming to a decision. "Listen," she said, propelling him by the arm in a new direction. "I know something you'd like to see. As a rigger. *Voluntary* workers. Come on."

Down a lifttube and along a winding ramp.

"It's early for me to show this to you, but I think you're ready for it. But before I do, I have to tell you that this is a top security area." She stopped and turned to look him squarely in the eye. "There will be security features there that you don't even see. Their order of business is to shoot first and ask questions later. Can you observe quietly and save *your* questions for later?"

Legroeder's voice caught. "Uh—sure, yes." What the hell else could he say? And why was he being taken to a top security area?

"Good."

A short distance farther on, they came to a door that said *Maintainer Staff Only.* The door was flanked by two guards bristling with sidearms. There were also various lenses in the walls. Cameras? Lasers? Legroeder opened his mouth to ask, then closed it. Tracy-Ace spoke briefly to the guards, who nodded deferentially but not without a close inspection of Legroeder.

The door paled at Tracy-Ace's touch. Legroeder followed her into an antechamber, where there were more guards and security instruments. Tracy-Ace had to establish two separate augment links with the security panels to get past this station, and Legroeder was scanned and then fitted with a security badge. It felt like a bulls-eye on his chest. With Tracy-Ace, he passed through another door into a large, semidarkened room. He blinked, looking around. The walls were dark; but in the center of the room, six heavily augmented Kyber men and women were seated around a circle of consoles. In the center of the circle, various holos were dancing and glowing, with views of the Flux. At the consoles were rapidly changing schematic readouts. Were these the riggers who kept the station anchored in the Flux?

At a nod from Tracy-Ace, Legroeder stepped forward cautiously, peering over the shoulder of the nearest crewman. One of the crew glanced up, then immediately returned her attention to her work. Legroeder could not follow all the information displayed on the screens, but he saw enough to be pretty sure: these weren't the maintainers. They were the people maintaining the maintainers, watching to ensure that whatever was happening out there in the Flux was satisfactory. Legroeder stepped back. Tracy-Ace angled her head to indicate that he should follow her through another door.

More security.

As they stepped into the next room, he was surprised to find that they were enclosed in a ghostly forcefield bubble. *To protect us from what's inside? Or to protect whatever's in here from us?* A glance from Tracy-Ace seemed to confirm the latter interpretation.

This was a very different sort of room: a cross between a holocinema and a medical intensive care ward. Abstract light impulses flashed around the walls of the room, in chaotic patterns, making him feel as if he were in a cinema watching the play of light, without seeing the actual images. Music filled the air; at least, he decided to think of it as music—a sort of atonal chant that he found vaguely disturbing.

In the center of the room were four—no, five—riggerstations, he guessed, though they resembled no riggerstations he had ever seen. They looked like a cross between scaffolds and exoskeletons. Ensconced within them were five humans. At least, he thought they were humans. To call them augmented would have been an understatement; they looked like Christmas trees. They were encased in what looked like clear gel sacks, with spider-webs of tubes, wires, and fibop cables running in and out of the sacks.

"The maintainers?" he asked.

"The maintainers," said Tracy-Ace.

For all their apparent confinement, the maintainers were constantly in motion: small movements—hands clenching and unclenching, arms swinging a few centimeters one way and then another, heads shifting this way and that. But looking at what?

A technician walked over in their direction; Legroeder decided it was a woman, though she was heavily suited, with a strange-looking helmet encasing her head. Tracy-Ace spoke to her briefly through a private com-link, then glanced back at Legroeder.

"Do they just stay here—constantly in the Flux?" Legroeder asked in amazement. The rigger-stations looked like permanent wombs. Were the maintainers even breathing air? It looked as if they were receiving their oxygen through some kind of amniotic fluid.

Tracy-Ace nodded absently. "Constantly," she murmured. Her voice sounded oddly distracted; she was looking off toward the flashing lights on the wall, as though she had forgotten why they were here. Were those lights hypnotizing her?

The technician spoke. "They *live* there. It's their life."

"Mm?" Legroeder said. He suddenly realized he was fighting the same distraction he'd noticed in Tracy-Ace. "But . . . what about *rest?*" He squinted at his own words; it took him a moment to realize that he was asking not about physical rest, but regeneration of the psyche. Connection with the real world.

"It all happens right here," said the tech, waving a gloved hand around. "All this provides cortical stimulation. It's only partly random. Plus there's other input, to modulate REM phase and so on."

Legroeder suppressed a shiver; the light-stimulus and the music were sending a strange glow through him. Was that why the tech was wearing a suit, to isolate her from this? He squinted at the flickering lights. Something nagged at him about that; there was something he wasn't seeing.

"They're not all actively monitoring the station at the same time, of course . . . they work in rotation . . ."

(Are you getting a handle on this?) he asked his implants, as the tech's voice droned.

◻ *We are . . . seeking to adapt . . . to the unfamiliar stimulus . . .* ◻

(What is it about . . . these lights? What am I missing?)

◻ *Patterns . . . complex patterns within . . .* ◻

He stopped listening, because he suddenly knew what it was. There were patterns in the lights, all right; there were whole images embedded in the patterns. If he could just see it. *Let go. Let it come.* His breath sighed out, and the pattern collapsed inward; and with a sudden perceptual transformation, he saw what was in there. It was a view of the Flux again. But it was a far more intimate view than the holos that the crew outside saw; it was the Flux as the maintainers saw it. The rest of his breath went out in a gasp, because he suddenly felt as though he were afloat in the Flux, stretched out in a net that extended much farther than any ship's net. It stretched out for a very long way . . . and down . . .

Far down . . . toward another layer . . . toward a network of moving shadows. It was like gazing into the depths of a fast-running river, and imagining falling in . . .

He drew back with a shudder, blinking.

"What is it?" Tracy-Ace asked.

"I don't—*Jesus*—these people are reaching all the way down—" He swallowed.

Tracy-Ace cocked her head. "Down to *what?*"

"Down to the *Deep Flux*," Legroeder whispered. "Why are they doing that? It's . . . it's . . ." He shook his head; it felt full of cobwebs.

"What did you see? Where?" Tracy-Ace demanded.

He breathed deeply, pointing vaguely into the room. "It's there—in the patterns on the walls—" He gulped for air; he was trembling, as though he'd made an emergency scram from a net. "I saw . . . currents down there—deep—dangerous—"

Tracy-Ace gazed at him, her face flickering. "I would not have expected you to be able to see that," she murmured.

"Even the maintainers barely see it. We're not *in* the Deep Flux. They monitor its location, to make sure we *don't* drift down there."

He gulped, only faintly relieved.

"They know the area very well," the tech said. "They spend a lot of their lives keeping watch on it."

"Good," Legroeder breathed. "What do they do when they're *not* watching that?"

The tech shrugged. "Living in whatever worlds they make for themselves out there, I suppose."

"That's their existence?"

"They're all volunteers," Tracy-Ace said, with an aggressive edge to her voice.

Legroeder gazed at her, trying to conceal his doubt.

The tech said in a more severe voice, "They have their reasons. Some of them are just drawn to it. Some have . . . severe physical handicaps. This gives them a way to serve."

"But to spend their *lives* . . . "

Tracy-Ace's eyes narrowed. "It's just another reality. I thought you, of all people, would understand."

"There's a reality to it, yes. But—" Legroeder shook his head. To spend their *lives* in it?

"Without them," Tracy-Ace said stiffly, "the station would be adrift in the Flux. This is a duty—and an honor— that they have chosen."

Legroeder didn't answer. *If you weren't an outlaw outpost that had to hide in the Flux, it wouldn't be necessary, would it?* But he knew he'd already said too much.

Tracy-Ace seemed to guess his thoughts. She spoke briefly to the tech, then turned and ushered Legroeder out.

In the corridor, with the cortical stimulation and the last security checkpoint behind him, Legroeder felt as if a blessed silence had descended around him. He felt his nervous system slowly coming down from whatever state it had been in.

Tracy-Ace was clearly experiencing some of the same effect. But she recovered quickly enough to say sharply, as they walked away, "You didn't approve of that, I take it."

Legroeder opened his mouth, and shut it. He wondered why she had even shown that to him.

"What I said was true, you know—about the maintainers being honored volunteers. It would hardly be in our interest to put unwilling draftees in the position of maintaining our station in the Flux."

He kept silent.

"They do lead interesting lives, you know, while they . . ." She hesitated.

"While they what?" Legroeder blurted. *"Live?"*

Her hesitation stretched a moment longer. "Yes."

He thought of how much it took out of *him* to stay in the Flux for an extended period, and he wondered how well the human mind and body could hold up to that kind of immersion. "How long *do* they live?" he asked, trying to sound merely curious, and knowing that he failed.

Tracy-Ace picked up her pace, avoiding his gaze. He thought she was going to avoid the question, as well. Then she said softly, "On average? About ten years, on the job."

Ten years. "And . . . how long after they retire?"

Another hesitation. "They don't usually retire . . . exactly."

"You mean, they die on the job?"

When Tracy-Ace didn't reply, he glanced sideways at her. Her temples were flickering, and she was scowling. It was a moment before he realized that she was nodding.

Oh.

She turned on him suddenly, her eyes flaring, but not from the glow of augments. Was she angry? He thought she was angry. "You think we're so heartless. Come with me." She grabbed his wrist and changed direction, down a side corridor. He practically had to run to keep up. There was surprising strength in those slender arms.

Was that a connection he felt between their implants? He focused inward. *(Are you connected to her?)*

◻ *No.* ◻

Then what the—? Her surge of anger, or passion, was so powerful he could have sworn it was a direct link. But no, it was just raw human emotion. She was boiling over with a need to do something and do it *now*, a burning that was working its way out from within. Was it always there, but under tighter control? Whatever it was she was burning to do, it was important and dangerous—and it involved him. Was this where Tracy-Ace the Law was going to reappear?

He swallowed back his apprehension. "Where, uh . . . can I ask where we're going?"

She didn't look at him, but her fingers tightened around his wrist. "Flicker-tube," was all she said. Grimly.

Chapter 24
JOININGS

FRE'GEEL PAUSED in his round of the detention cell area and peered out through the gate. Nothing, no sign even of the guards. He resumed his tireless walk among the crew. Most sat on the floor, or on benches, muttering to themselves or each other. Fre'geel gave an occasional hiss of encouragement as he passed among them. They needed it, especially those who did not understand what their human shipmate was trying to do, under the guise of betraying the Narseil.

Soon it would be time for another exercise period. Fre'geel intended to make sure they kept moving and active. It was the best he could do. It had been too long since any of them had had a proper soak in a pool. They were all drying out, and he was seeing far too much rubbing at sore and itchy skin, and scratching at neck-sails. He'd asked the Kyber guards, politely, if something could be done. The guard had laughed—a particularly ugly human laugh—and sauntered away. It had occurred to Fre'geel afterward that perhaps he should have asked to speak to a superior. He was not thinking all that clearly himself.

Cantha drifted his way, and they paused to confer. "I am told that the crew in the next compartment are becoming agitated," Cantha murmured. "Some of them are blaming Legroeder for turning us in, and they're beginning to vent their anger."

Fre'geel blinked his gritty eyes. Were his people forgetting their training? "We all knew it could happen this way," he sighed, as much to himself as to Cantha. It would only get worse if he didn't find a way to control it. "Perhaps the guards will permit me to go in and speak to them."

As he turned toward the security door, he was surprised to see it opening. Two Kyber guards stepped into the detention cell. "Where is the commander?" one of the guards called, in a barely comprehensible Kyber Anglic.

Fre'geel went forward. "I'm the commander."

"Someone to see you," said the guard. He motioned to Fre'geel to follow him out of the room.

The guards left him alone in a holding room with a human Kyber female. She was standing at a one-way glass staring into the prison cell. Fre'geel allowed her a slight nod—and suddenly saw Rigger Legroeder standing on the other side of her. For a moment, he was caught speechless—overjoyed to see Legroeder alive, and apparently healthy. Then, with a mental jerk, he remembered his role. He turned toward Legroeder and hissed: "You. Traitor. Human."

Legroeder's eyes widened, and for an instant he too seemed nonplused. "Fre'geel," he said, his voice cracking slightly. "I'm glad to see you. Are you all right? What about the others?"

"They haven't killed us yet, if that's what you mean." Fre'geel flexed a long finger threateningly. "You lying—murderous—"

"Are you the commander of these forces?" interrupted the Kyber woman.

Fre'geel bit off his words and made a head-inclining gesture of acknowledgment. "I am. And I should address you as—?"

"Tracy-Ace/Alfa." The female, dressed in gold and black, with considerable cyber augmentation on her face, appeared to be examining Fre'geel from head to toe. He wondered if she found him satisfactorily alien. "Commander Fre'geel, we are here on a courtesy call, to inquire as to your condition. I must tell you that there are others who will wish to speak to you soon. In spite of the destruction you have caused, I believe it is possible that we might find ways to work together."

Fre'geel let his breath out in a slow hiss. "We did not come here to collaborate with you. Ma'am." He flicked his eyes over to Rigger Legroeder, wishing fervently that he could read the human's mind, or speak privately with him.

"No?" she responded. "Well, then, perhaps you'll be able to explain why you *did* come here. In the meantime—" she crossed her arms over her chest and furrowed her brow "—tell me—is sufficient care being extended to your people?" Her gaze seemed both to invite complaint and to challenge it.

Fre'geel refused to rise to the bait. Complain? That he would not do. Despite his determination to address the question of—

"You look all dried out," Legroeder said, interrupting his thought.

"What do you mean?" the female asked, turning to Legroeder.

Legroeder gestured toward Fre'geel. "They need a pool they can soak in, for their skin. They're amphibians, you know."

"A *pool*? You think we keep pools in the detention area?"

"If not a pool, then bathing areas. Showers. Something. They'll get sick and be of no use to you, otherwise."

"Is this true?" Tracy-Ace/Alfa asked Fre'geel.

The Narseil nodded.

Tracy-Ace/Alfa looked thoughtful. Rings only knew what was going on in her augmented mind. But whatever it was, she astonished Fre'geel by saying, "All right, then—it will be done." She cocked her head. "Is there anything else you need, to maintain your health?"

Fre'geel overcame his surprise enough to decide he might as well take advantage of the opportunity. "A bit of room to exercise in would be helpful," he allowed. With a twitch of his eye, he glanced at Rigger Legroeder. The human was wearing a stony expression. But was that an approving twinkle in his eye?

"Exercise." Tracy-Ace/Alfa peered through the one-way pane at the crowded detention cell. It was just one of three that the Narseil were crammed into. "Very well." She turned back to Fre'geel. "You may return to your cell, Commander. You will be called when the time comes." With that, she gave a nod that was not quite dismissive, and the guards reappeared immediately.

As Fre'geel turned away, Legroeder murmured a farewell, and Tracy-Ace/Alfa said, "Think constructively, Commander. Think constructively."

Fre'geel said nothing, but was thoughtful as he walked back to rejoin his crew.

"I WANTED you to know," Tracy-Ace said, biting her words as they made their way back to the flicker-tube, "that we do have some ability to take care of people here. Even our prisoners."

Legroeder had no immediate answer; he was stunned by her assertion. *Is that why you were in such a rush to take me to see the Narseil? Because you were afraid of what I thought, after the maintainers?*

"Thank you," he said finally. He was pleased by her concessions to the needs of the Narseil, but a little worried, too. Had he betrayed too much interest in their well being?

Tracy-Ace said nothing more about it, as they got into the tubes. She didn't speak during the ride, and Legroeder, his head already spinning, used the *stop* command to turn off the flicker-feed. The silence was restful.

Stepping out at the end, he rejoined a troubled-looking

Tracy-Ace. "What is it?" he asked, falling in beside her as she strode away. He realized that he'd felt a sudden impulse to reach out to her. What was he going to do, take her by the hand? Put an arm around her shoulder? *Jesus.* He clasped his hands behind his back, to keep them out of trouble.

Keeping pace with her wasn't easy. She kept turning abruptly, and hurrying him along. Her temples were flickering madly; her mouth was pursed in concentration.

"Can I ask where we're going?" he said finally.

She stopped at an intersection, frowning. It must have been time for a shift change, because the corridors were bustling with people. "We need to talk," she said. Eyeing the crowds around them, she added, "In private."

Legroeder remained silent, wondering at the sudden urgency. Was this still about his remarks about the maintainers, or was something else going on? *You can still blow this, you know.*

She seemed to take his silence for assent, not that it mattered. Peering at him with sudden intense concentration, she rubbed at the corner of her mouth with a knuckle, as though to stop a tic. "Let's show you where the law lives." She grabbed his arm and pulled him along again. There was something dark in her tone that reminded him that he was a prisoner.

En route to wherever they were going, they passed a heavily guarded sector. SECTION 29, said a sign over the entrance. A tall, red-skinned man had walked into the area just a few seconds before, and Legroeder could feel Tracy-Ace tense up beside him. The man hadn't seen her, but she waited until he was out of sight before hurrying Legroeder along. "The command center," she muttered as they passed the entrance. "We'll get to that later."

"Who was that guy?"

Her breath hissed out. "Someone you won't need to worry about, I hope. This way."

Legroeder followed, uneasily. Some distance farther on, she stopped at a food-plaza, where she picked up a carton of Asian noodles and broc, plus something to drink. A few minutes later, they were in a sector that looked more like living quarters. Tracy-Ace's hand found its way to his arm again; this time he felt the slight twinge of a data-connection, though nothing came through the connection to tell him why she was tense.

He suddenly knew where they were going, though.

The corridor outside Tracy-Ace's apartment was more decorative than the one outside his; it was rose colored and obviously more recently refinished. This was the abode of the Law? Her hand touched the door. Unlike his, it opened with a click and swung inward: a solid door. Legroeder followed her in. The room was three times the size of his, finished in a russet two-tone. The basic appointments were similar: bunk in one corner, desk in another, counter with cupboards, doorway to the bath. The bunk was larger, but more striking was the modified com-console over the head of the bed, with linkup arms folded like a spider's legs against the wall. "Do you *sleep* hooked up to that thing?" he asked, with perhaps more distaste in his voice than he'd intended.

Tracy-Ace grunted noncommittally and set the food cartons on the counter.

On the pillow directly under the console was a brown plush animal. *Teddy bear?* Legroeder turned, refraining from comment. On the wall were two pieces of framed hol-oart: one an alien landscape, orange and smoky-looking with a huge, luminous red sun; the other a terrestrial farmhouse standing beside a woods. He peered at the two pictures. Some intuition told him that the farmhouse had some meaning to her, and something else told him not to ask just now. Below the farmhouse holo, her lounge chair was festooned with even more cyber-attachments than the bed; it was a smaller version of the command seat in which he'd first met her. "Is all this stuff for business or pleasure?" he asked, keeping his voice neutral.

Her eyebrows went up halfway, and for the first time in a while, she allowed herself half a grin. "Both, I suppose."

Her expression darkened again. "We can talk here," she said. "It's private. It's safe." She hesitated a moment. "That's why I brought you here."

Not an attempted seduction, then. Probably just as well. Greta the Enforcer was not so far in his past. But then, Tracy-Ace didn't seem anything like Greta, or so his instincts told him. And wasn't he, as a rigger, supposed to trust his instincts? And weren't his instincts telling him . . .

Jesus, get a grip. He exhaled tightly. It had been a *long* time since he'd been with a woman, and just being in this room with her made his groin ache. Even tense, she was surprisingly attractive. "Would this be a good time to tell me what's wrong?" he said suddenly, to take his mind off the subject. "*Something* is, isn't it?"

She looked at him sharply for a moment, and he had a sudden terrifying vision of her hissing, *Yes, we've just figured out that you're a spy. And you know what we do with spies . . .*

Then her gaze shifted, and she seemed to study the blank wall over his shoulder for a while. "Correct me if I'm wrong," she said finally, in a voice that was metered and precise. "I get the impression that you don't exactly approve of everything we do here at Ivan. Is that true?"

His throat constricted, until it was all he could do to manage a husky rasp. "Well, I—"

Her gaze shifted to probe his. "In addition, you seem to have a highly developed sympathy for the Narseil—and Rings knows who else, on the outside."

He swallowed. His vision was turning out to be frighteningly accurate.

Tracy-Ace pressed a finger to her lips, as one of those infuriating expressions that he couldn't identify flashed across her face. "Furthermore—when you first made your presence known here at Ivan, you were seen following a data-thread that indicated a connection to—"

He could hear nothing now except blood rushing in his ears. *To the underground. Admit it.* The knot in his stomach tightened. He tried not to let it show on his face. But hadn't she hinted earlier—?

Tracy-Ace seemed to be reading his thoughts. She nodded and completed her sentence: "—a connection to some of us who are dissatisfied with certain practices of this outpost, and of the Kyber Republic."

Huh? Legroeder started. "Dis . . . satisfied—?"

"With the treatment of certain groups of people, for example. And with the way we . . . pursue some of our goals."

Legroeder tried to swallow.

There was a catch in Tracy-Ace's voice as her expression softened. "As it happens, Legroeder, *I* am one of those people. One of those . . . hoping to change things."

His pulse was pounding now. He felt as if he might fall over in a faint. Was this a trap? It was, wasn't it? *Tell me it's not a trap.*

"You probably think I'm trying to trap you," she said. "I'm not. Really. It's no coincidence, you know, that you were brought to my attention when you explored that particular thread. And if you are looking to be put in touch with others . . ." She paused. "I can do that for you."

He tried to draw a breath, but someone was sitting on his chest. "I—"

"It will have to be set up carefully, of course."

"Uh—"

"Which I will do. But in the meantime—"

For all the speed of their direct connection, he felt as if he could barely keep up here. He hadn't been expecting anything at all like this. And that expression on her face— he was blinking at her, trying to understand; it looked like something he'd never seen on her face before. *Vulnerability.* She was taking a risk. She was afraid. But of what?

"You must speak of this to no one outside this room," she continued. "Not your friends. Not even me, unless I tell you it's safe." She rubbed one of her now-darkened implants. Meaning . . . others might be privy to what her implants heard?

"Do you understand?" she asked, and he nodded slowly.

"Good." She sighed, her breath a long, slow whisper, and the tension seemed to drain out of her. She glanced at him with a hint of a smile, then looked away, as though embarrassed.

It seemed impossible. Legroeder frowned, caught for an instant between impulses. *If she's another Greta, you are in deep, deep trouble.* Without allowing himself another thought, he reached out. She met his hand halfway, took it with surprising strength. His implants came to life, and he felt a shock of surprise at the intensity of the connection. Understanding flowed through the link and blossomed in his mind; and suddenly he realized *why* she felt vulnerable. Tracy-Ace, the dreaded node-commander, was appalled by the Kyber methods. But any attempt to change the system could backfire at once. For an instant, he glimpsed Tracy-Ace as a troubled young woman, caught in a maelstrom of shifting currents of power. Then the glimpse was gone, replaced by the confidence of Tracy-Ace/Alfa, the node-commander. But he had seen it; it was there.

If he could believe it. If she was telling the truth.

What would she gain by lying? She already had him as a prisoner, if that was what she wanted.

He squeezed her hand; she squeezed back, hard. Then she was up, padding across the room in her bare feet. When had she taken her shoes off? "Are you hungry?" she asked. Without waiting for an answer, she opened a cabinet door and took out bowls and a pair of slender glasses. Legroeder watched silently as she served the noodles; his head was still ringing like a bell from that contact. What had it touched in *him?*

"Glass of wino?" Tracy-Ace asked.

He barked a laugh. "Glass of what?"

She brandished a semiclear carton of red liquid. "Wino. It's synthetic, but it's not too bad. What's so funny?"

"Nothing," he said, suppressing a chuckle. "Sure, I'd love some."

She opened the carton and poured. Legroeder accepted a glass and held it up to the light. Clear burgundy color. He sniffed at the liquid. Could it be worse than what he'd drunk at DeNoble? He held his glass up to hers. "Clink them together," he said. Tracy-Ace looked puzzled, but clinked. It felt satisfying. He took a sip, hoping it would taste as good as the gesture had felt. It didn't, not even remotely; but somehow that didn't seem to matter. Tracy-Ace was watching him for a reaction, and when he smiled, it felt genuine.

She handed him a bowl and fork and gestured to the only place for them both to sit. They perched together on the edge of the bed—not too close together, but close enough to make him wonder what he was doing here. What he was doing about his mission. *Quite a lot, dammit,* he snarled to himself. *The Narseil are getting a bath, and we've met the underground. That's not too bad.* And it wasn't, really. But it didn't answer the question of what he was doing sitting on a bed with Tracy-Ace/Alfa. What did it mean that he *liked* sitting on the bed with her—liked it quite a lot, now that he thought about it?

He took a quick bite of noodles, then a sip of wino, then stole a glance at Tracy-Ace. It wasn't as if it had been love, or even lust, at first sight. And yet . . . he was aware now, almost hungrily aware, of her physical attractiveness: her lanky grace and energy, the almost elfin delicacy of her face. The vulnerability. Funny, that a woman who controlled so many lethal weapons should seem vulnerable.

And then there was the connecting touch they had shared, not just once but several times. As he gazed at her—no longer a stolen glance, but a steady gaze—he had the dizzying feeling that he had known her for years.

She smiled, and the effect was electrifying. Putting her fork down, she stretched out a hand. He watched the gesture in detached silence for a moment, then took her hand in his. He knew at once that this was something more than a handshake. "Pleased to know you, Tracy-Ace/Alfa," he said in a husky voice.

"Pleased to know you, Renwald Legroeder."

The tingle this time started not at the juncture of their hands, but at his toes. It moved up his body in a languid wave, more a physical sensation than a joining of minds. He felt a brief flash of fear—but a quick glance inward at his implants showed only a faint sparkling against darkness where he expected to see an active connection. This felt less like an uplink/downlink than like lowering himself into a tub of hot water, the heat flowing up his body. It wasn't exactly sexual; it was more like a rising awareness on multiple sensory levels. It was as if his connectors were being tuned, enhanced, made ready for a heightened response. But a response to what?

The wave moved up through his loins with a fleeting tingle, then into his torso. He gasped as it passed his diaphragm; Tracy-Ace let out a little sigh at the same time. He blinked and focused on her. She seemed to be staring at nothing, at space, through him or past him. *Is she who she seems?* She noticed his gaze then—and her eyes sharpened. Her lips turned up, in a smile that took his breath away.

The final rush came quickly, like a vapor filling his skull. He felt a sudden, euphoric clarity, as though he had breathed in a lungful of clear mountain air.

He peered down at their clasped hands and found he wanted to squeeze her hand tighter, to renew the sensation of physical touch. Her eyes brightened as he squeezed, and he felt a second wave pass through him. This time it came from his hand and went straight up his arm. It was accompanied by a strange *itch*.

It took him a moment to realize that the itch was a tremendous spike of uplink/downlink. They were exchanging knowledge in a great exhilarating rush . . .

Snippets of his childhood play, on the long rolling beaches of Claire Marie—pleasure darkened by a certain melancholy, and by his unease with the water. Flashes of the joy and release of an unrestrained dash through the streams of the Flux . . .

Entwined with his flashes were hers—early memories of a farmhouse and grandparents, then coming of age in an utterly alien place, a culture in hiding. Achieving at an early age, mastering the inner life of the intelnet, of the implants and the knowledge systems . . .

Legroeder was filling like a vessel with her challenges and fears, and also her excursions into hopefulness. And against that, his own joys and friendships blazed into relief—Janofer and Gev and Skan—and hints of bitterly dark times . . .

Legroeder was teetering on the edge of a complete surrender to the exchange. He felt a sharp pang of fear; *this is stupid, I'm going to betray everything!* Or his implants would; or hers would somehow find everything he was hiding. But she already knew that he wanted to meet the underground; the only question was whether she was lying to him. His fear was countered by a silent reassurance from his implants: *You're not an open book if you don't want to be.* But his implants had slipped up before.

He was more aware of outward signals now, as he peered at her through half-closed eyes: the body language that he might otherwise have missed, or misread: her eye movements, beckoning, the pressure of her hand, the angling of her legs toward him, a certain openness, a readiness.

I don't think she's lying about this.

She wanted him. And he wanted her. He hadn't been sure before, but now he was. There was not yet a feeling of urgency, but something was happening between them, and quickly. In an extraordinary way, it did not feel rushed at all, but a naturally flowing development. In this strange communion, all of the courtship and wondering and mutual exploration were passing in a blur, a blending of pigments on a living canvas, colors glowing and shifting and fusing. And through it all a slowly rising breath of desire . . .

"Renwald," he heard, and wondered for a moment if he had heard the sound through the air, or through the joining. *My name is Legroeder*, he murmured with mock indignation, the thought slipping out through their joined hands.

"I know," she whispered, "I know." *But I like Renwald, I like the way it rolls off my tongue, I like the way I feel when I say it, the way I'll feel when I hold you in my . . .*

And suddenly she broke off with an embarrassed inner laugh, as though she had not meant to let all of that slip.

You can call me Renwald, any time you want, he murmured, intending to speak it aloud . . . but no, it was another thought slipping through the link. There in front of him now was his hand, almost like a separate entity, moving up her arm; it paused, squeezing her shoulder, before sliding back down to clasp her hand with a tingle. Out of the blue, before he could stop it, the thought floated up out of his mind and into the connection: *Are you the face of the enemy?*

For an instant he feared that she had heard, and would be furious; and indeed she had heard, but her response was a soft laugh: *Do you think I'm your enemy?* And before he could even think that through, her other hand was running up his arm, and then kneading the back of his neck; and he wasn't really even sure how he got to this point, but they were kissing, and he was tasting her lips and shuddering a little from her tongue darting here, and there, and now his breath and hers were both coming faster.

The stream flowing through them was more than just knowledge now; it was like a song, its notes and phrases echoing round as if they had been leading up to this for a year, perfecting this song. And yet he also knew now of the three men and one woman she had made love to before, and of her desire for *him*; and she knew of the scattering of women he had known, only one with genuine love; and the next time he was aware of his left hand, it was stroking her bare right breast (how had it become bare?), caressing and squeezing the swollen red nipple, and feeling a tingle there between the tip of her nipple and the palm of his hand. Another pathway opened, and a memory came to him through her nipple, an image of a bright red sun breaking through a bank of clouds on the only planetary world she had ever known, as a young girl, a world called Carrie's Dream . . . and he squeezed again, and a new image came, this time a memory of her first trembling orgasm . . . and he felt slipping out through his fingers, into the firmness of her breast a memory of his own, the first time he had slipped into the warmth of a woman, a woman three years older than his nineteen years, and his own shuddering . . .

She sighed into his neck and pressed his head down, and he took her hard nipple in his mouth, and for an instant felt as if he were inside her skin looking out, and he reached out and touched himself, her, himself . . . momentarily confused as to which body he was in.

Now. I want you now . . .

He was aware of her augment-controlled immune protections sliding into place. *It is safe . . . no need to worry . . .*

He heard the sigh, and for a moment wasn't sure whose . . . but whichever, or both, their bodies were beginning to move in concert. Their remaining clothing was coming off, hands were darting and exploring; there was some awkwardness, and then everything was off, and they were entwined, not just in thought but in body as well; and she was holding his hardness, and he was stroking her softness; and a little later her mouth was on him hotly, and he was breathing her musky fragrance; then as he slipped into her warm center, the connecting tingle began from that piercing point and flowered outward . . .

*

Implants flickering, blazing with exhilaration, heart pounding, his net of awareness stretched out beyond her . . . but toward what? For a frozen, pulsing moment he felt as though he were joined to a far greater network, the intel-net . . .

*

That sensation flickered away, and in its place was something different, the web of his senses stretching out into time, into the past and future; *her* past and *his* past, and visions of the future . . . two futures, like thin silver ribbons interweaving toward a place that couldn't be seen . . .

*

And behind it all, the joining that was like a choir, given physical shape by sound and music, and urgent movement, joined harmonies rising and straining and falling, the sweet sounds of harp and deep thrumming of bass, all growing, building toward a climax . . .

*

The brightness at their center flared with desire and urgency. For an instant that seemed disconnected in time, his gaze caught her deep green eyes and there was a breathtaking, liquid connection between them. Their movements joined, growing faster. Her heat was building around him, drawing him out farther and harder, breath coming sharper and sharper . . . and for a moment they were suspended in time, electrified . . . and then they came together, in expanding circles of fire against darkness; she was squeezing him in shuddering gasping release, and around them in the darkness of space were bursts of light and sharply drawn breath, and sounds wrapped in silence; and the web blossomed out and exploded with liquid light, raining crimson and gold and pearly white, pulsing until all of the fire was gone. And then a great quilt of darkening comfort closed around them, and they collapsed in quiet release.

"JESUS, ACE," he whispered, his face against her cheek. "How did you do that?"

"Do what?" She laughed softly, trying to keep him from pulling free, but it was too late.

"Fireworks?" He shifted, propping his head, and looked down at her. "I mean, really—*fireworks*?" He gazed appreciatively over her body, which he'd hardly had a chance to do the entire time they were making love. He drew a deep breath, awed by her long-limbed beauty. He stroked her hipbone, cupping the angles.

"I want you to know I don't do that with every new arrival who comes into my node," she murmured, kissing his ear. "Did you like it?"

"Like it?" He laughed softly, pressing his lips to her temple, beside the flickering augment. Her hair was damp with sweat. "Did I just die and go to Heaven?" He paused in reflection. (*Have I just made love, with deep-cyber augment, to the Kyber Law? What have I done?*)

◻ *Isn't that how spies are supposed to do it, according to your folklore?* ◻

He gazed into space, considering. Maybe so, but that was just in crazy male fantasies.

"Good," said Tracy-Ace, pushing him up with a hand on his chest so she could see his face. She grinned, kissed her own fingertip and touched it to his lips. Rolling out from beneath him, she slipped out of his reach and stood up facing him. She was breathtaking, naked, staring down at him. He thought his heart might jump out of his chest. Crazy fantasies were beginning to crowd his thoughts. Along with the fears. (*You're being set up, used.*) *But what a way to be used.*

"I'm glad you liked that," Tracy-Ace said. "Really glad. Because I like you, Renwald Legroeder." She bent down, leading with her nipples, and kissed his forehead, lips, chin. His heart pounded as she straightened up again, then almost stopped as she whispered, "I think pretty soon we're going to have to go introduce you to the Boss, don't you?"

Chapter 25
YANKEE-ZULU/IVAN

To HIS relief, Tracy-Ace hadn't meant *now*. One thing led to another, and they were busy for a while longer after that.

They fell asleep half tangled together. Or rather, Tracy-Ace did. Legroeder drifted in and out of an uneasy sleep, his thoughts reverberating between a blissful euphoria and a terrifying conviction that he had blundered in the most appalling way. He awoke once with a start, imagining Kyber guards breaking down the door and thundering in to drag him away. His heart pounding, he peered across the room in the glow of tiny indicator lights, and saw nothing moving. Nothing except the slow rise and fall of Tracy-Ace/Alfa's breathing. He sighed and closed his eyes.

Doubts crowded in, warring for his attention. How could he have let himself do this? Was he a complete idiot? How could he know he wasn't being used? Manipulated. Set up.

He glanced in her direction. She was sound asleep with her back to him, but snuggled close. Peaceful as a lamb.

What's the matter with you? Can't you just enjoy, without wrecking it by worrying?

Enjoy what—sleeping with the enemy?

His ears were ringing as he drifted back off to sleep.

He awoke to find Tracy-Ace's arm flung over him, her face against his shoulder, her hair against his cheek. She stirred, pressing a leg against him before flickering an eye open and murmuring, and any thought he'd had of drawing away vanished instantly.

She pulled him out of bed and into the shower. Engulfed in a haze of warm mist, Tracy-Ace was just drawing him close again, sending a rush of arousal up his spine, when a memory surfaced in his thoughts, a conversation with Com'peer back at the Narseil station. The surgeon and her team had just finished changing the DNA in his gonads. *"That's where raiders like to do their testing . . . more humiliating that way . . ."*

He swallowed and tried to divert his thoughts, but there was no hiding the loss of arousal.

"You okay?"

"Uh, yes—fine!" he wheezed. He forced a grin, then seized her in a fierce hug. *What have I done? Thinking with my gonads. What have I done?*

She nuzzled his neck, but clearly wasn't fooled. "Let's get dressed and get something to eat," she said, hurrying out of the shower. "Then let's go talk business with the Boss."

"Yes, let's," he muttered, trying not to sound as if he had just been punched in the solar plexus.

* * *

THE BOSS. The single syllable, even in the silence of his thoughts, made him shiver.

After a barely-touched breakfast, they walked to Section 29, which they had passed yesterday. It was, she said, the nerve center of the station, and indeed of the entire Outpost Ivan organization. The security at the entrance was just as threatening as at the maintainers' facility.

Inside, though, the operations center had a surprisingly cobbled-together look, with a great deal of electronic equipment, and people sitting at stations of indeterminate function. Legroeder tried to cover his apprehension by peering over some shoulders, but Tracy-Ace pulled him onward. "This way," she said, heading to the back of the room.

This way. Legroeder kept his eyes open for anyone who looked like a Boss. Would he be a walking display case of augmentation? Tracy-Ace brought him to a semicircular alcove in back, several steps up on a kind of dais, where a swivel chair sat in the middle of a cluttered array of at least fifty tiny console monitors. The chair was facing away from them; blue smoke billowed up from it. Tobacco smoke, with a sharp, pungent sweetness. Legroeder wrinkled his nose. He hadn't smelled that since DeNoble. He hated it.

The chair rotated to face them. A bald-headed man without a trace of augmentation rose, waving a cigar in his right hand, as Tracy-Ace led Legroeder up the steps. "Legroeder, this is our Boss, Yankee-Zulu/Ivan. YZ/I, Rigger Renwald Legroeder."

"Legroeder," said the Boss. "We meet at last." He puffed from his cigar and blew a cloud of smoke upward.

At last? Legroeder wondered, staring at the Boss. *Why—was I expected?* And where had he seen this man before? Yankee-Zulu/Ivan was extremely pale-skinned, especially on his bald pate, slightly heavy of build, and a few centimeters taller than Legroeder. He did not seem particularly augmented. Not at first. A moment later, Legroeder's impression of that changed. The Boss's eyes were cerulean blue, glowing from within. But it was not just his eyes; his face was suddenly aglow, as well, with a pale golden light.

And now his hands—and through his silken shirt and pants, the rest of his body.

An illuminated man.

Now he remembered where he had seen this man before. It was in the joe shop, where Tracy-Ace had first debriefed him. The Boss had been quietly observing, from the back of the room. And for one instant, Legroeder had seen him aglow.

Yankee-Zulu/Ivan stuck out a hand, and as Legroeder shook it uneasily, waves of light rippled up the Boss's arm, shining through the shirt sleeve as though it were gauze. Legroeder could not keep his eyes off the moving light. As it passed over the Boss's shoulder and torso, it disappeared. But a moment later, pulsing threads of green, blue, and red became visible beneath the Boss's skin.

"Are you wondering if you should run away?" Yankee-Zulu/Ivan asked, with a rumble that grew into a hard-edged laugh.

Legroeder drew himself taller, but didn't answer.

The Boss turned to Tracy-Ace/Alfa. "You didn't prepare him for our meeting," he said.

"Oh, we did some preparation," Tracy-Ace murmured, with a sideways glance at Legroeder that made him flush.

"Is that so?" said another voice, behind the Boss. A tall man, dark haired with red skin, stepped out of an unnoticed shadow in the back of the alcove. "Will you introduce me to your friend?"

Tracy-Ace tensed; her expression turned sour. This was the man they had seen walking into the command center yesterday. *Someone you won't need to worry about.* "Hello, Lanyard," Tracy-Ace said. "How nice to see you here. Rigger Legroeder, I'd like you to meet a colleague of mine—"

"Come on, now," said the tall man. "You can call me a friend."

Tracy-Ace ignored the comment and continued speaking to Legroeder, taking him by the wrist as though to lead him through the room. "This is Group Coordinator Lanyard, who is a member of Outpost Ivan's Ruling Cabinet."

Legroeder felt his implants flicker to life as information flowed to him through his wrist. □ *Lanyard/GC is not just a member of the Cabinet, which oversees Outpost policy, but also of the current political opposition to this Boss. There may be a balance-of-power struggle here; he is considered a potential threat. Tracy-Ace was not expecting Lanyard/GC to be present, and isn't pleased. He formerly had a . . . relationship . . . with Tracy-Ace/Alfa, which ended badly.* □

Legroeder did his best to hide his scowl.

"Lanyard is here as—?" Tracy-Ace paused and stretched out an inquiring hand.

"An observer," said Yankee-Zulu/Ivan at once, which seemed to bring a frown—quickly concealed—to Lanyard's face.

Legroeder's augments flashed him a quick schematic. □ *The command hierarchy places Yankee-Zulu/Ivan at the top of the power structure. However, he remains in power at the pleasure of the Cabinet, which does not make day-to-day decisions, but grants him authority. YZ/I oversees the outpost from this operations center, through direct feeds to his internal augments as well as visual information in this room.* □

Legroeder nodded inwardly. Here it was, then. All this way he had come, to learn what he could about the operation of the fortress; and here was the man who ran it—if he really *was* a man, under all that glowing skin. Except, apparently his power was not absolute.

YZ/I was watching Legroeder with evident amusement. He puffed out three smoke rings and watched them disperse, then glanced back at Lanyard before asking Legroeder, "So—have you found our world here to your liking?"

Legroeder opened his mouth, and closed it, moving his head to avoid the smoke. He glanced at Tracy-Ace, but she had turned poker-faced.

As his gaze shifted back to Yankee-Zulu/Ivan, Legroeder drew a sharp breath. Instead of a man, he was gazing at a man-shaped holo, an image of the Kyber armada coursing through the swirls of the Deep Flux. The colony fleet. Was it underway already? Bound for . . . ? He wanted to ask, but YZ/I the man seemed to have utterly vanished into the image. Legroeder glanced to the side and suddenly realized that all the monitors around him were filled with images of space, forming a mosaic curtain. It was a picture he recognized: the Sagittarian Dust Clouds, inbound across the galactic sea. It was a course toward the rich star clusters known by various names in the Centrist Worlds, the clusters a war had been fought over.

The Cloud of a Thousand Suns.

The Well of Stars.

"YZ/I, I already told him about the fleet," Tracy-Ace said, with an edge of impatience in her voice.

"Is hearing the same as seeing?" boomed a voice that seemed to come from the deeps of space where the pirate fleet was hurtling. The image of the fleet rotated until it seemed that the ships were flying straight toward Legroeder. The holo blinked off, and Yankee-Zulu/Ivan was standing there as a man again. He stuck the cigar back in his mouth.

Behind him, Lanyard looked annoyed. "Do you really think it's wise to show him that, as if it's your personal toy?"

YZ/I shrugged. "What's he going to do with it, Lanyard? He's here, with us. Anyway, he's going to have to know that we're serious—and why. Is that okay with you, Rigger Legroeder?"

Legroeder, unsure what to say, jerked his head toward the monitors, where the image remained. "Is that where the fleet is headed? The Well of Stars?"

"That's right." YZ/I's voice grew deeper. "It's the biggest colonizing fleet in the history of the human race! And it's going to be launched within the year!" His lips suddenly curled into what at first looked like a sneer, then seemed to be a wince of pain. *"If* we can solve a few little problems." He stroked his lips as though to rub away the previous expression. "What do you think of it, Rigger Legroeder?"

What Legroeder thought was that he was having trouble

breathing. It was a magnificent fleet. Setting out to populate the galaxy with pirates. It would be a really fine thing if he could think of a way to stop it. But how?

YZ/I was still waiting for an answer. Legroeder moistened his lips, then asked, "Why did you show that to me? Were you thinking I might want to join up?"

YZ/I stared at him for a moment with those glowing eyes—and suddenly broke into a long, iron-hard guffaw. "No, Rigger Legroeder, I didn't really think you'd want to join up. Not after your experience at Barbados—or should I say, *your seven years of captivity at DeNoble*." Legroeder froze in sudden terror. YZ/I's eyes gleamed. "DeNoble. What a goddamn scum-pit of humanity. To think they're part of our Republic."

Legroeder felt paralyzed like an icecat in a spotlight.

"And you're mad as hell about it," YZ/I continued sourly, "and you've come to see what you can do to try to wipe us all out for good. Do I have it right?" He puffed smoke in a stream toward the ceiling, where a vent fan seemed to push it back downward rather than draw it away.

Legroeder struggled to draw a breath. How did YZ/I know about him and DeNoble? What else did he know? He closed his eyes to a squint, focusing inward in fury. *(Did you betray that information—when I was with Tracy-Ace—?)*

◻ We did not. We carefully monitored the passage of information. ◻

(Then—) He blinked his eyes open.

Tracy-Ace was touching his arm. He glared at her in silent indignation. He was afraid to think . . . didn't want to ask . . . or to admit . . .

Do you feel bad because you lied to her and then made love to her . . . or because you got caught?

He got his breath back at last, but felt her gaze burning back at him.

"Oh, for chrissake, Legroeder, don't try to deny it," YZ/I said.

Legroeder jerked his eyes back to the Boss.

"Legroeder," Tracy-Ace murmured in a strained voice, "I've known all along. *We've* known."

He jerked his eyes back to her. The world was tilting under him. *How could you have known?* But Tracy-Ace had already turned to YZ/I, her implants flaring. "Did you have to drop it on him like that?"

Legroeder slowly followed her gaze, and saw that the man had ripples of light flickering up in waves from his feet to the top of his head. YZ/I shrugged. "He can take it." He glanced at Lanyard, and in a voice that seemed calculatedly casual, continued, "Rigger Legroeder, there are a great many things that we know—things on the outside, in the Centrist Worlds. But you must not assume that we are like those who held you captive at DeNoble. We're not."

Aren't you? Legroeder felt his face stinging with humiliation. His cover was gone, had never been there in the first place.

But YZ/I wasn't gloating over the revelation. Instead, he was turning to speak to Lanyard. "I believe you had another appointment, Group Coordinator? Don't let us keep you."

Lanyard stiffened ever so slightly. "I think, given the circumstances, that it's probably more important that I hear—"

"What's *important*," YZ/I interrupted, "is that we conclude these sensitive discussions in private, for now."

Lanyard's eyes flashed dangerously. "Don't try to shut us out, YZ/I. If you go too far along this course, you might find—"

"I promise to give you and the Cabinet a full report," YZ/I said soothingly. "I assure you, we will not go too far along this or any other course. But just now . . . well, I'm sure you understand. Rigger Legroeder is on the spot—and he doesn't need to hear about our internal concerns. Compre-hendo?"

For a moment, it looked as if Lanyard would argue further. Whatever went between them did so in silence. Lanyard closed his eyes, and a line of augments flickered on his earlobes. Abruptly, he blinked his eyes open, nodded brusquely, and strode away.

As soon as he was gone, a privacy forcefield shimmered into place, enclosing the three of them. YZ/I laughed quietly. "I wouldn't laugh too hard," said Tracy-Ace, with a distinctly unhappy look on her face. "He could cause us trouble."

"Well, you'd know that about him, wouldn't you?" YZ/I said with a little chuckle, causing her face to darken even further. "No, Lanyard is okay; he's just fond of poking his nose where it doesn't belong. We're going to have to be careful of that." YZ/I paused, then said to Legroeder as if they had not been interrupted, "Rigger Legroeder, Tracy-Ace/Alfa did not betray you to me."

Legroeder stirred, filing the Lanyard encounter away. "Then who did?"

YZ/I rubbed his jaw. "If you must know, *I'm* the one who told *her*. We've known from the beginning about your escape from DeNoble. For Rings' sake, we *brought* you here. We have things to discuss with you."

"What do you mean you *brought*—"

YZ/I waved a hand in the air. "Our contacts with the Narseil indicated an interest in communication."

The underground. Legroeder swallowed, not speaking.

"We had things to talk about—but we couldn't be too obvious about it." YZ/I nodded to Tracy-Ace. "We have appearances to maintain. Very important. Power structures and so on."

Lanyard. The Ruling Cabinet.

"But you sent out . . . I mean, your ship tried to *destroy* us," Legroeder protested. "Destroy the Narseil."

YZ/I's breath hissed between his teeth. "That idiot, Te'Gunderlach. If he hadn't been killed in the fight, I'd do it myself. He was ordered to *find* you. *Capture* you. Not kill you. That's why Freem'n Deutsch was programmed to—"

"Deutsch? Programmed?"

"Must you interrupt? It didn't work. Deutsch was supposed to get a priority override if the captain got carried away." YZ/I shook his head. "Damn augments are probably what drove Te'Gunderlach berserk, and by then Deutsch's override was too little, too late. Fortunately, you made it here nevertheless—so everything worked out—"

"Not for the dead people we left behind," Legroeder interrupted.

"That is true," YZ/I said flatly. "I do not like losing ships *or* crew."

I wasn't thinking of your crew.

"In any case," YZ/I said, steepling his fingers, "due credit to you for a well-executed infiltration. We must guard our perimeter better, in the future. We had no idea that *Flechette* was being flown by you and the Narseil. But you came—wisely probing through the intelnet, and you triggered one of our signal points—and so we made contact. And here we are." YZ/I spread his hands.

Legroeder took a moment to absorb it all. There seemed no point in further denial. He exhaled slowly. "What about the—" he hesitated, struggling to say the word, *"under-ground?"*

White light rippled up YZ/I's shoulders and neck. He puffed from the cigar. "As I said—here we are."

Legroeder's mouth opened, closed. "You?"

YZ/I extended his hands. "Us. The underground—such as it is. Ready to undertake change for the betterment of the Republic, and so on. But—" he cautioned "—not too publicly. There are people"—and for an instant, the monitors behind him filled with faces; one of them was Lanyard—"who might regard this as sedition, and use it as a pretext for attempting to seize power." YZ/I raised his chin. "Question. Are *you* ready to talk?"

Legroeder let his breath out, stunned. He glanced at Tracy-Ace; in her eyes there was only serious business, no sign of the playful lover. "Why did—you wait so long?" he stammered finally. "Why didn't you talk to me right away? Why are the Narseil down there in jail, while I'm—?" He didn't finish the question.

YZ/I's face flickered. "Do you feel that the Narseil are being mistreated, after what you've seen elsewhere?"

Legroeder swallowed. It was true that they, and he, were being treated far better than anything he'd ever seen at DeNoble.

"We don't accommodate everyone so well. But we needed time. Time to get to know you. Find out what kind of a man you were. TA here was entrusted with that job." He grinned, all teeth.

Legroeder felt blood rushing to his face. Tracy-Ace gave her head an almost imperceptible shake. *It wasn't just that,* she seemed to be saying. Or was it, *You fool . . .*

"We brought you here," YZ/I continued, "partly to talk to you and your Narseil friends on matters of common interest—and partly because we have a job we think might interest you."

Legroeder barked a laugh. "Why would you think I'd be interested in a *job*, if you knew what I went through at DeNoble?"

YZ/I carefully stuck the cigar back in his mouth and talked around it. "But there was also what came after, yes?"

"Meaning what?"

YZ/I shrugged. "All those attempts on your life on Faber Eridani? Who do you think was responsible for that? And for your being framed for the attack on *Ciudad de los Angeles*? And the attack on Robert McGinnis?"

Legroeder felt weakness and rage mixed into one. "Are *you* claiming responsibility?" He wanted to look at Tracy-Ace, and found he could not. *Say no. At least say* she *wasn't involved.*

"Me?" YZ/I replied. "Rings, no! Not my way of operating. Not at all. And certainly counterproductive to what I hope to do."

Legroeder slowly began to breathe again. "Then who? I take it you know."

"I know in general terms." YZ/I waved his cigar in a circle. "For starters, I imagine it was Centrists, not Free Kybers, who did the actual deeds. Kyber-*sympathizing* Centrists, mind you. *Not* connected with Ivan."

"Then who were they connected with?"

YZ/I extended a hand toward the back of his working alcove. A holoimage appeared in the wall, showing a raider stronghold. Not Ivan. It was reminiscent of the stronghold from which Legroeder had escaped, in Golen Space. "This particular outpost is run by a boss by the name of Kilo-Mike/Carlotta," said YZ/I. An image of a dark-haired, heavily augmented woman appeared, giving Legroeder a shudder. YZ/I nodded toward the image. "KM/C and I don't get along too well. But KM/C has a great many connections in the Centrist Worlds—particularly, as it happens, on Faber Eridani. She—"

"Wait a minute," Legroeder said. "Connections I could see. But why would *anyone* on the Centrist Worlds have the slightest sympathy for pirates? Unless they're getting a kickback—"

YZ/I snorted. "Of course, they're getting kickbacks. But that's not what turned them into sympathizers."

"Then what—?"

YZ/I took a puff on his cigar. "Betrayal."

Legroeder remembered El'ken recounting the Centrist betrayal of the Narseil. But he didn't think that was what YZ/I meant. "What do you mean?"

"Betrayal of their own world's vision and purpose!" YZ/I thundered. He interrupted himself. "Christ, I'm being a poor host. TA, could you grab a couple of chairs for yourself and the rigger? Thank you." He paused again to study the burning end of his cigar. "A fanatical sense of betrayal. And they're right. The Centrist Worlds defeated the Kyber worlds—not *us*, but the worlds our ancestors came from—in the War of a Thousand Suns. You know that, right?"

Legroeder nodded, ignoring the implied insult.

"And then, having won among other things the right to be first out to the Well of Stars, what did they do?" YZ/I shook with rage. "You tell me!"

Legroeder hesitated. "Not much, I guess. There were some surveys." And meanwhile, drawing inward while rebuilding, regaining prosperity. And then . . . nothing. Isolationism.

YZ/I snorted contemptuously. "They won their racist war, then congratulated themselves and sat on their fat asses! Did they take risks to explore the worlds they *claimed* they were fighting for the right to colonize? *NO!*" He stuck the cigar back between his teeth again. "So that is what our fleet is going to do now. Seems pretty clear they've abdicated any right—" He stopped and glared. "What?"

Legroeder wondered why he was even arguing with this man. Nevertheless . . . "The Centrists wouldn't even have *won* that war—if you can call it winning—if they hadn't betrayed the Narseil. Turned their backs on an ally and made a deal with the enemy." *The enemy they hated. The enemy that was more implant than human.* "And if they hadn't broken up their rigging partnership with the Narseil, maybe we *would* be on our way to the Well of Stars right now."

YZ/I grinned. "You *learned* from El'ken and McGinnis. Very good. You know, I was sorry to learn of McGinnis's death. He was a worthy man."

"Yes, he was," Legroeder snapped. "And if you knew what those people were doing, why didn't you stop them?"

YZ/I stubbed out his cigar in a receptacle behind him. "I didn't say I could *control* them, for Almighty's sake. Just that I knew about them. KM/C has a lot more people on Faber Eridani than I do. And believe me—those sympathizers are very angry about their world's failure to act. Angry enough to collaborate with their supposed enemies, the Free Kyber. Imagine that."

Yes, imagine, Legroeder thought numbly. Imagine consorting with the Free Kyber. He met Tracy-Ace's gaze for a fraction of a second and jerked his eyes back to YZ/I.

"Some of them are in positions of authority, where they can make a pretty good show of opposing Free Kyber activity—"

"You mean piracy?" Legroeder asked carefully.

"Whatever." YZ/I waved a translucent hand. "All the while turning a blind eye to it. How do you think the Free Kyber fleets have been assembled so quickly? These are isolated outposts—many of them embedded in the Flux as we are, with practically no access to raw materials! That's why we need to colonize! *We* know we're living on borrowed time!" He paused. "You know, there's an old proverb, 'Where there's no vision, the people die.' Well, all the vision has gone out of the Centrist leaders. But there are others who haven't lost it."

"You mean people like Centrist Strength?" Legroeder asked sarcastically.

YZ/I shrugged. "They're not someone *we* deal with, but yeah. Same principle. Lemme ask you—why do you think, for *decades* now, the Free Kyber have drawn their tax from the wealthy planets, almost without opposition?"

"*Tax?*" Legroeder echoed sarcastically.

"Let's not quibble over terminology." YZ/I waved his hand in annoyance. He looked as if he missed the cigar, now that he'd put it out. "The point is they've been helping the Free Kyber build the colonizing fleet. Most of the ships in that fleet came from the Centrist Worlds—with the help of Centrists who'd rather see Free Kyber colonists move out to the Well of Stars than no one at all. Plus"—YZ/I waggled his hand —"there's the smell of profit for them. Of course."

"Of course," Legroeder murmured.

YZ/I gazed at him for a moment. "I believe someone you once knew is among them. A Captain Hyutu, formerly of the *Ciudad de los Angeles*?"

Legroeder was stunned. "Captain Hyutu!"

"A captain now in the fleet of Kilo-Mike/Carlotta. A nasty, mendacious son of a bitch, by reputation."

Legroeder swallowed back bile.

YZ/I's eyebrows went up. "You know, neither Hyutu—nor, for that matter, KM/C—will much like what I'm going to suggest. I suspect there could be some personal satisfaction in it for you, though."

Legroeder raised his chin. "What are you going to suggest?"

"Oh, nothing much." YZ/I focused on his fingertips for a moment. "Just that I thought you might want to go out and find *Impris* for us and see if you can bring her back in one piece."

Legroeder stopped breathing. He heard blood pounding in his ears and felt suddenly detached from reality. Was his heart still beating? Had this man just said what he thought he'd said?

"You okay there?" said Yankee-Zulu/Ivan, in a voice that seemed to echo in Legroeder's skull.

Breathe in, breathe out. Breathe in . . . yes, I am okay. He nodded, not trusting his voice.

"I was afraid I'd given you a heart attack or something."

You damn near did, Legroeder thought.

"What do you think? Want to do it?"

Legroeder cleared his throat. "You want me to find *Impris*—"

"Find her, see if anyone's still alive on her, make contact, do a full investigation. Bring her back, if you can."

The feeling of dizziness was passing, but slowly. "I didn't, uh, realize that *Impris* was lost. From your point of view, I mean."

"Well, not completely. KM/C knows more or less where she is, no doubt. They're the ones currently using her as a siren lure to bring in ships. But *I* don't where she is . . . precisely. And even KM/C can't *reach* her."

"Then why—"

"Because I want, very badly, to know why she disappeared."

Legroeder stared at him. "Why do you care?"

Yankee-Zulu/Ivan rose from his seat and stretched out a hand. The image of the fleet reappeared behind him. *"See this fleet?"* he rumbled. *"This fleet is the pride of our Republic!"* He was actually breathing hard from the apparent intensity of emotion, and it took him a moment to get his breath back. "And I don't want this fleet disappearing the way *Impris* did!"

Legroeder shook his head. "Why would it?"

YZ/I's face turned into a glowing network of veins and arteries. "Because . . . we have suffered losses. Unexplained losses. Not just Ivan, but other outposts." He turned his hands palms up.

Tracy-Ace tapped her feet impatiently. "Why don't you just tell him, YZ/I?"

Legroeder looked from one to the other.

YZ/I seemed annoyed. "Well, all right—for one thing, ships have been lost that were shadowing *Impris* too closely."

And you want me to fly close to her? Legroeder thought. He drew a breath, stretching his lips over his teeth. "Maybe you guys have just been shooting each others' ships up. Anyway, why don't you just stop flying so close to her?" *And why don't you stop using her for piracy, while you're at it?*

"Well, the shooting part isn't as far-fetched as you might think," YZ/I said thoughtfully. "But no—we're pretty sure whatever's happened to them is related to what happened to *Impris*. And we need to find out what the hell that is."

This time Tracy-Ace looked annoyed. "Tell him, YZ/I."

YZ/I sighed and rubbed his jaw, setting off little sparkles of color in his cheeks. "All right, it's not just ships near *Impris*. In the last three years, we've lost four probe ships headed to the Sagittarian Clouds. Advance ships for the fleet . . ." His voice trailed off, as he waved a hand back at the monitors. "I'm used to losing ships, but . . . with the whole fleet getting ready to go . . ."

"Tell him about your brother," Tracy-Ace said.

A flash of light went up YZ/I's face. With obvious irritation, he said, "And men who are like brothers to me are commanding ships in that fleet. All right?" Tracy-Ace stared, and he growled. "Anyway, it's not just that. We're going to commit an entire *fleet* to the Deep Flux. We need to know what's going on."

Tracy-Ace continued staring at YZ/I. "Tell him about your brother!"

YZ/I put his fingertips to his temple, as his face flashed dark and light. "All right," he said, as though suppressing a pain. "Come on." Rising, he led them across the dais and down the steps to a large holotank monitor. It took him a few seconds to get the image he wanted: an outpost floating in the reddish mists of the Flux. Not Ivan, not DeNoble, not KM/C. It was shaped rather like a skyscraper tower, but with its lower end simply fading into the Flux. "This is . . . was . . . Outpost Juliette."

"Was?" Legroeder asked.

"Yeah. It was anchored in the Flux, like Ivan. Only it had its foundation in the slow layers. They thought it would be safer that way, keep it anchored better."

"Only it didn't," Legroeder guessed.

YZ/I changed the image. "This holo was taken by a ship coming in from patrol, just as *this* happened." As he spoke, the image suddenly began to quiver and dance, as though they were looking at it through heat waves rising up off a desert floor.

"What's that? What's happening?"

"Watch."

The quivering worsened, and the recording became jerky, as though the camera were moving. The surrounding mists flickered and then darkened, and in that moment the tower suddenly became transparent. One heartbeat it was solid; the next it was a ghost. And then it vanished altogether, leaving behind the blood-red mist.

"Just like that," YZ/I said. "It was gone before the ship could approach for docking. They felt turbulence in the Flux, and sheared off. And then the outpost was just . . . gone." YZ/I suddenly looked old and care-worn. "Never found so much as a trace of it. And my pain-in-the-ass kid brother was on it at the time." He rubbed his forehead, wincing, then straightened as Legroeder absorbed that blow. "I can tell you, no other outposts are anchored in the lower layers now. *Impris*, as far as I know, is the only one of these ships that's ever reappeared where we can see it."

Legroeder regarded him in horror and fascination, thinking of all those people caught, perhaps for all of eternity, in a ghost realm that no rigger knew how to navigate. *Impris* had been . . . half a legend, and half a terrible, isolated reality. Just one. But now . . . *So many ships? And an outpost?*

"If I knew where to look, I'd send you after my own ships," YZ/I said.

"But you think they all somehow strayed into the Deep Flux, and couldn't get out?"

"If I knew, I wouldn't have to ask you to go find out, would I?"

"I guess not. But why me?"

"Why *not* you?"

Legroeder stirred angrily. "Give me a reason!"

YZ/I raised his eyebrows. "All right. You're a rigger, and you've seen the ship, and you have good reason to want to find it again. Don't you?"

Legroeder shook his head stubbornly. "Maybe I do. But why did *you* bring *me* here to do this? It wasn't for my benefit. Why don't you send your own riggers to find it?"

YZ/I took a deep, hoarse breath. *"Do you think we haven't tried?"* His voice softened to a growl. "And we've lost two more ships trying. So no, we didn't go to all this trouble just for the fun of it."

"You still haven't answered my question. What do you think I can do that your riggers can't? I told the Narseil that your riggers have tricks *we* could learn from."

YZ/I looked pained. "Our rigging may be *different* from yours. But that doesn't necessarily make it better."

Legroeder was startled by the admission. "All right, then—different. I don't know how your people function with all that augmentation, to be honest." Legroeder rubbed the implant on his right temple. "I'm lucky these things didn't ruin my ability to function in the net. I'm sure it's only because they stayed in the background."

"Exactly," said YZ/I.

"Huh?"

"Sure, we have AI augmentation that can run rings around yours, and it's very useful. We couldn't take on the Deep Flux without it. But we also have riggers who are dependent on it, who I think have lost skills that you take for granted. The intuitive element, the *human* element.

They're starting to lose it." YZ/I jabbed a thumb at himself. "You think I'm crazy, saying that? I'm just telling you what's happening."

He paused. "So let's talk about Renwald Legroeder—who not only has *had* an encounter with *Impris*, but escaped from Fortress DeNoble, escaped through a passage that to anyone else would have been suicide alley. We had a ship visiting there at the time—they saw the whole thing. Do you remember it? What do they call it, the Chimney?"

Legroeder shivered at the memory: the frantic, terrifying dash through the minefield, and then the Chimney, the Fool's Refuge . . . chased by raiders and flux torpedoes and fear, and somehow finding his way. He hadn't thought much about *how* he had gotten through, except to be grateful that he'd been so monumentally lucky.

"You think other riggers could have done that? I understand quite a few have tried, and died."

Tracy-Ace, Legroeder realized, was gazing at him with a strangely penetrating expression, and a hint of a smile on her lips. He shrugged, not to her but to YZ/I.

"And according to Rigger Deutsch's report, you led a pretty good chase through the bottom layers of the Flux when you were engaging *Flechette*. Well, okay—maybe some other riggers could have done that." YZ/I was staring unblinking at him now, ripples of light running down his arms and torso. "But I don't know *any* riggers—except maybe a couple of our maintainers—who could have seen those features of the Deep Flux that you picked out in the maintainers' net. And you weren't even in the net! You were just watching an image on the wall!"

Legroeder felt a sudden dizziness, remembering. Yes, he had seen those features. But so what? What did that mean?

"You don't even *know* that you're unusual, do you? At DeNoble, they were too dumb to recognize what they had." YZ/I cocked his head and gestured to Tracy-Ace. "Why do you think she took you into a high-security area like that? For your health?"

Open-mouthed, Legroeder turned to Tracy-Ace. "I

thought it was—I don't know—that you were trying to gain my trust."

She inclined her head. "Yes, I was. But that part didn't work so well, did it?"

YZ/I chuckled. "Of course she wanted to gain your trust. But *I* also wanted to know what you would see there. And what you saw . . . tells me you're worth taking a gamble on." His voice became almost solemn. "You have the vision. You see *deeper* than my people. Or at least, differently. That's why I want you to go."

"Well, I—"

"And I want you to take some of your Narseil friends with you."

Legroeder closed his open mouth. For a few seconds, he was speechless. "You want the Narseil to go?"

"Yes, because they'll see things that no human will see. Don't you get it? I want to send out the full spectrum—my people with their augments, you, the Narseil. Everyone together."

Legroeder's voice caught. "I'm having just a little trouble believing this. You want to work with the Narseil?"

"That's what I said, didn't I? Do I have to repeat everything?" YZ/I reached into a compartment on his chair. "Do you want a cigar?"

"No. Thank you."

Looking disappointed, YZ/I withdrew his hand. "Anyway, yes—I think it's time we and the Narseil talked. It might be very useful for us to exchange information."

Legroeder gave a harsh laugh. "And it might be useful if you stopped raiding innocent shipping!"

YZ/I grimaced and reached into his cigar compartment again. His hand seemed to war with his mind for a moment, before he snapped the compartment shut, empty-handed. He drew himself up. "As a matter of fact . . . that could be on the table, too."

Legroeder blinked, startled.

YZ/I looked pained and angry, and not eager to say more. Tracy-Ace looked as if she wanted to kick him. Instead, she turned to Legroeder. "The free ride. YZ/I, unlike some of the other bosses, has begun to recognize what some of us have been saying for a long time—the free ride may be coming to an end. The raiding. The *tax*. We've been living on it so long now—"

"It's made us *soft*," YZ/I growled. "Soft and lazy. And we're supposed to go out and colonize the Well of Stars?" He snorted.

"I think what YZ/I is trying to say," Tracy-Ace said slowly, "is that, in addition to making us soft, all the raiding has made us vulnerable."

Legroeder didn't hide his confusion.

"Look, we know that there are some, like the Narseil, who are getting ready to come looking for us. With guns. The ship you came on was just a start."

"Well—"

"We know you came here to talk, if you could," Tracy-Ace said. "But you also came to gather intelligence to wipe us out, if you could. We're not idiots."

"Oh hell," YZ/I muttered. "If you're going to tell him everything. Don't get cocky, Legroeder. We could fight your fleets. But sometimes—" sparks of light shot through his face, as though it hurt to say it "—sometimes, it makes more sense to talk. And that's what I want to do with the Narseil. Talk. And . . . go after something of mutual benefit. So, are you interested?" He rocked back in his chair.

"I'm interested," Legroeder said. "But what are you offering in return? Besides some vague promise to talk?"

"Why, you—" YZ/I cursed in a tongue Legroeder didn't recognize, but there was no mistaking the tone. He reached into his seat compartment, grabbed a cigar, and snapped the end of it alight. He blew an enormous cloud of smoke into the air. "Isn't *Impris* enough? I send you home with your friends, and you get to clear your name. Plus we open lines of talk. Isn't that enough?"

Legroeder held his breath until the smoke cleared, thinking, it wasn't as if he was in a position of power here; but on the other hand, YZ/I had gone to a lot of trouble to enlist him. "Seems to me," he said, with a cough, "that there's more at stake here. You mentioned a willingness to end the piracy."

"Rings!" YZ/I shouted. *"I didn't say I would discuss it with you!"*

Legroeder shot back, "You didn't say you wouldn't." He took a breath, gestured with one hand. "Look, you're telling me all about how you want to *talk* with the Narseil, and *share* with the Narseil, and give up the free ride."

YZ/I waved the burning tip of his cigar. "Your point?"

"And you've told me all about Carlotta conspiring with the Centrists, and Carlotta this and Carlotta that, but you haven't said a word about yourself. How do I know you're not as involved in piracy as she is? Not to mention slavery." A rush of memories from DeNoble threatened to overwhelm him. He forced them back down, and glanced at Tracy-Ace out of the corner of his eye. *How do I know* you *aren't involved in it, too?* he wanted, and didn't want, to say.

YZ/I shrugged. "We keep our ear to the deck on the Centrist Worlds, if that's what you mean. But we don't have our hooks in their governments, like KM/C. The raiding—okay. *I* see it can't last. Carlotta, she doesn't see it. Neither do some of the other bosses. We've got a disagreement in that regard." YZ/I raised his right hand and held it so that he could look into his own palm, as though studying the threaded pattern of light there. "With all the things we don't agree on, it's a wonder we've gotten this fleet assembled at all."

He eyed Legroeder. "So if we *do* this thing, KM/C isn't going to like it. And she isn't going to like our collaborating with the Narseil. These are things I have to think about. I don't live in isolation. Carlotta likes her cozy arrangement."

"But wouldn't it be to everyone's benefit to find out why ships are disappearing?" Legroeder asked. *And wouldn't it also be to the benefit of that Kyber fleet that I want to stop? Hell and damnation.*

"Yeah, but it wasn't Carlotta's probe ships that got lost, so what's she care? You rescue *Impris* and that'll interfere with a lucrative raiding setup." YZ/I shrugged. "Couldn't happen to a nicer person."

Legroeder thought about getting KM/C even angrier at him than she was already . . .

"So needless to say, I'm taking one hell of a risk just underwriting the mission. So don't give me a lot of crap about what other risks I ought to be taking on."

Legroeder closed his eyes. Had he pushed as far as he could push? Probably he would be smart to stop here, and just agree to it. Bring *Impris* back, clear his name, get people talking. What were Harriet and Morgan up to now? And Maris? They seemed a universe away, another lifetime. He was supposed to ask about Bobby Mahoney. Jesus Christ, he'd almost forgotten. But this wasn't the time . . .

"And yet," he found himself saying, "you continue to fly, and fight, with forced labor."

YZ/I glared in astonishment. "Christ, you don't give up, do you, boy?" He coughed on the cigar smoke; the stench was making Legroeder dizzy. "Yeah, we fly with captives. It's part of our history. What do you want me to do about it?"

"Give it up."

YZ/I gave a long, sputtering laugh. "Give it up!" He snapped his fingers. "Just like that!"

"You said you were the underground. You want things to change."

"Yeah, we're the underground," YZ/I said slowly. "And the reason we're the *under*ground is you don't just change things overnight. People like Lanyard—they've got friends."

Legroeder felt as if he were sliding on ice, unable to stop. "You're getting soft and lazy, preying on the innocent."

YZ/I stood up and shouted, *"Fuck . . . you . . . boy!* Don't you talk to me that way!"

Legroeder realized he had involuntarily raised an arm to ward off a blow.

YZ/I stood before him, his face a meteor shower of fury.

Then he shifted his glare to Tracy-Ace. "What are you looking at?" he shouted.

Tracy-Ace raised her eyebrows.

"*Rings.*" YZ/I chomped his cigar and turned his back to them for a moment. Then he sat and shook his head. "You have to understand some history here, for chrissake. *Jesus!* You don't know what it was like."

But I'm about to find out . . .

"The Centrists cut us off. Treated us like scum, like nonhumans. Sure, they made peace. *Peace.*" YZ/I snorted. "Peace with no future, peace as long as no one with *hardware* in their brains had a planet to live on, or worlds to conquer. They cast us off, cut us off, and sent us to live in Golen Space. And you wonder why the Free Kyber started raiding shipping, three generations ago? What else were they supposed to do?"

Legroeder opened his mouth, closed it. "But you said you want to change it."

"*Yes!* We need each other! I know that! But it can't be done overnight. There's just no way."

Legroeder leaned forward. "So make a start. Start it here. This is your chance to make history."

YZ/I glared, his anger clearly rising.

Tracy-Ace rubbed the flickering augments by her left eye, and said softly, "He's saying what I've been saying, YZ/I."

"Do me a favor," Legroeder said, "and put up that image of the fleet again. The colony fleet."

The monitors changed to the fleet image.

"Big fleet. Must be hundreds of ships."

"Over a thousand," YZ/I said.

Legroeder nodded. "And it means a lot to you to have the fleet get through safely. A lot of effort. Resources. Lives." Legroeder pressed his lips together. *What am I talking about trading here?* His head was pounding.

YZ/I stared at him furiously.

"End the piracy."

YZ/I spat to one side. "We'll talk about it later."

"You're asking me to risk my life. And you want me to

trust that we'll *talk* about it? Send me and the Narseil home with *Impris*. You can have all the information we get from her. It could save your fleet."

YZ/I snarled and blew smoke at him.

Legroeder let the smoke pass. "If we're going to deal, make it real."

YZ/I flung down his cigar. "Guards!" he shouted.

Before Legroeder could finish drawing a breath, there were four heavily armed and augmented Kyber soldiers surrounding him on the dais. Tracy-Ace was staring at YZ/I, wide-eyed. Legroeder's heart was pounding so hard he could barely hear YZ/I's next words.

"You think you can just waltz in here and tell me what to do! Guards, take this man to—" YZ/I suddenly broke off and jerked his gaze over to Tracy-Ace. They stood facing each other with silent glares, joined as though by a high-voltage charge. Legroeder watched them in numb bewilderment, trying not to think about the neutraser muzzles that were pointing at his chest. Tracy-Ace's implants were pulsing at a frantic rate; YZ's face looked like a contained explosion. What the devil was going on between them?

Suddenly Tracy-Ace cried out in pain, staggering. YZ/I turned with a curse to one of the soldiers. "Stand down your men. I'll call you if I need you."

The soldiers melted away. Tracy-Ace rubbed her temple and stood straight again, scowling.

YZ/I looked down at the floor where his cigar lay smoldering. Then he looked up at Legroeder. "I will negotiate—not with you, but with the Narseil commander—on a timetable for ceasing hostilities. If we come to agreement—and I think we will—you'll do the mission. Agreed?"

Legroeder forced himself to draw a breath. "One more thing."

YZ/I's eyes danced with fire. "*What*, damn it?"

"A small thing—to you. There's a boy . . ." He told YZ/I about Bobby Mahoney and Harriet. "Would you try to find him? See if he's okay? Release him?"

YZ/I's gaze softened and he sighed. "All right. I'll see what I can do."

Legroeder nodded thanks, his head spinning.

"Any agreement we reach is for Ivan only," YZ/I continued. "I can't speak for the other bosses."

Legroeder nodded again. "What about information about *Impris*, and a ship?"

"You'll go with the best we've got. KM/C could cause us trouble, so we'll have to send some escort." YZ/I rubbed his temple in thought. "Not too much, though. Can't have it looking like an armada."

Legroeder's heartrate was slowly easing. "Who are you sending with me?"

"I think . . . two or three Narseil riggers of your choice, and—Freem'n Deutsch, as well. He will represent our own rigger force. You, however, will be the lead rigger."

"Me?"

"You have the experience and the will to see the job done right. Don't you want it?"

Legroeder shrugged. "All right."

"Good. We'll begin preparations immediately." YZ/I called an aide from the ops room and began muttering in the man's ear.

Tracy-Ace stepped closer and squeezed Legroeder's hand. He felt a surge of the link, and a bewildering array of emotions, triumph and gratitude among them. This struggle had been as much between her and YZ/I as between the Boss and Legroeder. He found himself wishing he were alone with her.

"Oh, yes," YZ/I said suddenly. "In case you're wondering, Tracy-Ace/Alfa will *not* be flying with you. I have other things I need her for. But what the hell—it'll give you something to look forward to when you get back, eh?"

Legroeder felt his face redden.

YZ/I laughed in satisfaction. "You'd better get going, if you want to be the one to break the news to your Narseil captain."

Tracy-Ace gave Legroeder a tug. It took no further persuasion to get him moving from YZ/I's presence.

THEY FINALLY got a chance to talk, on the way to the detention area. "I misled you about what I knew," Tracy-Ace said, when they were in a corridor with no one around. "I'm sorry." She turned to face him.

He swallowed, licking his lips. "You, uh, weren't the only one to do that, I guess."

"No." A smile flickered across her face. "But, you know, we might not have gotten a chance to know each other . . . the same way . . . if we hadn't."

Legroeder remembered the anger he'd felt when he first realized that *she* had deceived *him*. He took her hand. "I guess not. I'm glad, anyway . . . about last night."

As their hands joined, he felt a tingle, and a flickering of augments. And . . . not quite a voice, but a presence. *Did it because I wanted* you . . . *couldn't help it . . . not just a job. Do you believe me?* I believe you, he thought; want to believe you. How could so much have happened, in such a short space of time? The answer was flowing through his fingertips, of course; it might otherwise have taken years. He felt a knot in his stomach, a vague dizziness. Like a lovesick puppy. Memories of a few hours ago were popping like camera flashes in the juncture between them, and his blood pressure was starting to rise.

"Let's get going to see Fre'geel," he said raspily, afraid he would lose all ability to control his thoughts.

She drew a slow breath and they turned and continued down the corridor.

Legroeder could not help chuckling as they hurried toward the detention center. Fre'geel and the others, he guessed, were going to be very, very surprised.

PART THREE

Deep into that darkness peering,
long I stood there wondering, fearing . . .
                                    —Edgar Allan Poe

Prologue

IMPRIS

In the shifting sands of time, the starship seemed always to be sliding, falling, never quite at a point where human intervention could bring it under control. It was not the slide of time itself that befuddled its occupants so much as the endless spinning pirouettes, the sideways shifts and turns that left them eternally breathless and anchorless.

And anchorless the starship was, in a network of splintered spacetime that stretched up and down the spiral arms of the galaxy, and from one end of time to the other . . .

JAMAL AWOKE with a start, sweating and shaking. He sat for a moment, staring into the darkness, listening to the sounds of *Impris* around him; then he growled to his cabin for a nightlight. As the pale orange glow came up, he peered around, breathing heavily, reassuring himself that everything in his cabin was normal. As normal as anything could be on the haunted ship.

Except in his head. The nightmare was back again, returned to plague him. *Damn you,* he thought. *Damn you damn you . . .*

Cursing the thing that lay in wait for them—great writhing monster of the Flux, lurking invisibly, waiting for them to move their net in the wrong direction . . .

Jamal shut his eyes, willing the image away. Poppy had been complaining of it two nights ago, and last week Sully.

Where the hell was this vision coming from? It couldn't be real.

The monster stretched in a tortuous line across the sky—a great threatening serpent, turning this way and that, looking for them. No question about that: it was looking for them. Looking to devour any living thing that fell within its reach. And they were falling . . . falling . . .

Jamal's eyes snapped open again. He took a deep breath and let it out slowly, counting to ten. Do not let it control you, he thought grimly. It's only a dream.

Only a dream.

A dream to fill an already nightmarish existence, stranded in a limbo without end, without hope. God, was it just his subconscious? Or was this realm of insanity finally becoming complete? No, surely it was just a nightmare.

Bad enough that one of them had it. But why *all* of them? Was it possible they were infecting each other with their fears—like a damn virus from the subconscious? If they weren't careful it would overwhelm them all.

Overwhelm us, but with what . . . what's worse than this kind of eternity?

He didn't mean to, didn't mean to close his eyes until he'd cleared his head of this image, but his brain was too tired, too desperately craving sleep, and before he even knew what was happening, he slipped helplessly back into the shifty, perilous world of his nightmare . . .

IMPRIS PATROL

JAKUS BARK had decided that few things were more tedious than being on a raider patrol. Lying in wait, the rigger-net stretched out into the void, the ship floating . . . *bor-r-r-rinnggg*. From time to time the riggers roused themselves from the tedium to scan the distant Flux for moving ships. The latter was almost unnecessary; when ships *did* come into view, they were noticed immediately by the AI component of the net. But in four weeks out here, it had only happened twice—for just one kill, and that a decrepit freighter not worth salvaging. The other sighting had disappeared without coming within range.

Jakus thought they were wasting their time here, drifting in hiding, keeping one eye out for the shadowy, intermittent trace of *Impris*—lost and unreachable in some weirdly separated pocket of the Flux—and another eye out for spaceship traffic that might be drawn toward the ghostly vessel. This was chickenshit piracy, dicking around waiting for ships to come along the Golen Space edge of the trade routes so that they could lure them in with distress calls. Why didn't they just go out and *get* the ships they wanted?

He supposed it worked, though, or the higher-ups wouldn't still be doing it this way. The distress calls seemed to work a kind of magic—both the real ones from *Impris* and the fake recorded ones from *Hunter*, which they used when the prey were too far away to pick up the real ones. What really made it work, of course, was the way *Impris* wandered around so unpredictably. Whatever realm she was in, its connection to this one was pretty freakish. Now it loomed into view over here; now it popped up over there. That made it pretty well impossible for the Centrist shippers to identify one region or another as unsafe for travel, even if they'd known for sure about *Impris*. It was also about the only thing that made patrol interesting for Jakus, when the old ship decided to take a hop and they had to follow. Well—that and the attack, of course.

Action was what Jakus wanted. Not the wait, but the hunt.

He hadn't always felt this way. He hadn't always been a pirate, not even at heart. But something had changed after his capture by the raiders of the DeNoble fortress. At first he'd merely been a prisoner working under duress in the nets of pirate ships. But to his surprise, he found exhilaration in the blood hunt, in the search for ships to conquer and capture, or to loot and destroy. This was especially true after his transfer from the backwater of DeNoble to the real powerhouse, Kilo-Mike/Carlotta. The augments helped, of course, urging him on whenever he felt his determination slipping. But it wasn't as if he were under the *control* of the augs; *he* was in command, not some goddamn little superconducting crystal.

By the time of his special assignment to Faber Eridani, he'd become a well-equipped soldier, trained in the arts of espionage and undercover activity. At least *he* thought so. And then—how incredibly annoying!—Renwald Legroeder, of all people, had somehow managed to escape from DeNoble. And not just escape: he'd come to Faber Eridani, and found Jakus, and challenged the perfect story he'd planted to explain the loss of the *L.A.*. Once that cover was compromised, his bosses had insisted on faking his death and getting him off Faber Eri. They should have just killed Legroeder, in Jakus's opinion, but the people at the Centrist Strength shop had been too damn slow on the uptake. They hadn't wanted to complicate matters by being implicated in a felony murder; never mind that they decided *later* to try and kill him, and then botched it . . .

But at least the whole fiasco had brought Jakus back to active duty with the raider fleet. And peering out into the quiet landscape of the Flux, he knew that it was better this way, even if he was bored right now. Because the time would come when they would strike. And his excitement this time would be not just for the thrill of the fight, but for the Free Kyber Alliance. For the colony fleets.

He could stand to wait awhile for their prey. When it came, they would strike like a cobra. Fast and deadly.

Captain Hyutu would see to that.

Chapter 26
FABER ERIDANI: HARRIET

"PETER, YOU are such a sight for sore eyes!" Harriet exclaimed, as the PI was conducted into the meeting room at the Narseil embassy.

The Clendornan seemed aglow with pleasure. "It is good to see you, too! Both of you."

"It feels like forever since we left," Harriet said.

"Since we got *back*," said Morgan. "We've been holed up in this embassy way too long."

The Clendornan chuckled. "It's only been a couple of weeks. Of course, by the time we finally get you out of here, it might *really* feel like forever." He chuckled at Morgan's groan, and then became serious. He looked as he always did when he had something important to say; his wedge-shaped head was slightly tilted, and his mouth was crinkled in a smile on one side, and tight and expectant on the other. "Are you ready for some encouraging news?"

Harriet laughed. "Believe me. We're ready."

"I thought you might be." The Clendornan opened his compad on the table, and as he looked up, his grin seemed almost human. "We finally got our hands on the preliminary McGinnis site report. It wasn't easy; it seemed to me that *someone* really didn't want us to see it."

"North?" asked Harriet.

Peter shrugged. "Hard to say for certain. But that's my guess."

"Why? What did it say?" asked Morgan. "If they didn't want us to see it, that must mean the results were in our favor."

The Clendornan nodded. "Nothing's official yet, but I think you can quit worrying about the arson charges against you. It turns out the house fire was caused by built-in incendiary devices."

Harriet drew back, stunned.

"What do you mean, *built-in* devices?" Morgan asked quietly.

Peter's eyes glimmered with purple fire. "Precisely as I said. Self-destruct devices, apparently. I didn't believe it, either, until I read the whole report. Why would a man build such things into his own home? It made no sense. But the investigators were most thorough, and that's what they found—along with evidence in the com logs that McGinnis triggered them himself."

Harriet lowered her eyeglasses, trying to find words. "Let me understand this. McGinnis booby-trapped his own home? Why would he—*unless*—"

"—unless he felt deeply threatened," Peter said. "A long-time threat, so grave that he was prepared to destroy himself, his home, and all of his records, rather than . . . *what?*" Peter gazed steadily at Harriet. "Of course, he didn't destroy his records. He gave them to you instead."

Harriet drew a deep breath, trying not to succumb to dizziness at the implications. "But what *was* the threat? Why was it so great that he was willing to take his own life?" She pinched her brow, thinking of the records now in their possession. She was more grateful than ever that they had secured copies in various safe locations. She looked at Peter again. "There's something you're waiting to tell me."

Peter gave a lopsided grin. "Not tell you. Show you. Remember the dog?"

"What dog?" asked Morgan.

"McGinnis's. Harriet remembers, don't you?"

"How could I forget?" Harriet shuddered at the memory of the dog convulsing outside McGinnis's house, and then bursting through the security forcefield to flee the fire. She still felt guilty for leaving it. But then, she'd left McGinnis, too.

"Well, one of my people has found it. Brought it back, alive and well."

Harriet felt her heart race, without quite knowing why. Morgan clapped her hands and cried, "And we get to adopt it?" Harriet eyed her, and Morgan shrugged. "Well, why not?"

Peter eyed Morgan balefully. "I'm pleased that I could amuse you. Perhaps, if all works out, you *will* get to adopt it. But as a matter of fact, the dog turns out to be carrying some extremely useful information. I brought a vid to show you." He pulled a cube from his pocket.

Harriet pointed to the player the Narseil had provided them. Popping in the cube, Peter said, "This first one was shot at a safe house outside the city, where we first brought the dog."

The recording was of moderately amateurish quality. It showed the brown dog, Rufus, in a sparsely furnished room, with two of Peter's assistants—one apparently controlling the camera, none too steadily. Harriet watched in silent fascination. The dog looked gaunter than she remembered, but seemed unharmed.

"That's my assistant Norman," Peter said, pointing to the man on screen who was crouched in front of the dog, trying to calm it. "Irv's doing camera. He's the one who caught it. Irv's afraid of dogs. I was proud of him."

Harriet nodded, fascinated by what was developing on the screen. The dog was clearly terrified, and growing more so every time it opened its mouth to bark. The reason quickly became obvious. Instead of a bark, what came out were garbled, but almost *human*, sounds. "What is that?" Harriet asked, leaning closer to hear. It was a husky, hissing voice. "It sounds like words!"

"Mhhusssst rrrr t-hhelll . . . ," rasped the dog.

"Is the dog *talking?*"

"Hrrrrr . . . musssst trrrrelll . . ."

"Must tell?" Harriet looked at Peter and demanded, "Is that what it's saying?"

Morgan was shaking her head. "You can't be serious."

But the look of skepticism on her face was evaporating as the dog strained to be heard—and then cringed, as though from the sound of its own voice.

"Very good, Harriet!" Peter said. "It took us much longer to figure it out. But look at this—" He pointed to the screen, where the dog was now pawing at something on the side of its head. The camera zoomed in, and something twinkled behind the dog's ear.

"An implant! I remember now, Legroeder noticed it."

"Exactly." Peter fast-forwarded the playback. "There's more of this stuff, which you can watch later if you want. But once we realized that it was *trying to get us to notice the implant*, then we started getting somewhere." The playback resumed, with Norman whispering soothingly to the dog and gently touching the implant. He murmured, almost inaudibly, "—get you hooked up. We'll get some equipment on you, boy." With those words, the dog's ears perked up and he began licking Norman's hand frantically.

"The dog understood," Morgan said in astonishment.

Peter stopped the playback and changed cubes. "Exactly. We didn't have the right equipment on hand, so we had to do some hunting around. Once we had him hooked up to the right implant com-gear, this is what we heard."

The second vid started with the dog being connected, with some difficulty, to a modified headset. Rufus remained calm during the hookup procedure, but as soon as the equipment was turned on, he became excited. He barked sharply, twice. And then—not from the dog but from the speaker on the nearby console—came a human voice. Strained and distorted, it was nonetheless recognizable as the voice of Robert McGinnis.

"If you can hear these words, know that the information I am about to give you is extremely urgent—and extremely dangerous. If possible, forward it to Rigger Renwald Legroeder, or attorney Harriet Mahoney—or failing that, anyone looking for the historical truth of the lost starship Impris. *Be aware—this information concerns not just* Impris, *but also present-day interference in local spacing af-*

fairs by agents of the so-called Free Kyber Republic.

"Time is short . . ."

Harriet felt her breath tighten, as Peter paused the playback. "McGinnis must have been recording this at the same time he was getting you out of the house," Peter said. He unpaused the vid. As the dog sat utterly still, with a strange look of intense concentration, McGinnis's voice continued:

"I do not know if I will survive the next minutes or hour. I am . . . under heavy attack from the Kyber pirates who installed these damnable implants in my skull. Thirty years ago they tried to make me their agent on Faber Eridani, and nearly succeeded. I have endeavored to make them believe that they succeeded, while safeguarding the Impris *records that they wanted destroyed or altered. With great difficulty, I have managed to deceive my own implants. But no longer.*

"I repeat: I am under attack from within—possibly driven by external transmission. The implants have discovered my deception. I am . . . resisting . . . under great duress . . . an almost irresistible command . . . to kill . . . Rigger Legroeder and Mrs. Mahoney, to whom I have just released the Impris *records. I made a hurried judgment as to their trustworthiness, and I pray I made the right decision. I must resist long enough to let them get clear. I wanted to tell them so much more. But I may have only minutes now before I must end this battle . . . for good . . . if I am to keep from destroying them.*

"I'll upload what I can into Rufus's implants, and hope that it may do some good, if it doesn't fall into the wrong hands. But if it does . . . to hell with . . . what can you do to me that you haven't done already?" The voice became terribly strained. *"You . . . bastards!"*

For a moment, there was silence, and then he seemed to regain strength.

"Do not allow this recording to fall into the hands of the Spacing Authority or the RiggerGuild. Both are under the influence of the Free Kyber, the Golen Space pirates. Insidious bastards! For years, they've distorted the events of his-

tory, betraying their own people to the Kyber. I do not know who to trust in positions of authority—or if you can trust anyone. I only know, the infestation goes very high . . ."

There was another break in the recording. The dog's ears twitched, and he seemed about to whine. Peter raised a finger to wait, and then came a last, gasping sentence.

"I will now upload the data log. Take care of Rufus for me . . ."

His voice trailed off, and there was a rasp of static. Rufus emitted a long howl. Then he lay down and rested his chin on his forepaws, seemingly oblivious to the com set strapped to his head.

Peter turned off the recording. "That was recorded yesterday. My people are working now to see if they can retrieve the data upload. It's some kind of neural-net recording—very difficult to decipher."

Morgan's eyes were wide. "There are some pretty damning statements in there."

Peter's eyes glimmered. "Yes, indeed. But no names, no dates, no events. Not yet. That's what I'm hoping we can get from the recording."

Harriet nodded, listening with only half her mind, as she remembered: *. . . pray I made the right decision.* She heard a voice, and only slowly became aware that it was her own. "He killed himself . . . so he wouldn't kill us . . ."

PETER WAS preparing to leave when a call came on his collar-com. It was Pew, his Swert associate. "What have you got?" Peter asked. And to Harriet and Morgan: "I sent him up to Forest Hills, near the Fabri preserve. Remember the car that took Maris O'Hare was spotted there . . . some sort of traffic thing?"

Harriet nodded, as Pew reported in a foghorn voice, distorted by the com. "Nothing from the traffic incident, Peter. But it transpires they made a fueling stop here. An attendant remembers them—that two people got out and walked around the car—the attendant does not recall looking inside the vehicle." But the attendant *did* remember their being joined by a local, someone new in town, who lived up in the hills nearby. The attendant was suspicious of newcomers and outsiders, including Pew. "But I persuaded him to tell me which way they headed."

"Do you have the location?" Peter asked.

"General area. Going to check further, now. I wanted to apprise you."

"Don't get too close," said Peter. "I'm going to send some backup. Where are you now?"

"At the hydrostop." Pew gave him the address and number.

"Stay put until I contact Georgio. I'll call you back."

Peter smacked a fist into his hand and gazed at Harriet and Morgan. "The rental car was returned two hundred kilometers west of here. But only after it went *north* to a rendezvous in this little town. Does that suggest anything to you?"

"It certainly does," said Harriet. "That's near the Fabri native lands. I wonder if Vegas has any connections there."

"I don't know about that. But it suggests to me that I'd better go with Georgio," Morgan said.

"Why, in Heaven's name?" asked Harriet, a knot tightening in her stomach. "You're not a detective."

"We've been over this before, Mother. If we find the people holding Maris, we're going to have to line up the legal case fast. You can't be there, but I can. I'll start by producing the hospital documentation showing that they *claimed* they were taking her to this other hospital in— wherever it was. Arlmont?" Morgan paused only momentarily as Harriet frowned at her. "Then we can call in the local or provincial police. If *they're* honest, we can at least get Maris into protective custody in another hospital." Morgan hesitated. "Assuming she's still alive, of course."

Harriet's heart sank as she thought of the attempt on her life and Legroeder's. And yet, Morgan was right. They just might have a chance to save Maris, after all.

"All right," she muttered at last. "You win. Go with Georgio—but you *by God be careful!*"

* * *

Adaria kept her wings close about her as she scurried from the Elmira Public Library, satchel held tightly in her arms. She blinked a trace of a tear from her eyes. She was going to miss the library, and her work. She would miss the friends she had made here. She would miss living in the company of interesting humans.

She would not miss the intimidation and fear, however.

She would not miss the insidious presence of Centrist Strength, and government officials who meddled in the business of truth preservation, which was a proper business of libraries.

It is not good, that people should be driven from such a calling—that the preservation of truth should be interfered with. But what can I do? One Fabri?

It seemed hopeless, and that was troublesome in itself. Adaria had never been one to give up hope. Her mentor would be sorry to hear that it had come to this. Perhaps there was *some* way to maintain this hope. Some way.

As she stepped off the transit platform near her apartment, the chill of memory set in. The memory of the night, ten days ago, when the agents of Centrist Strength had come calling. Terrorist agents, as far as she was concerned. Come to *her* home. Why hers?

The knock was not loud, but sharp. It was foolish of her to open the door, but somehow the knock seemed commanding. The two men who stood there spoke softly at first, and then with veiled threat in their voices: ". . . know that there are people you care for, back in the forest . . . it would be sad if evil came to them. But what you are doing, information you are giving to people who have no right to it, trying to make political gold out of a foolish legend—it has cost one man his life, already. How unfortunate if it cost more lives . . ."

Even that might not have been enough to cause her to leave her job. No, it was the change at work, her own boss acting as though Adaria had somehow done wrong to provide information to a patron, to Mrs. Mahoney. The chill had set in, not long after Mrs. Mahoney had come to the library asking about *Impris*; and it had grown steadily deeper, until Adaria simply could stand it no longer.

She let herself into the apartment with a whuffing sigh. Letting down her satchel, she turned and relocked the door with great deliberation. For a moment, she could not move, but just stood back from the door, arms and wings wrapped around herself, shivering. Then she went to the kitchen and put tea water on to heat. While she waited for the water to boil, she went to the com.

"Vegas . . ."

"Ffff—Adaria. Hello." Mrs. Mahoney's housekeeper sounded subdued, but pleased to hear from her. They were more *kefling*—acquaintances—than truefriends; and yet, in a city with so few Fabri natives, the distinction seemed less important.

Adaria fluttered her wings, trying to think what to say. She'd simply had the impulse to call, without knowing what she would say. "I've left my job at the library. It's just become too . . . uncomfortable." *Dangerous.*

"I'm sorry to hear that," said Vegas, who'd lived with her own share of danger in recent weeks. "Are you going to move back home?"

Back with our own people? "Perhaps later," Adaria admitted, trying not to feel it as a defeat. Driven from human society by racist elements. Was it racism? Or a simpler evil? "Have you heard anything from your employer?"

"Ffff—Mrs. Mahoney and Morgan have returned, and taken refuge in the Narseil embassy."

"The Narseil?" Adaria asked in surprise. "That's . . . most unusual, isn't it? I was not aware that the Narseil were prone to such hospitality."

"Unusual, indeed. But there are strange things happening at the Spacing Authority, apparently, and they cannot come home. Plus, there's the missing woman I told you about before. Mrs. Mahoney just called me, in fact. They think this woman might have been taken to a place up in the home province. They'd like us to put the word out . . . they don't know who's behind it . . ." The concern, edged with fear, was audible in Vegas's voice.

Adaria's own fear was rising again. *Centrist Strength . . . meddling in our land again?* "Are you all right, Vegas?"

"Yes—yes, I think I'm safe enough here. Mrs. Mahoney's people are looking out for me."

"Good." Adaria was silent a moment, thinking. "You know, maybe I should think about returning home sooner, rather than later . . ."

"Will you take word about the woman? Mrs. Mahoney is very worried."

"Of course. Yes. Send me all the details."

"I will. And Adaria? Ffff—take care."

MAJOR JENKINS Talbott read the intelligence reports with a curled lip. He still hadn't gotten over the way *someone* had snatched this woman Maris O'Hare out of the hospital before *his* people could get to her. And he still didn't know who the hell they were, or why they had done it. Someone trying to muscle in on Strength? But who else would care, or want to put the squeeze on Rigger Legroeder? Not that *that* mattered now, since Legroeder had fled the planet. But Command—and especially, it seemed, the Kyber affiliates—were even more upset than he was. They wanted her found. It seemed the affiliates didn't take well to people getting away from their outposts, even podunk backwater outposts.

But at last he had some good news. His people—well, okay, Colonel Paroti's people, but they were all part of the same division—had tracked her down. It seemed her abductors had gotten a little careless in their driving, and run someone off the road, way up north of here. They'd fled the scene, but a tracker on the other car had made the ID. So now Talbott knew where they were: basically in the middle of nowhere. Which was fine with him. All the easier to get in, make a snatch, and get out—without any hassle from the police or need to involve North and the planetary authorities.

Talbott looked up with a frown as the agent who'd

brought him the report entered his cubicle. "Good work, Corporal," Talbott said, slapping the report down. "Give yourself a pat on the ass for it."

"Thank you, sir," said Corporal Sladdak, with a crisp nod.

Talbott chuckled. A loyal Strength soldier, this one. Might make good officer material, some day—if he ever, for chrissake, learned to loosen up a little. So goddamn earnest. Talbott squinted at the wall above Sladdak's left shoulder, then blinked and picked up a document wafer. "Corporal, I need a message taken over to field ops. We're asking them to lend us a field action agent. *I* don't figure we need the extra body, but Command's got a bee in their bonnet about it." He paused, then yanked his gaze back to his man. "Corporal, how'd you like to join me on a little mission? We need to liberate this woman from captivity and take care of her ourselves."

"I sure would, sir," the corporal said, without blinking.

"Good. Damn straight. Well, after you deliver this message for me, you go home and get yourself ready for a little field operation. It's an important one, you hear?"

"Yes, *sir . . .*"

Chapter 27

IN SEARCH OF *IMPRIS*

THE FLUX felt different to Legroeder this time, as they flew down the light-years, far from the outer boundaries of Outpost Ivan. A part of him that had grown intensely attached to Tracy-Ace/Alfa was struggling to find a way to fill the emptiness where, against all odds, he had found something to treasure. Or at least *want* to treasure. Was it real, the thing that had happened to him with Tracy-Ace? He wasn't quite sure anymore. The Flux—perhaps acting in concert with his heart—felt more tenuous than usual, with a less clearly defined feeling of movement. He couldn't quite tell if the difference was in him or in the Flux itself—or maybe in the peculiarities of the Kyber ship *Phoenix*. Despite the lack of *feeling* of movement, they were speeding along briskly, as though in a planetary jetstream—thin, high-altitude winds.

The primary rigger crew consisted of Legroeder, Deutsch, Palagren, and Ker'sell—with Kyber riggers taking the secondary crew slots, a fact that did not sit well with the Kyber crew. Legroeder, per YZ/I's orders, was the command rigger in the net; but the ship itself was under the authority of a rugged Kyber captain named Jaemes Glenswarg, a man in his forties, with only modest augmentation. He seemed to have a tough disposition, and likely a willingness to take some risks—but also a predisposition toward conservative flying. That last was some reassurance to Legroeder, who was torn between excitement and fear as he thought of what lay ahead. He was grateful for the trio of Kyber escort ships that had departed along with them. The escort had already dropped back out of visual contact, to a distant shadowing position; but Legroeder was glad they were there—the first time in his life he'd ever welcomed the presence of pirate ships.

Any hope had evaporated for anything like a return to "old times." He and the Narseil and Deutsch worked well in the net together, as always—but it could never be quite the same, operating under a Kyber flag. If he wasn't sure whom to trust, the Narseil were even more uncertain. He had vivid memories of going to Fre'geel with the proposed mission . . .

"Send my people to fly with the Kyber? I'd as gladly send them out the airlock. What did you tell them, anyway?"

"I didn't have to tell them anything, Fre'geel. They knew all about us, the whole plan!"

It was hard to tell whether Fre'geel's indignation was real or staged. "What do you mean, they knew—?"

"They were waiting for us. They knew who I was the whole time. They were the ones who sent the feelers to El'ken. The whole thing was a setup to get us here! Not just me; they wanted your people, too!"

The Narseil's face was transformed by a series of expressions as he struggled to absorb this new information. "You're saying they brought us here to help them look for Impris?"

Legroeder appealed to Tracy-Ace, who nodded confirmation. "Don't forget it's one of the things we came here for, Fre'geel. We have a chance now to try to bring Impris in. Rescue her. Learn the truth."

Fre'geel glanced back through the window into the holding cell, where a set of portable mist-showers had recently been installed. The Kyber had kept their word on that, at least. But Legroeder could imagine him thinking, how would his crew react if he sent his best riggers out on a Kyber-run operation?

"Perhaps," Tracy-Ace said dryly, "you would like to hear the actual terms Ivan is offering."

"Terms!" Fre'geel said, not quite snorting. "Since you have us as your prisoners, you may be able to dictate terms. But you cannot command our actions. Why do you want Impris, anyway?"

Legroeder threw up his hands. "Why don't you listen to them and find out?"

Fre'geel looked stunned, but in the end he went along to discuss the matter with Yankee-Zulu/Ivan . . .

And in the end, if Fre'geel did not exactly *trust* Ivan, he did decide that the Narseil's prospects for achieving their goals were better with the deal than without. Even if there was no guarantee that YZ/I would uphold the bargain if they rescued the ship, they were at least pursuing contacts and gaining information. Fre'geel argued for the inclusion of Cantha and Agamem as bridge specialists to help analyze the structure of the Deep Flux, and although YZ/I had not originally intended to send non-rigger Narseil, he agreed.

They'd gotten underway without delay, despite signs of

considerable wariness between the Narseil team and the Kyber crew. Ker'sell, whom Legroeder suspected had never quite trusted him in the first place, seemed more guarded than ever. Legroeder couldn't tell if Ker'sell regarded him as a traitor, or if he simply distrusted everyone. Agamem, whom the Narseil really had wanted along for security, rather than Flux analysis, seemed to accept Legroeder's loyalty; but even so, Legroeder felt he was being watched. As far as he could tell, Palagren and Cantha still accepted him as a friend and crewmate.

Phoenix's heading was set for upper northeastern Golen Space, where Kyber tracking was last known to have followed *Impris*. The information at their command was scant; Kilo-Mike/Carlotta, whose ships were currently shadowing *Impris*, provided only the minimum tracking data required by the Kyber Republic commonality agreements. However, YZ/I's people had purchased some additional information—they hoped more than just rumor—from a third outpost that had deeper sources than Ivan's within KM/C.

While Cantha worked with the Kyber crew at the plotting computers, trying to project *Impris*'s possible locations from the information they had, Legroeder and the rigger team flew on a course traversing the narrow waist of the so-called Golen Space Peninsula. They were aiming for an area not too far from several important routes that skirted Golen Space just a few light-years to the galactic south of the star-birthing region of the Akeides Nebula. The nebula, just outside Golen Space on the route between Karg-Elert 4 and Vedris IV, was a passage of tremendous beauty, but also an area of turbulence, where a number of Centrist ships had been lost over the years.

The nebula was well known to Kyber worlds, too—but for another reason. It was a boundary point of *Impris*'s wanderings. The ship seemed to meander chaotically, appearing in ghostly fashion in one place and then another, at unpredictable intervals. Its movements seemed limited to a zone a few dozen light-years in length, and a dozen wide and high. The region of the Akeides Nebula marked one end point of that zone.

"Are you saying," Legroeder heard Cantha asking a Kyber navigator named Derrek, "that there's a *force* in the nebula that turns the ship back when it gets too close?"

Derrek's return gaze seemed to deny all recognition of Cantha's authority or position. His electronic eyes glanced at Captain Glenswarg, as if to ask, *How much do you want me to say?*

Legroeder watched in silence. When the captain didn't speak, Cantha explained, "If we want to locate the ship, we need to understand its behavior. If you have knowledge that bears on our search . . ." He appealed with a gesture to the captain.

Glenswarg moved his chin up and down a centimeter, nodding.

The Kyber navigator's mouth pursed as he struggled to accept this. "The answer is, we don't know."

Legroeder thought, *Was that so hard to say?*

"Don't know what—whether or not the nebula turns *Impris* back?" Cantha asked.

Derrek shrugged. "For all we know, the nebula just happens to be there. Maybe there's no connection." He pressed his lips together, making clear there was nothing else he would offer willingly.

Cantha looked thoughtful as he turned back to the simulation console.

AT THE end of the fourth day of flying, Cantha and the riggers gathered in the plotting room just aft of the bridge. "I find it interesting," Cantha said, "that even the Kyber— with all of their ships tracking *Impris*—cannot accurately predict her course, or even define its limits very precisely." Cantha gestured to the holo-image floating in the center of the room, where he'd traced out his projections of their course aboard *Phoenix*. From the net, their course had seemed like a fairly straight line; but from Cantha's plot of the Flux-layers, it looked more like a mangled corkscrew penetrating the Golen Space Peninsula.

"What are these lines here?" Legroeder asked, reaching out to trace glowing threads that crisscrossed under the path of *Phoenix*. "Why do they zigzag like that?"

Cantha picked carefully at his teeth. "That's something you should regard as extremely tentative. I'm trying to sketch out some possible routes of *Impris* through the—" he hesitated "—underflux."

"*Underflux?*" Legroeder asked, cocking an eye at him. "Do you mean the Deep Flux?"

"Only partially." Cantha's neck-ridge quivered; he seemed a little reticent, even defensive, as he continued. "Our Institute has been examining a theoretical series of spacetime layerings that we term the 'underflux.' We don't have enough data to confirm or deny our theories, and it's . . . not discussed much outside the Institute."

Legroeder frowned. "Meaning, it's for Narseil eyes only?"

Cantha shrugged at the implied reproach. "Essentially, yes. Until now. The underflux *includes*—as nearly as I can tell—the layer that the Kyber refer to when they say the Deep Flux."

"As nearly as you can *tell?*"

Deutsch floated forward. "Is there a question about terminology?"

Cantha displayed an uncharacteristic annoyance. "Not just that. No offense, Freem'n, but your Kyber crewmates would sooner open their veins than share their knowledge about the Deep Flux with us. And *somebody* had better start sharing information. Why'd they bring us along, if they're not willing to pool knowledge?"

Palagren stirred. "They probably think we'll use whatever they tell us to try to stop that colony fleet of theirs."

"And are they wrong?" Deutsch asked. Before anyone could answer, he added, "Don't forget, these guys are not entirely playing with their own decks here." He tapped the side of his head. "I don't *think* I'm being programmed to respond to you in any particular way, but I'm not sure the same thing is true of the *Phoenix* crew. There may be low-level safeguards against the spilling of information."

Legroeder opened his mouth, closed it. If the augments were keeping the Kyber crew hostile . . . "I'd better talk to Captain Glenswarg about that. If they want us to find *Impris*, and there's a chance she's actually lost in the Deep Flux . . ."

"It would be very helpful," said Cantha, "if you could use your influence with the captain."

That drew a low hiss from behind Legroeder, and he turned to see Ker'sell's eyes narrowed to thin vertical slits. Legroeder sighed impatiently. "Look, Ker'sell. Unless we cooperate with the Kyber, we'll never find the ship. I didn't sell out to them." *At least, I don't think I did.*

Ker'sell blinked slowly, looking like a large, dangerous lizard. "Perhaps not," he said. "But remember that *our* interests are not the same as the *Kyber's.*" He almost spat the word as he flexed his long-fingered hands. Had his nails grown long and sharp when Legroeder wasn't watching, or had they always been that way? "I will be watching to see whose interests you serve."

"Please do," Legroeder said softly, trying to sound merely annoyed rather than alarmed. He drew a breath. "And now, if you'll all excuse me, I think I'll go have that talk with the captain."

GLENSWARG CROSSED his arms over his chest, facing Legroeder in the commander's wardroom. "What do you expect me to do about it? I can't *make* my men like the Narseil. As long as they're doing their jobs—"

"But that's just it. They're not—" Legroeder caught himself.

"Are you suggesting they're *not* doing their jobs?" Glenswarg asked in a low voice. *Are you questioning my leadership?*

Legroeder steeled himself. "They're not sharing information," he said slowly. "At least, not freely enough to enable our riggers, and researchers—" *brought to you at enormous cost, across many light-years* "—to do what's necessary to complete our mission. To find *Impris.*"

"I am aware of our mission, Rigger."

"Yes, sir." Legroeder paused. "If you don't mind my asking, Captain—are these crew under . . . augment control?"

Glenswarg's gaze narrowed even more. "I don't see what concern that is of yours."

"Yes, well—" Legroeder cleared his throat "—let's just say, if they're *intentionally* being made to be suspicious of us, perhaps there is some adjustment that could be made . . ." His voice trailed off, as the captain's eyes grew more and more slitted.

"You're treading very close to accusing me of incompetence, or sabotage," Glenswarg growled.

Legroeder kept very still for a moment, holding the captain's gaze. "I don't mean to, sir," he said evenly, at last.

There was another pause that seemed to last a dozen heartbeats. "I'll see what can be done," Glenswarg said. "Dismissed."

"Thank you, Captain . . ."

LEGROEDER'S REQUEST seemed to bear fruit. During the following days, he often saw Cantha working at the sim console with one or more of the Kyber bridge crew; and the Narseil reported in private that the Kyber navigators were becoming a little less grudging in cooperating with his requests. No one was declaring the end of mutual suspicions, but at least he had a sense that they were working together. Of all those on the ship, Cantha clearly had the deepest understanding of the subtleties of the underflux—and even the Kyber crew were coming to recognize that fact, or were being permitted to recognize it.

Days passed, as they flew within distant view of the Great Barrier Nebula, a ghostly green wall that stretched for many light-years along the edge of Golen Space. They were passing to the galactic north of the region known as the Sargasso, where Robert McGinnis had once been shipwrecked.

Legroeder fervently hoped that they would have no need to fly any closer to the Sargasso than they were now.

He might as well have wished for a moon.

When Cantha called the riggers together for a look at his latest mapping displays, they were joined by the Kyber crew and captain. As everyone gathered around the floating holo of nearby space, Cantha raised a wand and shone a thin pointer of light into the display. "What I've been trying to establish is a track of where *Impris* has been seen, and ultimately where we might *expect* to see her—or better yet, have a chance of breaking through to *reach* her."

"Explain," said the captain, the light of the holo playing over his frowning face.

Cantha moved the pointer-beam through the glowing display. "The ships that are out there shadowing *Impris* apparently pick up only intermittent ghost traces—so at best, even with the extra information you obtained, we have only bits and pieces of her course."

"So what's the *good* news?" said Glenswarg.

"I've been making new projections, based not just on *Impris* sightings, but on what we think we know of the structure of the underflux." Cantha caused the holo to rotate in mid-air, then pointed out their current destination, not far from the Akeides Nebula. "Here's where the most recent intelligence places *Impris*, based on KM/C's movements." He touched a handheld controller, and something changed in the display: previously unfocused details came into focus, as though they were peering deeper into a multidimensional display. "Now, observe these green lines." He traced a series of spidery threads, through the newly focused region. "These are routes that I believe *Impris* could have followed in recent months." He peered through the display at the others. "These are not paths through the *known* Flux, but projections into the *under*flux—possibly into the lowest layers, what you call the Deep Flux. These are projections only. It is a poorly mapped region, to say the least."

Legroeder squinted, trying to visualize the elusive layer in which *Impris* might be trapped. Cantha's lines zigzagged to the south and radially out on the galactic meridian—converging in one region before spreading out again in other directions. "What's that area of convergence?" he asked—uneasily, because he thought he knew the answer. "Is that the Sargasso?"

"Indeed," said Cantha, with a tone of satisfaction that gave Legroeder a shiver. The Narseil's gaze pierced him for a moment, then shifted suddenly to Captain Glenswarg. "I believe, if we wish to catch up with *Impris*, the place to do it is in the Sargasso."

Legroeder's heart sank.

"That is," Cantha continued, over the muttering of the Kyber crewmen, "if we don't merely want to catch sight of her, but want to actually find her and rendezvous with her." Cantha looked around the room, the display shining on his vertical amphibian eyes, to see if he'd gotten everyone's attention.

Legroeder closed his eyes for a moment, trying to shut out the protests of the others. The Sargasso: a dead zone, where the currents of the Flux dwindled to a stop. Who knew why? And who knew how many ships were stranded there right now—not in the strange, ghostly immortality of *Impris*, but just stranded in the motionless Flux, dying like animals caught in quicksand. If they went in with *Phoenix*, looking for *Impris*, what were their chances of coming out again?

Not good, he thought.

Except that Cantha was suggesting it. And he trusted Cantha's opinion as much as he trusted his own rigging.

"I think, Narseil Cantha," said the captain in a tight, flat voice, "that you have a great deal of explaining to do. Are you seriously recommending that we take this ship into the Sargasso?"

"Yes, Captain," Cantha said. He pointed to the place where the green tracings converged, and altered the focus slowly to a higher level of the Flux, and then back down. The map changed in texture and color as he shifted the display. Cantha's pointer-beam traced green paths through the layers. "Here is what I want you to see. I don't know which of these paths *Impris* has followed—perhaps none of them precisely. But the important thing is that they come together, and *rise very close to the level of the normal Flux*—here in the Sargasso." He peered through the display at the captain. "That's the key. If we want to reach *Impris*, we have to break through into the level where she's trapped. And the Sargasso is the only place I see to do it."

"You're out of your mind," muttered a Kyber crewman.

"Why the hell are we listening to this?" said another.

Christ Almighty, Legroeder thought, gazing into Cantha's eyes. He felt despair.

"It could be a very dangerous course to take," Deutsch rumbled, breaking through the grumbling.

"Yes," said Glenswarg, commanding silence with an arch of his bristly eyebrows. "It sounds extremely dangerous." He paused, allowing Cantha to continue.

"That is true," Cantha said. "And that is why we need to talk about the underflux. And about the *spatial flaws* I believe may underlie it."

"*What* spatial flaws?" growled a Kyber rigger.

Cantha placed his hands together, forefingers pointing into the holo. "The Flux, generally speaking, displays a fairly smooth progression of dimensionality as we move through descending layers. But, from layer to layer, we may encounter differing currents of movement—yes?" He glanced sharply at Derrek, the Kyber navigator, who shrugged.

"As you go deeper and deeper, you may reach a point where the movement slows too much; and if you're using standard rigging techniques, you lose the ability to maneuver. Or, you simply come to a halt—like getting stuck in silt at the bottom of a river."

"Like in the Sargasso," Deutsch said.

"Almost." Cantha raised a finger. "There's a crucial difference. The Sargasso is a place where currents seem to lose their energy—but there it happens in the *normal* levels of the Flux, which is what makes it such a hazard. But *why* do the currents lose energy? Is it just a cancellation effect of converging currents? Or is it something more?"

Palagren's neck-sail stiffened. "Cantha, are you sure you should tell them—?"

"Why not?" Cantha asked. "We've demanded that they share their knowledge with us."

Palagren's mouth tightened. "But this information—"

"Is essential to finding *Impris*. How else can we do it?"

Palagren's eyes seemed filled with uncertainty; but finally he gestured acquiescence.

"So what's the explanation?" Legroeder prompted.

Cantha hissed softly. "The Narseil Rigging Institute believes there are flaws—*fractures*, if you will—in the structure of spacetime in the Sargasso. We believe that currents may be leaking *out* of the normal layers of the Flux into a deeper substrate . . . into the underflux." He gestured to Legroeder. "You've read the Fandrang Report. It talked about regions of high 'EQ.' We don't use that terminology anymore—but this may be a related phenomenon."

"These fractures—are you talking about openings that go all the way down into the Deep Flux?" Glenswarg asked, looking troubled.

"Possibly," Cantha said. "We don't *know* how deep they might go. In the Narseil understanding of the Deep Flux, there are layers far down in the underflux—" the holo shifted to a deeper level, and many of the star systems still visible as ghostly images seemed to draw closer together "—where extremely long routes in normal-space are shortened and compacted, but at the cost of becoming far more unpredictable." The threads marking starship routes became blurred and wavering. "Too unpredictable, in our view, for safe travel."

Cantha walked around the display, pointing here and there. "We can only guess at the details. But we have identified places where subsurface *cusps* or *folds* in the Flux *may* occur. Places where movement along hidden boundaries can result in abrupt transitions." The display flickered with topographic shifts and folds as his pointer beam moved along the indistinct route-threads. "It may happen so abruptly that an unsuspecting crew might not know how to make the transition back."

Legroeder blinked. "And you think this is what happened to *Impris*?"

Cantha steepled his long-fingered hands together. "Quite likely. I also believe this is how she can be *found*."

Glenswarg cleared his throat. "And that's why you're asking me to risk this ship in the Sargasso?"

"It is a risk," Cantha agreed. "But if these flaws exist, as we believe, in the Sargasso, then they could provide openings where we could break through into the underlying layers."

Glenswarg waved his arm through the holo. "But *Impris* isn't there. As far as we know, she's up here." He pointed to what was now the far corner of the display, at the point marking their present destination.

"Indeed," Palagren said, stirring. "She was last seen up there. But that doesn't mean we can *reach* her from there. Legroeder—when you encountered *Impris* seven years ago, did you have any sense that you could have physically reached her?"

"You mean, if we hadn't been attacked?" Legroeder shook his head. "I don't think so. We saw it, heard her riggers in the net . . . and then it faded, just as the attacking ship—" He shuddered, and allowed the inner hands of the implants to close off that memory for him.

"Exactly. It's there, but it's insubstantial . . . and then in a matter of seconds, it's gone again. Cantha, can you show the folds more clearly?" As the display changed to highlight the features, Palagren traced with his hand along the irregularities in the Flux. "We suspect that *Impris* may have become trapped somehow inside one of these folds in the underflux. Trapped in a parallel channel—seemingly close to us, and yet isolated." Palagren glanced around. "She does seem to move very quickly from one location to another."

"So," said Cantha, "we can look for *Impris* up here—" he rotated the image and highlighted their present destination "—under the nose of KM/C, where we won't be able to reach her anyway. Or we can try to *enter* that fold down here—" he rotated it again, highlighting the Sargasso region "—where the pathways converge and there may be openings that will let us reach her *from within the fold*. Where, I might add, Kilo-Mike/Carlotta will see much less of what we're doing."

"Carlotta will love that when she finds out," whispered a Kyber rigger.

He was silenced by a look from Glenswarg. The captain's eyebrows looked like two caterpillars trying to merge. He scowled into the display. "It's an interesting idea. But it'll be dangerous as hell, won't it?"

Cantha shrugged. "The Kyber are known for their courage, yes?"

Glenswarg's scowl darkened even further. "These paths in the folds—are they fast moving?"

Cantha cleared his throat with a rumble. "If they are Deep Flux, they may be *very* fast. Or short. So if you're asking, could we hope to make our way to her quickly once we're in the fold—"

"Not just that," said Glenswarg. "Are we going to be able to find our way out again?"

The Narseil hesitated.

"*Impris* couldn't find *her* way out. What makes you think we're different?"

The blood pounding in Legroeder's ears competed with Palagren's answer. "*Impris* probably didn't know *why* she was trapped. We will. We're going to have to *look* for a way in. Which means we'll be noting exactly where and how we enter. That'll make us better equipped to find our way out again." Palagren turned to Legroeder, then the captain. "With your permission, we would perform some retuning of the rigger-net—to take maximum advantage of our versatility. Human, Kyber, Narseil. All together. That's another advantage we have that *Impris* didn't."

Glenswarg rubbed his chin. "And assuming we make it out of this fold of yours, what about getting out of the Sargasso itself—once we're back in the normal Flux?"

"The Sargasso has extremely slow and tricky movement," said Palagren. "Not *no* movement. If we plan ahead and map with care, we should be able to manage. I won't deceive you, though. There's a degree of risk."

"*High* risk, if you ask me," said Navigator Derrek, leaning into the holo and craning his neck as though trying to extract more information from it.

Glenswarg turned to stare at Legroeder, who was responsible for the rigging decisions. Legroeder took a deep breath. "It has to be the Sargasso?" he asked the Narseil.

First Cantha, then Palagren nodded. "It's the only place we see an opening," Cantha said, unfolding his fingers in a humanlike palm-up gesture. "If we want to find *Impris*, that's where we have to go.

Legroeder closed his eyes, asking the implants if they had any wisdom. They didn't. He gazed at Glenswarg and sighed. "I'm afraid I must recommend, Captain, that we take this ship to the Sargasso."

Glenswarg's gaze bored into him, as though waiting to see if he would change his mind. When Legroeder held his gaze, the captain grunted and turned to his exec. "Prepare a message to the escort ships. And tell the bridge crew, we're changing course."

Chapter 28
GHOST HUNTING

IT WAS hard to be sure precisely when they entered the Sargasso, but soon enough the signs became unmistakable. The net softened around them like sails gone limp, as the currents of space slowed to a crawl. Legroeder gazed out at a tenuous skyscape of ocher clouds, and felt the image changing of its own accord to a vision of water. The mists flattened to become the foggy surface of a still sea, with a half-shrouded sun burning overhead.

Nothing moved. Even the water lapping at the side of the ship sounded like something caught in a time warp, the chuckling slap of listless waves drawn out into a croaking sound, like the monotonous drone of some primordial, throaty-voiced creature.

The riggers scanned in all directions. Legroeder half expected to see the cluttered flotsam of drifting ships; instead, what he saw was a profound and oppressive emptiness. It seemed to permeate not just the outward scene, but the mood inside the net, as well. All four riggers were silent, as though a single word might destroy the fragile magic that held it all together.

The Narseil had spent hours working with the Kyber crew, carefully retuning the flux reactor, adjusting the sensitivity of the net in painstaking increments. Palagren and Cantha were trying to make the net more responsive to emotional fluctuations among the riggers. That was easy; what was hard was to do it without losing the usual buffers against mood shifts. The other riggers, especially the Kyber who flew the alternate shifts, felt uneasy about the changes—and even Ker'sell seemed uncertain—but Legroeder and the captain had allowed Palagren and Cantha to try. They were convinced that, by heightening their sensitivity to fainter stirrings of the Flux, they could improve their maneuverability in the Sargasso. And Legroeder was very much in favor of being able to maneuver out of the Sargasso.

Right now, he couldn't see much except the stillness. He found himself thinking of Com'peer, the Narseil surgeon, quoting from the book of Psalms. How had one of them gone? *He leads me beside the still waters . . .* Yes, Legroeder thought. Still waters, indeed.

An unfamiliar inner voice offered a comment:

□ *The quote refers to "safe" waters, actually. Are these waters safe?* □

(I doubt that,) Legroeder muttered. *(Who are you? Do I know you?)*

◻ *I am an analytical subroutine. My exegetical database includes many of the known galaxy's religions.* ◻

(Oh. Well, what do you analyze about this place?)

◻ *Difficult to know . . .* ◻ said the implant.

(Yah.)

◻ *But I am working on it.* ◻

As are we all, Legroeder thought. But perhaps the implant was right about one thing: it would be very helpful to keep in mind an image of these waters as safe—particularly since the net was far more sensitive now to fear or anxiety. But they were also looking for evidence of any opening in the underflux, any opening through which a ship might pass into a hidden fold—a ship such as *Impris*. Or *Phoenix*. Legroeder wondered where their escort ships were by now. They had been unable to make contact; and though *Phoenix* had transmitted their intentions, they had no way of knowing if the escort had received the message.

Legroeder watched his crew watching the Flux. While commanding the rigger crew, Legroeder occupied his customary stern position, with Palagren at the bow and Ker'sell at top gun. Deutsch, at the keel, seemed intent on something. *Freem'n. What are you picking up?*

Deutsch didn't answer at once. He seemed to be processing through his augments. Finally: *Nothing that I can describe clearly. For a moment, I thought I'd sensed some ghost traces . . . I don't know of what. Like shadows. Maybe echoes from the underflux. Not clear.* Deutsch fell back into silence, but he seemed more emotionally connected to the imagery than usual.

Legroeder, for his part, felt a strange, listless foreboding, as if he were floating under a tropical sun, awaiting the arrival of some vaguely defined enemy. So far, though, he'd seen nothing; he found it hard even to focus on the features of the Flux. The ship was drifting sideways, very slowly. The only visible features on the sea were the fog banks, and if you watched them carefully you could see that they too were shifting with dreamy slowness, as if stirred by convection currents rising from the still surface of the water.

Turning to watch Palagren and Ker'sell, he noted their unstirring poses. He did not interrupt them; they were stretching out through the tessa'chron, probing as far into the future as their senses would allow, seeking any whorls or eddies in the flow of time, anything that might suggest the presence of a change or a flaw in the local fabric of spacetime. So far, they'd seen nothing suggestive of the entry point they were looking for. The net sang like a charged high-tension wire as Palagren came to and peered back at Legroeder.

I'd like to retune further, Palagren said. *I think we need more sensitivity.*

Legroeder frowned. The net was already a roomful of suppressed emotions waiting to erupt. With increased output from the flux reactor, they would shift even farther into an experimental operating regime. He wasn't sure how much more he wanted to experiment. *Cantha? Agamem?* he called to the bridge. *Are you picking up anything useful?*

From the bridge, the two Narseil replied in the negative. *No movement visible,* Cantha said. *Not much energy gradient of any kind.*

If they wanted to be able to maneuver, they had to do better. Legroeder glanced at the ethereal vision of Palagren, waiting at the front of the net for an answer, then called to Deutsch. *Freem'n, will it interrupt your AI scans if we increase the sensitivity further?*

I don't think so.

Was that a trace of nervousness in Deutsch's voice? Well, they were all nervous. *All right, Palagren, let's go ahead.*

Commencing now, replied the Narseil.

Legroeder felt a momentary tingle, followed by a heightened awareness of . . . what? His heartbeat, pulsing in his ears? Light and shadow, boredom and fear?

It seemed to fluctuate through a variety of responses, as Palagren made cautious adjustments—backing off here, enhancing there. Legroeder's implants flickered, joining in a circle with the others', as Palagren gauged the new settings. Legroeder became aware of a smell of the sea that he hadn't noticed before, of brine and seaweed. *Everyone okay with this?* he asked softly.

As the others agreed, he disengaged his augments from the circle. The others could use their augments for flying, but he was going to stick with his human senses. *Begin cycling the images.*

The plan was to try a variety of image types, in hopes of revealing patterns or movement beneath the surface. If the patterns were there, they might well manifest as different images for different individuals.

The first was an undersea vision: a clear and still place, with sunlight slanting down through the water as far as the eye could see. Far off, Legroeder saw floating tufts of seaweed and detritus—perhaps areas of altered density, or mass concentrations in nearby normal-space.

Legroeder was surprised to feel a profound sadness welling up in him for no apparent reason, a feeling of indescribable loss. His thoughts flickered to Tracy-Ace, and he felt himself on the verge of tears. Would he ever see her again? Had she deceived him to get him on this mission? Was he on a fool's errand? No . . . he remembered the intimacy of their joining, and refused to believe that it was false.

He drew a sharp breath, startled by the power of the emotion. *Good Lord.* Glancing around, he realized that everyone in the net seemed preoccupied. Palagren appeared wistful and distracted; Deutsch was concentrating fiercely on the Flux beneath him. Only Ker'sell showed any awareness of Legroeder, and he was staring down at the human with apparent suspicion. Legroeder looked away, hoping he had not let actual images of Tracy-Ace into the net.

Focus outward, he thought. We're here to fly, not gaze at our navels.

The silence was interrupted by: *This is Cantha. Nothing visible on instruments out here.*

Nothing here, Deutsch said.

Nothing, said Legroeder.

Ker'sell didn't answer.

Palagren changed the image again.

The crystal clarity of the seascape closed in, and *Phoenix* was transformed to an aircraft flying straight and level through solid cloud; the forward motion, of course, was purely an illusion. Legroeder felt his feelings changing with the image. At first he was oppressed by the clouds, but that gave way to a sense of freedom and exhilaration. Not everyone in the net shared the feeling, however. Palagren was focused deeply, as though pondering a mystery. Deutsch's mood was inscrutable. Ker'sell was snapping his gaze around with angry energy.

Before Legroeder could learn what was bothering Ker'sell, the Narseil changed the image—as though he could not bear the clouds any longer. Dark forms loomed in the fog, then faded back, like dream-shapes. What were *those*—something they needed to see? Too late: the fog dissipated and the surroundings changed to night. Now they were floating in a glass bubble over a dark, featureless plain.

Featureless plain like the featureless sea.

But was it? Legroeder sensed that something was building beneath the surface. The plain below was not altogether still and motionless; it was smoldering with sulfurous fire. Once he realized that, the fire seemed to spread. In just a few heartbeats, the plain was sprinkled with burning pools of sulfur, reddish orange, like a collection of portals into Hell. Legroeder's pulse quickened. *What do you all see down there?* he whispered.

Looks pretty featureless to me, said Deutsch.

Also to me, murmured Palagren.

Was he the only one who saw the fire? Legroeder glanced up at Ker'sell, and knew the answer. The Narseil was staring down from the top gun position, not at the landscape, but at Legroeder. Those weren't portals down there; that was Ker'sell's anger. Flickers of fire, of suspicion and rage.

Legroeder spoke softly to Ker'sell. *What is it? What's bothering you?*

What's to tell? Ker'sell's eyes seemed to say. The Narseil was eaten up by distrust of Legroeder, but he wasn't going to speak it aloud.

If you think I betrayed you, I did not. Legroeder was surprised by his own calm, in contrast to the smoldering sulfur. *I see your anger down there. That's you, not the Flux, isn't it?*

Ker'sell didn't answer, but Palagren glanced back at Legroeder in surprise. Palagren clearly didn't know what Legroeder was seeing, but he also seemed to be struggling with something else. Self doubt? Uncertainty about whether he could fulfill his promise to bring them through this place? *Is everything all right with you two?* Palagren asked. Then he grunted, as if he suddenly understood.

Perhaps he was glimpsing a moment or two into the future, because Ker'sell suddenly hissed to Legroeder, *You work with the enemy, you make friends with them. Do you make love to them, too?*

Legroeder was speechless. He had to grope for words to reply. *I did not betray you. I did my job. What would we have learned about Impris if we had not come here with this crew?*

Something in the Narseil's eyes brightened and then went dark, and Legroeder couldn't gauge the effect of his words. But below the ship the image suddenly changed again—the seething landscape dissolving to reveal something moving beneath it, a shadow under the molten surface.

Wait! Legroeder cried, as the image began to fade away. *Did you see that?*

The others looked, but whatever he had seen was gone now, and the sulfur with it. Perhaps it was just a reflection of all the disturbances in the net.

He shook his head as the images continued to evolve. They were high above ground in night flight, a weblike array of thousands of tiny nodes of liquid light sprawled out on the surface below. The array seemed to loom out of an infinity of darkness, as though they might fall down through the spaces between the threads, into some other universe altogether. *This reminds me of our homeworld,* Palagren said suddenly, with wistful longing in his voice. From Ker'sell, there was an even stronger reaction. He seemed to be struggling with a desire to break out of the net, to dive into that world and leave all of them behind.

A heartbeat later, a similar homesickness hit Legroeder, as if his own homeworld might be hidden somewhere below.

Something's there. I feel it, Deutsch said quietly from the keel position. For a moment, Legroeder could not identify the emotion disguised by Deutsch's metallic voice. And then he had it: fear.

Why fear?

What do you see, Freem'n?

Not sure. Not sure.

Legroeder peered, but could see nothing to be afraid of. *What does it look like? I don't see anything at all.*

Not sure. Shadows. Just a glimpse of something. Gone now, said Deutsch. His voice reverberated with increasing fear.

I felt it, too, said Palagren. *A presence, I don't know what.* He seemed to be catching some of Deutsch's fear, overlaid with a deep and troubling need. *Do we dare go closer?*

Deutsch tensed perceptibly at the suggestion.

Let's be careful here, said Legroeder. *What do we hope to find?*

Movement, Palagren said. *If there is movement . . .*

Then we shouldn't turn away from it, Legroeder thought. But that doesn't mean we should plunge right in, either. *All right,* he said. *But cautiously.*

It felt as if the image simply swelled up to engulf him. It was dark and mysterious, drawing him into something beautiful and exciting . . .

With a rush of memory, he felt himself becoming aroused as the shadows resolved into a powerful image of Tracy-Ace/Alfa, unclothed, reaching out, open to him at her center, eyes filled with inexpressible longing. Legroeder fell toward the image with a muted groan, unable to resist the hunger . . .

What's this? Ker'sell hissed, wheeling around to glare at him.

With a jerk of recognition, Legroeder tried to veer away from the thought; this was the last thing he wanted any of the others in the net to see. He strove to banish it, but Tracy-Ace was moving toward him, fingers closing around his shoulder blades, mouth closing on his . . .

Exactly as I thought! Ker'sell hissed, his anger flaring in the net like a pale, crackling flame.

No—it's not—! Legroeder protested as he struggled to change the image. Did Palagren and Deutsch see it, too? *(Help me!)* he whispered to the implants.

◻ *Initiating change,* ◻ they answered, and began a swift reweaving of the image.

Tracy-Ace was transformed in an eyeblink into another woman . . .

(Not you!) he whispered, as the beautiful, raven-haired pirate from DeNoble beckoned to him, augments flickering with sinister delight. *(Christ, not Greta!)*

◻ *Changing again . . .* ◻

(Just help me wipe it—!)

There was a flicker, and the image changed abruptly. The female form turned into a luminous wire figure and spun away from him, moving out across the darkness with a final sparkle. Legroeder gasped in relief.

I'm not sure I understand what's happening here, Palagren said slowly, as though rousing himself from a daze.

Ker'sell was still hissing, but his outrage seemed to ebb as he was distracted by changes in the scene below. The spiderweb pattern of lighted cities was turning into a cyberlandscape of cyan and crimson webbing suspended over black, illuminated from within by speeding pulses of sapphire and orange. They were dropping toward it as though moving through an intelnet. *We must not fly through this!* Ker'sell cried.

Legroeder reacted with annoyance. *Why not? Does anyone else see a problem?*

Not here, said Deutsch.

Palagren glanced backward, gesturing in the negative.

Then what was Ker'sell alarmed at?

(What do you see?) Legroeder asked his augments.

□ *Analyzing . . . the activity below is very regular and rhythmic, as if all activities balance other activities. No net gain . . .* □

Activity in the Sargasso . . . balancing and canceling . . . ?

(Can you filter it, let me see the component movements?)

□ *Attempting . . .* □

The augment matrix began to blur through its analyzing and filtering routines. At the same time, he felt the image begin to shift; one of the other riggers was changing it. *Leave it a moment!*

It's making me dizzy, Ker'sell complained, continuing to change the image.

Legroeder reached to stop him. *Why are you afraid? I need to know what's happening.* Then, a little too sternly: *I'm in command here! Freem'n, help me!*

Deutsch reacted in some unseen way, meshing his augmentation with the Kyber net to block the change.

No! Ker'sell protested. *We can't!*

What are you afraid of? Legroeder shouted, his annoyance growing. *Don't keep trying to change it! Tell me!*

The Narseil's fear was palpable, radiating throughout the net. *There are things down there—things out of time—past, future—all mixed up! I can't see . . .*

What things? Legroeder tried to probe the image, but it was all entangled with the Narseil's fear. *You've got to—*

NO! Cracks in time! Splinters! Things moving—!

Ker'sell, said Palagren suddenly. *Pull out of the tessa'chron! You're losing objectivity!*

Instead of answering, Ker'sell made a desperate attempt to bypass Deutsch's blocks. The net quaked from his efforts.

This was becoming dangerous. *You are relieved!* Legroeder commanded. *Ker'sell—leave the net.*

What—? squawked the Narseil.

Get out of the net! At once!

For an instant, no one moved. Then Palagren said to his fellow Narseil, *Follow his instructions.*

Ker'sell abruptly vanished from the net.

Legroeder's heart was pounding. He tried to concentrate on the landscape below, the virtual cyberimage of a world. *All right.* He gulped. *Let's all calm down.* He took three deep breaths, focusing on the flickering movements. *Palagren—get on the com and talk to Ker'sell. Find out what he saw, why he was so alarmed.*

As Palagren obeyed, Cantha called from the bridge. *We're picking up a lot of strange quantum effects. I can't quite follow it. And Ker'sell is quite upset. Captain wants to know, are things under control?*

Legroeder was breathlessly trying to assess that very question. What had Ker'sell seen that the others could not? Was he just hallucinating, or were there really—?

Legroeder's heart nearly stopped as he saw a shape begin to form among the threads of light below. What was that— and why did *he* feel alarmed by it, even before he knew what it was?

Legroeder, are you doing something? Deutsch asked worriedly.

Not intentionally. I've got my implants trying to sort out energy flows that are canceling each other . . .

Well, yeah—so am I, Deutsch said. *But I'm not getting anywh—*

His words broke off as the new image suddenly came to life. An enormous, spiderlike thing rose up out of the crisscrossing threads of light. Its body was an illuminated shape of transparent glass. It was moving across the landscape with a slow, undulating movement. Streaming out from it were faint wavelets in the Flux, moving backward like the wake of a boat.

What is that? Palagren whispered in fascination. *Is it alive?*

Legroeder shrugged, watching it with a creeping horror.

He struggled to control his emotions; he didn't know where they were coming from. *Look at the wake moving back from it. Is that canceling its energy?*

Let's find out, Deutsch said darkly, as if disapproving of this strange manifestation.

Legroeder nodded uneasily. Was he wrong to have sent Ker'sell away? Had Ker'sell been the first to see a real danger? Palagren was beginning to steer the ship away from the spider thing. *Wait, Palagren. I think we need to investigate this,* Legroeder said, feeling afraid even as he said it.

If we could probe the thing's wake, Deutsch muttered. He seemed charged with a dark kind of excitement. *If we could reach down . . .* As he spoke, he stretched a long arm down from the keel of the ship, trolling it in the wavelets far below.

The ship suddenly began to descend.

Alarmed, Legroeder said, *That may not be a good idea. Pull your arm out.*

I can't!

Look, Palagren said. The spider thing had turned and begun to stretch out toward them, as though it were a living thing. The wake streaming out from it was becoming more energetic.

Do you hear that? Palagren asked.

Legroeder's heart was pounding. *What?*

Voices. Below us.

Legroeder strained. At first, nothing; but as the glassy spider loomed toward them, he felt a sudden shiver. Something was happening to the spider; it was melting into a ghostly haze of light. Faces were forming in the haze, faces of light. Human, or nearly human, faces. Ghost faces . . .

That's what I heard. Their voices, Palagren whispered.

Legroeder's stomach knotted. The ghostly faces, drawn thin as though with desolation and anguish, were peering up at him, rising from the auroral glow to meet the ship. Were they images from his subconscious, or from Deutsch's?

The voices grew louder. Cries, and groans of distress.

Jesu, Legroeder whispered. He felt from Deutsch a horror like his own. They were only images, weren't they? But why here, why now?

Something strange is happening in the tessa'chron, Palagren whispered. *It's slipping away from me . . .*

The ghosts veered away just before reaching the ship. Their passage sent shock waves through the net.

What the hell was going on? Legroeder tried to focus . . .

His implants spoke. □ *Freem'n is remembering . . . we glimpsed it in his matrix . . . faces of death.* □

Faces of death? But from where?

More ghost-faces rose on shimmering waves. One flew so close its cry sent a poker through Legroeder's heart. He thought he recognized the voice. But how could that—? *Freem'n!* Was it Deutsch's memory of people he had watched die on starships, victims of piracy? *Freem'n!*

Legroeder, are you all right?

That was Palagren, nearly drowned out by the wail of the specters whirling around the ship.

Legroeder?

I'm not . . . sure, he whispered. *Holy MOTHER OF—*

HEL-L-L-P US-S-S! cried a spirit flashing past. For an instant Legroeder saw a young man's rictus-face pressed against the net like a window pane. It was no one he knew; yet he was overwhelmed by a sense that he had met this man before.

HEL-L-L-P US-S-S . . . !

The ghost veered away, and as Legroeder and Deutsch flinched, the ship rocked dangerously. Fly the ship, Legroeder thought desperately; but he couldn't control his fear. Palagren was trying to compensate. *Ker'sell—come back into the net! We need you!* the Narseil called into the com.

Another ghost hissed by. Palagren seemed utterly unaffected. As his fellow Narseil returned to the net, he reported, *Legroeder and Freem'n are seeing something I'm not— some sort of third-ring entities. They're losing control. You and I need to steer!* He was working urgently to level the ship, oblivious to the ghosts about his head.

□ *We've identified the voice,* □ murmured an implant in Legroeder's head. □ *It's from your memories of the Impris encounter. You heard the crew calling out to you on the L.A.—and at least one of those voices is the same.* □

Impris! Legroeder whispered aloud.

Yes? said Palagren. *If these are real voices and not just your memories, we must follow them. They may be showing us the way.*

Or, Legroeder thought desperately, it may be my subconscious taking us through some delirious hallucination.

Captain Glenswarg wants to know what the hell we're doing, Ker'sell said as he helped Palagren fly. He appeared to have shaken off whatever was alarming him; like Palagren, he was calm as ice now. *What shall we tell him?*

That we're onto something important and we need to see it through, Palagren said. *With your permission, Legroeder—?*

Legroeder struggled. Palagren was right; he had to overcome his fear. He finally grunted, *Permission granted,* and watched with dread as Palagren and Ker'sell steered them toward the waves of light from which the ghosts had emerged. The place that had once been a spider was now boiling and curling over with waves of light, ghosts whirling and diving through the curls. The ship wallowed like an overloaded airplane, dropping toward it. *You aren't intending to go through!* Legroeder whispered. I'm supposed to be in control; I'm supposed to be in control . . .

This is amazing! said Palagren. *I see glimpses forward and backward, as if time has flowered into beautiful petals. And Legroeder! I see the entities emerging. Some of them are from you and Freem'n—but some are not. Some are from down below, from the underflux! Legroeder, these voices came through that opening. We must go!*

All right, Legroeder managed, praying he was not condemning them to *Impris*'s fate. *Take us down!* And to his implants: *(Map everything!)*

Palagren banked the ship into a dive.

The waves grew, until the curling crests turned into coiling tunnels of darkness, lit by the glow of flying spirits. Legroeder held his breath, as the ship flew into one of the cresting wave tunnels, along with half a dozen of the faces.

Deutsch cried out in terror.

Legroeder, suppressing his own fear, felt a surge of unreasoning hope. *It's all right,* he gasped, as the starship plunged through the spectral glow after the whirling ghosts.

The passage seemed to take a long time, and no time at all. The tunnel blossomed open to reveal bright, golden-orange clouds: the clouds of the underflux, he felt certain. He didn't know why, but his fears had begun to melt away.

What is this? Palagren cried.

Legroeder blinked, then saw what Palagren meant—a great, clear orb floating toward them. The ghostly faces were gathering near the orb, their voices fading to a monotonous buzz. One after another, like bees, they plunged into the orb and vanished.

Legroeder's heart was still thundering in his chest, but he forced himself to focus as the ship drifted toward the shimmering sphere. He realized now what it was.

It was a giant raindrop.

And through the raindrop, magnified and distorted as though through an ethereal telescope, he saw something that took his breath away.

A starship, long and silver.

Impris.

FOR A moment, no one stirred. They all saw it, through the raindrop: the spaceship, like an insect caught in amber. Legroeder's pulse raced. He shifted his vantage point from one side of the net to the other, trying to get a clear view of the length of the starship. *I guess the only way to reach it is to go through,* he murmured, as much to himself as to the others.

The Narseil peered through the raindrop with expressions of wonderment. But at the keel position, Deutsch was quaking in terror. *You can't! It's a graveyard ship! Let it rest in peace!*

Legroeder looked down toward the keel. *What is it, Freem'n? What's wrong?*

Deutsch shuddered wordlessly.

Legroeder searched for the source of Freem'n's terror. What did Deutsch see that he didn't? He spoke to his own implants. *(Can you connect me to Freem'n's augments? Without exposing me to whatever he's going through?)*

◻ Attempting . . . ◻

Palagren called out at that moment, *I was wrong. Those are not third-ring entities! They are as alive as we are!*

They're coming from Impris, Legroeder said. *I know those voices.*

No! cried Deutsch. *They're not alive!*

◻ We have a connection, ◻ reported the implants.

Legroeder followed the augment prompts. It was like peering through a telescope, glimpsing what Deutsch saw. Legroeder was astounded by the difference in the view.

Deutsch was staring through the raindrop at a broken hull, filled with lifeless bodies. And ghosts, twirling in and out of view.

(This is insane. Why is he seeing this?)

◻ *Unsure . . .* ◻

(Is he viewing it through his augmentation?)

◻ *Yes.* ◻

Damn. Legroeder called out to his companions, *Listen, everyone! We're not all seeing the same image. Freem'n, can you change your view?*

No! Deutsch cried in anguish.

Legroeder spoke to his implants. *(Do you still have that connection—?)*

Before he could finish the question, he was suddenly gazing across a dark gulf—at Deutsch on a lighted stage, crouched down in terror. He called across to the stage. *(Freem'n! Disconnect from your augments!)*

(I can-n-n't!) Deutsch wailed.

Legroeder thought he knew what was happening. It was the damned raider augments, programmed to instill terror. *(Freem'n, your augments are distorting your view of the Flux! You've got to disconnect!)*

◻ *Try showing him this . . .* ◻

Legroeder's implants displayed his view of *Impris*, its net still active, an automated distress beacon flashing a monotonous plea for assistance. Then a translucent overlay slid across the image . . . and it was transmogrified into a ghost ship full of corpses and tormented spirits.

◻ *This is what he's seeing.* ◻

(Yes! Freem'n!) Legroeder called. *(Look at this!)* Legroeder's augments flashed the living-ship image above the stage, where Deutsch could see it.

For a moment, Deutsch seemed dazed. *(What are you saying—this isn't—)*

(It is, Freem'n! Look with your own eyes!)

(I don't have eyes of my own. Don't you understand? Without my augments, I'm blind!)

(Then find the ones that are doing this, and turn those

off. They're programmed to make you afraid!) Could he do it? Legroeder wondered. Or had he been living with the implants too long?

(*I don't dare. They'll come, they'll kill me . . .*)

(*Who will, Freem'n? Who will come and kill you?*)

(*They . . . will. I can't . . .*)

(*Won't the augments let you?*)

Deutsch was stammering now. (*It's not—not that. They'll come, I tell you.*)

(*Who, Freem'n? The ghosts?*)

(*Yes! YES!*)

(*NO,*) Legroeder said with difficulty. (*They won't. Freem'n, can you trust me on this? Do . . . you . . . trust . . . me?*) Dear God, were Deutsch's implants under Glenswarg's control? They weren't supposed to be. But what if the controls were malfunctioning?

Legroeder, what's going on? Palagren asked, his voice intruding on the inner connection. *We need to decide what to do. Our position isn't stable. If we're going to pass through that bubble, we should go!*

Legroeder tried to control the pounding of his heart. *Yes. Yes, I know. I have to work this out with Freem'n.* He gulped another breath. (*Freem'n, listen to me. You may be having an augment malfunction. You've GOT to check it.*)

Deutsch stared at him from across the stage, as if trying to comprehend what Legroeder was saying.

(*I'm . . . afraid.*)

(*I know you are. You've got to trust me. Do you trust me?*)

(*I . . . I'll try.*) A terrible tension filled the augment connection.

Then Legroeder's implants said softly, □ *He has control of his augments.* □

The Deutsch on the stage rose partway from his crouch and reached up to a large control panel. He fingered the switches hesitantly, before turning one off . . . then back on. There was no effect on the Flux image. (*It's not helping,*) he whispered.

(Don't stop! Try the rest.)

He continued flicking the switches off, then back on, one at a time. None seemed to have much effect, except in color and clarity and sound. He moved to the second row of switches, his hand shaking. OFF. The image changed abruptly. The bodies were gone. The terror was gone. Through the raindrop floated a living ship.

He flicked it back on.

The ghost ship loomed, spirits crying out.

OFF. The terror vanished.

(I'll be God damned,) he breathed. He looked across the stage at Legroeder. *(How did you know?)*

(Later,) Legroeder sighed, as the stage darkened and vanished. Back in the normal net view, he saw the Narseil waiting at their stations with a strange mix of patience and agitation. They reminded him of horses stamping restlessly, breath steaming. Through the raindrop, the other ship was beginning to drift out of his view. Palagren was right; they were going to lose it if they didn't hurry. *We have to go through,* Legroeder said. *And quickly. Are we agreed?*

The Narseil agreed with almost unnerving speed. Deutsch was still nervous, but didn't object. *Palagren,* Legroeder said. *What are our chances of finding our way back out?*

Palagren's hesitation sent a chill through his blood. *We can't be sure until we're on the other side, can we?*

Legroeder cursed, as the other ship drifted a little farther to the side.

A com-window opened from the bridge, and Glenswarg called, *Riggers, report! That looks like a ship in our monitors. Is that Impris?*

Legroeder's heart was in his throat. *Yes, Captain. We believe it is. She appears to be in a separate fold in the underflux. But we believe we can . . . reach her.* His voice caught. *Request . . . permission . . . to make a final transition to the next layer of the underflux. Sir.*

The captain's voice was sharp. *Final transition! Are you telling me we're already in the underflux? When did we cross over?*

We—just a few minutes ago, Captain. It was an . . . extremely hectic moment. Too hectic to communicate with the bridge? he could hear the captain thinking. *Captain, I'm afraid we had a tiger by the tail, and there was really no chance to explain.*

Glenswarg sounded as if he was torn between fury and disbelief. *You mean you took it upon yourselves to risk this ship—? Hold on.* Seconds passed, and the riggers in the net looked at each other and looked at *Impris,* slowly sliding away. Legroeder forced himself to breathe slowly, wondering what he would do if Glenswarg said no.

The com came to life again. *Cantha has shown me where we are and what you've done. Or what he thinks you've done. What he can't tell me is what our chances are of getting out the way we came in.*

Legroeder blinked. Only a third of *Impris* was visible now. *Captain, we're doing everything we can to chart our course in. It took our combined efforts to find this entry point. But we did find it, so we have that over the Impris crew. But I can't tell you it's a sure thing.* Legroeder peered at Palagren, who shook his neck-sail: nothing to add.

How soon do we have to go through? We're losing the view of the ship out here.

Legroeder felt flushed with urgency. *You're seeing what we're seeing, Captain. It may be now or never. We think it's worth the risk.*

Goddamn alien riggers, he imagined the captain thinking. But Glenswarg surprised him. *Proceed, then. Permission given.*

Permission to proceed, Legroeder echoed, then called to the others, *Let's go before we lose her.*

Palagren reached far out from the bow of the ship and touched the shimmering surface of the raindrop. It quivered as his hand went through. It was no longer possible to see *Impris.*

All together now, Legroeder whispered. There was very little movement of the ship, and the surface tension of the raindrop was just strong enough to resist even that motion.

If we can all just relax and let it pull us through . . . His heart was pounding. *(Help me relax . . .)*

The implants gave him a soothing chant . . . and he breathed deeply and felt himself calming . . .

And the ship began to ease forward into the drop of water. The raindrop dimpled inward, stretching for a dozen heartbeats. Then, with a sudden release, the drop shimmered open and flashed closed around them. For a whirling moment, Legroeder had a dizzy sensation of time and space being stretched and twisted and folded in some utterly incomprehensible manner. He felt the ship speeding and somehow *blurring* . . . and yet seemingly not moving at all. And then suddenly all of those feelings drained away, and he was floating in a warm, clear sea. It looked like the Sargasso they had just left, but glowing a deep, enveloping cyan.

Some distance off their port bow floated a ship, long and silver, like a dolphin frozen in the act of leaping.

There she is! Deutsch breathed.

Impris, Palagren said, his voice laced with wonder.

Ker'sell was dumb with amazement.

As Legroeder tried to find his voice, a call came from the bridge. *We've got it on the screen here!* Cantha called excitedly. *We somehow bridged a dozen light-years to Impris. I'm analyzing now. We had a big spike in the quantum wave flux readings.*

Before Legroeder could answer, Captain Glenswarg's voice cut in. *Can you bring us alongside?*

Attempting to do so now, Legroeder answered. *But there's almost no moving current. It's going to be tricky.*

Use extreme care, Glenswarg said, quite unnecessarily.

FOR A while, they hardly managed to move at all. The *Phoenix* net simply could find no purchase in the Flux. While they were preoccupied trying, Legroeder was startled by a small voice calling:

Ahoy there! Ahoy, ship!

Legroeder looked up.

It was not one voice but several—distant, haunting, echoing across the still, silent surface of the sea. Legroeder scarcely dared breathe. *Did you all hear that?* he asked his companions.

I heard it. It sounded human, said Palagren.

Human, yes. Legroeder peered across the empty sea between the ships. *Impris!* he called. *Can you hear me?*

The response was distorted, as if from over-amplification. Finally Legroeder made out the words, —*hear you! We hear you!*

Legroeder called back, *This is Phoenix, Impris. Please stand by!* He reported to Glenswarg: *We have contact, Captain, we have voice contact.* After all these years, the *Impris* crew was still alive! His heart raced with excitement. Now, if they could just find a way to bring the ships together.

Palagren, let's trade positions. I'd like to try something at the bow. The Narseil rigger acknowledged, and blinked instantaneously to the stern, while Legroeder blinked to the bow. Legroeder drew a breath, settling into position. Testing the flexibility of the bow net, he began to stretch forward from the bow, out into the stillness of the Flux. *Let's see how far I can reach . . .*

Hold on, Deutsch said, making an adjustment in the net. A moment later, Legroeder found himself stretched out as though on a tremendously long bowsprit. He managed to reach about a tenth of the way to the other ship before it began to feel unstable.

May I try? asked Deutsch, as Legroeder drew himself back in. *My augments might prove useful here.*

Legroeder frowned at the thought of Deutsch's augments, but perhaps Freem'n was right. *All right. Do you want to switch positions?*

Deutsch shook his head. *Right here is fine.* From the keel position, beneath the bowsprit, he stretched a long arm—a ridiculously exaggerated version of his mechanical telescoping arm—out over the sea toward the marooned starship.

Legroeder shouted from the bow: *Impris—we are trying to reach you! Can you stretch your net out farther?*

There was an indistinct return shout from *Impris*. Deutsch continued telescoping his arm—and the net, with his tuning, stretched out like a slow-motion sunbeam. On *Impris*, after a moment, Legroeder saw a tiny flash of gold light, then a halo growing around the ship's bow. Three tiny shadows moved in the glowing halo: human figures.

Legroeder felt a rush of hope, as the figures grew in size. Eventually he began to make out their faces across the distance. He became aware that Deutsch was having a difficult moment as the faces became more distinct; they were the same faces Legroeder and Deutsch had seen earlier as ghost images. Legroeder murmured reassuringly to his friend: *It was their faces we saw, Freem'n—live men, not dead men.*

Deutsch grunted acknowledgment. *See if you can get them to do what I'm doing,* he said.

Legroeder called out again to the *Impris* riggers. He had a sudden, eerie vision of being adrift on a life raft, trying to reach out and lock hands with survivors on another raft.

Even as he thought it, the net changed to reflect the image; and across the water, seconds later, he could see the *Impris* riggers reaching out shadowy hands. Deutsch's long reach lengthened even farther. But the ships were just too far apart, and in the end they pulled back, frustrated.

Legroeder glanced back at the Narseil. *Any ideas?*

Well, I wouldn't want to try the long-range grapplers, not without knowing how they'd behave in this underflux fold, Palagren said. *It's unfortunate we can't just throw them a line.*

That's it! Deutsch rasped.

Legroeder peered down at him.

Excuse me? said Ker'sell, with an edge of puzzlement. At least he no longer sounded hostile; the appearance of *Impris* seemed to have allayed his suspicions.

We'll throw them a line! Deutsch explained. *If we focus together . . .* As he spoke he crafted the image: a huge coil of line to be hurled out over the water. It would be net-stuff, of course, just a way of coaxing the net into stretching out beyond its ordinary limits. *We'll have to do this together. On the count of three.*

The four riggers jostled for position to exert their influence on the image. Finally four arms held the coil of line together. They swung it forward and backward.

One . . . two . . . THREE!

Their release was uncoordinated, and the coil tumbled away and sank like a stone.

Deutsch pulled it back in, zzzzzip. *Try it again. Focus, people. Timing is everything.*

He counted to three. This time Ker'sell held on an instant too long, and the coil flew up over their heads. Deutsch brought it back for a third attempt.

A voice broke into the net: *What are you doing in there? Are we getting any closer?* The coil vanished, the image broken.

Legroeder explained to the captain.

Can you do this without damaging the net? Glenswarg asked.

We'll have to watch the stresses if we do make contact. But right now we see no other way.

Glenswarg's reluctance was palpable. *Very well, since we can't seem to raise their captain on the flux-com. Is there anything you need us to do here?*

No, we just need to concentrate. With your permission . . . Freem'n? One more time?

Deutsch recreated the coil.

After two more tries, they finally came together on the rhythm and direction. The coil sailed out toward the glittering net of the other starship. *Catch it!* Legroeder shouted.

The shadow figures in the other ship's net moved and shifted, and stretched their own net . . .

And missed.

Two more failures followed. And then, at last, the shadows in the other net moved together, and caught it.

The line snapped taut. The sudden strain in *Phoenix*'s net left them all gasping. The net was stretched out like a nylon stocking with a boulder in its toe.

As they struggled, a voice reverberated down the net. *Are you guys for real-l-l?*

Startled, Legroeder sharpened the focus. He nearly jumped out of his skin at the sight of two, no three, faces peering back through the net at him. *Hello, Impris,* he called. *We're Phoenix. We've been looking for you. What is your condition?*

Our condition? said a different *Impris* voice, this one tinged with hysteria.

The first voice: *We're stranded!*

I know. We've been—

Are you stranded, too? cried the *Impris* rigger.

No, we're—Legroeder hesitated—*the rescue party.*

RESCUE? There was stunned silence in the joined nets. *Do you know how to get us out of—*

It's impossible! interrupted the second voice. *We've been here forever!*

You've been here for a very long time, Legroeder said. *But we're hoping to help you. We need to bring our ships together. If we can draw both of our nets in VERY GRADUALLY, we might be able to do it.*

The *Impris* rigger acknowledged. There was a sudden jerk on the net.

EASE OFF! Legroeder shouted.

The pressure eased.

Legroeder glanced back at his alarmed rigger-mates, and together they began to draw the net in slowly. Deutsch soon got on the com to the bridge, asking for as much power to the net as the flux-reactor could give them. The effort was difficult and unnerving. What would happen if they overstrained the net?

Behind him, the Narseil worked with dark, silent determination. As the riggers hauled in the line, like sailors on some ancient sailing ship pulling with their backs, the two ships drew slowly, almost imperceptibly, closer together.

ON THE bridge of starship *Impris*, Captain Noel Friedman stood with his hands on his hips, glaring from one control station to another. A strange, slow-motion pandemonium seemed to have taken hold of his crew—and truthfully, he wasn't in much better shape himself. A glance at his own reflection had shown a white-haired man, wild-eyed and un-kempt, scarcely a man Friedman would have wanted to trust with his ship. When the summons to the bridge had echoed through the ship, he had been jarred out of a dazed stalk through the corridors. How long had he been doing that? And how long had his bridge crew looked like escapees from an asylum?

Tiegs, the sanest of the bunch, had been on duty for most of this eternity as rigger-com; he was darting urgently back and forth among the com-console and the various bridge officers. Johnson, the navigator, was running around shout-ing like an evangelist that rescue was at hand. Gort and Fenzy, on systems, looked like two old drunks trying to decipher whether or not it was all a hallucination. The rest of them looked as though they were dreaming and happy to have it that way.

Friedman stared at the image in the monitor, reflecting on Tiegs's report. Voice contact with another ship. The question was, were they in contact with spirits, or flesh-and-blood humans? That ship in the monitor looked awfully solid. But so had the other ships down through the years . . . all the ships that had turned out to be nothing but vapor, jests of a malicious universe.

Or had they? Tiegs had maintained all along that those were real ships they'd seen, real voices of real riggers. *Soho . . . Mirabelle . . . Ciudad de los Angeles . . . Centauri Adventurer . . .* Friedman had never been sure himself. One way or another, they'd all slipped back into the night like dreams. But this one . . . could be different, he thought, rub-bing his stubbly chin.

Captain Friedman felt it in his gut, though he couldn't have said why. That black and gray ship out there, with its net stretched out toward *Impris* like a piece of ethereal taffy: Could this really be their rescuer?

"Tiegs," said Friedman to his earnest young officer, "is

that thing actually in physical contact with our net? Can you confirm that?"

Tiegs hesitated. "Well—actually, Poppy says it is, and Jamal agrees. But—"

Friedman frowned.

"—Sully says it isn't, and they're arguing about it right now." Tiegs touched his ear, listening to the conversation in the net. "Sounds like Sully's getting a bit worked up. Claims they're hallucinating, and wants Poppy and Jamal to leave the net."

Friedman closed his eyes, pondering through the haze of a sudden migraine. It was beyond him how the rigger crew had lasted this long together, after all the times their visions had turned to dust. The headache still thudding, he opened his eyes and studied the monitor again. The image of the other ship had grown noticeably. "That's no goddamn hallucination," he muttered. "Tell Sully to get out of there before he screws up the whole operation. If they need someone else, get Thompson."

Tiegs pressed his throat mike. "Sully, Captain's orders are to come out of the net. Do you read me on that, Sully?" He touched his ear. "Did you hear me on that, Sully?" Tiegs shook his head. "We may have a problem getting him out."

Friedman strode to the rigger-station where Sully was reclined behind a scratched and smudgy window. He rapped on the window, then pressed the com-key. "Sullivan, get your ass out here on the bridge!" After a moment's thought, he added more gently, "We need your help on something."

He stepped back, waiting. The window opened, and Sully squinted out at him as if he'd just emerged from a cave. Staggering, Sully climbed out of the station. He was a big man, with sandy hair. He looked as if he'd been in the rigger-station for days.

Friedman steadied him with one hand. "Sully, I want you to keep an eye on the monitor here and keep me informed about what's happening." And stay out of trouble, for God's sake.

Sully looked around in puzzlement, then shrugged and

went to stand in front of the monitor. "I see we have the hallucination up here on the screen," he said matter-of-factly.

"That's right," said Friedman. "That's exactly the sort of thing I need you to tell me. Let me know if it gets any closer." He turned to Tiegs. "Find out if those two need help in there. And find me my backups."

Tiegs nodded and returned to the com.

Friedman stabbed a finger at Fenzy, a lanky fellow who had gotten up from his station to stare open-mouthed at the screen. "You—fire up the fluxwave and see if you can put me in contact with that ship's captain out there."

THROUGH THE joined nets, the faces of the *Impris* riggers were growing larger and clearer. There was definitely a haunted look about them, Legroeder thought; the ghost images earlier had not been all wrong. While the spectral faces staring back did not necessarily reflect the physical appearance of the men in the other net, they undoubtedly echoed the men's states of mind. Was it surprising that they looked this way, if they had spent the last hundred twenty-four years in the net, waiting hopelessly for rescue?

There was some inaudible crosstalk in the net.

Say again? said Legroeder.

I said, don't do that.

Do what? Legroeder asked, then realized that some argument was going on in the *Impris* net. Maybe that explained the jerky hold the *Impris* crew was exerting on the line.

The *Phoenix* crew continued to draw in the net, slowly but steadily. The effort was becoming somewhat less difficult as the reach of the net shortened.

Cantha's voice cut in from the bridge. *We're getting a call on fluxwave. It's from the captain of Impris.*

Legroeder wanted to cheer. *Can you let us hear it?*

Stand by, said Cantha, and then a new voice filled the net.

—is Noel Friedman, captain of Faber Eridani starliner Impris. To whom am I speaking?

Glenswarg's voice filled the com. *This is Captain Jaemes Glenswarg of Kyber-Ivan Phoenix. Captain, we are extremely pleased to have found you. Are you in need of assistance?*

Are we—? The other skipper's voice was choked with emotion. *Captain, we are* very *much in need . . .*

As the captains conferred, Legroeder and his rigger-mates continued drawing *Impris* closer. Progress grew faster as the nets shortened and became stronger. Sooner than Legroeder would have imagined, the ships were nearly alongside each other. Legroeder signaled his fellow riggers to begin reaching all the way around *Impris* with the *Phoenix* net. It felt to him as if they were about to embrace a long-lost, estranged family.

As his crewmates handled the net, Legroeder called across to the *Impris* crew, *I'm Rigger Legroeder. We met once, years ago. I was aboard Ciudad de los Angeles then.*

Ciudad de los Angeles! echoed an astounded voice. *Have you come back to haunt us, then?*

Legroeder blinked in astonishment. They *had* heard the L.A. riggers! With sudden exultation, he remembered his own first reason for being here. He had witnesses! *Are you recording all this, Cantha?* he shouted into the com. *Get it all! Every word!* As Cantha muttered an acknowledgment, he called, *Impris—we heard your distress call seven years ago, on Ciudad de los Angeles. We couldn't help you then— but we've come back to get you!*

The confusion in the other net was palpable.

What do you mean—?

Seven years—?

Deutsch murmured to Legroeder, *It might be better not to try to explain too much right now.*

Legroeder nodded agreement. *Impris, you're caught in a fold of the underflux. We will do our very best to get you out. May we grapple and dock?*

At that moment Glenswarg came on the com to tell the

rigger crew that they had permission to dock with *Impris*. Legroeder drew a deep breath of triumph and relief.

As the riggers began to enfold *Impris* in their net, he had a sudden unsettling vision of the joined nets echoing with manic laughter.

Chapter 30
GHOST SHIP

THE GRAPPLING with the net turned out to be more difficult than Legroeder expected, despite *Phoenix*'s net having been built for just such operations. Just as they were about to close around *Impris*, the passenger liner began to ripple in their grasp like a great silver fish. Afraid they might lose it, Legroeder called for more power to the flux-reactor. The shimmying became worse; it was like trying to hold onto a frightened whale. A low groan began to reverberate through the net. *Everyone, stop!* Legroeder cried. His pulse thudded in his ears as the net relaxed. Gradually, over several seconds, the reverberations subsided.

Impris—what just happened? he called. *Do you know what caused that instability?*

What instability? came the answer.

Legroeder blinked. *You didn't feel yourselves shimmying in our net a moment ago?*

Pause. *We didn't feel anything.*

Legroeder turned to his crewmates. *Did* you *feel it?*

Indeed, said Palagren. *Give me a moment to speak with Cantha . . .*

As the Narseil turned his attention to the com, Legroeder asked Ker'sell, *What did you feel?*

Ker'sell's voice sounded sluggish, as though he were in

a daze. *Time,* he said slowly. *There's something wrong with it.*

What do you mean, wrong? asked Legroeder. *Do you mean the tessa'chron? Is there something in the immediate future?*

Ker'sell hesitated, as if embarrassed. *It's not that. It's as though it's . . . blurred,* he said finally.

Was this a Narseil admission of a weakness? Legroeder wondered. Ker'sell turned away, avoiding his gaze. Legroeder glanced down at Deutsch, who simply looked annoyed at the situation.

Palagren spoke again. *Cantha thinks what we were seeing was a temporal flutter. They measured no spatial anomalies from the bridge, but all of the Narseil felt a blurring in the tessa'chron.*

That's what Ker'sell said. What's it mean?

Palagren took a moment to readjust himself in the net. *I'm not seeing a clear window on past, present, and future. It's difficult to explain. My viewframe is smeared out, as if something's . . . vibrating the spacetime continuum.* He looked closely at his fellow riggers. He did not appear to share Ker'sell's embarrassment about the subject. *We may be feeling continuing quantum effects from our passage into this layer.*

Legroeder shivered. *How much do we know about that?*

Palagren answered cautiously. *Cantha and Agamem are studying it.*

Well, if you figure it out, don't forget to tell us, Deutsch muttered.

Palagren looked at him wordlessly for a moment. *Cantha suggests that we pull tight for a hard dock without actually encircling Impris with the net. He believes a physical joining might keep the two ships in better synch.*

I concur, said Captain Glenswarg, coming onto the com circuit. *Pull us in as close as you can. We'll fire tethers across.*

Legroeder signaled the other riggers, and they began drawing the two ships together as before. When the gap had closed to a hundred meters, the captain ordered magnetic tethering cables launched across to anchor on *Impris*'s hull. Bumper forcefields were turned on, to keep the ships from colliding, and the tethers drawn in. Finally Glenswarg ordered a boarding tube stretched between the ships. Before sending anyone through, he asked Legroeder if there was a chance of bringing the two ships out into normal-space.

Legroeder hesitated before answering. The captain's desire was understandable; they all wanted to know that they had done more than just join *Impris* in eternal limbo. And yet . . .

If I may interject, said Cantha, *I believe it would be unwise to try. Until we understand better how we got into this fold, we could run the risk of burrowing ourselves in deeper.*

Glenswarg's silence sounded like a curse.

Captain, said Legroeder, *I think the sooner we get over there to talk to their crew, the better.*

All right, then—stabilize the net and come on out, Glenswarg said. *I'll send in the backups.*

"Fine work," he said, when the four riggers were standing on the deck with him. "Now I want you to go get some rest."

Legroeder started to protest, then saw the other ship begin to ripple in the monitor with a slow-motion distortion. He held his breath.

"Don't worry, I'll call you when it's time for you to go over," Glenswarg said, reading his thoughts. "But first, we need to establish safe passage. That's going to take time. And I'm not about to risk *you* people until I have to. You're the only ones who have any hope of getting us out of here again."

The captain was being smarter than he was, Legroeder realized. They were all exhausted. Very definitely, the smartest thing they could do right now was to go get some sleep.

SLEEP, UNFORTUNATELY, did not come easily. Legroeder kept thinking about *Impris*, floating beside them. He was desperately eager to cross over and physically touch the ship, and at the same time, the prospect filled him with fear. Several times, as he was just drifting off, he awoke again with a sudden, burning sense of dread—an inexplicable feeling that something was waiting to haunt him in his sleep. He told himself not to be foolish; he was just overtired.

Something out there . . . hidden . . .

Go to sleep.

In the end, with some help from the implants, he did sleep; but even in the depths of sleep, he remained aware of an irrational fear . . . a feeling that there was a monster in this realm, lurking just out of sight.

When he awoke, he felt as though he had not slept at all. He had the strangest sense that he had somehow *slipped through time* as he slept. *(I don't feel quite right,)* he murmured to his implants, as he was getting dressed.

◻ *We register an inconsistency in your biological clock, compared with our clock mechanism.* ◻

(Explain.)

◻ *We cannot.* ◻

Cannot, he thought, frowning to himself as he looked in the mirror and gave his umbrella-cut hair a quick swipe. His eyes looked bleary. He sighed and went to find the others.

It wasn't long before the riggers were gathered, with rolls and cups of murk, in the briefing room off the galley. "I just spoke to the captain," Deutsch reported. "They're about to open the boarding tunnel to *Impris*. Let's see if we can get it on the monitor here." Deutsch made some adjustments to the wall screen, and soon had a picture of three Kyber crew members, including the first officer, making their way through the *Phoenix* airlock and then into the tunnel-shaped boarding tube. As the three men floated toward *Impris*, half the screen showed them dwindling down the tube and half showed a view, apparently from a shoulder-mounted camera, of the other ship drawing near. The *Impris* airlock opened as they approached.

Legroeder realized he was holding his breath, and forced himself to exhale.

"We're in the airlock now," reported the first officer on the comlink. *"Airlock's closing."* The image became shadowy as the other ship's hull came between the men and *Phoenix*, but the voice transmission was still clear enough to hear: *"Cycling and opening on the inside . . ."*

Standing in the briefing room, they could make out the door sliding open, and a large group waiting inside *Impris*.

"Hello!" called the first officer.

The *Impris* crew surged forward, engulfing the contact party. At first, their voices were indistinct; and then Legroeder heard: *"MY GOD, ARE YOU GUYS REAL? OH, MY GOD—!"* And then it was a total chaos of greetings and introductions, as the bewildered crew of the lost ship met the first humans from outside their hull in over a century.

Legroeder and the others watched for a while, then turned back to their part of the business at hand, which was to try to figure out a way to get both ships the hell out of this place.

"I think," said Cantha, "that we've pretty well confirmed where we are. But we still don't know how *Impris* got here, and or even for sure how *we* got here."

"Oh, that's great," said Derrek, the Kyber rigger, who seemed alternately impressed by and resentful of the Narseil success.

Cantha's neck-sail stiffened. "We appear to have passed through a quantum fluctuation as we entered the underflux fold. Unfortunately, it interfered with our ability to map what was happening. We really need to talk to the *Impris* riggers."

"The raindrop—was that the quantum fluctuation?" Legroeder asked.

"We believe so," Palagren said. "It was most likely a wave function connected to something deeper in the spacetime structure. We're still trying to understand why we found *Impris* right here when we passed through, instead of a dozen light-years away, where we thought she was."

"Are you saying we traveled that distance instantaneously—or was she actually here all along?" Legroeder asked.

"We're not sure the question actually has meaning in this context," said Cantha. "I'm not sure what the concept of *distance* means in the fold. But a more immediate question is, can we find a way back *out* through the quantum fluctuation, or is it a one-way passage?"

Derrek looked ill.

Legroeder prompted Palagren, who said, "To answer either question, we have to understand exactly what went on when we came through. We need to put our flight recordings through some intensive processing—which Cantha has already begun."

"I'm sure of this," said Cantha. "It's related to the phenomenon of quantum linkage across spacetime. We've always known that individual particles can be quantum-linked across vast distance—but no one's ever seen such a large-scale effect before, that I know of."

Legroeder mulled that over. "What about the problem we had grappling *Impris*? Was that quantum fluctuation, too?"

"Probably," said Cantha. "We know that the time flow is altered here. We've measured shifts in simultaneity, and all of us—" he gestured to the other Narseil "—have felt disturbances in the tessa'chron. But I still don't know how to interpret—"

He was interrupted by a call on the intercom. It was Captain Glenswarg, and he sounded annoyed. *"Researchers and contact personnel report to the boarding area at once. Riggers Legroeder and Deutsch—for the third time, dammit, report to the bridge!"*

Legroeder exchanged a mystified glance with Deutsch. "Have you heard him call before?"

"Nope," said Deutsch. "But I'm acknowledging now. Shall we go?"

"Keep us updated," Legroeder said to the Narseil, as he and Deutsch headed out of the room.

In the corridor he heard another call from the captain—this time saying, "Riggers Legroeder and Deutsch, stand by to go aboard *Impris*. Please acknowledge and report to the bridge for your instructions."

Legroeder looked at Deutsch, puzzled.

They found Glenswarg stalking back and forth before the consoles. "Call Legroeder and Deutsch again," he was instructing the com officer. Then he turned around. "Oh— there you are. Good of you to make it, for Rings' sake."

"We came as soon as you called," Legroeder said.

Glenswarg looked annoyed. "I called *four times*."

"Four—?" Legroeder began—and suddenly realized what was happening. They'd heard the captain's first call *after* the third one. *We're in trouble.* "Captain, I think you'd better get your people mapping everything they can on temporal instabilities in the area." He explained what they had heard, and when.

Glenswarg's scowl deepened as the implications sank in. "Just what we need," he muttered. "Well, until we find something we can *do* about it, I suppose we should go ahead with our plans. You need to talk to the riggers over there. Make damn sure you report back regularly," He stuck a finger into Legroeder's breastbone. "Err on the side of calling too often. If anything like this happens again, I want to know. And don't stay long. Got that?"

"Yessir."

"Get going."

ON THE boarding deck, they found that a number of Kyber crewmen had already gone back and forth between the two ships. The *Impris* crew were reportedly eager to speak with their rescuers. "Captain said to conduct you straightaway to *Impris*," said the Kyber lieutenant in charge of transfer operations.

Legroeder peered out at the long, transparent tube stretched out between the two ships' airlocks. He shivered at the thought of that frail protection between him and the naked Flux; but there was no help for it, and now the lieutenant was waving them into the airlock.

"After you," said Deutsch, telescoping an arm forward.

Legroeder grunted, then realized that Deutsch was probably ushering him ahead out of genuine consideration. After all, he had been looking for *Impris* far longer than Deutsch had. He nodded and stepped into the airlock.

Ship's gravity ended at the outer airlock door, and they floated out into the tube with a lurch. Two Kyber crewmen were waiting in the tube to escort them through. Legroeder was embarrassed but grateful. The weightlessness was disconcerting enough—but that became incidental when he looked out through the clear wall of the tube.

It was like gazing into another reality. They were the same swirling mists he saw in the rigger-net; but here, viewed with the human eye, they looked far more perilous, as though at any moment they might engulf him in their churning energies. What would happen if the ships moved apart and the boarding tube came loose, spilling him and Deutsch into the Flux? What horrifying death would they encounter?

Legroeder shuddered and headed for the far airlock. But Deutsch seemed fixated by the Flux; he was floating at the tube wall, peering out, his head a Christmas tree of flickering augments. "Freem'n, c'mon!" Legroeder shouted.

Deutsch followed reluctantly.

Legroeder sighed with relief as they floated into the *Impris* airlock. He grabbed a handhold, but stumbled nonetheless as the *Impris* gravity-field brought him to the deck with a lurch. Deutsch, effortless on his levitators, reached out to steady his friend. The Kyber crewmen checked to see they were secure, then launched themselves back toward *Phoenix*.

The airlock closed, and the inner hatch opened. Standing before them were two more Kyber, plus a pair of unfamiliar crewmen wearing rumpled *Impris* uniforms. The starliner crewmen looked haggard, but eager. "Sirs!" cried óne. "Welcome aboard!"

"Thank you," said Legroeder. "We'd like to see your riggers and captain as soon as possible."

"He said to bring you right away," said the crewman in a strangely halting voice.

Legroeder started. Had that crewman just *winked out* for an instant, like a faulty holo? He wasn't a holo, though; Legroeder's nose told him that the crewman was overdue for a mist-shower.

"This way," said the other.

Legroeder glanced at Deutsch. A tickle from his implants told him that Freem'n had seen it, too. *Not good,* he thought, as he turned to follow the crewmen down the ship's corridor and—he hoped—toward the bridge.

VOICES CLAMORED as the bulkhead door opened. "Tiegs! Did you tell Poppy and Jamal to come out of there?"

"I told them, Captain."

"Tell them again! Tell them I said *now*."

As Deutsch and Legroeder stepped onto the bridge, they saw crew members scattered among various posts. The bridge itself looked different enough from modern designs to be noticeable—it had more silver and chrome, for one thing—and yet, it bore more similarities than differences. Apparently, ship design had been stable awhile. A tallish, white-haired man turned to greet them. He wore a tattered uniform jacket over rumpled leisure pants. His bright blue eyes looked more than a little wild. "You're the riggers from *Phoenix?*" he demanded. It was more a shout than a greeting.

"Uh—yes—" began Legroeder.

The escorting crewman cleared his throat. "This is Captain Friedman—Noel Friedman. Captain, Riggers Legroeder and Deutsch."

"Welcome aboard!" the captain roared. "We're sure as hell happy to see you people! How the hell did you find us, out here?"

"That's a long story, Captain. I'd like to tell you about it when we have more—" Legroeder faltered, as he realized that Friedman was staring at Deutsch and not listening to a word. "Captain," he said hastily, "Rigger Deutsch is from the Free Kyber worlds."

"Free Kyber!"

"Yes, and I'm—well, from several worlds, I guess. Most recently, Faber Eridani."

"Faber Eri?" Friedman barked. "*We're* out of Faber Eri. Is that where *Phoenix* is from? I thought they said someplace named Ivan."

"Yessir. *Phoenix* is a Free Kyber ship, from Outpost Ivan. We've a mixed crew, including myself of the Centrist Worlds, and several Narseil members."

"Narseil! Kyber!" Friedman exclaimed. "Are you all working together? Is the war over?"

"Yes—for more than a hundred years."

"A hundred years!" Friedman looked from one to the other in astonishment. "Good Christ! Your captain said you'd been looking for us a long time, but . . . a *hundred years?*"

"A hundred twenty-four, actually. I'm afraid a lot has happened since you left Faber Eridani."

Friedman looked stunned. "I'm surprised anyone still remembers us," he said softly.

"Well, that's—"

"And yet, you came looking for us. Incredible." Friedman frowned. "What about Fandrang? Gloris Fandrang. Is he still working?"

Legroeder shook his head. "No, sir, I'm afraid he died many years ago. But it was his report that got me started in *my* search. There have been—" he hesitated, not wanting to get sidetracked by complicated explanations "—searches for you before. You have been *seen* by other ships. But no one has ever figured out how to *get to you.*"

"Fandrang dead?" Friedman said thoughtfully. "Sweet Jesus. Pen Lee will be distressed to hear that. He's already pretty shaky. He was Fandrang's assistant, you know." Friedman shook his head. "Has it really been—what did you say?—a hundred twenty years?"

"A hundred twenty-four," said Deutsch, speaking for the first time.

Friedman gazed around his bridge, frowning. In one corner of the center monitor, *Phoenix* was visible, large against the Flux. Legroeder tried to imagine what the captain was thinking. How many friends, family members, loved ones had he left behind when he'd set out on his journey? None were left to greet him at home.

"So." Friedman drew himself up and turned back to Legroeder and Deutsch. "Well, let me introduce you to my crew." He brushed at his rumpled uniform. "I'm afraid our hospitality has gotten a little rusty. If you'd like to see the ship, we can arrange—"

Legroeder raised a hand to cut him off. "If we could do that later—right now, we want to talk to your riggers, to see if we can find out what happened to strand you here. We're still working on the best way to get *out* of here— we're in a fold in the underflux, you know, in a layer of the Deep Flux."

"Deep Flux?" Friedman blinked. "Let me get my riggers. Tiegs! Have those men come out yet?"

"Coming now, skipper."

"Good." Friedman turned back to Legroeder and Deutsch. "We are more grateful then I can tell you. There are four hundred eighty-six men, women, and children passengers aboard, plus seventy-four crew."

"Yes, we—"

"It means a lot to know that we weren't forgotten."

Legroeder swallowed as he thought about the lies told about the ship over the years. "You have an almost . . . *legendary* status," he said finally.

The captain's eyes widened. "Is that so? Well, what now, then? Can you get us out? Lead us back to civilization?" His gaze was filled with sudden intensity. "You should know that this ship is still fully functional." For an instant, the message blazed unmistakable in his eyes: *Don't make me abandon my command.*

Deutsch made a soft clicking sound. "Captain, we're

compiling information about the quantum structure of the Flux here. We have experts with us from the Narseil Rigging Institute. And people from *Phoenix* to go over your ship with a fine-toothed comb for any evidence of what happened."

"You can try—but we went over the ship with a fine-toothed comb a hundred years ago and it didn't help." Friedman's eyes flashed. "Do you know the way out, or don't you?"

"We won't know until we try," said Legroeder. "That's why we really need to talk to your riggers."

Friedman spun around. "Where *are* those two?"

Across the bridge, a panel slid open on a rigger station. "Did you want me, skipper?" said a bearded, black-skinned man as he rolled out slowly, shaking his head. On the next station, another panel creaked open and a thin, pale, blond-haired man climbed out, blinking in the bright light.

"We've been calling you for half an hour," said Friedman. "Come say hello to the riggers from *Phoenix*. They came a long way to find us."

"That's an understatement, I guess," said the first rigger. "Let me tell you—for a while there, I thought you guys were ghosts or something. But ghosts don't *pull* like that."

"Rigger Jamal," said Captain Friedman, and then gestured to the blond "—and Rigger Poppy. Meet Riggers Legroeder and Deutsch."

Legroeder stuck out a hand in greeting.

Poppy peered at him. "You the one from the *Los Angeles?*"

Legroeder nodded, memories cascading in his skull.

"And you—" Poppy cocked his head at Deutsch "—you look just like a guy I saw in the net of some ship—jeez, it was like a damn *pirate* ship or something. It came out of nowhere and started shooting up *another* ship that looked like they were trying to help us."

Deutsch was silent a moment. "That was not me. But I think I know the people you mean."

Poppy frowned in puzzlement.

"We came to try to help you," Deutsch said softly.

"Well, what are we waiting for?" said Jamal. "Can you lead us out of here? I'm ready when you are."

"It's a little more complicated than that," said Legroeder.

"These two gentlemen need to sit down and talk to you," Friedman said. "Riggers Legroeder and Deutsch want to know about *your* experience."

"That's right," Legroeder said. "Everything you can tell us about how you got here. Anything that might help us avoid blind alleys or mistakes getting out again."

Deutsch interjected, "If you don't mind my asking, how have you managed to *survive* all this time?"

Friedman's brows went up. "We've done all right. We've . . . taken good care of the passengers, all things considered. We had to expand our hydroponics and recyclers and so on, of course." He pressed his lips together; he was trembling a little. "But you know—this time thing. It sure hasn't—well, it hasn't been any hundred and twenty-four years, here."

"More like an eternity," muttered Jamal.

Legroeder nodded, sensing the strain they were all under. "Is there someplace we can talk?" he asked gently.

THE CORRIDORS of the passenger liner were starting to fill up with crewmen from *Phoenix*, working with *Impris* officers to interview the passengers and crew, and see to any immediate needs or medical problems. The captain emptied a nearby conference room for the riggers to confer.

They had barely gotten settled around the table, however, when a call came to Legroeder on his collar-com from *Phoenix*, via relays set up through the boarding tube. It was Captain Glenswarg, wondering why the hell he hadn't reported in.

"We just got here," Legroeder said, surprised. "We've only just sat down to talk."

"Just sat down? You've been over there for six hours," said Glenswarg.

Legroeder's heart froze. "Excuse me, Captain? It's been less than half an hour, our time."

There was silence on the com. Then: "*Christ.* All right—look. Stay there absolutely not a minute longer than you have to. And report back to me in *ten* minutes, your time. Understood?"

"Understood," Legroeder echoed. He exchanged troubled glances with Deutsch, then turned to the *Impris* officers. "It looks like we're having some problems—*Captain, are you all right?*"

Friedman looked startled. "I'm fine. Why?"

"You seemed to *blink out* for a moment."

Friedman winced. "That sort of thing happens. We don't really know why. But the whole ship is riddled with time distortions. It seems to affect some of us more than others."

"What exactly do you mean?" Legroeder shifted his gaze from the captain to the riggers and back again. He was afraid to take his eyes off any of them.

"From one part of the ship to the next?" Friedman looked puzzled, as if unsure what should be obvious and what not. "As if the time seems to flow in these ripples and eddies, you know. Fast one place, slow another. Depending on where you are in the ship, you're aging faster, or more slowly." He rubbed his chin thoughtfully. "We've got one couple spending their time in a damn *closet* together, because time is slow there. They've been gambling on being rescued. But who knows if they're right? Because if we *weren't* rescued, they'd just be prolonging their lives so they'd be left behind when the rest of us finally die."

Legroeder shivered.

"Not to mention," Poppy interjected, "that boy who tried to kill hims—"

"*Here* now—no need to talk of that," Friedman chided. "We're here to think constructively."

Legroeder drew a deep breath. "We'd better concentrate on the rigging issues. Let's start by finding out what you know about how you got here. How much do you remember?"

Jamal snorted. "What's to remember? We were rigging along just fine, and when the time came to get out, we couldn't."

Legroeder glanced at Deutsch. "You didn't notice anything along the way? Any hint of problems?"

Poppy waved his hand in agitation. "Jamal, you're forgetting—there was that whole business of when we went through a sort of *funnel*. It wasn't such a big deal—except we all thought the Flux felt *different* afterward."

"Oh yeah," said Jamal, scratching his head. "But it's not like we thought anything was *wrong*, then."

"Not wrong. But different."

"Different, how?" Legroeder asked.

Poppy grimaced, as though trying to recall something from very long ago. "Different, like it was harder to get a grip. A purchase. We were still flying, but there was some *slippage*, if you know what I mean. Not enough to clue us that something was really wrong. But then, later, when we tried to come out . . ."

"What happened then?" Legroeder asked, wondering, was the funnel just another image of the raindrop *Phoenix* had gone through?

"*Nothing* happened!" Poppy and Jamal cried together.

"Do you mean, there was no response from the net?"

"It was as if it had gone dead," said Poppy. "I don't mean dead: it still worked. But we couldn't *do* anything, couldn't change our position or speed . . . couldn't even change the image much. And that's more or less how it's been ever since."

"Did you check the reactor? Try increasing the output?"

"Oh, yeah." Jamal chuckled grimly. "Of course. We gave it a real good goosing."

"And?"

Poppy gestured around the room. "That's when this *time* business started—"

"That's when people started *blinking out*." Jamal studied the opposite wall for a moment, rubbing with a thumb and forefinger at his lips. He looked back at Legroeder. "Let me tell you. That scared us real good. *Real* good." His eyes filled with fear as he spoke.

Legroeder remembered their effort to increase power when they were trying to grapple *Impris* with the net. It had only made the problem worse.

"So do you know how to get us out or not?" Poppy asked.

Legroeder hesitated, and Deutsch spoke instead. "We have thoughts on the matter," he said.

Jamal burst into bitter laughter. "You have *thoughts?* Well, isn't that a relief! Rings, man—*we've* had *thoughts!*"

Legroeder flushed. "He means that the Narseil riggers who got us *in* also think they can get us *out*. But—"

"But they don't know, is that it?" Jamal's laugh gave Legroeder a shiver. "Hell, man, don't tell me you came all this way just to sit and rot with us!"

"Not that we don't appreciate the company," Poppy added.

Legroeder exhaled softly. "We hope our situation is somewhat improved from yours. For one thing, we have the benefit of more than a hundred years of rigger science since you flew. Plus, we have a hybrid crew—with and without augmentation."

"I see *you've* got some augmentation yourself," Poppy said pointedly, reminding Legroeder that in *Impris*'s time the Kyber were a dreaded enemy, considered barely human.

Legroeder frowned. "I do have augments, but I don't use them much while rigging—unlike Rigger Deutsch here, who uses them extensively. So we're pairing our skills. Plus, we have two excellent Narseil riggers, who have a good understanding of the latest research."

"If they understand it so well—"

"What I'm trying to say is, we have a variety of different viewpoints—"

Legroeder was interrupted by the movement of a dark shadow over his head. He glanced up in alarm. It looked like a large ocean breaker, rising over him from behind. It was not a shadow on the walls, but a darkness in the air itself. It curled over, well above his head, and came down past the far side of the table, before curling under the conference table. Then it stopped, hovering, enclosing the conference table in the tube of its curling wave of blackness. *"What the hell?"* Legroeder whispered.

Deutsch rose on his levitators and approached the leading edge of the shadow. He rotated in midair, inspecting it from various angles, his regular eyes and his cheekbone eyes swiveling. "I can't tell *what* it is," he murmured. The augments on the side of his head were afire with activity. Floating forward, he telescoped his left hand out toward the phenomenon.

"Freem'n, wait—"

Deutsch reached *into* the wave until his hand disappeared. Then he pulled it back out. "Seems okay," he said, turning his hand over. "Whatever it is, it didn't hurt me. Let's have a closer look."

"Freem'n, wait!"

Deutsch floated forward and leaned into the shadow. " 'S okay . . ." His voice became muffled, then cut off. Abruptly, as though yanked, he toppled headfirst into the shadow.

"Freem'n!" Legroeder yelled, jumping up. But his friend was gone, lost in the wall of darkness. Legroeder swung to Captain Friedman and the *Impris* riggers. *"What's going on?"*

Jamal and Poppy were shaking their heads.

A heartbeat later, the wave of darkness surged forward. Before he could move, it engulfed him, too.

LEGROEDER BLINKED, stunned. He was sitting on a cold metal deck, in a very deep gloom. "Captain? Freem'n?" There was no answer. As his eyes slowly adjusted to the darkness, he realized he was no longer in the meeting room. Then where was he? There was some illumination: emergency or night-lighting, emanating from hidden sources spaced along the base of the walls. His eyes adjusted slowly. He was in a corridor. He could hear a distant ticking sound, and a noise like the closing of a door. "Hello?" he called.

There was no answer.

(What can you tell me?) he asked the implants.

□ *We registered a discontinuity in all readings. Our chronometry is totally desynchronized.* □

(In other words, you don't know much.)

□ *Acknowledged.* □ The implants sounded almost rueful.

Legroeder groaned to his feet and looked both ways down the corridor. There was nothing to indicate where in the ship he was, so he chose a direction at random and started walking. In due course, he came to a series of doors outlined in a pale luminous blue. A hum was audible behind the wall. He tried two of the doors, but they didn't budge. Probably an engineering area—ventilation or hydroponics or something.

He continued walking, but his feelings of unease grew steadily. Was anybody here? He felt as if he were on a ghost ship, the only one still alive.

He drew a breath, cupped his hands, and bellowed down the corridor, "HALLOOO! ANYBODY HER-R-RE?" He turned and called the other way.

At first there was no answer. Then he heard an amplified voice calling back, *"Legroeder? Is that you?"*

His heart quickened. "Yes! This way!"

Deutsch appeared around a corner, some distance down the corridor. He was an eerie sight, floating toward Legroeder on his base with his augments winking slowly on the sides of his head. "Are you all right?" he called.

"Yah." Legroeder hurried to meet his friend. "Thank God! I thought I was the only one left." He stopped and turned around. "Do you have any idea what happened? I was—was—" He suddenly stopped, shaking his head. He had completely lost his train of thought.

"Time," Deutsch said. "That's all I know. There was a time fluctuation. My internal clocks are all scrambled. It's ship's night now." The Kyber's eyes, glowing in the dark, made him seem more robot than human. "Did we just *lose* a bunch of hours?"

Legroeder blinked. "Weren't we just—?" He shook his

head; he was having trouble remembering where he had been. "We were . . . talking . . . in the meeting room."

"Yes," Deutsch said.

"And that wave of shadow—"

"Temporal displacement wave, I think," Deutsch said slowly.

"It pulled you right out of the meeting room—and then hit the rest of us—"

"Which, by my reckoning, was about ten minutes ago. I've been wandering the passageways," Deutsch said.

"Did you see *anyone?*"

"A couple of people. When they saw me, they ran the other way. I think they thought I was a ghost." Deutsch scanned the corridor. "Do you know what I'm wondering?"

"*I'm* wondering a lot of things."

"Well, I'm wondering where we were, physically, between the time we were in that meeting room, and now."

Legroeder cleared his throat uneasily. "You have any thoughts on that?"

"Yeah, but you won't like it."

"I already don't like it."

"Yeah, well, I'm thinking maybe we were *far* away . . . especially if this quantum fluctuation that Palagren and Cantha talk about is spread out over a large area. Or maybe we weren't exactly in existence at all." Deutsch's round glass eyes seemed to loom in the near-darkness.

Legroeder chewed his knuckles for a moment, trying to focus constructively. Before he could come to any conclusions, he was startled by a strange-sounding cry behind him in the corridor. He turned and saw three people walking toward him. Or not so much walking as *rippling* toward him, stretching through the air like ghostly time-lapse holos, then contracting forward. They were talking, or possibly shouting; their voices were distorted, incomprehensible.

As they drew close, it became clear they did not see Legroeder and Deutsch before them. "Excuse me!" Legroeder called, stepping out to get their attention. They *still* appeared not to see him, and he flattened himself to the wall to get out of their way.

The nearest, a heavyset man, brushed against him; the man passed through him as if he were a ghost. Legroeder turned to gape as the trio receded down the passageway. Their voices dopplered down to a distorted bass rumble.

"That was very interesting," Deutsch remarked, floating out into the center of the corridor again. "What do you suppose just happened?"

"I don't know," Legroeder said. "But I hope we can find someone on this ship who can talk to us."

"Or on *Phoenix*," Deutsch said. "I'm not getting a com-signal. Are you?"

Legroeder felt a sudden chill; he'd not thought to check. *(Are we?)*

□ *There is no com-signal.* □

He shook his head. "You don't suppose it could just be our implant function messed up?"

"Maybe. Or maybe we haven't quite made it all the way back to our own space," Deutsch said softly.

Legroeder's jaw muscles tightened. If *Impris* could be trapped in its own space, floating like a specter out of contact with others, what was to prevent individuals from being similarly trapped? He squeezed his hands into fists. *Don't jump to conclusions.* "Do you know which way to the bridge?"

"This way, I think."

They walked awhile, and finally found a directional map showing them to be aft of the passenger's recreational area. Once they located the main corridor, they moved quickly along its deserted length. Were there any real people here?

The answer came finally when they passed through a large passenger lounge and found a scattering of people, as one might on a large ship, late at night. "I wonder if *these* folks will see us," Deutsch murmured.

Seated at a coffee table, two women were playing cards. One, blonde, looked to be in her twenties; the other was a brunette, somewhat older. The brunette sat with her blouse partly open in back—as if she had been interrupted in process of dressing and transported to this spot, with no memory of what she had been doing. The blonde, sitting opposite, was absorbed in her hand of cards. As Deutsch and Legroeder approached, she looked up at them. She seemed to focus on Legroeder's face and started to speak. For a moment he thought she was going to address him; then the older woman said something, and the blonde looked back down at her cards.

Legroeder frowned, stepping close to the table. He peered at the cards and asked, "What are you playing?"

The younger woman held out a card, placing it on the center of the coffee table—and as Legroeder bent for a better look, she peered right through him. She spoke again, and her voice was incomprehensibly distorted.

"They don't see you," Deutsch said. "Let's go."

Passing along the length of the lounge, they came to a young man absorbed in a stand-up holo-game of twisting lights and strange sounds, all contained within a ghostly shadow-curtain. Was this what the game was supposed to look like? Legroeder wondered—or was it, too, being distorted? He stepped up beside the young man. "Good game?"

"Mrrrrk-k-k-k-ll . . ."

"Can you *hear* me?"

The man, reaching out to fiddle with a control on the game board, put his hand through Legroeder's left arm. Legroeder drew a deep breath. *If there's a way to get here, there has to be a way to get out,* he told himself, as though chanting a mantra. Only half believing it, he followed Deutsch onward.

At the end of the lounge, an old man was sitting with his feet propped on the table, reading a book. As they went by, the man looked up, arching his eyebrows. "Don't recall seeing you two here before," he said. "You must be off a' that other ship, the one that's knockin' us off kilter—"

Legroeder could scarcely breathe. "You can see us?"

"I'm talking to you, aren't I?"

"Yeah, but . . . well, you're the first person who's—"

"Wait a minute," said Deutsch. "You said *we're* knocking *you* off kilter?"

The man chuckled. "Well, begging your pardon—things have gone from bad to worse since you got here, what with the time waves and all." He marked his place in the book and closed it. "Don't get me wrong. But I hear people saying your arrival must have upset something in the continuum. Not that I understand how things could *possibly* be worse—except if we take you along with us."

Legroeder stared at him open-mouthed.

◻ *If we might interject—it could be very important to determine whether or not this is true.* ◻

(No kidding,) Legroeder thought.

"We passed through an instability ourselves, not long ago," Deutsch said.

The man laughed. "You're in good company. Twice now, since I been reading my book here, I found myself having dinner again last night." He grimaced. "The first time was bad enough. They *used* to have good food on this ship. That was before everything came from the recyclers."

"Do you have any idea where we might find the captain?" Legroeder asked. "We were meeting with him, and then this wall of darkness—"

The old man waved him to silence. "If the same thing happened to him, he could be most anywhere. But you're headed in the right direction for the bridge and crew section. Just keep going till you get to the royal blue doors."

"Thank you," Deutsch said, his face flickering with augment activity. He peered up the corridor with his primary eyes, while his cheekbone eyes remained fixed on the man. "Any chance you might come with us? Help us if we get lost?"

"Jesus, that's weird. Your eyes, I mean. No offense." The man shook his head. "No, I'd rather just read my book, if that's okay with you. It's a happier way to go."

"All right," said Legroeder. "Thanks, then."

They continued quickly on.

* * *

It seemed only a dozen heartbeats later when Legroeder suddenly shivered, blinked . . .

—*wave of shadow passing over*—

. . . grabbed for Deutsch, didn't find him, felt a rush of disorientation, his vision swimming . . .

He refocused with an effort and found himself in the meeting room with Captain Friedman, Jamal, and Poppy. He struggled for breath as he peered around the room. No Deutsch.

"What the hell are you doing?" Friedman asked.

Legroeder couldn't tell if the captain was angry or just surprised. "I'm—not sure—" Legroeder gasped. "I think I just got transported to . . . *tonight*. At least . . . some night. There was a passenger lounge, and hardly any people. Most of them couldn't see me."

Friedman grunted.

"A passenger told us that things had grown more unstable since our arrival—"

"Told *us?* Who's us?"

"Rigger Deutsch. I found him back there, and then we got separated again. Have you seen him since—?"

"I'm right here," said Deutsch, beside him.

Legroeder jumped, startled.

"I have not seen Rigger Deutsch since—oh, there he is," Friedman said, squinting. He shook his head. "What were you saying?"

"That the instabilities may be worse as a result of our presence here. May I take a moment to contact my ship?"

"Certainly. Do you need a com-unit?"

Legroeder shook his head. *(Connect me to the ship, please?)*

□ *Trying . . . connecting . . .* □

A moment later, Cantha's voice squawked from the collar-com: "Legroeder, this is *Phoenix*. We've been trying to reach you for hours. What's wrong? Do you have a report?"

"Sort of," Legroeder said, and described briefly what had happened. "Have you been observing anything like this?"

"We certainly have," said Cantha. "Including the fact that you seem completely out of time synch with us. More importantly, we've mapped some movement in the quantum flux, and we have some ideas about what might be causing it."

"Such as—?"

"We believe that we may be sitting on top of a very large flaw in the quantum structure of the Deep Flux. We suspect its influence is reverberating upward through the layers of the underflux. And by the way, at least three riggers on this ship have reported having dreams—all with a similar thread. Frightening dreams, mostly."

"Dreams!" Legroeder barked, suddenly remembering the fears he'd felt trying to sleep the night before.

"Yes, have you—?"

"Hold a moment, Cantha." Legroeder realized that Jamal and Poppy had swung to face him, the word *dream* on both of their lips. "Does this mean something to you?"

The two *Impris* riggers looked wide-eyed. Jamal was crouching slightly in his chair, a grimace on his face. "Something coming," Jamal whispered. "I keep dreaming that it's coming. Coming to get me. To get all of us."

"What is? What's coming to get you?"

Jamal shook his head. "Don't know. Monstrous thing. It sounds crazy. But it's like there's a big *serpent* or something in the sky . . ."

Legroeder shifted his gaze. "You, too, Poppy?"

Poppy nodded, biting his lip. "For me, it's like . . . the Gates of *Hell* or something," he whispered. "Something real bad. I can't sleep at all when I've been dreaming about it. Sully too. Sully's had it, too."

"Okay," Legroeder said. "I want to know everything you can tell me about it. Cantha, did you hear that?"

"Yes, I did," came the Narseil's voice. "Get the details, please. We've got to piece it together quickly. Palagren thinks we need to get out of here before the instability gets uncontrollable."

"Do you know yet what's causing it?"

"We think it's an entropic effect of the two overlapping flux-reactor fields, in the presence of the quantum fluctuations. There are signs it's getting progressively worse."

Legroeder felt faint. "Meaning, if we don't get out soon, we won't get out at all?"

"Precisely."

"And have you come up with a way to do it? To get out?"

"Possibly. That confirmation of the dreams might be an important clue. If there *is* a deeper structure . . . and people, riggers, are somehow sensing it subconsciously . . ."

Legroeder frowned.

"Hold on a moment, Legroeder. Palagren wants to talk to you."

Legroeder waited, drumming his fingers on the table. Finally he heard Palagren's voice. "Are you there? Did Cantha tell you that we have to move fast?"

"Yes. But he didn't say how we were going to do it."

"We think we have a way. But we nee-e-e-d to-o-o ta-a-a-a-l-l-l-k-k . . ." Palagren's answer suddenly stretched out into a long distortion of his voice, then faded away.

"Palagren? *Palagren?*"

◻ *We have lost the connection.* ◻

(Can you get it back?)

◻ *We are trying, but there is no longer a com-signal.* ◻

"What is it, Legroeder?" Deutsch asked.

Legroeder gestured sharply. "See if you can raise the ship."

Deutsch became very still, then shook his head.

Friedman reached for his own com-set. "Bridge! Has there been any change in the other ship?"

"Excuse me, sir?" came the answer.

"The other ship. *Phoenix.* Is there a change in its condition."

There was a pause. "I'm not sure what you mean, sir. What other ship?"

"The ship that docked with us a few hours ago!" Friedman shouted.

"Sir?" said the voice on the bridge. "We haven't had contact with another ship in at least a month. Is there . . . a problem, sir?"

"With *me?* No." Friedman snapped off the com in frustration, then snapped it back on. "Bridge, give me a time and date check."

"Certainly," said the bridge officer, sounding relieved to have a question that could be answered. "It's now 1730 hours. And we're showing, let's see, day six hundred fifty-two."

Friedman stiffened. "Thank you." He snapped off the com.

"What?" Legroeder said.

"The bridge is two days behind us. Your ship hasn't arrived, as far as they're concerned." Friedman's face was ashen. "This has never happened before. It's definitely getting worse, isn't it?"

Legroeder took a deep breath. "Yes," he whispered. "Yes, it is."

Chapter 31
SPLINTERS IN TIME

"I WOULD like to suggest," Deutsch said, "that we forget about what day it is, or whether our ship happens to be out there right now."

"Excuse me?" said Jamal. "Are you aware of what's happening here?" *You Kyber,* his eyes seemed to say.

"I *do* understand," said Deutsch. "We must assume that, at some point, our ship will reappear. When that happens, we should be ready to move."

"Agreed," Legroeder said. He had been running through

various scenarios in his head, and the one that scared him the most was the one where they waited too long and found they'd missed their opportunity to escape. "It's clear Palagren has a plan for attempting to fly out."

"Great. What good does that do, if we don't know what it is?" Poppy muttered.

"But we should be ready to act when we *do* find out what it is. And—" Legroeder focused inward for a moment "—the first question is whether we should try to fly the two ships out together, which could be very difficult and dangerous, or instead just get everyone over to *Phoenix*." He turned to Captain Friedman, whose eyes he'd been avoiding. "I'm sorry, Captain. We must consider the possibility."

Friedman's face had turned even whiter, if that was possible. "You don't know what you're saying," he whispered. "We have passengers who are hiding, crewmen disappearing and reappearing . . ." He shook his head, and appeared to regain strength as he drew a deep breath. "I don't think we could ever be sure we had them all. And some people would never willingly leave the ship."

Including you? Legroeder wondered.

"We cannot assume that everyone will be rational about it."

"Well," said Deutsch, "I think we would all prefer to bring *Impris* out, if we can do it safely. Our people very much want to study it."

Jamal's voice was a flat twang of skepticism. "I don't know how we're going to get *one* ship, let alone two, out of this—whatever you called it—fold in the underflux." His nostrils flared. *Prove it to me,* his gleaming white eyes seemed to say.

Legroeder couldn't; he could only guess what Palagren had been about to say. But it had something to do with the hidden structure in the Flux. "The Narseil seemed to think that those dreams of yours might be an important clue in how to get out."

Jamal shuddered. "Man—if you are trying to *reassure* me, that's not the way to do it."

Legroeder persisted. "I think the dreams *may* be trying to tell us something about the Deep Flux. And the more you can tell us about them, the better."

Jamal glanced at his crewmates, shrugged, and began talking.

". . . I DON'T always see the same *thing*, but it's always the same *feeling*—you know what I'm saying? That there's something out there." Jamal's voice fell to a murmur, straining. "Something that . . . *devours*."

Legroeder suppressed a shiver as his own memories surfaced. "Suppose," he said, following a sudden hunch, "that you had to *confront* this thing—whatever it is. To get your ship out. Could you do that? Could you face it?"

Jamal shook his head. "I just want to get *away* from it, man."

"But suppose *it's* what's keeping you here." Legroeder's voice became husky. "Suppose, to find your way past it, you had to make it real. In the net. Could you?"

Beads of sweat were forming on Jamal's forehead.

Legroeder felt a sudden wave of dizziness, and leaned heavily on his elbows for support. *(What's happening?)*

◻ We have contact with the ship. ◻

"Thank God!" he gasped.

"For *what?*" said Poppy, who had been sitting tightlipped since giving a terse description of his dreams.

"Our ship is back," Legroeder said. He held up a hand. *(Put me through.)*

◻ We have a voice channel— ◻

"*Phoenix*," Legroeder snapped. "Can you hear me?"

"Legroeder?" called Cantha. "Are you there? For a few minutes, it looked like you flickered out. Not *you*—the whole ship."

"Tell me about it. Look, Cantha—we have a crew here that's ready to do whatever's necessary to get out." *Right?* he asked with his eyes, of the *Impris* riggers. Jamal scowled, while Poppy looked as if he had been drained of emotion. After a moment, Jamal nodded reluctantly; then Poppy.

Good. "I think I should probably get back over to *Phoenix* to plan with you and Palagren," Legroeder said to Cantha.

Jamal sneered at that. "What, you're going to cut and run now? And leave us here?"

"I'm doing-nothing of the kind," Legroeder said, with annoyance. "But we've got a lot of planning to do." He turned in his seat. "Freem'n, what do you think?"

Deutsch raised his chin. "Okay—but how about I stay and work with these guys. That okay with you?" He surveyed Friedman and the two *Impris* riggers, who looked frightened at the prospect. "Flying out of here is going be a real bitch, you know. Anyone else think formation flying, through instabilities and quantum fluctuations, might be hard?"

Poppy squinted hard at him. "You've got those—" He jerked his chin at Deutsch.

"Augments? Yes. I do." Deutsch raised a hand to stop Poppy's protest. "Look—if you guys want your ship to fly out with us, then we *have* to link the two nets together. I only know one way to do that. That's for Legroeder and me to link ship-to-ship through our augments." Ignoring their reluctance, he turned back to Legroeder. "Yes, I think that's probably the way to do it."

Legroeder nodded, lips tight. This was bound to be unnerving to the *Impris* riggers. It was unnerving to him, too. "If it's okay with everyone, I'll inform Captain Glenswarg and head back over." He rose. "Could someone show me the way out?"

STEPPING INTO the airlock, Legroeder peered uneasily through the outer hatch window. The connector to *Phoenix* was still there, still intact. But one of the *Impris* crewmen on watch was saying in a trembling voice, "A few minutes ago, that whole thing was gone. The ship and everything. I hope you know what you're doing."

Legroeder tried not to show the fear that was tying his stomach in knots. What if one of the ships winked out while he was in the connecting tube?

Before he could reconsider, he slapped the hatch control. The inner hatch hissed shut, and the outer hatch hissed open. He stepped out into the tube.

He'd forgotten about the weightlessness. His first step sent him tumbling into flight. With a gasp, he caught a handhold and brought himself up short. Behind him, the hatch slid shut with a *thunk*. He was alone in the tunnel between the two ships. Where were the Kyber escort crewmen who had brought him over? He tried not to look at the Flux swirling around him, just beyond the transparent wall of the tube.

He pulled himself along quickly, but it was impossible to ignore the Flux; it was a magnet, drawing his gaze outward, to its vapors of blood. He was breathing in short, quick gasps; he could smell his own acrid fear. Jesus. He had to get across before he went crazy, just get across . . .

*

. . . but there was a tapping sound that blurred his concentration, and a strange, ringing vibration in the air . . . it was becoming impossible to think . . .

*

The tapping was in the walls, all around him. He was in a shipboard compartment; he wasn't sure for a moment *which* ship. *What's happening to me?* Turning, he realized he was in an engineering section, and it didn't look like the Kyber ship. He was surrounded by panels of controls, and the hulking shapes of enormous coils that hadn't changed much in a hundred years, just enough to notice.

He was inside *Impris*'s fluxfield reactor, in one of the interstitial spaces . . . and he wasn't wearing a shielded suit . . .

His vision was blurring, knees buckling; he couldn't last here for long . . .

IN THE briefing room, Deutsch felt a sudden dizziness; in the same instant, his inner monitors told him that the connection to *Phoenix* had been lost again. He wondered where Legroeder was; had he made it back to the Kyber ship?

A com unit was chirping somewhere in the room, a voice rasping something about the other ship having flickered out again, and the connector tube . . .

Deutsch leaned forward and shouted, "Was Rigger Legroeder in that connector when it went out?"

"Gone, they're just gone . . ."

THE FLUX was pulling at him as he tumbled. He was back in the connecting tube. Legroeder lunged for a handhold and missed, then finally grabbed another. What the hell was happening? Thank God that reactor had been at low power, or he'd have been fried.

He fought his way toward the hatch—then stopped. *Wrong way. Damn. Turn around.* The Flux tore at his eyes, a living, devouring thing. Had the fluxfield lines caught him, pulled him into a quantum fluctuation? His heart was pounding; he could feel the sweat as he struggled, hand over hand, down the tube toward *Phoenix.* The coils of the Flux were wrapped around the tube like a cosmic boa constrictor, squeezing. He gave a last mighty shove from a handhold, and crashed into the *Phoenix* hatch.

It was closed. He grunted, terror crawling up his neck as he groped for the switch.

What if it didn't open?

What if the ship blinked away again?

He choked back a scream—suddenly realizing he might *trigger* the unthinkable with his own emotions. He was a rigger . . . he was a rigger . . . *damn it, think like a rigger . . .*

He pounded on the hatch switch. *Open, for God's sake—open!*

The hatch slid open, and he tumbled into the airlock. He slapped clumsily at the inner switch, and the hatch slammed shut. He clung, gasping, to a handhold, hanging by his arms. Finally, as the inner hatch opened, he sank to his knees. Gravity had never felt so good.

* * *

HIS HEART was still hammering as he stumbled onto the bridge. Palagren and Cantha were hunched over one of the computers. "That was fast," Palagren said, looking up—and then his eyes narrowed as he registered the strain on Legroeder's face. "Are you all right?"

"You look like hell," said Captain Glenswarg. "Where's Deutsch?"

Legroeder struggled to catch his breath. "He stayed. He wants to work with the *Impris* riggers, and try to fly it out with them. With us."

Palagren's gaze was dark. "That could be risky."

"But can we do it?" asked Glenswarg.

"Captain—"

"Our orders," said Glenswarg, "are to bring *Impris* out if we can. We want the ship, not just the people. We need every bit of information we can get from her." He glanced at Legroeder.

"That's right," Legroeder gulped. "And from what Captain Friedman says, even if we *tried* to get all of her passengers over here, we probably couldn't." He explained.

"Well," said Palagren, "it's an open question: *Can* we fly the two ships out in formation? Or once we power up the two fluxfield generators, will the interaction between them and the quantum fluctuation throw the whole thing out of control?"

Legroeder remembered all too clearly what had just happened to him in the connecting tube. "First tell me how we're going to get *one* ship out."

"Ah." Palagren scratched the base of his neck sail. "We have developed a plan, Cantha and I. It will not be easy, and it involves a degree of risk."

"Which is—?"

"On the one hand, that we lodge ourselves permanently in the underflux; on the other, that we disappear in a spray of neutrinos."

"Oh."

Palagren swung back to the console. "Here, let me show you what we have in mind. We have been looking at this business of the dreams, and we've found evidence of a physical feature that correlates with it . . ."

WHAT THE Narseil had found, from a careful mapping of the Flux lines of force, was an indication of what they called a *deep quantum flaw*, a fracture not just in local space as they had thought before, but in the primordial fabric of spacetime itself, situated beneath even the present level of the Deep Flux. Though they could not say much about its size or extent, they believed it was the source of the fluctuations that had drawn *Impris* and *Phoenix* into this trap in the underflux. It was entirely possible that similar flaws were the bane of other ships lost in the Deep Flux, as well.

The influence of the flaw could be felt well beyond its actual location. This, Cantha believed, could explain the dreams of the riggers. They, of all the souls on the two ships, were the ones whose psyches were most directly exposed to the Flux. It was no coincidence that they shared the fears about, and possibly a subconscious awareness of, a great monster lurking deep within the Flux. "There really is a monster there," Cantha said. "That's why you're feeling it."

"In order to get out," said Palagren, "we must locate the quantum flaw. The opening that brought us *into* the Deep Flux does not appear to offer an exit. To find another way, we must seek the point of origin of the openings . . ."

Legroeder listened in sober silence. The Narseil plan was audacious—and not a little desperate. They would try to make the ships sink *deeper still*—by suppressing even further the action of the nets, by bringing them to a state of controlled, meditative stillness. They hoped to accomplish two things: one, to reduce the dangerous interactions between the two ships' fluxfields; and two, to allow the natural eddies and ripples to draw the ships down into the lowest layers of the Deep Flux. There, they hoped, they would find not just a clearer view of the underlying quantum flaw, but also a pathway out.

"There are no guarantees," Palagren noted.

Legroeder remembered the Narseil's warning about vanishing in a spray of neutrinos. But he couldn't think of a better idea. And remaining where they were was unthinkable.

Captain Glenswarg was already persuaded; Captain Friedman was a little tougher to sell on the proposal. By the time they reached him by com, on the *Impris* bridge, there had already been one more time dislocation aboard *Impris*. "How do we know it won't make matters worse?" Friedman asked.

Before Legroeder could answer, Deutsch, on the other bridge with Friedman, pointed out that they were already on a nonstop course toward chaos; and surely it was better to try even a risky course of action than none at all. Before *he* could finish talking, Jamal stepped into view. His eyes were wide as he said, "You're going to deliberately take us *toward* that thing that we've been dreaming about?" Turning, he gesticulated toward Poppy, who was standing still as a statue, fear frozen on his face.

"We talked about it before, remember?" asked Legroeder, thinking, *it wasn't much more than an hour ago.*

"Yeah, but I didn't think we were going to fly right into the thing's face!" Jamal protested. "It's not like we exactly *agreed* to it."

"No, we didn't," Poppy whispered, behind him.

Legroeder drew a breath, wanting to close his eyes and go somewhere far, far away. "We talked about the fact that it might be necessary."

Palagren stepped up beside him to speak into the com. Jamal's eyes grew even wider at the sight of the Narseil. "You are right, that this is a dangerous plan," Palagren said. "But we know what will happen if we stay. The situation will grow steadily more desperate. We won't have saved you; we will have doomed you, and us, to watching each other die . . . very slowly."

"But—" *You Narseil,* Jamal seemed about to say. He didn't complete the thought aloud.

Friedman faded out of the image, then reappeared. "If I

may point out—we have watched people die here, and it is not pleasant."

By now, they had all heard the story: the boy who in despair had poisoned himself with a fast-acting poison—or so he had thought. Due to the time distortions, he had died for almost a year, ship's time. The captain had finally moved him to the bridge, where time seemed to move faster, to complete the process.

The two *Impris* riggers stood silent. They had no answer.

"I don't know about you," Friedman continued, "but I think a hundred and twenty-four years are enough. Let's do it."

Poppy and Jamal looked at each other, then at Deutsch. "Will *he* be flying with us?" Jamal asked.

"You can't ask for a better rigger on board with you," said Legroeder.

"He has those . . . *things*," Poppy said.

Legroeder drew a deep breath. "Yes. And those *things* may be what enable us to get you out. Give him a chance. I think you'll be surprised. Right, Freem'n?"

Before Deutsch could reply, Friedman said, "Consider it done. Riggers, make ready to sail."

Poppy and Jamal frowned. But if they were tempted to argue, something in the captain's expression persuaded them otherwise. One after another, they turned reluctantly toward their stations.

DEPARTURE HAD to await the engineers' completion of their work on the *Impris* powerplant. Legroeder's anxieties mounted with the delay, but they didn't dare fly without ensuring that *Impris*'s flux-reactor and field components were properly tuned. Twice more, the other ship flickered out, leaving those on the *Phoenix* bridge holding their breaths. But when it reappeared the second time, they got the all-clear call from the Kyber engineers on *Impris*, and the riggers hurried to their posts.

As the rigger station closed around him, Legroeder thought of how tired he felt, and how much he longed for a good night's sleep. It was foolhardy to fly while exhausted. But it would be worse to wait while things deteriorated. (*Whatever else you guys do, make sure I stay alert, okay?*).

◻ *Roger wilco,* ◻ he heard in reply.

Legroeder was joined in the *Phoenix* net by Palagren and Ker'sell, and Cantha in Deutsch's place. They had decided that Cantha's inexperience in the net was outweighed by his knowledge of the quantum flaw. Cantha would ride in the top gun position, as observer and advisor. Legroeder, while still in command of the net, would fly in his accustomed sternrigger spot; Palagren was in the lead position, and Ker'sell was at the keel. If Ker'sell still harbored any suspicions about Legroeder, he was keeping them to himself.

In the *Impris* net, Freem'n Deutsch would be the commanding rigger. There had been some argument about that; the *Impris* riggers had not been eager to relinquish control. But Captain Friedman had agreed that it was the best way to fly the ships in formation—with Deutsch's and Legroeder's augments linked by flux-com.

Is everyone ready? Legroeder asked across the joined nets, as the connecting tube was drawn back to the Kyber ship. Deutsch murmured acknowledgment, as did the Narseil. Jamal and Poppy muttered ambiguously to themselves, probably trying not to show their fear.

We are disconnecting from hard-dock now, came the voice of Glenswarg. *Riggers, you may begin your flight.* As he spoke, the tethers were released and the ships were gently pushed apart by the forcefield bumpers. The two nets separated, and the connection between Legroeder's augments and Freem'n Deutsch's switched to a flux-com link.

Prepare to descend, Legroeder called. *All riggers, begin to still your thoughts. Let's start with a standard meditation.* He drew a breath and let it out slowly, and allowed his vision to go to soft focus. Drawing on exercises from his earliest rigger training, he began to allow conscious thought to drain from his mind. Around him, the others were doing the same.

Through the connection Legroeder became aware of the *Impris* riggers jittering around. *Relax, everyone,* he called softly.

They began to form images, underwater at first. Legroeder exhaled, watching his breath bubble away. Reduce buoyancy . . . sink . . . *This okay with everyone?* As soon as the words were out, he realized that the *Impris* riggers were struggling.

I can't swim! Jamal cried.

Startled, Legroeder let the image dissolve. *Is this better?* He spun forth an old standby for meditations: a hillside sprinkled with wildflowers. He reclined in the grass and gazed up into a deep cerulean sky. *Fill it in however seems best to you.*

That seemed to work better for Jamal and Poppy. Sighing, Legroeder closed his eyes halfway. He too was having trouble calming down.

◻ *Would you like assistance? An alpha-field?* ◻

(No, let me take it the same way as Jamal and Poppy. I need to know how they're feeling.)

◻ *Understood.* ◻

He tried to let his thoughts go. Banks of pastel mist floated overhead, became clouds drifting in a cyan summer sky. *What color sky do you see, everyone?*

Ah, deep purple, said Palagren.

Blue, shading off to green. Deutsch.

Blue. Pale blue. That was Poppy.

I feel, said Ker'sell, *as if I am back home, waiting for the rain to fall and bring the brinies up to the surface.*

You are indeed relaxed, Palagren murmured, *if you can think of eating at a time like this.*

Legroeder let a small chuckle escape. He was beginning, just beginning, to let go of his anxieties. He glanced over at *Impris*, a ghostly silver presence on the hillside . . .

The other ship winked out.

◻ *Loss of signal.* ◻

He cursed. *(Time fluctuation?)*

◻ *Most likely.* ◻

Palagren seemed not to have noticed. Legroeder called to him and the Narseil looked around in puzzlement. *What do you mean? Impris is right there. They're starting to look a little transparent, though.*

Legroeder stared, where the ghostly shape of the other ship had just been. *All right,* he said softly. *If you see it, I'm going to count on you to keep track. As far as I can tell, it's gone.* He drew a breath and let it out slowly, thinking: It'll come back again. Just believe that.

He had lost all semblance now of a meditative state. *(Maybe you'd better give me that shot of alpha-wave, after all,)* he muttered to the implants. An instant later, he felt himself calming down. He relaxed his grip on the stern tiller, allowing the ship to drift wherever the Flux wanted to take them.

There was only the slightest movement of cloud in the sky. He focused on his breath. Just be. Feel. He began to enter a deeper state of relaxation, and to let go of some of his deeper anxieties.

After what seemed a very long while, he realized that the ship was *sinking.*

It felt like a softening in the hillside, as if he were sinking into the earth, easing his way down into some subterranean kingdom where hidden thoughts and possibilities lurked, and invisible currents ran. He noted that his rigger-mates were in similar attitudes of meditation. As one, they appeared to be sinking into the image of the hillside; and now, beside them again was the ghostly presence of *Impris.* Overhead, the clouds were starting to move, to drift upward and across.

Movement.

Legroeder drew a slow breath. It's working. Don't stop now; just keep doing what you're doing. The clouds were scudding overhead now. They were leaving the area of doldrums. But going where? Did they know what they were doing? Could they control their fears?

Just the thought was enough to distract him. The calm

was starting to slip away again; feelings and memories were bubbling up unbidden . . .

A memory of his old riggermate, Janofer—more beautiful than ever. Not now, of all times! Despite himself, he was becoming aroused at the memory, the memory of desire. He'd always been half in love with her . . .

Legroeder, the ghostly Janofer whispered, brushing back her long hair, brushing her lips on his neck. No, he thought, this isn't right . . .

It's very right, she whispered back to him, turning into Morgan Mahoney.

The sudden change left him breathless. Morgan . . . Morgan, how are . . . where are . . . have you found Maris yet?

Morgan turned to Maris, with a little smile that seemed to say, We hardly even knew each other. But if we'd had the time . . .

As Legroeder struggled to follow, he seemed to hear his mother's voice echoing the familiar refrain: *If you would take the opportunities life puts in front of you* . . . from a woman who had taken perhaps one too many opportunities in the form of Legroeder's father, who hadn't stayed around to meet his son. Legroeder felt his old protest rising in his throat. But his mother was long gone; there was no one here to talk to now.

□ *Warning: this train of thought . . .* □

Was not good. Letting his thoughts get away from him . . .

But Tracy-Ace/Alfa was here now, as he had somehow known she would be, as if her spirit had always been present, moving through the terrain of his subconscious. She was beckoning to him . . . her head cocked to one side, augments twinkling, watching him from a position in space, just out of reach. *Hurry and come back*, she said softly. *We have a lot to talk about.*

Yes. Yes! But first they had to get back . . .

IN THE net of *Impris*, Deutsch had been laboring to match his efforts with those of his crewmates over on *Phoenix*. He was leading Poppy and Jamal in a maneuver that ran counter to everything they had been trained to do. He wanted them to suppress their inputs; let themselves flow; allow the ship to drift like a cork into a whirlpool. He wanted them to float helpless toward a terror hidden deep in the Flux. So far, he'd been keeping their input to a minimum—for all practical purposes flying the ship himself.

For Deutsch, it was old hat to drift in the Flux; he'd done it as a Kyber raider countless times, like a predatory sea creature camouflaged as seaweed. But to Poppy and Jamal, it was unthinkable. They didn't trust him *or* this plan of falling toward their worst nightmare. They hadn't yet refused an instruction, but they were like two kettles about to blow their lids.

Gentlemen, if we're to stay with Phoenix, we need to follow her precisely. Which means—

We're clear on what it means, said Jamal, in a mutinous tone.

If we go limp the way you want us to, Poppy said stiffly, *how are we going to keep from falling right in?*

Deutsch drew the net more firmly about himself, thinking, we sure won't fall in if we stay stuck here in the underflux. *Phoenix* had already flickered away for a couple of minutes; now that it was back, he didn't want to lose it again. But when things got more energetic, he wouldn't be able to manage *Impris* alone.

He was not going to win this by arguing. He spoke to his augments. *(Bring up some alpha-wave; amplify and broadcast it into the net.)* On further reflection, he decided to add music, and chose a selection from his augment archives, something soothing.

What's that—*hospital music?* Poppy asked, with thinly disguised annoyance.

Well, damn, Deutsch thought. It had always worked on the riggers in the raider ships. Maybe musical tastes had changed more than he thought. He riffled through his play list and tried something different, with a little more bass beat and movement, and some horn. It wasn't as soothing to his ears, but he could manage. *Better?*

First Poppy, then Jamal shrugged. Deutsch kept an eye on them, and after a few minutes they began to relax. Now, if they just unwound enough for the alpha-waves to start having an effect . . .

The silvery shape of *Phoenix* shimmered; it began to sink into the hill of mist it was resting on. Deutsch nudged the alpha-field up a little more.

As the net of *Impris* grew calmer, Deutsch thought he felt the tug of the lower underflux, pulling them downward also.

HAVE TO get back.

Heaven and sky. Legroeder had gotten so absorbed in the vision of all these women, like a testosterone dream, that he'd nearly forgotten what he was doing. He was in the net of a starship, trying to fly out of an impossible situation.

Gazing through the fading image of Tracy-Ace, he saw myriad stars. The ship was falling through space like a stone now. Around him, the Narseil riggers were deep in meditation; only Cantha seemed alert, and Cantha wasn't actively influencing the net. He looked scared, actually. *Everything okay?* Legroeder murmured.

Cantha's neck-sail was quivering; his eyes were darting downward, and back up again. *Thank heaven you're conscious,* he said. *Look down there.*

Legroeder looked—and for a moment, had trouble drawing a breath. Below them, through the faint glitter of the net, he saw the starry darkness change to just plain darkness . . . and far down, embedded in the deepest part of the darkness, was a writhing thread of fire.

The quantum flaw? he whispered.

They were falling toward it like a body tumbling from a cliff.

I think we've left the dead zone behind, said Cantha. He looked at his fellow Narseil. *Should we disturb them?*

Yes! Wake them! Do whatever you have to. Legroeder wheeled around. *Where is Impris?*

Far off to the port side, he saw the other ship, tumbling and twinkling. They should bring the two ships back together while they still could. He needed help. *Palagren!* he shouted. *Snap out of it!*

The Narseil rigger was slowly turning his head. His neck-sail was glowing a delicate yellowish green along its outer rim; the glow faded as his eyes focused. *By the deeps,* he sighed, *that took me farther than I expected. Were we in entirely separate meditations?*

I think so, Legroeder murmured. *But never mind that. Impris is over there*—he pointed to the tiny, distant ship—*and we're falling fast, toward that.* He pointed down, toward the malevolent light of the quantum flaw. It had grown in the last minute.

Palagren gasped. *We've succeeded!*

I think so, Legroeder said. *But what the hell do we do now?* He felt Deutsch connecting with his implants, asking the same question.

Cantha turned from rousing Ker'sell. *I've been searching for Flux currents leading away from the flaw.*

And? said Palagren.

What have you found? Legroeder demanded.

Cantha had links set up to the bridge sensors, and now they flashed a rippling series of lines across the darkness of the Flux below. The lines spiraled and spiked as different measurements were highlighted; it was difficult to discern an overall pattern. But one thing Legroeder did *not* see was anything like a path emerging from the vicinity of the flaw, a path that would take them away from it.

This isn't working the way we'd hoped, is it? Palagren asked softly.

Legroeder squinted downward. *Do we have any idea what lies* inside *that thing?*

I imagine, said Cantha, almost casually, *that it bears some resemblance to a singularity.*

Legroeder felt his heart stop. He swallowed and peered

across at *Impris*, still twinkling at a distance. They were both still falling, the thread of light growing beneath them. Palagren, having roused Ker'sell from his trance, was stretching his arms into the invisible streams like a high-diver.

I really had hoped it would all become clearer once we approached the quantum flaw, Cantha muttered, adjusting the sensor-displays.

Legroeder tried to keep the desperation out of his voice. *Do you have any more data? Anything at all?*

I'm trying, but I—wait, let me do something.

Legroeder waited, for an endless couple of heartbeats.

Cantha made another adjustment, causing a sudden change as all the space around them suddenly filled with what looked like a blue Cherenkov glow. *Can you see it better now?*

Unfortunately, Legroeder could. The space around them had suddenly taken on a discernible shape and form. Now he could see all the streams of movement in the region. They were all flowing, twisting, spiraling . . . all in one direction.

Toward the quantum flaw.

Into the quantum flaw.

Chapter 32

SAILING THE QUANTUM FLAW

WHAT THE bleeding hell are we doing? Poppy screamed shrilly, deafening Deutsch. *You aren't taking us into that thing!*

No choice, Poppy. That's where we're headed.

No-o-o-o!

Deutsch cut off the music and jacked up the alpha-field. *It's the only way. You've got to forget the dreams. Those are your fears speaking.*

Jamal shouted, *You're damn right my fears are speaking. And they're saying, don't go into that thing!*

Deutsch called on a series of authority-routines to deepen his voice and projection. *We can't NOT go into it. The question is, are we going to fly in like riggers, or drop like stones? GENTLEMEN, I NEED YOUR ASSISTANCE!* His words rang in the net like a gunshot across a valley.

Jamal's voice was muted, frightened. *You don't suppose the dreams were telling us we have to go meet it, do you, Pop? You think Legroeder mighta' been right?*

Deutsch held his breath, as Poppy wailed wordlessly—and after gulping a few times, finally calmed down enough to say, *You really think so—?*

Maybe. 'Cause we're goin' down, anyway, said Jamal. *Shall we go out in glory?*

Deutsch began to breathe again. Whether it was his words or the calming effects of the alpha-field, the two riggers seemed to be finding the foothold they needed to climb out of their hysteria. *Excellent, gentlemen. Now, let's see if we can get this ship under control . . .*

IF THEY were going to do anything, they would have to do it fast, Legroeder thought. The quantum flaw was a *lot* closer now, their movement toward it visible to the eye. *Cantha—are you getting any information on what to expect?*

Pretty fragmentary, Cantha said from the top gun position. *But I believe the flaw has a greater than infinitesimal aperture, which I take as a hopeful sign.*

Jesus, Legroeder thought. If that's what you call hopeful . . .

It may be, said Cantha, *that we can fly through it. It's possible that the flaw itself is the exit path we're looking for. I don't see any other hope.*

Legroeder blinked in fear. He turned to Palagren, who

was watching the growing thread of fire. *Let's see if we can close the range with Impris.*

Are you in contact with Freem'n? Palagren asked.

Legroeder could hear little sputters of static from his implants. He shook his head as he asked, *(Anything—?)*

▫ Getting stronger fragments of transmission now . . . ▫

The net flexed alarmingly as Palagren stretched it, trying to find a shape that would give them better control. It was like trying to steer in a waterfall. But if they could at least converge on a course with the other ship . . .

Let's see if we can reach across, link the nets again, Legroeder said.

At that moment, his implants found their signal lock, and he felt sudden input from Deutsch's streaming in. *(Freem'n—can you hear me?)*

(Right here. Are we going down into that thing, then?)

(We seem committed. Cantha thinks maybe we can go through it and out. Otherwise we die. We should go in formation or God knows where we'll be scattered. Can you extend your net toward us?)

(I'll try. Let me see if—hey, watch it, Poppy!) Deutsch's voice suddenly went elsewhere.

Legroeder swallowed hard. But he saw a tendril of light stretching out toward them from *Impris*.

Legroeder focused on flying *Phoenix*, as Palagren and Ker'sell stretched their end of the *Phoenix* net toward *Impris*. It was still too long a reach. But the ships were drawing closer. Could they link in time?

Below, the quantum flaw was growing faster than ever, its diamond-white glare brightening. Legroeder clicked in a filtering routine and peered at the flaw through darkened glass. If they were going to fly headlong through it, was there any way to control the outcome? Was it all up to Nature and the structure of the flaw? Maybe not. This was the Flux, and if there was any chance of influencing their passage by changing their entry, it was now or never.

Legroeder felt a tremor, and looked up to see a tenuous

link between the two ships. Palagren and Ker'sell were slowly reeling in the joined net.

Cantha spoke up. *I recommend going in one after another. These readings are all very strange, my friends. I don't know what's going to happen, but I feel it's going to be interesting.*

Interesting!

If you can't hold it together, Cantha called to Deutsch, *then fall in behind us and break contact just before we enter. Try to follow as precisely as possible.*

Are you going in and leaving us here? Poppy screeched.

No one's leaving anyone, Cantha answered. *But our time perceptions may give us a better chance to find the way.*

I approve of your plan, said another voice. It took Legroeder an instant to recognize Captain Friedman. He had almost forgotten about the captains. Not that any orders from them could make much difference at this point.

Everyone prepare, Legroeder called, *to enter the quantum flaw.*

From somewhere deep within the strained fabric of the net came the rumbling voice of Captain Glenswarg: *Permission granted. Godspeed, gentlemen . . .*

THE QUANTUM flaw dominated the sky now, nearly encircling them. It was no longer a smoothly curved line, but a finely jagged thing, fractal in nature. Deep within Legroeder's implants, a furious analysis of the flaw was taking place. Was it a relic of the primordial universe, like a cosmic string of normal-space? It was a discontinuity in the structure of spacetime, for certain. One moment, it looked like an opening across half the universe; the next, it was a one-way passage into oblivion.

The answers would soon become clear.

With *Impris* swinging around behind them, the joined nets were becoming more difficult to control. The attraction of the flaw was beginning to fluctuate as they drew near. Were they feeling the effects of its fractal shape?

Cantha looked increasingly worried. He peered across the

net at Legroeder, his face lit by the ghostly glare of the quantum flaw. *Uncertainty-readings are off the scale. Even if you find a way to maneuver, I can't give you any guidance on a course.*

Legroeder nodded.

The fractal nature of the flaw was becoming increasingly pronounced, as finer and finer details of jaggedness came into view. Would their passage be determined by how they intersected with those jagged elements at the boundary? How could he possibly control that? But there had to be a way to influence their passage. It was not a matter of evidence, but of faith.

The Narseil were peering this way and that. What were they seeing in the tessa'chron? His own sense of time and reality was singing and twanging like a violin string. *If any of you sees a way through this, don't be shy about telling me. Freem'n—can you still hear me?*

Like you're at the end of a tunnel. You ready to go through?

Ready, Legroeder lied. He could feel the other ship pulling from side to side like a boat in tow. *It'll be soon now. If we get separated going through...*

I'll be looking for you on the other side. Tell Palagren to have one of those Narseil beers ready for me.

Yah, said Legroeder, wishing he could think of something more to say.

Palagren suddenly exclaimed, *By the Three Rings, would you look at that!*

And then the bottom fell out from under Legroeder, and he could feel the net suddenly stretching ahead like a spiderweb in a breeze, and one particular fractal angle in the flaw blossomed. And in a single, strangely prolonged instant of time, the flaw yawned open and swallowed them.

THE NET was turned inside out. The Narseil voices distorted into a sound like an electronic malfunction, and Legroeder's stomach went into freefall. His head felt distended like a child's soap bubble. As he brought his gaze around behind, to where *Impris* was following, he glimpsed a flicker of silver and a crazed opening in the sky. He heard Deutsch's voice—a heart-rending shriek, tearing off into silence. Then the jagged opening closed, with a blinding flash that billowed out in slow motion.

That had been . . . *Impris* . . . enveloped by the blinding flash.

Legroeder cried out: *Frrreeemm'nnn . . . Faarrrraaeeee mmmmaaauuu . . .*

His voice was incomprehensible, even to him. Focusing inward, trying to reconnect with Deutsch through his implants, he found instead an enormous inner vista of space, spangled with stars and galaxies. He tried to draw breath; he could not; dizzily he searched for the implants; they were circling him like flickering stars, doing he knew not what. There was no connection left with *Impris*.

His vision ballooned out again. Where the flash had been there was now a coiling darkness, webbed with lines of force.

Dear Christ! he whispered, and his voice moaned out into the net, joining with the incomprehensible groans of the Narseil. Had they just watched *Impris* die?

Palagren's arms were stretched out, distended and transparent; all the riggers were turning transparent. All of their voices were dying away; but new sounds were rising . . .

*

An impossibly deep rumble . . . a thrum of incredible power . . . and, it seemed, sadness. Legroeder was hypnotized, unable to turn his attention, as the thrum filled with deeper and deeper harmonics. It was a choir of unimaginable size and proportion, a choir of space and time, and yet seemingly almost a living thing.

Was he hearing the shifting and creaking of the very fabric of spacetime itself? He was stunned, awed, terrified. For a moment, he wondered: was *he* even still alive? The quantum flaw could have wrenched them apart into constituent particles, puffing them out of existence in a cloud of neutrinos and gamma rays. Were these the dying thoughts of a haze of neutrinos, soon to dissipate like the morning dew?

They had lost *Impris*. Deutsch. Legroeder wanted to experience all that he could before he too vanished. Maybe it was pride. Or longing. Or grief. Or stubbornness. He focused all of his being on trying to perceive the sounds that welled around him. If only he could form a picture from them.

As if in response, coiling out of the darkness came distorted lines of force, turbulent traceries of fire, the body of the quantum splinter, surrounding them. Before them stretched a long, jagged avenue of fire and darkness, reaching out into the deeps of space . . . from infinity at one end to infinity at the other.

He stared at it and thought dumbly, it's either the road to Heaven or the road to Hell . . .

*

He viewed its majesty through sound, an embryonic music of the spheres, heartbreakingly mournful. But this was not just the music of a handful of stars and star clouds. This was something very different, something far, far greater . . .

. . . wheeling majestically in space . . .

. . . enveloped by the sound of an expanding universe . . .

. . . very close to the instant of its origins . . . the sound of an infant spacetime continuum struggling to establish itself in the . . . place? . . . time? . . . where there had been no place, no time, nothing at all.

Through his astonishment, Legroeder knew . . . if he could reach out just a little farther, he might hear the sound of the Genesis Moment itself. There was a sound coming at intervals: a great *CLUNGGGG* ringing through the choir of origins, like a vast bass string being struck with percussive force. He thought he knew what that was: fractures forming in the expanding continuum, splinters, flaws in space and time . . . fractures forming in the deep quantum structures of reality.

How he knew all this, he did not know. But he was aware of the perceptions of the Narseil overlapping his own, like layers of transparency. What they saw, he saw, in shimmering shadows.

And in his head, the implants were furiously recording.

*

Before him now was a broad ribbon of fire, reaching jaggedly, with streamers and fractal fingers, in both directions. It was not simply a blaze of light through a fracture, but something roiling with inner chaos and change, like a long window into the surface of a sun. It hurt the eye to behold; something about the perspective was all wrong. This was not Einsteinian space or even Chey-Kladdian . . . it was something different . . .

And then he knew what it was. This was the heart of the temporal discontinuities. This aspect of the flaw stretched through *time* rather than space, deep into the past at one end, and impossibly far into the future in the other. Stretching toward its birth . . . and its death.

The birth and death of the *universe?*

Legroeder was dumb with awe and terror, gazing down a rent in spacetime that stretched from one end of existence to the other. Would he next gaze into the face of God? Surely he would fall dead even if the flaw itself did not kill him . . .

But stirring in him now were other strange and wonderful and frightening emotions, emotions not human; and yet contained within them were human feelings—joy and determination and rage and reverence. It was the Narseil emotions; they were seeing this as he was—the terrible beauty and peril of the quantum flaw, the groans of birth and death, linked together in a single instant.

It was changing, though, sparkling at the edges, splinters of light streaming out into infinity . . . and at the same time, turning his thoughts inside out . . .

*

Visions of places he had been . . . present . . . past . . . future . . . Outpost Ivan . . . DeNoble . . . Maris and Jakus and Harriet . . . his mother carrying him as a small child, crying, in a shopping valley on New Tarkus . . . Tracy-Ace/Alfa standing with YZ/I, proposing a mission . . . in flight, speeding toward fabulous clouds of stars . . .

All these images gathered and then blew away like smoke, leaving him staggered by the vastness around him, the power of cosmic creation. What meaning could *his* existence have here, where elemental forces flowed like rivers? What possible influence could he have?

Insignificance.

The word flickered in his awareness like a sparkle of light at the boundaries of infinity. It danced, twinkling, along the great ribbon of light . . .

*

It was, Palagren knew, the most astounding thing he would ever see, the quantum flaw stretched out in multicolored glory: at one end the past, dwindling into the deepest infrared, and at the other end the future, vanishing into an ultraviolet diamond. The present loomed in a golden haze, within which possibilities danced like motes of dust against time and space.

Among the possibilities, Palagren saw a precious few that contained images of himself. He felt unutterably lonely as he glimpsed those. How could a single Narseil matter in the face of such cosmic history?

Something tattered was billowing around him; it was the rigger-net, coming undone. Electroquantum technology did not work well here; and yet *something* had been holding the net together. But if it wasn't the fluxfield generators . . .

Palagren saw the net quiver, as though in response to his uncertainty. And then a fragment of the Wisdoms echoed in his thoughts:

"The Whole survives in unity with the One, and the One with the Whole. In all of the Rings, nothing can exist apart from the Circle except that which would break it . . . the Destroyer . . ."

The Destroyer . . .

The quantum flaw?

Or his own doubt?

Palagren drew a breath and stretched his arms wide, and turned his will toward holding the net together . . .

*

Who are these beings that you are mindful of them . . .

The question sparkled in Legroeder's thoughts like a sunbeam through a window; it was a line from an ancient human text . . . but he hadn't heard it from a human, had he? It had been Com'peer, the Narseil surgeon.

But hadn't he heard it somewhere else, long ago? The memory was beginning to come:

What is man that you are mindful of him?

That was it: an earlier form. A poem, or a psalm. But what did it mean?

Skating across the sea of spacetime, his thoughts spun around, and the word "insignificance" twinkled back to face him. He laughed suddenly, and then cried. Who was he, *what* was he, to be here in the midst of this—surrounded by a shimmering net that was beginning to come apart like an old spiderweb?

The net . . . if they couldn't hold it together, they would cease to exist.

What is man—?

He was man, human, individual—like his fellows, and yet one of a kind, unique. Did that matter, his uniqueness?

He gazed into the sea of eternity, churning with chaos and uncertainty, and thought perhaps it did matter, very much so, right now.

*

To Palagren, the waves of uncertainty brought hope. Hope for the integrity of his own being, and of the net itself. He thought of the old human story: Schrödinger's cat in the box, its life or death decided by a single quantum event. And more than that, the life and death coexisting in one; it took the glance of an observer to force reality to crystallize.

Just as a rigger's thoughts forced the uncertainty of the Flux to transmute into the desired form . . .

That's it, Palagren thought. *We must see ourselves holding the net together . . . finding our way through . . .*

*

Around Legroeder, the net was twanging out of tune as it shredded. He was aware of the thoughts of the other riggers, but all in a jangling chaos. He was in a sea of consciousness, struggling to pick out the voices closest to him. He had to; only *they*, together, could hold the net together . . .

Was it even *possible* to contest infinity this way?

Why shouldn't they? If quantum events could link across spacetime—why not their own thoughts reaching out to critical points in this zigzag ribbon of spacetime? Perhaps they could even steer themselves through a window of their choosing in this cosmic chaos.

It came to him in a rush of understanding as he gathered the net around him like an enormous billowing bubble, and pulled it in close . . . and peered down and out through the beautiful and mysterious ribbon of fire, looking for the place to fall through . . . first riggers to sail the quantum flaw . . .

Alongside him, Palagren did likewise . . . and at last, following their lead, Cantha and Ker'sell.

*

And fire blossomed around them, filling the net with a cosmic glare. . . .

Chapter 33

HUNTED

IT WAS the damnedest thing.

With the other riggers and crew on KM/C *Hunter*, Jakus Bark had been keeping an eye on the intermittent signs of the snark, *Impris*—mostly just the occasional ghostly glimmer on the deep-layer instrumentation. Every once in a great while the riggers in *Hunter*'s net caught the even more ghostly glimmer of the actual ship, or heard the low, mournful trill of its distress beacon. They followed it relentlessly as it wandered on its erratic course, presently taking it back toward Golen Space. But lately, the readings just hadn't seemed right. It was as though something were disturbing it in its ghostly flight. And now . . .

Jakus strained to focus into the distance. *What the hell is that over there?* he asked his co-riggers, pointing down through the gauzy layers of the Flux. There was something in those layers that looked like a ship. But it didn't look like *Impris.*

Another ship? said Cranshaw. *It looks like another ship!*

Don't it just, Jakus breathed. *What's another ship doing down there?* That was not a layer of the Flux where any other ship should be. How would it even get there? Jakus called on the bridge com: *What are you guys gettin' on the deep-layer, thirty down and twenty t' port? Do you see what we see?*

As he waited for an answer, Jakus tried to adjust the image. Now the ship was gone, like a puff of vapor. But there was no question he'd seen it. Right in the fold haunted by *Impris.* And so had Cranshaw and the others.

This is really strange, said Nockey, from the bridge instrumentation crew. *We've lost it now, but there was definitely another ship there for a few seconds. Not in our layer. Down there with the snark. Someone call Captain Hyutu.*

Yah, said Jakus. *I wonder if someone else got lost like Snarkie. Maybe we've got two of them now.* He chuckled at the thought. Even as one who thought this was a pretty wimpy way to snatch targets, it was amusing to think of another lure just dropping into their laps.

We're trying to refine the signal, said Nockey. *Maybe we can get some kind of an ident on the thing. The captain will love it.*

Yah, said Jakus, settling back into watchful mode. He checked the time. He'd be going off shift soon. If the normal pattern of sightings held true, that was all the excitement they could expect for a while.

* * *

BY ALL accounts, nothing new had happened in the meantime, but when Jakus stepped into Captain Benadir Hyutu's office before his next shift, Hyutu was scowling. That in itself didn't mean much, since Hyutu had generally the disposition of a Kargan rattler; but it didn't take long to deduce that the captain was even more displeased with life than usual.

"What's wrong, Ben?" Jakus asked, dropping into a seat across from the captain. Having known Hyutu since the old days on the *L.A.*, he allowed himself more familiarity than most of the crew.

Hyutu's right eyebrow twitched fiercely. The old man was a stiff prig, anyway—and under strain, his augments tended to go a little flaky. Jakus was sure it was some kind of a malf, but Hyutu refused to have them looked at. "You see the report on that sighting?" Hyutu said sharply.

Jakus shrugged. "I've been off duty. Why, is there something new?"

Hyutu's face tightened with disdain, which was a good trick with that eyebrow still going. He muttered something under his breath that Jakus couldn't quite hear, then grunted, "Bark, that's why you're never going to get ahead in this organization. An ambitious man is *never* 'off duty.' "

Jakus shrugged at the rebuke. He hated it when Hyutu got on his high horse. He'd been like that even back on the *L.A.*, before any of them were pirates. But it had gotten worse since Hyutu'd become an augmented captain in the KM/C navy. Still, the man was a powerhouse, and Jakus had good reason to stay loyal to him. "Okay, okay—so what did they find out?"

"You tell me. They got some readings on that ship you saw."

"Yeah?"

"It's *Kyber*," Hyutu said impatiently.

Jakus stared at him, stunned. "Kyber?"

"Not just Kyber." Hyutu turned away for a minute, rubbing his eyebrow. He swiveled back. "It looks like it's one of Ivan's."

Jakus whistled.

"I presume that means something to you? You've paid that much attention, anyway?"

"Of course it means something," Jakus said defensively. He didn't actually know much about Ivan, but he knew KM/C and Ivan together spelled bad blood. Not that anyone ever briefed him on this stuff. "I work to find out these things," he added. "We and Ivan don't like each other. At all."

Hyutu almost smiled for the first time. "Don't like each other. That's one way to put it. How about, what other Kyber boss'd be—if I may be vulgar for a moment—*asshole* enough to mess with *Impris* when it's not his turn." Hyutu paused, and for a moment actually broke into a grin. "And I can't think of anything that would make Carlotta smile more than for Ivan to get caught out here with his genitalia where they don't belong." He chuckled, and his other eyebrow started twitching.

Jakus frowned. "What d'you think they're up to? Some kind of sabotage? Maybe they got caught by accident."

"Well, what do *you* think? Why else would they be sneaking around out there? Of course, they're probably regretting it now. They'll never get out, any more than *Impris* did. But if they do . . ."

Jakus waited.

For a moment, Hyutu looked like a cruise ship captain getting ready to make nice with the passengers. "If he does come out again?" Hyutu's phony smile broadened. "I'll put a flux-torpedo up his shiny ass."

Jakus grinned.

Hyutu's sharp black eyes focused inward in contemplation. "Because I think it's time," he said, "that we made an example of people who interfere with the rightful order of things in the Kyber Republic. Wouldn't you agree, Rigger?" He nodded decisively, not waiting for a reply. "Of course you agree. Now, let's go to work, shall we?"

Jakus got up and followed Hyutu out of the office.

As they approached the rigger-stations, Jakus heard a shout from the instrumentation section. "We're getting some activity out there! I don't know what's happening, but it's pretty damn strange. Skipper, I think there may be something coming *out* of the underlayer!"

"Move it, people!" Hyutu snapped, clapping his hands. "Sound battle stations! This could be the fun we've been waiting for."

THE FIRE roared around *Phoenix*, a diamond inferno. They were falling, burrowing through the inferno, a storm of tangled thoughts enveloping them as intensely as the fire itself. For a moment, an eternity, it was impossible to tell whose thoughts were whose, and where any of them were going. *We're alive alive are we third ring second ring alive first alive burning can't hold on . . .*

Am I palagren? . . . legroeder . . . ?

It was beginning to sort out. Legroeder saw images flickering explosively around him, little windows opening through the flaw, the Flux, maybe reality itself—not memories this time, but something else. The glimpses came so fast he could not absorb them instantly, but only a heartbeat or two after—

—an unfamiliar nebula, roiling with fire and starlife—

—*where is that? did you see—? yes, I—*

—a place of deep stillness, where the streams of space came to a stop—

—*where we were? or are? a singularity? no, I don't—*

—a startling array of connections, flashing open like wildfire across the cosmos, light splintering off into infinity—

—*everywhere? riddled with them, space is riddled—*

—loops of movement, a circuit of motion in timelessness, an eternal damnation in which four hundred and some souls had been trapped—

—*look, the openings—*

—scattered like shards of light, hidden nexus points—

—through! we can go through!—

—in the shifting layers, a rigger ship, visible for an instant, then gone . . . mists of endless Flux . . .

—and somehow in the shower of images, Legroeder registered something about that glimpse of a ship; there'd been something Kyberlike about it; and he thought, *One of the escort ships?* Not quite right . . . and yet such a fleeting glimpse, who could tell. But it hit him again, just possibly they could exert some control over where they were going if not headlong into insanity . . .

And if that *had* been one of their ships? They'd lost contact way back before turning to the Sargasso, but what if—?

Focus on that ship! Focus on it! We're riggers, damn it—riggers!

And even as he thought it, he felt them beginning to find a course through the twisted tangle of spacetime, through the unraveling skein . . .

And then the inferno suddenly blew itself out, and the ship fell through darkness for endless heartbeats, leaving the quantum splinter behind. Legroeder and the Narseil felt their minds and bodies and souls reconverging, knitting themselves back together again, becoming whole.

Phoenix fell like a meteor out of the folds of the underflux, and burst into the normal Flux with a blinding flash. The net was shaking like an aircraft on the verge of stress failure, the four riggers nearly paralyzed by the shock of the passage. Legroeder shouted hoarsely, *Where are we?*

And Palagren, *I can't tell!*

And *when* were they? They'd touched the ends of eternity . . .

Cantha and Ker'sell cried out incoherently as they struggled to bring themselves back to the present, as they all strained to focus on the waves and currents of the Flux battering past them.

Legroeder took short, sharp breaths. We're alive, he cried silently. *Alive!* For a fleeting moment, he tried to wrap his memory around the passage—the glimpse of eternity—but it was all coming apart in his mind, like a dream.

Gulping air, he took a quick look around in the net. There was still a net. But what about *Impris*? And where were they? The normal Flux, but where?

We're out! We made it through! shouted a Narseil voice, Cantha's. The voice, and the answering cries from Palagren and Ker'sell, were almost surreal after the bizarre melding of the passage. *Find Impris!* he shouted, and his own voice sounded flat and empty of resonance, no longer reverberating against infinity.

He looked around frantically—and suddenly remembered. *Impris* had been torn from them. Destroyed in the quantum flaw. *Impris* was gone. Freem'n Deutsch gone. *No—!* Legroeder started to bellow, then choked and could not finish the cry.

The com came alive again, sputtering. *Riggers, report! Can you hear me?* It was the captain calling through a hash of static.

Legroeder drew a sharp breath. Get hold of yourself. Let's go, now; but felt himself moving in molasses. *Captain, we're here—give us a moment*—he whispered to the com.

The net was a tattered shambles, barely functional, but power was starting to flow back into it now. Had they really held it together with not much more than the force of will in the quantum flaw? Palagren was starting to reshape the net from the bow backward, and Legroeder took up the trailing threads to strengthen the stern position.

The com crackled insistently. Captain Glenswarg's voice finally punched through. *Legroeder, report! Where are we? Where is Impris?*

Legroeder began to explain that he didn't know where they were, that *Impris* had gotten separated from them. He couldn't bear to say what he knew to be the truth. Gone! Dead! Neutrinos. Nothing left; all a terrible waste. *We . . . got separated during the passage through the quantum flaw . . .*

Yes, yes—what the hell HAPPENED then? I thought my head was going to explode! I couldn't tell . . . I mean all of us . . . the whole crew was immobilized.

Legroeder struggled to explain. *That's . . . going to take time to figure out, Captain. It was . . . God, it was like . . .* He could not piece together the words. It was as if his mind had stretched from one end of the universe to the other, but without getting any smarter . . .

All right, never mind that. Are you searching for Impris?

Searching for what—the neutrinos? *Yes, of course,* he whispered. *But try to get as much instrumentation working as you can. We can't see a lot right now.*

Palagren glanced back and stared at Legroeder with an expression full of—what? Sorrow? Sympathy? Legroeder couldn't tell. But this ship was hurtling through the mists of the Flux and there was no time to dwell on the question. They had to bring the ship under control, and find out where they were.

Another voice came on. *This is nav. My first reading puts us south of the Akeides Nebula. I think we've come out near our original prime target, in the KM/C patrol area.*

Oh, no.

Attention, everyone! barked a Narseil voice, interrupting the nav officer. It was Agamem, with the weapons and tactics crew. *We've got a ship coming in fast, heading three-one-two-slash-three-seven. Not Impris. Not one of ours. Coming directly toward us.*

No, Legroeder thought.

Glenswarg, with the comlink still open, called at once for general quarters. *Have you got an ident on it?* he asked the tactical crew.

Negative—but I think it's Kyber—not one of ours.

Must be KM/C, then. Dammit, put me on the fluxwave to it. Am I on? There was some static, and then, *Kyber ship, this is Kyber-Ivan Phoenix. We've just made an emergency exit from the Deep Flux. Who are you, please. Kyber ship, Kyber ship . . .*

Legroeder and the other riggers were still trying to spot the other ship, but so far all they could see was swirling mist. They were moving fast; that quantum passage must have given them one hell of a kick.

I've got signs of weapons powering up, Agamem warned. Legroeder blinked in dismay.

He heard a shout from the bridge crew, and then Glenswarg snapping: *Flux-torpedoes incoming! Riggers, prepare for countermeasures!*

Christ! Legroeder thought, still trying to locate the other ship. There it was, ahead of them. It had moved in *fast.* Three tiny twinkling lights were streaking through the Flux toward *Phoenix.* About four seconds to impact.

Riggers, hard to port! Captain Glenswarg shouted. *Prepare to launch countermeasures . . . launch countermeasures!*

No time for thought. Legroeder fell into a smooth motion with Palagren, Ker'sell, and Cantha. The net had returned to about half strength, and they warped it carefully, forming the ship into a stubby-winged aircraft. They banked sharply left, as a swarm of decoys shot out from the ship's stern and billowed away like swarming bees. Some clouds passed between them and the incoming torpedoes, and for several seconds, they were blind to both the enemy ship and the torpedoes.

They dove, banked right, then left again, and climbed. As they passed around a cloud bank, there were two bright flashes behind the clouds, and concussions: **thump! thump!** Legroeder glanced back and saw one remaining torpedo, streaking in a long arc toward them. *One incoming behind us!* he called out.

Hold your course, Glenswarg said calmly. Then: *Neutrasers—fire.*

A bright streak lanced out from the tail of *Phoenix,* caught the torpedo, and destroyed it. The concussion wave shook *Phoenix,* but the riggers held tight and rode it out.

Damage report! Glenswarg called. *Riggers, do you have the enemy in sight?*

Negative, Legroeder replied. They had lost sight of it during their evasion. They brought *Phoenix* around now and passed beneath a puff of cloud . . .

Mother of—Legroeder recoiled as a dazzling white light

split through the vapors far off to their right. *What the hell is that?* Legroeder squinted, shielding his eyes. *Bridge, is that more incoming fire?*

He heard a lot of shouting, with Agamem's voice among them. But even as the captain replied in the negative, he saw the flash fading, and something streaking away—another ship, moving fast through the Flux.

Hell's bells. Was that ship coming out of the folds of the underflux? Legroeder felt his implants suddenly buzzing back to life. *It's IMPRIS!* Legroeder bellowed. He couldn't hear anything comprehensible from the implants, but he could feel them seeking a connection. *IMPRIS! IMPRIS! They made it through!*

His heart threatened to pound out of his chest, as the other riggers and the bridge crew shouted at once. Glenswarg broke through finally. *Have you got a lock yet on the enemy ship? Are you sure that's Impris?*

Yes! No—no lock. Palagren—Cantha—Ker'sell—any sign of that Kyber?

The implant link opened up, interrupting him, and he felt Deutsch at the other end of it, and he shouted silently, *(Freem'n, you're alive—are you there?)*

Find me that Kyber! demanded the captain.

Still searching, called Palagren.

The reply from Deutsch was shaky and bewildered. *(What—? What—? Legroeder? Is that you?)*

(Yes, we—)

He was interrupted by a thunderous flash across the bow of *Phoenix*. The attacking ship—a Kyber raider twice the size of *Phoenix*—had just streaked out of the clouds, moving at tremendous speed. Had it missed them? Or was it on another errand now? It was arrowing straight for *Impris,* whose riggers were almost certainly dizzy and disoriented from their passage. The link with Deutsch was flickering out, probably interference from the attacker.

Captain, I had a link with Impris, but I've lost it! We've got to warn them! Legroeder shouted. *Impris* probably had no armament, and was certainly in no shape to deal with a surprise attack. *(Freem'n!)* he called urgently. *(Impris! If you can hear me, flee for cover!)*

An instant later, Glenswarg's voice boomed out through the Flux, amplified by the net: *ATTACKING SHIP, IDENTIFY YOURSELF! YOU ARE WARNED AWAY FROM OUR COMPANION! THIS IS CAPTAIN GLENSWARG OF KYBER-IVAN PHOENIX!* He snapped to tactical, *How soon can we get a torpedo off?*

We've got problems here. Not for a few minutes, came the answer.

Legroeder drew a steady breath. Glenswarg was inviting a renewed attack on *Phoenix* with his challenge—but at the same time, he'd warned the captain and riggers of the starliner. *Impris* was already altering course, with slow, difficult movements.

Riggers, stand by for battle, Glenswarg ordered.

The attacker, dwindling in the direction of *Impris*, answered Glenswarg's challenge with a sternward volley of torpedoes, streaking back toward *Phoenix*.

Legroeder and the Narseil hurled their ship at once into violent, evasive course changes. The Flux came alive suddenly with **DROOM, DROOM, DROOM**, the drums of a raider ship in full attack, and then the voice of the raider captain, booming through the clouds:

THIS IS HYUTU OF KM/C HUNTER! YOU ARE IN VIOLATION OF A DESIGNATED HUNTING SPACE. YOU ARE INTERFERING WITH OUR MISSION, IVAN! EXPECT NO CONSIDERATION.

Legroeder choked. Hyutu! On the com from the bridge, there was an angry outcry. The captain was shouting instructions, but Legroeder barely heard him. The name was ringing in his ears, threatening to drown out all other thought.

Hyutu . . .

—launch countermeasures!

Legroeder, follow!

That last was Palagren, jerking him back to the present.

Legroeder struggled to keep up with the Narseil on a barrel-rolling dive.

Hyutu—the murdering—!

Legroeder, move it! What's the matter?

That bastard—Hyutu! he sputtered, late with his rudder movement.

Palagren had to compensate. *What?*

The bastard who betrayed the L.A.!

Worry about him later! Palagren shouted. *Let's stay alive!*

The Narseil was right. They were straining the net with their diving and twisting. The torpedoes were sparkling closer, turning to match their turns. The countermeasures hadn't worked—the torpedoes had adapted. *Up and left!* Legroeder snapped, suddenly seeing a way to do it. *Palagren, give me the image!*

Are you s—?

Do it!

In the blink of an eye, he changed the ship to a fluttering bat, blindingly quick and maneuverable. The image helped them fly the same way—darting up, sideways, down, wings flicking in a blur. Was Weapons ever going to get a shot off at those things? The spread of torpedoes swept around, following, gaining. But the torpedoes were taking the turns a little wider than *Phoenix.*

Stabs of light went out from *Phoenix* in a machine-gun burst, catching the lead torpedo. It detonated—**thump!**—and as the others were caught by the explosion, they went off, too. ***Thump! Th-kump! BM-BOOM!***

Too close. The shock wave rippled through the Flux and hit *Phoenix.* The net shook and lost its hold, and the ship tumbled. The net was ablaze. *Get it out! Get the fire out!* Legroeder cried, trying to dampen the net. It wasn't a literal fire, but energy was flooding through the damaged net and the feedback pain was incredible. It slowly subsided as they damped the net down and began to reshape it; and as they regained a measure of control, the pain became more tolerable. They were skidding in a slow turn now . . . coming back around . . .

We just lost our torpedo launchers, called a voice on the bridge.

And there was the Kyber *Hunter*, turning from *Impris* to loop back toward *Phoenix*.

Legroeder could not contain himself. Without even thinking about it, he amplified his voice and bellowed out into the Flux, *HYUTU, YOU STUPID MURDERING BASTA-A-A-RD!*

JAKUS BARK'S blood was hot with fever, the fever of battle. The augments thrummed exhortation through his skull. The drumming that boomed through the net heightened his fever, and that of his fellow riggers. Most powerful of all, his own exultation bubbled up like a geyser of champagne, unstoppable. How long had he waited for this? How long to watch his ship belch fire and death? How long to watch KM/C triumph?

Jakus owed everything to Kilo-Mike/Carlotta. It was KM/C who had brought him from DeNoble, KM/C who beefed up his implants to make him a valued member of their forces . . . no longer a half-baked captive impressed into service, but a *member of the force,* who talked to the right people, and moved with the shakers and thinkers. KM/C had trusted him and put him to work undercover on Faber Eri; and when things had gone wrong there through no fault of his own, moved him right on to his next assignment. They'd put him where he belonged, in the net of a Kyber marauder. And now he had a chance to show his worth.

That Ivan interloper was hurt—it was obvious from the way she was maneuvering. Once the captain gave the word, they would put the final stake through its heart—but first they needed to complete this pass on the second ship that had come out. Find out who the hell it was.

A heartbeat later, Hyutu's voice sounded through the net like a klaxon, and a curse: *The ship is the snark. It's Impris.*

A murmur of dismay filled the net, led by Jakus. Their lure had been pulled out by Ivan!

We'll find out how they did it later, Hyutu growled. *Leave it here for now. Rigger Bark, bring us around to finish off that Ivan!*

Jakus signaled his fellow riggers to come around for another attack dive. He heard a cry, echoing across the Flux—a shout of rage and defiance from the enemy. He grinned broadly at the outrage—and then, with astonishment, recognized the voice. It couldn't be! *Legroeder? Jakus gasped. Legroeder—here?*

Stunned, he called to Hyutu, *Captain! Captain, you aren't going to believe this . . .*

RIGHT ABOUT now, Legroeder thought, they could have used some Free Kyber riggers in the net, to help them contend with these insane KM/C pirates. The net was straining with every maneuver. The Ivan riggers knew the ship better from a tactical standpoint, and knew the enemy, too. But there was no time to switch riggers. Palagren had *Phoenix* in the shape of a dashing, speeding fish, and they were fighting to make the ship live up to its image. But with the damage to their net slowing them down, *Hunter* had drawn inexorably closer, until their only means of evasion was to keep changing directions, twisting through clouds in hopes of shaking the enemy off.

Captain—any chance of getting a shot off soon? Legroeder called anxiously.

Launchers are still down, Glenswarg answered tightly. *You've got to keep us out of their reach—or if you can't do that, get us close enough for the neutrasers.*

Legroeder acknowledged; they were spinning and turning, reaching the limits of what their net could do, but also forcing *Hunter* to maneuver tightly to follow. Ker'sell spotted an opening—and at his shout, they turned, and with several fast directional changes, shot perilously close to the enemy—exchanging neutraser fire as they flew past. *Phoenix* trembled, taking several hits; but it kept going. As the KM/C ship came around, Legroeder looked for damage, but saw little sign that their efforts against *Hunter* were having any effect.

He heard something—what was that?—his name echoing across the Flux: *Rigger Legroeder . . . so good to see you again . . .*

For a moment, Legroeder was speechless. It was Hyutu . . . calling out across the Flux to gloat. Legroeder bit his tongue to keep silent. Keep silent. But he couldn't. *Hyutu, you bloodsucking traitor!*

Hyutu's answer was a laugh—but Legroeder had no time to answer, because Palagren and Ker'sell had just dumped them into a spinning dive, away from *Hunter*, and Legroeder helped them by instinct alone. Glenswarg was snapping orders—among them, telling Legroeder to shut the hell up. But another new voice filled the net from the remoteness of the Flux, and again it was a voice that Legroeder recognized. Jakus Bark!

—really fallen into it this time, Legroeder. What did you think you were doing? There's no way you're going to get out of this one! Bark's voice was utterly scornful.

You bastard! I thought you were dead! Legroeder whispered.

Did you think we were going to lie down and die? Bark said, and then burst into a roar of laughter. *Well, guess who's going to do the dying!*

At that moment, the KM/C ship seemed to find a favorable new current, because it came overhead in a loop far too fast for *Phoenix* to follow and bore down directly down on the Ivan ship, like a hawk swooping on its prey. Legroeder and the others strained to maneuver out of its path, but they couldn't fight the natural movements of the Flux, and this time the winds were against them. All they could do was fire their neutrasers futilely, and wait for the volley of torpedoes.

(Impris, get clear!) Legroeder called, his inner voice desperate, filled with despair at the thought of being killed by his traitorous old shipmates—and at the thought that they had brought *Impris* out only to be killed, too.

Bark's laughter echoed. *So long, Legroeder, baby-y-y . . .*

Before Legroeder could think of a word to say, he felt a sudden shudder through the Flux and heard, **K-B-BOOM-M-M!**

And he heard Agamem cry from the bridge, *Flux torpedoes—but they're not coming at us!*

K-B-BOOM-M-M!

There was a second explosion, and Legroeder kicked the stern of *Phoenix* around for a better look. He was astonished to see the KM/C raider targeted by a cluster of bursting flux torpedoes. Where the hell had they come from? Surely not from *Impris*. Then where?

The next voice was Jakus's again—howling in a splutter of confusion and rage. The KM/C ship was taking a beating. But from whom? It was turning with evident difficulty— attempting, for the first time, its own evasive maneuvers. Hyutu's voice screamed, *WHO IS THAT ATTACKING US? COME OUT AND IDENTIFY YOURSELVES!* Streams of neutraser fire radiated from Hyutu's ship, seemingly aimed at random.

The only response was the glow of a converging swarm of new, incoming torpedoes.

JAKUS BLINKED as he heard the warning cry from the other side of the net. The flickering glare of the torpedoes was almost hypnotic; there were so many of them, from several directions, but all converging on the same point.

On *Hunter.*

How could this *be?*

Captain Hyutu, what now? he whispered. His implants were savagely stoking his blood lust, but they couldn't change reality. *Hunter* was pinned, trapped; nowhere to turn. His fury had nowhere to turn, either, except inward, on himself and his captain. *You stupid bastard captain . . .*

EVASIVE ACTION, YOU MORONS! EVASIVE ACTION! Hyutu screamed. *COUNTERMEASURES AWAY! NEU-TRASERS SHOOT! SHOO-O-O-OT—!*

The captain's voice shook with rage, and the riggers wrenched the ship into wild gyrations trying to shake the torpedoes. But it was hopeless; Jakus Bark knew it was hopeless even as his augments drove him onward, trying to save the ship.

The first wave of torpedoes loomed, their sparkle glaring against the Flux. Jakus let go of the net with a loud cry, heedless of his captain screaming, *TURN, YOU IDIOTS, TURRRRNNN—!* and Jakus felt a sudden terror and then an utterly insane release as he grinned out into the Flux, directly into the dazzling glare of the exploding warheads.

As THE rigger-crew of *Phoenix* watched dumbfounded, the torpedoes converged on the KM/C ship and flashed with great pulses of light. *Hunter*'s net blazed like a torch, and a heartbeat later the entire raider ship crumpled inward, then exploded.

The ***BOO-O-OM-M-M*** reverberated with ghostly echoes from the clouds.

No one in the *Phoenix* net spoke. They could hear mutters of amazement from the bridge, as though Glenswarg were holding the com open, intending to speak, but too stunned to know what to say. Legroeder's heart was pounding so hard, he could scarcely hear himself think.

What the hell was that? he whispered finally. *Who was—?*

Phoenix! called a voice, distant but strong across the Flux. *This is Kyber-Ivan Freedom. Are you all right?* A silver ship slipped out of the clouds high above the expanding debris field that had been *Hunter*. Had it been there all along?

My left nut, I'm glad to see you! Captain Glenswarg boomed. *How the hell did you find us? Where were you?*

Two other ships appeared—one from beyond and one from beneath the debris field. It was the escort squadron. They'd had *Hunter* bracketed; the bastard hadn't stood a chance. The same voice answered, and there was laughter in it this time. *Where were* you *is my question! We lost you halfway to the destination point. Did you change course?*

Yes!—yes!—didn't you get our transmission? Glenswarg's voice was shaking with relief.

Got no transmission, said the other captain. *We kept going and hoped we'd find you here. The next time we picked you up, it looked like you'd popped out of some kind of Flux anomaly—and then KM/C came out of nowhere and started shooting at you. It took us a few minutes to get in close enough to help.*

Rings! muttered Glenswarg, seemingly at a loss for words. Finally he sighed, *Thank you. Your timing couldn't have been better.*

You're welcome, said Freedom. *Now, did we or did we not see a ship that looked like Impris? I think it disappeared into those clouds.*

Yes, where did they go? Legroeder thought, peering around dizzily. They'd been so busy staying alive, he'd become totally disoriented. He queried his implants; but the comlink was still down.

We're here, called a new voice, breaking the momentary silence. *We've been wondering if we should come out. Captain Glenswarg?* It was Friedman of *Impris.*

Legroeder let out a great cry of relief.

Please come out now, answered Glenswarg. *Let's group up this fleet.*

As Legroeder and his crew slowly brought their ship around toward the escort fleet, the long, stately shape of *Impris* emerged from a dense layer of cloud beneath them and rose to join the group. Legroeder felt the implant connection coming back to life. *(Freem'n!)* he cried silently. *(Are you there?)*

(We're here. We're here,) came the reply, like a whisper down the length of an acoustically perfect auditorium.

(Can you still fly? Are you in one piece?)

(Just barely, and more or less,) said Deutsch. *(I don't know how, and I don't know why, but somehow we came through the quantum flaw on your coattails. How did you do that, Legroeder?)*

(I just thought like a rigger, Freem'n. I just thought like a rigger.)

At that, Deutsch began chuckling, softly at first and then louder, until the inside of Legroeder's head echoed with his friend's laughter.

THE SQUADRON formed up quickly around *Phoenix* and *Impris*, and the order was given to set course for Outpost Ivan.

Has it occurred to anyone that we're all exhausted, and we need time for repairs? Legroeder asked Glenswarg, as he and the Narseil strained to bring the ship into formation.

Sure, answered the captain. *We'll do something about that just as soon as we get the hell out of here. Our friend the Hunter might have buddies, you know.*

Ah, Legroeder said, not arguing. But oh, how he wanted some sleep!

The squadron, like a naval armada from some long-ago holodrama, rose slowly through the colored mists until the clouds scattered and cleared, and the smooth waters of a mystical, ethereal ocean stretched before them. The two ships in the middle, *Phoenix* and *Impris*, wobbled but held their positions. And as a grand, if battered fleet, they set sail for Outpost Ivan.

PART FOUR

Eternity waits at the crossway of the stars.
—Jorge Luis Borges

Prologue

AWAKENING

THE KYBER agent turned from the briefcase console to peer at the comatose young woman lying in the bed. "Is she okay?"

"How the hell should I know?" his partner snapped, glancing down to check her sidearm. "I've got to go make sure the perimeter's safe."

The man scowled at his partner and squinted at the medical monitors attached to the captive woman. "I'm sure the perimeter's fine. I need you here right now."

"How do *you* know the perimeter's fine?"

"Look, just trust the security system for five minutes, will you? The woman's no good to us dead. This is a tricky operation, and I need you to monitor her condition. All right?"

It was not all right, his partner's expression made clear. But she grunted and stepped close to the monitors. "She's still alive."

The Kyber nodded. He frowned at the captive's skin color, which was pale, and checked her pulse. It seemed a little weak, but what did he know; he was no doctor. "All right," he said. "Hang in there, Miss O'Hare. With any luck, this won't kill you."

He made a final check of the electrodes attached to the back of the woman's neck, then returned to the console and, with one last hesitation, initiated the program. The data-collecting subroutines began running; it all looked good so far. But then, he wasn't an implant programmer, either. For all he knew, he could be killing her.

Contacting implant, opening command kernel . . .

He watched, hands clenched, as the program moved through several increasingly invasive stages to the critical one.

Disabling autonomic intervention routines . . .

He held his breath.

Deleting command kernel . . .

He let his breath out slowly as the program completed its cycle and terminated. He checked the monitors. "All right, I guess we can let her sleep." He had done what he could. Only time would tell if he had succeeded.

VOICES JABBERING. The hissing crackle of neutraser fire. Shouting billowing urgency, dragon's breath of plasma, run run, no time. Struggling for breath, consciousness slipping away. A baby crying . . . why . . . mother, are you there? Is baby Jessica there?

Mother? Mother's not here. She died ten years ago. And Jessica . . . a hundred light-years away.

Golen Space, fleeing Golen Space. What happened?

Sunlight pouring through a curtained window. Wood framework around the window. *Wood?*

Alien sun.

Any sun was an alien sun.

Her eyes blinked several times, then opened. Stayed open. Peering at the curtains.

Why curtains—?

Remembered running for her life. Leaning on Legroeder. Why Legroeder? They were fleeing . . . pirates in pursuit.

Maris groaned softly. She tried to sit up, and failed. Her head was on a pillow. She turned it slightly to look around. *Where am I?* she wanted to ask, but swallowed the words. *Don't talk yet; don't know where you are.* She remembered excruciating pain—and footsteps, pounding. Pursuit. Must hide. But where? Nowhere to hide.

She wondered if she could move now; maybe just a hand.

Slowly, forcing every inch of movement, she dragged her left hand across her chest and brought it to touch the hurt on her right shoulder and neck. What was it? *Neutraser fire . . . there was shooting . . .* Probing under the loose fabric, she felt a spray-on bandage; and under the bandage, the ridges and bumps of a wound. At first there was no sensation from the touch of her fingers; then the fire flashed up her neck. She rasped in a sharp, agonized breath and lay trembling, clutching her arms together.

A wooden door to her right burst open.

She blinked, trying to focus. A man and a woman stood in the doorway, staring at her in astonishment. "You're awake!" the woman said.

Maris struggled to find her voice. She couldn't; couldn't even swallow. Her throat was dry and cracked.

"Here, now," said the man, pushing past the woman. "Don't try to sit up, you're not ready for that." He stepped to Maris's side and bent to peer at a medical monitor.

She tried to move her right arm and felt a new pain. She was tied to a monitor and a set of IV's. Was she in a hospital?

The man urged her to lie still, and she didn't argue; she was dizzy anyway. But not too dizzy to wonder, Who are these people? Had she made it away with Legroeder? Where was she? And where was Legroeder?

She tried once more to swallow, then heard the man send the woman for a glass of water. Good. Good. The water arrived, and the man lifted her head as she tried to drink. She sipped greedily, water splashing down her chin, soaking her neck. With a gasp, she sank back as the woman dabbed at her with a towel. "Take it easy, now," the man was saying. "You've had a tough time of it."

Tough time of it . . .

The woman was muttering something she couldn't quite make out, and the man replied, "We really should get her seen by a doctor."

"No doctor!" the woman said sharply.

"Look at her, Lydia. You can see she needs help."

No doctors. Not a hospital, then. Maris listened with growing alarm. *Where am I? What's happened to Legroeder?*

"What's she saying?"

"Legroeder," the woman said. "She's calling for Legroeder. Her boyfriend. The one who skipped bail."

Had she spoken out loud? *No—you have it wrong. What do you mean, he skipped bail?*

"Watch what you say, now she's awake," the man murmured. He leaned in closer. "Miss O'Hare—can you hear me?"

Maris drew a breath, and with an almost superhuman effort, shouted: *"Where—am—I—?"*

"She said something," said the woman. "What'd she say?"

"I'm not sure," said the man. "Miss O'Hare?"

She grunted in frustration and tried again, harder. This time words came out. "Where . . . am . . . I?" Her voice sounded harsh and unnatural.

"I think she said, 'Where am I?'"

"Huh," said the woman. "Don't worry about—"

"Wait," said the man, cutting her off. He moved around the bed, to where Maris could see him more easily. "Miss O'Hare, you've been in a coma for weeks. We finally managed to deactivate your implants—"

Implants. Of course, the pirates had put them in the back of her neck. How had she been able to escape? There'd been a plasma leak . . .

"—which were keeping you unconscious."

She tried to focus. The pirates had told her that escape was impossible; the programming in her implants was like a knife at her throat.

"Damn near killed you, as far as I could tell. But I guess they were rigged to incapacitate, rather than kill."

Maris strained. "Where—?"

"You're in the North Country. Away from the city."

Maris shook her head weakly.

The man finally seemed to catch on. "On Faber Eridani."

Maris's breath caught. "Faber—" She'd made it out, then. Made it back to civilization. Or had she? She squinted at the man and woman, and thought with a shiver, *Why won't they let me see a doctor?*

"You're safe here," the man continued reassuringly. "You're among friends." He smiled and turned away.

Chapter 34
THE CENTRIST CONNECTION

"BUT HARRIET—we can record the whole thing on VR and bring it to you here in the embassy. There's no need to risk your going out." Peter stretched his big hands out pleadingly.

Harriet fixed the Clendornan PI with her gaze. "I don't *want* to see it on the VR, Peter. I want to see it in person. You can bring me right back when we're done. But if I'm going to use this for a legal case, I need to know everything. How it sounds, how it feels, how it smells. And not through some damn electronic reproduction!"

The light in the back of the Clendornan's eyes flickered as he gazed at her.

"Peter, I appreciate your concern. But I've got to do this." *Besides, if I don't get out of this embassy soon, I'm going to lose my mind. How can such a beautiful place feel like such a prison?*

Peter gave in at last. "All right. But at least let me talk to the embassy staff. Maybe they'll let us travel in one of their vans. Less likely to be intercepted that way."

"I knew you'd understand." Harriet grabbed Peter's arm. "Come on, let's go find the assistant ambassador . . ."

ALL THE way in the Narseil floater-van, Harriet found herself checking the security sensors, and peering back through the darkened windows to see if they were being followed. Her courage of an hour ago had evaporated. She sank back in her seat with a sigh. "Harriet, there's no reason to think we've been seen," Peter said, glancing back from the front seat.

"I'm sure you're right," she murmured. She glanced to her right at the tall form of Dendridan, the embassy attaché. He had come along to observe, as well as to lend diplomatic legitimacy to their use of the Narseil vehicle. Dendridan's vertical eyes gleamed, but he said nothing.

Leaving the city proper, they glided through the northeast suburbs, past an area Harriet barely knew even though she'd lived in Elmira all her adult life. The Narseil driver followed Peter's directions flawlessly, and twenty minutes later they were parked between two other vehicles in back of a peeling white wood-frame house.

"Stay here a moment while I do a check," Peter said. He ducked out of the van, leaving Harriet with Dendridan and the Narseil driver. He reappeared a few minutes later, with one of his men. "The coast is clear. Let's go inside."

Leaving the driver with the van, they entered the house through the kitchen and made their way upstairs to a large bedroom that had been converted into a makeshift VR studio. There were cameras on tripods everywhere, and a large white screen across one wall. Peter introduced his assistants Norman and Irv, whom Harriet recognized from the earlier holo. There was no need to introduce Rufus the dog, who lay on a small cot, panting slowly. He was wired up like a marionette with optiwire feeds. The dog's tail twitched when he saw Harriet—was it possible he remembered her?—but everything about him seemed in slow motion. "He's under a relaxation field," Peter explained. He cocked his head, studying the setup. "Downloading information from a dog is not as easy as you might think."

"Oh, really," Harriet said dryly.

"I'm afraid I don't quite follow," said the Narseil.

"Well," said Peter, "since the data in Rufus's implants was a direct memory feed from McGinnis, a lot of it isn't necessarily in verbal form. Some of it's visual, some of it's sound and smell and touch; some of it's pure emotion. To be valid in court, it must be read and interpreted by a certified intermediary."

"One of your people?"

Peter shook his head. "We hire the Kell, who make this something of a specialty. I've brought one in from the city of Port Huron."

"On the other side of the continent."

"Right. She's not well known here, but she's one of the best." Peter paused to survey the setup. "If everyone's ready, I'll go get her." Peter disappeared into another room, while Harriet and Dendridan waited uncomfortably.

"Irv here's the one who found Rufus, at the McGinnis place," Norman said, nodding. Norman was a large man who seemed comfortable around the dog. Irv, on the other hand, was skinny and nervous looking. Harriet remembered Peter saying that Irv was afraid of dogs. Apparently he had gotten over his fear; he paused to scratch Rufus's head as he made some adjustments to the hookup.

"Everyone," said Peter, returning with the blue-robed Kell, "may I introduce the interpreter who will be assisting us today? This is Counselor Corellay. She is certified for Level-three implant reading and Level-two telepathic extraction."

Counselor Corellay was just over a meter tall, with silken grey fur and a hamster-like face. Her eyes were black with bright silver dots slightly off-center. She nodded to the observers and then walked, with a rippling gait, across the room to the dog. She touched Rufus on the head and murmured to him for a moment. Then she turned. "Are we ready to begin?"

"Quadrocam?" Peter asked Irv.

"Ready."

"Sensory feed? Data storage?"

"Ready."

Peter nodded to the Kell. "You may begin your certification." Corellay bent to examine the wiring attached to the dog. As she made her inspection, Peter explained to the Narseil, "We've made test tracings, but this will be the first court-certified reading. I'll ask you and Harriet to sign off as witnesses." Dendridan agreed, and Peter produced a small retinal scanner-recorder into which the two of them would make their attestations.

When Corellay was satisfied, she adjusted her own collar, which looked a bit like a cervical brace glinting with opticom processors. She stepped to the center of the room, in front of the white screen. Drawing a lightwand out of her robe, she faced Peter and the others. "Begin recording. This is Counselor Corellay of Kell, licensed to the courts of Faber Eridani in Port Huron. Here begins my translation of memory-data presently stored in the cortical implants of Mr. Robert McGinnis's dog, Rufus . . ."

The formal preface went on for a while. Suddenly Corellay's voice deepened. She raised the lightwand. *"This is the record of Robert McGinnis. I may have only minutes left in which to live."* She waved the lightwand in a sudden blur in front of the screen. A sketch appeared in midair, first in black and white, then color. Harriet marveled at the speed of the rendering while focusing on the image: a room with flames licking through the walls and a bank of consoles glowing. Robert McGinnis appeared in the foreground, his face contorted with pain.

Corellay's voice changed to her own. "This is how Robert McGinnis looks to me as he uploads. He is fighting for his life. The flames are in his mind only; but he expects their physical presence soon." Corellay's voice dropped again; she sounded startlingly like McGinnis, even to the cadence and inflection.

"What will follow is a list of crimes that I hereby attest have been committed by Kyber agents and certain representatives of the RiggerGuild and the Spacing Authority over the past thirty years. I have compiled this record in deliberate isolation from my implants, which have otherwise prevented me from coming forward. It is my hope that this record will now be used to bring the guilty to justice." Corellay paused a moment, then waved the wand rapidly in the air. A holoimage took shape, surrounding her as though she were standing in a cavern. Faces appeared in the blur of the wand, flickering with streaks of light that flashed onto Corellay's face. The Kell winced in pain. Suddenly she gestured urgently to Harriet and Dendridan to step forward, into the image.

The Narseil looked unsure, but Harriet grasped his elbow and propelled him forward. As she stepped into the hologram, Harriet's breath went out; she felt as if she'd been punched. She gasped in fear and looked around wildly for an instant. Threatening faces glared from the walls of the holographic image, and Harriet felt a sudden wash of fear of what would happen if she revealed the truths that she knew. Who were these people? Some had implants on the sides of their heads; others didn't. The faces were indistinct; her feelings of vulnerability and fear were so powerful it was difficult to focus on the images. The Corellay/McGinnis voice was rapidly running down a long list of dates, and coercive threats, and instructions he had been given for undercover activities. The instructions ranged from espionage to destruction of evidence to creation of false navigational data for use by riggers. He could not always successfully resist . . .

After a moment, the images began to spin, until they were gathered into a whirlpool. As Harriet watched, stunned, they drained down into a holographic box on the floor.

Corellay's voice sounded like her own again. "Those details have been stored in the permanent record. Step out now, please."

With a sigh of relief, Harriet and Dendridan moved back to a safe distance. Harriet could see that Dendridan was confused about their role in this. "We were just witnessing McGinnis's emotional responses to the physical details embedded in the recording," Harriet whispered to the Narseil. "That becomes part of the testimony, and it can be used to support the claim of intimidation via implant—which is criminal assault under Faber Eridani law."

McGinnis's voice returned.

"It was not just Kyber agents behind these actions, I am convinced—but the Spacing Authority itself. And the RiggerGuild—betraying its charge to protect the life and liberty of riggers, by sending its members into areas of known pirate activity . . ."

Harriet felt a knot tightening in her stomach as she watched Corellay's hand speed up to a blur again. A long written list of ships scrolled down the middle of the holo. Was the *L.A.* one of them? *Bobby?* It was scrolling too fast to read. The list funneled down into the data storage and vanished.

"The Guild," Corellay/McGinnis continued, "has collaborated with a raider organization known as Carlotta. It was Carlotta who salvaged me when I was shipwrecked in the Sargasso, and Carlotta who put these accursed implants into me . . ." The Kell interpreter spun a new hologram, this time of McGinnis's face twisted with pain as shiny implants appeared in his temples. "It was Carlotta who planted me on Faber Eridani as one of their agents. It is Carlotta who preys upon ships and their crews near the edges of Golen Space, sometimes using the lost ship *Impris* as a lure." Harriet shut her eyes, suddenly feeling physically ill. Through the rushing of blood in her head, she thought, *This is exactly what I need. Finally.* But the thought gave her no pleasure.

". . . and it is Carlotta who for years has been wielding her influence over the Guild of Riggers and the Spacing Authority of Faber Eridani." The image changed to a sketch of RiggerGuild headquarters on the left, and Spacing Authority headquarters, on the right. McGinnis's voice softened. "I don't accuse all who work for these organizations—or even the majority. Most employees probably know nothing of the crimes, many of which were carried out through intermediaries. One of those intermediaries is the paramilitary organization that tried to control me. Its name is Centrist Strength."

Harriet drew a sharp breath. *Centrist Strength.*

The Corellay/McGinnis voice became hollow and strained: "They had visions of using my military expertise . . ."

THE STORY that emerged was a confusing one. But after all she had learned from El'ken and McGinnis, Harriet was able to fit the pieces together fairly readily.

Centrist Strength was building an underground military force on Faber Eridani. No surprise; they seemed bent on achieving power through intimidation masquerading as self-defense. Their stated motives were ambiguous: they claimed to be working for the destiny of the Centrist Worlds, reawakening the leaders of Faber Eridani and other worlds to the once-common vision of a grand-scale exploration of the galaxy. So far, so good. But for a group dedicated to the destiny of the Centrist Worlds, they had far too many surreptitious dealings with a pirate group called the Free Kyber Republic—a group diametrically opposed to the expansion of the Centrist Worlds. According to McGinnis, Centrist Strength had decided that any human expansion—and the power and profit that would flow from it—was better than none. And any means would do to achieve it.

But who was behind their secret military buildup here? Over a period of some years, McGinnis had made cautious investigative forays into the system to which his implants were connected. And he'd learned some names.

It was a long list, funneling down into data-storage as McGinnis spoke them aloud. Some individuals were clearly implicated; others were connected to Centrist Strength only through shadowy intermediaries and front organizations. It was through those indirect connections that the more familiar names appeared, just at the periphery of clear culpability. Among them were officials of the RiggerGuild and Spacing Authority.

It had taken many careful traceroutes, but McGinnis had found the chain of evidence. The Spacing Commissioner's office had quietly signed off on a transfer of retired Spacing

Authority armaments—not directly, but through carefully laundered transactions—to the private arsenal of Centrist Strength.

Harriet found herself holding her breath. Was Commissioner North involved in a paramilitary conspiracy? If so, who were his real bosses?

Corellay stroked her wand through the air, leaving a ghostly image of McGinnis's face, surrounded by a curtain of emotional fire—and in the fire the faces of his enemies, an image of the forces assailing him through his implants.

"This is their final attempt to coerce me," said McGinnis with a strained voice. " '*Kill the visitors. Destroy the* Impris *records. Do not let them leave!*' This is the order I finally had to openly disobey."

Corellay urged Harriet and Dendridan back into the holo, as the images intensified: indistinct faces barking commands at McGinnis. Harriet felt McGinnis's anger, held back and masked as long as humanly possible. "For thirty years," McGinnis whispered, "I've kept my true thoughts hidden from my implants. For thirty years, I've deceived them." Harriet felt the rage pounding in her own temples as she saw McGinnis painstakingly ignoring the orders to destroy the *Impris* records while seeming to comply with them.

Harriet prayed she would never have to face such a battle. She could not imagine how the man could deceive implants lurking right inside his own skull. The control that must have taken . . .

But the images were slipping now toward the fatal end. The implants had learned of McGinnis's deception, and were using all their power to regain control. The voice grew short and raspy. *"Not much time—Jesus, it hurts! They're trying to make me kill you! Take this information. Use it!"* Harriet felt her own breath grow ragged with fear.

"I must destroy this place now! Disconnect—forever—!"

Corellay cried out, and Harriet felt a shocking blow of pain as real flames erupted from the walls, and then emptiness as McGinnis's face dissolved in a sparkling cloud of glitter.

Corellay waved them out of the holo. As Harriet and Dendridan staggered away, Corellay's voice became her own again. "Here ends that section of the data-upload. But there are images that follow—of explosion, fire—" flames engulfing the holo "—and the vision now is from the view-point of the dog, Rufus, outside the house."

On the cot, the real Rufus was whimpering now, his legs twitching as he tried to run.

The last image Corellay painted was of the dog running in terror from the burning house. Then the holo faded, and she spoke soberly into the recording equipment. "This con-cludes the Robert McGinnis reading. I present this interpre-tation with a confidence level of nine. This is Counselor Corellay." The Kell lowered the wand and stood swaying, her eyes closed. "You may turn off the recording."

Harriet groped for a chair, overcome with emotion. There was a great emptiness in her, from McGinnis's death. For a time, she felt as if nothing could change that emptiness; it was so real, so painful.

And then the details of the revelations began to filter back into place in her mind. And she began to recoil with horror at what the conspirators had done . . .

RIDING BACK in the Narseil van, Harriet and Peter debated where to go next with the information. A notarized copy of the recording had already been placed for safekeeping on the worldnet. Another copy had been transmitted to El'ken, the Narseil historian.

"I think," said Dendridan, glancing thoughtfully out the window, "that if there was any doubt about whether you still need our protection at the embassy, it is gone now. You've just implicated one of the most powerful officials on this planet in a conspiracy to conceal the truth. About *Impris*—and about the Narseil." He turned to Harriet, and there was a sharp gleam in his eye. "We'll most certainly grant you every protection we can."

Harriet nodded her thanks. A certain satisfaction was starting to settle in. She now had an important piece of evidence that would help to exonerate Legroeder, if he ever returned. The interpreter's confidence rating of nine was very high, almost as strong in court as direct verbal testimony. But the evidence against North and the other officials was still shy of what they would need to convict anyone.

"We've got to go after North," said Peter. "If we unmask North, the whole conspiracy will unravel."

Harriet agreed. But how to go after him? North was in power, and she was in hiding. Whose word would carry the greater weight? Still, it was all recorded and notarized, and ready to be released on a moment's notice. Perhaps it could be used to force North's hand.

"Excuse me," said Dendridan, craning his neck suddenly to look behind the van and up. "But I think we're about to have an emergency. Driver, could you speed up, please?"

Peter angled a glance into the security monitors. "What's that? Is this your time sen—? Hold on. Yes, I think someone's following us from overhead. It's a flyer."

Dendridan seemed to look inward. "And they're about to give chase. Begin evasive driving, please."

Peter grimaced as he tied his compad into the security monitors. "I'm trying to get a registration on it. It's too far away."

"It won't be for long," Dendridan murmured.

Peter seemed to read the Narseil's tone of voice. He glanced at Harriet with eyes aflame, then said to the driver, "You might want to speed up a *lot*."

Harriet shut her eyes and held her breath as the sudden acceleration slammed her back into her seat. *Dear God.*

"Don't worry, Harriet. I'm sure we can shake them," said Peter, in a voice that was not at all reassuring.

Chapter 35
MARIS

THE LOCAL airbus left a cloud of dust as it disappeared around the bend of the old road. Adaria, watching the bus vanish, gave a whistling sigh of relief. She stretched her flightless wings, picked up her bag, and started down the path into the woods.

It had been a long journey, but Adaria was nearly home now, back with her own people, the Fabri. In the end, there was nothing like the company of the homefolk. Especially after the last few months of life among humans. Adaria still shivered at the memories of the coolness and fear that had insinuated their way into her life at the library, and that late-night visit by Centrist Strength, with their half-veiled threats. Centrist Strength made her extremely uneasy, even at a distance—with their known caching of weapons on Fabri land, their proclamations of Destiny Manifest . . .

Better to leave all that behind, if one could.

The path was not long, but it wound in serpentine fashion through the woods. She felt her own inner tensions unwinding as she followed the path's twisty course among the penalders and fragrant ellum trees to the village. Someone called out to her as she approached, and she whistled a greeting in return. She didn't go straight to the village center, though; instead she detoured to a cabin at the edge of the village. She had someone to visit, an old friend.

Adaria paused, gazing with a shake of her feathers at her friend's house, a low wooden structure. It seemed in poorer repair than she remembered, the bark clapboard cracked and desiccated. "Telessst?" she called through the bead curtain that hung over the front door. She ducked her head and entered, the beads brushing back over her wings. The room was dim; the only light came from two small windows with curtains drawn. It was a modest den, with a raised wooden floor, cushions, and a low table. Adaria whistled.

"Adaria? Is that you?" cried a voice from the shadows of the back room. An old female Fabri stepped out to greet her with a feathery embrace. "*Iiiirrrrrrlllll*," Telest sighed, squeezing her with pent-up affection. "It is good to see you, my friend!"

Adaria didn't answer for a moment, but just held the old Fabri's arms. So much to think about, so much to say. "I am back," she said finally.

"So you are. And how are you?"

Adaria gazed at her old mentor before answering. Telest's curving neck, which the humans might have called swan-like, was a little more bent, a little frailer than when she'd last seen her. Telest's eyes were bright, though the fine feathers covering her cheeks looked thin and worn. It was so good to be back. But there was no time for sentiment just yet.

Adaria drew a breath. "There is trouble, Telest. Word from Vegas and the Mahoney people. They need our help if we can give it. They need it now . . ."

I AM *Maris O'Hare. I may be a prisoner, but I am not without control.*

Maris opened her eyes and leaned forward in the living room recliner. With a glance at her two captors, she raised her cup of tea from the side stand and took a tiny sip. The pain in her shoulder and neck was lessening; she could manage a teacup now. She set it down with trembling hands and rested her head back. "You still haven't told me who you're working for," she murmured. Moving only her eyes, she glanced around the living room. She was still getting used to the idea of being planetside, in a house. But in the hands of pirates. Right where she'd started.

The woman turned from the security console she was

always checking. "We told you. Ivan. That's all you need to know."

"Who is *Ivan?*"

"A friend," the woman grunted, and walked out of the room.

The man put down a beam rifle he'd been cleaning and peered out the window. "Don't worry about it. Just work on getting better."

Maris pressed her lips together. For perhaps the twentieth time, she surveyed what she could see of the house: Living room. Kitchen. Short hallway with bedrooms. And two captors. Dennis and Lydia. Dennis, who hardly talked. And Lydia, the bitch. They didn't seem like lovers, just partners—though Maris could have sworn she'd heard grunting and moaning in the other room last night. Why the hell wouldn't they tell her what was going on? Maris sighed and closed her eyes against a rush of lingering dizziness. Coma. She'd been in a coma. She'd woken, what—three days ago? Four? She could walk a little now, from room to room, or into the shower—but always with help. She thought she could probably walk unassisted if she had to. But maybe she didn't need to advertise that—at least until she knew more.

Dennis had promised to fill her in when she was stronger. Right now he was rubbing at his temples, as though waiting for some instruction. He didn't have visible implants, but Maris was pretty sure he had them. Lydia, too. Maris closed her eyes, picturing the back of her neck where her own implants were mercifully silent. Dennis claimed to have deactivated them. Crude things they were, used only for sadistic control by her captors at DeNoble.

But they have implants, these two. They're pirates. What more do I need to know about them?

She couldn't stop the hatred from welling up; couldn't stop the memories. The slavery, the rapes and attempted rapes, the degradation. She couldn't stop any of it from coming back. But she could keep it inside. Her hand shook on the teacup, and she put her hand in her lap and held one fist clenched tightly together with the other. She waited until the wash of nausea subsided and she could breathe again.

She grunted softly, looking over at the window. She wondered if she had any chance of running away. Hah. She'd be lucky to make the door. Or maybe the backyard. She had no idea *where* she was, other than the planet Faber Eridani. But why would pirates hold her here? If she'd been recaptured, why didn't they just take her back? Were they waiting for a ship? That was probably it; they were awaiting transport, and when it came, they'd whisk her away. All this anguish for nothing. Where was Legroeder? Everything after their escape was a blank. Her only friend; she barely knew him; but as far as she was concerned, he was her best friend in the world. If he was alive.

If I get a chance, I must . . . must . . .

She drew a slow breath. She had to make a break if the opportunity arose. But she needed to know more. "It might help me recover faster," she said to Dennis, "if you told me what was going on."

Lydia walked in with sandwiches and a carafe of tea. "Christ, doesn't she ever give up?"

"Sign of recovery," Dennis said with a shrug.

"Great. So glad you're feeling better," Lydia said sarcastically. She handed Maris a sandwich and slid back onto the bench in front of her security console.

Maris frowned and took a bite. The sandwich had a pungent, unidentifiable taste. She swallowed the first bite with difficulty and washed it down with some tea. To Dennis she said, "You're with the Kyber. Are you planning to take me back?" As soon as the words were out, she regretted them.

If Dennis was surprised, he didn't show it. He looked noncommittal and said simply, "We're just keeping you out of the way."

"Excuse me?"

"It's *for your own good,*" Lydia said, with her back still turned.

"For my own good?" *That's why you took me out of a hospital?*

"Yes." Dennis propped his beam rifle against the wall. As if reading her thoughts, he added, "It was necessary. Before *others* got to you."

"What—others—?" Maris whispered, trying not to tremble. She'd escaped, fair and square. She shouldn't have to be going through this. *Where am I, damn you? Where is Legroeder?* "What others?" she repeated.

Dennis rubbed a scar on the side of his nose. "The Spacing Authority, for one."

Maris stared at him. She was being protected from the planetside authorities? So they *were* planning to take her back to the pirate stronghold.

"They do not welcome raider escapees."

Maris nodded slowly. "Who else?"

Dennis shrugged and picked up the rifle again. "Various interests. There are many, on this planet."

Maris opened her mouth, closed it.

"None in our backyard at the moment, though," Lydia muttered, leaning over the console. "At least I don't think so. There was a bit of a blip there for a second, but nothing on the sensors now."

Looking from one to the other, Maris tried to comprehend. "What does that mean? Who is your enemy? Who are you fighting?"

"Not fighting anyone," Dennis said. "We're hiding."

"And that's why you have all these guns?"

"There are bad people out there—all right?" Lydia snapped. Standing, she flexed her right hand. A palm beamer appeared in it, and she checked its charge. "You ask too many damn questions. We're here to protect you, and that's all you need to know." To Dennis, she said, "I'm taking a walk around the grounds."

"It's raining."

Lydia snorted. "So that means we don't keep a watch?" Dennis shrugged.

"But—" Maris said, then fell silent as Lydia banged the door on her way out.

Dennis began breaking down his rifle again.

Maris sighed, reclined her chair, and closed her eyes to try to nap.

MORGAN MAHONEY stood in the rain with Pew and Georgio, peering down the wooded hillside. They were somewhere outside the rural community of Forest Hills. The house below the tree line was the one that Pew had identified as the supposed residence of a Mr. Lerner—the newcomer in town who was reported to have been seen meeting the car used in the abduction of Maris. Morgan pulled her rain cloak tighter, thinking, anyone who would kidnap a woman in a coma probably wouldn't greet her and her friends with open arms.

Georgio, the Gos'n, could not seem to stand still. He was constantly stretching his three long tentacle-ended arms in restless movement. His short-stalked eyes swiveled constantly, taking in the surroundings. He was not an easy person to hide, ordinarily, but he was very good at observing. Fortunately, there was plenty of cover here, and they had a sensor-defeating camouflage mesh drawn across the bushes in front of them. The wooded surroundings that made the house inconspicuous from the road also made it relatively easy to set up for observation.

"I've identified six probable surveillance sensors on the outside of the building," said Pew, keeping his foghorn voice muffled. The Swert dipped his horselike snout as he put away his remote detection gear. "There's no telling what weapons they might have. At the verrry least, I expect they carry sidearms."

"Like that one?" said Georgio, pointing down the hill with his third arm-tentacle.

"Eh?" said Pew.

Morgan saw a woman coming out of the house, crouching in the rain as she circled the clearing, peering one direction and then another—probably checking for intruders. The woman's hand flexed, revealing a palm weapon. For a moment, she stared in their direction; but the camouflage screen seemed to hide them, because she moved on, circling the house. She disappeared around the far side of the house and did not reappear.

"So they *ar-r-re* armed," Pew murmured.

"No charging in, then," said Georgio.

Morgan scowled. "What should we do?"

"Well, I suppos-s-se that we could amble peaceably up to the front door," said Pew.

"Without the police?"

The Swert scratched his great head with a long-nailed hand. "I would prefer-r-r to keep the police out of this for as long as possible. The other option is to wait and see whether there's any actual sign of Miss O'Hare."

"You know what I think?" Georgio said suddenly, rising in alarm. He pointed with a tentacle at a point beyond the house. "I think we'd better find out who *those* people are."

Morgan suddenly felt chilled to the bone by the rain. *Who—?* Then she saw the movement. There were two—no, three—people in the woods on the far side of the house, apparently also watching the property. Now, who the hell would *they* be?

"Do you suppose the police followed the same leads we did?" Pew murmured.

"I don't believe it's the police," said Georgio, his eyes shifting from side to side as he used his natural zoom lenses. "They're not in uniform. Human, though."

"Let's have a look." Pew raised a pair of high-powered binocs. He peered for a few moments, then handed them to Morgan.

The binocs were too large for her, but she managed to sight through one lens. She pressed the RELOCATE button, then clicked in for a sharp closeup—or as sharp as she could get, filtered through the rain. Two men and one woman. She frowned. One of the men looked familiar.

"I think I recognize one of them," she said, lowering the glasses.

"Indeed?" said Pew, taking the binocs from her and touching them to his compad for download.

Morgan squinted across the distance. "I can't be certain.

But I remember looking over some reports on Centrist Strength with my mother—and someone who looked like one of those men was in the pictures."

Georgio made a *tssk*ing sound. "Why would Centrist Strength care about—"

"Just a moment and I'll tell you," Pew interrupted. A moment later, he looked up from his compad. "She's right." He nodded to Morgan. "Well done, Miss Mahoney. The images match. Both of those men, in fact, are in the Centrist Strength database. The woman I don't know."

"Then that means someone *else* is holding Maris," Morgan said.

"It also means we'd better be figuring out how to get her out of there," said Georgio.

"But how?" said Pew. "That's the question. How?"

Morgan looked from one to the other, but saw no answer. She shivered and hugged the rain cloak to her neck as she gazed down at the silent house.

MAJOR TALBOTT used his spy-glasses to study the house through the trees. There'd been no sign of activity except for the occasional circuit of the house by the Kyber woman. Kyber woman! He still didn't understand what was going on here. Somehow everything had gotten turned around. The Kyber were supposed to be the ones he was working with. And now it turned out they were set to raid a house *held* by Kyber agents! Well, it was on the authority of the frigging Joint Command—meaning the Carlotta people and people like Hizhonor North—but it still didn't make any sense. Weren't the Kyber supposed to be working together? It sure as shit didn't seem like it, the way those guys down there had nabbed the O'Hare woman before Strength could get to her.

All these years of putting his balls on the line for the cause, and he still wasn't sure he trusted the Kyber "alliance." He had to work with Joint Command, but more and more he wondered if the loonies weren't in charge of the asylum.

Damn it all . . . if he didn't believe so much in . . .

"So, Major, what are we going to do here?" grumbled the raven-haired woman crouched beside him. "Just stand around taking in the view all day?"

Talbott glared at her. Lieutenant Cassill. Good-looking bitch, but a pain in the ass. Supposed to be a top "field action-group" operative—code for act first, think later, as far as he was concerned. Too bad; he could think of better uses for someone with her looks. "We'll move when I say we move," he muttered finally. "If we botch it, we'll be worse off than before." He glanced at their third member. "You understand that, right, Corporal?"

Corporal Sladdak shrugged. "Right."

Lieutenant Cassill checked her ion rifle. "I don't see what's so important about this woman, anyway."

"She belongs to our sponsors, that's what's important about her."

"Belongs?"

Talbott shrugged in annoyance. "Supposed to be one of their people. She got away. Defected. Whatever."

Lieutenant Cassill looked unconvinced.

"You don't have to understand; you just have to do it."

"Yes, *sir*," she said stiffly.

Talbott suppressed a snarl and raised his spy-glasses again.

THE TWO Fabri natives slipped silently through the trees, moving with urgent speed. The word had come from their village leader, backed up by the informal Fabri intelligence network. Centrist Strength agents were on the move in connection with a kidnapping, and help was requested. A homefolk friend was involved—Harriet Mahoney, who had aided the Fabri on more than one occasion. *Look for a human woman with a Swert and a Gos'n. Help them help the offworlder woman, if you can.* The Fabri were not exactly freedom fighters, but they weren't afraid to step forward when necessary.

The Fabri reconnoitered carefully as they approached the

house in the woods. The taller one, the leader, searched the area around the clearing. "Fffff—two parties," he murmured softly, with a shiver of his wings.

The other set down a ventilated leather case and joined the first in peering. "Those three, they are Strength," he murmured, focusing on three humans about a third of a circle around the house to the right. "They are known to us."

"And over there?" murmured the leader.

The second Fabri shifted his gaze to the left of the clearing. "Ah—the two aliens and the woman. They are Mrs. Mahoney's people. They are here for the missing one."

"Shall we make contact, then?"

GEORGIO WAS the first to see them. He muttered something guttural, and Morgan turned her head and nearly jumped out of her skin at the sight of two approaching Fabri natives, clad in white. *How did they move so silently?* She placed a hand on Georgio's tentacle-arm, the one with the weapon. "They've come to talk," she said quietly.

Pew's foghorn voice was surprisingly soft as he addressed the two Fabri males, "May we help you?"

One of the two fluttered his wings slightly. "That's precisely what we intended to ask. Are you the friends of Vegas?"

Morgan's heart raced. "She works for my mother."

"Then you are here to attempt to free the offworlder woman?" asked the second Fabri.

"We are."

"Then may we offer our assistance—?"

THE SHORTER Fabri opened the leather case he was carrying and hoisted out a sinuous white animal. "This is a ferrcat," he said softly, cradling the animal in his arms. "Its name is N'tari." He was silent a moment, peering into the ferrcat's eyes. There seemed to be a wordless exchange between the two. The ferrcat rolled its head from side to side, hissing softly. "She senses the woman," the Fabri said. "Alive. And conscious. Weak, but well."

The other Fabri unslung his weapon, a thistlegun. "Quickly, then. Before we are seen." He bowed briefly to the others. "With your permission, I will move to another position, to offer additional protection." Without waiting for a reply, he melted into the trees.

His companion spoke softly to the ferrcat, touching the glowing jewel hanging from its collar. Then he set the cat down. It stretched languorously for a moment, then suddenly flashed into motion, darting down through the brush in a fast zigzag, and out of the woods. It paused at the edge of the lawn, peering up into the treetops as though checking for birds; then it sauntered on toward the house.

"I have asked N'tari to find the woman and lead her to us. Now, we shall have to wait and see . . ." With those words, the Fabri raised his own thistlegun to the ready.

MARIS WOKE up wondering why she was suddenly hearing voices. Or imagining voices, a soft mewling in her mind . . .

This way, Maris . . . this way to a friend . . .

She shivered, wondering if her captors had reactivated her implants. They'd claimed to have saved her life by turning them off; but what was to prevent them from switching them back on to keep her under *their* control?

But this hadn't felt like a controlling force; it was more like a living voice. Not hostile. Friendly.

Come to the window. Come and you'll see me . . .

There it was again.

Come to the window.

Like a purring in her mind. *Come . . .*

She rubbed her forehead. Well, why not? She could make it if she moved carefully. She heard Dennis clattering in the kitchen, and Lydia down the hall. If she got up slowly, now . . . if anyone saw her, she was just . . . going to the window.

Maris pushed herself to her feet, staggering a little. She caught her balance and stepped away from the chair. Dennis was clinking glassware. No sign of Lydia. Three more steps.

She reached the living room window and gripped the sill.

Hello . . . there you are . . .

She peered through the curtain at an overgrown lawn, leading out to a woods. A light rain was falling.

A small face popped up on the other side of the glass. She stifled a cry. It wasn't a human face; it was an animal. White. Like a large cat or weasel . . . wearing a collar with something glowing on it . . .

I can show you the way out.

Maris drew back, startled. Was the thing speaking in her mind? Maybe that glowing thing on its collar was doing it. The animal dropped out of sight. Maris leaned forward to peer out and down. The animal was on all fours on the ground. It was the size of a large house cat, with a bushy tail. It glanced up at her, then trotted toward the back door. To meet her?

Maris drew a breath. What was this all about? Faber Eridani was apparently full of hostiles. It would be insane to trust this animal. Wouldn't it?

She remembered her determination to run, if she could.

The touch of the animal's mind was reassuring. She sensed an earnestness. *This way. My friends sent me. Your friends. Friends of Harriet. Friends of Legroeder. You know Legroeder?*

Maris stiffened. Had she heard right? She pressed her face to the window again. The animal was standing outside the back door, staring up at it expectantly.

"What are you doing?"

Maris jerked back from the window, staggering a little. Lydia glared from the hallway.

"I'm just—"

"Well, you shouldn't be—"

"Shouldn't be up without help," said Dennis, interrupting Lydia as he came in from the kitchen. "Still, can't blame you for being curious, I suppose."

"We're supposed to be keeping her safe!" Lydia snarled. She pointed a finger at Maris. "Do *not* expose yourself like that!"

"But I was just—"

"Miss O'Hare," said Dennis, "please stay away from the windows. We don't know who might be out there."

Maris allowed herself to look more confused than she felt. "But you're keeping an eye out with all these sensors, aren't you?" She shot a glance at the console.

Dennis opened his palms. "True. There's no need to get all worked up."

Lydia scowled. "Look—just be more careful, all right?" She hooked a thumb at Dennis. "Let's talk."

Dennis shrugged and followed Lydia out into the kitchen.

Maris's pulse quickened. Her chance? Was she crazy?

Friends of Harriet and Legroeder—come quickly!

Her heart was pounding like a drum. What the hell was she thinking? But if this was for real . . .

Voices came from the kitchen:

"She's not a goddamn house guest, you know!" Lydia sounded furious.

"Look, the orders were just that she's to be held—"

"*Held*, you moron. Held."

"But for safety—"

Lydia's voice dropped in volume, but the contempt was sharper than ever. ". . . are we going to keep her safe if she's sticking her goddamn face out the goddamn window—?"

Maris was surprised to realize that she'd crossed half the distance to the door while listening to the exchange from the kitchen. Her hand was reaching out.

Be quick! To safety! Before the others get here!

An image filled her mind of people approaching in the woods, strangers even less friendly than her captors here in the house. Maris shuddered, and pulled her hand back.

". . . keep her the same way we'd keep any prisoner!"

"But the commander said we could—"

"What? The less she knows the better. You know that."

"You were the one who said—"

I sense your fear. I can lead you to help.

Maris squeezed the door handle. *What am I doing? What will happen if I stay?*

You don't want to meet the others.

There was a bang in the kitchen. "We better not leave her alone in there."

"Well, it's not as if she can—"

Maris yanked the handle and staggered out of the house. Raindrops struck her face. Fragments of memory of her escape from the outpost cascaded into her mind—the confusion, the urgency and fear, the need to escape *now*. Blood rushed in her ears.

Quickly . . . quickly . . .

The animal was waving its front paws like an excited dog. The pendant on its collar was pulsing with pink light. *Now, Miss Maris! Follow!*

"Okay," she whispered, surrendering all reason, except that this creature had spoken the name of Legroeder, the only friend she knew. The creature sprang to the right, away from the house. Maris followed on shaky legs.

An alarm was trilling.

"She's gone out!"

"Hey! Where do you think you're going?"

There was a pounding of footsteps.

"MAJOR," said the corporal, "who's that coming out of the house?"

Talbott peered down through the woods.

"There she is!" shouted Lieutenant Cassill. "It's her."

Jezu. "Let's get moving! *Get her!*" Talbott shoved the underbrush aside with his rifle as he leaped downward toward the clearing.

"THERE SHE is—!" shouted an unfamiliar woman's voice.

Maris hesitated, turning her head.

"Get her!" called a man's voice from the same direction.

No! cried the animal. *Follow me!*

Maris ran dizzily after the scurrying creature.

"You stupid bitch!" screamed Lydia.

A plasma beam crackled across the wet grass behind her, and there was a muffled shriek of pain.

* * *

"WHAT'S THE ferrcat doing—*look!* There's a woman coming out!" rasped Georgio, pointing a tentacle-arm.

Morgan rose from behind the bushes, stunned. "That's *her*, that's Maris! She's alive. She's *running!*"

"She's following the animal," Pew boomed in his foghorn voice.

"There she is!" shouted a voice from the far side of the clearing. Morgan blinked, then realized that it was one of the Centrist Strength people. Another voice shouted, and then a door banged, and a different woman's voice: ". . . *stupid bitch!*"

"We've got to move!" Morgan hissed. *"Now!"* She jumped up to shout to Maris, but Pew's large, horny hand shoved her back down. A shot crackled across the lawn; the flash had come from the far side of the clearing. A woman screamed in pain. Not Maris.

"NOW!" boomed Pew, leaping out to crash downward through the bushes. A weapon had materialized in his hand. Georgio leaped after him, and Morgan scrambled to follow. Maris was running in their direction, after the ferrcat.

More shots. From the house, from the woods; it was dizzying, and Morgan couldn't tell who was shooting at whom. But the woman she'd seen circling the house earlier was down in a heap, and the Centrist Strength trio were crashing down through the brush across the way. Morgan cupped her hands and shouted, *"Maris—KEEP GOING! Stay down!"*

Pew and Georgio dropped for cover, and Pew's great hand swung up, aiming his weapon across the clearing.

The fleeing Maris saw the movement of the gun and dove into the grass even as Pew shouted, *"Get down, Miss O'Hare!"*

Morgan sucked a breath, expecting to see fire erupt from Pew's weapon. The three Centrists, bursting into the clearing, were exchanging fire not with Pew but with someone in the house. But before Pew could fire, Morgan heard the *zzzip* of a thistlegun. She saw the Fabri in the trees to her right taking another aim. One of the Centrist Strength men was down, and the other was staggering back. The Centrist Strength woman grabbed the second man and pulled him back toward cover.

Another man, apparently from inside the house, came around the corner—and fell face down with a smoking hole in his back. The Centrist Strength woman swung her weapon around, looking for another target, then retreated before a hail of thistledarts.

The Fabri who had fired gestured to Morgan and her friends, waving them forward. Morgan launched herself down through the brush, and out onto the lawn.

Maris was crawling along the ground now. The ferrcat was leading her straight toward Morgan. "Maris!" Morgan gasped, sliding to her knees on the wet grass beside the woman. "We're here to help. To take you to safety."

"Who are you?" whispered Maris fiercely, struggling to rise. "Are you—"

"Friends of Legroeder. Friends of Legroeder. Come with us now, quickly."

Maris gasped and forced herself up. "How do I know you're—"

"You've got to trust us. Come on. Just a little farther." Pew and Georgio were at her side now. Pew lifted Maris effortlessly and carried her up into the forest at a run.

Glancing back, Morgan saw one of the two Fabri standing watch, thistlegun at the ready. The closer one whistled in a shrill tone, and the ferrcat ran back to him, a streak of white through the brush. Morgan gasped her thanks to the Fabri. He merely nodded, catching the ferrcat. Georgio kept his weapon raised, covering her retreat.

Morgan beat a fast path up through the woods to Pew and Maris, then fled with them across the ridge toward the waiting car.

Chapter 36
RETURN TO IVAN

"WHAT THE hell happened to you?" Glenswarg demanded.

Legroeder was standing in front of a mirror, wondering the same thing. The face that looked back at him was thin, dark-haired, and olive-skinned. The eyes were blue. It was *his* face, the face he'd had all his life, until the Narseil surgeons ran their camouflage job on him. There was no hint at all of the pale skin or the umbrella-cut white hair. Which probably explained why half the bridge crew had stared at him as he'd left the rigger station after the battle.

Something happened during the quantum passage. Had a part of him gone back in time?

▢ *Our internal records are incomplete for that period. But there may have been spontaneous activity by the residual plastic-surgical agents in your bloodstream . . .* ▢

Legroeder grunted to himself and turned to the captain. "This is what I look like. What I'm *supposed* to look like." The three Narseil were standing behind the captain, and they appeared to be suppressing laughter—Cantha and Palagren, anyway. Ker'sell merely looked perplexed, his vertical eyes slightly crossed.

Glenswarg was scowling, though. "Do you intend to explain?"

Legroeder sighed. (*You really don't know what happened?*) he asked the implants.

▢ *Negative. Internal recordkeeping failed during the passage. Or rather, was crowded out by a massive influx of data concerning the structure of the flaw—which, by the way, you will find very interesting.* ▢

(Yeah? What kind of data?) He was aware of Glenswarg staring at him, still waiting for an answer.

◻ *We're still analyzing. But you saw more during that passage than you might have realized. We must consider very carefully how to use it . . .* ◻

Thoughts spinning, Legroeder forced a grin at Glenswarg and began stammering out an explanation. "What I looked like before . . . was a form of camouflage, you might say. It was before we were all working together . . ."

Glenswarg's frown only deepened, as Legroeder continued.

DURING THE flight back, Legroeder thought often about what the implants had said about the quantum flaw data. He could never quite get them to elaborate clearly; they were always still analyzing. But his own memories were beginning to come back in flickering bursts. *Splinters of light fracturing off in all directions, like the needles of a newborn ice crystal . . . quantum flaws entwined through the Flux . . .* The visions gave him shivers of awe and fear. Just how closely had his implants traced the positions of those flaws, anyway?

He debriefed with Glenswarg, and discussed the passage with his rigger-mates. The Narseil were absorbed in their own detailed studies of the instrumentation data. They weren't sure what to make of Legroeder's observations— they had caught intimations of the sprawling proliferation of the flaw, but few details; but then each of them had seen features no one else had seen. Legroeder found himself wondering how long it would take his implants to complete their own analysis. He missed Deutsch, who was still aboard *Impris*, flying in formation with the fleet. They spoke on flux-com from time to time, but that wasn't the same thing as sitting down together. Legroeder wanted to know what Deutsch had *really* gone though during the passage.

He also wondered what kind of reception they were going to receive from Yankee-Zulu/Ivan. YZ/I, of course, should be delighted to see them pull in with *Impris*; but would he be as happy to keep his end of the bargain once *Impris* was parked in his dock? And what about Tracy-Ace/Alfa? His thoughts veered one way and then another as he thought about her: remembering her eyes, her touch, the flowing connection between them . . . and then thinking, what if she had only been used to set him up? Would she still be there for him, now that the job was done?

And what of Maris, and Harriet—and Harriet's grandson? And now that he'd found *Impris*, would he succeed in clearing his name at last?

No wonder he felt so damned anxious.

WATCHING FROM the bridge as *Phoenix* docked at Outpost Ivan, Legroeder struggled with a new set of mixed emotions. He could not believe, watching as the Kyber riggers brought the ship in to the outer docks of the Kyber fortress, how much like home Outpost Ivan looked to him. The last thing he wanted was to feel at home here. With luck, that wouldn't be a problem for long.

Cantha appeared at his side. "Troubled?" the Narseil asked. Legroeder nodded. "Well, if you're thinking what I'm thinking . . . we are not entirely without resources."

Legroeder turned and gazed at the stocky Narseil.

Cantha scratched under the neck of his Narseil khakis; he hadn't had a decent soak in a pool since leaving *H'zzarrelik*, and the thick crest on the back of his neck was looking pretty flaky. "I was just thinking," Cantha said as he turned to view the fleet movement in the monitors, "that we learned an awful lot of new rigging science out there, and we haven't really even sorted it all out among ourselves." His slitted, vertical eyes shifted to catch Legroeder's gaze. "But it could be very useful—to many people. If you know what I mean."

Legroeder glanced around at the Kyber crewmen on the bridge. *Useful, indeed.* "I think I do, yes," he said, drawing a deep breath. "I think I do."

* * *

The escort ships fell back to allow tugs to bring *Impris* into dock; *Phoenix* docked alongside the passenger liner. The procedure seemed to take forever, but eventually Captain Glenswarg called, "Shut down engines." Nodding in satisfaction, he turned to Legroeder and the Narseil. "Gentlemen, you've discharged your duties well. You may collect your things and go stationside." He shook each of their hands. "Good work, riggers. It's been one hell of an experience having you aboard, that's for sure." It was the closest thing to levity Legroeder had ever heard from Glenswarg.

"It's been an experience working with you, too, sir," Legroeder said, cracking half a smile. "I suppose we might see you around the station?"

"I suppose we might," Glenswarg agreed. With a brisk salute, he turned back to his bridge duties. Legroeder and the Narseil trooped off to the airlock.

If Legroeder was hoping they might be greeted by Tracy-Ace in the docking bay, he was unsurprised to find a security escort instead. The leader of the escort, ears bristling with augments, bowed. "Riggers, Yankee-Zulu/Ivan welcomes you back, and requests a meeting at the earliest opportunity."

"Um—" Legroeder said, squinting at the man's name badge. Lieutenant Zond, it looked like. "Certainly. But do you mind if we see our colleagues off *Impris* first? We've had quite a time of it."

"Of course," the lieutenant said, gesturing down the platform. "That was the next thing I was going to say. We're about to have the formal opening of the *Impris* hatch. First time in a hundred years, I understand. Of course we want all of you to be on hand."

Not quite the first time, Legroeder thought dryly, but confined himself to saying, "A hundred twenty-four years, actually."

Lieutenant Zond gave no sign of having heard, but led the way around to the *Impris* docking platform. A clear wall afforded a breathtaking view of the ship, like a great silver whale. About a third of the way down its hull, a circle of security people surrounded the main hatch. In the middle of the circle stood Tracy-Ace/Alfa.

Legroeder's heartbeat quickened as he saw her gesturing and giving orders. Lieutenant Zond brought them through the circle. It took Tracy-Ace a few moments to notice them; she turned with a big grin, her eyes shining—and did a double take when she saw Legroeder's hair. She didn't say a word about it, but strode forward with an outstretched hand to greet him. "Rigger Legroeder! Welcome back to Outpost Ivan!"

Legroeder had been wondering how he should greet her. Taking her cue, he clasped her hand in an official welcome. He felt an electric tingle at her touch, and her beaming if slightly unfocused smile. For a moment, he felt a giddy desire to enfold her in his arms; but then the tingle fled, and her smile and hand moved on, leaving him empty as she turned to his Narseil friends. "Welcome back, all of you! And congratulations! You've accomplished an astounding feat!" Tracy-Ace made a sweeping gesture to the starliner. "*Impris!* You brought her back safely! Who would have believed it?"

As she marveled, Legroeder found himself feeling ignored by Tracy-Ace. *Is it because we're in public? Or is something going on?* He cleared his throat. *Don't be a fool; she could hardly hug you in front of everyone, could she? I don't care; I don't like being ignored.* He cleared his throat again. "Did you get our preliminary report?"

"Indeed, we did," boomed a voice beside him, and Legroeder turned to see a larger-than-life holo of Yankee-Zulu/Ivan floating beside him. "It's an incredible story. Simply incredible. We want to hear every detail."

Legroeder inclined his head in acknowledgment, wondering why YZ/I had chosen to appear in holo, rather than in person.

"We're expecting the *Impris* officers to emerge momentarily," Tracy-Ace said, her temple implants racing with activity. For an instant Legroeder thought he caught the familiar twinkle in her eye, and he suppressed a flutter of excitement. "We have people standing by to give *Impris* a royal welcome. We've got medical teams, engineering teams, hospitality teams . . ."

Hospitality teams? Legroeder suddenly saw a new holo—a large brass ensemble poised just outside the circle. *Okay . . .* He let out a long, slow breath, waiting for the hatch to open. Trying to ignore Tracy-Ace. Focus on *Impris* . . . on the mysteries of the ghost ship, the Flying Dutchman of space. It would soon be crawling with Kyber techs. He felt a sudden surge of resentment. Damn it, these were *his* mysteries to reveal, his and the others who had gone through it with him.

A shout went up. A dark opening appeared in the airlock. The brass ensemble played a triumphant fanfare. And now, emerging ahead of the other officers and crew, were Captain Noel Friedman and Rigger Freem'n Deutsch. The captain's face looked as if it were about to crack, straining between joy and solemnity; but Deutsch, though his facial expressions were concealed behind metal skin, appeared to Legroeder to be grinning from ear to ear.

"Welcome back to civilization!" boomed the voice of YZ/I.

"Thank you," Friedman whispered, looking around.

Legroeder could not contain himself. He strode forward to greet Friedman and Deutsch. "Captain!" he cried. "Freem'n! Am I glad to see you!"

The solemnity on Captain Friedman's face finally cracked. *"Halleluiah!"* he cried, raising his hands joyfully. *"Landfall!* By God, I never thought I'd see the day again!" He cocked his head in puzzlement, as he pumped Legroeder's hand. "Is that you, Legroeder? What the hell's happened to your hair, man?"

"Well, it's, uh—" Legroeder gestured helplessly "—I'll have to explain later." He suddenly realized he wasn't observing any kind of protocol here. "Captain Friedman, may I introduce you to the leader of the Outpost, Yankee-Zulu/Ivan?" He gestured to the holo of YZ/I, who was lit up like a Christmas tree. "And Tracy-Ace/Alfa, YZ/I's right-hand assistant."

"Welcome to Outpost Ivan of the Free Kyber Republics," Tracy-Ace said smoothly, stepping forward. "We're delighted to see *Impris*, and to extend our hospitality to you, to your crew, and to all of your passengers."

The brass ensemble struck up another welcoming tune.

Friedman bowed with obvious relief. "Thank you. Thank you all for coming to the aid of my ship and crew. We are honored to accept your hospitality." He gestured to the emerging officers. "Needless to say, we are eager to get back to our home port. But we would be most grateful for your assistance with repairs and supplies and so on."

Freem'n Deutsch stood just behind Friedman, looking inscrutable. Legroeder held his breath, watching Tracy-Ace.

Tracy-Ace bowed. "Captain, we will assist you with medical treatment and whatever else you need."

"Indeed," said YZ/I's holo. "And after all the time you've been away, we hope you might enjoy a look at our modest outpost. I think you'll find it rather different from Faber Eridani."

"Yes, of course," Friedman said. But a shadow had crept over his face. "We certainly appreciate the offer of help. Including the medical—though I'm afraid for many of our people, the needs are more psychological than medical. It has been . . . a difficult ordeal."

"We understand—and we'll do our best," Tracy-Ace promised.

"Some of them," Friedman continued, "might be reluctant to leave the ship. It is difficult to explain . . ."

"Then our people will go to them," Tracy-Ace said. "Captain, we would very much like to study your ship. We hope to find some explanation for what you and your crew have gone through."

"Certainly, you may look," Friedman said. "But I think you'll learn more from the riggers who brought us out. Rigger Deutsch here. Rigger Legroeder. The Narseil."

Legroeder suddenly knew why he felt a slowly tightening

knot in his stomach. Yes, it was the riggers who knew; the ship would tell them nothing. And it was he and the Narseil who knew most of all. And that made them a valuable—perhaps dangerously valuable—commodity. Was it his imagination, or was Deutsch peering at him with eyes that seemed to reflect his own thoughts?

He spoke suddenly, to release the tension. "I believe you're right, Captain. It's not the ship we need to understand; it's the Flux. My Narseil colleagues and I have been working very hard to formulate answers—for all of us." He turned to YZ/I and Tracy-Ace. "We'll be happy to go over it all with you at your earliest convenience." *But I don't know how you're going to take what we have to say.*

"The sooner the better," rumbled the image of YZ/I. "Why don't you come on down now?"

Tracy-Ace's implants flickered with intense activity. She cocked her head and raised a hand. "Excellent idea. Lieutenant Zond, would you care to escort—?"

IT WAS probably just as well that Tracy-Ace wasn't with them, Legroeder thought as they approached YZ/I's operations center. He had enough to think about right now without wondering what was going on in her mind. Freem'n was at his side, but they'd had no chance to talk privately. Behind them walked all of the Narseil except Agamem, who'd been sent to report back to Commander Fre'geel. Legroeder's thoughts were starting to percolate with memories of the passage, and a flood of further questions, many of them coming from the implants in his skull. It was going to be hard to keep his head clear for this meeting.

A man was just leaving YZ/I's command platform as they approached—a dark-haired, red-skinned man. It took Legroeder a moment to place him; he was the one who'd argued with YZ/I and Tracy-Ace during their previous meeting. He searched his memory for the man's name. Lanyard/GC. Old boyfriend of Tracy-Ace's or something. A pain in the ass. Legroeder was glad he was leaving, not arriving.

"Thank you for sharing your concerns with me," YZ/I called after Lanyard, who seemed to give a silent snort. As he passed, Lanyard glanced at Legroeder and the Narseil with what seemed a mix of curiosity and derision.

Legroeder forgot Lanyard as YZ/I boomed out, "Wonderful to see you! All of you! Come in, come in!" The glowing man greeted Legroeder with a hearty handshake. "I was afraid I'd never see you again. And here you are! Incredible mission—just fantastic!" YZ/I's face rippled with light as he waved them all into the command section of his operations center. He sealed the section off with an opaque force-screen. "So, Legroeder. How's it feel to be back?"

Legroeder laughed, in spite of himself. "Glad to be here. Glad to be alive."

"I can imagine," said YZ/I. He studied Legroeder for a moment. "Nice haircut, by the way. Did you do that yourself?"

Legroeder sighed deeply. He thought he heard the Narseil chuckling behind him. "You could say that, I suppose." He cleared his throat. "Anyway—we're here, and we're ready to report."

"Excellent." YZ/I rubbed his hands together expectantly. "I wish I could have been there at the docks in person. But I'm afraid that . . . well, certain political concerns precluded that. I do apologize. Now, tell me everything. Everything that happened. Everything you learned." His face and body shimmered with moving patches of color. YZ/I spread his hands and looked piercingly at Legroeder.

Legroeder frowned, trying to frame words. "I can tell you what happened," he said finally. "But telling you what we learned—that's going to be more difficult."

"Then let's start with what's easy," YZ/I said.

Legroeder felt momentarily at a loss; he gestured helplessly to his fellow riggers.

"Come, gentlemen," YZ/I laughed. "*Impris* is sitting in my docking port. You found her." He clapped his hands together. "Don't be bashful. Tell me how you did it."

"Perhaps I can summarize," said Cantha. And in a husky

murmur, the Narseil gave a recap of the search for and discovery of *Impris*. He paused for breath, then briefly explained how the time instabilities had forced their hasty departure.

YZ/I's eyes were intense with interest. "So the key discovery in all of this was the spacetime . . . 'quantum flaw.' Is that right?" He rummaged in his seat pockets until he found a cigar. He inspected it thoughtfully, as though by mulling over the cigar he might comprehend the meaning of the phrase, *quantum flaw*.

"Yes," Legroeder said, finding his voice again. "And we can't explain it fully, because we don't understand it fully. We can tell you how we got into the flaw, and how we got out, but I'm not sure we can tell you *why*."

YZ/I stopped in the middle of lighting his cigar. "You don't know why you did what you did?"

"We know why we made certain decisions. But in the larger sense—it all happened so fast that by the end we were operating almost wholly on instinct."

YZ/I puffed. "And once it was over, and you had some time to reflect back on it?"

Legroeder snorted. "Once we got out of the flaw, we had a little something else to think about—a ship named *Hunter*. I presume Captain Glenswarg informed you about our brush with KM/C?"

"Yes, he did," YZ/I said. "It was exactly as we feared— Carlotta did not take kindly to having their prize lure taken out of the water."

"No." Legroeder reflected back on the discovery that his former captain was trying to kill him. "No, they did not."

"Well, I'm glad our people were able to take care of it without too much trouble," YZ/I said casually. "I understand you people were very good in the fight, too."

"Thank you," said Palagren with, Legroeder noted, a dry Narseil sarcasm that YZ/I almost certainly missed.

"But back to what you were saying—about your findings."

"Well—" Legroeder drew a deep breath "—we don't

have a definitive picture of the quantum flaw yet. We do have a huge amount of information that we're still analyzing." *And mapping? Is that what's going to come out of all this?*

YZ/I stared at him for a moment. "Still analyzing. Okay. But tell me this: are my ships in danger of disappearing into the quantum flaw the way *Impris* did? If you recall, that was one of the things I sent you to find out." He rippled with white light, flicking his gaze from one rigger to the next.

Legroeder's head hurt, buzzing with a sudden burst of activity from the implants. "I think they are," he said at last.

"You *think* they are? You *think* they're in danger?"

Legroeder drew another slow breath under YZ/I's glare, and caught a slight nod from Palagren and Cantha. "Let me rephrase. The danger exists, definitely. It can happen again, and probably will. But I can't tell you—*yet*—exactly *where* the dangers exist . . ." He shook his head; it suddenly felt full of cobwebs. He wasn't purposely being vague. And yet his thoughts . . . what the devil was going on?

"Why not?" YZ/I demanded, puffing smoke. "Are you saying you don't *have* the knowledge? Or that you aren't planning to *share* it with us?" His voice was suddenly full of needles.

"Uh—"

Palagren raised a hand to interrupt. "May I be so bold as to ask a question in return?"

YZ/I cocked his head, frowning. "You may ask."

"Thank you. I was just wondering, what would we expect in return for providing that kind of information?"

YZ/I's eyes narrowed. He clicked his teeth together, though whether in surprise or admiration of Palagren's bluntness wasn't clear. "Well, I promised you the ship, and your freedom, didn't I?"

He paused a beat, and Palagren said, "When?"

"*Eventually.* What do you want? Some kind of preferred treatment?"

Palagren opened his mouth and closed it. "Could you

define 'eventually'? And 'preferred treatment'?"

YZ/I glared around his cigar. "Better than nonpreferred treatment. Let's quit screwing around. How useful *is* your information?"

Legroeder felt his own lips tighten, as Palagren made a soft hissing sound. *Useful isn't the right word,* he thought. *Indispensable is more like it, if it's what I think it is.*

"Look," YZ/I said. His eyes flicked from one to another. "You all went out and risked your lives to bring this ship back, on the strength of my promise to release you. Right? Well, if I repeated that promise now, would it make any difference? I could still renege just as easily, if that's what you're afraid of."

How reassuring, Legroeder thought, noting that YZ/I had *not* repeated the promise. The Narseil seemed to be waiting for Legroeder to respond; this was human psychological territory. He cleared his throat.

"What?" YZ/I asked.

Legroeder let his breath escape. "We're not trying to hold out on you. But until the information is processed—which we cannot do overnight—there's only so much we *can* share. Right, Palagren? Cantha?"

Palagren's neck-sail rippled in agreement.

YZ/I squinted through the cigar smoke. "All right, then— let's back off a little. Tell me what you *do* know. Tell me what it felt like." He waved his hands, inviting elaboration. "You were caught in this fold. Tell me what your *instincts* told you was going on . . ."

Palagren made a hissing sound, and began to describe the riggers-eye view of their flight out through the quantum flaw . . .

"THE PASSAGE was utterly harrowing," the Narseil concluded.

"To say the least," Legroeder muttered.

Palagren glanced at him. "And I don't know how repeatable it would be. I think we were very, very lucky."

YZ/I looked troubled, as they by turns described their

experiences. He questioned each of them with urgency, and a surprising degree of technical understanding. Legroeder was struck by how similar their impressions were in general, and yet how different in detail. Deutsch, in some ways, had the most interesting experience, since he'd been leading a team of human riggers who were wholly unprepared mentally. "Those men had some images during the transit that I would not want to see again in the net," Deutsch murmured, the modulated tones of his synthetic voice belying the emotions that Legroeder guessed he was feeling. "If we had not been so closely linked to *Phoenix*, I doubt we'd have made it through."

"I must speak with these *Impris* riggers," YZ/I mused, when Deutsch finished. "But gentlemen—I'm still waiting to hear what caused *Impris* to fall into the fold in the first place. Was it just bad luck—or did they do something wrong, eh?" He squinted through the cigar smoke boiling in the air, and suddenly his manner seemed to suggest that they were old friends, catching up. "Was it because they'd rigged together too many times? Or was it their route?" He held out his hands. *"Tell me why."*

It was Cantha who replied. "We don't know for sure. We had only a brief time with the *Impris* riggers, before the time distortions forced us to act." Cantha's dark-green cheeks puffed out, and his oval eyes stretched even farther vertically, making him look like a large cobra.

"You have no opinion on why she was trapped, then?"

Cantha flicked his fingers. "If you want my *opinion*—I believe there was an element of bad luck in the route they followed. They may have frequented a route that took them—perhaps over and over—close to the folds, and the underlying flaw, without their ever being aware of it. They may have been perilously close on those occasions when they reported difficulty. And then, one time, they didn't just come close."

"They fell in?"

"Precisely." Cantha paused. "This flaw is extremely long, and possibly infinite, and branches through several dimensions. I doubt it's an isolated cosmological phenomenon. Other flaws may be closer to the surface in some places and farther in others. But in any case, difficult to detect, with our current state of knowledge."

Legroeder stirred. "Cantha's being way too conservative. Coming out of the flaw, I saw *quite clearly* . . . that space is *full* of these things." He gazed hard at YZ/I. "If you want to find them the hard way, the surest thing you can do is send a whole fleet through the underflux."

A long silence followed, during which YZ/I seemed frozen. Then he breathed again, and rose slowly to his feet. "Gentlemen," he said, "I want to show you something." As he turned, the back wall of his command center paled, and a doorway opened. "If you would follow me, please . . ."

Legroeder and the others exchanged glances as they followed YZ/I down a darkening passageway. The only light, for a few seconds, came from YZ/I's body, and the tip of his cigar. Then all the darkness around slowly came to life with stars, a sprinkling at first, and then a multitude. The stars were below them as well as above, and on all sides. They seemed to be standing on a narrow catwalk, suspended in space. Legroeder's pulse quickened as he saw the swirl of the galactic spiral arm; then the stars slowly wheeled until they were looking directly into the Sagittarian sector, in the direction of the galactic core. Out in those clusters of stars and nebulas, he knew, lay the Well of Stars, the next great sector of space to be colonized. By the Free Kyber, if YZ/I had his way.

"You know why I've brought you here?" YZ/I asked, his voice reverberating softly among the stars. No one answered. YZ/I raised a hand, and the stars slowly softened to a blur, until they were looking at a vast chart of the Flux, of the territory between where they were now, and the Well of Stars. The view changed gradually, reflecting a descent into ever-deeper levels of the Flux. "Gentlemen, I have only one overriding interest. And that is for you to show me: where are the quantum flaws that endanger my fleet?" He turned and his eyes burned with light. "Rigger Legroeder, you say you saw them. Can you put them on the map for me?"

Legroeder hesitated. He thought about the information that the implants had displayed to him—arrays of spacetime splinters that stretched out toward infinity through the underflux. He felt his implants continuing to buzz as they sifted through the mountains of information. He felt near-certainty that he would, in time, be able to produce just such a map. But not yet. Not until the implants finished their work. For a moment he reached out, as though to touch the Flux. Then he stopped and shook his head. "Not yet. But later, I think—after we've analyzed the information—"

"Later," YZ/I echoed. "I see. And where *is* all this raw data that you need to analyze?"

Legroeder felt himself unable to speak.

"Some of it is in our data records," Cantha volunteered. "But most—"

"Is where?" YZ/I growled.

Legroeder felt a shortness of breath. Why couldn't he just say it?

Freem'n Deutsch floated forward. "It is in our minds, YZ/I. And our augments. That is probably where the most important part of it is." He glanced at Legroeder. "And Legroeder here . . . well, you seem to have seen more of it than the rest of us. That talent of yours . . ."

Legroeder started to speak, but something caught in his mind. He felt as if a fog were settling back around his brain, as if some part of him were resolutely determined not to share with anyone.

"I believe," Cantha said, "that the only way to wholly clarify the information is to bring *Impris* and her crew to the Narseil Rigging Institute for study. There, I am certain, we will find the answers we need."

A circlet of light slid up YZ/I's body like a ring on a pole. "The Narseil Institute." YZ/I looked as if he were involved in a long inner dialogue, against the swirling colors of the Flux. He was silent a long time. Finally he said, "No, I don't believe that will do. I believe what we will do is study the ship *here*, quite thoroughly. And see if we can't learn the answers ourselves. Eh?"

The Narseil riggers stiffened. Legroeder tried not to betray the tension in his own throat as he said carefully, "You did promise to release the ship to return home."

YZ/I looked faintly amused. "And so I shall . . . in due course. But we have extremely capable people here, and here is where the study will be done. After all—would you expect me to believe that the Narseil Institute, if it had custody of *Impris*, would gladly hand over all of its findings to the Free Kyber Republic?"

The Narseil were silent.

YZ/I leveled a gaze at Legroeder. "And what about the knowledge in *your* head?"

Legroeder studied the palms of his hands for a moment. "I've . . . already told you what I saw and felt." *Threads of light, a web work of flaws . . . the beginnings of the map that would come . . .*

"But the rest of it . . . the *hard data* . . ."

Legroeder swallowed.

YZ/I was flickering like a ghost come alive.

Legroeder felt behind his ears. That buzzing vagueness . . . a feeling of cotton stuffed between himself and the implants. "I don't . . . know. These are Narseil implants. I'm . . . having a little trouble getting access to some of the information myself." His voice sounded stupid even to himself, as he said it. *What are these damn implants doing to me?*

YZ/I pulsed as if he were about to explode. "You're having difficulty gaining access? Well, then—" he glanced at the Narseil "—maybe we can *help* you get access. We have people here who are quite expert in that sort of work." Legroeder recoiled in alarm, as YZ/I closed his eyes for a moment and appeared to subvocalize. His eyes opened. "Some of my people will be coming to take you to our labs. We'll see what we can do, eh?" He took a puff from his cigar, blew the smoke out into the Flux. "*Just helping*, you understand. All right?"

Legroeder stared at him, appalled. *Helping,* he thought, images of DeNoble flashing in his mind. Indoctrination . . . reinforcement . . . punishment . . . *I know how the Kyber like to help.* "Oh, no you don't," he whispered, barely aware of his own voice speaking.

YZ/I smiled chillingly. "Oh, yes I do." He raised his chin slightly and spoke past him. "Yes, Lieutenant—in here with your men."

Chapter 37

FINAL ANALYSIS

THE ROOM didn't look that terrible, really; it was a plain white laboratory, with a couple of high-backed, padded seats that might have been in a dentist's office. But when the tech pointed toward one of the seats, Legroeder found himself thinking of the outpost's maintainers working in their little artificial world in a vault, and the guards and med-techs who kept them there.

Legroeder kept his gaze implacable and stood unmoving in the center of the room. He wished to hell now he'd fought this business in YZ/I's office, but it hadn't seemed a smart idea at the time. And now his Narseil friends had been whisked away elsewhere, supposedly to report to their own commander. *I may have no choice about this, but I'll be damned if I'm going to just step into it for them.*

"Please sit, Rigger," said the tech, in a tinny voice that came from a speaker embedded in the front of his throat.

"Go fuck yourself."

The tech squinted at him, as if unsure how to proceed in the face of opposition. After a moment, the tech twitched an eyebrow; one of the guards grasped Legroeder's arm to move him toward the seat, and Legroeder yanked it away. "Get your hands off me." The guard grabbed *both* arms, this time with augmented strength, and lifted him straight into the seat. Before Legroeder could get his breath back, two other guards were strapping him in with restraints that seemed to come out of nowhere. "You bastards," he hissed, gasping for wind. "Are you *trying* to screw up the data?"

"Certainly not," said the tech, in an admonishing voice. "The Boss said that you needed some help in opening access to your augment stores. It may be that your resistance here is being mediated by the augments themselves, so we'll just move things along and do our best not to cause any pain or discomfort. You'll probably find it easier to cooperate once the procedure's underway."

"Like hell I will," he grunted. He found himself suddenly thinking of Bobby Mahoney—who, if he was still alive at all, was probably living a life full of this kind of crap. Legroeder hadn't gotten a chance yet to ask again about the boy. *Where the hell's Tracy-Ace when I need her?*

The tech smiled faintly. "Bear with me for one moment."

There was a soft whine, and Legroeder just glimpsed out of the corner of his eye a set of padded flaps rotating up from the headrest. Before he could react, his head was clamped in a vice. He felt a tingle in his temples, and an instant paralysis, leaving him with heartbeat, breath, and eye movement—and little else. He saw Lieutenant Zond off to one side, looking studiously indifferent.

"Put your implants into handshake mode," the tech said.

Legroeder tried to snarl, but what came out was a mumble.

"All right, let's see if this works." The tech drew an opaque visor down over Legroeder's eyes.

Legroeder felt a sheet of white noise slide across his consciousness like an ocean wave. *Drowning—!* His thoughts blurred and lost coherence; he watched his own conscious thought vanish into a haze, like milk swirling into coffee.

He was gasping; his *neurons* were gasping.

He was twisting on a synaptic connection; something was

trying to illuminate the way into the implants attached to his brain. It was finding no entry, but the effort filled him with a sense of violation, and danger. He could not speak . . .

An external voice rasped and *scree*ed, and another voice answered from within . . .

◻ *No connection is possible at this time . . .* ◻

The screeing voice changed pitch, dropped to a growl.

◻ *No connection is possible . . .* ◻

A metallic resonance.

◻ *No connection is possible . . .* ◻

There was a brief, sharp interaction that set his teeth chattering. Then, with an abrupt *thunk*, the pressure against his thought let up.

Legroeder tried to refocus; he felt a rush of claustrophobia, his heart racing. There was a rasping sound in his ears, rhythmic and urgent, frightening. His breath.

He tried to cry out. *What—are you—doing—to me?*

The tinny voice of the tech: "This isn't working. Let's try something else here . . ."

There was a *twang*, and then the world went away . . .

*

Incessant heartbeat.
Scratching, a bird's feet on metal.
Pulsing shocks of fear.
Muttering voices, incomprehensible.
Time passing like molasses . . .

*

More voices, in another time and place, discussing the possibility of surgical extraction of implants . . . but they were too deeply interwoven into his neural matrix; the risk of killing him was too great . . .

A pity . . . it might have been so quick, so easy . . .

*

When he came to, Legroeder felt dizzy and nauseous, with ringing memories of voices clashing like armies. But the visor was off; he could see. "What . . . how long . . . ?" he rasped.

A different tech came forward. A woman this time; she had a flesh-and-blood face, thin and birdlike. Her voice was deeper than the previous tech's. "You were out for twelve hours. We couldn't get a thing. You aren't holding your augments back, are you? The Boss assured us you were trying to get access."

Legroeder blinked furiously. His eyes were gritty; his head hurt from the clamp pads. But it hurt even more on the inside.

"We'll keep trying," muttered the tech. "There are some other approaches that might—"

The nearby door slid open. A female voice shouted, "Get him out *now*, I said!"

Legroeder tried to turn.

"Miss Alfa," said the tech in apparent surprise.

"Do you understand *now?*" Tracy-Ace/Alfa, in her black work outfit, strode into view, gesturing angrily. The tech seemed frozen in alarm. Tracy-Ace peered down at Legroeder. "My God, what are they doing to you?" She slapped an open palm down on one of the controls. The clamp-pads fell away, releasing him abruptly. Legroeder gasped, his head rolling on the headrest. He could barely control the movement.

A hand on his shoulder, Tracey-Ace bent to peer into his eyes. "Are you all right?"

"Uh . . ." His lips felt as though they'd been anesthetized.

Tracy-Ace yanked open a drawer and snatched out a handheld paramedical probe. She thrust it against his chest. "Hold still. Okay—you're not having a cardiac event—but your cortical activity looks scrambled." Muttering under her breath, she peered into his eyes again. Her augments flickered, illuminating her face. "Rings, Legroeder, I wish I'd gotten here sooner."

"I. . . . it's . . ." *It's all right.*

No, it's not all right. Where the hell were you?

"Christ, I'm sorry."

"Been here . . . twelve hours . . ." His voice was a whisper.

"*Damn* that fucker! I was with *Impris*. YZ/I didn't *tell* me he was sending you here. I'll kill him." Tracy-Ace's brow was furrowed, her gaze deep and probing as she studied him.

Was she telling the truth? He had to steel himself not to be drawn into those eyes. Not until he knew.

She released the straps. "Come on, we're getting out of here." She turned and hollered, "Lieutenant Zond!"

BACK AT his quarters, Tracy-Ace fed him a dinner that she'd sent Zond to fetch. Some kind of noodles; he swallowed without noticing the taste. When Tracy-Ace was satisfied that he wouldn't keel over, she said, "You need rest and I need to talk to YZ/I. I'll leave Zond outside, with orders to let no one in except by my authorization."

Legroeder tried to choke back an angry reply. It bubbled up anyway. "A lot of good Zond will be. He's the one who *took* me to that place. How do I know he won't take me back there the minute you leave?"

Tracy-Ace bristled. "He will obey my orders."

Legroeder flushed. "Were those your orders, for me to be worked over by the inquisition?"

Her eyes widened in shock. "Is that what you think?"

"Well, you just said—"

"*Damn*. That *is* what you think, isn't it?" She studied Legroeder with narrowed eyes. "I did *not* send you there. YZ/I did it, without letting me know. I have now transferred authority over Zond back to me."

"And YZ/I can't take it right back?"

Tracy-Ace stared at him hard, the flickering around her eyes slowly dying down. "He won't," she said softly. "I will see to that. Believe me, I will."

Before he could respond, she leaned forward as though to kiss him on the cheek. Instead, she gripped his shoulders and squeezed, giving him a quick hug. Then she was out the door, leaving him reverberating with a welter of confused images from the contact.

Legroeder finished his meal in a state of shock. How

much of that was he supposed to believe? He ought to call Deutsch, or the Narseil. But he was so exhausted. He needed to stretch out on his bunk to rest. Just for a few minutes . . .

When sleep came over him it was deep and filled with angry dreams.

HE DREAMED of distant, crackling contact through his implants . . . flickering images of Tracy-Ace and Yankee-Zulu/ Ivan . . . and echoes of shouting voices . . .

Fucking bastard! WHY DID YOU HIDE THAT FROM ME?

Am I supposed to show you everything?

When it matters like that—yes, dammit! You deliberately—

Spared you a distraction when you had other responsibilities. I think you're letting your personal feelings—

Fuck my personal feelings!

Now, Tracy-Ace/Alfa, I suggest you calm down . . .

CALM DOWN? I'll calm down after I've wrung your miserable neck, you lying manipulative sonofabitch!

Watch your tone, Node Alfa . . .

It's about the stupidest thing I've ever seen you do.

I said, watch your tone . . .

The connection hissed and faded . . .

LEGROEDER WAS awakened by Tracy-Ace, bringing breakfast. He sat up, holding his head, trying to sort dream from reality. He could not. "What the devil's going on?" he gasped.

"A lot," she said tightly. "How are you feeling?"

"Lousy." He drew a slow, painful breath. Memories of the inquisition were already crowding out whatever remained of the fragments of his dreams. "I guess returning-hero status is pretty short-lived around here."

"I have just had a long and unpleasant talk with YZ/I about that very question," she said severely, pouring him a cup of murk from a thermal pitcher. She put a plate with a breakfast roll and a citromelon slice in front of him. "Let's just say, your status has been restored."

He squinted, shouting voices echoing in his mind. "Yeah? How wonderful."

She frowned. "You don't believe me."

He didn't look at her. "I didn't say that. Thanks for breakfast."

"Legroeder . . ." She frowned harder. "You *don't* believe me, do you?"

He didn't answer, or look up.

"Legroeder, I would have stopped it sooner if I'd known. I really would have. I'm *sorry*."

He finally raised his eyes, and tried not to sound too acid. "I thought you were this all-fired powerful *node*. How could you not have known?"

She stared at him, open-mouthed.

"I thought so. Maybe you should leave now."

"*Legroeder*. Look, I know you're mad at me, and I don't blame you. I should have been there to look out for you. But YZ/I blindsided me; he kept me from seeing what was happening until after you'd been worked over."

He remained silent.

"Will you please believe me?" When he didn't answer, she pulled up a chair and sat directly in front of him. She grasped both of his hands in hers. The sudden electric connection took his breath away. He felt her gaze, and her presence . . .

And then, as suddenly, the connection ebbed away. Tracy-Ace drew back, her augments winking. "What are you doing? Are you blocking me?" she whispered. "Talk to me. What's going on?"

Legroeder stared down at her hand grasping his. He felt no sensation except the physical pressure, and that seemed a million miles away. He searched inward. The implants had been there for an instant, allowing the connection; but now they were gone. Without the implants there could be no link with Tracy-Ace. And he had a distinct feeling— perhaps they had left him a subtle message—that they had shut themselves down for the duration. Meaning, until they were in a place of safety. A Narseil place of safety. *Oh, Jesus.*

Tracy-Ace was squeezing his hand harder, as if she could force the connection. "What's *wrong*, Legroeder? What's wrong with your implants?"

He shook his head. "They've closed down. It's not me. I don't know why."

Tracy-Ace rocked back in consternation, still holding his hand. "Are they damaged?"

"I don't think so. No."

She looked at him for a long moment, disheartened. Then she drew a breath. "Legroeder—can I tell you this? I *missed* you. I'm very glad to have you back. And not just for *Impris*."

He couldn't react; his thoughts were too tangled.

Tracy-Ace pursed her lips together; finally she nodded and drew herself erect. "As soon as you're ready, we're going to have a very interesting talk with YZ/I. We'll be joining a few people there."

"A few people?"

"You know them."

"LEGROEDER, I'M so glad to see you're ... unharmed! Come in," YZ/I said, breathing sincerity from every pore. Before Legroeder could reply, YZ/I extended a hand past him. "And Commander Fre'geel—thank you for coming! And Riggers." Legroeder turned to see that Fre'geel, the Narseil riggers, and Deutsch had come in right behind him. "And ... Tracy-Ace/Alfa! How good of you to join our meeting." YZ/I's gaze at Tracy-Ace suggested he was less than happy to see her.

"I wouldn't miss a chance to help out with the debriefing," Tracy-Ace said coldly. She turned to greet the others. Then she gave a brief nod to the man Legroeder just now noticed standing to one side and little behind YZ/I's chair. Lanyard/GC. What was he doing here?

"And," Tracy-Ace continued, "I thought perhaps I should

be here to help make sure nothing *else* went wrong." She stared hard at YZ/I.

Legroeder glanced at his fellow riggers, wishing he could convey with his eyes what had happened.

YZ/I sighed heavily. "Rigger Legroeder, please allow me to apologize. I did not intend for you to be treated roughly by my analysts. My instructions were to try to release the information—but to treat you only with courtesy and respect. I regret . . . that you had such a difficult time of it."

Legroeder considered being diplomatic—then thought, the hell with it. "You lying asshole sonofabitch. What *were* you trying to do—make sure *nobody* could get the information from my implants?"

YZ/I raised his hands in the air. "Heavens no. I merely told my people to try to set up an interface with your implants." He shook his head sorrowfully. "I have since learned that they were neither as gentle nor as successful as I'd hoped."

Legroeder glared. "*Not as gentle or successful as you'd hoped?* Is this the way you always treat people who go out and do the impossible for you?"

YZ/I winced, gesturing apologetically. He seemed to be groping for appropriate words, and failing. YZ/I glanced back at Lanyard, whose face was creased by a dark frown. "Do you folks all know my associate?" he barked suddenly, gesturing at Lanyard. "This is Group Coordinator Lanyard— a member of Outpost Ivan's Ruling Cabinet. He's here to observe, and to learn what he can do to help out." YZ/I's expression became unreadable for a moment, as Lanyard nodded stiffly to the assembled group.

Fre'geel spoke up, not letting YZ/I change the subject. "I take it you tried, and failed, to force information from Legroeder's implants."

YZ/I flickered a shade of pink. "Not *force*, Commander. We did try to encourage a sharing with his implants."

"And in so doing, you risked grave harm to him," Fre'geel replied, his voice light, yet hard as steel.

"Not intentionally, I assure you. Legroeder, my people didn't do serious harm to you, did they?"

Legroeder gathered himself for another angry statement, but was interrupted by Fre'geel saying in a dry, flinty voice, "I must say, it would be a great shame if you *lost* all of this information that has been gathered, at such risk—because you tried to *extract* it, rather than *cooperate* with us." The Narseil commander stood with his two hands clasped at his breast. Only a slight twitching of his gill slits, and a widening of his vertical eyes betrayed his anger.

YZ/I waved a hand in agitated reassurance. "That's not at all the case, Commander Fre'geel. Look—your people did an outstanding job in rescuing *Impris*. Outstanding. I'm deeply grateful, and I intend to cooperate with you in every way we can. But—" YZ/I gestured, as though struggling with an inescapable fact "—here's the ship, right in our docks, available for study by our techs. And here's Legroeder, carrying some very important data in his head. Possibly—I think I heard you saying—a map of this network of quantum flaws. Right?"

Legroeder nodded slowly, silently.

"Except," Fre'geel said dryly, "that it's locked away in Rigger Legroeder's implants."

"Exactly. And you surely can understand our position. Once he leaves here, a lot can happen between his departure and our receipt of the analyzed data."

"I *do* understand that. But do *you* understand that his implants were designed by the Narseil security forces?" Fre'geel said pointedly. "You *can't* get the data, and neither can Legroeder. For that matter, neither can I. Only Narseil Security—or the Narseil Rigging Institute—can extract the information! Any effort on your part not only risks harm to Legroeder—but also jeopardizes the integrity of the data itself. Do you realize *that*, Yankee-Zulu/Ivan?"

YZ/I's eyes shone abruptly with surprise and fury.

Behind him, there was a sharp intake of breath. Lanyard's eyes were narrowed, and his lips appeared to be moving subvocally. YZ/I snapped a look back at him; his gaze darkened further.

"Double cross . . ." Lanyard whispered.

YZ/I face flickered several shades of crimson and orange. "Let's not make hasty judgments," he muttered to Lanyard. To Legroeder and the others, he said sternly, "Have you known this all along?"

Legroeder was dumbstruck. He *should* have known it, or guessed it. How could he have been so naive? But none of the Narseil had ever intimated, and even the implants themselves had been tightlipped. *(You bastards, why didn't you tell me?)*

There was no answer.

Christ. All that time he'd sat in YZ/I lab, being worked over.

"Only Mission Command knew," Fre'geel said, making a hissing sound that approximated a clearing of the throat. "There was no reason to share that point with my other officers."

"And were you," YZ/I said, almost too softly to hear, "planning to share the rigging data with us once *you* had extracted it?" His eyes had a deadly sparkle to them now.

"Of course," Fre'geel said calmly.

Of course . . .

"But I'm sure you understand why we wanted to ensure our own access to the data," Fre'geel continued. His Narseil eyes blinked slowly.

YZ/I slammed his fist down on the arm of his chair. *"You amphibian bastards! You got that information on MY SHIP, flying MY MISSION!"*

The Narseil commander made a side-to-side gesture with his right hand. "Come, Yankee-Zulu/Ivan. We were merely protecting our interests. After all, our riggers were instrumental in effecting the rescue. Do you deny *our* rights?"

YZ/I's skin rippled. "I do not deny that your riggers were an asset to the mission."

"If I'm not mistaken," Tracy-Ace interjected, "the Narseil

riggers were indispensable. In fact, all of the participants were indispensable."

"That is correct," Legroeder said. "The Narseil. The Kyber. The Centrist. All of us."

"Damn it," YZ/I hissed furiously at Tracy-Ace. "*You* know what's at stake here. What are you trying to do?"

"One thing that's at stake," Legroeder said in a soft drawl, "is *our* future ability to map the hazards that *your* fleet will face when it travels to the Well of Stars. And it would seem that *that* depends on your cooperating with us."

For a moment YZ/I looked as if he had stopped breathing altogether. Finally he whispered, as though speaking to some demon dwelling deep within himself, *"I'll be a goddamned sonofabitch . . ."*

In the discussion that followed, Lanyard/GC hovered close to YZ/I, and it was clear that a sharp conflict was playing itself out beneath the surface between them. YZ/I was asking the Narseil commander, curtly, just what he expected in exchange for sharing the information.

"Not too much," Fre'geel said. "Safe passage for all of my crew. An unconditional end to raiding on our shipping—"

"*All* of our shipping," Legroeder snapped. "Centrist as well as Narseil."

Fre'geel looked nonplused. "Well, I can only speak for the Narseil Navy—"

"Well, *I'm* speaking for the Centrist worlds. In case you've forgotten, the data's in *my* head," Legroeder said coldly.

Fre'geel bobbed his head in acquiescence. He had no reason to object.

"One other thing," Legroeder said. "*Impris* goes home first, to Faber Eridani. From there, we can request her loan to the Narseil Rigging Institute."

"Now, excuse me, Rigger," Fre'geel began.

"Excuse me, my ass, Fre'geel. You're the best equipped to study her, so Captain Friedman should agree. But if not—

were you thinking of replacing one form of piracy with another, and just hijacking her?"

Fre'geel stiffened, puffing air through his gills. "We were intending no such thing. But let me ask this. Do *you* trust the Faber Eridani authorities?"

Legroeder swallowed hard. *Touché.* "I guess we'll have to cross that bridge when we come to it. But in any case, *I'm* the one you need, more than the ship."

Fre'geel didn't contradict him.

YZ/I gazed at Legroeder for a long time, with what seemed a new degree of respect. He shot a glance at Deutsch, floating in silence. "How much did you know about this?"

"Not a thing," Deutsch said. "I've been learning a lot, listening to this conversation."

"And so have I," Lanyard interrupted icily. "YZ/I, it's starting to sound as if you're giving away the whole store here."

YZ/I turned to Lanyard with an expression of calculated calm. "Not at all, my friend. And if you are thinking to put out false claims on that score, you had better think very carefully indeed."

"I make no false claims," Lanyard said rigidly.

"Let us be clear, then," YZ/I said. "You know my position on strengthening Ivan and the Kyber Republic— through *self reliance*. Perhaps we've taxed the outworlds enough, eh? My position is that anything we can do to aid the colony fleet, we will. Now, you tell me a better bargain than one that will *gain us a map of the quantum flaws that can ensure the safety of our fleet.*"

Lanyard's mouth grew tight; he was clearly taken aback. Legroeder could only marvel at the way YZ/I worked to turn what a few moments ago was a setback, into a political triumph. Lanyard strained to protest, "But what about the others? Carlotta . . . ?"

"Ah," YZ/I said. "There, you are right. There is Carlotta to be considered." He turned back to Legroeder. "You met our friends from KM/C."

"Yes. We met them. Including a couple of old colleagues of mine," Legroeder replied grimly.

YZ/I nodded. "I did not know that you would actually meet your old shipmates. I am sorry. But you found our response satisfactory?"

Legroeder shrugged. "The escort squadron saved our lives. But it seems you took a big risk, provoking one of your allies."

YZ/I glanced in amusement at Lanyard, who seemed startled to find himself in agreement with Legroeder. "You mean, why didn't we negotiate with them beforehand?"

"Well, yeah."

"They would not have agreed. Sometimes they just can't seem to see what's in their own best interest. They *really* didn't want to see *Impris* rescued. Or revealed. You, Legroeder, may be the only person ever to have escaped from one of the KM/C outposts, much less to have taken word of *Impris* back to the Centrist Worlds."

Legroeder shook his head. "But I wasn't captured by KM/C. I escaped from—"

"DeNoble—a KM/C satellite."

Legroeder blinked. "Oh."

"So, KM/C had great visions of using *Impris* for the last four years of her term of exclusive use." YZ/I shrugged. "They were going to be annoyed, no matter how we cut it. I probably would have been, too, in her place."

"So now what?"

"So now I persuade Carlotta that she needs this map even more badly than she needed *Impris*. And you know what?" YZ/I glanced back at Lanyard. "I think she's going to see the wisdom." When his gaze came back to the others, it was full of fire. "Especially if this information of yours is as valuable as you've been claiming. Eh?"

"It is," Legroeder said. He looked inward, in vain, for reassurance on that score. "I'm sure of it," he said.

YZ/I ignored Lanyard's obvious doubt, behind him. His face split into a mirthless grin. The room darkened, and around him and *through* him, images blazed up of the Kyber colony fleet, making ready for the pilgrimage. YZ/I's voice reverberated. "Oh, it had *better* be. Because we'll know where to find you. And, I might add, so will Carlotta."

"I'M SENDING Freem'n Deutsch with you, as my personal representative," YZ/I said, three days later. "He will be authorized to carry back the data, as it becomes available. And he will be capable, I think, of conveying *my* needs."

The half-metal man nodded, his glass eyes glowing momentarily. "I look forward to the opportunity."

Legroeder remembered Deutsch's previous ambition to escape from Ivan altogether. Was this a happy compromise? He tried to imagine how the average citizen of Faber Eridani would react to the half-metal man.

"You will admit Rigger Deutsch into your Narseil Institute?" YZ/I asked Fre'geel, with only a hint of an edge to his voice.

Fre'geel assured him that Deutsch would be welcomed. All three interests—Narseil, Centrist, and Kyber—would be entitled to representation in the study of the data.

Over the last three days, they'd met several times to discuss such matters as future espionage and piracy. The Narseil promised not to attempt to lead ships back to Ivan as long as its location remained secret. In return, YZ/I would end piracy as far as Outpost Ivan was concerned. In fact, the time was coming, he said, when the Free Kyber might be interested in trying to normalize relations with the outer worlds. That time was not yet here, perhaps, but equal participation in the *Impris* data was a step in the right direction.

Legroeder finally had a chance to bring up the subject of Harriet's grandson. "Remember the matter I asked you to look into? The boy—Bobby Mahoney?"

"What boy?"

Damn. "Have you forgotten? The boy who was captured at the same time I was, on the *Ciudad de los Angeles*."

YZ/I focused inward for a moment. "Oh yes—six or seven years old, wasn't he?"

"At the time. He'd be about . . . fourteen now, I guess."

Legroeder leaned forward. "This is *important*, YZ/I. He's the only grandson of someone I owe a lot to. Can you find him? Find out if he's still alive? Get him released, if possible?"

YZ/I raised an eyebrow. "Tracy-Ace?"

Tracy-Ace was already working at the console. "I began a search when you asked before. There was nothing in our system about him." She looked up at Legroeder. "But you were captured by DeNoble. YZ/I?"

The Boss rubbed his chin. "We have some connections on DeNoble. It'll be awkward, what with your having escaped from there and all—but sure, we'll make some discreet inquiries for you. If we can help the boy, we will. Fair enough?"

Legroeder felt the knot in his chest ease. "Fair enough. And thank you."

"Anytime," said YZ/I.

WHILE *IMPRIS* was studied by Kyber techs, her passengers and crew were treated as guests of Outpost Ivan. For many of the passengers, it was almost irrelevant where they were; the mere fact of emerging a century and a quarter in their future was clearly disorienting. Quite a number opted to remain on the ship, venturing out only for short exploratory trips into the outpost. Captain Friedman was among those who spent more time aboard the ship than not.

Freem'n Deutsch, during the voyage back, had developed a friendship with the *Impris* riggers, and also with Pen Lee, the one-time assistant to Inspector Gloris Fandrang. Lee, having been trapped years ago in his vain effort to understand what was happening to *Impris* and her crew, now seemed trapped in another kind of incomprehensible world, inside his own mind. Deutsch had somehow made an empathic connection where others had failed. If anyone was going to be able to help Pen Lee find his way back out of that interior world, Deutsch was a good candidate, Legroeder thought.

Legroeder himself was growing increasingly anxious,

waiting for departure. He had no trouble imagining all the things that might go wrong and interfere with his return to Faber Eridani. Every passing hour seemed an invitation to trouble. Tracy-Ace was extremely busy overseeing much of the activity around *Impris*, and in her absence Legroeder spent most of his time with the Narseil, or Freem'n Deutsch, or the *Impris* crew. His *H'zzarrelik* shipmates now had a certain degree of freedom to move about the outpost. An elaborate story was going around the outpost, a web of lies and truths and near-truths, about how the Narseil had come here under cover to collaborate with the Kyber in going after *Impris*, and only a terrible misunderstanding had resulted in the battle with *Flechette*. The story made Legroeder uneasy, but he wasn't about to contradict it.

As for Tracy-Ace, he was at a loss as to what to think. She remained his primary helper and guide; she was still his friend, but he wasn't sure if she was still his lover. His implants remained silent, and without the implant connection, it seemed impossible to know her mind or her desires. They hadn't made love since his return, and he felt awkward and frustrated, and even more disconnected. Half the time Legroeder felt helplessly in love with her, and half the time he feared that he had fallen into a hopeless infatuation. Could he hope to share a life, really, with a pirate? It seemed unlikely.

Over dinner in her quarters, one evening, Tracy-Ace seemed to be reading his thoughts, as she produced a bottle of wine—*real* wine, apparently—and began to open it. "Legroeder, you're tense. You've *been* tense."

"Well—"

She popped the seal and squinted at him. "Let me guess. You think there's a contradiction between the person you thought I was, and the person you're afraid I am. Is that it?"

Legroeder didn't answer. He took the wine bottle from her and studied it instead. The label was in an unfamiliar language. Where'd they get real wine here on Fortress Ivan? Did they have their own vineyards? It seemed unlikely. He handed it back and sat beside her on the edge of the bunk.

"Well, you're right," she said, pouring a glass and holding it up to the light. The wine had a robust claret color. Heaven knew what it was going to taste like, if it was home grown. She handed it to him.

Nervously, he took a sip, and at once felt depressed. It was much too good to be locally made. He was drinking the booty of piracy.

"YZ/I did all of the things you're thinking of," Tracy-Ace said. "And I'm guilty of complicity."

"Yes?" he whispered, his voice choked off by pain.

"I'm no angel," she said pointedly.

"But—" his voice caught "—you didn't order—"

"Fleets out to raid shipping? No. But I worked with him; I've sentenced people to captivity; I can't say I wasn't involved."

Guilty, Legroeder thought silently. He stared at the floor, his heart aching. And what were *his* needs, *his* secret agendas? What would he hate to admit to her?

For a moment, he wished desperately for the implant connection, so that he could get it all over with in one big exchange of confessions. A moment later, he was deeply, fervently grateful for the lack. Bad enough this way, he thought.

"YZ/I hates to admit it, Legroeder—but he's *tired* of living this way. And I'm more than tired of it. Legroeder? *I want the raiding to stop!* YZ/I does, too—it's just that his reasons are more pragmatic." She waved her wine glass. "He'd say something like, 'It makes us lazy—we'd be stronger if we made do for ourselves.' " She sniffed, and he couldn't quite tell what emotion she was feeling.

"Do you believe that?" he asked.

"Sure, I believe it. But I also *just want out of it.* I'm sick of it." She pressed her lips together, then said more softly, "*It's wrong and I'm sick of it.* Never mind the fancy reasons." She gazed at him, and he suddenly realized that her implants were dark and her eyes were welling with tears. For a moment, she sat crying silently, her wine glass quivering in her hand. Wiping an eye on her sleeve, she whispered, "Before you came, I didn't like it—but I wasn't sure why. Then I caught a glimpse of how *you* see it, what *you* went through."

Legroeder frowned. "But I didn't show . . . *did* I show that to you?"

"Yes, you did. I don't think you meant to. But I'm glad you did, because it showed *me* what was wrong." She seemed about to say more, then shook her head and looked away with a sigh.

Legroeder's heart ached. He took the glass from Tracy-Ace's hand and set it, with his own, on the end table. He gently enfolded her in his arms. She sat stiffly, and for the first time in a while he remembered that she was taller than he was. Finally she softened and sank against him, putting her head on his shoulder, shaking as she let her feelings tumble out with her tears. After a while, she lay down with her head in his lap. He stroked her hair, saying nothing.

Not long after, he realized she was asleep. He gently stretched her out on the bed and pulled a cover over her. He sat watching her for the better part of an hour, thinking about what she had told him. Thinking about his own actions.

He didn't know what he thought. That he had succeeded in his mission and become a hero? That he had sold out to pirates—and was now paving the way for them to colonize the stars? That he had fallen for a woman whose existence was so utterly alien that he was an idiot even to dream of a common ground between them? That he didn't care, because he loved her anyway?

He lay awake for a long time; he lay in the near darkness beside Tracy-Ace, wishing he had his old pearlgazers to use as a focus to make sense of it all. Finally he pretended that he was with Deutsch and his gazing crystals, and he carried on a long dialogue with himself on a lighted stage, imagining his implants as silent spectators. He debated the merits of collaboration with the enemy versus fighting versus fleeing, and in the end, as the curtain closed, he fell asleep, exhausted, having decided nothing.

HE WOKE just before Tracy-Ace did. As he was attempting to sort out his blurry morning thoughts, Tracy-Ace sat up abruptly and threw off the covers. "Uh—" he said, still trying to bring last night back into focus "—Trace, you okay?"

She turned her head to gaze down at him, as if she didn't know why he was here. Her augments were flickering madly. She seemed to be light-years away. He sat up beside her. "Ace?"

"Hi," she said. The powerlessness and self-doubt were gone from her voice, but he wasn't sure what had taken their place. Her silver-green eyes were alert but distracted. She seemed to focus on him for a moment. "I have to go," she said, jumping out of bed. "Something I've got to have out with YZ/I. Right now." She glanced down, brushing at the clothes she'd slept in. She grabbed a bottle of juice from the fridge, took a swallow and handed the bottle to Legroeder, then headed for the door.

"Ace, wait!"

"I'll see you la—" And then the door clicked behind her, cutting off her voice.

Legroeder stared silently after her, turning the bottle slowly in his hands.

WHEN SHE hadn't called by lunchtime, Legroeder buzzed her quarters from his own, without success. He put in a general call for her on the intelnet, and got back a brusque message saying that she was in conference, and would he please get his ass to YZ/I's operations center, if he could find it. He presumed the latter was a reference to operations, not his ass, so he headed off to the flicker-tube.

He found YZ/I and Tracy-Ace in the middle of a shouting match. Tracy-Ace was doing most of the shouting; actually, all of the shouting. "You say you want to change things, but you don't have the guts to just up and *do* it, do you?" she yelled, striding back and forth like a pacing wildcat. YZ/I's face showed only a low, emberlike glimmer. "I hear all this goddamn *talk* about shaking things up, but what you mean is you want to shake up just as much as you feel *comfortable* with! You want to be *comfortable* in your virtue, don't you, YZ/I?"

"Hello, Legroeder," said YZ/I, nodding.

"Don't change the goddamn subject!"

"Legroeder's here," YZ/I said, pointing.

Tracy-Ace turned, startled, her temple implants going like crazy. "Legroeder. Hi."

"Hi."

"We were just—" Tracy-Ace shook an exasperated fist at YZ/I.

"So I gathered. Just out of curiosity, may I ask—"

"No," Tracy-Ace snapped.

A flicker of light went up YZ/I's face. "Why not tell him?"

"Tell me what?" Legroeder asked.

YZ/I answered. "That we're inviting some people to leave if they want to, and sending them to Faber Eridani with you. People you might call . . . prisoners."

"What?" Tracy-Ace screamed.

Legroeder looked back and forth between them in confusion.

"You mean you've been planning to do it all along? You lying, devious sonofabitch! You've been toying with me all this time, claiming you can't do it because it would be admitting guilt!"

YZ/I reached out with a hand that didn't quite touch her arm. "Let's say you made a very convincing argument."

She glared at him, temples blazing.

YZ/I shrugged. "I needed you to give me persuasive arguments to use on Lanyard and his crew."

"Fuck Lanyard and his crew!"

YZ/I grinned. "Not for me to do, dear. But I do have to watch my backside. If I'm not careful to justify it, he could make a move against me in the Cabinet. We're not invulnerable, you know."

"You'd annihilate him."

"Maybe. But it would be messy. And it doesn't pay to be overconfident."

Tracy-Ace snarled, "So what justification *are* you using?"

"Why, just what you said. If we want the Centrist Worlds to play ball with us, we need to make a good-faith gesture. And it'll send a signal to our own people that things are changing." YZ/I cocked his head, eyes alight. "You always say these things better than I do. That's one reason I promoted you." He grinned again. "You know, Carlotta bet me I wouldn't do it. I can't wait to hear her reaction."

Tracy-Ace turned to Legroeder. "I cannot believe this."

"Believe it," YZ/I said. "Now, both of you clear out of here and let me do my work, okay?"

As he left with Tracy-Ace, Legroeder said in puzzlement, "I don't get it. Aren't you glad he's doing it?"

"Of *course* I'm glad. But the sonofabitch was *toying* with me. I don't know how he gets away with it, honestly." Tracy-Ace paused in her stride and closed her eyes for a count of three, her lips twitching as she subvocalized. Her eyes popped open again. "I'm going to have to call him on that, sooner or later. Anyway—" she drew a breath and pursed her lips in a frown. "I'm glad we're sending some people home, I'm glad we're pressuring KM/C, I'm glad of all except one thing."

"What's that?"

She turned, her eyes dark. "You're leaving tomorrow."

THEY SPENT most of that day together, and most of it in silence. Or if not silence, then in conversation about matters technical and administrative. How to prepare and organize the *Impris* passengers and crew; how to present the Kyber bargain to the Fabri authorities, and the Narseil authorities.

Dinner was almost as silent; they hardly ate, pushing aside a savory meal ordered specially by YZ/I for them for the occasion. They sat on the edge of Tracy-Ace's bed, looking at the walls, glancing at each other, scarcely touching. Then her hand went out, and his. They clasped tentatively; then hard. He touched her hair, stroked it. They began to kiss.

They made love in a frantic, almost wordless coupling. His implants remained silent; it was just the two of them, undressing each other in awkward haste. There was so much he wanted to say—and he could only say it in whispers and sighs, with his hands on her and their bodies pressing together. Her hands were all over him, drawing out his pent-up fears and his streaming, billowing desires all at the same time; and woven through it were her desires, not through the implants but through sound and scent and touch and murmured half-words. She moaned as he touched her; she didn't want him to leave, now or tomorrow or the next day; he didn't want to leave her at all. Their desire was bubbling over; he was already inside her in a way, but it wasn't enough. He was holding her naked breasts, and her hands were moving on him, and he was breathing so fast he couldn't think.

It was fast and slow, all at the same time. He rose against her, and she pushed back, crying out; and when they came, it was with a cascade of pain and gladness and sorrow. And then they subsided into a tangled heap, whispering and murmuring without saying a word, and yet meaning everything.

SHE STOOD with him as the entire Narseil crew filed past onto *Impris*. They were the last to board, except for Legroeder. "I will come and see you," Tracy-Ace said softly. "When I can."

"How? When?" he murmured. He was having trouble talking, with the lump in his throat.

She looked away. "I can't say, exactly. When I can."

He nodded, but it was hard to believe. Node Alfa of Fortress Ivan, visiting Faber Eridani?

She grabbed his arm suddenly. "Legroeder! I almost forgot! *Rings!*"

"What?"

"That boy—Bobby Mahoney?"

His pulse quickened. "What about him?"

Tracy-Ace had a look of intensity on her face; she was focused inward, on her augments. "A source on DeNoble found a record of the boy being taken from DeNoble to another outpost."

"*Yes?*"

"The trail ended there, from his point of view. But he thought that someone more highly placed might be able to pick it up."

Legroeder frowned. "Which leaves us where? Do you have someone more highly placed?"

"Well—KM/C is pretty highly placed."

Legroeder opened his mouth, closed it. "I thought you guys were practically mortal enemies!"

"Well . . . you'd be surprised how much we can compartmentalize our agreements and disagreements. There's a certain . . . I guess you could call it a code of—" She hesitated.

"What? Honor among thieves?"

Tracy-Ace reddened. "Basically, yes. I mean, a ship here and a ship there . . . it's almost like chips in a board game. That may sound cruel—"

"It *is* cruel."

"Yes, it is. But it's their way. You heard YZ/I talking about a bet he had with KM/C? Well, I've been leaning on him to include finding that boy and giving him his freedom, as part of the payoff when we win."

Legroeder was astounded. "Do you really think there's hope?"

"There's *always* hope."

"Harriet will be very happy to hear that," Legroeder said softly, almost to himself. Cocking his head, he asked, "Do you mind if I ask—what exactly *is* this bet?"

She shrugged, a little smile on her face. "You'll find out soon, I imagine."

"What's *that* supposed to mean?"

"You'll see. Promise."

"Rigger Legroeder," called one of the ship's officers from the hatch. "The captain is ready for departure."

"They need you." Tracy-Ace swallowed, gazing at him.

"I hate this," he said hoarsely.

"I do, too," Tracy-Ace whispered. She leaned into him and kissed him earnestly. "I love you, I think. Good-bye."

Legroeder still felt the pressure of her lips as he turned and boarded *Impris*.

Chapter 38
GOING PUBLIC

THE PURSUIT was getting faster. The Narseil driver, flying low through the suburban streets, had put some distance between the embassy van and their overhead pursuit; but another floater-van, a white one, had appeared out of no-where to their left and was trying to pull alongside them.

"Stay down!" Peter ordered Harriet, before snapping an-other street direction to the Narseil driver.

My God, not again, Harriet thought, recalling the attack on their approach to the McGinnis house. Could these peo-ple know about the McGinnis data? They'd already shown their willingness to kill.

Assistant Ambassador Dendridan had been on the com to the embassy. He leaned forward and spoke to the driver, then said to Harriet, "We're on our own for the next few kilometers. But we've got the edge, eh? I doubt *their* drivers can see into the future. Brace yourself."

An instant later, the restraint-field kicked on as the driver spun the van violently around an acute right turn, thrusters whining. The white van missed the turn, and could be heard, shrieking, trying to avoid other vehicles as it braked. The Narseil driver veered past two ground-cars and rocketed up a ramp onto a high-speed glideway. Before Harriet could catch her breath, they'd hurtled down the next ramp *off* the glideway, then careened around to get back on it, headed in the other direction.

"Carefully," Dendridan cautioned.

"Absolutely," said the driver.

"Hit it," said Peter. As they shot down the expressway, he craned his neck to look skyward for possible attack from above. "Our flyer friend is staying with us. Dendridan, you said they'd pick us up at Third and Park?"

"That's right," Dendridan said calmly. He looked at Harriet, his eyes widening. "Breathe, Mrs. Mahoney."

Harriet gasped; she hadn't realized she'd been holding her breath.

Minutes passed. "About three seconds now," Peter said. They veered suddenly to the left and came down off a ramp into the downtown area. "There they are!" They were abruptly flanked by three green floaters similar to their own van. One cut directly behind them; the other two closed in on either side.

"Yours?" Harriet wheezed.

"Ours," Dendridan murmured. "Now, let's proceed home with all due speed, shall we?"

Peter peered back from the front seat with a crooked Clendornan grin. "I see we have police coming up behind. I wonder if they're here to stop us or protect us."

Harriet glanced back uneasily. She was still technically a fugitive for helping Legroeder jump bail; she didn't want to deal with the police right now. The diplomatic protection was no doubt causing strains in higher echelons; it might have its limits. She turned forward again. "Don't let the police stop us. How much farth—?"

Her question was cut off as the Narseil driver punched in full power, blasting through an intersection where the white van had just reappeared from the right. Peter started to say something, but was drowned out by a scream of thrusters and a sickening *CRUNCH!* Harriet looked back, horrified to see the right-flanking Narseil floater spinning around in the air, twisted together with the white van. "Mother of God," she breathed.

The sight was cut off as their own driver took one last turn, then blazed the final block to the entry gate of the Narseil Embassy. "We're in!" Peter cried, as the embassy gates opened to receive them. He craned his neck to look up, as the pursuing flyer peeled off into the sky.

"Very good," Dendridan said, as the van slowed to a stop in the underground parking garage. "Are you all right, Mrs. Mahoney?"

Harriet let her breath out with a shudder. "I'm fine. But what about your people back there?"

Dendridan was listening to the com. "We have help on the scene. Several of our staff members were hurt—apparently none seriously. I can assure you a protest will be filed. But in the meantime, we are safely back and I think we should get inside as quickly as possible."

Harriet looked out the window, where one of their escort-floaters had followed them into the compound. She sighed in gratitude. "Your people, they know how to provide a rescue squad, don't they?"

Dendridan's face creased in a Narseil smile. "If those people were willing to threaten a diplomatic floater, they must be very frightened of what we can do. Please, Mrs. Mahoney—let us go see how we can help you use this information you have gained."

As THE embassy staff brought in beverages and platters of seafood and fruit, Peter set up equipment to replay the McGinnis-implant reading. "Counselor Corellay gave this reading a confidence level of nine," he explained to high-level embassy officials who had come in to see what the excitement was about. "That means we can use it in court. It carries roughly the weight of a notarized deposition—almost as much as verbal testimony."

"Let's view it," said Dendridan, who had just returned from briefing Ambassador Nantock.

Harriet set aside her cup of tea and took a seat. During

the live reading, she had been absorbing impressions and getting the general picture. This time her lawyer's mind would be running at full speed.

The replay took two hours, with numerous pauses and backtrackings. But when it was done, Harriet's mind was afire with the import of what they had learned. They might not be able to convict anyone solely on the basis of this evidence, but it could be the wedge they needed to crack the whole conspiracy open. If they could get new investigations started, especially in the press, and if other sources could be persuaded that the conspiracy was crumbling and they should talk . . .

Harriet turned to speak to Dendridan and realized for the first time that Ambassador Nantock had joined them. He was an old Narseil, probably El'ken's contemporary. His grey-green scaled face was wrinkled in thought. He inclined his head toward her. "Mrs. Mahoney, I believe you've got some damning evidence here. It could strengthen the Narseil position on several matters that have concerned us for a long time." His gill openings billowed. "Spacing Authority collaboration with Centrist Strength—who openly advocate discord with our people? And possible links to the Kyber pirates?" The Narseil shook his head in amazement.

"Are you going to take an official position on this?" Harriet asked. "Or is there anything in particular you would like *me* to do?"

Ambassador Nantock raised his hands. "We will protest the entire chain of events—and all of the implications that go with it. We may attempt to enlist the help of Secretary General Albright. It is hardly a secret that Commissioner North and others have been pressuring us to give you up into their custody."

"No. Not a secret," Harriet said softly. Gratefully.

"Have no fear, Mrs. Mahoney. If your work is so dangerous to them that they have to resort to sending outlaw groups to stop you—"

"We don't actually have proof yet that there was any

official involvement in that pursuit, Mr. Ambassador," Peter reminded him.

"Perhaps not," said the ambassador. "But we have good holo evidence of the vans that were pursuing you, and we have already linked one of them to Centrist Strength. And one link does tend to lead to another." Ambassador Nantock paused in thought. "If you were to publish your findings on the worldnet—and solicit information from anyone who might be willing to come forward—" he paused again, his neck-sail stiffening "—especially concerning the sale of weapons to Centrist Strength—"

"Then we just might flush the vermin into the light," Peter said.

Harriet nodded, thinking out loud. "Mr. North and his friends must be quite alarmed right now. And if they can be pressured into making a mistake—"

"Exactly," said the ambassador.

THE DETAILED plan took the rest of the day to work out. Rather than posting the entire text of Counselor Corellay's reading for public view, they decided to create a summary, with a request for reply from anyone with direct knowledge of the facts. In addition, they would put up a discussion space for anyone who wanted to comment. By creating massive public awareness of the accusations, they hoped to generate as much pressure as possible on North, the Spacing Authority, and the RiggerGuild to come forward with a response. Harriet generally disapproved, in principle, of prosecution by publicity—and even now she felt a certain uneasiness in taking that route. But her reservations paled in light of the two attempts on her life.

As their preparations neared completion, Peter excused himself to take a call. When he returned, his eyes were lit up like tiny violet lanterns, and he wore a dazzling, crinkly grin on his face.

Harriet looked up from her compad. "What is it? You look like you've seen an angel."

"Almost that good," Peter said. "They have Maris! Morgan and Georgio and Pew. They're on their way back with her right now!"

Harriet whooped in delight. She jumped up and grabbed Peter and danced him in a circle. When she let go of Peter, she turned dizzily to Dendridan. "Do you think we could bring them here? Would you mind?"

"Mind?" said Dendridan. "We'd be delighted. Please send word to your people, and ask if they'd like a diplomatic escort."

Peter laughed. "I can already tell you, the answer is yes. But the way Pew drives, I wouldn't be surprised if they got here before your escort reached them."

Dendridan hissed a chuckle and spoke into his com-unit. "It is on its way," he said with a nod.

"Thank you," Harriet whispered.

"And now," said the Narseil, "weren't you almost ready to make that posting to the net?"

Harriet forced her gaze back to the screen, scanning the work they had done. "Yes," she said softly, and reached out to begin the transmission.

JENKINS TALBOTT poured himself a double shot of lace-bourbon and sat back in front of the com-console in his living room. The news feeds were coming in, and they were damned depressing.

Especially after his dressing down today, with Colonel Paroti and a few others, right there in the Strength offices . . .

". . . *What the hell's the matter with you people? You call yourselves soldiers? Officers? I send you on a few errands, and you can't get even the simplest, most basic things done right!*" It was Ottoson North at his most arrogant—and since the man usually never even let himself be seen or associated with them in any way, you knew he was pissed. *He'd been lighting into one of them after another. Now it was Talbott's turn. "You!" North pointed a finger right at Talbott's face. "You can't grab a comatose woman without getting shot to pieces—and then you come away empty-*

handed? Are you just incompetent, or were you trying *to screw up?"*

"Well, it wasn't quite like that—"

"And you!" North, ignoring Talbott's protests, turned next on Paroti. "I ask you to stop a van— a fucking van! How hard can that be? *And you botched that one, too, even though I told you it was urgent, but you fucked it up, and now I've got this Mahoney bitch spreading lies about me all over the fucking worldnet!"*

"We did our best, Commissioner," Paroti said, his face as red as a beet. "But since we were forbidden to use weapons . . ."

"Excuses! Don't give me excuses," North said in disgust. "Well, now we're knee-deep in shit. Listen, if I need your help, I expect you to be ready to jump when I say jump. Let's see if you morons can do it right, next time."

"Of course, sir," Paroti muttered. "If I might say—"

But North's holoimage had already winked out, leaving Paroti, Talbott, and other loyal Strength officers standing stunned . . .

Humiliated.

Angry.

They didn't deserve this kind of crap.

Talbott squinted, sighing, looking around his living room as if he'd never seen it before. God, what a shithole. Had it always been this bad? Empty food cartons, dirty clothes, and data-cubes everywhere—not quite the military spit and polish. The damned place looked like it was going to seed. But then, so the fuck what? His living room was no one's business.

Talbott was still angry, very angry. And why shouldn't he be? North wasn't even the worst of it. Everything just kept going from bad to worse. His shoulder hurt like christo from the thistlegun wound. *Thistlegun*, for chrissakes! The Fabri dinks! Who'd've expected *them* to butt in? They'd damn near killed him. And though he'd bite off his tongue before he'd admit it in public, he owed his life to Lieutenant Bitch, who'd pulled him to safety.

His pride hurt more than his shoulder, though. All these years he'd worked to get where he was in the org; and just when it was starting to count—they finally had the makings of a decent assault fleet for when the time came to use it—everything just went to shit. Not just his personal pride, either; his pride in Strength, too. They'd failed to grab Maris O'Hare; they'd failed the grab of Harriet Mahoney; and now Mahoney was just warming up with her skewering of Ottoson North, who could spill a hell of a lot more than those yokels on the outside knew. Talbott never did trust the bastard. But if North went down talking, he could take a lot of people with him—Talbott included. He'd managed to keep from being publicly connected with Strength so far (not counting that horseshit a couple years ago about the arms sales, but that had blown over). The heat was on now, though. With Mahoney putting that stuff out on the net, people were coming out of the woodwork to back it up.

Talbott paged grimly through some of the accusations that were making the rounds. Bad stuff. With the vultures of the press on it, Strength could be in some serious trouble. They weren't ready yet to make their move for control of the government—and now it might never happen.

He paused to take a long pull on his lace-bourbon. Shuddering as it went down, he morosely turned the glass in his hand, glaring at the reddish-orange liquid, waiting for the burning to subside. Why the hell did he drink this stuff, anyway? *Because it feels good, once you get over that first belt* . . . He shrugged and took another swallow.

Come to think of it, he reflected through the numbness, North was the cause of a *lot* of Strength's troubles—besides just being a supercilious asshole. No one in command wanted to talk about it, but it was true. Ever since that rigger escaped from Carlotta—and North blew it as far as keeping Legroeder out of trouble—everything had gone to hell in a handcart. Everything the *dedicated* Strength members had been working for, for years and years . . . just slipping away like sand through your fingers.

Christ, look at this stuff on the net . . .

Talbott didn't mind if North himself went down. But somebody was going to have to watch *real close*, to make sure the rest of them didn't go with him.

He drew a deep breath, pulled the keypad into his lap, and began typing instructions to his group leaders. Maybe Command was paralyzed by this—he'd gotten no answers to his questions about what the hell they should be doing to respond—but at least he could get his own crews ready. *". . . Essential to be prepared for any eventuality. If group security is compromised, we must be ready to act independently. All militia units, ground and space, are to be at full state of readiness. This is what we trained for, people . . ."*

When you got right down to it, Talbott reflected, it was possible that someone would have to be prepared to silence North. The thought gave him goose bumps; he didn't like the idea of removing a commanding officer, even one who fucked up this bad. But it might have to be done. And it would take someone who cared more about mission and destiny, and about Centrist Strength, than about his own life.

Jenkins Talbott had never been afraid of sacrifice. That was really what it was all about, right? Damn straight.

He squirted the message and scanned more of the news feeds with growing gloom, and hardening determination.

He took another swallow of lace-bourbon.

Yeah, sacrifice is what it's all about. No guts, no glory . . .

MARIS O'HARE arrived that evening, brought in by Morgan and Peter's men. She looked pretty shaky, and more than a little wary, but Morgan had spent the trip back to Elmira briefing her on what their relationship was to Legroeder— and why they'd had to take refuge in the Narseil embassy. Maris was a dark-haired, muscular woman; but she looked hurt, and walking was obviously an effort. Her face was lined, her neck bandaged, her eyes tired and wary. It was a wonder she was alive at all. She followed the embassy staff to a room where she could rest while they all got acquainted. The rapid appearance of a robodoc and a Narseil physician seemed to reassure her.

"I'm very happy to meet you at last," Harriet said, squeezing her hand as the robodoc began fussing over her. "Legroeder was worried sick about you. He went to see you whenever he could, while you were in the hospital in a coma."

Maris drew a slow breath, clearly making an effort to relax. She looked both bewildered and touched to find herself surrounded by friends; at least, that's how Harriet hoped Maris saw them. Even the tentacled Gos'n and the Swert had solicitously remained nearby. "I've been worried about Legroeder, too," Maris said finally. "Where *is* he?"

Harriet glanced at Morgan. "You didn't tell her?"

"She told me he'd gone off-planet," Maris said. "Looking for information to clear his name."

Morgan smiled ruefully. "I didn't want to hit her with too much at once."

"Too much *what?*" demanded Maris, pushing the robodoc out of the way to sit forward.

Harriet winced a little. "It's complicated. He *did* go off planet looking for information. You see, they were going to throw him in jail here—"

"Morgan told me that."

"Yes. Well, you see—" Harriet swallowed "—he's gone on a somewhat . . . risky . . . mission with the Narseil."

"The Narseil? To do what?"

"To, uh, go back to Golen Space—"

"*What?*"

"—to try to infiltrate a pirate stronghold."

Maris looked as if she might faint. "He went *back to the pirates?*"

"Well, not to the same stronghold—but yes," Harriet muttered, remembering all too well whose advice Legroeder had been following. "It sounds crazy, I know. But it seemed the only way to make good *this* escape. To prove he was innocent of the trumped up charges he was facing here." Harriet shook her head. It sounded utterly mad, now. What could they have been thinking? Her voice trembled as she continued, "That was about eight weeks ago. The last report we had was that they had met and captured a pirate ship, and were going to attempt to penetrate the raider's home port."

"But why?" Maris whispered.

Harriet felt her voice growing heavy. "To try to gain intelligence about the pirates' use of starship *Impris* to prey on shipping. Do you know about *Impris*?"

Maris closed her eyes, nodding, then shaking her head. "I've heard of it, sure. I never knew if it was real, though." She opened her eyes, staring up at Harriet, then glancing at all the others, as though wondering if she had fallen into the hands of yet another group of crazies.

"Oh, it's real," Harriet said. "Maris, dear, there's a *lot* we have to tell you . . ."

THE POSTING on the net had attracted attention at once, both from the news media and the public at large. Peter and Harriet used their connections in the news business to the fullest; stories about the implant reading and the car chase were in the late-night news, and in the morning there were news analyses of the legal status of Level 9 implant interpretations. By noon, the first denials from Commissioner North's office had replayed endlessly, and several news groups had exhumed file holos and data on Centrist Strength and begun a fresh round of investigative reporting.

Harriet found the process at once sobering and exhilarating. It was astounding how fast the press could move in response to a whiff of corruption and vulnerability in high office. And on the net, anecdotal stories poured in. Peter hired additional people to search and sort, trying to separate the wheat from the chaff. It was mostly typical net ranting . . .

****
BREAKER29: If he's guilty, we ought to GET HIM OUTA THERE. I mean, here the guy's RUNNING THE WHOLE FRICKIN' WORLD!
****

JUDYJOHN: Excuse me, could we do with a little less exaggeration? He's not running the world, he's running the Spacing Authority. And all we have is rumors. Are we going to convict somebody on the basis of rumors?

****

CAN-DO: Well, the Spacing Authority is practically the world. I mean, it's the most powerful agency in the world. Shouldn't we have someone there we can trust?

****

SKIPJACK: Trust???? You trust a lawyr whose on the lamb from the law? Give me an f'in' break. . . .

****

Even the talk in North's favor seemed to increase the pressure on him to make a response. The day after Harriet's posting, North issued a strong denial. But he had not yet made a personal appearance.

In the embassy lounge, news reports played nonstop. To Harriet the reports were almost hypnotic . . .

Newscaster: " . . . Joran Philips, live with two professors from the Sota University Policy Institute. Jonathan Dutt is a longtime specialist in political history, and Professor Daniel Marshall has been studying the fringe group Centrist Strength for more than ten years. Gentlemen, what about these accusations against Commissioner North? Is there any substance to them?"

Professor Dutt: "None that I can see. You have to understand, accusations of this sort pop up in any administration. If Ms. Mahoney has some real evidence against the Commissioner, why doesn't she come out and present it in a court of law, instead of hiding behind the Narseil Embassy? Maybe we should be asking what role the Narseil are playing in all this."

Newscaster: "But we have an affidavit, apparently admissible in court, that Commissioner North has been involved in illicit weapons deals with the fringe group Centrist Strength. Don't you think that's something of a bombshell?"

Professor Marshall: "Joran, it sure could be."

Dutt: "*If* they can prove it's true."

Marshall: "Of course. But some of these claims are pretty indicative—including a couple that have surfaced on the net in the last twelve hours, that there may have been more weapons deals. I've been saying for years that there needs to be more accountability. No question, if North *wanted* to make those weapons deals, he could have."

Newscaster: "And if he did? Centrist Strength—for all its rhetoric about building up Faber Eridani—has been rumored to have connections with outlaw worlds of the Kyber alliance."

Dutt: "Rumors! Allegations! Why would North *want* to make deals with Centrist Strength? He's hardly an apologist for them. And he's been a vocal opponent of any rapprochement with the outlaw worlds."

Marshall: "Vocal, yes. But when you look at the people he's appointed to serve in the Spacing Authority, you find no fewer than four known extremist sympathizers."

Dutt: "Well, that's just a gross generalization . . ."

Marshall: "Plus there's evidence that he owes a significant personal debt to Centrist Strength . . ."

****

LIKEMINDED: 'S'not just this one guy, you know. You gotta drill down. He's got people under him, and I wouldn' be surprised if the whole damn place was rotten to the core.

****

HACKWOMAN: If anyone's interested, I've got a list of all the places North contacted by secure channel in the last two years. A friend of mine burrowed in and got some VERY interesting data. Y'know, I wonder if that lawyer lady might like to see it . . .
****

SAMSAM: What is this, a godd*mn lynch mob?
****

TRUTHWILLRULE: Dunno about a lynch mob, but isn't it true what I read, that North had this lover—not a human—I think it was a Delta Aeregian . . .
****

JIM824: Old news . . . years ago . . . died of an incurable neuron fungus.
****

TRUTHWILLRULE: I know it died. But Centrist Strength paid for some kind of experimental treatment, before it died . . . that's what I read, anyhow . . .
****

[Newscaster . . .]

"Here at FaberNews, we're going live with Commissioner Ottoson North in his first public statement since the potentially damning accusations were released. The commissioner is apparently ready to speak now . . ."

[An angry North, in full dress uniform . . .]

" . . . nothing but vicious, unfounded rumor. Let me state flatly that I am completely innocent of *all* the charges that have been slung about. I remind you that not a single accusation has been made where it counts—in a court of law. If anyone has evidence, let them confront me with it in person, instead of this cowardly hiding in a foreign embassy and leaking libelous trash to the net. In fact, I call right now upon the Narseil Embassy to turn Mrs. Mahoney over to the police, and let *her* face the legal charges that stand against her.

"In the meantime, let me assure *all* the citizens of Faber Eridani that I will tolerate no interference in the affairs of this Spacing Authority by any outsider, including and *especially* members of any fringe group or the Kyber alliance."

[Finger stabbing at the camera . . .]

"If they want to interfere in our business, let 'em come and see how we deal with outsiders. Let 'em come—"

*

Harriet froze the screen. For a long time, she stared thoughtfully at that angry, righteous image. Was it intuition, or wishful thinking, on her part? It seemed to her that the longer North protested, the more those angry eyes betrayed the soul of a man with a great deal to hide. . . .

Chapter 39
RETURN TO FABER ERIDANI

IMPRIS EMERGED from the Flux just inside the orbit of Janus, the largest of the gas giants of the Faber Eridani system. Their destination, the planet that shared the name of its sun, lay half a billion kilometers farther in. Legroeder and Deutsch grinned across the net at each other, and Palagren and Ker'sell hooted a Narseil cheer. They left the net together and gathered on the bridge with Captain Friedman and the rest of the *Impris* crew. "Welcome home," Legroeder said to the captain.

"Thank you," Friedman answered softly, his voice trembling with emotion. He gazed silently at the monitors, nodding as the nav officer confirmed the star system and their orbital path. Legroeder could see it on Friedman's face: *Home, at last.* Friedman sighed finally, and broke into a smile. "Thank you for everything," he said to the riggers, extending his gesture to Fre'geel and the other Narseil officers. Solemnly he went around the bridge, shaking hands.

Impris was alone now on the final leg of her return, back in normal-space for the first time since the start of her illfated journey one hundred twenty-four years ago. The Ivan escort had stopped at the edge of Faber Eridani territorial space. The time might come when Free Kyber ships could enter that space freely, but it wasn't here yet.

Legroeder wondered what Captain Friedman and the others were feeling as they approached their home port after a century away. To say that Legroeder himself felt mixed emotions would have been an understatement. His thoughts veered from Tracy-Ace, and a time on Ivan that already seemed a lifetime away, to growing apprehension about his return to Faber Eridani. He presumed he was still a fugitive, and it was possible he was walking right back into captivity. Was it too much to hope that in bringing *Impris* back from limbo he had exonerated himself in the eyes of the law?

Captain Friedman finished logging the ship's status, then turned to the Narseil commander. "If you'd like to contact your colleagues now, you may go ahead and do so."

Fre'geel signaled Cantha, who had been working with Com Officer Tiegs throughout the flight. Cantha placed the call to El'ken's asteroid.

The plan was to report first to El'ken, and through him to the Narseil Naval authorities. Captain Friedman felt that the Narseil should be the first to learn the results of the mission that they had taken the risk of mounting; and while it would undoubtedly annoy the Faber Eri Spacing Authority not to be told first, Legroeder suspected that it might be to his advantage to have the Narseil already behind him.

"On the com now," Cantha reported.

"El'ken!" Fre'geel called.

"Is that you, Fre'geel? Are you really still alive?" said a husky voice from the console. Legroeder was surprised how good it was to hear the voice of the Narseil historian.

"This is Fre'geel—and I have Rigger Legroeder with me, and Palagren, and all of the surviving crew that penetrated raider Outpost Ivan. Have you heard from *H'zzarrelik?* We weren't able to contact them again."

"*H'zzarrelik* returned safely to base," said El'ken. "We knew about your battle with a Kyber ship, and that you were attempting the penetration. But that was the last we heard. What success did you have?"

Fre'geel glanced at Legroeder and cracked an almost human smile. "Better than you can imagine."

"Please elaborate!" El'ken cried, his excitement audible through the com-link. "What ship are you in now? The captured raider?"

"No, not the raider." Fre'geel started to say more, then waved Legroeder over instead. "Would you like to tell him?"

Legroeder laughed and leaned toward to the console. "El'ken, this is Legroeder! Speaking to you from the deck of a legend . . ."

THE CONVERSATION with El'ken was a lengthy one. After bringing El'ken up to date, the Narseil on both ends voiced concerns about whether *Impris*—or for that matter, Legroeder—would be free to continue on from Faber Eridani to the Narseil Rigging Institute. El'ken proposed that Legroeder be picked up by a Narseil diplomatic ship and brought to his asteroid for safety, a suggestion endorsed by Fre'geel. Legroeder was sorely tempted, but in the end he refused. Perhaps he was being stupid; but having come this far with *Impris*, he was determined to bring her the rest of the way home. *Impris* was of Faber Eridani registry and carried nearly four hundred Faber Eri citizens. It seemed unlikely that the ship itself would be in danger, whatever he personally might have to endure. And as for himself, he'd lived under a cloud long enough. It was high time this business was settled.

"Do I still have a lawyer on Faber Eridani?" he asked El'ken.

The historian hesitated, clearly reluctant to give up on his proposal. "Yes, you do," he said finally. "She has been living in our embassy on Faber Eridani, and working diligently on your behalf. She's compiled a sizable brief on the misdeeds of your authorities, in fact. Shall I send her word of your return? I can perhaps send more secure messages from here than you can from a civilian liner."

"Please do," Legroeder answered, thinking with a pang, *Harriet, living in the Narseil embassy? To stay out of jail, on my account?*

"And Rigger Legroeder—" El'ken said, interrupting his thoughts. "You might like to know, you've been cleared in the matter of Robert McGinnis's death. At least you won't have *that* hanging over you."

Legroeder closed his eyes and breathed a silent prayer of thanks.

"Rigger Legroeder? Did you hear me?"

"Yes. *Yes.* Thank you, El'ken. That's very good news." He grunted and straightened up from the console, feeling a sudden lump in his throat. Somehow that last item had brought it all back with a sharp jolt of reality. McGinnis's death, and all the threats that awaited him on Faber Eridani.

Fre'geel spoke a while longer with El'ken, discussing ways they might protect Narseil interests in information gleaned from the rescued starship, including dispatching a Narseil diplomatic ship to follow *Impris* in. Legroeder left them to work that out among themselves. But as *Impris* continued its long fall inward toward Faber Eridani, he felt his anxieties rising. Was he a fool not to have taken the Narseil up on their offer of protection?

Soaring toward the golden-white sun and the planet of Faber Eridani, Legroeder could only imagine how the passengers must be reacting, as they watched the growing image of Faber Eri on their viewscreens. Captain Friedman stood for long periods of time on the bridge with his hands clenched, eyes focused on the growing orb of his ship's home port. Soon they would be calling for a tow to guide them into final planetary orbit.

As they passed the outer markers for inbound starships, Captain Friedman gave the order to contact Approach Control. Com Officer Tiegs made the call. "Outer Orbit Approach, this is Starship *Impris*, Faber Eridani registry Sierra Alfa Niner-Four-Two-Seven-Two, with you at half a million kilometers. Transponder ident active on eight-niner-one Alfa . . ." A newer ship would have made the contact automatically, but they were lucky *Impris*'s com systems were compatible at all.

The reply from Approach Control shocked Legroeder: *"Ship identifying as Impris, Outer Orbit Approach One. Change to vector three-two-seven Tango Charlie and proceed to holding orbit at four hundred thousand kilometers. Do NOT approach any closer to Faber Eridani."*

Tiegs glanced up in surprise. He adjusted the com settings. "Outer Approach, say again?"

The instructions were repeated. *"Any attempt to approach this planet will result in immediate police action . . ."*

THE CAPTAIN summoned his officers to a hurried conference. Legroeder could only admit his surprise and advise the captain to go along with the orders.

They were not alone for long in the holding orbit. Two interplanetary destroyers were approaching at high acceleration. The lead destroyer contacted them with a curt: *"Ship identified as Impris, this is Spacing Authority Destroyer Vigilant. Prepare to be boarded for inspection. You are ordered to shut down all propulsive systems. Any unauthorized maneuvers will be considered hostile and subject to immediate response."*

Legroeder stared at the warships in dismay and disbelief. Was this to be a replay of his first arrival, only worse?

"What the hell is going on?" Captain Friedman asked in bewilderment, with a tinge of anger in his voice. "This is our home planet! Do they think we're an enemy? A threat?"

"They're quarantining us, I think."

"Why? Do they think we have some kind of space disease?"

Legroeder shook his head. "I think this is political, not medical." Were they after *him?* This would be overkill, even if they knew he was aboard. But who knew what might have gone on in his absence? "Captain, I'm worried about who's in charge down there. Given what happened to me last time, I would be . . . reluctant . . . to let them board us way out here, if we can avoid it."

But what could they do? They couldn't fight—though for a moment, he fantasized having his finger on the button of *H'zzarrelik*'s concealed weapons. He shivered. A glance at Agamem, the Narseil weapons officer, suggested that he was not the only one harboring fantasies.

"Got to be a misunderstanding," Friedman muttered. "Tiegs, send our ident again." He paced the deck for a moment, then strode to the com. "This is Captain Noel Friedman of *Impris*. We are Faber Eridani citizens. We have been stranded in space for one hundred and twenty-four years. We are a registered starliner of Faber Eridani, with civilians on board. I demand you explain this treatment."

"We are aware of your claim," answered the destroyer. *"You are being detained under Special Provision, Section 128-d of the Spacing Authority Code, by order of the Commissioner. Match orbit and turn off your space inductors. This is your final warning."*

Friedman muttered orders to the maneuvering crew, then glanced at Legroeder. "Looks as though we're going to be boarded, like it or not."

Legroeder thought furiously. Why the hostility? Confusion, he'd expected—or skepticism. Even caution might be called for—a prudent medical quarantine, perhaps—but that could be done in a far less bellicose fashion. That left one possibility that he could think of: someone in the Spacing Authority didn't want *Impris* coming home. Did they really have that much stake in perpetuating a lie? "Captain, if you can find any way to stall—and see if we can get a signal out onto the worldnet on Faber Eri. Make some kind of broadband announcement of who we are and what's happening . . ." He frowned, wondering if they could somehow reach Harriet.

"Tiegs, did you hear that? Get on it!"

"Captain, I don't know how to tie in—"

Cantha slid into place beside him. "I'll help. I know the Centrist nets."

"Good. Legroeder, do we have any allies on the ground? Any remnant of Golden Star Lines? Any surviving officers? Anyone who might have a legal interest in our return?"

Legroeder rubbed his jaw. "Besides my lawyer, none that I know of. There was chaos after the war, and then a deliberate cover-up. But people still know about you. I think the worldnet is our best bet. Try to get picked up on the news." He pointed to the destroyers moving against the stars, like two sharks in the night. "This far from the planet, that's probably our best protection against our friends out there opening fire and asking questions later."

Fre'geel stepped forward in agitation. "Captain, it was clearly a mistake to come here without advance preparation—but it's not too late to get a message off to our diplomatic ship. And our embassy. They can apply some pressure." Fre'geel shot Legroeder an enigmatic glance. Annoyance, for rejecting El'ken's plan?

"By all means," Friedman said, gesturing to the com. He leaned over Tiegs. "How are you doing on that announcement?"

"Sending a first burst now, Captain. We didn't have time to say anything fancy—"

"We don't need fancy—just get word out that we're here!"

"First announcement away. Cantha, are you ready with the next?—oh hell!—Captain, message from destroyer *Vigilant*."

"Put it on."

"Ship identifying as Impris, you are ordered to cease your transmissions at once—"

Friedman jabbed a finger. "Don't answer. Finish those messages! Fre'geel, have you gotten your messages out yet?"

"I'm sending blind," said the Narseil. "No replies yet."

Friedman reached across Tiegs to open a third channel. *"Vigilant,* this is *Impris.* Say again? Your signal was garbled. Did you say—-?"

"Look out!" cried several of the Narseil at once.

An instant later, there was a flash of blue-green light from the lead destroyer.

"They've *fired* at us!" cried Johnson, on the nav console. His voice held steady. "Tracking now—it's a missile, aimed for our bow!"

"Reverse space inductors!" Friedman shouted. "Sound collision alarms!"

Legroeder grabbed for support as he felt a momentary change in gravity.

The missile billowed into a prolonged, exploding swath as it streaked past the ship's bow, only a few kilometers wide. It had obviously been intended as a warning—but a deadly clear one.

Fre'geel hissed a stream of Narseil epithets. Legroeder didn't say a word; he stared into the monitor, feeling his eyes bulge. Had he brought *Impris* home only to see it destroyed?

The com crackled to life again. *"Ship identifying as Impris, if you do not cease transmissions, the next shot will not miss."*

"They're jamming now," reported Tiegs.

"Cease transmission," said Friedman. "And open my response channel." Friedman raised his voice. "Destroyer *Vigilant,* I remind you that this ship carries several hundred citizens of Faber Eridani. How dare you fire upon us! I hold you responsible for the safety of—"

His voice broke off as a sudden tremor passed through

the deck of the starship, causing Legroeder to grab for another handhold.

"What the hell was that?" Friedman barked.

"There!" cried Johnson, pointing to the long-ranger scanner. "Look at that!" A dozen or more ships were materializing out of the Flux—an entire armada—directly into orbit around Faber Eridani. They were far too close to the planet for safety, and the bridge continued quaking as waves of gravitational disturbance passed through *Impris*.

Legroeder shuddered. If those riggers had miscalculated even a little, those ships could have slammed into the planet's crust like cannon balls.

"Are those people idiots? Who *are* they?" Friedman demanded.

"They're Kyber ships!" Deutsch said. "Look at them!"

Four or five of the ships were almost as close to them now as the two Faber Eri destroyers. They were moving *fast*—and they appeared to be maneuvering to surround *Impris*. But for what purpose? To capture her?

"Whose? Ivan's?" Legroeder asked.

Deutsch was studying the screen. "I don't think so. I'm not sure, but—"

He was interrupted by a yell from Tiegs. "Captain, they're sending a warning to the destroyers to keep their distance!"

"Well, that's good—I think. Isn't it?"

"I'm not sure—wait." Tiegs made some adjustments to the display, trying to make sense of a barrage of incoming information. "Listen to this. It's coming from that fleet. Going out on regular com, but also onto the worldnet!"

A metallic-sounding voice filled the bridge, apparently coming from one of the Kyber ships. "*. . . here to guarantee starship Impris's safe passage home. We are Kilo-Mike/Carlotta, of the Free Kyber Republics. We're not here to bother anyone, as long as you let this ship through to her home port—now. It is carrying—*" the voice hesitated, as though fumbling through a script "*—information vital to* *riggers of all worlds. Any interference with Impris could have dire consequences ..."*

There was more of that, followed by a challenge from the Faber Eridani destroyers. In response, the Kyber ship repeated its intention to guarantee *Impris*'s unimpeded passage.

On the *Impris* bridge, they listened to the exchange in stunned silence. This was altogether too bizarre. Legroeder felt as if events were slipping entirely out of his control.

"Captain!" Tiegs called. "We're picking up some response on the worldnet! A lot of it. A whole series of . . . what did you call them, Cantha?"

"Response trees," said the Narseil. "People are picking up on it—amazingly fast, and in large numbers. A lot of them seem to want to know if we're who we say we are." He put a rapidly scrolling stream of messages up on one of the com-screens. "*And* the news nets are starting to pick up the story. Captain, we're becoming news all over the planet!" He touched another control, and on a second screen, multiple frames showed talking heads chattering excitedly. One, and then others, switched to high-powered telescope images of the spaceships.

"Do they know about the Kyber fleet, too?" Friedman asked.

"Yes—but I'm not sure anyone knows what to *make* of it. There seems to be a lot of confusion."

"Well, *I'm* certainly confused," Friedman said. He turned to Legroeder. "How much do they know about the Kyber on Faber Eridani?"

Legroeder opened his mouth and closed it. "Well . . . they know about the old Kyber worlds. But the Free Kyber Republic is just a fancy name for what they'd call the Golen Space pirates."

Friedman frowned, perhaps reflecting on the nature of their recent stopover at Ivan. "Then these people . . . no . . ." He shook his head, and just watched and listened for a while.

Legroeder, looking over Tiegs' shoulder, tried to follow

the worldnet display erupting in a streaming chaos of instant messages. Did they have any filtering software that could help them make sense of this?

Before he could ask, the Kyber captain's voice intruded again. *"We're making this port call for another reason, as well. Commissioner North of the Spacing Authority—are you listening? Our captain has a message for you."*

Commissioner North! Legroeder remembered YZ/I's comments about Carlotta's tentacles extending deep into Eridani affairs. Did they reach as high as the Spacing Authority Commissioner?

Apparently North *was* listening. After a brief delay, a voice responded on another thread: *"This is Commissioner North. I don't know you, but if you are indeed of the so-called Free Kyber, then this commissioner has just one thing to say to you: Turn your fleet around and get out of our solar system at once."* A visual image flickered onto one of the screens. It was North, glaring into a camera, with what looked like a control center in the background. *"We will tolerate no interference from pirates of Golen Space."*

The channel switched back to the Kyber transmission, catching a different speaker in a laugh. A visual snapped on of a heavyset male, encrusted with augmentation, including a metal ring around his skull. *"This is Captain Arden of KM/C Farhawk. Our fleet will be staying just a little longer, thank you. Hello, Ottoson—it's good to see you again. It's been too long, hasn't it?"*

North's eyes blinked in dismay. Or was it recognition? Whatever the emotion was, it vanished beneath a mantle of unmistakable anger. *"Do not assume familiarity with me, Kyber—"*

His transmission was stepped on by the Kyber's. *"Commissioner North—no need to apologize for our past history. This seems as good a time as any to thank you for your excellent work on behalf of Kilo-Mike/Carlotta and the Free Kyber Republic."*

Legroeder exchanged glances with his shipmates as

North's voice strained unsuccessfully to penetrate the static created by the Kyber transmission.

The Kyber voice rose. *"Citizens of Eridani, this is Captain Arden of the Kyber fleet, here to safeguard starship Impris. We mean no threat to your world. But it is time you were told: Commissioner North has been assisting us for years, with skill and devotion. Please do not blame him. His diversion of resources to our fleet has been in answer to a higher calling—reaching out to the stars, for all of humanity. We assure you, what little it has cost you will be more than offset by the gains yet to come."*

North's voice was barely audible, his transmission hissing through the jamming. *". . . enough lies, you are trespassing and threatening our territory. Your presence here is an act of war."*

"Come now, Commissioner . . ."

Cantha murmured, above the confusion, "We're picking up some other official transmissions here. Your Secretary General Albright has issued a plea for calm . . ." Cantha touched a switch, and in one corner of the main viewscreen, a heavyset, bearded man was speaking in front of the emblem of the Faber Eridani world government. Cantha started to raise the audio on that, but Captain Friedman waved it off; the Kyber captain was speaking again.

"Commissioner, you and your colleagues in the Rigger-Guild performed beautifully in keeping Impris protected for us—and her history hidden, while that was necessary. We regret that you, or perhaps some of your people, became overzealous and threatened the life of Rigger Legroeder. That was never our intention—"

Legroeder frowned. It was getting harder and harder to sort out the lies, here . . .

*"Fortunately Rigger Legroeder escaped, and has since acquitted himself with great courage in the rescue of Impris. Commissioner, there is no need for you to threaten Impris. These are returning heroes—*your *heroes, citizens of your world. We all have an interest in learning why she suffered the terrible fate that she did."*

The Kyber captain's face was now on many of the news channels, as the direct transmission was fed through the nets to the entire planet. *"Good people of Faber Eridani—the safety of Impris is of paramount importance to us. Your rigger scientists will no doubt want to examine her. But we also ask that she be made available to—"* and was it Legroeder's imagination or did the Kyber choke a little *"—the Narseil Rigging Institute. The Narseil played a great role in her rescue, and they have a role to play yet in unlocking her secrets."*

That's it, Legroeder thought. KM/C knows their operations are on the skids here, so they're cutting their losses. They can't seem like enemies, or they'll be cut out of the findings from the mission. How long do they think they can play the innocent?

"We also request—insist upon!—safe passage for Rigger Legroeder, whose role will be no less important . . ."

Legroeder was aware of all eyes on the bridge turning to him. He pressed his lips together grimly.

On the com-console, messages streaming from the world-net had become a blur, impossible to follow with the eye. Tiegs increased the number of frames on the viewscreen, until it was filled with an array of tiny faces of excited newscasters, all talking about the confrontation in space. Cantha glanced over from his attempt to filter the message stream and remarked, with wry Narseil humor, "I believe the planet knows about you now, my friend. Are you ready to fulfill your destiny?"

Legroeder grimaced.

Cantha hissed a Narseil chuckle. "I'm making some progress here. Your computer was good in its time, Captain. But the newsnets are ahead of us. Here's one analysis of worldnet opinion . . ." On the main screen, a large frame showed a graphic representation of worldnet message streams, branching and growing with the live public debate. "The largest stream there represents people who want *Impris* brought in safely. It overlaps with people claiming Commissioner North is a Kyber collaborator. And *that's* about the same size as the stream supporting him . . ."

Captain Friedman squinted at the display. "What's that big band smearing across the whole frame?"

Cantha hummed. "There you have the people who are— what is the term?—scared witless about an invasion fleet in their—"

"Reply coming from North," Tiegs interrupted.

"*. . . these ridiculous claims! If you came to provoke a confrontation, we'll give you one. We hold you completely responsible for any harm that may come to Impris, or any other—*"

His signal again disappeared under the hiss of the stronger Kyber transmission.

"*Commissioner—we mean no harm to Impris or anyone else. In fact, we have an offer to make. We invite you to come personally to our flagship for a conference, a parlay. We have worked together before; there is no reason for threats and posturing. Let us put mistakes of the past behind us.*"

A break in the static. "*The mistakes are yours, Kyber—*"

"*We feel, in light of your past service to our cause, that we owe you a place here with us . . .*"

From the North channel there was only silence.

Freem'n Deutsch floated close to Legroeder. "Was North really working for KM/C the way they're claiming?"

Legroeder closed his eyes, thinking about the conspiracy against him. Had that been orchestrated from the very top, by North—at the behest of KM/C? How many others were involved, and how long would it take to flush them out?

The Kyber captain concluded, "*. . . if you accept our offer, notify us when your ship has reached orbit. We will escort Impris inward, and meet you for safe transit in low orbit. For the sake of peace, we urge you to accept. Far-hawk out.*"

Captain Friedman glanced at Tiegs. "Any official reaction?"

Tiegs shook his head. "Nothing from the world government yet. But listen to this news commentary . . ."

One of the frames containing a talking head was magnified, and a newscaster's voice came up. ". . . Analysts have been comparing the Kyber statements with evidence released last week by attorney Harriet Mahoney. And they're finding some startling points of agreement."

Legroeder stood open mouthed. *Harriet Mahoney?*

On the main display, the Spacing Authority destroyers were edging away from *Impris* as several of the Kyber ships completed their protective gauntlet around the starliner.

"Impris, this is KM/C Kyber Farhawk. Are you able to make normal-space headway?"

Friedman answered, *"Farhawk, Impris.* Affirmative— though we were about to request a tow for final approach."

"Well, follow us on in. We'll see if anyone wants to screw with us. All right?"

Friedman's eyes closed to slits as he contemplated this turn of events. He was clearly thinking, Do I want to fall in with a KM/C fleet? Do I have a choice? Friedman said to Tiegs, "Get me the Spacing Authority ships." When Tiegs nodded, he said, *"Vigilant,* this is *Impris.* Do you intend to interfere with our movement?"

There was a long pause before the destroyer replied, *"Impris, you are cleared to establish a one-thousand kilometer orbit."*

Captain Friedman's eyebrows went up, as the two Spacing Authority destroyers began to accelerate away from them, toward the large, blue-and-white orb of Faber Eridani.

As THEY moved inward with the Kyber ships, Legroeder had for a time the surreal feeling that all spacing activities around the planet had simply frozen in a state of panic. Planetary defenses were at a state of high alert, monitoring the approaching fleet. Ships moved in their orbits, of course, but most ordinary departures and arrivals had been put on hold as traffic control waited to see if hostilities would erupt. From Spacing Commissioner North, there had been no further word.

Cantha continued to monitor net transmissions. According to the news channels, messages on the public net were coming in at a rate of half a million a minute, and were deeply divided between fear of the Kyber fleet and ambivalence over North. "Everyone's wondering what the World Protectorate and the secretary general will have to say," Cantha observed. So far, there had been no further official statement.

Captain Friedman, pacing nervously between the com station and the nav and helm who were flying formation with the Kyber ships, seemed to be working himself up to a dangerous level of tension. Finally he stopped and cried out, "Would someone, for God's sake—" and he hesitated a moment, as everyone stared at him in alarm.

"Sir?" said crewman Fenzy.

"—*please* go and get us all some coffee?"

"Yes, *sir.*"

"And sandwiches. Call the galley for some sandwiches."

The tray of food arrived just as Cantha called out, "Legroeder! We've reached your friend Harriet—at the Narseil Embassy!"

"Harriet!" Legroeder cried, practically throwing himself onto the com-console. "Can you hear me?"

"Legroeder—is that you? You're really there, with Impris? My God, I can't believe it!"

"It's really me. Have you been following what's happening?"

"Yes, of course! Good Lord, Legroeder, what sort of a ploy are these Kyber up to?"

"I wish I knew. What's this about your releasing evidence on North? Is it true, what the Kyber captain said about him?"

"Quite true. We have not been Mr. North's favorite people lately. Robert McGinnis left a breathtaking record of Kyber meddling, and of North's complicity. I'm not sure I understand why this Kyber captain is proclaiming it, as if he ought to get credit."

"I can probably explain that, but it's—"

"Wait a minute, something new's coming over the net. From the secretary general . . ."

"Here it is," Tiegs interrupted, and put it on the main screen.

A voiceover was saying, ". . . statement from Secretary General William Albright."

The bearded world leader was standing at a podium, and speaking with a drawn face. ". . . to announce that I have relieved Spacing Commissioner North of his duties, without prejudice, pending a full investigation. I am naming Deputy Commissioner Ahmed to the position of Acting Commissioner, and am instructing him to take all proper precautions in dealing with the incoming fleet of ships . . ."

"Whoa," said Tiegs, lowering the audio slightly. "This is coming in at the same time." Two large frames appeared in the main screen, one showing the secretary general, and the other North. The latter appeared to be outside now, standing with an aide next to an aircar. The Spacing Authority headquarters were visible behind him.

North was hemmed in by a crowd of newscasters. "—I'll not comment on the secretary general's statement—"

"Commissioner North—"

"No comment."

"But Commissioner—"

"Whatever I have to say to Mr. Albright, I'll say to his face."

"Commissioner North!" a newscaster shouted. "What about the claims of the Kyber captain—"

"Reckless fabrications!" North snapped. "I have ordered our forces to full alert." North edged toward the car as his aide attempted to force an opening.

The newscasters yielded only reluctantly, with shouts of: "But the Kyber say—" "What about the accusations—?"

"No comment!"

The camera view moved up jerkily, practically into North's face. A rapid-fire voice asked, "Commissioner, the accusations of the Kyber captain seem consistent with those brought by Attorney Mahoney—"

Something in North's gaze seemed to snap at the sound of Mahoney's name. He stabbed an angry finger into the camera lens. "You mean, *ex*-attorney Mahoney. If you want to investigate something, investigate how a fugitive hiding out in an alien embassy can put out this kind of trash and get away with it. You're all so bent on crucifying Centrist Strength, which is only trying to *make* something of this world, when you *could* be exposing criminals. Well, if I have anything to do with it, we'll be making an example of Ms. Mahoney, very soon. Now, if you'll excuse me, I have an important conference to get to." He snapped inaudibly at his aide, who was trying to maneuver him into the car. Pressed by reporters, North swung his elbows to make room.

As the reporters fell back, one shouted, "What about Mrs. Mahoney's standing and reputation—?"

"Commissioner!" shouted another. "Who are you going to confer with? Are you going to see the secretary general?"

The car door slammed and the vehicle came to life with a thunderous whine. As journalists scattered back in alarm, a reporter turned into the camera and said, "That's Commissioner North's statement."

In the other frame, Secretary General Albright was stepping away from his podium, ignoring his own cacophony of shouted questions.

Legroeder leaned over the com. "Did you hear those announcements, Harriet?"

"Yes, I did, and I—just a moment. Legroeder, let me get right back to you. I have so much to ask you."

Legroeder nodded and stared with balled fists at the still-talking newscasters.

HARRIET TURNED to Peter, who was plugged into the net monitor. His top-heavy head was tilted in thought, a crinkled smile on his face. "What are you thinking, Peter? Is it time to lean on our friend the A. G.?" They now had the McGinnis report, plus the Kyber captain's accusations, plus new allegations that had come in of armed Centrist Strength ships harbored in Elmira. The release on the worldnet, and investigative journalism in response, had turned up a raft of new information.

"More than time," Peter said.

Harriet turned back to her console. "All right, we're cued up to send." It wasn't as if the attorney general didn't have the information already—they'd been passing it to him as it came in—but so far he'd resisted taking action. Not enough evidence, he said. He'd known Harriet for years, and professed the greatest respect for her—but claims from an acknowledged fugitive required extraordinary evidence. Well, if he didn't call this extraordinary . . .

She pressed SEND.

After a count of five, she said, "You handle the press release, Peter." Then she keyed the voice-com. "Attorney General Dulley, please. Harriet Mahoney. I'll wait . . . yes . . . thank you. Frank? Harriet Mahoney. Yes, I have been. Mr. Attorney General, you've got a large packet sitting in your in-box, and I strongly recommend that you give it your *immediate* attention. The citizens are counting on you, Frank . . ."

Chapter 40
POWER PLAY

URGENT . . . PROCEED at once to spaceport hangar . . . urgent . . .

Major Talbott had gotten the call on his personal com while en route to a strategy meeting. It wasn't a secure line, so he had to wait until he got there to hear the rest. He'd changed course at once and made a beeline to the launch control center in the basement of Centrist Strength's east ramp hangar. On his way to the spaceport, he'd glimpsed a Spacing Authority patrol ship lifting under emergency thrust from the main field. What the hell was *that* all about? And in the Strength hangar, there was furious activity around one of the pursuit craft. *Arming weapons.* "What's going on?" he called, striding into the control center. The sound of his voice hurt his head; too much lace-bourbon last night.

Jerry the tech looked up. "Haven't you been following the news?"

Of course he'd been following. One disaster after another. What the hell was going *on* out there in orbit? Carlotta's people were blowing the whole thing open. Had they decided North was more of a liability than an asset? Were they getting ready to betray Centrist Strength, too?

"I've been out of touch for a few minutes. Anything new on North?"

The tech laughed. "You could say so. He headed off for a 'conference'—only instead of going to see the SecGen, he shook the press and came to the spaceport."

"And then?" Talbott prompted impatiently. He dropped into a seat and slapped his hand down on the DNA-reader to release the coded message waiting for him. "What did he do?"

"Took off in a police cruiser. No flight plan. They're halfway to orbit now, and Spacing Authority is going nuts."

Talbott grunted and hooded himself to the screen. The message flared up; it was from Kyber Command Contact. This was serious indeed; the Kyber liaison would not contact him directly unless drastic action was needed.

"Talbott!" someone shouted from across the room. "*Red Knight*'s ready to launch. Are you taking command?"

He read quickly, not answering.

"*. . . launch fastest available pursuit craft. Code Blue. Acknowledge at once.*"

Talbott drew a deep breath. Code Blue. That was what he'd been preparing for. Command was not deserting them, after all. He turned and shouted, "Get the crew aboard! We launch *now!*"

* * *

LEGROEDER WAS blowing on a cup of hot coffee when a shout brought his attention back to the newscast on the main screen.

"—major evidence just filed with Attorney General Dulley by Harriet Mahoney reportedly confirms claims made by the Kyber captain about Spacing Commissioner North. The commissioner's whereabouts have been unknown since shortly after he was relieved of duties by Secretary General Albright—though reports have come in of a mysterious launch at Elmira Spaceport. North last spoke to the press as he was leaving Spacing Authority headquarters for what he described as a high-level conference. Speculation has been rife about the possible nature of that conference, some believing it to be with the secretary general . . ."

Legroeder blew a kiss at the console. "Love you, Harriet!"

Captain Friedman, standing behind him, murmured, "Rigger Legroeder, you certainly have brought us back to interesting times."

Legroeder nodded. "Haven't I just?"

Some time later, Nav Officer Johnson reported a course change by the Spacing Authority destroyers.

"What are they doing?" Friedman asked.

"I'm not sure."

"Captain," Tiegs said, "there's a report of a high-speed ship making orbit from Elmira spaceport. A small one."

"So?"

"Apparently Commissioner North is aboard. Wait—here it is." A news loop displayed an image of a small vessel streaking into the sky above the spaceport. It was not assisted by a tow, which meant that it was most likely military or police. A voiceover was now giving it a tentative identification as a Spacing Authority police cruiser commandeered by North.

Good God, Legroeder thought.

"Can we see it?" Friedman demanded, as the main screen switched back to the outside view. *Impris* was presently at two thousand kilometers, and moving inward. The globe of the planet was much larger now, its horizon a gentle curve across the viewscreen.

"Not yet, sir," said Johnson. "But it should be coming over the horizon soon. The two destroyers are moving to intercept, I think. Maybe to protect it?"

"Captain, Cantha's picked up some of the military com-chatter off the net," Tiegs said. "Someone's decoded the secure freqs and they're rebroadcasting it!" Tiegs was chortling as he switched on the audio.

A voice that Legroeder recognized as North's came through, slightly distorted. *"Vigilant, I am en route to an emergency parlay with the intruders. I require you to deploy your ships to ensure my safe passage. This is a top security mission . . ."*

The signal broke up; then another voice replied: *"Commissioner North, we have no authorization for your flight. Technically, you are no longer in command. If we can obtain confirmation—"*

There was a hiss, as if the commissioner were stepping on their transmission. Then his voice again. *". . . no time, there is no time. These Kyber are treacherous. If you permit Impris to dock, there may be very serious consequences. Time is of the essence . . ."*

Freem'n Deutsch floated alongside Legroeder. "Is he making this up as he goes? Why's he trying to keep us from docking?"

Legroeder shook his head helplessly. Was North just scared now, scared and running to Carlotta, and trying to distract everyone in the meantime? Legroeder felt a growing sense of unreality. Too many incomprehensible actions . . .

"Captain, a call coming in from the Kyber," said Tiegs. Friedman frowned, as the Kyber captain's face appeared in a small frame at the corner of the screen.

"Impris, this is Arden of Farhawk. We've received an interesting proposal from Commissioner North. He says he can make new arrangements for your ship. If we escort you directly to the Narseil Rigging Institute, we can avoid a

great deal of entanglement here. We are contacting the Narseil directly to confirm this arrangement. In the meantime, prepare for a course change . . ."

Legroeder drew a breath, his blood suddenly cold. If KM/C had a chance to hijack *Impris*, he didn't doubt they would take it. Who would there be to stop them, if they left the Faber Eri system? "Captain, no—" he whispered "—don't do it."

Friedman was already scowling over the com board. "Get me that Narseil diplomat ship," he snapped to Tiegs. Cantha stirred uneasily at the com-console, while at the back of the bridge, Fre'geel was looking increasingly alert. "Narseil courier," Friedman barked. "Have you received any messages from Commissioner North or the Kyber ship? Please respond."

Fre'geel was moving forward, toward Captain Friedman.

There was a long delay. Then a reply from the Narseil ship: *"This is Narseil Diplomat Vessel Essling. We have received messages from both parties. Although the Narseil government has no wish to be a party to hostilities in any form, we do guarantee shelter and asylum, if you choose to bring your vessel to our Rigging Institute."*

Captain Friedman cleared his throat. "Are you saying that you intend to cooperate with North and the Kyber ship?"

"We will cooperate with whatever action provides your ship the greatest protection and security."

Cleverly put, Legroeder thought. Especially since the Faber Eri authorities had hardly been welcoming. He felt his throat tighten. Were the Narseil about to have a change of heart here, to get *Impris* sooner? Legroeder glanced at Fre'geel, whose neck-sail was quivering. The Narseil commander seemed ready for the possibility; he was avoiding Legroeder's gaze. Legroeder frowned and edged toward Freem'n Deutsch. Freem'n met his eyes with a steady, glowing gaze.

"What's that?" asked Friedman, pointing. "Is that North's ship, coming over the horizon?" On the screen, a point of light was moving just above the delicate boundary line between the planet's atmosphere and the black of space.

"That's him," said Johnson. "He's not the only one, though. There's another ship following him up. I wonder who that is."

Tiegs interjected, "A second ship took off from Elmira, shortly after North. Unauthorized and identified as belonging to something called Centrist Strength. What the hell does *that* mean? Are they pursuing him?"

In the left-hand frame of the screen was a magnified view of the two Spacing Authority warships that earlier had been threatening *Impris*. Their space inductors blazed as they accelerated on an intercept course. Were they moving to help the commissioner's ship or hinder it? This, Legroeder thought, could very quickly get out of control.

Cantha switched an audio channel, and appeared to be picking up an eavesdropped, rebroadcast military frequency.

"—is Commissioner North the only one aboard the launch?"

"—negative—pilot, and traveling with one aide—Berkhauer—"

"Do we have any confirmation from HQ?"

"Negative. He may be acting on his own."

There was a sound of muttered imprecations. Then: "All right. We'd better give him some protection. But let's see if we can slow up his rendezvous a little, until we get word from command."

"Aye, aye."

"Whoops," said Johnson, and Legroeder looked up as four ships of the Kyber fleet abruptly shot out ahead of the formation, streaking inward as though to join the impending fray. Was everybody trying to get to North first? Was *Farhawk* really hoping to make a deal with him?

"Here's a different thread," said Cantha.

A scratchy hiss, then: "I must meet with them alone, Vigilant. Repeat, there may be jeopardy to Impris if I cannot conclude this parlay successfully. Please keep your ships at a distance to avoid inflaming the situation . . ."

Hiss.

"Commissioner North—this is Captain Sanspach of Vigilant. We have no verification of your authority for this mission. Please stabilize your orbit until we receive confirmation."

The commissioner's voice was edged with desperation. *"You don't understand. There may be an attack from other Kyber forces if I don't meet with this fleet. Break off your approach and let me proceed."*

Sanspach sounded skeptical. *"Commissioner, can you identify the ship following you? We have information that it is registered to Centrist Strength."*

"Do not—repeat, do NOT—allow that ship to approach! I am uncertain of its purpose!"

"But Commissioner—" Sanspach paused, then muttered, *"Damn—!"* before cutting his transmission.

For two long minutes, there was near-silence on the bridge of *Impris* as everyone watched the movements of the ships. The Kyber ships were hurtling toward a possible rendezvous, but the two Spacing Authority destroyers were closer. And the Centrist Strength ship was closer still, and gaining . . .

A new transmission came in on a tight beam from the Kyber commander. *"This is Kyber Farhawk. Impris, you are to lay in the following course and prepare to boost out of orbit as soon as negotiations are complete."* A series of instructions followed.

"No!" Legroeder shouted.

Friedman looked defeated. "They have the weapons, Rigger. I can't refuse, if they order us."

"No, you must not resist," Commander Fre'geel said in a soft hiss.

Legroeder hesitated. The Narseil were desperately eager to get *Impris*—and him—to their institute. Would they be willing to abduct him and the passengers and crew of *Impris* to do it? They owed no allegiance to Faber Eridani. But how about him? Did they owe it to him? He glanced at Cantha and saw a torn expression. Shit. If only he had a weapon.

To do what with?

Deutsch floated closer, almost protectively. Legroeder blinked. He leaned into Deutsch and whispered into his friend's ear. A moment later, Deutsch's telescoping arm shot out with blinding speed and put something in Legroeder's hand. He gripped it before his eyes had a chance to focus on it.

A tiny neutraser pistol, a one-shot. Legroeder snapped it up into view, for all to see. "Listen to me, people—"

Fre'geel's eyes narrowed.

"Rigger Legroeder, what are you doing?" Friedman protested. "Raising a weapon against friends?"

"No," Legroeder said, and drew a sharp breath. He raised the gun and placed its muzzle to his own head. To the slight bump of the implant in his temple. "Not against friends."

Fre'geel let out a low hiss.

"All right? Back me up, Freem'n." Keeping the gun to his head, Legroeder stepped forward so that all on the bridge could see him, and to let the captain of the Kyber ship see him on the monitor. "You all get it? This ship does not leave Faber Eri orbit. If it does, it goes without the information you all want so badly. Captain Arden, I suggest you back off and forget that little change of plans of yours. And Fre'geel?" He faced the Narseil commander. "Do you wish to say something to the good Captain Arden?"

He had never seen a Narseil's eyes shrink so narrow.

TALBOTT'S FACE held a grim expression as *Red Knight* streaked into space, but his heart was racing. Somehow he had known that it would fall to him, in the end, to stop the former Spacing Commissioner. At last he was *doing something* instead of waiting, always waiting—this was why he had joined Centrist Strength—to act, and to make a difference.

They would make a difference, all right. The three of them—Talbott, his pilot Hanson, his weapons officer Manny. They would make clear that you do not kick sand in the eyes of Centrist Strength. And they would do it not just on behalf of Strength, but of all the people of this world who believed in the *destiny,* in the *future.*

One of their own leaders had fallen away, and it was the task of *Red Knight* to bring him in. To stop a disaster from happening. Ottoson North, fleeing like a jackrabbit when the going got tough, and risking the security of all they had worked for.

The planetary horizon had spread out in a round arc beneath them, glowing against the eternal black of space. "How long to weapons lock?"

Manny replied, "Long shot, in about four minutes. Tighter shot, and more options, about seven. Major, I'm picking up a couple of destroyers moving toward intercept. Must be *Vigilant* and *Forte.*"

"Message coming in from them now," Talbott muttered, adjusting the com.

"Vigilant to unidentified Centrist Strength vessel. Discontinue your pursuit at once. Repeat—call off your pursuit. We warn you not to interfere with Spacing Authority business."

Talbott didn't answer, but snorted as he punched up a secure transmission to Command. Text only—not as classy as what the Authority used, maybe, but more secure. He sent: *Range in four to seven minutes. Have received a warning from Authority destroyers. Estimate they will be a factor in six minutes. Awaiting final instructions.*

As he waited for a response, he watched Faber Eridani turn beautifully beneath them. They were still in high acceleration, their space inductors pulling them around the planet in a guided path at about twice standard orbital velocity. If their power shut down, they'd fly off into space like a stone from a sling.

"What's the word, Major?" Hanson asked, eyes glued to the controls.

"Coming now." Talbott held his breath as their orders scrolled across.

Code Blue confirmed. Take your prey, and good hunting.

Talbott's voice caught. He'd trained for this for years,

but he'd never actually been in ship-to-ship combat. It was time to prove his mettle. Those two Authority destroyers weren't going to play games. Should he say something to his crew?

He drew a breath. *Sacrifice is the name of the game,* he whispered silently. *No guts, no glory.* He glanced left, right. His voice was gravel. "You know what we're here for. They're going to try to stop us. Let's go get the job done."

FOR A long moment, no one on the *Impris* bridge spoke, or even seemed to breathe. Then Fre'geel, stiffly, moved toward the screen. "Captain of the Kyber. I must inform you that the Narseil Navy—" he hesitated, just a heartbeat "—stands in support of our colleague Rigger Legroeder. We cannot cooperate with the coerced removal of *Impris* from her home system." He looked back at Legroeder, his eyes drawn with tension.

The Kyber captain spoke forcefully. "You *must* cooperate . . . and you will . . ."

"And what?" answered Fre'geel. "Bring back a dead man, with dead implants? Will that advance your cause?"

The first hint of uncertainty entered the Kyber commander's voice. "You may regret not taking this opportunity."

"I'll regret it more," Fre'geel said flatly, "if Rigger Legroeder pulls that trigger."

Legroeder strained to keep his hand from shaking. "Captain Friedman," he murmured to the horrified *Impris* skipper, "I'm sorry to have to do it this way. But if you went with the KM/C fleet . . . I'm not sure you would ever reach the Narseil Institute. These are pirates, the same ones who tried to destroy you *and* us, once before."

"Skipper," Tiegs said urgently, "there's an awful lot of coded com activity among the Kyber ships. I can't read any of it, but there's some heavy-duty discussion going on."

Friedman squinted, and suddenly pointed to the center of the screen. "What's *that?*" Seven ships were converging on

North's launch from above, in front, and behind. The pursuing ship was closest, and gaining rapidly.

"North's ship has increased power," Johnson said. "He's trying to get away from the Centrist Strength ship and join up with—*oh my God,* what are they doing?"

There were several flickers of light on the screens.

"What's happening?" Friedman snapped.

Johnson worked frantically at the controls. The image on the screen shifted left and right, then snapped to a higher magnification. "It's weapons fire! Centrist Strength has fired a missile at North! Now one of the destroyers is firing at the Centrist—"

Blast of static, then North's voice: *"Stop! What are you—?"*

North's words were cut off as a burst of white light ballooned out like a small sun on the near side of the planetary horizon. It was followed by a second, more distant sunburst.

Legroeder, stunned, had to struggle to keep the neutraser to his head. Cold, hard metal against his temple.

"Mother of—"

"Johnson, was that what I think it was?"

"Yeah, Captain. It was North's launch. They blew him. The Centrist Strength ship blew him." The nav officer looked up, dazed. "He's smoke, Captain. And so is the Centrist."

Friedman whispered, "This Centrist Strength blew him to keep him from going to the Kyber?"

The com crackled. *"Terrible, terrible,"* said the Kyber captain, on a public channel. *"This violence was totally unnecessary. We came here in the hope of preventing such tragedies."*

"No," Legroeder said, with sudden understanding. "The Centrist Strength ship *was* Kyber—they were *all* KM/C agents."

"KM/C wanted North dead, so he wouldn't talk," said Deutsch. They were just baiting him to get him up here. Right, Legroeder? And then they let Spacing Authority take care of his killers, so *they* wouldn't talk. They sacrificed their own agents to conceal the extent of their complicity. They're determined to look clean." Deutsch turned slowly to Legroeder. "My friend, I think you can lower that gun now. I don't think they'll take you by force."

No one on the bridge spoke, as Legroeder stood nearly motionless, slowly shifting his eyes to Fre'geel. "Commander," he said softly. "Do I have your word on what you just told the Kyber captain?"

Fre'geel was breathing raspily. But a hint of what could almost have been a human smile fluttered at his mouth. "You have my word," he said huskily. "And my . . . apology." He inclined his head forward.

Legroeder sighed and lowered the weapon.

"Thank you," the captain said.

Legroeder nodded, gazing down at the gun, turning it slowly in his hand. Lifeless metal. But one squeeze of the trigger . . . He handed it back to Deutsch. It disappeared into Deutsch's metal side.

"I trust you'll turn that weapon in later," Captain Friedman murmured, staring at the image in the screen, where the explosion and the debris had faded from visibility. The Kyber detachment had broken off its run and was now returning to the main Kyber fleet. Legroeder suddenly felt utterly drained. He wondered whose move it was now.

Tiegs spoke. "*Vigilant* is warning *Farhawk* not to interfere with orbital operations, and *Farhawk* is warning everyone not to interfere with *Impris*."

Captain Friedman pursed his lips. "Hell of a thing—bastards like that being our protection. But better them, I guess, than no one."

To which Legroeder whispered a silent amen.

THEY WERE approaching their parking orbit when the message arrived from El'ken, addressed to Secretary General Albright via an open broadcast on the net. The statement made no mention of the clandestine near-hijacking of *Impris* by the Kyber ships. But it hailed the return of *Impris* as vindication of the Narseil's century-old claim dating back to the War of a Thousand Suns. El'ken urgently requested safe passage for the ship and full participation by the Narseil Rigging Institute in the investigation of her disappearance. *"We also applaud critical contributions made by Rigger Legroeder in the rescue of Impris—and call for guarantees of his safety and freedom, as well . . ."*

Fre'geel's bright, vertical eyes gazed at Legroeder as El'ken spoke. *Will you let it go at that?* he seemed to be asking. Legroeder gave a slight nod.

The answer from the secretary general came a few minutes later. *"We respect and appreciate the Narseil interest in this matter. Rest assured that your recommendations will receive the highest level of attention. In the meantime, we guarantee free passage for Impris, and welcome her home after a long absence. We are dispatching a tow, with escort, and clearing Impris for immediate docking at Outer Terminus Three. As for the Kyber fleet in our skies, we thank you for such helpful role as you may have played in her safe return. Now, it is time for you to leave."*

Tiegs fussed at the com-console for a few minutes. "Lots of coded message traffic again. The Kyber are talking up a storm among themselves. I think they're talking to someone outside the Faber Eri system."

Though it seemed forever, it was only a few minutes before the Kyber ship responded, *"Our conditions have been met. Since we have no further business at this time, we will be on our way. But you can count on us to stay in touch about the progress of the Impris investigation."*

"They're pulling away," Johnson murmured.

Everyone stared at the main screen. The rings and outriggers on the KM/C ships were starting to glow, as they powered up their Circadie space inductors. Legroeder's heart was pounding as he watched the Kyber break from formation around *Impris*. They began to accelerate outward from the planet, their space inductors blazing sapphire. He felt it coming before he saw it: the ships vanishing into the Flux—once again, recklessly close to the planet, shaking *Impris* with the gravitational turbulence. The

KM/C riggers were good at that, he had to admit. But he wished to hell they'd cut it out.

Now they were gone, all of the Kyber ships.

He blinked and looked again.

All of them except one.

Chapter 41

REUNION

THE REMAINING Kyber warship glided into formation alongside *Impris*. "What the hell?" Captain Friedman muttered. "Is that *Phoenix?*"

Legroeder's heart did a couple of flips. *Phonenix* had not been part of the original escort. But confirmation came a few moments later. *"Impris, this is Ivan ship Phoenix. Please stand by while we contact local authorities."*

Legroeder laughed joyfully at the sound of the voice.

"Faber Eridani Defense Command, this is Yankee-Zulu/ Ivan ship Phoenix, Tracy-Ace/Alfa speaking for Kyber Outpost Ivan. We are here to provide continuing escort for Impris, and to seek diplomatic contact on behalf of Yankee-Zulu/Ivan. We are not, repeat not, connected with the Kilo-Mike/Carlotta fleet, just departed. Our mission is entirely peaceful, and—"

A burst of static interrupted the transmission.

"Pirate ship Phoenix, this is Captain Sanspach, of Vigilant." He sounded exasperated. *"You are instructed to turn your ship around and depart this system at once. We have no need of further Kyber interference."*

Legroeder hurried to speak to Cantha. "Can you get Harriet back on the line for me?"

While Cantha was working, Friedman snapped his fingers

at Tiegs. "Transmit on that frequency." When Tiegs nodded, the captain raised his voice, "*Vigilant*, this is Captain Friedman of *Impris*. Be advised that we owe this Ivan ship our lives. She and her crew brought us back from a living death in the Flux. In addition, they saved us from destruction at the hands of a hostile fleet."

"*Impris, Vigilant. Are you saying you want this ship to come in with you?*"

"That's affirmative."

Pause. "*Impris, please stand by . . .*"

While they were standing by, Legroeder got a nod from Cantha. He stepped to the com. "Harriet? Are you there?"

"Here, Legroeder. What's this new ship?"

"Friends, Harriet. We've got to make Spacing Authority understand that. It's the ship that took us to rescue *Impris*. And Harriet . . . we've got a raider organization here that wants to make peace."

"Make peace? You're certain of that?"

"I'm certain, Harriet. I know what you're thinking. But these are not the people who took Bobby. You've got to trust me on this."

If Harriet hadn't been thinking of Bobby before, the reminder seemed to give her even greater pause. "What are you telling me, Legroeder? Did you find out anything about—?"

"Some leads, yes. And these people from Ivan are working on it for me. I'll explain later."

Harriet seemed to accept that with difficulty. "All right. I'll see what I can do."

Legroeder turned to Friedman. "Maybe she can persuade them, if they don't believe you."

Friedman looked ready to believe anything, and nothing.

APPARENTLY THE authorities were persuaded, either by Friedman's claim or by Harriet's intervention, or both, because eventually a directive came down from the secretary general to the Spacing Authority, and both ships were granted clearance to enter orbit near the docking terminal.

Phoenix settled into a parking orbit under the watchful eyes of a small squadron, while *Impris*, aided by a tow, was brought into an arrival dock.

There was growing excitement aboard *Impris* as they awaited permission to debark. They were told that arrangements were being made for lodging, medical exams, and preparation for transport to the surface. After endless delays, a decontamination tunnel was put in place. When at last the passengers and most of the crew were given permission to go "ashore," the ship's corridors resounded with cheers. The exodus began at once—though Fre'geel ordered his Narseil crew to remain on board until the Narseil diplomats arrived, from the *Essling* and from the embassy on Faber Eri.

Legroeder and Deutsch went out through the checkpoint and stood in the receiving area with a knot of officials, watching as the *Impris* passengers crowded off the ship. It was a lot like the debarkation at Outpost Ivan; many of the passengers looked dazed. And yet, it was different: this world was home for them, or at least their point of departure a century and a quarter ago. Legroeder suspected that for many of them, the stopover at Ivan had been more like a dream than a return to civilization as they had known it. He wondered if they'd recognize the society they were about to encounter here.

He had little time to think about it, before one of the station security agents approached. "Rigger Legroeder, you're wanted in the station administrator's office. Follow me, please." The agent looked at Deutsch. "Are you here as an official representative of the Kyber?"

Deutsch hummed thoughtfully. "In the absence of Tracy-Ace/Alfa, I could be considered official, I suppose."

"He should come along," Legroeder said.

The agent still looked unsure, but waved them on together.

They were ushered into a room with more Faber Eridani officials than he could keep track of. Events began to blur from that point on. The most senior government officials had not yet arrived, but those who were there wanted to hear the entire story. Legroeder gave the brief version, knowing he was going to be telling it many times over. No one seemed to know quite what to do with Deutsch, and he sat silent most of the time, only occasionally answering a direct question or offering a small elaboration.

After what seemed hours, Legroeder was drawn aside and informed he had a visitor. For a moment, he fantasized that it might be Tracy-Ace, but that seemed unlikely; her ship wasn't even in dock. Curiosity overcoming weariness, he followed the aide out to the anteroom.

"There you are!" said a grey-haired lady.

"Harriet!" he cried, and ran past the startled aide to embrace Harriet in a bear hug.

"Don't crush me, dear!" she pleaded, laughing.

Legroeder held her at arm's length. "How did you get here so fast?"

Harriet's eyes twinkled as she readjusted her glasses. "I grabbed the first Narseil shuttle up. I'm still technically under their wing. What, did you think you don't need a lawyer anymore?"

Legroeder practically danced her around the room. "How could I doubt? Harriet, what's been happening here? Tell me everything! How are you—and how is Morgan? And did you find Maris?"

"Stop. *Stop*, before I get dizzy!" she laughed. "Yes, Morgan and Maris will be very happy to see you."

"You found her!"

"About a week ago. Alive and well."

Legroeder closed his eyes and breathed a deep sigh of gratitude.

"I knew you'd be glad to hear that. But now, Legroeder"—Harriet put a hand on his arm—"before you say anything else—tell me what you found about Bobby."

Legroeder felt his throat tighten. Harriet saw his hesitation, and her face fell at once. He put a hand on hers. "We haven't found *him* yet, but we found his trail. He was taken alive from the *L.A.*, and later transferred from DeNoble to another outpost. When I left Ivan, they were still trying to track him down." He squeezed her hand. "There's hope, Harriet. Don't give up."

Harriet drew a deep breath. "All right. I can hold out a little longer, I guess." She forced a smile. "My word, but it's good to see you in one piece." She glanced toward the door where the aide was waiting for Legroeder to return to the debriefing. "How are they treating you in there?"

Legroeder shrugged. "They haven't hung me out to dry yet."

"We'll do much better for you than that, dear. Your lawyer's with you now . . ."

WHETHER OR not it mattered to anyone else that his lawyer was with him, it certainly made him feel better. By the time they broke for dinner, it was apparent that he could look forward to a lot more of the same. It would start all over again tomorrow, once the people with real power had arrived. At that point, they'd bring in Captain Friedman and the Narseil, as well. Legroeder was grateful for a chance to get away for dinner with Harriet, in the station administrator's dining room. "I feel so out of touch with what's been happening here," he said, wrapping his fingers around a glistening stein of beer.

Harriet laughed. "*You* feel out of touch! Which one of us went flying off to be captured by space pirates, was gone for ten weeks without a word, and then came back standing at the wheel of the legendary Flying Dutchman of the stars?" She peered over the tops of her glasses. "I was afraid I'd never see you again. And I never dreamed you'd *fly the bloody ship back to us!*"

"Well, I was a little surprised myself," Legroeder admitted. He glanced out through the doorway of the dining room. "Freem'n! Come on in here! Harriet, I'd like you to meet a friend of mine." The cyborg floated in through the doorway and greeted Harriet with an amplified rumble and an outstretched metal hand. "I don't think you were ever properly introduced back there."

"No," said Harriet, rising. "I know you were together on the rescue mission—"

"A major understatement. Freem'n's—" Legroeder hesitated. "Well, besides being a friend, he's an outstanding rigger. And a goodwill representative . . ." The rest of the words caught in his throat. *Of Ivan. Of the Kyber pirates.*

Harriet stiffened, as she shook Deutsch's hand. It didn't take a mind-reader to guess what she was thinking.

Legroeder hastened to add, "He started out as a captive, impressed into service just like me, Harriet. And I couldn't have done any of this without him."

Harriet relaxed a little. "So," she murmured to Deutsch, "what is your role here at Faber Eridani?"

Deutsch's eyes were no doubt unreadable to Harriet, but Legroeder could have sworn he saw them twinkle as he answered, "I'm here to see if I can mend some fences. And—" he chuckled softly "—to see that nothing bad happens to Legroeder and all that information he's carrying in his head."

Harriet cocked her head in puzzlement.

"I still have to explain about that," Legroeder said. "It's sort of complicated."

Harriet nodded. "Then I guess this is where I should say, any friend of Legroeder's—" She opened her palm.

"Just what I was thinking," Deutsch said. "In any case, I'm hoping to provide you with some information about the Kyber worlds, while I'm here."

"I look forward to hearing it."

"And I could probably use a good lawyer, if you happen to know of one."

"Actually," Legroeder said thoughtfully, "there are a *lot* of people coming in here who are going to need help. Of all kinds. Being in limbo for a century hasn't left all of them in such good shape. Can you use some more *pro bono* work, Harriet?"

His lawyer raised her eyebrows. "It may be time for me to impose upon the goodwill of some of my colleagues . . ."

* * *

After dinner, Harriet excused herself to make a couple of calls. When she returned, said, "You know, the press is on the verge of breaking down the doors to see you, and I'm going to let them, if our hosts here will allow it. But there are a couple of people I want you to see first, okay?"

Legroeder shrugged. "Okay."

"Follow me." Harriet led him out of the dining room, down a short hallway past several guards, and into an anteroom. Morgan Mahoney whirled at his approach and with a cry of joy ran toward him with open arms. Hugging Morgan, Legroeder saw the second woman, waiting with her.

"Maris?" he gasped, releasing Morgan and reaching out to catch Maris's hand. He held her at arm's length, looking her up and down. "I wasn't sure I'd ever see you alive again! I thought you were gone. I really did." She grinned back at him, and finally he drew her into a long bear hug.

Maris looked healthier than she ever had as a prisoner; there was a flush to her cheeks and a light in her eyes that almost made up for the scar on the side of her neck. The change was remarkable. She'd had her auburn hair styled, probably for the first time in years. Looking at her now, it felt like an eternity since they'd fled DeNoble together; and it felt like yesterday.

The grin on Maris's face turned to sober amazement. "I didn't know if *you'd* be alive, Legroeder. When your friends rescued me, I couldn't believe what they'd done to you at the RiggerGuild. And then to hear you'd gone back to a pirate camp. *My God*, Legroeder!" She shook her head and squeezed his hands.

"Well, *I* knew you'd be back," Morgan interjected. "Pirates or no pirates. No man can stay away from me forever."

Legroeder laughed. "Thanks, Morgan. But where did you *find* her? Where *were* you, Maris?"

"Held by pirates," Morgan said darkly.

"KM/C agents? Kilo-Mike/Carlotta?"

Maris glanced at Morgan and shrugged. "I never heard that name. They kept talking about Ivan—Yankee, someone?"

"Yankee Zulu Ivan is what you said before," said Morgan. "Have you heard of them, Legroeder?"

He felt a sudden rushing in his ears. He closed his eyes. *Yankee-Zulu/Ivan?* For a moment he stood there, trying to will the thought away. *Not Ivan. Please.* He tried to answer, but couldn't find his voice.

Morgan's words finally cut through the fog in his head. "Does that mean yes or no? Hey, who's your friend here?"

Legroeder grunted and blinked his eyes open. Deutsch was floating beside him, augments flickering. Before Legroeder could answer, Deutsch said, "Legroeder, you seem to gather women around you everywhere you go, don't you?"

Legroeder winced. "Maris and Morgan, my friend Freem'n Deutsch." *Break this to them slowly* . . . "I think maybe I'd better tell you from the beginning what's happened since I left El'ken's asteroid . . ."

"WAIT A minute—*wait a minute!*" Morgan was waving a hand in the air. He'd just gotten to the part about YZ/I's sending him to search for *Impris*—leaving out a few details, such as his relationship with Tracy-Ace/Alfa. "These people who helped you find *Impris*—what did you say they were called—*YZ/I?* You don't mean—" the color drained from her face "—you don't mean Yankee . . . Zulu . . ."

Legroeder nodded, feeling his own face flush.

"What?" Maris whispered.

"Wait—let me explain—"

"Explain *what?*" snapped Morgan. "Why they kidnapped Maris? Do I have that right? Yankee Zulu Ivan are the creeps who kidnapped you, right, Maris?"

Maris's mouth was open in hurt bewilderment. "Yes," she said, without looking back at Morgan. "That's what they said. Yankee Zulu—Ivan, right. What's this all about, Legroeder? Are *these* the people you've been making friends with?" She turned and stared penetratingly at Deutsch.

Legroeder face was afire. "YZ/I is Yankee-Zulu/Ivan,

yeah. And I don't *know* what they were doing with you, Maris. But I intend to find out. Very soon."

"Legroeder," Morgan said. "We're talking kidnappers, here. *Pirates.*"

He swallowed, his blood turning to ice. Fire and ice. "Yes. Apparently so," he whispered. He cleared his throat with difficulty. "And . . . they're the ones I'm going to be asking you—and Faber Eridani—to work with." *Tracy-Ace, what have you people done? Why?* He felt a drum thumping in the center of his forehead.

"Murdering thugs," Morgan said.

Legroeder struggled. "Some of them—yes, they are. But not all. There's a confederation of Kyber outposts out there—and—" He cut off his own words. *Dear God, better not mention just yet that they're getting ready to expand into the galaxy . . .*

"And what?"

"And—" his eye caught Harriet's incredulous look, and that made it even harder "—and we've got a boss who wants to *talk* to us, wants to stop the hostilities."

"And we're supposed to believe them?" Morgan asked disdainfully.

He drew a breath. "We have to at least listen to them. I can't vouch for the other outposts. But these people from Ivan . . . they helped us find *Impris*, and got us back safely to Faber Eri. They *escorted* us. As a gesture of good faith."

Deutsch, beside him, murmured a metallic affirmation.

"They sent Freem'n here as an envoy to share information. *And—*" Legroeder gasped dizzily, hoping all these promises would be kept "—there's a shipload of repatriated prisoners on their way back here right now. Right behind us."

"What are you talking about, Legroeder?" Maris said, holding her head as if it hurt just trying to take in his words. "Repatriated prisoners? Are you serious?"

"I am. Look, I know this is all very confusing. Maris, I don't know the explanation for what happened to you. But I know someone who does, or can find out. I'm just asking you right now to keep an open mind. When you hear the rest of the story . . . Do we have time, Harriet?"

"We'll make time. I'll have them send in some coffee."

"Good. Then let me finish telling you what happened . . ."

EVEN RECOUNTING the events of the *Impris* rescue in brief, he found his emotions stirring at the memories. "The passage through the flaw was the most astounding experience of my life," he said in a near whisper, as the rush of dizziness that he'd felt in the retelling slowly subsided. He'd allowed himself to relive the feelings far more intensely in the presence of his friends than he had before. At least for those few minutes, he'd forgotten his other problems.

Morgan and Maris were dumbstruck. Harriet, who had heard the gist of the story before, was the first to stir. "It's an amazing story. Simply amazing. And I think now you need to tell it again—this time to the ladies and gentlemen of the press."

Legroeder groaned.

Harriet was not to be put off, however. As she took his arm and propelled him toward a conference room where he could hear the sounds of a crowd, she said, "You might hate this, but if you want to clear the air about everything that's happened, and you want the Spacing Authority and RiggerGuild off your back, you've got to get it all out in public."

"What do you want me to do?" he mumbled.

She put a hand on his shoulder. "Just tell it the way you did to us. You'll knock 'em dead."

THE PRESS conference was every bit as chaotic as he'd expected; but through the chaos, he managed somehow to give a coherent summary of his adventure, and convey it as a triumph not only for himself, but for *Impris* and Faber Eridani as well. His lawyer deftly deflected all but a very few questions, and got him out of the room as quickly as she'd gotten him in. They left the reporters with ample fodder for many days of sensational stories, and the promise of more details to come.

"Superbly done," Harriet said, as they rejoined his friends in the guest suite he'd been assigned on the station. "You've got a big day tomorrow. So I think we'd better all clear out of here and let you get some sleep."

Legroeder didn't argue. After everyone left, he threw himself down onto the bed. For a time he felt as if he wouldn't sleep a wink, but instead would spend the entire night with one thought racing against the next, and most of all remembering the shock in the eyes of his friends as he'd revealed the name of YZ/I.

When he rolled out of bed in the morning, he realized he had, in fact, slept like the dead. Even after rejoining his friends for breakfast, he was still groggy. He drank his coffee in near-silence, trying to reconstitute himself before the start of the formal hearings.

The Special Envoy to the Secretary General, one Martha Clark, had arrived during the night, as had a number of Narseil diplomats. They were all eager not just to hear the details of the mission but to put a shape on it in anticipation of drawing conclusions. The arrival of *Impris* was not a problem for them; the arrival of the Kyber was another matter. Legroeder was joined by Captain Friedman and by his Narseil shipmates, and he was grateful for the company and the support.

It was astounding how long it could take to tell even the most basic points of a story when one was interrupted and questioned at every turn, and when there were no fewer than three human and four Narseil viewpoints to be told.

The first day of hearings stretched into three, and by then Legroeder was ready for just about anything except another day of questions. Every time he spoke with Harriet, Morgan, or Maris, he imagined the suspicion and betrayal he'd seen in their eyes that first night.

For their part, they seemed at least to be trying to give him the benefit of the doubt. Morgan seemed the angriest and most inclined to think he was an idiot for believing anything the Kyber told him. Harriet, perhaps hiding at times behind her professional facade, seemed to be working hardest at trying to maintain an open mind. Maris was still just trying to make sense of the whole thing.

Legroeder was beginning to wonder if he would ever hear from Tracy-Ace/Alfa, who as far as he knew was still in a parking orbit somewhere well out of sight of the station. As the hearings neared their completion on the fourth day, he was stunned to hear her voice coming through the door of the meeting room. Tracy-Ace herself appeared a few moments later, flanked by Captain Glenswarg. They were followed closely by armed Spacing Authority guards.

"Ah," said Envoy Clark, "our guests from the Kyber vessel have arrived."

"Thank you for permitting us to address you," Tracy-Ace said with a bow. "It's a pleasure to be here representing the Kyber outpost of Yankee-Zulu/Ivan." She was dressed much as she had been the first time Legroeder met her—spectacular in black and gold. She seemed, if anything, to be taller than before; probably it was his imagination. Her eyes searched the room until she found Legroeder. A smile creased her face.

Legroeder started to rise, then caught himself and made do with a blush and a grin. He was aware of Harriet, beside him, and he cleared his throat.

"Friend of yours?" Harriet murmured. "Very pretty . . ."

Legroeder nodded, not trusting his voice.

"I see . . ."

Which was exactly what he was afraid of. He had gone, after all, to gather intelligence against the pirates, not to make love to them. But if Harriet was interpreting his discomfort accurately, she said nothing more.

At the front of the room, Tracy-Ace addressed the panel of officials. "A shipload of repatriates is en route, and should be here in a few days," she said, causing an immediate stir. "We'll have names and other information for you at that time."

"Miss Alfa," said Special Envoy Clark in surprise, "are you saying—"

"That we are serious about establishing meaningful relations with your world? Yes, we are . . ."

It was another hour before the session was called for the day and Legroeder got a chance to speak with her. He hurried to the front of the room as people dispersed, feeling a flash of worry that this would be like their arrival back at Ivan, all business. Which perhaps would have been for the better; but never mind that . . .

Tracy-Ace embraced him, hard. "Am I glad to see you, babe!" she murmured, kissing him on the cheek, then pulling back to gaze at him. "We were worried, back when you first arrived, that things weren't going too well."

Legroeder gazed back at her in wonderment. "Were you there the whole time?"

One corner of her mouth curled in a grin. "What do you think? Now, if they'll let me go with you, do you think you're ready to take me to meet your friends?"

IT TOOK some intervention on Harriet's part to get that much freedom of movement for Tracy-Ace; and even then, guards were never far away. The officers of *Phoenix* and *Impris* joined Legroeder, Harriet, and Deutsch in the dining room, and that was where Tracy-Ace and Harriet first had an opportunity to talk. Tracy-Ace was frowning, the corners of her eyes flickering. Finally she stabbed the air with her finger. "Harriet Mahoney—*Bobby Mahoney!* I almost forgot to tell you, Legroeder—I got news from YZ/I on the way in. They found him! They found Bobby. One of Carlotta's outposts has him, and YZ/I is negotiating for his release." She turned to Harriet. "Bobby is your grandson, yes?"

Harriet looked faint, her eyes wide with shock and joy. "Yes," she whispered. "Is it true? He's really alive?"

Tracy-Ace's face was alight. "He really is."

Harriet leaned across the table. "Will he be freed?"

Tracy-Ace breathed out slowly. "He's not in our hands yet, so I can't promise. But I believe there's a good chance.

YZ/I can strike a pretty hard bargain." She glanced around the table with a grin. "And if YZ/I can't do it, maybe we could send in the Narseil."

Legroeder winced a little at the joke, but was filled with gratitude on Harriet's behalf. Harriet was weeping openly now, dabbing at her eyes with a handkerchief. Legroeder took her hand, and she squeezed back fiercely. Then, to Legroeder's surprise, Harriet reached across the table and squeezed Tracy-Ace's hand, too. "Thank you," she whispered. "I just can't tell you . . ."

INTRODUCING TRACY-ACE to Morgan and Maris was a different matter. After dinner, Tracy-Ace was permitted to come to his suite along with other visitors, and she was there when Maris and Morgan arrived. In fact, she was standing with her hand on Legroeder's shoulder as the two women walked in.

Legroeder blushed as he saw Morgan stiffen. "Hi," he said, managing not to stammer. "Ladies, I'd like you to meet my friend, Tracy-Ace/Alfa." He turned, as Tracy-Ace's hand dropped from his shoulder, and awkwardly completed the introductions. He glanced at Harriet, but she merely raised her eyebrows slightly.

Tracy-Ace stepped forward to meet the other two. "I'm pleased to meet you both at last," she said. "Legroeder has been very eager to get back here to rejoin you. He's told me a lot about you all." Legroeder pressed his lips together and said nothing.

"I'm sure he has," Morgan said brusquely. "Pleased to meet you. Hi, Mom."

"Hello, dear," Harriet said, and appeared to decide to help Legroeder out a bit, after all. "Legroeder's friend Miss Alfa—"

"Please. Tracy-Ace."

"Tracy-Ace, sorry. Tracy-Ace has brought some wonderful news. They've found Bobby, and there's a good chance he'll be freed." Harriet waved to a small sofa and a side table. "Please sit. Get yourself a glass of wine."

Morgan blinked, and seemed to be struggling to recompute.

"That's right," Tracy-Ace said, taking a seat in a chair, while Legroeder joined Harriet on the other sofa. "Bobby's not at our outpost, but we're hopeful." She explained what she had told Harriet.

"That's . . . *terrific*," Morgan said, her eyes implying that it would have been even more terrific if Bobby had never been captured in the first place.

"Bobby is what—your nephew?" Tracy-Ace asked.

Morgan bobbed her head. "And I'm extremely grateful—really—for the news."

Tracy-Ace took a sip of wine. "But you're not so sure about me, I take it."

"Well, it's not—"

"I think," said Maris, speaking for the first time, "that we're both wondering . . . well . . . are you here with Legroeder in a purely *official* capacity, or . . ."

"We're friends," Tracy-Ace said quickly.

"Good friends," Legroeder echoed, in a voice that seemed exceedingly hollow.

"Ah-hah," Maris said, nodding.

Morgan also nodded, more slowly. "Then we should—" *Regard you as a friend? Claw your eyes out? What?* her eyes seemed to say.

Legroeder cleared his throat. "You should treat her as a friend of mine," he said softly. "As someone I trust, and someone who has helped me tremendously. If it weren't for her, I wouldn't be back here now." He could feel the flush in his face as he said it—annoyance, defensiveness, guilt. Love for Tracy-Ace, and embarrassment about it.

"Perhaps," Harriet said, in an even voice, "we could let Tracy-Ace speak. I'm sure she'd like to answer some of our questions."

"I would be happy to answer your questions," Tracy-Ace said softly.

* * *

ANSWERING THEIR questions was no trivial matter; and as Tracy-Ace talked about Ivan's scheme to draw first the Narseil and Legroeder—and later the Centrist Worlds—into talks, Morgan grew increasingly restless. "That's all very well," she said, "but what about the kidnapping of Maris? And those attacks on my mother and Legroeder? They almost *died* getting to McGinnis, you know. Are you going to explain those away?"

Tracy-Ace looked a little startled by the ferocity of the question. She closed her eyes for a moment; her cheek implants flickered frenetically. She muttered something under her breath before opening her eyes again. "We certainly had nothing to do with those attacks. I believe it was the local group Centrist Strength, under orders from Kilo-Mike/Carlotta."

"If you knew that, why didn't you do something to stop it?" Morgan demanded.

Tracy-Ace turned her palms up. "We didn't know in *advance*. Understand, we have a few people here, but nothing like Carlotta. She has agents everywhere, including—well, we know where, now. All the way at the top of the Spacing Authority. We did what we could." She turned to Maris. "I didn't know until just now about your ... protective custody. But yes—it was our people who took you."

Maris's face tightened.

"Our field commander had learned of the attack on Legroeder and Harriet," Tracy-Ace continued. "It was his judgment that you were in grave danger, Maris, and that you very likely would not have left that hospital alive, or free, if they did not take action at once." Tracy-Ace opened her hands in apology. "I'm sorry they treated you like a prisoner. *Very* sorry. Our agents truly were ordered to protect you. But they were insufficient, as it turned out. And they both paid with their lives. I'm very glad that your friends came to rescue you." She nodded toward Morgan.

For a moment, no one seemed to know what to say, Legroeder least of all. Maris stared at Tracy-Ace with an uncertain expression. She seemed to be trying to process this latest twist, and coming up short. Finally Legroeder cleared his throat. "Maris, Tracy-Ace and her people saved my life, more than once. If she says that's what happened, you can believe her."

Maris did not shift her gaze from Tracy-Ace. But after a moment she nodded decisively. "Very well. Since you are a friend of Legroeder's, I will allow that you may be telling the truth." She glanced at Legroeder with a trace of a grin. "Seeing as how *you* saved my life, too, eh?"

Legroeder allowed a smile to tickle at his lips.

Tracy-Ace drew a deep breath. "That was one time when we managed to act ahead of Carlotta. But don't misunderstand—even with North dead, Carlotta still has plenty of agents here, and they've managed to disassociate themselves from Centrist Strength with that attack on North's ship. But don't believe for a minute that they're not still pulling strings in that group. They can cause plenty of trouble."

"What do you intend to do?" Harriet asked.

Tracy-Ace opened her hands. "What *can* I do? It's your world, not mine. I'll help if I can—but my help won't matter much if we don't get *Impris*, and Legroeder and his implants, to the Narseil Rigging Institute."

"Do you want to explain that to the others?" Harriet asked.

Tracy-Ace looked to Legroeder, who sighed. "When the Narseil fitted me with these implants—" he rubbed at his temples and behind his ears "—I didn't know that they were going to end up recording some of the most crucial data in the history of starship rigging—and then treat it as a Narseil state secret." *(You bastards. Are you still there? Answer me, damn you.)*

▢ *Awaiting release codes.* ▢

Stunned, Legroeder drew a sharp breath. *(You're there?)* No answer.

"You okay?" Tracy-Ace asked, cocking her head, as if she'd caught an echo of it.

Legroeder nodded slowly. "And so right here," he continued, tapping the implants, "is where the data remain, even as we speak."

Morgan and Maris stared at him. *"What data?"* Morgan demanded.

Legroeder closed his eyes with a shiver. "When we came out of the underflux with *Impris*, my implants mapped it all. It's the most astounding, and beautiful, and deadly thing I've ever imagined—this network of quantum flaws woven through the whole galaxy, through spacetime." He opened his eyes. "Every rigging world, and every rigger, needs to know about this." He drew a breath. "And only the Narseil Rigging Institute can get at the data."

Morgan and Maris sat stunned.

"So," said Harriet, who had already had a chance to grasp the political implications, "it's crucial that we get you to the Narseil Institute in one piece . . . along with *Impris*."

"An understatement."

"And . . . is this what the future peace is going to hinge upon?"

"That is almost certainly the case," Tracy-Ace said softly. "Our mutual friend here—" her gaze drifted meaningfully to Legroeder "—has a long road still ahead of him." Her eyes twinkled in contact with his. "Don't you, babe?"

Legroeder grunted and tried not to notice the raised eyebrows all around him.

Chapter 42
BEGINNINGS

IT WAS another two days before Tracy-Ace was permitted to make her full presentation on behalf of Outpost Ivan. Though Special Envoy Clark made clear that a formal response from the government would take time, she acknowledged that the secretary general was open-minded on the subject of establishing relations with the Kyber outposts. "This does not in any way imply that we condone piracy," she said sternly. "But we recognize that we have to *consider* being willing to move on. If you are serious about repatriating citizens—"

Tracy-Ace raised a hand. "Our first shipload of repatriates has just called in. They've entered the Faber Eri system."

The officials in the room stirred as Clark replied, "Then we may indeed have something to talk about."

The Narseil ambassador leaned forward. "That is good news, indeed." He turned to the envoy. "May I ask if we might also talk about moving forward with the *Impris* investigation, and getting Rigger Legroeder to our Institute for study? In the interests of maintaining good relations with a people who have been forgiving of certain transgressions for these many years?"

Special Envoy Clark, with a faint smile, bowed her head slightly. "I think, my friend Mr. Ambassador, that it may be time to talk about that, as well."

IT WAS late that night, station time, when Legroeder finally got some time alone with Tracy-Ace, with watchful station guards standing a discreet distance away. Tracy-Ace clearly felt the strain of being around his friends—something he could only hope would pass, in time—and she gripped his hand tightly as they walked along the station's observatory deck, watching the largest Faber Eri moon set behind the planet's horizon.

"You'll let me know the instant you hear from YZ/I about—"

"Harriet's grandson? Of course. But you know, Legroeder . . ." Her words caught, and he felt a sudden chill. "There's something you ought to know."

He cocked his head, waiting uneasily.

Tracy-Ace hesitated, pressing her lips together. "Well—it's just that not everyone will necessarily *want* to return."

He tugged her around to face him. "What are you saying?"

Her gaze was unflinching. "Some of the people we offered repatriation to, for example. I know, I know—but Legroeder, for some people it becomes their way of life, to be with us. I'm not saying it *should* be that way, or that it'll happen with Bobby. But it is possible." She shrugged, and suddenly chuckled. "Although it's hard to imagine why anyone would want to stay with KM/C, if they could help it." She squeezed his hand. "I'm sorry—I shouldn't worry you about that. I'm sure it'll work out."

Legroeder nodded, and tried not to worry. There was more than enough to worry about already. He kept trying not to think about the quantum-flaw data, for one thing. He was taking it on faith that meaningful answers to the rigging hazards would be found within those maps in his head. It was a lot to stake on faith.

He drew a deep breath, and for a moment simply enjoyed standing on the deck of a space station—in normal-space— with Tracy-Ace at his side.

"When are you planning to tell them about the Kyber colonizing plans?" he asked, after a while. "That could be pretty explosive news, you know."

Tracy-Ace chuckled. "That's why I figured, one thing at a time. I thought I'd bring it up along with the negotiations for the *Impris* investigation"—she squeezed his hand and grinned—"meaning, the Rigger Legroeder implant investigation."

How reassuring. "There's no telling how they'll react, you know."

Tracy-Ace shrugged. "Maybe they *need* to be shaken out of their complacency and timidity. But one thing has to be clear—and that's that we, and Carlotta, are deadly serious about getting the full report on the quantum flaws. Without that, everything falls apart."

"Carlotta. Huh. You know, I was wondering why they just up and left, rather than sticking around to make sure things went the way they liked."

"Well, now, that was part of their agreement with YZ/I. They got a chance to make a little demonstration of force, but still appear to be good guys." Tracy-Ace snorted. "Or as good as they know how to be. They knew *we* were there, of course."

"Ah. Of course."

"And I wouldn't assume that they've gone too far away. They're almost certainly around somewhere."

Legroeder absorbed that in silence. It would not do to become complacent about Carlotta's future behavior, either. It wouldn't take much, here on Eridani, for the analysis of *Impris*—and the data he carried—to become mired in disputes. "Tell me something, Trace. Is this all part of that bet between YZ/I and KM/C you told me about earlier?"

"Of course. All part of YZ/I's plan to get Carlotta to start thinking about doing things differently. While keeping her own best interests in mind, naturally. She'd already lost *Impris*, but YZ/I convinced her that she could get something better. So she was willing to flush out some of her spies here, if it helped to ensure that she'd get access to this." Tracy-Ace gently touched the side of Legroeder's head.

He shivered at the reminder. "Will she stick to it? Will she stop the raiding? Is this where the honor among thieves kicks in?"

Tracy-Ace's eyebrows went up. "We'll find out, won't we? She wouldn't do it if she didn't need the information from the Narseil as badly as we do. YZ/I let them save face here, but it's in everyone's interest to make sure Carlotta doesn't wind up feeling conned. They did, after all, refrain from going after *Impris*—and you—while you were en route here."

Legroeder felt that knot in his stomach again. He gazed at Tracy-Ace, and something else in his stomach told him there was more for him to ask. "And you . . . came to make sure Carlotta's ships behaved themselves?"

"That, and other reasons." Tracy-Ace looked out at the stars and laughed. *Nervously?* She turned to face him again, and clasped his hands between her own. "I was thinking . . . I might stay on a while."

Legroeder felt a rushing in his ears.

Tracy-Ace looked down at their clasped hands. "For one thing, YZ/I wants to maintain a presence here. Through me."

"Yes?" he murmured. "And the other?"

She let her breath out slowly and raised her eyes to meet his. Her implants were afire. "The other is, I'd like to stay with you. If you want me."

His breath escaped with searing slowness.

"Do you want me?"

Legroeder's eyes were blurring. "You mean that? Really?"

"I just *said* it, didn't I?"

"Yeah, but—"

She stepped closer, until their bodies were just touching. "But what?"

He had trouble meeting her eyes. "Well—you have a life with—the Kyber, right? And I've got this history, where the Kyber are concerned. What about that?"

Tracy-Ace slipped her arms around him and hugged him wordlessly. She pressed her face to his shoulder.

He wanted, desperately, to be satisfied with that. "Trace," he murmured, squeezing her, "what if YZ/I doesn't live up to *his* promise?"

"Which promise?" she whispered.

"The promise to stop piracy."

She chuckled into his shoulder. "I have a pretty good idea what promises he can be expected to keep, and why. I'm *connected* to YZ/I, Legroeder. I'm *part* of him." She drew back and peered at him. "You mean you never suspected?"

Legroeder stared at her, feeling utterly stupid. "Do you mean that you're—of course, you're connected to him. Your augments . . ." He suddenly remembered his dream—or had it been a dream—of *his* augments connected to Tracy-Ace's, while he slept and she fought with YZ/I.

Tracy-Ace chuckled. "Yes, love. Not *now*. But when I'm

there, in the intelnet. At certain times, you could say that I'm a significant component of his consciousness. Didn't you ever wonder why he understood your views so well?"

Legroeder flushed. "Do you mean to say—" he glanced around and lowered his voice "—that when we were making love—"

"No, dear, not then. He might have been *interested*—but no. I'm *me*, Legroeder, not some hybrid. YZ/I, now—he's a different story."

He stared at her. "I won't argue with that. What other tricks does he have for me? Or should I say, do *you* have for me?"

Tracy-Ace grinned. "Touché."

He raised his eyebrows.

"No tricks," she promised. "There's a lot I have to do here, though. When our returnees start arriving, there's going to be pressure on Carlotta to follow suit—especially if she thinks we're benefiting from relations with the Centrist Worlds. On the other hand, if she thinks we're betraying them, and convinces the Republic of that—anything could happen." She turned to peer out at the curved edge of the planet. "By God, though, Legroeder, I'm going to make it work. Damn if I'm not."

There was an adamance in her voice that he liked, and admired.

They walked arm in arm to the opposite end of the observation deck, away from the planet, where all they could see was the dark of deep space. They stood awhile, peering into the measureless infinity of stars. "There's a lot to do at Outpost Ivan, before the first fleets can leave for the Well of Stars," Tracy-Ace murmured. "I'll need to go back eventually to join them. But right now my work is here, I think." She gazed at Legroeder for several heartbeats. "You never answered my question. Do *you* want me here? Do you want me *with* you?"

He smiled out at the stars.

"Legroeder?"

He turned. "What exactly is it you want to do here with

me, Trace? Besides making sure that I'm delivered in one piece to the Narseil?"

"Besides *be with* you? I'm not sure, I guess. Are you still in legal trouble?"

"I dunno yet. But I've got Harriet. I think we'll be able to handle it."

"But can *I* help you?"

Legroeder drew her close. "You helped me come back on the deck of *Impris*. I don't know what more you could possibly do."

Tracy-Ace's augments were gleaming like jewels. She closed her arms around his neck. "How about if I do this?" she whispered, and kissed him. It was a long, slow kiss that flickered between his lips, and seemed to stretch out time itself. He imagined his implants tickling themselves to life, joining with hers; imagined them all talking back and forth, like an echo in a canyon.

◻ . . . *love you . . . love you . . . love you . . .* ◻

He held her close and thought, *Maybe you can, at that. Maybe you just can.*

"Are you going to answer me?"

He felt a foolish grin crack his face before the words came. "Sorry—I thought I already had . . ." And he kissed her again as, outside the viewport, the stars shone bright and beckoning.

About the Author

Jeffrey A. Carver is the author of fourteen popular science fiction novels, including *The Infinity Link* and *The Rapture Effect*. His books combine hard-SF concepts, deeply humanistic concerns, and a sense of humor, making them both compellingly thought-provoking and emotionally satisfying. Previous novels set in the Star Rigger universe include *Star Rigger's Way, Dragons in the Stars,* and *Dragon Rigger*.

In recent years, he has penned the first three volumes of *The Chaos Chronicles*, a grand scope hard-SF series inspired by the science of chaos. *Science Fiction Chronicle* named *Neptune Crossing* one of the best science fiction novels of the year, while *Kirkus Reviews* called *Strange Attractors* "dazzling, thrilling, innovative." He is currently at work on *Sunborn*, the fourth volume of the series.

Carver has taught science fiction writing both through educational television and as the author of *Writing Science Fiction and Fantasy*, a CD-ROM and web-based course that teaches the fundamentals of storytelling and writing.

A native of Huron, Ohio, Carver graduated from Brown University with a degree in English. He has been a high school wrestler, a scuba diving instructor, a quahog diver, a UPS sorter, a private pilot, a freelance instructional designer, and a stay-at-home dad. He lives with his family in the Boston area, where he is a member of the Science Fiction and Fantasy Writers of America, and The Authors Guild.

More information about the author can be found on his web site at *www.starrigger.net*, and he can be reached by email at *jeff@starrigger.net*.